MASTER OF THE GAME

will have you rushing through its pages to find out what happens next. Just as he did in his bestselling novels, *The Other Side of Midnight, A Stranger in the Mirror, Bloodline* and *Rage of Angels,* Sidney Sheldon holds you in thrall to the final words of this book. Read now a tale of one hundred years of a family that climbs from obscurity to opulence—the story of:

Jamie McGregor— a young Scot whose diamond fortune is built on guts, grit and pure, unadulterated hate.

Kate Blackwell— his extraordinary daughter who converts wealth into world-wide dominance—a legacy for her son, whether he wants it or not.

Tony Blackwell— with the talent to be a great painter and the misfortune to be Kate's son.

Eve and Alexandra Blackwell— Kate's twin granddaughters, two facets of the same diamond—one gleaming with the light of love, the other consumed with burning jealousy.

Books by Sidney Sheldon

*Master of the Game
*Rage of Angels
*Bloodline
*A Stranger in the Mirror
The Other Side of Midnight

*Published by
WARNER BOOKS

SIDNEY SHELDON

MASTER OF THE GAME

WARNER BOOKS

A Warner Communications Company

WARNER BOOKS EDITION

This Warner Books Edition is published by arrangement with
William Morrow and Company, Inc.,
105 Madison Avenue,
New York, N.Y. 10016

Cover design by Honi Werner

Warner Books, Inc.,
666 Fifth Avenue,
New York, N.Y. 10103

A Warner Communications Company

Printed in the United States of America

First Warner Books Printing: August, 1983

10 9 8 7 6 5

For my brother,
Richard
the Lion-Hearted

My appreciation goes to Miss Geraldine Hunter for her endless patience and assistance in preparing this manuscript.

"And hence one master-passion in the breast,
Like Aaron's serpent, swallows up the rest."

—ALEXANDER POPE,
Essay on Man, Epistle II

"Diamonds resist blows to such an extent that an iron hammer may be split in two and even the anvil itself may be displaced. This invincible force, which defies Nature's two most violent forces, iron and fire, can be broken by ram's blood. But it must be steeped in blood that is fresh and warm and, even so, many blows are needed."

—PLINY THE ELDER

PROLOGUE

Kate
1982

The large ballroom was crowded with familiar ghosts come to help celebrate her birthday. Kate Blackwell watched them mingle with the flesh-and-blood people, and in her mind, the scene was a dreamlike fantasy as the visitors from another time and place glided around the dance floor with the unsuspecting guests in black tie and long, shimmering evening gowns. There were one hundred people at the party at Cedar Hill House, in Dark Harbor, Maine. *Not counting the ghosts,* Kate Blackwell thought wryly.

She was a slim, petite woman, with a regal bearing that made her appear taller than she was. She had a face that one remembered. A proud bone structure, dawn-gray eyes and a stubborn chin, a blending of her Scottish and Dutch ancestors. She had fine, white hair that once had been a luxuriant black cascade, and against the graceful folds of her ivory velvet dress, her skin had the soft translucence old age sometimes brings.

I don't feel ninety, Kate Blackwell thought. *Where have all the years gone?* She watched the dancing ghosts. *They know. They were there. They were a part of those years, a part of my life.* She saw Banda, his proud black face beaming. And there was her David, dear David, looking tall and young and handsome, the way he looked when she first fell in love with him, and he was smiling at her, and she thought, *Soon, my darling, soon.* And she wished David could have lived to know his great-grandson.

Kate's eyes searched the large room until she saw him. He was standing near the orchestra, watching the musicians. He was a strikingly handsome boy, almost eight years old, fair-haired, dressed in a black velvet jacket and tartan trousers. Robert was a replica of his great-great-grandfather, Jamie McGregor, the man in the painting above the marble fireplace. As though sensing her eyes on him, Robert turned, and Kate beckoned him to her with a wave of her fingers, the perfect twenty-carat diamond her father had scooped up on a sandy beach almost a hundred years ago scintillating in the radiance of the crystal chandelier. Kate watched with pleasure as Robert threaded his way through the dancers.

I am the past, Kate thought. *He is the future. My great-grandson will take over Kruger-Brent Limited one day.* He reached her side, and she made room for him on the seat beside her.

"Are you having a nice birthday, Gran?"

"Yes. Thank you, Robert."

"That's a super orchestra. The conductor's really *bad.*"

Kate looked at him in momentary confusion, then her brow cleared. "Ah. I presume that means he's good."

Robert grinned at her. "Right. You sure don't seem ninety."

Kate Blackwell laughed. "Just between the two of us, I don't feel it."

He slipped his hand in hers, and they sat there in a contented silence, the eighty-two-year difference between them giving them a comfortable affinity. Kate turned to watch her granddaughter dancing. She and her husband were without doubt the handsomest couple on the floor.

Robert's mother saw her son and grandmother seated together and she thought, *What an incredible woman. She's ageless. No one would ever guess all she has lived through.*

The music stopped, and the conductor said, "Ladies and gentlemen, it's my pleasure to present young Master Robert."

Robert squeezed his great-grandmother's hand, stood up and walked over to the piano. He sat down, his face serious and intent, and then his fingers began to race across the keyboard. He played Scriabin, and it was like the rippling of moonlight on water.

His mother listened and thought, *He's a genius. He'll grow up to be a great musician.* He was no longer her baby. He was going to belong to the world. When Robert finished, the applause was enthusiastic and genuine.

Earlier, dinner had been served outdoors. The large and formal garden had been festively decorated with lanterns and ribbons and balloons. Musicians played from the terrace while butlers and maids hovered over tables, silent and efficient, making sure the Baccarat glasses and Limoges dishes were kept filled. A telegram was read from the President of the United States. A Supreme Court justice toasted Kate.

The governor eulogized her. ". . . One of the most remarkable women in the history of this nation. Kate Blackwell's endowments to hundreds of charitable causes around the world are legendary. The Blackwell Foundation has contributed to the health and well-being of people in more than fifty countries. To paraphrase the late Sir Winston Churchill, 'Never have so many owed so much to one person.' I have had the privilege of knowing Kate Blackwell . . ."

Bloody hell! Kate thought. *No one knows me. He sounds like he's talking about some saint. What would all these people say if they knew the real Kate Blackwell? Sired by a thief and kidnapped before I was a year old. What would they think if I showed them the bullet scars on my body?*

She turned her head and looked at the man who had once tried to kill her. Kate's eyes moved past him to linger on a figure in the shadows, wearing a veil to conceal her face. Over a distant clap of thunder, Kate heard the governor finish his speech and introduce her. She rose to her feet and looked out at the assembled guests. When she spoke, her voice was firm and strong. "I've lived longer than any of you. As youngsters today would say, 'That's no big deal.' But I'm glad I made it to this age, because otherwise I wouldn't be here with all you dear friends. I know some of you have traveled from distant countries to be with me tonight, and you must be tired from your journey. It wouldn't be fair for me to expect everyone to have my energy."

There was a roar of laughter, and they applauded her.

"Thank you for making this such a memorable evening. I shall never forget it. For those of you who wish to retire, your rooms are ready. For the others, there will be dancing in the ballroom." There was another clap of thunder. "I suggest we all move indoors before we get caught in one of our famous Maine storms."

Now the dinner and dancing were over, the guests had retired and Kate was alone with her ghosts. She sat in the library, drifting back into the past, and she suddenly felt depressed. *There's no one left to call me Kate,* she thought. *They've all gone.* Her world had shrunk. Wasn't it Longfellow who said, "The leaves of memory make a mournful rustle in the dark"? She would be entering the dark soon, but not yet. *I still have to do the most important thing of my life,* Kate thought. *Be patient, David. I'll be with you soon.*

"Gran . . ."

Kate opened her eyes. The family had come into the room. She looked at them, one by one, her eyes a pitiless camera, missing nothing. *My family,* Kate thought. *My immortality. A murderer, a grotesque and a psychotic. The Blackwell skeletons. Was this what all the years of hope and pain and suffering had finally come to?*

Her granddaughter stood beside her. "Are you all right, Gran?"

"I'm a little tired, children. I think I'll go to bed." She rose to her feet and started toward the stairs, and at that moment there was a violent roar of thunder and the storm broke, the rain rattling against the windows like machine-gun fire. Her family watched as the old woman reached the top of the stairway, a proud, erect figure. There was a blaze of lightning and seconds later a loud clap of thunder. Kate Blackwell turned to look down at them, and when she spoke, it was with the accent of her ancestors. "In South Africa, we used to call this a *donderstorm.*"

The past and present began to merge once again, and she walked down the hallway to her bedroom, surrounded by the familiar, comfortable ghosts.

BOOK ONE

Jamie
1883–1906

1

"By God, this is a real *donderstorm!*" Jamie McGregor said. He had grown up amid the wild storms of the Scottish Highlands, but he had never witnessed anything as violent as this. The afternoon sky had been suddenly obliterated by enormous clouds of sand, instantly turning day into night. The dusty sky was lit by flashes of lightning—*weerlig,* the Afrikaners called it—that scorched the air, followed by *donderslag*—thunder. Then the deluge. Sheets of rain that smashed against the army of tents and tin huts and turned the dirt streets of Klipdrift into frenzied streams of mud. The sky was aroar with rolling peals of thunder, one following the other like artillery in some celestial war.

Jamie McGregor quickly stepped aside as a house built of raw brick dissolved into mud, and he wondered whether the town of Klipdrift was going to survive.

Klipdrift was not really a town. It was a sprawling canvas village, a seething mass of tents and huts and wagons crowding the banks of the Vaal River, populated by wild-eyed dreamers drawn to South Africa from all parts of the world by the same obsession: diamonds.

Jamie McGregor was one of the dreamers. He was barely eighteen, a handsome lad, tall and fair-haired, with startlingly light gray eyes. There was an attractive ingenuousness about him, an eagerness to please that was endearing. He had a light-hearted disposition and a soul filled with optimism.

He had traveled almost eight thousand miles from his father's farm in the Highlands of Scotland to Edinburgh, London, Cape Town and now Klipdrift. He had given up his rights to the share of the farm that he and his brothers tilled with their father, but Jamie McGregor had no regrets. He knew he was going to be rewarded ten thousand times over. He had left the security of the only life he had ever known and had come to this distant, desolate place because he dreamed of being rich. Jamie was not afraid of hard work, but the rewards of tilling the rocky little farm north of Aberdeen were meager. He worked from sunup to sundown, along with his brothers, his sister, Mary, and his mother and his father, and they had little to show for it. He had once attended a fair in Edinburgh and had seen the wondrous things of beauty that money could buy. Money was to make your life easy when you were well, and to take care of your needs when you were ailing. Jamie had seen too many friends and neighbors live and die in poverty.

He remembered his excitement when he first heard about the latest diamond strike in South Africa. The biggest diamond in the world had been found there, lying loose in the sand, and the whole area was rumored to be a great treasure chest waiting to be opened.

He had broken the news to his family after dinner on a Saturday night. They were seated around an uncleared table in the rude, timbered kitchen when Jamie spoke, his voice shy and at the same time proud. "I'm going to South Africa to find diamonds. I'll be on my way next week."

Five pairs of eyes stared at him as though he were crazy.

"You're goin' chasing after diamonds?" his father asked. "You must be daft, lad. That's all a fairy tale—a temptation of the devil to keep men from doin' an honest day's work."

"Why do you nae tell us where you're gettin' the money to

go?" his brother Ian asked. "It's halfway 'round the world. You hae no money."

"If I had money," Jamie retorted, "I wouldn't have to go looking for diamonds, would I? Nobody there has money. I'll be an equal with all of them. I've got brains and a strong back. I'll not fail."

His sister, Mary, said, "Annie Cord will be disappointed. She expects to be your bride one day, Jamie."

Jamie adored his sister. She was older than he. Twenty-four, and she looked forty. She had never owned a beautiful thing in her life. *I'll change that,* Jamie promised himself.

His mother silently picked up the platter that held the remains of the steaming haggis and walked over to the iron sink.

Late that night she came to Jamie's bedside. She gently placed one hand on Jamie's shoulder, and her strength flooded into him. "You do what you must, Son. I dinna ken if there be diamonds there, but if there be, you'll find them." She brought out from behind her a worn leather pouch. "I've put by a few pounds. You needn't say nothin' to the others. God bless you, Jamie."

When he left for Edinburgh, he had fifty pounds in the pouch.

It was an arduous journey to South Africa, and it took Jamie McGregor almost a year to make it. He got a job as a waiter in a workingman's restaurant in Edinburgh until he added another fifty pounds to the pouch. Then it was on to London. Jamie was awed by the size of the city, the huge crowds, the noise and the large horse-drawn omnibuses that raced along at five miles an hour. There were hansom cabs everywhere, carrying beautiful women in large hats and swirling skirts and dainty little high-button shoes. He watched in wonder as the ladies alighted from the cabs and carriages to shop at Burlington Arcade, a dazzling cornucopia of silver and dishes and dresses and furs and pottery and apothecary shops crammed with mysterious bottles and jars.

Jamie found lodging at a house at 32 Fitzroy Street. It cost ten shillings a week, but it was the cheapest he could find. He spent his days at the docks, seeking a ship that would take him to South Africa, and his evenings seeing the wondrous sights of London town. One evening he caught a glimpse of Edward, the Prince of Wales, entering a restaurant near Covent Garden by the side door, a beautiful young lady on his arm. She wore a large flowered hat, and Jamie thought how nice it would look on his sister.

Jamie attended a concert at the Crystal Palace, built for The Great Exposition in 1851. He visited Drury Lane and at intermission sneaked into the Savoy Theatre, where they had installed the first electric lighting in a British public building. Some streets were lighted by electricity, and Jamie heard that it was possible to talk to someone on the other side of town by means of a wonderful new machine, the telephone. Jamie felt that he was looking at the future.

In spite of all the innovations and activity, England was in the midst of a growing economic crisis that winter. The streets were filled with the unemployed and the hungry, and there were mass demonstrations and street fighting. *I've got to get away from here,* Jamie thought. *I came to escape poverty.* The following day, Jamie signed on as a steward on the *Walmer Castle,* bound for Cape Town, South Africa.

The sea journey lasted three weeks, with stops at Madeira and St. Helena to take on more coal for fuel. It was a rough, turbulent voyage in the dead of winter, and Jamie was seasick from the moment the ship sailed. But he never lost his cheerfulness, for every day brought him nearer to his treasure chest. As the ship moved toward the equator, the climate changed. Miraculously, winter began to thaw into summer, and as they approached the African coast, the days and nights became hot and steamy.

The *Walmer Castle* arrived in Cape Town at early dawn, moving carefully through the narrow channel that divided the great leper settlement of Robben Island from the mainland, and dropped anchor in Table Bay.

Jamie was on deck before sunrise. He watched, mesmerized,

as the early-morning fog lifted and revealed the grand spectacle of Table Mountain looming high over the city. He had arrived.

The moment the ship made fast to the wharf, the decks were overrun by a horde of the strangest-looking people Jamie had ever seen. There were touts for all the different hotels—black men, yellow men, brown men and red men frantically offering to bear away luggage—and small boys running back and forth with newspapers and sweets and fruits for sale. Hansom drivers who were half-castes, Parsis or blacks were yelling their eagerness to be hired. Vendors and men pushing drinking carts called attention to their wares. The air was thick with huge black flies. Sailors and porters hustled and halloaed their way through the crowd while passengers vainly tried to keep their luggage together and in sight. It was a babel of voices and noise. People spoke to one another in a language Jamie had never heard.

"*Yulle kom van de Kaap, neh?*"
"*Het julle mine papa zyn wagen gezien?*"
"*Wat bedui'di?*"
"*Hulstoel!*"

He did not understand a word.

Cape Town was utterly unlike anything Jamie had ever seen. No two houses were alike. Next to a large warehouse two or three stories high, built of bricks or stone, was a small canteen of galvanized iron, then a jeweler's shop with hand-blown plate-glass windows and abutting it a small greengrocer's and next to that a tumble-down tobacconist's.

Jamie was mesmerized by the men, women and children who thronged the streets. He saw a kaffir clad in an old pair of 78th Highland trews and wearing as a coat a sack with slits cut for the arms and head. The kaffir walked behind two Chinese men, hand in hand, who were wearing blue smock frocks, their pigtails carefully coiled up under their conical straw hats. There were stout, red-faced Boer farmers with sun-bleached hair, their wagons loaded with potatoes, corn and leafy vegetables. Men dressed in brown velveteen trousers and coats, with broad-brimmed, soft-felt hats on their heads and long clay pipes in their mouths, strode ahead of their *vraws,* attired in black, with thick black veils and large black-silk poke bonnets. Parsi washerwomen with large bundles of soiled clothes on their heads pushed past soldiers in red coats and helmets. It was a fascinating spectacle.

The first thing Jamie did was to seek out an inexpensive boardinghouse recommended to him by a sailor aboard ship. The landlady was a dumpy, ample-bosomed, middle-aged widow.

She looked Jamie over and smiled. *"Zoek yulle goud?"*

He blushed. "I'm sorry—I don't understand."

"English, yes? You are here to hunt gold? Diamonds?"

"Diamonds. Yes, ma'am."

She pulled him inside. "You will like it here. I have all the convenience for young men like you."

Jamie wondered whether she was one of them. He hoped not.

"I'm Mrs. Venster," she said coyly, "but my friends call me 'Dee-Dee.'" She smiled, revealing a gold tooth in front. "I have a feeling we are going to be very good friends. Ask of me anything."

"That's very kind of you," Jamie said. "Can you tell me where I can get a map of the city?"

With map in hand, Jamie went exploring. On one side of the city were the landward suburbs of Rondebosch, Claremont and Wynberg, stretching along nine miles of thinning plantations and vineyards. On the other side were the marine suburbs of Sea Point and Green Point. Jamie walked through the rich residential area, down Strand Street and Bree Street, admiring the large, two-story buildings with their flat roofs and peaked stuccoed fronts—steep terraces rising from the street. He walked until he was finally driven indoors by the flies that seemed to have a personal vendetta against him. They were large and black and attacked in swarms. When Jamie returned to his boardinghouse, he found his room filled with them. They covered the walls and table and bed.

He went to see the landlady. "Mrs. Venster, isn't there anything you can do about the flies in my room? They're—"

She gave a fat, jiggling laugh and pinched Jamie's cheek. "*Myn magtig.* You'll get used to them. You'll see."

The sanitary arrangements in Cape Town were both primitive and inadequate, and when the sun set, an odoriferous vapor covered the city like a noxious blanket. It was unbearable. But Jamie knew that he would bear it. He needed more money before he could leave. "You can't survive in the diamond fields without money," he had been warned. "They'll charge you just for breathin'."

On his second day in Cape Town, Jamie found a job driving a team of horses for a delivery firm. On the third day he started working in a restaurant after dinner, washing dishes. He lived on the leftover food that he squirreled away and took back to the boardinghouse, but it tasted strange to him and he longed for his mother's cock-a-leekie and oatcakes and hot, fresh-made baps. He did not complain, even to himself, as he sacrificed both food and comfort to increase his grubstake. He had made his choice and nothing was going to stop him, not the exhausting labor, or the foul air he breathed or the flies that kept him awake most of the night. He felt desperately lonely. He knew no one in this strange place, and he missed his friends and family. Jamie enjoyed solitude, but loneliness was a constant ache.

At last, the magic day arrived. His pouch held the magnificent sum of two hundred pounds. He was ready. He would leave Cape Town the following morning for the diamond fields.

Reservations for passenger wagons to the diamond fields at Klipdrift were booked by the Inland Transport Company at a small wooden depot near the docks. When Jamie arrived at 7:00 A.M., the depot was already so crowded that he could not get near it. There were hundreds of fortune seekers fighting for seats on the wagons. They had come from as far away as Russia and America, Australia, Germany and England. They shouted in a dozen different tongues, pleading with the besieged ticket sellers to find spaces for them. Jamie watched as a burly Irishman angrily pushed his way out of the office onto the sidewalk, fighting to get through the mob.

"Excuse me," Jamie said. "What's going on in there?"

"Nothin'," the Irishman grunted in disgust. "The bloody wagons are all booked up for the next six weeks." He saw the look of dismay on Jamie's face. "That's not the worst of it, lad. The heathen bastards are chargin' fifty pounds a head."

It was incredible! "There must be another way to get to the diamond fields."

"Two ways. You can go Dutch Express, or you can go by foot."

"What's Dutch Express?"

"Bullock wagon. They travel two miles an hour. By the time you get there, the damned diamonds will all be gone."

Jamie McGregor had no intention of being delayed until the diamonds were gone. He spent the rest of the morning looking for another means of transportation. Just before noon, he found it. He was passing a livery stable with a sign in front that said MAIL DEPOT. On an impulse, he went inside, where the thinnest man he had ever seen was loading large mail sacks into a dogcart. Jamie watched him a moment.

"Excuse me," Jamie said. "Do you carry mail to Klipdrift?"

"That's right. Loadin' up now."

Jamie felt a sudden surge of hope. "Do you take passengers?"

"Sometimes." He looked up and studied Jamie. "How old are you?"

An odd question. "Eighteen. Why?"

"We don't take anyone over twenty-one or twenty-two. You in good health?"

An even odder question. "Yes, sir."

The thin man straightened up. "I guess you're fit. I'm leavin' in an hour. The fare's twenty pounds."

Jamie could not believe his good fortune. "That's wonderful! I'll get my suitcase and—"

"No suitcase. All you got room for is one shirt and a toothbrush."

Jamie took a closer look at the dogcart. It was small and roughly built. The body formed a well in which the mail was stored, and over the well was a narrow, cramped space where a person could sit back to back behind the driver. It was going to be an uncomfortable journey.

"It's a deal," Jamie said. "I'll fetch my shirt and toothbrush."

When Jamie returned, the driver was hitching up a horse to the open cart. There were two large young men standing near the cart: One was short and dark, the other was a tall, blond Swede. The men were handing the driver some money.

"Wait a minute," Jamie called to the driver. "You said *I* was going."

"You're all goin'," the driver said. "Hop in."

"The *three* of us?"

"That's right."

Jamie had no idea how the driver expected them all to fit in the small cart, but he knew he was going to be on it when it pulled out.

Jamie introduced himself to his two fellow passengers. "I'm Jamie McGregor."

"Wallach," the short, dark man said.

"Pederson," the tall blond replied.

Jamie said, "We're lucky we discovered this, aren't we? It's a good thing everybody doesn't know about it."

Pederson said, "Oh, they know about the post carts, McGregor. There just aren't that many fit enough or desperate enough to travel in them."

Before Jamie could ask what he meant, the driver said, "Let's go."

The three men—Jamie in the middle—squeezed into the seat, crowded against each other, their knees cramped, their backs pressing hard against the wooden back of the driver's seat. There was no room to move or breathe. *It's not bad,* Jamie reassured himself.

"Hold on!" the driver sang out, and a moment later they were racing through the streets of Cape Town on their way to the diamond fields at Klipdrift.

By bullock wagon, the journey was relatively comfortable. The wagons transporting passengers from Cape Town to the diamond fields were large and roomy, with tent covers to ward off the blazing winter sun. Each wagon accommodated a dozen passengers and was drawn by teams of horses or mules. Refreshments were provided at regular stations, and the journey took ten days.

The mail cart was different. It never stopped, except to change horses and drivers. The pace was a full gallop, over rough roads and fields and rutted trails. There were no springs on the cart, and each bounce was like the blow of a horse's hoof. Jamie gritted his teeth and thought, *I can stand it until we stop for the night. I'll eat and get some sleep, and in the morning I'll be fine.* But when nighttime came, there was a ten-minute halt for a change of horse and driver, and they were off again at a full gallop.

"When do we stop to eat?" Jamie asked.

"We don't," the new driver grunted. "We go straight through. We're carryin' the mails, mister."

They raced through the long night, traveling over dusty, bumpy roads by moonlight, the little cart bouncing up the rises, plunging down the valleys, springing over the flats. Every inch of Jamie's body was battered and bruised from the constant jolting. He was exhausted, but it was impossible to sleep. Every time he started to doze off, he was jarred awake. His body was cramped and miserable and there was no room to stretch. He was starving and motion-sick. He had no idea how many days it would be before his next meal. It was a six-hundred-mile journey, and Jamie McGregor was not sure he was going to live through it. Neither was he sure that he wanted to.

By the end of the second day and night, the misery had turned to agony. Jamie's traveling companions were in the same sorry state, no longer even able to complain. Jamie understood now why the company insisted that its passengers be young and strong.

When the next dawn came, they entered the Great Karroo, where the real wilderness began. Stretching to infinity, the monstrous veld lay flat and forbidding under a pitiless sun. The passengers were smothered in heat, dust and flies.

Occasionally, through a miasmic haze, Jamie saw groups of men slogging along on foot. There were solitary riders on horseback, and dozens of bullock wagons drawn by eighteen or twenty oxen, handled by drivers and *voorlopers,* with their sjamboks, the whips with long leather thongs, crying, "Trek! Trek!" The huge wagons were laden with a thousand pounds of produce and goods, tents and digging equipment and wood-burning stoves, flour and coal and oil lamps. They carried coffee and rice, Russian hemp, sugar and wines, whiskey and boots and Belfast candles, and blankets. They were the lifeline to the fortune seekers at Klipdrift.

It was not until the mail cart crossed the Orange River that there was a change from the deadly monotony of the veld. The scrub gradually became taller and tinged with green. The earth was redder, patches of grass rippled in the breeze, and low thorn trees began to appear.

I'm going to make it, Jamie thought dully. *I'm going to make it.*

And he could feel hope begin to creep into his tired body.

They had been on the road for four continuous days and nights when they finally arrived at the outskirts of Klipdrift.

Young Jamie McGregor had not known what to expect, but the scene that met his weary, bloodshot eyes was like nothing he ever could have imagined. Klipdrift was a vast panorama of tents and wagons lined up on the main streets and on the shores of the Vaal River. The dirt roadway swarmed with kaffirs, naked except for brightly colored jackets, and bearded prospectors, butchers, bakers, thieves, teachers. In the center of Klipdrift, rows of wooden and iron shacks served as shops, canteens, billiard rooms, eating houses, diamond-buying offices and lawyers' rooms. On a corner stood the ramshackle Royal Arch Hotel, a long chain of rooms without windows.

Jamie stepped out of the cart, and promptly fell to the ground, his cramped legs refusing to hold him up. He lay there, his head spinning, until he had strength enough to rise. He stumbled toward the hotel, pushing through the boisterous crowds that thronged the sidewalks and streets. The room they gave him was small, stifling hot and swarming with flies. But it had a cot. Jamie fell onto it, fully dressed, and was asleep instantly. He slept for eighteen hours.

Jamie awoke, his body unbelievably stiff and sore, but his soul filled with exultation. *I am here! I have made it!* Ravenously hungry, he went in search of food. The hotel served none, but there was a small, crowded restaurant across the street, where he devoured fried snook, a large fish resembling pike; carbonaatje, thinly sliced mutton grilled on a spit over a wood fire; a haunch of bok and, for dessert, *koeksister,* a dough deep-fried and soaked in syrup.

Jamie's stomach, so long without food, began to give off alarming symptoms. He decided to let it rest before he continued eating, and turned his attention to his surroundings. At tables all around him, prospectors were feverishly discussing the subject uppermost in everyone's mind: diamonds.

". . . There's still a few diamonds left around Hopetown, but the mother lode's at New Rush. . . ."

". . . Kimberley's got a bigger population than Joburg. . . ."

". . . About the find up at Dutoitspan last week? They say there's more diamonds there than a man can carry. . . ."

". . . There's a new strike at Christiana. I'm goin' up there tomorrow."

So it was true. There were diamonds everywhere! Young Jamie was so excited he could hardly finish his huge mug of coffee. He was staggered by the amount of the bill. Two pounds, three shillings for one meal! *I'll have to be very careful,* he thought, as he walked out onto the crowded, noisy street.

A voice behind him said, "Still planning to get rich, McGregor?"

Jamie turned. It was Pederson, the Swedish boy who had traveled on the dogcart with him.

"I certainly am," Jamie said.

"Then let's go where the diamonds are." He pointed. "The Vaal River's that way."

They began to walk.

Klipdrift was in a basin, surrounded by hills, and as far as Jamie could see, everything was barren, without a blade of grass or shrub in sight. Red dust rose thick in the air, making it difficult to breathe. The Vaal River was a quarter of a mile away, and as they got closer to it, the air became cooler. Hundreds of prospectors lined both sides of the riverbank, some of them digging for diamonds, others meshing stones in rocking cradles, still others sorting stones at rickety, makeshift tables. The equipment ranged from scientific earth-washing apparatus to old tub boxes and pails. The men were sunburned, unshaven and roughly dressed in a weird assortment of collarless, colored and striped flannel shirts, corduroy trousers and rubber boots, riding breeches and laced leggings and wide-brimmed felt hats or pith helmets. They all wore broad leather belts with pockets for diamonds or money.

Jamie and Pederson walked to the edge of the riverbank and watched a young boy and an older man struggling to remove a huge ironstone boulder so they could get at the gravel around it. Their shirts were soaked with sweat. Nearby, another team loaded gravel onto a cart to be sieved in a cradle. One of the diggers rocked the cradle while another poured buckets of water into it to wash away the silt. The large pebbles were then emptied onto an improvised sorting table, where they were excitedly inspected.

"It looks easy," Jamie grinned.

"Don't count on it, McGregor. I've been talking to some of the diggers who have been here a while. I think we've bought a sack of pups."

"What do you mean?"

"Do you know how many diggers there are in these parts, all hoping to get rich? Twenty bloody thousand! And there aren't enough diamonds to go around, chum. Even if there were, I'm beginning to wonder if it's worth it. You broil in winter, freeze in summer, get drenched in their damned *donderstormen,* and try to cope with the dust and the flies and the stink. You can't get a bath or a decent bed, and there are no sanitary arrangements in this damned town. There are drownings in the Vaal River every week. Some are accidental, but I was told that for most of them it's a way out, the only escape from this hellhole. I don't know why these people keep hanging on."

"I do." Jamie looked at the hopeful young boy with the stained shirt. "The next shovelful of dirt."

But as they headed back to town, Jamie had to admit that Pederson had a point. They passed carcasses of slaughtered oxen, sheep and goats left to rot outside the tents, next to wide-open trenches that served as lavatories. The place stank to the heavens. Pederson was watching him. "What are you going to do now?"

"Get some prospecting equipment."

In the center of town was a store with a rusted hanging sign that read: SALOMON VAN DER MERWE, GENERAL STORE. A tall black man about Jamie's age was unloading a wagon in front of the store. He was broad-shouldered and heavily muscled, one of the most handsome men Jamie had ever seen. He had soot-black eyes, an aquiline nose and a proud chin. There was a dignity about him, a quiet aloofness. He lifted a heavy wooden box of rifles to his shoulder and, as he turned, he slipped on a leaf fallen from a crate of cabbage. Jamie instinctively reached out an arm to steady him. The black man did not acknowledge Jamie's presence. He turned and walked into the store. A Boer prospector hitching up a mule spat and said distastefully, "That's Banda, from the Barolong tribe. Works for Mr. van der Merwe. I don't know why he keeps that uppity black. Those fuckin' Bantus think they own the earth."

The store was cool and dark inside, a welcome relief from the hot, bright street, and it was filled with exotic odors. It seemed to Jamie that every inch of space was crammed with merchandise. He walked through the store, marveling. There were agricultural implements, beer, cans of milk and crocks of butter, cement, fuses and dynamite and gunpowder, crockery, furniture, guns and haberdashery, oil and paint and varnish, bacon and dried fruit, saddlery and harness, sheep-dip and soap, spirits and stationery and paper, sugar and tea and tobacco and snuff and cigars . . . A dozen shelves were filled from top to bottom with flannel shirts and blankets, shoes, poke bonnets and saddles. *Whoever owns all this,* Jamie thought, *is a rich man.*

A soft voice behind him said, "Can I help you?"

Jamie turned and found himself facing a young girl. He judged she was about fifteen. She had an interesting face, fine-boned and heart-shaped, like a valentine, a pert nose and intense green eyes. Her hair was dark and curling. Jamie, looking at her figure, decided she might be closer to sixteen.

"I'm a prospector," Jamie announced. "I'm here to buy some equipment."

"What is it you need?"

For some reason, Jamie felt he had to impress this girl. "I—er—you know—the usual."

She smiled, and there was mischief in her eyes. "What is the usual, sir?"

"Well . . ." He hesitated. "A shovel."

"Will that be all?"

Jamie saw that she was teasing him. He grinned and confessed, "To tell you the truth, I'm new at this. I don't know what I need."

She smiled at him, and it was the smile of a woman. "It depends on where you're planning to prospect, Mr. ——?"

"McGregor. Jamie McGregor."

"I'm Margaret van der Merwe." She glanced nervously toward the rear of the store.

"I'm pleased to meet you, Miss van der Merwe."

"Did you just arrive?"

"Aye. Yesterday. On the post cart."

"Someone should have warned you about that. Passengers have died on that trip." There was anger in her eyes.

Jamie grinned. "I can't blame them. But I'm very much alive, thank you."

"And going out to hunt for *mooi klippe.*"

"*Mooi klippe?*"

"That's our Dutch word for diamonds. Pretty pebbles."

"You're Dutch?"

"My family's from Holland."

"I'm from Scotland."

"I could tell that." Her eyes flicked warily toward the back of the store again. "There are diamonds around, Mr. McGregor, but you must be choosy where you look for them. Most of the diggers are running around chasing their own tails. When someone makes a strike, the rest scavenge off the leavings. If you want to get rich, you have to find a strike of your own."

"How do I do that?"

"My father might be the one to help you with that. He knows everything. He'll be free in an hour."

"I'll be back," Jamie assured her. "Thank you, Miss van der Merwe."

He went out into the sunshine, filled with a sense of euphoria, his aches and pains forgotten. If Salomon van der Merwe would advise him where to find diamonds, there was no way Jamie could fail. He would have the jump on all of them. He laughed aloud, with the sheer joy of being young and alive and on his way to riches.

Jamie walked down the main street, passing a blacksmith's, a billiard hall and half a dozen saloons. He came to a sign in front of a decrepit-looking hotel and stopped. The sign read:

> R-D MILLER, WARM AND COLD BATHS.
> OPEN DAILY FROM 6 A.M. TO 8 P.M.,
> WITH THE COMFORTS OF A NEAT
> DRESSING ROOM

Jamie thought, *When did I have my last bath? Well, I took a bucket bath on the boat. That was—* He was suddenly aware of how he must smell. He thought of the weekly tub baths in the kitchen at home, and he could hear his mother's voice calling, "Be sure to wash down below, Jamie."

He turned and entered the baths. There were two doors inside, one for women and one for men. Jamie entered the men's section and walked up to the aged attendant. "How much is a bath?"

"Ten shillings for a cold bath, fifteen for a hot."

Jamie hesitated. The idea of a hot bath after his long journey was almost irresistible. "Cold," he said. He could not afford to throw away his money on luxuries. He had mining equipment to buy.

The attendant handed him a small bar of yellow lye soap and a threadbare hand towel and pointed. "In there, mate."

Jamie stepped into a small room that contained nothing except a large galvanized-iron bathtub in the center and a few pegs on the wall. The attendant began filling the tub from a large wooden bucket.

"All ready for you, mister. Just hang your clothes on those pegs."

Jamie waited until the attendant left and then undressed. He looked down at his grime-covered body and put one foot in the tub. The water was cold, as advertised. He gritted his teeth and plunged in, soaping himself furiously from head to foot. When he finally stepped out of the tub, the water was black. He dried himself as best he could with the worn linen towel and started to get dressed. His pants and shirt were stiff with dirt, and he hated to put them back on. He would have to buy a change of clothes, and this reminded him once more of how little money he had. And he was hungry again.

Jamie left the bathhouse and pushed his way down the crowded street to a saloon called the Sundowner. He ordered a beer and lunch. Lamb cutlets with tomatoes, and sausage and potato salad and pickles. While he ate, he listened to the hopeful conversations around him.

"... I hear they found a stone near Colesberg weighin' twenty-one carats. Mark you, if there's *one* diamond up there, there's plenty more. ..."

"... There's a new diamond find up in Hebron. I'm thinkin' of goin' there. ..."

"You're a fool. The big diamonds are in the Orange River. . . ."

At the bar, a bearded customer in a collarless, striped-flannel shirt and corduroy trousers was nursing a shandygaff in a large glass. "I got cleaned out in Hebron," he confided to the bartender. "I need me a grubstake."

The bartender was a large, fleshy, bald-headed man with a broken, twisted nose and ferret eyes. He laughed. "Hell, man, who doesn't? Why do you think I'm tendin' bar? As soon as I have enough money, I'm gonna hightail it up the Orange myself." He wiped the bar with a dirty rag. "But I'll tell you what you might do, mister. See Salomon van der Merwe. He owns the general store and half the town."

"What good'll that do me?"

"If he likes you, he might stake you."

The customer looked at him. "Yeah? You really think he might?"

"He's done it for a few fellows I know of. You put up your labor, he puts up the money. You split fifty-fifty."

Jamie McGregor's thoughts leaped ahead. He had been confident that the hundred and twenty pounds he had left would be enough to buy the equipment and food he would need to survive, but the prices in Klipdrift were astonishing. He had noticed in Van der Merwe's store that a hundred-pound sack of Australian flour cost five pounds. One pound of sugar cost a shilling. A bottle of beer cost five shillings. Biscuits were three shillings a pound, and fresh eggs sold for seven shillings a dozen. At that rate, his money would not last long. *My God,* Jamie thought, *at home we could live for a year on what three meals cost here.* But if he could get the backing of someone wealthy, like Mr. van der Merwe . . . Jamie hastily paid for his food and hurried back to the general store.

Salomon van der Merwe was behind the counter, removing the rifles from a wooden crate. He was a small man, with a thin, pinched face framed by Dundreary whiskers. He had sandy hair, tiny black eyes, a bulbous nose and pursed lips. *His daughter must take after her mother,* Jamie thought. "Excuse me, sir . . ."

Van der Merwe looked up. *"Ja?"*

"Mr. van der Merwe? My name is Jamie McGregor, sir. I'm from Scotland. I came here to find diamonds."

"Ja? So?"

"I hear you sometimes back prospectors."

Van der Merwe grumbled, *"Myn magtig!* Who spreads these stories? I help out a few diggers, and everyone thinks I'm Santa Claus."

"I've saved a hundred and twenty pounds," Jamie said earnestly. "But I see that it's not going to buy me much here. I'll go out to the bush with just a shovel if I have to, but I figure my chances would be a lot better if I had a mule and some proper equipment."

Van der Merwe was studying him with those small, black eyes. *"Wat denk ye?* What makes you think *you* can find diamonds?"

"I've come halfway around the world, Mr. van der Merwe, and I'm not going to leave here until I'm rich. If the diamonds are out there, I'll find them. If you help me, I'll make us both rich."

Van der Merwe grunted, turned his back on Jamie and continued unloading the rifles. Jamie stood there awkwardly, not knowing what more to say. When Van der Merwe spoke again, his question caught Jamie off guard. "You travel here by bullock wagon, *ja?"*

"No. Post cart."

The old man turned to study the boy again. He said, finally, "We talk about it."

They talked about it at dinner that evening in the room in back of the store that was the Van der Merwe living quarters. It was a small room that served as a kitchen, dining room and sleeping quarters, with a curtain separating two cots. The lower half of the walls was built of mud and stone, and the upper half was faced with cardboard boxes that had once contained provisions. A square hole, where a piece of wall had been cut out, served as a window. In wet weather it could be closed by placing a board in front of it. The dining table consisted of a long plank stretched across two wooden crates. A large box, turned on its side, served as a cupboard. Jamie guessed that Van der Merwe was not a man who parted easily with his money.

Van der Meerwe's daughter moved silently about, preparing dinner. From time to time she cast quick glances at her father, but she never once looked at Jamie. *Why is she so frightened?* Jamie wondered.

When they were seated at the table, Van der Merwe began,. "Let us have a blessing. We thank Thee, O Lord, for the bounty we receive at Thy hands. We thank Thee for forgiving us our sins and showing us the path of righteousness and delivering us from life's temptations. We thank Thee for a long and fruitful life, and for smiting dead all those who offend Thee. Amen." And without a breath between, "Pass me the meat," he said to his daughter.

The dinner was frugal: a small roast pork, three boiled potatoes and a dish of turnip greens. The portions he served to Jamie were small. The two men talked little during the meal, and Margaret did not speak at all.

When they had finished eating, Van der Merwe said, "That was fine, Daughter," and there was pride in his voice. He turned to Jamie. "We get down to business, *ja?*"

"Yes, sir."

Van der Merwe picked up a long clay pipe from the top of the wooden cabinet. He filled it with a sweet-smelling tobacco from a small pouch and lighted the pipe. His sharp eyes peered intently at Jamie through the wreaths of smoke.

"The diggers here at Klipdrift are fools. Too few diamonds, too many diggers. A man could break his back here for a year and have nothing to show for it but *schlenters.*"

"I—I'm afraid I'm not familiar with that word, sir."

"Fools' diamonds. Worthless. Do you follow me?"

"I— Yes, sir. I think so. But what's the answer, sir?"

"The Griquas."

Jamie looked at him blankly.

"They're an African tribe up north. *They* find diamonds—big ones—and sometimes they bring them to me and I trade them for goods." The Dutchman lowered his voice to a conspiratorial whisper. "I know where they find them."

"But could you nae go after them yourself, Mr. van der Merwe?"

Van der Merwe sighed. "No. I can't leave the store. People would steal me blind. I need someone I can trust to go up there and bring the stones back. When I find the right man, I'll supply him with all the equipment he needs." He paused to take a long drag on the pipe. "And I'll tell him where the diamonds are."

Jamie leaped to his feet, his heart pounding. "Mr. van der Merwe, *I'm* the person you're looking for. Believe me, sir, I'll work night and day." His voice was charged with excitement. "I'll bring you back more diamonds than you can count."

Van der Merwe silently studied him for what seemed to Jamie to be an eternity. When Van der Merwe finally spoke, he said only one word. *"Ja."*

Jamie signed the contract the following morning. It was written in Afrikaans.

"I'll have to explain it to you," Van der Merwe said. "It says we're full partners. I put up the capital—you put up the labor. We share everything equally."

Jamie looked at the contract in Van der Merwe's hand. In the middle of all the incomprehensible foreign words he recognized only a sum: *two pounds*.

Jamie pointed to it. "What is that for, Mr. van der Merwe?"

"It means that in addition to your owning half the diamonds you find, you'll get an extra two pounds for every week you work. Even though I know the diamonds are out there, it's possible you might not find anything, lad. This way you'll at least get something for your labor."

The man was being more than fair. "Thank you. Thank you very much, sir." Jamie could have hugged him.

Van der Merwe said, "Now let's get you outfitted."

* * *

It took two hours to select the equipment that Jamie would take into the bush with him: a small tent, bedding, cooking utensils, two sieves and a washing cradle, a pick, two shovels, three buckets and one change of socks and underwear. There was an ax and a lantern and paraffin oil, matches and arsenical soap. There were tins of food, biltong, fruit, sugar, coffee and salt. At last everything was in readiness. The black servant, Banda, silently helped Jamie stow everything into backpacks. The huge man never glanced at Jamie and never spoke one word. *He doesn't speak English,* Jamie decided. Margaret was in the store waiting on customers, but if she knew Jamie was there, she gave no indication.

Van der Merwe came over to Jamie. "Your mule's in front," he said. "Banda will help you load up."

"Thank you, Mr. van der Merwe," Jamie said. "I—"

Van der Merwe consulted a piece of paper covered with figures. "That will be one hundred and twenty pounds."

Jamie looked at him blankly. "W—what? This is part of our deal. We—"

"Wat bedui'di?" Van der Merwe's thin face darkened with anger. "You expect me to *give* you all this, and a fine mule, and make you a partner, and give you two pounds a week on top of *that?* If you're looking for something for nothing, you've come to the wrong place." He began to unload one of the backpacks.

Jamie said quickly, "No! Please, Mr. van der Merwe. I—I just didn't understand. It's pefectly all right. I have the money right here." He reached in his pouch and put the last of his savings on the counter.

Van der Merwe hesitated. "All right," he said grudgingly. "Perhaps it was a misunderstanding, neh? This town is full of cheaters. I have to be careful who I do business with."

"Yes, sir. Of course you do," Jamie agreed. In his excitement, he had misunderstood the deal. *I'm lucky he's giving me another chance,* Jamie thought.

Van der Merwe reached into his pocket and pulled out a small, wrinkled, hand-drawn map. "Here is where you'll find the *mooi klippe*. North of here at Magerdam on the northern bank of the Vaal."

Jamie studied the map, and his heart began to beat faster. "How many miles is it?"

"Here we measure distance by time. With the mule, you should make the journey in four or five days. Coming back will be slower because of the weight of the diamonds."

Jamie grinned. *"Ja."*

When Jamie McGregor stepped back out onto the streets of Klipdrift, he was no longer a tourist. He was a prospector, a digger, on his way to his fortune. Banda had finished loading the supplies onto the back of a frail-looking mule tethered to the hitching post in front of the store.

"Thanks." Jamie smiled.

Banda turned and looked him in the eye, then silently walked away. Jamie unhitched the reins and said to the mule, "Let's go, partner. It's *mooi klippe* time."

They headed north.

Jamie pitched camp near a stream at nightfall, unloaded and watered and fed the mule, and fixed himself some beef jerky, dried apricots and coffee. The night was filled with strange noises. He heard the grunts and howls and padding of wild animals moving down to the water. He was unprotected, surrounded by the most dangerous beasts in the world, in a strange, primitive country. He jumped at every sound. At any moment he expected to be attacked by fangs and claws leaping at him from out of the darkness. His mind began to drift. He thought of his snug bed at home and the comfort and safety he had always taken for granted. He slept fitfully, his dreams filled with charging lions and elephants, and large, bearded men trying to take an enormous diamond away from him.

At dawn when Jamie awakened, the mule was dead.

2

He could not believe it. He looked for a wound of some kind, thinking it must have been attacked by a wild animal during the night, but there was nothing. The beast had died in its sleep. *Mr. van der Merwe will hold me responsible for this,* Jamie thought. *But when I bring him diamonds, it won't matter.*

There was no turning back. He would go on to Magerdam without the mule. He heard a sound in the air and looked up. Giant black vultures were beginning to circle high above. Jamie shuddered. Working as quickly as possible, he rearranged his gear, deciding what he had to leave behind, then stowed everything he could carry into a backpack and started off. When he looked back five minutes later, the enormous vultures had covered the body of the dead animal. All that was visible was one long ear. Jamie quickened his step.

It was December, summer in South Africa, and the trek across the veld under the huge orange sun was a horror. Jamie had started out from Klipdrift with a brisk step and a light heart, but as the minutes turned into hours and the hours into days, his steps got slower and his heart became heavier. As far as the eye could see, the monotonous veld shimmered flat and forbidding under the blazing sun and there seemed no end to the gray, stony, desolate plains.

Jamie made camp whenever he came to a watering hole, and he slept with the eerie, nocturnal sounds of the animals all around him. The sounds no longer bothered him. They were proof that there was life in this barren hell, and they made him feel less lonely. One dawn Jamie came across a pride of lions. He watched from a distance as the lioness moved toward her mate and their cubs, carrying a baby impala in her powerful jaws. She dropped the animal in front of the male and moved away while he fed. A reckless cub leaped forward and dug his teeth into the impala. With one motion, the male raised a paw and swiped the cub across the face, killing it instantly, then went back to his feeding. When he finished, the rest of the family was permitted to move in for the remains of the feast. Jamie slowly backed away from the scene and continued walking.

It took him almost two weeks to cross the Karroo. More than once he was ready to give up. He was not sure he could finish the journey. *I'm a fool. I should have returned to Klipdrift to ask Mr van der Merwe for another mule. But what if Van der Merwe had called off the deal? No, I did the right thing.*

And so, Jamie kept moving, one step at a time. One day, he saw four figures in the distance, coming toward him. *I'm delirious,* Jamie thought. *It's a mirage.* But the figures came closer, and Jamie's heart began to thud alarmingly. *Men! There is human life here!* He wondered if he had forgotten how to speak. He tried out his voice on the afternoon air, and it sounded as if it belonged to someone long dead. The four men reached him, prospectors returning to Klipdrift, tired and defeated.

"Hello," Jamie said.

They nodded. One of them said, "There ain't nothin' ahead, boy. We looked. You're wastin' your time. Go back."

And they were gone.

Jamie shut his mind to everything but the trackless waste ahead of him. The sun and the black flies were unbearable and there was no place to hide. There were thorn trees, but their

branches had been laid waste by the elephants. Jamie was almost totally blinded by the sun. His fair skin was burned raw,
and he was constantly dizzy. Each time he took a breath of air,
his lungs seemed to explode. He was no longer walking, he was
stumbling, putting one foot in front of the other, mindlessly
lurching ahead. One afternoon, with the midday sun beating
down on him, he slipped off his backpack and slumped to the
ground, too tired to take another step. He closed his eyes and
dreamed he was in a giant crucible and the sun was a huge,
bright diamond blazing down on him, melting him. He awoke in
the middle of the night trembling from the cold. He forced himself to take a few bites of biltong and a drink of tepid water. He
knew he must get up and start moving before the sun rose, while
the earth and sky were cool. He tried, but the effort was too
great. It would be so easy just to lie there forever and never have
to take another step. *I'll just sleep for a little while longer,* Jamie
thought. But some voice deep within him told him he would
never wake up again. They would find his body there as they
had found hundreds of others. He remembered the vultures and
thought, *No, not my body—my bones.* Slowly and painfully, he
forced himself to his feet. His backpack was so heavy he could
not lift it. Jamie started walking again, dragging the pack behind him. He had no recollection of how many times he fell onto
the sand and staggered to his feet again. Once he screamed
into the predawn sky, "I'm Jamie McGregor, and I'm going to
make it. I'm going to live. Do you hear me, God? I'm going to
live. . . ." Voices were exploding in his head.

*You're goin' chasin' diamonds? You must be daft, son. That's a
fairy tale—a temptation of the devil to keep men from doin' an
honest day's work.*

*Why do you nae tell us where you're gettin' the money to go? It's
halfway 'round the world. You hae no money.*

*Mr. van der Merwe, I'm the person you're looking for. Believe
me, sir, I'll work night and day. I'll bring you back more diamonds
than you can count.*

And he was finished before he had even started. *You have two choices,* Jamie told himself. *You can go on or you can stay here and die . . . and die . . . and die . . .*

The words echoed endlessly in his head. *You can take one more step,* Jamie thought. *Come on, Jamie boy. One more step. One more step . . .*

Two days later Jamie McGregor stumbled into the village of Magerdam. The sunburn had long since become infected and his body oozed blood and sera. Both eyes were swollen almost completely shut. He collapsed in the middle of the street, a pile of crumpled clothes holding him together. When sympathetic diggers tried to relieve him of his backpack, Jamie fought them with what little strength he had left, raving deliriously. "No! Get away from my diamonds. Get away from my diamonds. . . ."

He awakened in a small, bare room three days later, naked except for the bandages that covered his body. The first thing he saw when he opened his eyes was a buxom, middle-aged woman seated at the side of his cot.

"Wh—?" His voice was a croak. He could not get the words out.

"Easy, dear. You've been sick." She gently lifted his swathed head and gave him a sip of water from a tin cup.

Jamie managed to prop himself up on one elbow. "Where—?" He swallowed and tried again. "Where am I?"

"You're in Magerdam. I'm Alice Jardine. This is my boarding house. You're going to be fine. You just need a good rest. Now lie back."

Jamie remembered the strangers who tried to take his backpack away, and he was filled with panic. "My things, where—?" He tried to rise from the cot, but the woman's gentle voice stopped him.

"Everything's safe. Not to worry, son." She pointed to his backpack in a corner of the room.

Jamie lay back on the clean white sheets. *I got here. I made it. Everything is going to be all right now.*

Alice Jardine was a blessing, not only to Jamie McGregor, but to half of Magerdam. In that mining town filled with adventurers, all sharing the same dream, she fed them, nursed them, encouraged them. She was an Englishwoman who had come to South Africa with her husband, when he decided to give up his teaching job in Leeds and join the diamond rush. He had died of fever three weeks after they arrived, but she had decided to stay on. The miners had become the children she never had.

She kept Jamie in bed for four more days, feeding him, changing his bandages and helping him regain his strength. By the fifth day, Jamie was ready to get up.

"I want you to know how grateful I am to you, Mrs. Jardine. I can't pay you anything. Not yet. But you'll have a big diamond from me one day soon. That's a promise from Jamie Mc-Gregor."

She smiled at the intensity of the handsome young boy. He was still twenty pounds too thin, and his gray eyes were filled with the horror he had been through, but there was a strength about him, a determination that was awesome. *He's different from the others,* Mrs. Jardine thought.

Jamie, dressed in his freshly washed clothes, went out to explore the town. It was Klipdrift on a smaller scale. There were the same tents and wagons and dusty streets, the flimsily built shops and the crowds of prospectors. As Jamie passed a saloon, he heard a roar from inside and entered. A noisy crowd had gathered around a red-shirted Irishman.

"What's going on?" Jamie asked.

"He's going to wet his find."

"He's what?"

"He struck it rich today, so he stands treat for the whole saloon. He pays for as much liquor as a saloon-full of thirsty men can swallow."

Jamie joined in a conversation with several disgruntled diggers sitting at a round table.

"Where you from, McGregor?"

"Scotland."

"Well, I don't know what horseshit they fed you in Scotland, but there ain't enough diamonds in this fuckin' country to pay expenses."

They talked of other camps: Gong Gong, Forlorn Hope, Delports, Poormans Kopje, Sixpenny Rush . . .

The diggers all told the same story—of months doing the backbreaking work of moving boulders, digging into the hard soil and squatting over the riverbank sifting the dirt for diamonds. Each day a few diamonds were found; not enough to make a man rich, but enough to keep his dreams alive. The mood of the town was a strange mixture of optimism and pessimism. The optimists were arriving; the pessimists were leaving.

Jamie knew which side he was on.

He approached the red-shirted Irishman, now bleary-eyed with drink, and showed him Van der Merwe's map.

The man glanced at it and tossed it back to Jamie. "Worthless. That whole area's been picked over. If I was you, I'd try Bad Hope."

Jamie could not believe it. Van der Merwe's map was what had brought him there, the lodestar that was going to make him rich.

Another digger said, "Head for Colesberg. That's where they're findin' diamonds, son."

"Gilfillans Kop—*that's* the place to dig."

"You'll try Moonlight Rush, if you want my opinion."

At supper that night, Alice Jardine said, "Jamie, one place is as big a gamble as another. Pick your own spot, dig in your pickax and pray. That's all these other *experts* are doing."

After a night of sleepless self-debate, Jamie decided he would forget Van der Merwe's map. Against everyone's advice, he decided to head east, along the Modder River. The following morning Jamie said good-bye to Mrs. Jardine and set off.

He walked for three days and two nights, and when he came to a likely-looking spot, he set up his small tent. Huge boulders lay along both sides of the riverbank, and Jamie, using thick branches as levers, laboriously moved them out of the way to get at the gravel that lay beneath.

He dug from dawn until dusk, looking for the yellow clay or the blue diamondiferous soil that would tell him he had found a diamond pipe. But the earth was barren. He dug for a week without finding a single stone. At the end of the week, he moved on.

One day as he walked along, he saw in the distance what looked like a silver house, glowing dazzlingly in the sun. *I'm going blind,* Jamie thought. But as he got closer, he saw that he was approaching a village, and all the houses seemed to be made of silver. Crowds of Indian men, women and children dressed in rags swarmed through the streets. Jamie stared in amazement. The silver houses glistening in the sun were made of tin jam pots, flattened out, fastened together and nailed over the crude shacks. He walked on, and an hour later, when he looked back, he could still see the glow of the village. It was a sight he never forgot.

Jamie kept moving north. He followed the riverbank where the diamonds might be, digging until his arms refused to lift the heavy pick, then sifting the wet gravel through the hand sieve. When it got dark, he slept as though drugged.

At the end of the second week, he moved upstream again, just north of a small settlement called Paardspan. He stopped near a bend in the river and fixed himself a meal of carbonaatje, grilled on a spit over a wood fire, and hot tea, then sat in front of his tent, looking up at the wheeling stars in the vast sky. He had not seen a human being in two weeks, and an eddy of loneliness washed over him. *What the hell am I doing here?* he wondered. *Sitting in the middle of a blasted wilderness like a bloody fool, killing myself breaking rocks and digging up dirt? I was better off at the farm. Come Saturday, if I don't find a diamond, I'm going home.* He looked up at the uncaring stars and yelled, "Do you hear me, damn you?" *Oh, Jesus,* he thought, *I'm losing my mind.*

Jamie sat there, idly sifting the sand through his fingers. They closed on a large stone, and he looked at it a moment, then threw it away. He had seen a thousand worthless stones like it in the past weeks. What was it Van der Merwe had called them? *Schlenters.* Yet, there was something about this one that belatedly caught Jamie's attention. He rose, went over to it and picked it up. It was much larger than the other stones and of an odd shape. He rubbed some of the dirt off it against the leg of his trousers and examined it more closely. It *looked* like a diamond. The only thing that made Jamie doubt his senses was the size of it. It was almost as large as a hen's egg. *Oh, God. If it is a diamond . . .* He suddenly had difficulty breathing. He grabbed his lantern and began searching the ground around him. In fifteen minutes he had found four more like it. None of them was as large as the first one, but they were large enough to fill him with a wild excitement.

He was up before dawn, digging like a madman, and by noon he had found half a dozen more diamonds. He spent the next week feverishly digging up diamonds and burying them at night in a safe place where no passers-by could find them. There were fresh diamonds every day, and as Jamie watched his fortune pile up, he was filled with an ineffable joy. Only half of this treasure was his, but it was enough to make him rich beyond anything he had ever dared to dream.

At the end of the week, Jamie made a note on his map and staked out his claim by carefully marking the boundaries with his pick. He dug up his hidden treasure, carefully stored it deep down in his backpack and headed back to Magerdam.

The sign outside the small building read: DIAMANT KOOPER.

Jamie walked into the office, a small, airless room, and he was filled with a sudden sense of trepidation. He had heard dozens of stories of prospectors who had found diamonds that had turned out to be worthless stones. *What if I'm wrong? What if—?*

The assayer was seated at a cluttered desk in the tiny office. "Somethin' I can do for you?"

Jamie took a deep breath. "Yes, sir. I would like to have these valued, please."

Under the watchful eye of the assayer, Jamie started laying the stones on his desk. When he was finished, there was a total of twenty-seven, and the assayer was gazing at them in astonishment.

"Where—where did you find these?"

"I'll tell you after you tell me whether they're diamonds."

The assayer picked up the largest stone and examined it with a jeweler's loupe. "My God!" he said. "This is the biggest diamond I've ever seen!" And Jamie realized he had been holding his breath. He could have yelled aloud with joy. "Where—" the man begged, "where did these come from?"

"Meet me in the canteen in fifteen minutes," Jamie grinned, "and I'll tell you."

Jamie gathered up the diamonds, put them in his pockets and strode out. He headed for the registration office two doors down the street. "I want to register a claim," he said. "In the names of Salomon van der Merwe and Jamie McGregor."

He had walked through that door a penniless farm boy and walked out a multimillionaire.

The assayer was in the canteen waiting when Jamie McGregor entered. He had obviously spread the news, because when Jamie walked in there was a sudden, respectful hush. There was a single unspoken question on everyone's mind. Jamie walked up to the bar and said to the bartender, "I'm here to wet my find." He turned and faced the crowd. "Paardspan."

Alice Jardine was having a cup of tea when Jamie walked into the kitchen. Her face lighted up when she saw him. "Jamie! Oh, thank God you're back safely!" She took in his disheveled appearance and flushed face. "It didn't go well, did it? Never you mind. Have a nice cup of tea with me, dear, and you'll feel better."

Without a word, Jamie reached into his pocket and pulled out a large diamond. He placed it in Mrs. Jardine's hand.

"I've kept my promise," Jamie said.

She stared at the stone for a long time, and her blue eyes became moist. "No, Jamie. No." Her voice was very soft. "I don't want it. Don't you see, child? It would spoil everything. . . ."

When Jamie McGregor returned to Klipdrift, he did it in style. He traded one of his smaller diamonds for a horse and carriage, and made a careful note of what he had spent, so that his partner would not be cheated. The trip back to Klipdrift was easy and comfortable, and when Jamie thought of the hell he had gone through on this same journey, he was filled with a sense of wonder. *That's the difference between the rich and the poor,* he thought. *The poor walk; the rich ride in carriages.*

He gave the horse a small flick of the whip and rode on contentedly through the darkening veld.

3

Klipdrift had not changed, but Jamie McGregor had. People stared as he rode into town and stopped in front of Van der Merwe's general store. It was not just the expensive horse and carriage that drew the attention of the passers-by; it was the air of jubilation about the young man. They had seen it before in other prospectors who had struck it rich, and it always filled them with a renewed sense of hope for themselves. They stood back and watched as Jamie jumped out of the carriage.

The same large black man was there. Jamie grinned at him. "Hello! I'm back."

Banda tied the reins to a hitching post without comment and went inside the store. Jamie followed him.

Salomon van der Merwe was waiting on a customer. The little Dutchman looked up and smiled, and Jamie knew that somehow Van der Merwe had already heard the news. No one could explain it, but news of a diamond strike flashed across the continent with the speed of light.

When Van der Merwe had finished with the customer, he nodded his head toward the back of the store. "Come, Mr. McGregor."

Jamie followed him. Van der Merwe's daughter was at the stove, preparing lunch. "Hello, Margaret."

She flushed and looked away.

"Well! I hear there is good news." Van der Merwe beamed. He seated himself at the table and pushed the plate and silverware away, clearing a place in front of him.

"That's right, sir." Proudly, Jamie took a large leather pouch from his jacket pocket and poured the diamonds on the kitchen table. Van der Merwe stared at them, hypnotized, then picked them up slowly, one by one, savoring each one, saving the largest until last. Then he scooped up the diamonds, put them in a chamois bag and put the bag in a large iron safe in the corner and locked it.

When he spoke, there was a note of deep satisfaction in his voice. "You've done well, Mr. McGregor. Very well, indeed."

"Thank you, sir. This is only the beginning. There are hundreds more there. I don't even dare think about how much they're worth."

"And you've staked out the claim properly?"

"Yes, sir." Jamie reached in his pocket and pulled out the registration slip. "It's registered in both our names."

Van der Merwe studied the slip, then put it in his pocket. "You deserve a bonus. Wait here." He started toward the doorway that led into the shop. "Come along, Margaret."

She followed him meekly, and Jamie thought, *She's like a frightened kitten.*

A few mintues later, Van der Merwe returned, alone. "Here we are." He opened a purse and carefully counted out fifty pounds.

Jamie looked at him, puzzled. "What's this for, sir?"

"For you, son. All of it."

"I—I don't understand."

"You've been gone twenty-four weeks. At two pounds a week, that's forty-eight pounds, and I'm giving you an extra two pounds as a bonus."

Jamie laughed. "I don't need a bonus. I have my share of the diamonds."

"Your share of the diamonds?"

"Why, yes, sir. My fifty percent. We're partners."

Van der Merwe was staring at him. "Partners? Where did you get that idea?"

"Where did I—?" Jamie looked at the Dutchman in bewilderment. "We have a contract."

"That is correct. Have you read it?"

"Well, no, sir. It's in Afrikaans, but you said we were fifty-fifty partners."

The older man shook his head. "You misunderstood me, Mr. McGregor. I don't need any partners. You were working for me. I outfitted you and sent you to find diamonds for me."

Jamie could feel a slow rage boiling up within him. "You gave me nothing. I paid you a hundred and twenty pounds for that equipment."

The old man shrugged. "I won't waste my valuable time quibbling. Tell you what I'll do. I'll give you an extra five pounds, and we'll call the whole thing quits. I think that's very generous.

Jamie exploded in a fury. "We'll nae call the whole thing quits!" In his anger his Scottish burr came back. "I'm entitled to half that claim. And I'll get it. I registered it in *both* our names."

Van der Merwe smiled thinly. "Then you tried to cheat me. I could have you arrested for that." He shoved the money into Jamie's hand. "Now take your wages and get out."

"I'll fight you!"

"Do you have money for a lawyer? I own them all in these parts, boy."

This isn't happening to me, Jamie thought. *It's a nightmare.* The agony he had gone through, the weeks and months of the burning desert, the punishing physical labor from sunrise to sunset—it all came flooding back. He had nearly died, and now this man was trying to cheat him out of what was his.

He looked Van der Merwe in the eye. "I'll not let you get away with this. I'm not going to leave Klipdrift. I'll tell everybody here what you've done. I'm going to get my share of those diamonds."

Van der Merwe started to turn away from the fury in the pale-gray eyes. "You'd better find a doctor, boy," he muttered. "I think the sun has addled your wits."

In a second, Jamie was towering over Van der Merwe. He pulled the thin figure into the air and held him up to eye level. "I'm going to make you sorry you ever laid eyes on me." He dropped Van der Merwe to his feet, flung the money on the table and stormed out.

When Jamie McGregor walked into the Sundowner Saloon, it was almost deserted, for most of the prospectors were on their way to Paardspan. Jamie was filled with anger and despair. *It's incredible,* he thought. *One minute I'm as rich as Croesus, and the next minute I'm dead broke. Van der Merwe is a thief, and I'm going to find a way to punish him. But how?* Van der Merwe was right. Jamie could not even afford a lawyer to fight his case. He was a stranger there, and Van der Merwe was a respected member of the community. The only weapon Jamie had was the truth. He would let everyone in South Africa know what Van der Merwe had done.

Smit, the bartender, greeted him. "Welcome back. Everything's on the house, Mr. McGregor. What would you like?"

"A whiskey."

Smit poured a double and set it in front of Jamie. Jamie downed it in one gulp. He was not used to drinking, and the hard liquor scorched his throat and stomach.

"Another, please."

"Comin' up. I've always said the Scots could drink anybody under the table."

The second drink went down easier. Jamie remembered that it was the bartender who had told a digger to go to Van der Merwe for help. "Did you know Old Man Van der Merwe is a crook? He's trying to cheat me out of my diamonds."

Smit was sympathetic. "What? That's terrible. I'm sorry to hear that."

"He'll nae get away with it." Jamie's voice was slurred. "Half those diamonds are mine. He's a thief, and I'm gonna see that everybody knows it."

"Careful. Van der Merwe's an important man in this town," the bartender warned. "If you're goin' up against him, you'll need help. In fact, I know just the person. He hates Van der Merwe as much as you do." He looked around to make sure no one could overhear him. "There's an old barn at the end of the street. I'll arrange everything. Be there at ten o'clock tonight."

"Thanks," Jamie said gratefully. "I won't forget you."

"Ten o'clock. The old barn."

The barn was a hastily thrown-together structure built of corrugated tin, off the main street at the edge of town. At ten o'clock Jamie arrived there. It was dark, and he felt his way carefully. He could see no one around. He stepped inside. "Hello . . ."

There was no reply. Jamie went slowly forward. He could make out the dim shapes of horses moving restlessly in their stalls. Then he heard a sound behind him, and as he started to turn, an iron bar crashed across his shoulder blades, knocking him to the ground. A club thudded against his head, and a giant hand picked him up and held him while fists and boots smashed into his body. The beating seemed to last forever. When the pain became too much to bear and he lost consciousness, cold water was thrown in his face. His eyes fluttered open. He thought he caught a glimpse of Van der Merwe's servant, Banda, and the beating began anew. Jamie could feel his ribs breaking. Something smashed into his leg, and he heard the crunch of bone.

That was when he lost consciousness again.

His body was on fire. Someone was scraping his face with sandpaper, and he vainly tried to lift a hand to protest. He made an effort to open his eyes, but they were swollen shut. Jamie lay there, every fiber of his being screaming with pain, as he tried to remember where he was. He shifted, and the scraping began again. He put out his hand blindly and felt sand. His raw face was lying in hot sand. Slowly, every move an agony, he managed to draw himself up on his knees. He tried to see through his swollen eyes, but he could make out only hazy images. He was somewhere in the middle of the trackless Karroo, naked. It was early morning, but he could feel the sun starting to burn through his body. He felt around blindly for food or a billy can of water. There was nothing. They had left him there for dead. *Salomon van der Merwe. And, of course, Smit, the bartender.* Jamie had threatened Van der Merwe, and Van der Merwe had punished him as easily as one punished a small child. *But he'll find out I'm no child,* Jamie promised himself. *Not anymore. I'm an avenger. They'll pay. They will pay.* The hatred that coursed through Jamie gave him the strength to sit up. It was a torture for him to breathe. How many ribs had they broken? *I must be careful so they don't puncture my lungs.* Jamie tried to stand up, but fell down with a scream. His right leg was broken and lay at an unnatural angle. He was unable to walk.

But he could crawl.

Jamie McGregor had no idea where he was. They would have taken him to some place off the beaten track, where his body would not be found except by the desert scavengers, the hyenas and secretary birds and vultures. The desert was a vast charnel house. He had seen the bones of men's bodies that had been scavenged, and there had not been a scrap of meat left on the skeleton. Even as Jamie was thinking about it, he heard the rustle of wings above him and the shrill hiss of the vultures. He felt a flood of terror. He was blind. He could not see them. But he could smell them.

He began to crawl.

He made himself concentrate on the pain. His body was aflame with it, and each small movement brought exquisite rivers of agony. If he moved in a certain way, his broken leg would send out stabbing pains. If he shifted his position slightly to favor his leg, he could feel his ribs grinding against each other. He could not stand the torture of lying still; he could not stand the agony of moving.

He kept crawling.

He could hear them circling above, waiting for him with an ancient, timeless patience. His mind started to wander. He was in the cool kirk at Aberdeen, neatly dressed in his Sunday suit, seated between his two brothers. His sister, Mary, and Annie Cord were wearing beautiful white summer dresses, and Annie Cord was looking at him and smiling. Jamie started to get up and go to her, and his brothers held him back and began to pinch him. The pinches became excruciating shafts of pain, and he was crawling through the desert again, naked, his body broken. The cries of the vultures were louder now, impatient.

Jamie tried to force his eyes open, to see how close they were. He could see nothing except vague, shimmering objects that his terrified imagination turned into feral hyenas and jackals. The wind became their hot, fetid breath caressing his face.

He kept crawling, for he knew that the moment he stopped they would be upon him. He was burning with fever and pain and his body was flayed by the hot sand. And still, he could not give up, not as long as Van der Merwe was unpunished—not as long as Van der Merwe was alive.

He lost all awareness of time. He guessed that he had traveled a mile. In truth, he had moved less than ten yards, crawling in a circle. He could not see where he had been or where he was going. He focused his mind on only one thing: Salomon van der Merwe.

He slipped into unconsciousness and was awakened by a shrieking agony beyond bearing. Someone was stabbing at his leg, and it took Jamie a second to remember where he was and what was happening. He pulled one swollen eye open. An enormous hooded black vulture was attacking his leg, savagely tearing at his flesh, eating him alive with its sharp beak. Jamie saw its beady eyes and the dirty ruff around its neck. He smelled the foul odor of the bird as it sat on his body. Jamie tried to scream, but no sound came out. Frantically he jerked himself forward, and felt the warm flow of blood pouring from his leg. He could see the shadows of the giant birds all around him, moving in for the kill. He knew that the next time he lost consciousness would be the last time. The instant he stopped, the carrion birds would be at his flesh again. He kept crawling. His mind began to wander into delirium. He heard the loud flapping wings of the birds as they moved closer, forming a circle around him. He was too weak now to fight them off; he had no strength left to resist. He stopped moving and lay still on the burning sand.

The giant birds closed in for their feast.

4

Saturday was market day in Cape Town and the streets were crowded with shoppers looking for bargains, meeting friends and lovers. Boers and Frenchmen, soldiers in colorful uniforms and English ladies in flounced skirts and ruffled blouses mingled in front of the bazaars set up in the town squares at Braameonstein and Park Town and Burgersdorp. Everything was for sale: furniture, horses and carriages and fresh fruit. One could purchase dresses and chessboards, or meat or books in a dozen different languages. On Saturdays, Cape Town was a noisy, bustling fair.

Banda walked along slowly through the crowd, careful not to make eye contact with the whites. It was too dangerous. The streets were filled with blacks, Indians and coloreds, but the white minority ruled. Banda hated them. This was his land, and the whites were the *uitlanders*. There were many tribes in southern Africa: the Basutos, Zulus, Bechuanas, the Matabele—all of them Bantu. The very word *bantu* came from *abantu—the people*. But the Barolongs—Banda's tribe—were the aristocracy. Banda remembered the tales his grandmother told him of the great black kingdom that had once ruled South Africa. *Their* kingdom, *their* country. And now they were enslaved by a handful of white jackals. The whites had pushed them into smaller and smaller territories, until their freedom had been eroded. Now, the only way a black could exist was by *slim,* subservient on the surface, but cunning and clever beneath.

Banda did not know how old he was, for natives had no birth certificates. Their ages were measured by tribal lore: wars and battles, and births and deaths of great chiefs, comets and blizzards and earthquakes, Adam Kok's trek, the death of Chaka and the cattle-killing revolution. But the number of his years made no difference. Banda knew he was the son of a chief, and that he was destined to do something for his people. Once again, the Bantus would rise and rule because of him. The thought of his mission made him walk taller and straighter for a moment, until he felt the eyes of a white man upon him.

Banda hurried east toward the outskirts of town, the district allotted to the blacks. The large homes and attractive shops gradually gave way to tin shacks and lean-tos and huts. He moved down a dirt street, looking over his shoulder to make certain he was not followed. He reached a wooden shack, took one last look around, rapped twice on the door and entered. A thin black woman was seated in a chair in a corner of the room sewing on a dress. Banda nodded to her and then continued on into the bedroom in back.

He looked down at the figure lying on the cot.

Six weeks earlier Jamie McGregor had regained consciousness and found himself on a cot in a strange house. Memory came flooding back. He was in the Karroo again, his body broken, helpless. The vultures . . .

Then Banda had walked into the tiny bedroom, and Jamie knew he had come to kill him. Van der Merwe had somehow learned Jamie was still alive and had sent his servant to finish him off.

"Why didn't your master come himself?" Jamie croaked.

"I have no master."

"Van der Merwe. He didn't send you?"

"No. He would kill us both if he knew."

None of this made any sense. "Where am I? I want to know where I am."

"Cape Town."

"That's impossible. How did I get here?"

"I brought you."

Jamie stared into the black eyes for a long moment before he spoke. "Why?"

"I need you. I want vengeance."

"What do you—?"

Banda moved closer. "Not for me. I do not care about me. Van der Merwe raped my sister. She died giving birth to his baby. My sister was eleven years old."

Jamie lay back, stunned. "My God!"

"Since the day she died I have been looking for a white man to help me. I found him that night in the barn where I helped beat you up, Mr. McGregor. We dumped you in the Karroo. I was ordered to kill you. I told the others you were dead, and I returned to get you as soon as I could. I was almost too late."

Jamie could not repress a shudder. He could feel again the foul-smelling carrion bird digging into his flesh.

"The birds were already starting to feast. I carried you to the wagon and hid you at the house of my people. One of our doctors taped your ribs and set your leg and tended to your wounds."

"And after that?"

"A wagonful of my relatives was leaving for Cape Town. We took you with us. You were out of your head most of the time. Each time you fell asleep, I was afraid you were not going to wake up again."

Jamie looked into the eyes of the man who had almost murdered him. He had to think. He did not trust this man—and yet he had saved his life. Banda wanted to get at Van der Merwe through him. *That can work both ways,* Jamie decided. More than anything in the world, Jamie wanted to make Van der Merwe pay for what he had done to him.

"All right," Jamie told Banda. "I'll find a way to pay Van der Merwe back for both of us."

For the first time, a thin smile appeared on Banda's face. "Is he going to die?"

"No," Jamie told him. "He's going to live."

Jamie got out of bed that afternoon for the first time, dizzy and weak. His leg still had not completely healed, and he walked with a slight limp. Banda tried to assist him.

"Let go of me. I can make it on my own."

Banda watched as Jamie carefully moved across the room.

"I'd like a mirror," Jamie said. *I must look terrible*, he thought. *How long has it been since I've had a shave?*

Banda returned with a hand mirror, and Jamie held it up to his face. He was looking at a total stranger. His hair had turned snow-white. He had a full, unkempt white beard. His nose had been broken and a ridge of bone pushed it to one side. His face had aged twenty years. There were deep ridges along his sunken cheeks and a livid scar across his chin. But the biggest change was in his eyes. They were eyes that had seen too much pain, felt too much, hated too much. He slowly put down the mirror.

"I'm going out for a walk," Jamie said.

"Sorry, Mr. McGregor. That's not possible."

"Why not?"

"White men do not come to this part of town, just as blacks never go into the white places. My neighbors do not know you are here. We brought you in at night."

"How do I leave?"

"I will move you out tonight."

For the first time, Jamie began to realize how much Banda had risked for him. Embarrassed, Jamie said, "I have no money. I need a job."

"I took a job at the shipyard. They are always looking for men." He took some money from his pocket. "Here."

Jamie took the money. "I'll pay it back."

"You will pay my sister back," Banda told him.

* * *

It was midnight when Banda led Jamie out of the shack. Jamie looked around. He was in the middle of a shantytown, a jungle of rusty, corrugated iron shacks and lean-tos, made from rotting planks and torn sacking. The ground, muddy from a recent rain, gave off a rank odor. Jamie wondered how people as proud as Banda could bear spending their lives in a place such as this. "Isn't there some—?"

"Don't talk, please," Banda whispered. "My neighbors are inquisitive." He led Jamie outside the compound and pointed. "The center of town is in that direction. I will see you at the shipyard."

Jamie checked into the same boardinghouse where he had stayed on his arrival from England. Mrs. Venster was behind the desk.

"I'd like a room," Jamie said.

"Certainly, sir." She smiled, revealing her gold tooth. "I'm Mrs. Venster."

"I know."

"Now how would you know a thing like that?" she asked coyly. "Have your men friends been tellin' tales out of school?"

"Mrs. Venster, don't you remember me? I stayed here last year."

She took a close look at his scarred face, his broken nose and his white beard, and there was not the slightest sign of recognition. "I never forget a face, dearie. And I've never seen yours before. But that don't mean we're not going to be good friends, does it? My friends call me 'Dee-Dee.' What's your name, love?"

And Jamie heard himself saying, "Travis. Ian Travis."

The following morning Jamie went to see about work at the shipyard.

The busy foreman said, "We need strong backs. The problem is you might be a bit old for this kind of work."

"I'm only nineteen—" Jamie started to say and stopped himself. He remembered that face in the mirror. "Try me," he said.

He went to work as a stevedore at nine shillings a day, loading and unloading the ships that came into the harbor. He learned that Banda and the other black stevedores received six shillings a day.

At the first opportunity, Jamie pulled Banda aside and said, "We have to talk."

"Not here, Mr. McGregor. There's an abandoned warehouse at the end of the docks. I'll meet you there when the shift is over."

Banda was waiting when Jamie arrived at the deserted warehouse.

"Tell me about Salomon van der Merwe," Jamie said.

"What do you want to know?"

"Everything."

Banda spat. "He came to South Africa from Holland. From stories I heard, his wife was ugly, but wealthy. She died of some sickness and Van der Merwe took her money and went up to Klipdrift and opened his general store. He got rich cheating diggers."

"The way he cheated me?"

"That's only one of his ways. Diggers who strike it lucky go to him for money to help them work their claim, and before they know it Van der Merwe owns them."

"Hasn't anyone ever tried to fight back?"

"How can they? The town clerk's on his payroll. The law says that if forty-five days go by without working a claim, it's open. The town clerk tips off Van der Merwe and he grabs it. There's another trick he uses. Claims have to be staked out at each boundary line with pegs pointing straight up in the air. If the pegs fall down, a jumper can claim the property. Well, when Van der Merwe sees a claim he likes, he sends someone around at night, and in the morning the stakes are on the ground."

"Jesus!"

"He's made a deal with the bartender, Smit. Smit sends likely-looking prospectors to Van der Merwe, and they sign partnership contracts and if they find diamonds, Van der Merwe takes everything for himself. If they become troublesome, he's got a lot of men on his payroll who follow his orders."

"I know about that," Jamie said grimly. "What else?"

"He's a religious fanatic. He's always praying for the souls of sinners."

"What about his daughter?" She had to be involved in this.

"Miss Margaret? She's frightened to death of her father. If she even looked at a man, Van der Merwe would kill them both."

Jamie turned his back and walked over to the door, where he stood looking out at the harbor. He had a lot to think about. "We'll talk again tomorrow."

It was in Cape Town that Jamie became aware of the enormous schism between the blacks and whites. The blacks had no rights except the few they were given by those in power. They were herded into conclaves that were ghettos and were allowed to leave only to work for the white man.

"How do you stand it?" Jamie asked Banda one day.

"The hungry lion hides its claws. We will change all this someday. The white man accepts the black man because his muscles are needed, but he must also learn to accept his brain. The more he drives us into a corner, the more he fears us because he knows that one day there may be discrimination and humiliation in reverse. He cannot bear the thought of that. But we will survive because of *isiko*."

"Who is *isiko*?"

Banda shook his head. "Not a *who*. A *what*. It is difficult to explain, Mr. McGregor. *Isiko* is our roots. It is the feeling of belonging to a nation that has given its name to the great Zambezi River. Generations ago my ancestors entered the waters of the Zambezi naked, driving their herds before them. Their weakest members were lost, the prey of the swirling waters or hungry crocodiles, but the survivors emerged from the waters stronger and more virile. When a Bantu dies, *isiko* demands that the members of his family retire to the forest so that the rest of the community will not have to share their distress. *Isiko* is the scorn felt for a slave who cringes, the belief that a man can look anyone in the face, that he is worth no more and no less than any other man. Have you heard of John Tengo Jabavu?" He pronounced the name with reverence.

"No."

"You will, Mr. McGregor," Banda promised. "You will." And Banda changed the subject.

Jamie began to feel a growing admiration for Banda. In the beginning there was a wariness between the two men. Jamie had to learn to trust a man who had almost killed him. And Banda had to learn to trust an age-old enemy—a white man. Unlike most of the blacks Jamie had met, Banda was educated.

"Where did you go to school?" Jamie asked.

"Nowhere. I've worked since I was a small boy. My grandmother educated me. She worked for a Boer schoolteacher. She learned to read and write so she could teach me to read and write. I owe her everything."

It was on a late Saturday afternoon after work that Jamie first heard of the Namib Desert in Great Namaqualand. He and Banda were in the deserted warehouse on the docks, sharing an impala stew Banda's mother had cooked. It was good—a little gamey for Jamie's taste, but his bowl was soon empty, and he lay back on some old sacks to question Banda.

"When did you first meet Van der Merwe?"

"When I was working at the diamond beach on the Namib Desert. He owns the beach with two partners. He had just stolen his share from some poor prospector, and he was down there visiting it."

"If Van der Merwe is so rich, why does he still work at his store?"

"The store is his bait. That's how he gets new prospectors to come to him. And he grows richer."

Jamie thought of how easily he himself had been cheated. How trusting that naïve young boy had been! He could see Margaret's oval-shaped face as she said, *My father might be the one to help you.* He had thought she was a child until he had noticed her breasts and— Jamie suddenly jumped to his feet, a smile on his face, and the up-turning of his lips made the livid scar across his chin ripple.

"Tell me how you happened to go to work for Van der Merwe."

"On the day he came to the beach with his daughter—she was about eleven then—I suppose she got bored sitting around and she went into the water and the tide grabbed her. I jumped in and pulled her out. I was a young boy, but I thought Van der Merwe was going to kill me."

Jamie stared at him. "Why?"

"Because I had my arms around her. Not because I was black, but because I was a *male*. He can't stand the thought of any man touching his daughter. Someone finally calmed him down and reminded him that I had saved her life. He brought me back to Klipdrift as his servant." Banda hesitated a moment, then continued. "Two months later, my sister came to visit me." His voice was very quiet. "She was the same age as Van der Merwe's daughter."

There was nothing Jamie could say.

Finally Banda broke the silence. "I should have stayed in the Namib Desert. That was an easy job. We'd crawl along the beach picking up diamonds and putting them in little jam tins."

"Wait a minute. Are you saying that the diamonds are just lying there, on top of the sand?"

"That's what I'm saying, Mr. McGregor. But forget what you're thinking. Nobody can get near that field. It's on the ocean, and the waves are up to thirty feet high. They don't even bother guarding the shore. A lot of people have tried to sneak in by sea. They've all been killed by the waves or the reefs."

"There must be some other way to get in."

"No. The Namib Desert runs right down to the ocean's shore."

"What about the entrance to the diamond field?"

"There's a guard tower and a barbed-wire fence. Inside the fence are guards with guns and dogs that'll tear a man to pieces. And they have a new kind of explosive called a land mine. They're buried all over the field. If you don't have a map of the land mines, you'll get blown to bits."

"How large is the diamond field?"

"It runs for about thirty-five miles."

Thirty-five miles of diamonds just lying on the sand . . . "My God!"

"You aren't the first one to get excited about the diamond fields at the Namib, and you won't be the last. I've picked up what was left of people who tried to come in by boat and got torn apart by the reefs. I've seen what those land mines do if a man takes one wrong step, and I've watched those dogs rip out a man's throat. Forget it, Mr. McGregor. I've been there. There's no way in and there's no way out—not alive, that is."

Jamie was unable to sleep that night. He kept visualizing thirty-five miles of sand sprinkled with enormous diamonds belonging to Van der Merwe. He thought of the sea and the jagged reefs, the dogs hungry to kill, the guards and the land mines. He was not afraid of the danger; he was not afraid of dying. He was only afraid of dying before he repaid Salomon van der Merwe.

On the following Monday Jamie went into a cartographer's shop and bought a map of Great Namaqualand. There was the beach, off the South Atlantic Ocean between Lüderitz to the north and the Orange River Estuary to the south. The area was marked in red: SPERRGEBIET—Forbidden.

Jamie examined every detail of the area on the map, going over it again and again. There were three thousand miles of ocean flowing from South America to South Africa, with nothing to impede the waves, so that their full fury was spent on the deadly reefs of the South Atlantic shore. Forty miles south, down the coastline, was an open beach. *That must be where the poor bastards launched their boats to sail into the forbidden area,* Jamie decided. Looking at the map, he could understand why the shore was not guarded. The reefs would make a landing impossible.

Jamie turned his attention to the land entrance to the diamond field. According to Banda, the area was fenced in with barbed wire and patrolled twenty-four hours a day by armed guards. At the entrance itself was a manned watchtower. And even if one did somehow manage to slip past the watch-tower into the diamond area, there would be the land mines and guard dogs.

The following day when Jamie met Banda, he asked, "You said there was a land-mine map of the field?"

"In the Namib Desert? The supervisors have the maps, and they lead the diggers to work. Everybody walks in a single file so no one gets blown up." His eyes filled with a memory. "One day my uncle was walking in front of me and he stumbled on a rock and fell on top of a land mine. There wasn't enough left of him to take home to his family."

Jamie shuddered.

"And then there's the sea *mis,* Mr. McGregor. You've never seen a *mis* until you've been in one in the Namib. It rolls in from the ocean and blows all the way across the desert to the mountains and it blots out everything. If you're caught in one of them, you don't dare move. The land-mine maps are no good then because you can't see where you're going. Everybody just sits quietly until the *mis* lifts."

"How long do they last?"

Banda shrugged. "Sometimes a few hours, sometimes a few days."

"Banda, have you ever *seen* a map of those land mines?"

"They're closely guarded." A worried look crossed his face. "I'm telling you again, no one can get away with what you're thinking. Once in a while workers will try to smuggle out a diamond. There is a special tree for hanging them. It's a lesson to everybody not to try to steal from the company."

The whole thing looked impossible. Even if he could manage to get into Van der Merwe's diamond field, there was no way out. Banda was right. He would have to forget about it.

The next day he asked Banda, "How does Van der Merwe keep the workers from stealing diamonds when they come off their shifts?"

"They're searched. They strip them down mother-naked and then they look up and down every hole they've got. I've seen workers cut gashes in their legs and try to smuggle diamonds out in them. Some drill out their back teeth and stick diamonds up there. They've tried every trick you can think of." He looked at Jamie and said, "If you want to live, you'll get that diamond field off your mind."

Jamie tried. But the idea kept coming back to him, taunting him. Van der Merwe's diamonds just lying on the sand waiting. *Waiting for him.*

The solution came to Jamie that night. He could hardly contain his impatience until he saw Banda. Without preamble, Jamie said, "Tell me about the boats that have tried to land on the beach."

"What about them?"

"What kind of boats were they?"

"Every kind you can think of. A schooner. A tugboat. A big motorboat. Sailboat. Four men even tried it in a rowboat. While I worked the field, there were half a dozen tries. The reefs just chewed the boats to pieces. Everybody drowned."

Jamie took a deep breath. "Did anyone ever try to get in by raft?"

Banda was staring at him. *"Raft?"*

"Yes." Jamie's excitement was growing. "Think about it. No one ever made it to the shore because the bottoms of their boats were torn out by the reefs. But a *raft* will glide right over those reefs and onto the shore. And it can get out the same way."

Banda looked at him for a long time. When he spoke, there was a different note in his voice. "You know, Mr. McGregor, you might just have an idea there. . . ."

It started as a game, a possible solution to an unsolvable puzzle. But the more Jamie and Banda discussed it, the more excited they became. What had started as idle conversation began to take concrete shape as a plan of action. Because the diamonds were lying on top of the sand, no equipment would be required. They could build their raft, with a sail, on the free beach forty miles south of the *Sperrgebiet* and sail it in at night, unobserved.

There were no land mines along the unguarded shore, and the guards and patrols only operated inland. The two men could roam the beach freely, gathering up all the diamonds they could carry.

"We can be on our way out before dawn," Jamie said, "with our pockets full of Van der Merwe's diamonds."

"How do we get out?"

"The same way we got in. We'll paddle the raft over the reefs to the open sea, put up the sail and we're home free."

Under Jamie's persuasive arguments, Banda's doubts began to melt. He tried to poke holes in the plan and every time he came up with an objection, Jamie answered it. The plan *could* work. The beautiful part of it was its simplicity, and the fact that it would require no money. Only a great deal of nerve.

"All we need is a big bag to put the diamonds in," Jamie said. His enthusiasm was infectious.

Banda grinned. "Let's make that *two* big bags."

The following week they quit their jobs and boarded a bullock wagon to Port Nolloth, the coastal village forty miles south of the forbidden area where they were headed.

At Port Nolloth, they disembarked and looked around. The village was small and primitive, with shanties and tin huts and a few stores, and a pristine white beach that seemed to stretch on forever. There were no reefs here, and the waves lapped gently at the shore. It was a perfect place to launch their raft.

There was no hotel, but the little market rented a room in back to Jamie. Banda found himself a bed in the black quarter of the village.

"We have to find a place to build our raft in secret," Jamie told Banda. "We don't want anyone reporting us to the authorities."

That afternoon they came across an old, abandoned warehouse.

"This will be perfect," Jamie decided. "Let's get to work on the raft."

"Not yet," Banda told him. "We'll wait. Buy a bottle of whiskey."

"What for?"

"You'll see."

The following morning, Jamie was visited by the district constable, a florid, heavy-set man with a large nose covered with the telltale broken veins of a tippler.

"Mornin'," he greeted Jamie. "I heard we had a visitor. Thought I'd stop by and say hello. I'm Constable Mundy."

"Ian Travis," Jamie replied.

"Headin' north, Mr. Travis?"

"South. My servant and I are on our way to Cape Town."

"Ah. I was in Cape Town once. Too bloody big, too bloody noisy."

"I agree. Can I offer you a drink, Constable?"

"I never drink on duty." Constable Mundy paused, making a decision. "However, just this once, I might make an exception, I suppose."

"Fine." Jamie brought out the bottle of whiskey, wondering how Banda could have known. He poured out two fingers into a dirty tooth glass and handed it to the constable.

"Thank you, Mr. Travis. Where's yours?"

"I can't drink," Jamie said ruefully. "Malaria. That's why I'm going to Cape Town. To get medical attention. I'm stopping off here a few days to rest. Traveling's very hard on me."

Constable Mundy was studying him. "You look pretty healthy."

"You should see me when the chills start."

The constable's glass was empty. Jamie filled it.

"Thank you. Don't mind if I do." He finished the second drink in one swallow and stood up. "I'd best be gettin' along. You said you and your man will be movin' on in a day or two?"

"As soon as I'm feeling stronger."

"I'll come back and check on you Friday," Constable Mundy said.

That night, Jamie and Banda went to work on the raft in the deserted warehouse.

"Banda, have you ever built a raft?"

"Well, to tell you the truth, Mr. McGregor, no."

"Neither have I." The two men stared at each other. "How difficult can it be?"

They stole four empty, fifty-gallon wooden oil barrels from behind the market and carried them to the warehouse. When they had them assembled, they spaced them out in a square. Next they gathered four empty crates and placed one over each oil barrel.

Banda looked dubious. "It doesn't look like a raft to me."

"We're not finished yet," Jamie assured him.

There was no planking available so they covered the top layer with whatever was at hand: branches from the stinkwood tree, limbs from the Cape beech, large leaves from the marula. They lashed everything down with thick hemp rope, tying each knot with careful precision.

When they were finished, Banda looked it over. "It still doesn't look like a raft."

"It will look better when we get the sail up," Jamie promised.

They made a mast from a fallen yellowwood tree, and picked up two flat branches for paddles.

"Now all we need is a sail. We need it fast. I'd like to get out of here tonight. Constable Mundy's coming back tomorrow."

It was Banda who found the sail. He came back late that evening with an enormous piece of blue cloth. "How's this, Mr. McGregor?"

"Perfect. Where did you get it?"

Banda grinned. "Don't ask. We're in enough trouble."

They rigged up a square sail with a boom below and a yard on top, and at last it was ready.

"We'll take off at two in the morning when the village is asleep," Jamie told Banda. "Better get some rest until then."

But neither man was able to sleep. Each was filled with the excitement of the adventure that lay ahead.

* * *

At two A.M. they met at the warehouse. There was an eagerness in both of them, and an unspoken fear. They were embarking on a journey that would either make them rich or bring them death. There was no middle way.

"It's time," Jamie anounced.

They stepped outside. Nothing was stirring. The night was still and peaceful, with a vast canopy of blue overhead. A sliver of moon appeared high in the sky. *Good,* Jamie thought. *There won't be much light to see us by.* Their timetable was complicated by the fact that they had to leave the village at night so no one would be aware of their departure, and arrive at the diamond beach the next night so they could slip into the field and be safely back at sea before dawn.

"The Benguela current should carry us to the diamond fields sometime in the late afternoon," Jamie said. "But we can't go in by daylight. We'll have to stay out of sight at sea until dark."

Banda nodded. "We can hide out at one of the little islands off the coast."

"What islands?"

"There are dozens of them—Mercury, Ichabod, Plum Pudding . . ."

Jamie gave him a strange look. *"Plum Pudding?"*

"There's also a Roast Beef Island."

Jamie took out his creased map and consulted it. "This doesn't show any of those."

"They're guano islands. The British harvest the bird droppings for fertilizer."

"Anyone live on those islands?"

"Can't. The smell's too bad. In places the guano is a hundred feet thick. The government uses gangs of deserters and prisoners to pick it up. Some of them die on the island and they just leave the bodies there."

"That's where we'll hide out," Jamie decided.

Working quietly, the two men slid open the door to the warehouse and started to lift the raft. It was too heavy to move. They sweated and tugged, but in vain.

"Wait here," Banda said.

He hurried out. Half an hour later, he returned with a large, round log. "We'll use this. I'll pick up one end and you slide the log underneath."

Jamie marveled at Banda's strength as the black man picked up one end of the raft. Quickly, Jamie shoved the log under it. Together they lifted the back end of the raft and it moved easily down the log. When the log had rolled out from under the back end, they repeated the procedure. It was strenuous work, and by the time they got to the beach they were both soaked in perspiration. The operation had taken much longer than Jamie had anticipated. It was almost dawn now. They had to be away before the villagers discovered them and reported what they were doing. Quickly, Jamie attached the sail and checked to make sure everything was working properly. He had a nagging feeling he was forgetting something. He suddenly realized what was bothering him and laughed aloud.

Banda watched him, puzzled. "Something funny?"

"Before, when I went looking for diamonds I had a ton of equipment. Now all I'm carrying is a compass. It seems too easy."

Banda said quietly, "I don't think that's going to be our problem, Mr. McGregor."

"It's time you called me Jamie."

Banda shook his head in wonder. "You *really* come from a faraway country." He grinned, showing even white teeth. "What the hell—they can hang me only once." He tasted the name on his lips, then said it aloud. "Jamie."

"Let's go get those diamonds."

They pushed the raft off the sand into the shallow water and both men leaped aboard and started paddling. It took them a few minutes to get adjusted to the pitching and yawing of their strange craft. It was like riding a bobbing cork, but it was going to work. The raft was responding perfectly, moving north with the swift current. Jamie raised the sail and headed out to sea. By the time the villagers awoke, the raft was well over the horizon.

"We've done it!" Jamie said.

Banda shook his head. "It's not over yet." He trailed a hand in the cold Benguela current. "It's just beginning."

They sailed on, due north past Alexander Bay and the mouth of the Orange River, seeing no signs of life except for flocks of Cape cormorants heading home, and a flight of colorful greater flamingos. Although there were tins of beef and cold rice, and fruit and two canteens of water aboard, they were too nervous to eat. Jamie refused to let his imagination linger on the dangers that lay ahead, but Banda could not help it. He had been there. He was remembering the brutal guards with guns and the dogs and the terrible flesh-tearing land mines, and he wondered how he had ever allowed himself to be talked into this insane venture. He looked over at the Scotsman and thought, *He is the bigger fool. If I die, I die for my baby sister. What does he die for?*

At noon the sharks came. There were half a dozen of them, their fins cutting through the water as they sped toward the raft.

"Black-fin sharks," Banda announced. "They're man-eaters."

Jamie watched the fins skimming closer to the raft. "What do we do?"

Banda swallowed nervously. "Truthfully, Jamie, this is my very first experience of this nature."

The back of a shark nudged the raft, and it almost capsized. The two men grabbed the mast for support. Jamie picked up a paddle and shoved it at a shark, and an instant later the paddle was bitten in two. The sharks surrounded the raft now, swimming in lazy circles, their enormous bodies rubbing up close against the small craft. Each nudge tilted the raft at a precarious angle. It was going to capsize at any moment.

"We've got to get rid of them before they sink us."

"Get rid of them with what?" Banda asked.

"Hand me a tin of beef."

"You must be joking. A tin of beef won't satisfy them. They want *us!*"

There was another jolt, and the raft heeled over.

"The beef!" Jamie yelled. "Get it!"

A second later Banda placed a tin in Jamie's hand. The raft lurched sickeningly.

"Open it halfway. Hurry!"

Banda pulled out his pocketknife and pried the top of the can half open. Jamie took it from him. He felt the sharp, broken edges of the metal with his finger.

"Hold tight!" Jamie warned.

He knelt down at the edge of the raft and waited. Almost immediately, a shark approached the raft, its huge mouth wide open, revealing long rows of evil, grinning teeth. Jamie went for the eyes. With all his strength, he reached out with both hands and scraped the edge of the broken metal against the eye of the shark, ripping it open. The shark lifted its great body, and for an instant the raft stood on end. The water around them was suddenly stained red. There was a giant thrashing as the sharks moved in on the wounded member of the school. The raft was forgotten. Jamie and Banda watched the great sharks tearing at their helpless victim as the raft sailed farther and farther away until finally the sharks were out of sight.

Banda took a deep breath and said softly, "One day I'm going to tell my grandchildren about this. Do you think they'll believe me?"

And they laughed until the tears streamed down their faces.

Late that afternoon, Jamie checked his pocket watch. "We should be off the diamond beach around midnight. Sunrise is at six-fifteen. That means we'll have four hours to pick up the diamonds and two hours to get back to sea and out of sight. Will four hours be enough, Banda?"

"A hundred men couldn't live long enough to spend what you can pick up on that beach in four hours." *I just hope we live long enough to pick them up....*

They sailed steadily north for the rest of that day, carried by the wind and the tide. Toward evening a small island loomed ahead of them. It looked to be no more than two hundred yards in circumference. As they approached the island, the acrid smell of ammonia grew strong, bringing tears to their eyes. Jamie could understand why no one lived here. The stench was overpowering. But it would make a perfect place for them to hide until nightfall. Jamie adjusted the sail, and the small raft bumped against the rocky shore of the low-lying island. Banda made the raft fast, and the two men stepped ashore. The entire island was covered with what appeared to be millions of birds: cormorants, pelicans, gannets, penguins and flamingos. The thick air was so noisome that it was impossible to breathe. They took half a dozen steps and were thigh deep in guano.

"Let's get back to the raft," Jamie gasped.

Without a word, Banda followed him.

As they turned to retreat, a flock of pelicans took to the air, revealing an open space on the ground. Lying there were three men. There was no telling how long they had been dead. Their corpses had been perfectly preserved by the ammonia in the air, and their hair had turned a bright red.

A minute later Jamie and Banda were back on the raft, headed out to sea.

They lay off the coast, sail lowered, waiting.

"We'll stay out here until midnight. Then we go in."

They sat together in silence, each in his own way preparing for whatever lay ahead. The sun was low on the western horizon, painting the dying sky with the wild colors of a mad artist. Then suddenly they were blanketed in darkness.

They waited for two more hours, and Jamie hoisted the sail. The raft began to move east toward the unseen shore. Overhead, clouds parted and a thin wash of moonlight paled down. The raft picked up speed. In the distance the two men could begin to see the faint smudge of the coast. The wind blew stronger, snapping at the sail, pushing the raft toward the shore at an ever-increasing speed. Soon, they could clearly make out the outline of the land, a gigantic parapet of rock. Even from that distance it was possible to see and hear the enormous whitecaps that exploded like thunder over the reefs. It was a terrifying sight from afar, and Jamie wondered what it would be like up close.

He found himself whispering. "You're sure the beach side isn't guarded?"

Banda did not answer. He pointed to the reefs ahead. Jamie knew what he meant. The reefs were more deadly than any trap man could devise. They were the guardians of the sea, and they never relaxed, never slept. They lay there, patiently waiting for their prey to come to them. *Well,* Jamie thought, *we're going to outsmart you. We're going to float over you.*

The raft had carried them that far. It would carry them the rest of the way. The shore was racing toward them now, and they began to feel the heavy swell of the giant combers. Banda was holding tightly to the mast.

"We're moving pretty fast."

"Don't worry," Jamie reassured him. "When we get closer, I'll lower the sail. That will cut our speed. We'll slide over the reefs nice and easy."

The momentum of the wind and the waves was picking up, hurtling the raft toward the deadly reefs. Jamie quickly estimated the remaining distance and decided the waves would carry them in to shore without the help of the sail. Hurriedly, he lowered it. Their momentum did not even slow. The raft was completely in the grip of the huge waves now, out of control, hurled forward from one giant crest to the next. The raft was rocking so violently that the men had to cling to it with both hands. Jamie had expected the entrance to be difficult, but he was totally unprepared for the fury of the seething maelstrom they faced. The reefs loomed in front of them with startling clarity. They could see the waves rushing in against the jagged rocks and exploding into huge, angry geysers. The entire success of the plan depended on bringing the raft over the reefs intact so that they could use it for their escape. Without it, they were dead men.

They were bearing down on the reefs now, propelled by the terrifying power of the waves. The roar of the wind was deafening. The raft was suddenly lifted high in the air by an enormous wave and flung toward the rocks.

"Hold on, Banda!" Jamie shouted. "We're going in!"

The giant breaker picked up the raft like a matchstick and started to carry it toward shore, over the reef. Both men were hanging on for their lives, fighting the violent bucking motion that threatened to sweep them into the water. Jamie glanced down and caught a glimpse of the razor-sharp reefs below them. In another moment they would be sailing over them, safe in the haven of the shore.

At that instant there was a sudden, tearing wrench as a reef caught one of the barrels underneath the raft and ripped it away. The raft gave a sharp lurch, and another barrel was torn away, and then another. The wind and the pounding waves and the hungry reef were playing with the raft like a toy, tossing it backward and forward, spinning it wildly in the air. Jamie and Banda felt the thin wood begin to split beneath their feet.

"Jump!" Jamie yelled.

He dived over the side of the raft, and a giant wave picked him up and shot him toward the beach at the speed of a catapult. He was caught in the grip of an element that was powerful beyond belief. He had no control over what was happening. He was a part of the wave. It was over him and under him and inside him. His body was twisting and turning and his lungs were bursting. Lights began to explode in his head. Jamie thought, *I'm drowning.* And his body was thrown up onto the sandy shore. Jamie lay there gasping, fighting for breath, filling his lungs with the cool, fresh sea air. His chest and legs were scraped raw from the sand, and his clothes were in shreds. Slowly, he sat up and looked around for Banda. He was crouching ten yards away, vomiting seawater. Jamie got to his feet and staggered over to him.

"You all right?"

Banda nodded. He took a deep, shuddering breath and looked up at Jamie. "I can't swim."

Jamie helped him to his feet. The two men turned to look at the reef. There was not a sign of their raft. It had been torn to pieces in the wild ocean. They had gotten into the diamond field.

There was no way to get out.

5

Behind them was the raging ocean. Ahead was unbroken desert from the sea to the foothills of the distant, rugged, purple mountains of the Richterveld escarpment, a world of kloofs and canyons and twisted peaks, lit by the pale moon. At the foot of the mountains was the Hexenkessel Valley—"the witch's cauldron"—a bleak wind trap. It was a primeval, desolate landscape that went back to the beginning of time itself. The only clue that man had ever set foot in this place was a crudely printed sign pounded into the sand. By the light of the moon, they read:

VERBODE GEBIED
SPERRGEBIET

Forbidden.

There was no escape toward the sea. The only direction left open to them was the Namib Desert.

"We'll have to try to cross it and take our chances," Jamie said.

Banda shook his head. "The guards will shoot us on sight or hang us. Even if we were lucky enough to slip by the guards and dogs, there's no way to get by the land mines. We're dead men."

There was no fear in him, only a resigned acceptance of his fate.

Jamie looked at Banda and felt a sense of deep regret. He had brought the black man into this, and not once had Banda complained. Even now, knowing there was no escape for them, he did not utter one word of reproach.

Jamie turned to look at the wall of angry waves smashing at the shore, and he thought it was a miracle that they had gotten as far as they had. It was two A.M., four hours before dawn and discovery, and they were both still in one piece. *I'll be damned if I'm ready to give up,* Jamie thought.

"Let's go to work, Banda."

Banda blinked. "Doing what?"

"We came here to get diamonds, didn't we? Let's get them."

Banda stared at the wild-eyed man with his white hair plastered to his skull and his sopping trousers hanging in shreds around his legs. "What are you talking about?"

"You said they're going to kill us on sight, right? Well, they might as well kill us rich as poor. A miracle got us in here. Maybe a miracle will get us out. And if we do get out, I damned well don't plan to leave empty-handed."

"You're crazy," Banda said softly.

"Or we wouldn't be here," Jamie reminded him.

Banda shrugged. "What the hell. I have nothing else to do until they find us."

Jamie stripped off his tattered shirt, and Banda understood and did the same.

"Now. Where are all these big diamonds that you've been talking about?"

"They're everywhere," Banda promised. And he added, "Like the guards and the dogs."

"We'll worry about them later. When do they come down to the beach?"

"When it gets light."

Jamie thought for a moment. "Is there a part of the beach where they *don't* come? Someplace we could hide?"

"There's no part of this beach they don't come to, and there's no place you could hide a fly."

Jamie slapped Banda on the shoulder. "Right, then. Let's go."

Jamie watched as Banda got down on his hands and knees and began slowly crawling along the beach, his fingers sifting sand as he moved. In less than two minutes, he stopped and held up a stone. "I found one!"

Jamie lowered himself to the sand and began moving. The first two stones he found were small. The third must have weighed over fifteen carats. He sat there looking at it for a long moment. It was incredible to him that such a fortune could be picked up so easily. And it all belonged to Salomon van der Merwe and his partners. Jamie kept moving.

In the next three hours, the two men collected more than forty diamonds ranging from two carats to thirty carats. The sky in the east was beginning to lighten. It was the time Jamie had planned to leave, to jump back on the raft, sail over the reefs and make their escape. It was useless to think about that now.

"It will be dawn soon," Jamie said. "Let's see how many more diamonds we can find."

"We're not going to live to spend any of *this*. You want to die *very* rich, don't you?"

"I don't want to die at all."

They resumed their search, mindlessly scooping up diamond after diamond, and it was as though a madness had taken possession of them. Their piles of diamonds increased, until sixty diamonds worth a king's ransom lay in their torn shirts.

"Do you want me to carry these?" Banda asked.

"No. We can both—" And then Jamie realized what was on Banda's mind. The one caught in actual possession of the diamonds would die more slowly and painfully.

"I'll take them," Jamie said. He dumped the diamonds into the rag that was left of his shirt, and carefully tied it in a knot. The horizon was light gray now, and the east was becoming stained with the colors of the rising sun.

What next? That was the question! What was the answer? They could stand there and die, or they could move inland toward the desert and die.

"Let's move."

Jamie and Banda slowly began walking away from the sea, side by side.

"Where do the land mines start?"

"About a hundred yards up ahead." In the far distance, they heard a dog bark. "I don't think we're going to have to worry about the land mines. The dogs are heading this way. The morning shift is coming to work."

"How soon before they reach us?"

"Fifteen minutes. Maybe ten."

It was almost full dawn now. What had been vague, shimmering patterns turned into small sand dunes and distant mountains. There was no place to hide.

"How many guards are on a shift?"

Banda thought for a moment. "About ten."

"Ten guards aren't many for a beach this big."

"*One* guard is plenty. They've got guns and dogs. The guards aren't blind, and we're not invisible."

The sound of the barking was closer now. Jamie said, "Banda, I'm sorry. I should never have gotten you into this."

"You didn't."

And Jamie understood what he meant.

They could hear voices calling in the distance.

Jamie and Banda reached a small dune. "What if we buried ourselves in the sand?"

"That has been tried. The dogs would find us and rip our throats out. I want my death to be quick. I'm going to let them see me, then start running. That way they'll shoot me. I—I don't want the dogs to get me."

Jamie gripped Banda's arm. "We may die, but I'll be damned if we're going to *run* to our deaths. Let's make them work for it."

They could begin to distinguish words in the distance. "Keep moving, you lazy bastards," a voice was yelling. "Follow me . . . stay in line. . . . You've all had a good night's sleep. . . . Now let's get some work done. . . ."

In spite of his brave words, Jamie found he was retreating from the voice. He turned to look at the sea again. *Was drowning an easier way to die?* He watched the reefs tearing viciously at the demon waves breaking over them and he suddenly saw something else, something beyond the waves. He could not understand what it was. "Banda, look . . ."

Far out at sea an impenetrable gray wall was moving toward them, blown by the powerful westerly winds.

"It's the sea *mis!*" Banda exclaimed. "It comes in two or three times a week."

While they were talking, the *mis* moved closer, like a gigantic gray curtain sweeping across the horizon, blotting out the sky.

The voices had moved closer, too. *"Den dousant!* Damn this *mis!* Another slowdown. The bosses ain't gonna like this. . . ."

"We've got a chance!" Jamie said. He was whispering now. "What chance?"

"The *mis!* They won't be able to. see us."

"That's no help. It's going to lift sometime, and when it does we're still going to be right here. If the guards can't move through the land mines, neither can we. You try to cross this desert in the *mis* and you won't go ten yards before you're blown to pieces. You're looking for one of your miracles."

"You're damned right I am," Jamie said.

The sky was darkening overhead. The *mis* was closer, covering the sea, ready to swallow up the shore. It had an eerie, menacing look about it as it rolled toward them, but Jamie thought exultantly, *It's going to save us!*

A voice suddenly called out, "Hey! You two! What the hell are you doin' there?"

Jamie and Banda turned. At the top of a dune about a hundred yards away was a uniformed guard carrying a rifle. Jamie looked back at the shore. The *mis* was closing in fast.

"You! You two! Come here," the guard yelled. He lifted his rifle.

Jamie raised his hands. "I twisted my foot," he called out. "I can't walk."

"Stay where you are," the guard ordered. "I'm comin' to get you." He lowered his rifle and started moving toward them. A quick look back showed that the *mis* had reached the edge of the shore, and was coming in swiftly.

"Run!" Jamie whispered. He turned and raced toward the beach, Banda running close behind him.

"Stop!"

A second later they heard the sharp crack of a rifle, and the sand ahead of them exploded. They kept running, racing to meet the great dark wall of the fog. There was another rifle shot, closer this time, and another, and the next moment the two men were in total darkness. The sea *mis* licked at them, chilling them, smothering them. It was like being buried in cotton. It was impossible to see anything.

The voices were muffled now and distant, bouncing off the *mis* and coming from all directions. They could hear other voices calling to one another.

"Kruger! . . . It's Brent. . . . Can you hear me?"

"I hear you, Kruger. . . ."

"There're two of them," the first voice yelled. "A white man and a black. They're on the beach. Spread your men out. *Skiet hom!* Shoot to kill."

"Hang on to me," Jamie whispered.

Banda gripped his arm. "Where are you going?"

"We're getting out of here."

Jamie brought his compass up to his face. He could barely see it. He turned until the compass was pointing east. "This way . . ."

"Wait! We can't walk. Even if we don't bump into a guard or a dog, we're going to set off a land mine."

"You said there are a hundred yards before the mines start. Let's get away from the beach."

They started moving toward the desert, slowly and unsteadily, blind men in an unknown land. Jamie paced off the yards. Whenever they stumbled in the soft sand, they picked themselves up and kept moving. Jamie stopped to check the compass every few feet. When he estimated they had traveled almost a hundred yards, he stopped.

"This should be about where the land mines start. Is there any pattern to the way they're placed? Anything you can think of that could help us?"

"Prayer," Banda answered. "Nobody's ever gotten past those land mines, Jamie. They're scattered all over the field, buried about six inches down. We're going to have to stay here until the *mis* lifts and give ourselves up."

Jamie listened to the cotton-wrapped voices ricocheting around them.

"Kruger! Keep in voice contact. . . ."

"Right, Brent. . . ."

"Kruger . . ."

"Brent . . ."

Disembodied voices calling to each other in the blinding fog. Jamie's mind was racing, desperately exploring every possible avenue of escape. If they stayed where they were, they would be killed the instant the *mis* lifted. If they tried moving through the field of mines, they would be blown to bits.

"Have you ever seen the land mines?" Jamie whispered.

"I helped bury some of them."

"What sets them off?"

"A man's weight. Anything over eighty pounds will explode them. That way they don't kill the dogs."

Jamie took a deep breath. "Banda, I may have a way for us to get out of here. It might not work. Do you want to gamble with me?"

"What have you got in mind?"

"We're going to cross the mine fields on our bellies. That way we'll distribute our weight across the sand."

"Oh, Jesus!"

"What do you think?"

"I think I was crazy for ever leaving Cape Town."

"Are you with me?" He could barely make out Banda's face next to him.

"You don't leave a man a lot of choice, do you?"

"Come on then."

Jamie carefully stretched himself out flat on the sand. Banda looked at him a moment, took a deep breath and joined him. Slowly the two men began crawling across the sand, toward the mine field.

"When you move," Jamie whispered, "don't press down with your hands or your legs. Use your whole body."

There was no reply. Banda was busy concentrating on staying alive.

They were in a smothering, gray vacuum that made it impossible to see anything. At any instant they could bump into a guard, a dog or one of the land mines. Jamie forced all this out of his mind. Their progress was painfully slow. Both men were shirtless, and the sand scraped against their stomachs as they inched forward. Jamie was aware of how overwhelming the odds were against them. Even if by some chance they did succeed in crossing the desert without getting shot or blown up, they would be confronted by the barbed-wire fence and the armed guards at the watchtower at the entrance. And there was no telling how long the *mis* would last. It could lift at any second, exposing them.

They kept crawling, mindlessly sliding forward until they lost all track of time. The inches became feet, and the feet became yards, and the yards became miles. They had no idea how long they had been traveling. They were forced to keep their heads close to the ground, and their eyes and ears and noses became filled with sand. Breathing was an effort.

In the distance was the constant echo of the guards' voices. *"Kruger . . . Brent . . . Kruger . . . Brent . . ."*

The two men stopped to rest and check the compass every few minutes, then moved on, beginning their endless crawl again. There was an almost overwhelming temptation to move faster, but that would mean pressing down harder, and Jamie could visualize the metal fragments exploding under him and ripping into his belly. He kept the pace slow. From time to time they could hear other voices around them, but the words were muffled by the fog and it was impossible to tell where they were coming from. *It's a big desert*, Jamie thought hopefully. *We're not going to stumble into anyone.*

Out of nowhere, a large, furry shape leaped at him. It happened so swiftly that Jamie was caught off guard. He felt the huge Alsatian's teeth sinking into his arm. He dropped the bundle of diamonds and tried to pry open the dog's jaw, but he had only one free hand and it was impossible. He felt the warm blood running down his arm. The dog was sinking its teeth in harder now, silent and deadly. Jamie felt himself begin to faint. He heard a dull thud, and then another, and the dog's jaw loosened and its eyes glazed over. Through the mist of pain, Jamie saw Banda smashing the sack of diamonds against the dog's skull. The dog whimpered once and lay still.

"You all right?" Banda breathed anxiously.

Jamie could not speak. He lay there, waiting for the waves of pain to recede. Banda ripped off a piece of his trousers and tied a strip tightly around Jamie's arm to stop the bleeding.

"We've got to keep moving," Banda warned. "If there's one of them around, there are more."

Jamie nodded. Slowly he slid his body forward, fighting against the terrible throbbing in his arm.

He remembered nothing of the rest of the trek. He was semi-conscious, an automaton. Something outside him directed his movements. *Arms forward, pull ... Arms forward, pull ... Arms forward, pull ...* It was endless, an odyssey of agony. It was Banda who followed the compass now, and when Jamie started to crawl in the wrong direction Banda gently turned him around. They were surrounded by guards and dogs and land mines and only the *mis* kept them safe. They kept moving, crawling for their lives, until the time came when neither man had the strength to move another inch.

They slept.

When Jamie opened his eyes, something had changed. He lay there on the sand, his body stiff and aching, trying to remember where he was. He could see Banda asleep six feet away, and it all came flooding in. The raft crashing on the reefs ... the sea *mis*

. . . But something was wrong. Jamie sat up, trying to figure out what it was. And his stomach lurched. *He could see Banda! That was what was wrong. The* mis *was lifting.* Jamie heard voices nearby. He peered through the thin mists of the dissipating fog. They had crawled near the entrance to the diamond field. There was the high guard tower and the barbed-wire fence Banda had described. A crowd of about sixty black workers was moving away from the diamond field toward the gate. They had finished their shift and the next shift was coming in. Jamie got on his knees and crawled over to Banda and shook him. Banda sat up, instantly awake. His eyes turned to the watchtower and the gate.

"Damn!" he said incredulously. "We almost made it."

"We *did* make it! Give me those diamonds!"

Banda handed him the folded shirt. "What do you—?"

"Follow me."

"Those guards with the guns at the gate," Banda said in a low voice, "they'll know we don't belong here."

"That's what I'm counting on," Jamie told him.

The two men moved toward the guards, drifting between the line of departing workers and the line of arriving workers who were yelling at one another, exchanging good-natured catcalls.

"You fellas gonna work your asses off, man. We got a nice sleep in the *mis.* . . ."

"How did you arrange for the *mis,* you lucky bastards . . . ?"

"God listens to me. He ain't gonna listen to you. You're bad. . . ."

Jamie and Banda reached the gate. Two huge armed guards stood inside, herding the departing workers over to a small tin hut where they would be thoroughly searched. *They strip them down mother-naked and then they look up and down every hole they've got.* Jamie clutched the tattered shirt in his hand more tightly. He pushed through the line of workers and walked up to a guard. "Excuse me, sir," Jamie said. "Who do we see about a job here?"

Banda was staring at him, petrified.

The guard turned to face Jamie. "What the hell are you doin' inside the fence?"

"We came in to look for work. I heard there was an opening for a guard, and my servant can dig. I thought—"

The guard eyed the two ragged, disreputable-looking figures. "Get the hell back outside!"

"We don't want to go outside," Jamie protested. "We need jobs, and I was told—"

"This is a restricted area, mister. Didn't you see the signs? Now get the hell out. Both of you!" He pointed to a large bullock wagon outside the fence, filling with the workers who had finished their shift. "That wagon'll take you to Port Nolloth. If you want a job, you have to apply at the company office there."

"Oh. Thank you, sir," Jamie said. He beckoned to Banda, and the two men moved out through the gate to freedom.

The guard glared after them. "Stupid idiots."

Ten minutes later, Jamie and Banda were on their way to Port Nolloth. They were carrying with them diamonds worth half a million pounds.

6

The expensive carriage rolled down the dusty main street of Klipdrift, drawn by two beautiful matched bays. At the reins was a slender, athletic-looking man with snow-white hair, a white beard and mustache. He was dressed in a fashionably tailored gray suit and ruffled shirt, and in his black cravat was a diamond stickpin. He wore a gray top hat, and on his little finger was a large, sparkling diamond ring. He appeared to be a stranger to the town, but he was not.

Klipdrift had changed considerably since Jamie McGregor had left it a year earlier. It was 1884, and it had grown from a camp to a township. The railway had been completed from Cape Town to Hopetown, with a branch running to Klipdrift, and this had created a whole new wave of immigrants. The town was even more crowded than Jamie remembered, but the people seemed different. There were still many prospectors, but there were also men in business suits and well-dressed matrons walking in and out of stores. Klipdrift had acquired a patina of respectability.

Jamie passed three new dance halls and half a dozen new saloons. He drove by a recently built church and barbershop, and a large hotel called the Grand. He stopped in front of a bank and alighted from the carriage, carelessly tossing the reins to a native boy.

"Water them."

Jamie entered the bank and said to the manager in a loud voice, "I wish to deposit one hundred thousand pounds in your bank."

The word spread quickly, as Jamie had known it would, and by the time he left the bank and entered the Sundowner Saloon, he was the center of interest. The interior of the saloon had not changed. It was crowded, and curious eyes followed Jamie as he walked up to the bar. Smit nodded deferentially. "What would you like, sir?" There was no recognition on the bartender's face.

"Whiskey. The best you have."

"Yes, sir." He poured the drink. "You're new in town?"

"Yes."

"Just passin' through, are you?"

"No. I've heard this is a good town for a man looking for investments."

The bartender's eyes lighted up. "You couldn't find better! A man with a hundred—A man with money can do real well for hisself. Matter of fact, I might be of some service to you, sir."

"Really? How is that?"

Smit leaned forward, his tone conspiratorial. "I know the man who runs this town. He's chairman of the Borough Council and head of the Citizen's Committee. He's the most important man in this part of the country. Name of Salomon van der Merwe."

Jamie took a sip of his drink. "Never heard of him."

"He owns that big general store across the street. He can put you on to some good deals. It'd be worth your while to meet him."

Jamie McGregor took another sip of his drink. "Have him come over here."

The bartender glanced at the large diamond ring on Jamie's finger, and at his diamond stickpin. "Yes, sir. Can I tell him your name?"

"Travis. Ian Travis."

"Right, Mr. Travis. I'm sure Mr. van der Merwe will want to meet you." He poured out another drink. "Have this while you're waitin'. It's on the house."

Jamie sat at the bar sipping the whiskey, aware that everyone in the saloon was watching him. Men had departed from Klipdrift wealthy, but no one of such obvious wealth had ever arrived there before. It was something new in their experience.

Fifteen minutes later, the bartender was back, accompanied by Salomon van der Merwe.

Van der Merwe walked up to the bearded, white-haired stranger, held out his hand and smiled. "Mr. Travis, I'm Salomon van der Merwe."

"Ian Travis."

Jamie waited for a flicker of recognition, a sign that Van der Merwe found something familiar about him. There was nothing. *But then, why should there be?* Jamie thought. There was nothing left of that naïve, idealistic, eighteen-year-old boy he had been. Smit obsequiously led the two men to a corner table.

As soon as they were seated, Van der Merwe said, "I understand you're looking for some investments in Klipdrift, Mr. Travis."

"Possibly."

"I might be able to be of some service. One has to be careful. There are many immoral people around."

Jamie looked at him and said, "I'm sure there are."

It was unreal, sitting there carrying on a polite conversation with the man who had cheated him out of a fortune and then tried to murder him. His hatred for Van der Merwe had consumed him for the last year, his thirst for vengeance was all that had sustained him, kept him alive. And now Van der Merwe was about to feel that vengeance.

"If you don't mind my asking, Mr. Travis, how much money were you planning on investing?"

"Oh, around a hundred thousand pounds to begin with," Jamie said carelessly. He watched Van der Merwe wet his lips. "Then perhaps three or four hundred thousand more."

"Er—you should be able to do very well with that, very well, indeed. With the right guidance, of course," he added quickly. "Do you have any idea what you might want to invest in?"

"I thought I'd look around and see what opportunities there were."

"That's very wise of you." Van der Merwe nodded sagely. "Perhaps you would like to come to dinner tonight and we can discuss it? My daughter's an excellent cook. It would be an honor to have you."

Jamie smiled. "I'd enjoy that, Mr. van der Merwe." *You have no idea how much I'd enjoy that,* he thought.

It had started.

The journey from the diamond fields of Namib to Cape Town had been uneventful. Jamie and Banda had hiked inland to a small village where a doctor treated Jamie's arm, and they had gotten a lift on a wagon bound for Cape Town. It was a long, difficult ride, but they were oblivious to the discomfort. At Cape Town, Jamie checked into the ornate Royal Hotel on Plein Street—"Patronized by HRH, the Duke of Edinburgh"—and was escorted to the Royal Suite.

"I want you to send up the best barber in town," Jamie told the manager. "Then I want a tailor and a bootmaker up here."

"At once, sir," the manager said.

It's wonderful what money can do, Jamie thought.

The bath in the Royal Suite was heaven. Jamie lay back in the hot water, soaking the tiredness out of his body, thinking back over the past incredible weeks. Had it been only weeks since he and Banda had built that raft? It seemed like years. Jamie thought about the raft sailing them to the *Sperrgebiet,* and the sharks, and the demon waves and the reefs tearing the raft to pieces. The sea *mis* and the crawling over the land mines, and the huge dog on top of him . . . The eerie, muffled cries that would ring in his ears forever: *Kruger . . . Brent . . . Kruger . . . Brent . . .*

But most of all, he thought of Banda. His friend.

When they had reached Cape Town, Jamie had urged, "Stay with me."

Banda smiled, showing his beautiful white teeth. "Life's too dull with you, Jamie. I have to go somewhere and find a little excitement."

"What will you do now?"

"Well, thanks to you and your wonderful plan about how easy it is to float a raft over the reef, I'm going to buy a farm, find a wife and have a lot of children."

"All right. Let's go to the *diamant kooper* so I can give you your share of the diamonds."

"No," Banda said. "I don't want it."

Jamie frowned. "What are you talking about? Half the diamonds are yours. You're a millionaire."

"No. Look at my skin, Jamie. If I became a millionaire, my life would not be worth a tickey."

"You can hide some of the diamonds away. You can—"

"All I need is enough to buy a morgen of farmland and two oxen to trade for a wife. Two or three little diamonds will get me everything I'll ever want. The rest are yours."

"That's impossible. You can't give me your share."

"Yes, I can, Jamie. Because you're going to give me Salomon van der Merwe."

Jamie looked at Banda for a long moment. "I promise."

"Then I'll say good-bye, my friend."

The two men clasped hands.

"We'll meet again," Banda said. "Next time think of something *really* exciting for us to do."

Banda walked away with three small diamonds carefully tucked in his pocket.

Jamie sent off a bank draft amounting to twenty thousand pounds to his parents, bought the finest carriage and team he could find and headed back to Klipdrift.

The time had come for revenge.

* * *

That evening when Jamie McGregor entered Van der Merwe's store, he was gripped by a sensation so unpleasant and so violent that he had to pause to regain control of himself.

Van der Merwe hurried out of the back of the shop, and when he saw who it was, his face lighted up in a big smile. "Mr. Travis!" he said. "Welcome."

"Thank you, mister—er—sorry, I don't remember your name ..."

"Van der Merwe. Salomon van der Merwe. Don't apologize. Dutch names are difficult to remember. Dinner is ready. Margaret!" he called as he led Jamie into the back room. Nothing had changed. Margaret was standing at the stove over a frying pan, her back to them.

"Margaret, this is our guest I spoke of—Mr. Travis."

Margaret turned. "How do you do?"

There was not a flicker of recognition.

"I'm pleased to meet you." Jamie nodded.

The customer bell rang and Van der Merwe said, "Excuse me, I'll be right back. Please make yourself at home, Mr. Travis." He hurried out.

Margaret carried a steaming bowl of vegetables and meat over to the table, and as she hurried to take the bread from the oven Jamie stood there, silently looking at her. She had blossomed in the year since he had seen her. She had become a woman, with a smoldering sexuality that had been lacking before.

"Your father tells me you're an excellent cook."

Margaret blushed. "I—I hope so, sir."

"It's been a long time since I've tasted home cooking. I'm looking forward to this." Jamie took a large butter dish from Margaret and placed it on the table for her. Margaret was so surprised she almost dropped the plate in her hands. She had never heard of a man who helped in woman's work. She lifted her startled eyes to his face. A broken nose and a scar spoiled what would otherwise have been a too-handsome face. His eyes were light gray and shone with intelligence and a burning intensity. His white hair told her that he was not a young man, and yet there was something very youthful about him. He was tall and strong and—Margaret turned away, embarrassed by his gaze.

Van der Merwe hurried back into the room, rubbing his hands. "I've closed the shop," he said. "Let's sit down and have a fine dinner."

Jamie was given the place of honor at the table. "We'll say grace," Van der Merwe said.

They closed their eyes. Margaret slyly opened hers again, so that she could continue her scrutiny of the elegant stranger while her father's voice droned on. "We are all sinners in your eyes, O Lord, and must be punished. Give us the strength to bear our hardships on this earth, so that we may enjoy the fruits of heaven when we are called. Thank you, Lord, for helping those of us who deserve to prosper. Amen."

Salomon van der Merwe began serving. This time the portions he served Jamie were more than generous. They talked as they ate. "Is this your first time out this way, Mr. Travis?"

"Yes," Jamie said. "First time."

"You didn't bring Mrs. Travis along, I understand."

"There is no Mrs. Travis. I haven't found anyone who'd have me." Jamie smiled.

What fool of a woman would refuse him? Margaret wondered. She lowered her eyes, afraid the stranger might read her wicked thoughts.

"Klipdrift is a town of great opportunity, Mr. Travis. *Great* opportunity."

"I'm willing to be shown." He looked at Margaret, and she blushed.

"If it isn't too personal, Mr. Travis, may I ask how you acquired your fortune?"

Margaret was embarrassed by her father's blunt questions, but the stranger did not seem to mind.

"I inherited it from my father," Jamie said easily.

"Ah, but I'm sure you've had a lot of business experience."

"Very little, I'm afraid. I need a lot of guidance."

Van der Merwe brightened. "It's fate that we met, Mr. Travis.

I have some very profitable connections. Very profitable, indeed. I can almost guarantee that I can double your money for you in just a few months." He leaned over and patted Jamie's arm. "I have a feeling this is a big day for both of us."

Jamie just smiled.

"I suppose you're staying at the Grand Hotel?"

"That's right."

"It's criminally expensive. But I suppose to a man of your means . . ." He beamed at Jamie.

Jamie said, "I'm told the countryside around here is interesting. Would it be an imposition to ask you to let your daughter show me around a bit tomorrow?"

Margaret felt her heart stop for a second.

Van der Merwe frowned. "I don't know. She—"

It was an iron-clad rule of Salomon van der Merwe's never to permit any man to be alone with his daughter. In the case of Mr. Travis, however, he decided there would be no harm in making an exception. With so much at stake, he did not want to appear inhospitable. "I can spare Margaret from the store for a short time. You will show our guest around, Margaret?"

"If you wish, Father," she said quietly.

"That's settled then." Jamie smiled. "Shall we say ten o'clock in the morning?"

After the tall, elegantly dressed guest left, Margaret cleared away the table and washed the dishes, in a complete daze. *He must think I'm an idiot.* She went over and over in her mind everything she had contributed to the conversation. Nothing. She had been completely tongue-tied. Why was that? Hadn't she waited on hundreds of men in the store without becoming a stupid fool? Of course they had not looked at her the way Ian Travis had. *Men all have the devil in them, Margaret. I'll not let them corrupt your innocence.* Her father's voice echoed in her mind. Could that be it? The weakness and trembling she had felt when the stranger had looked at her? Was he corrupting her innocence? The thought of it sent a delicious thrill through her body. She looked down at the plate she had dried three times and sat down at the table. She wished her mother were still alive.

Her mother would have understood. Margaret loved her father, but sometimes she had the oppressive feeling that she was his prisoner. It worried her that he never allowed a man to come near her. *I'll never get married,* Margaret thought. *Not until he dies.* Her rebellious thoughts filled her with guilt, and she hurriedly left the room and went into the store, where her father sat behind a desk, working on his accounts.

"Good night, Father."

Van der Merwe took off his gold-framed spectacles and rubbed his eyes before he raised his arms to embrace his daughter good-night. Margaret did not know why she pulled away.

Alone in the curtained-off alcove that served as her bedroom, Margaret studied her face in the small, round mirror that hung on the wall. She had no illusions about her looks. She was not pretty. She was interesting-looking. Nice eyes. High cheekbones. A good figure. She drew nearer to the mirror. What had Ian Travis seen when he looked at her? She began getting undressed. And Ian Travis was in the room with her, watching her, his eyes burning into her. She stepped out of her muslin drawers and camisole and stood naked before him. Her hands slowly caressed the swell of her breasts and felt her hardening nipples. Her fingers slid down across her flat belly and his hands became entwined with hers, moving slowly downward. They were between her legs now, gently touching, stroking, rubbing, harder now, faster and faster until she was caught up in a frantic whirlpool of sensation that finally exploded inside her and she gasped his name and fell to the bed.

They rode out in Jamie's carriage, and he was amazed once more at the changes that had taken place. Where before there had been only a sea of tents, now there were substantial-looking houses, constructed of timber with roofs of corrugated iron or thatch.

"Klipdrift seems very prosperous," Jamie said as they rode along the main street.

"I suppose it would be interesting for a newcomer," Margaret said. And she thought, *I've hated it until now.*

They left the town and drove out toward the mining camps along the Vaal River. The seasonal rains had turned the countryside into an enormous, colorful garden, filled with the luxuriant bush Karroo, and the spreading Rhenoster bush and heaths and diosmas plants that could be found nowhere else in the world. As they drove past a group of prospectors, Jamie asked, "Have there been any big diamond finds lately?"

"Oh, yes, a few. Every time the news gets out, hundreds of new diggers come pouring in. Most of them leave poor and heartbroken." Margaret felt she had to warn him of the danger here. "Father would not like to hear me say this, but I think it's a terrible business, Mr. Travis."

"For some, probably," Jamie agreed. "For some."

"Do you plan to stay on a while?"

"Yes."

Margaret felt her heart singing. "Good." Then added quickly, "Father will be pleased."

They drove around all morning, and from time to time they stopped and Jamie chatted with prospectors. Many of them recognized Margaret and spoke respectfully. There was a warmth to her and an easy friendliness that she did not reveal when she was around her father.

As they drove on, Jamie said, "Everyone seems to know you."

She blushed. "That's because they do business with Father. He supplies most of the diggers."

Jamie made no comment. He was keenly interested in what he was seeing. The railroad had made an enormous difference. A new combine called De Beers, named after the farmer in whose field the first diamond discovery was made, had bought out its chief rival, a colorful entrepreneur named Barney Barnato, and De Beers was busily consolidating the hundreds of small claims into one organization. Gold had been discovered recently, not far from Kimberley, along with manganese and zinc. Jamie was convinced this was only the beginning, that South Africa was a treasure-house of minerals. There were incredible opportunities here for a man with foresight.

When Jamie and Margaret returned, it was late afternoon. Jamie stopped the carriage in front of Van der Merwe's store and said, "I would be honored if you and your father would be my guests at dinner tonight."

Margaret glowed. "I'll ask Father. I do so hope he'll say yes. Thank you for a lovely day, Mr. Travis."

And she fled.

The three of them had dinner in the large, square dining room of the new Grand Hotel.

The room was crowded, and Van der Merwe grumbled, "I don't see how these people can afford to eat here."

Jamie picked up a menu and glanced at it. A steak cost one pound four shillings, a potato was four shillings and a piece of apple pie ten shillings.

"They're robbers!" Van der Merwe complained. "A few meals here and a man could eat himself into the poorhouse."

Jamie wondered what it would take to put Salomon van der Merwe in the poorhouse. He intended to find out. They ordered, and Jamie noticed that Van der Merwe ordered the most expensive items on the menu. Margaret ordered a clear soup. She was too excited to eat. She looked at her hands, remembered what they had done the night before and felt guilty.

"I can afford dinner," Jamie teased her. "Order anything you like."

She blushed. "Thank you, but I'm—I'm not really very hungry."

Van der Merwe noticed the blush and looked sharply from Margaret to Jamie. "My daughter is a rare girl, a rare girl, Mr. Travis."

Jamie nodded. "I couldn't agree with you more, Mr. van der Merwe."

His words made Margaret so happy that when their dinner

was served, she could not even eat the soup. The effect Ian Travis had on her was incredible. She read hidden meanings into his every word and gesture. If he smiled at her, it meant he liked her a lot; if he frowned, it meant he hated her. Margaret's feelings were an emotional thermometer that kept going up and down.

"Did you see anything of interest today?" Van der Merwe asked Jamie.

"No, nothing special," Jamie said casually.

Van der Merwe leaned forward. "Mark my words, sir, this is going to be the fastest-growing area in the world. A man would be smart to invest here now. The new railway's going to turn this place into a second Cape Town."

"I don't know," Jamie said dubiously. "I've heard of too many boomtowns like this going bust. I'm not interested in putting my money into a ghost town."

"Not Klipdrift," Van der Merwe assured him. "They're finding more diamonds all the time. And gold."

Jamie shrugged. "How long will that last?"

"Well, nobody can be sure of that, of course, but—"

"Exactly."

"Don't make any hasty decisions," Van der Merwe urged. "I wouldn't like to see you lose out on a great opportunity."

Jamie thought that over. "Perhaps I am being hasty. Margaret, could you show me around again tomorrow?"

Van der Merwe opened his mouth to object, then closed it. He remembered the words of Mr. Thorenson, the banker: *He walked in here and deposited a hundred thousand pounds, cool as you please, Salomon, and he said there'd be a lot more comin'.*

Greed got the better of Van der Merwe. "Of course she could."

The following morning, Margaret put on her Sunday dress, ready to meet Jamie. When her father walked in and saw her, his face turned red. "Do you want the man to think you're some kind of fallen woman—dressin' up to attract him? This is business, girl. Take that off and put on your workin' clothes."

"But, Papa—"

"Do as I say!"

She did not argue with him. "Yes, Papa."

Van der Merwe watched Margaret and Jamie drive away twenty minutes later. He wondered if he could be making a mistake.

This time Jamie headed the carriage in the opposite direction. There were exciting signs of new developments and building everywhere. *If the mineral discoveries keep up,* Jamie thought—and there was every reason to believe they would—*there is more money to be made here in real estate than in diamonds or gold. Klipdrift will need more banks, hotels, saloons, shops, brothels . . .* The list was endless. So were the opportunities.

Jamie was conscious of Margaret staring at him. "Is something wrong?" he asked.

"Oh, no," she said, and quickly looked away.

Jamie studied her now, and noticed the radiance about her. Margaret was aware of his closeness, his maleness. He sensed her feelings. She was a woman without a man.

At noon Jamie drove off the main road down to a wooded area near a stream and stopped under a large baobab tree. He had had the hotel pack a picnic lunch. Margaret put down a tablecloth, unpacked the basket and spread out the food. There was cold roast lamb, fried chicken, yellow saffron rice, quince jam and tangerines and peaches and *soetekoekjes,* almond-topped spice cookies.

"This is a banquet!" Margaret exclaimed. "I'm afraid I don't deserve all this, Mr. Travis."

"You deserve much more," Jamie assured her.

Margaret turned away, busying herself with the food.

Jamie took her face between his hands. "Margaret . . . look at me."

"Oh! Please. I—" She was trembling.

"Look at me."

Slowly she lifted her head and looked into his eyes. He pulled her into his arms, and his lips found hers and he held her close, pressing his body against hers.

After a few moments she struggled free, shook her head and said, "Oh, my God. We mustn't. Oh, we mustn't. We'll go to hell."

"Heaven."

"I'm afraid."

"There's nothing to be afraid of. Do you see my eyes? They can look right inside you. And you know what I see, don't you? You want me to make love to you. And I'm going to. And there's nothing to fear, because you belong to me. You know that, don't you? You belong to me, Margaret. You say it. I belong to Ian. Go on. I—belong—to—Ian."

"I belong—to Ian."

His lips were on hers again, and he began to undo the hooks on the back of her bodice. In a moment she stood naked in the soft breeze, and he lowered her gently down to the ground. And the tremulous passage from girlhood to womanhood became an exciting, soaring experience that made Margaret feel more alive than she had ever felt in her life. *I'll remember this moment forever,* she thought. The bed of leaves and the warm caressing breeze on her naked skin, the shadow of the baobab tree that dappled their bodies. They made love again, and it was even more wonderful. She thought, *No woman could ever love anyone as much as I love this man.*

When they were spent, Jamie held her in his strong arms, and she wished she could be there forever. She looked up at him and whispered, "What are you thinking?"

He grinned and whispered back, "That I'm bloody starving."

She laughed, and they rose and had their lunch under the shelter of the trees. Afterward they swam and lay down to let the hot sun dry them. Jamie took Margaret again, and she thought, *I want this day to go on forever.*

That evening, Jamie and Van der Merwe were seated at a corner table at the Sundowner. "You were right," Jamie announced. "The possibilities here may be greater than I thought."

Van der Merwe beamed. "I knew you were too clever a man not to see that, Mr. Travis."

"What exactly would you advise me to do?" Jamie asked.

Van der Merwe glanced around and lowered his voice. "Just today I got some information on a big new diamond strike north of Pniel. There are ten claims still available. We can divide them up between us. I'll put up fifty thousand pounds for five claims, and you put up fifty thousand pounds for the other five. There are diamonds there by the bushel. We can make millions overnight. What do you think?"

Jamie knew exactly what he thought. Van der Merwe would keep the claims that were profitable and Jamie would end up with the others. In addition, Jamie would have been willing to bet his life that Van der Merwe was not putting up one shilling.

"It sounds interesting," Jamie said. "How many prospectors are involved?"

"Only two."

"Why does it take so much money?" he asked innocently.

"Ah, that's an intelligent question." He leaned forward in his chair. "You see, they know the value of their claim, but they don't have the money to operate it. That's where you and I come in. We give them one hundred thousand pounds and let them keep twenty percent of their fields."

He slipped the twenty percent in so smoothly that it almost went by unnoticed. Jamie was certain the prospectors would be cheated of their diamonds and their money. It would all flow to Van der Merwe.

"We'll have to move fast," Van der Merwe warned. "As soon as word of this leaks out—"

"Let's not lose it," Jamie urged.

Van der Merwe smiled. "Don't worry, I'll have the contracts drawn up right away."

In Afrikaans, Jamie thought.

"Now, there are a few other deals I find very interesting, Ian."

Because it was important to keep his new partner happy, Van der Merwe no longer objected when Jamie asked that Margaret show him around the countryside. Margaret was more in love with Jamie every day. He was the last thing she thought of when she went to bed at night, and the first thing she thought of when she opened her eyes in the morning. Jamie had loosed a sensuality in her that she had not even known existed. It was as though she had suddenly discovered what her body was for, and all the things she had been taught to be ashamed of became glorious gifts to bring pleasure to Jamie. And to herself. Love was a wonderful new country to be explored. A sensual land of hidden valleys and exciting dales and glens and rivers of honey. She could not get enough of it.

In the vast sweep of the countryside, it was easy to find isolated places where they could make love, and each time for Margaret was as exciting as the first time.

The old guilt about her father haunted her. Salomon van der Merwe was an elder of the Dutch Reformed Church, and Margaret knew if he ever found out what she was doing, there would be no forgiveness. Even in the rough frontier community where they lived, where men took their pleasures where they found them, there would be no understanding. There were only two kinds of women in the world—nice girls and whores—and a nice girl did not let a man touch her unless she was married to him. So she would be labeled a whore. *It's so unfair,* she thought. *The giving and taking of love is too beautiful to be evil.* But her growing concern finally made Margaret bring up the subject of marriage.

They were driving along the Vaal River when Margaret spoke. "Ian, you know how much I—" She did not know how to go on. "That is, you and I—" In desperation she blurted out, "How do you feel about marriage?"

Jamie laughed. "I'm all for it, Margaret. I'm all for it."

She joined him in his laughter. It was the happiest moment of her life.

On Sunday morning, Salomon van der Merwe invited Jamie to accompany him and Margaret to church. The Nederduits Hervormde Kerk was a large, impressive building done in bastard Gothic, with the pulpit at one end and a huge organ at the other. When they walked in the door, Van der Merwe was greeted with great respect.

"I helped build this church," he told Jamie proudly. "I'm a deacon here."

The service was brimstone and hellfire, and Van der Merwe sat there, rapt, nodding eagerly, accepting the minister's every word.

He's God's man on Sunday, Jamie thought, *and the rest of the week he belongs to the devil.*

Van der Merwe had placed himself between the two young people, but Margaret was conscious of Jamie's nearness all through the service. *It's a good thing*—she smiled nervously to herself—*that the minister doesn't know what I'm thinking about.*

That evening, Jamie went to visit the Sundowner Saloon. Smit was behind the bar serving drinks. His face brightened when he saw Jamie.

"Good evenin', Mr. Travis. What will you have, sir? The usual?"

"Not tonight, Smit. I want to talk to you. In the back room."

"Certainly, sir." Smit scented money to be made. He turned to his assistant. "Mind the bar."

The back room of the Sundowner was no more than a closet, but it afforded privacy. It contained a round table with four chairs, and in the center of the table was a lantern. Smit lit it.

"Sit down," Jamie said.

Smit took a chair. "Yes, sir. How can I help you?"

"It's you I've come to help, Smit."

Smit beamed. "Really, sir?"

"Yes." Jamie took out a long, thin cigar and lighted it. "I've decided to let you live."

An uncertain look flickered over Smit's face. "I—I don't understand, Mr. Travis."

"Not Travis. The name is McGregor. Jamie McGregor. Remember? A year ago you set me up to be killed. At the barn. For Van der Merwe."

Smit was frowning now, suddenly wary. "I don't know what—"

"Shut up and listen to me." Jamie's voice was like a whiplash.

Jamie could see the wheels turning in Smit's mind. He was trying to reconcile the face of the white-haired man in front of him with the eager youth of a year before.

"I'm still alive, and I'm rich—rich enough to hire men to burn this place down and you with it. Are you with me so far, Smit?"

Smit started to protest his ignorance, but he looked into Jamie McGregor's eyes and saw the danger there. Smit said cautiously, "Yes, sir . . ."

"Van der Merwe pays you to send prospectors to him so he can cheat them out of what they find. That's an interesting little partnership. How much does he pay you?"

There was a silence. Smit was caught between two powerful forces. He did not know which way to jump.

"How much?"

"Two percent," he said reluctantly.

"I'll give you five. From now on when a likely prospect comes in, you'll send him to me. I'll finance him. The difference is that he'll get his fair share and you'll get yours. Did you really think Van der Merwe was paying you two percent of what he made? You're a fool."

Smit nodded. "Right, Mr. Trav—Mr. McGregor. I understand."

Jamie rose to his feet. "Not completely." He leaned over the table. "You're thinking of going to Van der Merwe and telling him about our little conversation. That way, you can collect from both of us. There's only one problem with that, Smit." His voice dropped to a whisper. "If you do, you're a dead man."

7

Jamie was getting dressed when he heard a tentative knock at the door. He listened, and it was repeated. He walked over to the door and opened it. Margaret stood there.

"Come in, Maggie," Jamie said. "Is something wrong?" It was the first time she had come to his hotel room. She stepped inside, but now that she was face to face with him, she found it difficult to speak. She had lain awake all night, wondering how to tell him the news. She was afraid he might never want to see her again.

She looked into his eyes. "Ian, I'm going to have your baby."

His face was so still that Margaret was terrified that she had lost him. And suddenly his expression changed to such joy that all her doubts were instantly wiped out. He grabbed her arms and said, "That's wonderful, Maggie! Wonderful! Have you told your father?"

Margaret pulled back in alarm. "Oh, no! He—" She walked over to the Victorian green-plush sofa and sat down. "You don't know Father. He—he would never understand."

Jamie was hurriedly putting on his shirt. "Come on, we're going to tell him together."

"Are you sure everything will be all right, Ian?"

"I've never been surer of anything in my life."

Salomon van der Merwe was measuring out strips of biltong for a prospector when Jamie and Margaret strode into the shop. "Ah, Ian! I'll be with you in a moment." He hurriedly finished with the customer and walked over to Jamie. "And how is everything this fine day?" Van der Merwe asked.

"It couldn't be better," Jamie said happily. "Your Maggie's going to have a baby."

There was a sudden stillness in the air. "I—I don't understand," Van der Merwe stuttered.

"It's very simple. I've gotten her pregnant."

The color drained from Van der Merwe's face. He turned wildly from one to the other. "This—this isn't true?" A maelstrom of conflicting emotions whirled through Salomon van der Merwe's head. The terrible shock of his precious daughter losing her virginity . . . getting pregnant . . . He would be the laughing stock of the town. But Ian Travis was a very wealthy man. And if they got married quickly . . .

Van der Merwe turned to Jamie. "You'll get married immediately, of course."

Jamie looked at him in surprise. *"Married?* You'd allow Maggie to marry a stupid bairn who let you cheat him out of what belonged to him?"

Van der Merwe's head was spinning. "What are you talking about, Ian? I never—"

"My name's not Ian," Jamie said harshly. "I'm Jamie McGregor. Dinna you recognize me?" He saw the bewildered expression on Van der Merwe's face. "Nae, a course you don't. That boy is dead. You killed him. But I'm not a man to hold a grudge, Van der Merwe. So I'm giving you a gift. My seed in your daughter's belly."

And Jamie turned and walked out, leaving the two of them staring after him, stunned.

Margaret had listened in shocked disbelief. He could not mean what he had just said. *He loved her! He—*

Salomon van der Merwe turned on his daughter, in the throes of a terrible rage. "You whore!" he screamed. *"Whore! Get out! Get out of here!"*

Margaret stood stock-still, unable to grasp the meaning of the awful thing that was happening. Ian blamed her for something her father had done. Ian thought she was part of something bad. *Who was Jamie McGregor? Who—?*

"Go!" Van der Merwe hit her hard across the face. "I never want to see you again as long as I live."

Margaret stood there, rooted, her heart pounding, gasping for breath. Her father's face was that of a madman. She turned and fled from the store, not looking back.

Salomon van der Merwe stood there watching her go, gripped by despair. He had seen what happened to other men's daughters who had disgraced themselves. They had been forced to stand up in church and be publicly pilloried and then exiled from the community. It was proper and fitting punishment, exactly what they deserved. But his Margaret had been given a decent, God fearing upbringing. *How could she have betrayed him like this?* Van der Merwe visualized his daughter's naked body, coupling with that man, writhing in heat like animals, and he began to have an erection.

He put a Closed sign on the front door of the store and lay on his bed without the strength or the will to move. When word got around town, he would become an object of derision. He would be either pitied or blamed for his daughter's depravity. Either way, it would be unbearable. He had to make certain no one learned about it. He would send the whore out of his sight forever. He knelt and prayed: *O, God! How could you do this to me, your loyal servant? Why have you forsaken me? Let her die, O Lord. Let them both die....*

The Sundowner Saloon was crowded with noon trade when Jamie entered. He walked over to the bar and turned to face the room. "Your attention, please!" The conversation tapered off into silence. "Drinks on the house for everybody."

"What is it?" Smit asked. "A new strike?"

Jamie laughed. "In a way, my friend. Salomon van der Merwe's unmarried daughter is pregnant. Mr. van der Merwe wants everybody to help him celebrate."

Smit whispered, "Oh, Jesus!"

"Jesus had nothing to do with it. Just Jamie McGregor."

Within an hour, everyone in Klipdrift had heard the news. How Ian Travis was really Jamie McGregor, and how he had gotten Van der Merwe's daughter pregnant. Margaret van der Merwe had fooled the whole town.

"She doesn't look like the kind, does she?"

"Still waters run deep, they say."

"I wonder how many other men in this town have dipped their wick in that well?"

"She's a shapely girl. I could use a piece of that myself."

"Why don't you ask her? She's givin' it away."

And the men laughed.

When Salomon van der Merwe left his store that afternoon, he had come to terms with the dreadful catastrophe that had befallen him. He would send Margaret to Cape Town on the next coach. She could have her bastard there, and there was no need for anyone in Klipdrift to know his shame. Van der Merwe stepped out into the street, hugging his secret, a smile pasted on his lips.

"Afternoon, Mr. van der Merwe. I hear you might be stockin' some extra baby clothes."

"Good day, Salomon. Hear you're gonna get a little helper for your store soon."

"Hello there, Salomon. I hear a bird watcher just spotted a new species out near the Vaal River. Yes, sir, a stork!"

Salomon van der Merwe turned and blindly stumbled back into his shop, bolting the door behind him.

At the Sundowner Saloon, Jamie was having a whiskey, listening to the flood of gossip around him. It was the biggest scandal Klipdrift had ever had, and the pleasure the townspeople took in it was intense. *I wish,* Jamie thought, *that Banda were here with me to enjoy this.* This was payment for what Salomon van der Merwe had done to Banda's sister, what he had done to Jamie and to—how many others? But this was only part payment for all the things Salomon van der Merwe had done, just the beginning. Jamie's vengeance would not be complete until Van der Merwe had been totally destroyed. As for Margaret, he had no sympathy for her. She was in on it. What had she said the first day they met? *My father might be the one to help you. He knows everything.* She was a Van der Merwe too, and Jamie would destroy both of them.

Smit walked over to where Jamie was sitting. "Kin I talk to you a minute, Mr. McGregor?"

"What is it?"

Smit cleared his throat self-consciously. "I know a couple of prospectors who have ten claims up near Pniel. They're producin' diamonds, but these fellas don't have the money to get the proper equipment to work their claim. They're lookin' for a partner. I thought you might be interested."

Jamie studied him. "These are the men you talked to Van der Merwe about, right?"

Smit nodded, surprised. "Yes, sir. But I been thinkin' over your proposition. I'd rather do business with you."

Jamie pulled out a long, thin cigar, and Smit hastened to light it. "Keep talking."

Smit did.

In the beginning, prostitution in Klipdrift was on a haphazard basis. The prostitutes were mostly black women, working in sleazy, back-street brothels. The first white prostitutes to arrive in town were part-time barmaids. But as diamond strikes increased and the town prospered, more white prostitutes appeared.

There were now half a dozen sporting houses on the outskirts of Klipdrift, wooden railway huts with tin roofs. The one exception was Madam Agnes's, a respectable-looking two-story frame structure on Bree Street, off Loop Street, the main thoroughfare, where the wives of the townspeople would not be offended by having to pass in front of it. It was patronized by the husbands of those wives, and by any strangers in town who could afford it. It was expensive, but the women were young and uninhibited, and gave good value for the money. Drinks were served in a reasonably well-decorated drawing room, and it was a rule of Madam Agnes's that no customer was ever rushed or short-changed. Madam Agnes herself was a cheerful, robust redhead in her mid-thirties. She had worked at a brothel in London and been attracted to South Africa by the tales of easy money to be picked up in a mining town like Klipdrift. She had saved enough to open her own establishment, and business had flourished from the beginning.

Madam Agnes prided herself on her understanding of men, but Jamie McGregor was a puzzle to her. He visited often, spent money freely and was always pleasant to the women, but he seemed withdrawn, remote and untouchable. His eyes were what fascinated Agnes. They were pale, bottomless pools, cold. Unlike the other patrons of her house, he never spoke about himself or his past. Madam Agnes had heard hours earlier that Jamie McGregor had deliberately gotten Salomon van der Merwe's daughter pregnant and then refused to marry her. *The bastard!* Madam Agnes thought. But she had to admit that he was an attractive bastard. She watched Jamie now as he walked down the red-carpeted stairs, politely said good night and left.

When Jamie arrived back at his hotel, Margaret was in his room, staring out the window. She turned as Jamie walked in.

"Hello, Jamie." Her voice was atremble.

"What are you doing here?"

"I had to talk to you."

"We have nothing to talk about."

"I know why you're doing this. You hate my father." Margaret moved closer to him. "But you have to know that whatever it was he did to you, I knew nothing about. Please—I beg of you—believe that. Don't hate me. I love you too much."

Jamie looked at her coldly. "That's *your* problem, isn't it?"

"Please don't look at me like that. You love me, too. . . ."

He was not listening. He was again taking the terrible journey to Paardspan where he had almost died . . . and moving the boulders on the riverbanks until he was ready to drop . . . and finally, miraculously, finding the diamonds. . . . Handing them to Van der Merwe and hearing Van der Merwe's voice saying, *You misunderstood me, boy. I don't need any partners. You're working for me. . . . I'm giving you twenty-four hours to get out of town.* And then the savage beating . . . He was smelling the vultures again, feeling their sharp beaks tear into his flesh. . . .

As though from a distance, he heard Margaret's voice. "Don't you remember? I—belong—to—you. . . . I love you."

He shook himself out of his reverie and looked at her. *Love.* He no longer had any idea what the word meant. Van der Merwe had burned every emotion out of him except hate. He lived on that. It was his elixir, his lifeblood. It was what had kept him alive when he fought the sharks and crossed the reef, and crawled over the mines at the diamond fields of the Namib Desert. Poets wrote about love, and singers sang about it, and perhaps it was real, perhaps it existed. But love was for other men. Not for Jamie McGregor.

"You're Salomon van der Merwe's daughter. You're carrying his grandchild in your belly. Get out."

There was nowhere for Margaret to go. She loved her father, and she needed his forgiveness, but she knew he would never—could never—forgive her. He would make her life a living hell. But she had no choice. She had to go to someone.

Margaret left the hotel and walked toward her father's store. She felt that everyone she passed was staring at her. Some of the men smiled insinuatingly, and she held her head high and walked on. When she reached the store, she hesitated, then stepped inside. The store was deserted. Her father came out from the back.

"Father . . ."

"*You!*" The contempt in his voice was a physical slap. He

moved closer, and she could smell the whiskey on his breath. "I want you to get out of this town. Now. Tonight. You're never to come near here again. Do you hear me? Never!" He pulled some bills from his pocket and threw them on the floor. "Take them and get out."

"I'm carrying your grandchild."

"You're carrying the devil's child!" He moved closer to her, and his hands were knotted into fists. "Every time people see you strutting around like a whore, they'll think of my shame. When you're gone, they'll forget it."

She looked at him for a long, lost moment, then turned and blindly stumbled out the door.

"The money, whore!" he yelled. "You forgot the money!"

There was a cheap boardinghouse at the outskirts of town, and Margaret made her way to it, her mind in a turmoil. When she reached it, she went looking for Mrs. Owens, the landlady. Mrs. Owens was a plump, pleasant-faced woman in her fifties, whose husband had brought her to Klipdrift and abandoned her. A lesser woman would have crumbled, but Mrs. Owens was a survivor. She had seen a good many people in trouble in this town, but never anyone in more trouble than the seventeen-year-old girl who stood before her now.

"You wanted to see me?"

"Yes. I was wondering if—if perhaps you had a job for me here."

"A job? Doing what?"

"Anything. I'm a good cook. I can wait on tables. I'll make the beds. I—I'll—" There was desperation in her voice. "Oh, please," she begged. "Anything!"

Mrs. Owens looked at the trembling girl standing there in front of her, and it broke her heart. "I suppose I could use an extra hand. How soon can you start?" She could see the relief that lighted Margaret's face.

"Now."

"I can pay you only—" She thought of a figure and added to

it. "One pound two shillings eleven pence a month, with board and lodging."

"That will be fine," Margaret said gratefully.

Salomon van der Merwe seldom appeared now on the streets of Klipdrift. More and more often, his customers found a Closed sign on the front door of his store at all hours of the day. After a while, they took their business elsewhere.

But Salomon van der Merwe still went to church every Sunday. He went not to pray, but to demand of God that He right this terrible iniquity that had been heaped upon the shoulders of his obedient servant. The other parishioners had always looked up to Salomon van der Merwe with the respect due a wealthy and powerful man, but now he could feel the stares and whispers behind his back. The family that occupied the pew next to him moved to another pew. He was a pariah. What broke his spirit completely was the minister's thundering sermon artfully combining Exodus and Ezekiel and Leviticus. "I, the Lord thy God, am a jealous God, visiting the iniquity of the fathers upon the children. Wherefor, O harlot, hear the word of the Lord. Because thy filthiness was poured out, and thy nakedness discovered through thy whoredoms with thy lovers. . . . And the Lord spake unto Moses, saying, 'Do not prostitute thy daughter, to cause her to be a whore; lest the land fall to whoredom and the land become full of wickedness. . . .' "

Van der Merwe never set foot in church again after that Sunday.

As Salomon van der Merwe's business deteriorated, Jamie McGregor's prospered. The expense of mining for diamonds increased as the digging got deeper, and miners with working claims found they were unable to afford the elaborate equipment needed. The word quickly spread that Jamie McGregor would provide financing in exchange for a share in the mines, and in time Jamie bought out his partners. He invested in real estate and businesses and gold. He was meticulously honest in his dealings, and as his reputation spread, more people came to him to do business.

There were two banks in town, and when one of them failed because of inept management, Jamie bought it, putting in his own people and keeping his name out of the transaction.

Everything Jamie touched seemed to prosper. He was successful and wealthy beyond his boyhood dreams, but it meant little to him. He measured his successes only by Salomon van der Merwe's failures. His revenge had still only begun.

From time to time, Jamie passed Margaret on the street. He took no notice of her.

Jamie had no idea what those chance encounters did to Margaret. The sight of him took her breath away, and she had to stop until she regained control of herself. She still loved him, completely and utterly. Nothing could ever change that. He had used her body to punish her father, but Margaret knew that that could be a double-edged sword. Soon she would have Jamie's baby, and when he saw that baby, his own flesh and blood, he would marry her and give his child a name. Margaret would become Mrs. Jamie McGregor, and she asked nothing more from life. At night before Margaret went to sleep, she would touch her swollen belly and whisper, "Our son." It was probably foolish to think she could influence its sex, but she did not want to overlook any possibility. Every man wanted a son.

As her womb swelled, Margaret became more frightened. She wished she had someone to talk to. But the women of the town did not speak to her. Their religion taught them punishment, not forgiveness. She was alone, surrounded by strangers, and she wept in the night for herself and for her unborn baby.

Jamie McGregor had bought a two-story building in the heart of Klipdrift, and he used it as headquarters for his growing enterprises. One day, Harry McMillan, Jamie's chief accountant, had a talk with him.

"We're combining your companies," he told Jamie, "and we need a corporate name. Do you have any suggestions?"

"I'll think about it."

Jamie thought about it. In his mind he kept hearing the sound of long-ago echoes piercing the sea *mis* on the diamond field in the Namib Desert, and he knew there was only one name he wanted. He summoned the accountant. "We're going to call the new company Kruger-Brent. Kruger-Brent Limited."

Alvin Cory, Jamie's bank manager, stopped in to visit him. "It's about Mr. van der Merwe's loans," he said. "He's fallen very far behind. In the past he's been a good risk, but his situation has drastically changed, Mr. McGregor. I think we should call in his loans."

"No."

Cory looked at Jamie in surprise. "He came in this morning trying to borrow more money to—"

"Give it to him. Give him everything he wants."

The manager got to his feet. "Whatever you say, Mr. McGregor. I'll tell him that you—"

"Tell him nothing. Just give him the money."

Every morning Margaret arose at five o'clock to bake large loaves of wonderful-smelling bread and sourdough biscuits, and when the boarders trooped into the dining room for breakfast, she served them porridge and ham and eggs, buckwheat cakes, sweet rolls and pots of steaming coffee and *naartje*. The majority of the guests at the boardinghouse were prospectors on their way to and from their claims. They would stop off in Klipdrift long enough to have their diamonds appraised, have a bath, get drunk and visit one of the town's brothels—usually in that order. They were for the most part rough, illiterate adventurers.

There was an unwritten law in Klipdrift that nice women were not to be molested. If a man wanted sex, he went to a whore. Margaret van der Merwe, however, was a challenge, for she fit into neither category. Nice girls who were single did not get pregnant, and the theory went that since Margaret had fallen once, she was probably eager to bed everyone else. All they had to do was ask. They did.

Some of the prospectors were open and blatant; others were leering and furtive. Margaret handled them all with quiet dignity. But one night as Mrs. Owens was preparing for bed, she heard screams coming from Margaret's room at the back of the house. The landlady flung the door open and rushed in. One of the guests, a drunken prospector, had ripped off Margaret's nightgown and had her pinned down on the bed.

Mrs. Owens was on him like a tiger. She picked up a flatiron and began hitting him with it. She was half the size of the prospector, but it made no difference. Filled with an overpowering rage, she knocked the prospector unconscious and dragged him into the hallway and out to the street. Then she turned and hurried back to Margaret's room. Margaret was wiping the blood off her lips from where the man had bitten her. Her hands were trembling.

"Are you all right, Maggie?"

"Yes. I—thank you, Mrs. Owens."

Unbidden tears sprang into Margaret's eyes. In a town where few people even spoke to her, here was someone who had shown kindness.

Mrs. Owens studied Margaret's swollen belly and thought, *The poor dreamer. Jamie McGregor will never marry her.*

The time of confinement was drawing close. Margaret tired easily now, and bending down and getting up again was an effort. Her only joy was when she felt her baby stir inside her. She and her son were completely alone in the world, and she talked to him hour after hour, telling him all the wonderful things that life had in store for him.

Late one evening, shortly after supper, a young black boy appeared at the boardinghouse and handed Margaret a sealed letter.

"I'm to wait for an answer," the boy told her.

Margaret read the letter, then read it again, very slowly. "Yes," she said. "The answer is yes."

The following Friday, promptly at noon, Margaret arrived in front of Madam Agnes's bordello. A sign on the front door read Closed. Margaret rapped tentatively on the door, ignoring the startled glances of the passers-by. She wondered if she had made a mistake by coming here. It had been a difficult decision, and she had accepted only out of a terrible loneliness. The letter had read:

> Dear Miss van der Merwe:
>   It's none of my business, but my girls and me have been dis-cussing your unfortunate and unfair situation, and we think it's a damned shame. We would like to help you and your baby. If it would not embarrass you, we would be honored to have you come to lunch. Would Friday at noon be convenient?
>
> Respectfully yours,
Madam Agnes
>
> P.S. We would be very discreet.

Margaret was debating whether to leave, when the door was opened by Madam Agnes.

She took Margaret's arm and said, "Come in, dearie. Let's get you out of this damned heat."

She led her into the parlor, furnished with Victorian red-plush couches and chairs and tables. The room had been deco-rated with ribbons and streamers and—from God knows where—brightly colored balloons. Crudely lettered cardboard signs hanging from the ceiling read: WELCOME BABY . . . IT'S GOING TO BE A BOY . . . HAPPY BIRTHDAY.

In the parlor were eight of Madam Agnes's girls, in a variety of sizes, ages and colors. They had all dressed for the occasion under Madam Agnes's tutelage. They wore conservative after-noon gowns and no makeup. *They look,* Margaret thought in wonder, *more respectable than most of the wives in this town.*

Margaret stared at the roomful of prostitutes, not quite know-ing what to do. Some of the faces were familiar. Margaret had waited on them when she worked in her father's store. Some of the girls were young and quite beautiful. A few were older and fleshy, with obviously dyed hair. But they all had one thing in common—they *cared.* They were friendly and warm and kind, and they wanted to make her happy.

They hovered around Margaret self-consciously, afraid of

saying or doing the wrong thing. No matter what the townspeople said, they knew this was a lady, and they were aware of the difference between Margaret and themselves. They were honored that she had come to them, and they were determined not to let anything spoil this party for her.

"We fixed you a nice lunch, honey," Madam Agnes said. "I hope you're hungry."

They led her into the dining room, where a table had been festively set, with a bottle of champagne at Margaret's place. As they walked through the hallway, Margaret glanced toward the stairs that led to the bedrooms on the second floor. She knew Jamie visited here, and she wondered which of the girls he chose. All of them, perhaps. And she studied them again and wondered what it was they had for Jamie that she did not.

The luncheon turned out to be a banquet. It began with a delicious cold soup and salad, followed by fresh carp. After that came mutton and duck with potatoes and vegetables. There was a tipsy cake and cheese and fruit and coffee. Margaret found herself eating heartily and enjoying herself immensely. She was seated at the head of the table, Madam Agnes on her right, and Maggie, a lovely blond girl who could have been no more than sixteen, on her left. In the beginning the conversation was stilted. The girls had dozens of amusing, bawdy stories to tell, but they were not the kind they felt Margaret should hear. And so they talked about the weather and about how Klipdrift was growing, and about the future of South Africa. They were knowledgeable about politics and the economy and diamonds because they got their information firsthand from experts.

Once, the pretty blonde, Maggie, said, "Jamie's just found a new diamond field at—" And as the room went suddenly silent and she realized her gaffe, she added nervously, "That's my *Uncle* Jamie. He's—he's married to my aunt."

Margaret was surprised by the sudden wave of jealousy that swept through her. Madam Agnes hastily changed the subject.

When the luncheon was finished, Madam Agnes rose and said, "This way, honey."

Margaret and the girls followed her into a second parlor which

Margaret had not seen before. It was filled with dozens of gifts, all of them beautifully wrapped. Margaret could not believe her eyes.

"I—I don't know what to say."

"Open them," Madam Agnes told Margaret.

There was a rocking cradle, handmade booteee, eaoques, embroidered bonnets, a long, embroidered cashmere cloak. There were French kid button shoes, a child's silver cup, gold-lined, and a comb and brush with solid sterling-silver handles. There were solid-gold baby bib pins with beaded edges, a celluloid baby rattle and rubber teething ring and a rocking horse painted dapple gray. There were toy soldiers, brightly colored wooden blocks and the most beautiful thing of all: a long, white christening dress.

It was like Christmas. It was beyond anything Margaret had ever expected. All the bottled-up loneliness and unhappiness of the past months exploded in her, and she burst into sobs.

Madam Agnes put her arms around her and said to the other girls, "Get out."

They quietly left the room. Madam Agnes led Margaret to a couch and sat there holding her until the sobs subsided.

"I—I'm so sorry," Margaret stammered. "I—I don't know what came over me."

"It's all right, honey. This room has seen a lot of problems come and go. And you know what I've learned? Somehow, in the end everything always gets sorted out. You and your baby are gonna be just fine."

"Thank you," Margaret whispered. She gestured toward the piles of presents. "I can never thank you and your friends enough for—"

Madam Agnes squeezed Margaret's hand. "Don't. You don't have no idea how much fun the girls and me had gettin' all this together. We don't get a chance to do this kind of thing very often. When one of *us* gets pregnant, it's a fuckin' tragedy." Her hands flew to her mouth and she said, "Oh! Excuse me!"

Margaret smiled. "I just want you to know that this has been one of the nicest days of my life."

"We're real honored that you came to visit us, honey. As far as I'm concerned, you're worth all the women in this town put together. Those damned bitches! I could kill them for the way they're behavin' to you. And if you don't mind my sayin' so, Jamie McGregor is a damned fool." She rose to her feet. "Men! It would be a wonderful world if we could live without the bastards. Or maybe it wouldn't. Who knows?"

Margaret had recovered her composure. She rose to her feet and took Madam Agnes's hand in hers. "I'll never forget this. Not as long as I live. Someday, when my son is old enough, I'll tell him about this day."

Madam Agnes frowned. "You really think you should?"

Margaret smiled. "I really think I should."

Madam Agnes saw Margaret to the door. "I'll have a wagon deliver all the gifts to your boardinghouse, and—good luck to you."

"Thank you. Oh, thank you."

And she was gone.

Madam Agnes stood there a moment watching Margaret walk clumsily down the street. Then she turned inside and called loudly, "All right, ladies. Let's go to work."

One hour later, Madam Agnes's was open for business as usual.

8

It was time to spring the trap. Over the previous six months, Jamie McGregor had quietly bought out Van der Merwe's partners in his various enterprises so that Jamie now had control of them. But his obsession was to own Van der Merwe's diamond fields in the Namib. He had paid for those fields a hundred times over with his blood and guts, and very nearly with his life. He had used the diamonds he and Banda had stolen there to build an empire from which to crush Salomon van der Merwe. The task had not yet been completed. Now, Jamie was ready to finish it.

Van der Merwe had gone deeper and deeper into debt. Everyone in town refused to lend him money, except the bank Jamie secretly owned. His standing instruction to his bank manager was, "Give Salomon van der Merwe everything he wants."

The general store was almost never open now. Van der Merwe began drinking early in the morning, and in the afternoon he would go to Madam Agnes's and sometimes spend the night there.

One morning Margaret stood at the butcher's counter waiting for the spring chickens Mrs. Owens had ordered, when she glanced out the window and saw her father leaving the brothel. She could hardly recognize the unkempt old man shuffling along the street. *I did this to him. Oh, God, forgive me, I did this!*

Salomon van der Merwe had no idea what was happening to him. He knew that somehow, through no fault of his own, his life was being destroyed. God had chosen him—as He had once chosen Job—to test the mettle of his faith. Van der Merwe was certain he would triumph over his unseen enemies in the end. All he needed was a little time—time and more money. He had put up his general store as security, the shares he had in six small diamond fields, even his horse and wagon. Finally, there was nothing left but the diamond field in the Namib, and the day he put that up as collateral, Jamie pounced.

"Pull in all his notes," Jamie ordered his bank manager. "Give him twenty-four hours to pay up in full, or foreclose."

"Mr. McGregor, he can't possibly come up with that kind of money. He—"

"Twenty-four hours."

At exactly four o'clock the following afternoon, the assistant manager of the bank appeared at the general store with the marshal and a writ to confiscate all of Salomon van der Merwe's worldly possessions. From his office building across the street, Jamie watched Van der Merwe being evicted from his store. The old man stood outside, blinking helplessly in the sun, not knowing what to do or where to turn. He had been stripped of everything. Jamie's vengeance was complete. *Why is it,* Jamie wondered, *that I feel no sense of triumph?* He was empty inside. The man he destroyed had destroyed him first.

When Jamie walked into Madam Agnes's that night, she said, "Have you heard the news, Jamie? Salomon van der Merwe blew his brains out an hour ago."

The funeral was held at the dreary, windswept cemetery outside town. Besides the burying crew, there were only two people in attendance: Margaret and Jamie McGregor. Margaret wore a shapeless black dress to cover her protruding figure. She looked pale and unwell. Jamie stood tall and elegant, withdrawn and remote. The two stood at opposite sides of the grave watching the crude pine-box coffin lowered into the ground. The clods of dirt clattered against the coffin, and to Margaret they seemed to say, *Whore! . . . Whore! . . .*

She looked across her father's grave at Jamie, and their eyes met. Jamie's glance was cool and impersonal, as though she were a stranger. Margaret hated him then. *You stand there feeling nothing, and you're as guilty as I am. We killed him, you and I. In God's eyes, I'm your wife. But we're partners in evil.* She looked down at the open grave and watched the last shovelful of dirt cover the pine box. "Rest," she whispered. "Rest."

When she looked up, Jamie was gone.

There were two wooden buildings in Klipdrift that served as hospitals, but they were so filthy and unsanitary that more patients died there than lived. Babies were born at home. As Margaret's time for delivery drew closer, Mrs. Owens arranged for a black midwife, Hannah. Labor began at three A.M.

"Now you just bear down," Hannah instructed. "Nature'll do the rest."

The first pain brought a smile to Margaret's lips. She was bringing her son into the world, and he would have a name. She would see to it that Jamie McGregor recognized his child. Her son was not going to be punished.

The labor went on, hour after hour, and when some of the boarders stepped into Margaret's bedroom to watch the proceedings, they were sent packing.

"This is personal," Hannah told Margaret. "Between you and God and the devil who got you into this trouble."

"Is it going to be a boy?" Margaret gasped.

Hannah mopped Margaret's brow with a damp cloth. "I'll let you know as soon as I check out the plumbin'. Now press down. Real hard! Hard! Harder!"

The contractions began to come closer together and the pain tore through Margaret's body. *Oh, my God, something's wrong,* Margaret thought.

"Bear down!" Hannah said. And suddenly there was a note of

alarm in her voice. "It's twisted around," she cried. "I—I can't get it out!"

Through a red mist, Margaret saw Hannah bend down and twist her body, and the room began to fade out, and suddenly there was no more pain. She was floating in space and there was a bright light at the end of a tunnel and someone was beckoning to her, and it was Jamie. *I'm here, Maggie, darling. You're going to give me a fine son.* He had come back to her. She no longer hated him. She knew then she had never hated him. She heard a voice saying, "It's almost over," and there was a tearing inside her, and the pain made her scream aloud.

"Now!" Hannah said. "It's coming."

And a second later, Margaret felt a wet rush between her legs and there was a triumphant cry from Hannah. She held up a red bundle and said, "Welcome to Klipdrift. Honey, you got yourself a son."

She named him Jamie.

Margaret knew the news about the baby would reach Jamie quickly, and she waited for him to call on her or send for her. When several weeks had passed and Margaret had not heard anything, she sent a message to him. The messenger returned thirty minutes later.

Margaret was in a fever of impatience. "Did you see Mr. McGregor?"

"Yes, ma'am."

"And you gave him the message?"

"Yes, ma'am."

"What did he *say*?" she demanded.

The boy was embarrassed. "He—he said he has no son, Miss van der Merwe."

She locked herself and her baby in her room all that day and all that night and refused to come out. "Your father's upset just now, Jamie. He thinks your mother did something bad to him. But you're his son, and when he sees you, he's going to take us to live in his house and he's going to love both of us very much. You'll see, darling. Everything is going to be fine."

In the morning when Mrs. Owens knocked on the door, Margaret opened it. She seemed strangely calm.

"Are you all right, Maggie?"

"I'm fine, thank you." She was dressing Jamie in one of his new outfits. "I'm going to take Jamie out in his carriage this morning."

The carriage, from Madam Agnes and her girls, was a thing of beauty. It was made of the finest grade of reed, with a strong cane bottom and solid, bentwood handles. It was upholstered in imported brocade, with piped rolls of silk plush, and it had a parasol hooked on at the back, with a deep ruffle.

Margaret pushed the baby carriage down the narrow sidewalks of Loop Street. An occasional stranger stopped to smile at the baby, but the women of the town averted their eyes or crossed to the other side of the street to avoid Margaret.

Margaret did not even notice. She was looking for one person. Every day that the weather was fine, Margaret dressed the baby in one of his beautiful outfits and took him out in the baby carriage. At the end of a week, when Margaret had not once encountered Jamie on the streets, she realized he was deliberately avoiding her. *Well, if he won't come to see his son, his son will go to see him,* Margaret decided.

The following morning, Margaret found Mrs. Owens in the parlor. "I'm taking a little trip, Mrs. Owens. I'll be back in a week."

"The baby's too young to travel, Maggie. He—"

"The baby will be staying in town."

Mrs. Owens frowned. "You mean *here*?"

"No, Mrs. Owens. Not here."

Jamie McGregor had built his house on a kopje, one of the hills overlooking Klipdrift. It was a low, steep-roofed bungalow with two large wings attached to the main building by wide verandas. The house was surrounded by green lawns studded with trees and a lush rose garden. In back was the carriage house and separate quarters for the servants. The domestic arrangements were in the charge of Eugenia Talley, a formidable middle-aged widow with six grown children in England.

Margaret arrived at the house with her infant son in her arms at ten in the morning, when she knew Jamie would be at his office. Mrs. Talley opened the door and stared in surprise at Margaret and the baby. As did everyone else within a radius of a hundred miles, Mrs. Talley knew who they were.

"I'm sorry, but Mr. McGregor is not at home," the housekeeper said, and started to close the door.

Margaret stopped her. "I didn't come to see Mr. McGregor. I brought him his son."

"I'm afraid I don't know anything about that. You—"

"I'll be gone for one week. I'll return for him then." She held the baby out. "His name is Jamie."

A horrified look came over Mrs. Talley's face. "You can't leave him here! Why, Mr. McGregor would—"

"You have a choice," Margaret informed her. "You can either take him in the house or have me leave him here on your doorstep. Mr. McGregor wouldn't like *that* either."

Without another word, she thrust the baby into the arms of the housekeeper and walked away.

"Wait! You can't—! Come back here! Miss—!"

Margaret never turned around. Mrs. Talley stood there, holding the tiny bundle and thinking, *Oh, my God! Mr. McGregor is going to be furious!*

She had never seen him in such a state. "How could you have been so *stupid*?" he yelled. "All you had to do was slam the door in her face!"

"She didn't give me a chance, Mr. McGregor. She—"

"I will not have her child in my house!"

In his agitation he paced up and down, pausing to stop in front of the hapless housekeeper from time to time. "I should fire you for this."

"She's coming back to pick him up in a week. I—"

"I don't care when she's coming back," Jamie shouted. "Get that child out of here. Now! Get rid of it!"

"How do you suggest I do that, Mr. McGregor?" she asked stiffly.

"Drop it off in town. There must be someplace you can leave it."

"Where?"

"How the devil do I know!"

Mrs. Talley looked at the tiny bundle she was holding in her arms. The shouting had started the baby crying. "There are no orphanages in Klipdrift." She began to rock the baby in her arms, but the screams grew louder. "Someone has to take care of him."

Jamie ran his hands through his hair in frustration. "Damn! All right," he decided. "You're the one who so generously took the baby. *You* take care of him."

"Yes, sir."

"And stop that unbearable wailing. Understand something, Mrs. Talley. I want it kept out of my sight. I don't want to know it's in this house. And when its mother picks it up next week, I don't want to see her. Is that clear?"

The baby started up with renewed vigor.

"Perfectly, Mr. McGregor." And Mrs. Talley hurried from the room.

Jamie McGregor sat alone in his den sipping a brandy and smoking a cigar. *The stupid woman. The sight of her baby is supposed to melt my heart, make me go rushing to her and say, "I love you. I love the baby. I want to marry you."* Well, he had not even bothered looking at the infant. It had nothing to do with him. He had not sired it out of love, or even lust. It had been sired out of vengeance. He would forever remember the look on Salomon van der Merwe's face when he had told him Margaret was pregnant. That was the beginning. The end was the dirt being thrown onto the wooden coffin. He must find Banda and let him know their mission was finished.

Jamie felt an emptiness. *I need to set new goals,* he thought. He was already wealthy beyond belief. He had acquired hundreds of acres of mineral land. He had bought it for the diamonds that might be found there, and had ended up owning gold, platinum and half a dozen other rare minerals. His bank held mortgages on half the properties in Klipdrift, and his landholdings extended from the Namib to Cape Town. He felt a satisfaction in this, but it was not enough. He had asked his parents to come and join him, but they did not want to leave Scotland. His brothers and sister had married. Jamie sent large sums of money back to his parents, and that gave him pleasure, but his life was at a plateau. A few years earlier it had consisted of exciting highs and lows. He had felt alive. He was alive when he and Banda sailed their raft through the reefs of the *Sperrgebiet.* He was alive crawling over the land mines through the desert sand. It seemed to Jamie that he had not been alive in a long time. He did not admit to himself that he was lonely.

He reached again for the decanter of brandy and saw that it was empty. He had either drunk more than he realized or Mrs. Talley was getting careless. Jamie rose from his chair, picked up the brandy snifter and wandered out to the butler's pantry where the liquor was kept. He was opening the bottle when he heard the cooing of an infant. *It! Mrs. Talley must have the baby in her quarters, off the kitchen.* She had obeyed his orders to the letter. He had neither seen nor heard the infant in the two days it had been trespassing in his home. Jamie could hear Mrs. Talley talking to it in the singsong tone that women used to talk to infants.

"You're a handsome little fellow, aren't you?" she was saying. "You're just an angel. Yes, you are. An angel."

The baby cooed again. Jamie walked over to Mrs. Talley's open bedroom door and looked inside. From somewhere the housekeeper had obtained a crib and the baby was lying in it. Mrs. Talley was leaning over him, and the infant's fist was tightly wrapped around her finger.

"You're a strong little devil, Jamie. You're going to grow up to be a big—" She broke off in surprise as she became aware of her employer standing in the doorway.

"Oh," she said. "I—is there something I can get for you, Mr. McGregor?"

"No." He walked over to the crib. "I was disturbed by the noise in here." And Jamie took his first look at his son. The baby was bigger than he had expected, and well formed. He seemed to be smiling up at Jamie.

"Oh, I'm sorry, Mr. McGregor. He's really such a good baby. And healthy. Just give him your finger and feel how strong he is."

Without a word, Jamie turned and walked out of the room.

Jamie McGregor had a staff of over fifty employees working on his various enterprises. There was not an employee from the mail boy to the highest executive who did not know how Kruger-Brent, Ltd., got its name, and they all took fierce pride in working for Jamie McGregor. He had recently hired David Blackwell, the sixteen-year-old son of one of his foremen, an American from Oregon who had come to South Africa looking for diamonds. When Blackwell's money ran out, Jamie had hired him to supervise one of the mines. The son went to work for the company one summer, and Jamie found him such a good worker that he offered him a permanent job. Young David Blackwell was intelligent and attractive and had initiative. Jamie knew he could also keep his mouth shut, which is why he chose him to run this particular errand.

"David, I want you to go to Mrs. Owens's boardinghouse. There's a woman living there named Margaret van der Merwe."

If David Blackwell was familiar with the name or her circumstances, he gave no indication of it. "Yes, sir."

"You're to speak only to her. She left her baby with my housekeeper. Tell her I want her to pick it up today and get it out of my house."

"Yes, Mr. McGregor."

Half an hour later, David Blackwell returned. Jamie looked up from his desk.

"Sir, I'm afraid I couldn't do what you asked."

Jamie rose to his feet. "Why not?" he demanded. "It was a simple enough job."

"Miss van der Merwe wasn't there, sir."

"Then find her."

"She left Klipdrift two days ago. She's expected back in five days. If you'd like me to make further inquiries—"

"No." That was the last thing Jamie wanted. "Never mind. That's all, David."

"Yes, sir." The boy left the office.

Damn that woman! When she returned, she was going to have a surprise coming. She was going to get her baby back!

That evening, Jamie dined at home alone. He was having his brandy in the study when Mrs. Talley came in to discuss a household problem. In the middle of a sentence, she suddenly stopped to listen and said, "Excuse me, Mr. McGregor. I hear Jamie crying." And she hurried out of the room.

Jamie slammed down his brandy snifter, spilling the brandy. *That goddamned baby! And she had the nerve to name him Jamie. He didn't look like a Jamie. He didn't look like anything.*

Ten minutes later, Mrs. Talley returned to the study. She saw the spilled drink. "Shall I get you another brandy?"

"That won't be necessary," Jamie said coldly. "What *is* necessary is that you remember who you're working for. I will not be interrupted because of that bastard. Is that quite clear, Mrs. Talley?"

"Yes, sir."

"The sooner that infant you brought into this house is gone, the better it will be for all of us. Do you understand?"

Her lips tightened. "Yes, sir. Is there anything else?"

"No."

She turned to leave.

"Mrs. Talley . . ."

"Yes, Mr. McGregor?"

"You said it was crying. It's not ill, is it?"

"No, sir. Just wet. He needed a change."

Jamie found the idea revolting. "That will be all."

Jamie would have been furious had he been aware that the servants in the house spent hour upon hour discussing him and his son. They all agreed that the master was behaving unreasonably, but they also knew that even to mention the subject would mean instant dismissal. Jamie McGregor was not a man who took kindly to advice from anyone.

The following evening Jamie had a late business meeting. He had made an investment in a new railroad. It was a small one, to be sure, running from his mines in the Namib Desert to De Aar, linking up with the Cape Town-Kimberley line, but it would now be much cheaper to transport his diamonds and gold to the port. The first South Africa Railway had been opened in 1860, running from Dunbar to the Point, and since then new lines had been run from Cape Town to Wellington. Railroads were going to be the steel veins that allowed goods and people to flow freely through the heart of South Africa, and Jamie intended to be a part of them. That was only the beginning of his plan. *After that,* Jamie thought, *ships. My own ships to carry the minerals across the ocean.*

He arrived home after midnight, undressed and got into bed. He had had a decorator from London design a large, masculine bedroom with a huge bed that had been carved in Cape Town. There was an old Spanish chest in one corner of the room and two enormous wardrobes which held more than fifty suits and thirty pairs of shoes. Jamie cared nothing about clothes, but it was important to him that they be there. He had spent too many days and nights wearing rags.

He was just dozing off when he thought he heard a cry. He sat up and listened. Nothing. Was it the baby? It might have fallen out of its crib. Jamie knew that Mrs. Talley was a sound sleeper. It would be dreadful if something happened to the infant while it was in Jamie's house. Then it could become his responsibility. *Damn that woman!* Jamie thought.

He put on a robe and slippers and went through the house to Mrs. Talley's room. He listened at her closed door and could hear nothing. Quietly, Jamie pushed open the door. Mrs. Talley was sound asleep, huddled under the covers, snoring. Jamie walked over to the crib. The baby lay on its back, its eyes wide open. Jamie moved closer and looked down. There *was* a resemblance, by God! It definitely had Jamie's mouth and chin. Its eyes were blue now, but all babies were born with blue eyes. Jamie could tell by looking at it that it was going to have gray eyes. It moved its little hands in the air and made a cooing sound and smiled up at Jamie. *Now, that's a brave lad,* Jamie thought, *lying there, not making any noise, not screaming like other babies would do.* He peered closer. *Yes, he's a McGregor, all right.*

Tentatively, Jamie reached down and held out a finger. The infant grabbed it with both hands and squeezed tightly. *He's as strong as a bull,* Jamie thought. At that moment, a strained look came over the infant's face, and Jamie could smell a sour odor.

"Mrs. Talley!"

She leaped up in bed, filled with alarm. "What—what is it?"

"The baby needs attention. Do I have to do everything around here?"

And Jamie McGregor stalked out of the room.

"David, do you know anything about babies?"

"In what respect, sir?" David Blackwell asked.

"Well, you know. What they like to play with, things like that."

The young American said, "I think when they're very young they enjoy rattles, Mr. McGregor."

"Pick up a dozen," Jamie ordered.

"Yes, sir."

No unnecessary questions. Jamie liked that. David Blackwell was going to go far.

That evening when Jamie arrived home with a small brown package, Mrs. Talley said, "I want to apologize for last night, Mr. McGregor. I don't know how I could have slept through it. The baby must have been screaming something terrible for you to have heard it all the way in your room."

"Don't worry about it," Jamie said generously. "As long as one of us heard it." He handed her the package. "Give this to it.

Some rattles for him to play with. Can't be much fun for him to be a prisoner in that crib all day."

"Oh, he's not a prisoner, sir. I take him out."

"Where do you take him?"

"Just in the garden, where I can keep an eye on him."

Jamie frowned. "He didn't look well to me last night."

"He didn't?"

"No. His color's not good. It wouldn't do for him to get sick before his mother picks him up."

"Oh, no, sir."

"Perhaps I'd better have another look at him."

"Yes, sir. Shall I bring him in here?"

"Do that, Mrs. Talley."

"Right away, Mr. McGregor."

She was back in a few minutes with little Jamie in her arms. The baby was clutching a blue rattle. "His color looks fine to me."

"Well, I could have been wrong. Give him to me."

Carefully, she held the baby out and Jamie took his son in his arms for the first time. The feeling that swept over him took him completely by surprise. It was as though he had been longing for this moment, living for this moment, without ever knowing it. This was his flesh and blood he was holding in his arms—his son, Jamie McGregor, Jr. What was the point of building an empire, a dynasty, of having diamonds and gold and railroads if you had no one to pass them on to? *What a bloody fool I've been!* Jamie thought. It had never occurred to him until now what was missing. He had been too blinded by his hatred. Looking down into the tiny face, a hardness somewhere deep in the core of him vanished.

"Move Jamie's crib into my bedroom, Mrs. Talley."

Three days later when Margaret appeared at the front door of Jamie's house, Mrs. Talley said, "Mr. McGregor is away at his office, Miss van der Merwe, but he asked me to send for him when you came for the baby. He wishes to speak with you."

Margaret waited in the living room, holding little Jamie in her arms. She had missed him terribly. Several times during the week she had almost lost her resolve and rushed back to Klipdrift, afraid that something might have happened to the baby, that he might have become ill or had an accident. But she had forced herself to stay away, and her plan had worked. Jamie wanted to talk to her! Everything was going to be wonderful. The three of them would be together now.

The moment Jamie walked into the living room, Margaret felt again the familiar rush of emotion. *Oh, God*, she thought, *I love him so much.*

"Hello, Maggie."

She smiled, a warm, happy smile. "Hello, Jamie."

"I want my son."

Margaret's heart sang. "Of course you want your son, Jamie. I never doubted it."

"I'll see to it that he's brought up properly. He'll have every advantage I can give him and, naturally, I'll see that you're taken care of."

Margaret looked at him in confusion. "I—I don't understand."

"I said I want my son."

"I thought—I mean—you and I—"

"No. It's only the boy I want."

Margaret was filled with a sudden outrage. "I see. Well, I'll not let you take him away from me."

Jamie studied her a moment. "Very well. We'll work out a compromise. You can stay on here with Jamie. You can be his—his governess." He saw the look on her face. "What *do* you want?"

"I want my son to have a name," she said fiercely. "His father's name."

"All right. I'll adopt him."

Margaret looked at him scornfully. "Adopt my baby? Oh, no. You will not have my son. I feel sorry for you. The great Jamie McGregor. With all your money and power, you have nothing. You're a thing of pity."

And Jamie stood there watching as Margaret turned and walked out of the house, carrying his son in her arms.

The following morning, Margaret made preparations to leave for America.

"Running away won't solve anything," Mrs. Owens argued.

"I'm not running away. I'm going someplace where my baby and I can have a new life."

She could no longer subject herself and her baby to the humiliation Jamie McGregor offered them.

"When will you leave?"

"As soon as possible. We'll take a coach to Worcester and the train from there to Cape Town. I've saved enough to get us to New York."

"That's a long way to go."

"It will be worth it. They call America the land of opportunity, don't they? That's all we need."

Jamie had always prided himself on being a man who remained calm under pressure. Now he went around yelling at everyone in sight. His office was in a constant uproar. Nothing anyone did pleased him. He roared and complained about everything, unable to control himself. He had not slept in three nights. He kept thinking about the conversation with Margaret. *Damn her!* He should have known she would try to push him into marriage. Tricky, just like her father. He had mishandled the negotiations. He had told her he would take care of her, but he had not been specific. Of course. *Money!* He should have offered her money. A thousand pounds—ten thousand pounds—more.

"I have a delicate task for you," he told David Blackwell.

"Yes, sir."

"I want you to talk to Miss van der Merwe. Tell her I'm offering her twenty thousand pounds. She'll know what I want in exchange." Jamie wrote out a check. He had long ago learned the lure of money in hand. "Give this to her."

"Right, sir." And David Blackwell was gone.

He returned fifteen minutes later and handed the check back to his employer. It had been torn in half. Jamie could feel his face getting red. "Thank you, David. That will be all."

So Margaret was holding out for more money. Very well. He would give it to her. But this time he would handle it himself.

Late that afternoon, Jamie McGregor went to Mrs. Owens's boardinghouse. "I want to see Miss van der Merwe," Jamie said.

"I'm afraid that's not possible," Mrs. Owens informed him. "She's on her way to America."

Jamie felt as though he had been hit in the stomach. "She can't be! When did she leave?"

"She and her son took the noon coach to Worcester."

The train sitting at the station in Worcester was filled to capacity, the seats and aisles crowded with noisy travelers on their way to Cape Town. There were merchants and their wives, salesmen, prospectors, kaffirs and soldiers and sailors reporting back for duty. Most of them were riding a train for the first time and there was a festive atmosphere among the passengers. Margaret had been able to get a seat near a window, where Jamie would not be crushed by the crowd. She sat there holding her baby close to her, oblivious to those around her, thinking about the new life that lay ahead of them. It would not be easy. Wherever she went, she would be an unmarried woman with a child, an offense to society. But she would find a way to make sure her son had his chance at a decent life. She heard the conductor call, "All aboard!"

She looked up, and Jamie was standing there. "Collect your things," he ordered. "You're getting off the train."

He still thinks he can buy me, Margaret thought. "How much are you offering this time?"

Jamie looked down at his son, peacefully asleep in Margaret's arms. "I'm offering you marriage."

9

They were married three days later in a brief, private ceremony. The only witness was David Blackwell.

During the wedding ceremony, Jamie McGregor was filled with mixed emotions. He was a man who had grown used to controlling and manipulating others, and this time it was he who had been manipulated. He glanced at Margaret. Standing next to him, she looked almost beautiful. He remembered her passion and abandon, but it was only a memory, nothing more, without heat or emotion. He had used Margaret as an instrument of vengeance, and she had produced his heir.

The minister was saying, "I now pronounce you man and wife. You may kiss the bride."

Jamie leaned forward and briefly touched his lips to Margaret's cheek.

"Let's go home," Jamie said. His son was waiting for him.

When they returned to the house, Jamie showed Margaret to a bedroom in one of the wings.

"This is your bedroom," Jamie informed her.

"I see."

"I'll hire another housekeeper and put Mrs. Talley in charge of Jamie. If there's anything you require, tell David Blackwell."

Margaret felt as though he had struck her. He was treating her like a servant. But that was not important. *My son has a name. That is enough for me.*

Jamie did not return home for dinner. Margaret waited for him, then finally dined alone. That night she lay awake in her bed, aware of every sound in the house. At four o'clock in the morning, she finally fell asleep. Her last thought was to wonder which of the women at Madam Agnes's he had chosen.

If Margaret's relationship with Jamie was unchanged since their marriage, her relationship with the townspeople of Klipdrift underwent a miraculous transformation. Overnight, Margaret went from being an outcast to becoming Klipdrift's social arbiter. Most of the people in town depended for their living in one way or another on Jamie McGregor and Kruger-Brent, Ltd. They decided that if Margaret van der Merwe was good enough for Jamie McGregor, she was good enough for them. Now when Margaret took little Jamie for an outing, she was met with smiles and cheery greetings. Invitations poured in. She was invited to teas, charity luncheons and dinners and urged to head civic committees. When she dressed her hair in a different way, dozens of women in town instantly followed suit. She bought a new yellow dress, and yellow dresses were suddenly popular. Margaret handled their fawning in the same manner she had handled their hostility—with quiet dignity.

Jamie came home only to spend time with his son. His attitude toward Margaret remained distant and polite. Each morning at breakfast she played the role of happy wife for the servants' benefit, despite the cool indifference of the man sitting across the table from her. But when Jamie had gone and she could escape to her room, she would be drenched in perspiration. She hated herself. Where was her pride? Because Margaret knew she still loved Jamie. *I'll always love him,* she thought. *God help me.*

* * *

Jamie was in Cape Town on a three-day business trip. As he came out of the Royal Hotel, a liveried black driver said, "Carriage, sir?"

"No," Jamie said. "I'll walk."

"Banda thought you might like to ride."

Jamie stopped and looked sharply at the man. "Banda?"

"Yes, Mr. McGregor."

Jamie got into the carriage. The driver flicked his whip and they started off. Jamie sat back in his seat, thinking of Banda, his courage, his friendship. He had tried many times to find him in the last two years, with no success. Now he was on his way to meet his friend.

The driver turned the carriage toward the waterfront, and Jamie knew instantly where they were going. Fifteen minutes later the carriage stopped in front of the deserted warehouse where Jamie and Banda had once planned their adventure into the Namib. *What reckless young fools we were,* Jamie thought. He stepped out of the carriage and approached the warehouse. Banda was waiting for him. He looked exactly the same, except that now he was neatly dressed in a suit and shirt and tie.

They stood there, silently grinning at each other, then they embraced.

"You look prosperous," Jamie smiled.

Banda nodded. "I've not done badly. I bought that farm we talked about. I have a wife and two sons, and I raise wheat and ostriches."

"Ostriches?"

"Their feathers bring in lots of money."

"Ah. I want to meet your family, Banda."

Jamie thought of his own family in Scotland, and of how much he missed them. He had been away from home for four years.

"I've been trying to find you."

"I've been busy, Jamie." Banda moved closer. "I had to see you to give you a warning. There's going to be trouble for you."

Jamie studied him. "What kind of trouble?"

"The man in charge of the Namib field—Hans Zimmerman—he's bad. The workers hate him. They're talking about walking out. If they do, your guards will try to stop them and there will be a riot."

Jamie never took his eyes from Banda's face.

"Do you remember I once mentioned a man to you—John Tengo Javabu?"

"Yes. He's a political leader. I've been reading about him. He's been stirring up a *donderstorm.*"

"I'm one of his followers."

Jamie nodded. "I see. I'll do what has to be done," Jamie promised.

"Good. You've become a powerful man, Jamie. I'm glad."

"Thank you, Banda."

"And you have a fine-looking son."

Jamie could not conceal his surprise. "How do you know that?"

"I like to keep track of my friends." Banda rose to his feet. "I have a meeting to go to, Jamie. I'll tell them things will be straightened out at the Namib."

"Yes. I'll attend to it." He followed the large black man to the door. "When will I see you again?"

Banda smiled. "I'll be around. You can't get rid of me that easily."

And Banda was gone.

When Jamie returned to Klipdrift, he sent for young David Blackwell. "Has there been any trouble at the Namib field, David?"

"No, Mr. McGregor." He hesitated. "But I have heard rumors that there might be."

"The supervisor there is Hans Zimmerman. Find out if he's mistreating the workers. If he is, put a stop to it. I want you to go up there yourself."

"I'll leave in the morning."

When David arrived at the diamond field at the Namib, he spent two hours quietly talking to the guards and the workers.

What he heard filled him with a cold fury. When he had learned what he wanted to know, he went to see Hans Zimmerman.

Hans Zimmerman was a goliath of a man. He weighed three hundred pounds and was six feet, six inches tall. He had a sweaty, porcine face and red-veined eyes, and was one of the most unattractive men David Blackwell had ever seen. He was also one of the most efficient supervisors employed by Kruger-Brent, Ltd. He was seated at a desk in his small office, dwarfing the room, when David walked in.

Zimmerman rose and shook David's hand. "Pleasure to see you, Mr. Blackwell. You should have told me you was comin'."

David was sure that word of his arrival had already reached Zimmerman.

"Whiskey?"

"No, thank you."

Zimmerman leaned back in his chair and grinned. "What can I do for you? Ain't we diggin' up enough diamonds to suit the boss?"

Both men knew that the diamond production at the Namib was excellent. "I get more work out of my kaffirs than anyone else in the company," was Zimmerman's boast.

"We've been getting some complaints about conditions here," David said.

The smile faded from Zimmerman's face. "What kind of complaints?"

"That the men here are being treated badly and—"

Zimmerman leaped to his feet, moving with surprising agility. His face was flushed with anger. "These ain't men. These are kaffirs. You people sit on your asses at headquarters and—"

"Listen to me," David said. "There's no—"

"You listen to *me*! I produce more fuckin' diamonds than anybody else in the company, and you know why? Because I put the fear of God into these bastards."

"At our other mines," David said, "we're paying fifty-nine shillings a month and keep. You're paying your workers only fifty shillings a month."

"You complainin' 'cause I made a better deal for you? The only thing that counts is profit."

"Jamie McGregor doesn't agree," David replied. "Raise their wages."

Zimmerman said sullenly, "Right. It's the boss's money."

"I hear there's a lot of whipping going on."

Zimmerman snorted. "Christ, you can't hurt a native, mister. Their hides are so thick they don't even feel the goddamned whip. It just scares them."

"Then you've scared three workers to death, Mr. Zimmerman."

Zimmerman shrugged. "There's plenty more where they came from."

He's a bloody animal, David thought. *And a dangerous one.* He looked up at the huge supervisor. "If there's any more trouble here, you're going to be replaced." He rose to his feet. "You'll start treating your men like human beings. The punishments are to stop immediately. I've inspected their living quarters. They're pigsties. Clean them up."

Hans Zimmerman was glaring at him, fighting to control his temper. "Anything else?" he finally managed to say.

"Yes. I'll be back here in three months. If I don't like what I see, you can find yourself a job with another company. Good day." David turned and walked out.

Hans Zimmerman stood there for a long time, filled with a simmering rage. *The fools,* he thought. *Uitlanders.* Zimmerman was a Boer, and his father had been a Boer. The land belonged to them and God had put the blacks there to serve them. If God had meant them to be treated like human beings, he would not have made their skins black. Jamie McGregor did not understand that. But what could you expect from an *uitlander,* a native-lover? Hans Zimmerman knew he would have to be a little more careful in the future. But he would show them who was in charge at the Namib.

Kruger-Brent, Ltd., was expanding, and Jamie McGregor was away a good deal of the time. He bought a paper mill in Canada and a shipyard in Australia. When he was home, Jamie spent all his time with his son, who looked more like his father each day. Jamie felt an inordinate pride in the boy. He wanted to take the child with him on his long trips, but Margaret refused to let him.

"He's much too young to travel. When he's older, he can go with you. If you want to be with him, you'll see him here."

Before Jamie had realized it, his son had had his first birthday, and then his second, and Jamie marveled at how the time raced by. It was 1887.

To Margaret, the last two years had dragged by. Once a week Jamie would invite guests to dinner and Margaret was his gracious hostess. The other men found her witty and intelligent and enjoyed talking to her. She knew that several of the men found her very attractive indeed, but of course they never made an overt move, for she was the wife of Jamie McGregor.

When the last of the guests had gone, Margaret would ask, "Did the evening go well for you?"

Jamie would invariably answer, "Fine. Good night," and be off to look in on little Jamie. A few minutes later, Margaret would hear the front door close as Jamie left the house.

Night after night, Margaret McGregor lay in her bed thinking about her life. She knew how much she was envied by the women in town, and it made her ache, knowing how little there was to envy. She was living out a charade with a husband who treated her worse than a stranger. If only he would notice her! She wondered what he would do if one morning at breakfast she took up the bowl that contained his oatmeal especially imported from Scotland and poured it over his stupid head. She could visualize the expression on his face, and the fantasy tickled her so much that she began to giggle, and the laughter turned into deep, wrenching sobs. *I don't want to love him any more. I won't. I'll stop, somehow, before I'm destroyed. . . .*

By 1890, Klipdrift had more than lived up to Jamie's expectations. In the seven years he had been there, it had become a full-fledged boomtown, with prospectors pouring in from every part of the world. It was the same old story. They came by coach and in wagons and on foot. They came with nothing but the rags they wore. They needed food and equipment and shelter and grubstake money, and Jamie McGregor was there to supply it all. He had shares in dozens of producing diamond and gold mines, and his name and reputation grew. One morning Jamie received a visit from an attorney for De Beers, the giant conglomerate that controlled the huge diamond mines at Kimberley.

"What can I do for you?" Jamie asked.

"I've been sent to make you an offer, Mr. McGregor. De Beers would like to buy you out. Name your price."

It was a heady moment. Jamie grinned and said, "Name *yours.*"

David Blackwell was becoming more and more important to Jamie. In the young American Jamie McGregor saw himself as he once had been. The boy was honest, intelligent and loyal. Jamie made David his secretary, then his personal assistant and, finally, when the boy was twenty-one, his general manager.

To David Blackwell, Jamie McGregor was a surrogate father. When David's own father suffered a heart attack, it was Jamie who arranged for a hospital and paid for the doctors, and when David's father died, Jamie McGregor took care of the funeral arrangements. In the five years David had worked for Kruger-Brent, Ltd., he had come to admire Jamie more than any man he had ever known. He was aware of the problem between Jamie and Margaret, and deeply regretted it, because he liked them both. *But it's none of my business,* David told himself. *My job is to help Jamie in any way I can.*

Jamie spent more and more time with his son. The boy was five now, and the first time Jamie took him down in the mines, young Jamie talked of nothing else for a week. They went on camping trips, and they slept in a tent under the stars. Jamie was used to the skies of Scotland, where the stars knew their rightful places in the firmament. Here in South Africa, the constellations were confusing. In January Canopus shone brilliantly overhead, while in May it was the Southern Cross that was near the zenith. In June, which was South Africa's winter, Scorpio was the glory of the heavens. It was puzzling. Still, it was a very special feeling for Jamie to lie on the warm earth and look up at the timeless sky with his son at his side and know they were part of the same eternity.

They rose at dawn and shot game for the pot: partridge, guinea fowl, reedbuck and oribi. Little Jamie had his own pony, and father and son rode along the veld carefully avoiding the six-foot holes dug by the ant bear, deep enough to engulf a horse and rider, and the smaller holes dug by the mere-cat.

There was danger on the veld. On one trip Jamie and his son were camped at a riverbed where they were almost killed by a band of migrating springbok. The first sign of trouble was a faint cloud of dust on the horizon. Hares and jackals and mere-cats raced past and large snakes came out of the brush looking for rocks under which to hide. Jamie looked at the horizon again. The dust cloud was coming closer.

"Let's get out of here," he said.

"Our tent—"

"Leave it!"

The two of them quickly mounted and headed for the top of a high hill. They heard the drumming of hooves and then they could see the front rank of the springbok, racing in a line at least three miles long. There were more than half a million of them, sweeping away everything in their path. Trees were torn down and shrubs were pulverized, and in the wake of the relentless tide were the bodies of hundreds of small animals. Hares, snakes, jackals and guinea fowl were crushed beneath the deadly hooves. The air was filled with dust and thunder, and when it was finally over, Jamie estimated that it had lasted more than three hours.

On Jamie's sixth birthday, his father said, "I'm going to take you to Cape Town next week and show you what a real city looks like."

"Can Mother go with us?" Jamie asked. "She doesn't like shooting, but she likes cities."

His father ruffled the boy's hair and said, "She's busy here, Son. Just the two of us men, eh?"

The child was disturbed by the fact that his mother and father seemed so distant with each other, but then he did not understand it.

They made the journey in Jamie's private railway car. By the year 1891, railways were becoming the preeminent means of travel in South Africa, for trains were inexpensive, convenient and fast. The private railway car Jamie ordered built for himself was seventy-one feet long and had four paneled staterooms that could accommodate twelve persons, a salon that could be used as an office, a dining compartment, a barroom and a fully equipped kitchen. The staterooms had brass beds, Pintsch gas lamps and wide picture windows.

"Where are all the passengers?" the young boy asked.

Jamie laughed. "We're all the passengers. It's your train, Son."

Young Jamie spent most of the trip staring out the window, marveling at the endless expanse of land speeding past.

"This is God's land," his father told him. "He filled it with precious minerals for us. They're all in the ground, waiting to be discovered. What's been found so far is only the beginning, Jamie."

When they arrived at Cape Town, young Jamie was awed by the crowds and the huge buildings. Jamie took his son down to the McGregor Shipping Line, and pointed out half a dozen ships loading and unloading in the harbor. "You see those? They belong to us."

When they returned to Klipdrift, young Jamie was bursting with the news of all he had seen. "Papa owns the whole city!" the boy exclaimed. "You'd love it, Mama. You'll see it next time."

Margaret hugged her son to her. "Yes, darling."

Jamie spent many nights away from home, and Margaret

knew he was at Madam Agnes's. She had heard he had bought a house for one of the women so that he could visit her privately. She had no way of knowing whether it was true. Margaret only knew that whoever she was, she wanted to kill her.

To retain her sanity, Margaret forced herself to take an interest in the town. She raised funds to build a new church and started a mission to help the families of prospectors who were in dire need. She demanded that Jamie use one of his railroad cars to transport prospectors free of charge back to Cape Town when they had run out of money and hope.

"You're asking me to throw away good money, woman," he growled. "Let 'em walk back the same way they came."

"They're in no condition to walk," Margaret argued. "And if they stay, the town will have to bear the cost of clothing and feeding them."

"All right," Jamie finally grumbled. "But it's a damn fool idea."

"Thank you, Jamie."

He watched Margaret march out of his office, and, in spite of himself, he could not help feeling a certain pride in her. *She'd make a fine wife for someone,* Jamie thought.

The name of the woman Jamie set up in a private house was Maggie, the pretty prostitute who had sat next to Margaret at the baby shower. It was ironic, Jamie thought, that she should bear his wife's name. They were nothing alike. This Maggie was a twenty-one-year-old blonde with a pert face and a lush body—a tigress in bed. Jamie had paid Madam Agnes well for letting him take the girl, and he gave Maggie a generous allowance. Jamie was very discreet when he visited the small house. It was almost always at night, and he was certain he was unobserved. In fact, he was observed by many people, but not one of them cared to comment about it. It was Jamie McGregor's town, and he had the right to do anything he pleased.

On this particular evening, Jamie was finding no joy. He had gone to the house anticipating pleasure, but Maggie was in a foul mood. She lay sprawled across the large bed, her rose-colored dressing gown not quite concealing her ripe breasts or the silky, golden triangle between her thighs. "I'm sick of stayin' locked up in this damned house," she said. "It's like I'm a slave or somethin'! At least at Madam Agnes's there was somethin' goin' on all the time. Why don't you ever take me with you when you travel?"

"I've explained that, Maggie. I can't—"

She leaped out of bed and stood defiantly before him, her dressing gown wide open. "Horseshit! You take your *son* everywhere. Ain't I as good as your son?"

"No," Jamie said. His voice was dangerously quiet. "You're not." He walked over to the bar and poured himself a brandy. It was his fourth—much more than he usually drank.

"I don't mean a damned thing to you," Maggie screamed. "I'm just a piece of arse." She threw her head back and laughed derisively. "Big, moral Scotchman!"

"Scot—not Scotchman."

"For Christ's sake, will you stop criticizin' me? Everythin' I do ain't good enough. Who the hell do you think you are, my bloody father?"

Jamie had had enough. "You can go back to Madam Agnes's tomorrow. I'll tell her you're coming." He picked up his hat and headed for the door.

"You can't get rid of me like this, you bastard!" She followed him, wild with anger.

Jamie stopped at the door. "I just did." And he disappeared into the night.

To his surprise, he found he was walking unsteadily. His mind seemed fuzzy. Perhaps he had had more than four brandies. He was not sure. He thought about Maggie's naked body in bed that evening, and how she had flaunted it, teasing him, then withdrawing. She had played with him, stroking him and running her soft tongue over his body until he was hard and eager for her. And then she had begun the fight, leaving him inflamed and unsatisfied.

When Jamie reached home, he entered the front hall, and as

he started toward his room, he passed the closed door of Margaret's bedroom. There was a light from under the door. She was still awake. Jamie suddenly began to picture Margaret in bed, wearing a thin nightgown. Or perhaps nothing. He remembered how her rich, full body had writhed beneath him under the trees by the Orange River. With the liquor guiding him, he opened Margaret's bedroom door and entered.

She was in bed reading by the light of a kerosene lamp. She looked up in surprise. "Jamie . . . is something wrong?"

" 'Cause I decide to pay my wife a l'il visit?" His words were slurred.

She was wearing a sheer nightgown, and Jamie could see her ripe breasts straining against the fabric. *God, she has a lovely body!* He began to take off his clothes.

Margaret leaped out of bed, her eyes very wide. "What are you doing?"

Jamie kicked the door shut behind him and walked over to her. In a moment, he had thrown her onto the bed and he was next to her, naked. "God, I want you, Maggie."

In his drunken confusion, he was not sure which Maggie he wanted. How she fought him! Yes, this was his little wildcat. He laughed as he finally managed to subdue her flailing arms and legs, and she was suddenly open to him and pulling him close and saying, "Oh, my darling, my darling Jamie. I need you so much," and he thought, *I shouldn't have been so mean to you. In the morning I'm gonna tell you you don't have to go back to Madam Agnes's . . .*

When Margaret awoke the next morning, she was alone in bed. She could still feel Jamie's strong male body inside hers and she heard him saying, *God, I want you, Maggie,* and she was filled with a wild, complete joy. She had been right all along. He did love her. It had been worth the wait, worth the years of pain and loneliness and humiliation.

Margaret spent the rest of the day in a state of rapture. She bathed and washed her hair and changed her mind a dozen times about which dress would please Jamie most. She sent the cook away so that she herself could prepare Jamie's favorite dishes. She set the dining-room table again and again before she was satisfied with the candles and flowers. She wanted this to be a perfect evening.

Jamie did not come home for dinner. Nor did he come home all night. Margaret sat in the library waiting for him until three o'clock in the morning, and then she went to her bed, alone.

When Jamie returned home the following evening, he nodded politely to Margaret and walked on to his son's room. Margaret stood staring after him in stunned bewilderment, and then slowly turned to look at herself in the mirror. The mirror told her that she had never looked as beautiful, but when she looked closer she could not recognize the eyes. They were the eyes of a stranger.

10

"Well, I have some wonderful news for you, Mrs. McGregor," Dr. Teeger beamed. "You're going to have a baby."

Margaret felt the shock of his words and did not know whether to laugh or cry. *Wonderful news?* To bring another child into a loveless marriage was impossible. Margaret could no longer bear the humiliation. She would have to find a way out, and even as she was thinking it, she felt a sudden wave of nausea that left her drenched in perspiration.

Dr. Teeger was saying, "Morning sickness?"

"A bit."

He handed her some pills. "Take these. They'll help. You're in excellent condition, Mrs. McGregor. Not a thing to worry about. You run along home and tell the good news to your husband."

"Yes," she said dully. "I'll do that."

They were at the dinner table when she said, "I saw the doctor today. I'm going to have a baby."

Without a word, Jamie threw down his napkin, arose from his chair and stormed out of the room. That was the moment when

Margaret learned she could hate Jamie McGregor as deeply as she could love him.

It was a difficult pregnancy, and Margaret spent much of the time in bed, weak and tired. She lay there hour after hour, fantasizing, visualizing Jamie at her feet, begging for forgiveness, making wild love to her again. But they were only fantasies. The reality was that she was trapped. She had nowhere to go, and even if she could leave, he would never allow her to take her son with her.

Jamie was seven now, a healthy, handsome boy with a quick mind and a sense of humor. He had drawn closer to his mother, as though somehow sensing the unhappiness in her. He made little gifts for her in school and brought them home, and Margaret would smile and thank him and try to lift herself out of her depression. When young Jamie asked why his father stayed away nights and never took her out, Margaret would reply, "Your father is a very important man, Jamie, doing important things, and he's very busy."

What's between his father and me is my problem, Margaret thought, *and I'll not have Jamie hating his father because of it.*

Margaret's pregnancy became more and more apparent. When she went out on the street, acquaintances would stop her and say, "It won't be long now, will it, Mrs. McGregor? I'll bet it's going to be a fine boy like little Jamie. Your husband must be a happy man."

Behind her back, they said, "Poor thing. She's lookin' peaked—she must have found out about the whore he's taken as his mistress . . ."

Margaret tried to prepare young Jamie for the new arrival. "You're going to have a new brother or sister, darling. Then you'll have someone to play with all the time. Won't that be nice?"

Jamie hugged her and said, "It will be more company for you, Mother."

And Margaret fought to keep back the tears.

*   *   *

The labor pains began at four o'clock in the morning. Mrs. Talley sent for Hannah, and the baby was delivered at noon. It was a healthy baby girl, with her mother's mouth and her father's chin, and black hair curling around her little red face. Margaret named her Kate. *It's a good, strong name*, Margaret thought. *And she's going to need her strength. We all are. I've got to take the children away from here. I don't know how yet, but I must find a way.*

David Blackwell burst into Jamie McGregor's office without knocking, and Jamie looked up in surprise. "What the hell—?"

"They're rioting at the Namib!"

Jamie stood up. "*What?* What happened?"

"One of the black boys was caught trying to steal a diamond. He cut a hole under his armpit and hid the stone inside it. As a lesson, Hans Zimmerman flogged him in front of the other workers. The boy died. He was twelve years old."

Jamie's face filled with rage. "Sweet Jesus! I ordered a stop to flogging at all the mines."

"I warned Zimmerman."

"Get rid of the bastard."

"We can't find him."

"Why not?"

"The blacks have him. The situation's out of control."

Jamie grabbed his hat. "Stay here and take care of things until I get back."

"I don't think it's safe for you to go up there, Mr. McGregor. The native that Zimmerman killed was from the Barolong tribe. They don't forgive, and they don't forget. I could—"

But Jamie was gone.

When Jamie McGregor was ten miles away from the diamond field, he could see the smoke. All the huts at the Namib had been set to the torch. *The damned fools!* Jamie thought. *They're burning their own houses.* As his carriage drew closer, he heard the sounds of gunshots and screams. Amid the mass confusion, uniformed constables were shooting at blacks and coloreds who were desperately trying to flee. The whites were outnumbered ten to one, but they had the weapons.

When the chief constable, Bernard Sothey, saw Jamie McGregor, he hurried up to him and said, "Don't worry, Mr. McGregor. We'll get every last one of the bastards."

"The hell you will," Jamie cried. "Order your men to stop shooting."

"*What?* If we—"

"Do as I say!" Jamie watched, sick with rage, as a black woman fell under a hail of bullets. "Call your men off."

"As you say, sir." The chief constable gave orders to an aide, and three minutes later all shooting had stopped.

There were bodies on the ground everywhere. "If you want my advice," Sothey said, "I'd—"

"I don't want your advice. Bring me their leader."

Two policemen brought a young black up to where Jamie was standing. He was handcuffed and covered with blood, but there was no fear in him. He stood tall and straight, his eyes blazing, and Jamie remembered Banda's word for Bantu pride: *isiko*.

"I'm Jamie McGregor."

The man spat.

"What happened here was not my doing. I want to make it up to your men."

"Tell that to their widows."

Jamie turned to Sothey. "Where's Hans Zimmerman?"

"We're still looking for him, sir."

Jamie saw the gleam in the black man's eyes, and he knew that Hans Zimmerman was not going to be found.

He said to the man, "I'm closing the diamond field down for three days. I want you to talk to your people. Make a list of your complaints, and I'll look at it. I promise you I'll be fair. I'll change everything here that's not right."

The man studied him, a look of skepticism on his face.

"There will be a new foreman in charge here, and decent working conditions. But I'll expect your men back at work in three days."

The chief constable said, incredulously, "You mean you're gonna let him go? He killed some of my men."

"There will be a full investigation, and—"

There was the sound of a horse galloping toward them, and Jamie turned. It was David Blackwell, and the unexpected sight of him sounded an alarm in Jamie's mind.

David leaped off his horse. "Mr. McGregor, your son has disappeared."

The world suddenly grew cold.

Half the population of Klipdrift turned out to join in the search. They covered the countryside, looking through gulleys, ravines and klops. There was no trace of the boy.

Jamie was like a man possessed. *He's wandered away somewhere, that's all. He'll be back.*

He went into Margaret's bedroom. She was lying in bed, nursing the baby.

"Is there any news?" she demanded.

"Not yet, but I'll find him." He looked at his baby daughter for an instant, then turned and walked out without another word.

Mrs. Talley came into the room, twisting her hands in her apron. "Don't you worry, Mrs. McGregor. Jamie is a big boy. He knows how to take care of himself."

Margaret's eyes were blinded by tears. *No one would harm little Jamie, would they? Of course not.*

Mrs. Talley reached down and took Kate from Margaret's arms.

"Try to sleep."

She took the baby into the nursery and laid her down in her crib. Kate was looking up at her, smiling.

"You'd better get some sleep too, little one. You've got a busy life ahead of you."

Mrs. Talley walked out of the room, closing the door behind her.

At midnight, the bedroom window silently slid open and a man climbed into the room. He walked over to the crib, threw a blanket over the infant's head and scooped her up in his arms.

Banda was gone as quickly as he had come.

It was Mrs. Talley who discovered that Kate was missing. Her first thought was that Mrs. McGregor had come in the night and taken her. She walked into Margaret's bedroom and asked, "Where's the baby?"

And from the look on Margaret's face, she knew instantly what had happened.

As another day went by with no trace of his son, Jamie was on the verge of collapsing. He approached David Blackwell. "You don't think anything bad has happened to him?" His voice was barely under control.

David tried to sound convincing. "I'm sure not, Mr. McGregor."

But he *was* sure. He had warned Jamie McGregor that the Bantus neither forgave nor forgot, and it was a Bantu who had been cruelly murdered. David was certain of one thing: If the Bantus had taken little Jamie, he had died a horrible death, for they would exact their vengeance in kind.

Jamie returned home at dawn, drained. He had led a search party of townspeople, diggers and constables, and they had spent the night looking without success in every conceivable place for the young boy.

David was waiting when Jamie walked into the study. David rose to his feet. "Mr. McGregor, your daughter has been kidnapped."

Jamie stared at him in silence, his face pale. Then he turned and walked into his bedroom.

Jamie had not been to bed for forty-eight hours, and he fell into bed, utterly exhausted, and slept. He was under the shade of a large baobab tree and in the distance across the trackless veld a lion was moving toward him. Young Jamie was shaking him. *Wake up, Papa, a lion is coming.* The animal was moving toward them faster now. His son was shaking him harder. *Wake up!*

Jamie opened his eyes. Banda was standing over him. Jamie started to speak, but Banda put a hand over Jamie's mouth.

"Quiet!" He allowed Jamie to sit up.

"Where's my son?" Jamie demanded.

"He's dead."

The room began to spin.

"I'm sorry. I was too late to stop them. Your people spilled Bantu blood. My people demanded vengeance."

Jamie buried his face in his hands. "Oh, my God! What did they do to him?"

There was a bottomless sorrow in Banda's voice. "They left him out in the desert. I—I found his body and buried him."

"Oh, no! Oh, please, no!"

"I tried to save him, Jamie."

Jamie slowly nodded, accepting it. Then dully, "What about my daughter?"

"I took her away before they could get her. She's back in her bedroom, asleep. She'll be all right if you do what you promised."

Jamie looked up, and his face was a mask of hatred. "I'll keep my promise. But I want the men who killed my son. They're going to pay."

Banda said quietly, "Then you will have to kill my whole tribe, Jamie."

Banda was gone.

It was only a nightmare, but she kept her eyes tightly closed, because she knew if she opened them the nightmare would become real and her children would be dead. So she played a game. She would keep her eyes squeezed shut until she felt little Jamie's hand on hers saying, "It's all right, Mother. We're here. We're safe."

She had been in bed for three days, refusing to talk to anyone or see anyone. Dr. Teeger came and went, and Margaret was not even aware of it. In the middle of the night Margaret was lying in bed with her eyes shut when she heard a loud crash from her son's room. She opened her eyes and listened. There was another sound. Little Jamie was back!

Margaret hurriedly got out of bed and ran down the corridor toward the closed door of her son's room. Through the door, she could hear strange animal sounds. Her heart pounding wildly, she pushed the door open.

Her husband lay on the floor, his face and body contorted. One eye was closed and the other stared up at her grotesquely. He was trying to speak, and the words came out as slobbering animal sounds.

Margaret whispered, "Oh, Jamie—Jamie!"

Dr. Teeger said, "I'm afraid the news is bad, Mrs. McGregor. Your husband has had a severe stroke. There's a fifty-fifty chance he'll live—but if he does, he'll be a vegetable. I'll make arrangements to get him into a private sanitarium where he can get the proper care."

"No."

He looked at Margaret in surprise. "No . . . what?"

"No hospital. I want him here with me."

The doctor considered for a moment. "All right. You'll need a nurse. I'll arrange—"

"I don't want a nurse. I'll take care of Jamie myself."

Dr. Teeger shook his head. "That won't be possible, Mrs. McGregor. You don't know what's involved. Your husband is no longer a functioning human being. He's completely paralyzed and will be for as long as he lives."

Margaret said, "I'll take care of him."

Now Jamie finally, truly, belonged to her.

11

Jamie McGregor lived for exactly one year from the day he was taken ill, and it was the happiest time of Margaret's life. Jamie was totally helpless. He could neither talk nor move. Margaret cared for her husband, tended to all his needs, and kept him at her side day and night. During the day, she propped him up in a wheelchair in the sewing room, and while she knitted sweaters and throw-robes for him, she talked to him. She discussed all the little household problems he had never had time to listen to before, and she told him how well little Kate was getting along. At night she carried Jamie's skeletal body to her bedroom and gently lay him in bed next to her. Margaret tucked him in and they had their one-sided chat until Margaret was ready to go to sleep.

David Blackwell was running Kruger-Brent, Ltd. From time to time, David came to the house with papers for Margaret to sign, and it was painful for David to see the helpless condition Jamie was in. *I owe this man everything,* David thought.

"You chose well, Jamie," Margaret told her husband. "David is a fine man." She put down her knitting and smiled. "He reminds me of you a bit. Of course, there was never anyone as clever as you, my darling, and there never will be again. You were so fair to look at, Jamie, and so kind and strong. And you weren't afraid to dream. Now all your dreams have come true. The company is getting bigger every day." She picked up her knitting again. "Little Kate is beginning to talk. I'll swear she said 'mama' this morning . . ."

Jamie sat there, propped up in his chair, one eye staring ahead.

"She has your eyes and your mouth. She's going to grow up to be a beauty . . ."

The following morning when Margaret awakened, Jamie McGregor was dead. She took him in her arms and held him close to her.

"Rest, my darling, rest. I've always loved you so much, Jamie. I hope you know that. Good-bye, my own dear love."

She was alone now. Her husband and her son had left her. There was only herself and her daughter. Margaret walked into the baby's room and looked down at Kate, sleeping in her crib. *Katherine. Kate.* The name came from the Greek, and it meant clear or pure. It was a name given to saints and nuns and queens.

Margaret said aloud, "Which are you going to be, Kate?"

It was a time of great expansion in South Africa, but it was also a time of great strife. There was a long-standing Transvaal dispute between the Boers and the British, and it finally came to a head. On Thursday, October 12, 1899, on Kate's seventh birthday, the British declared war on the Boers, and three days later the Orange Free State was under attack. David tried to persuade Margaret to take Kate and leave South Africa, but Margaret refused to go.

"My husband is here," she said.

There was nothing David could do to dissuade her. "I'm going to join with the Boers," David told her. "Will you be all right?"

"Yes, of course," Margaret said. "I'll try to keep the company going."

The next morning David was gone.

The British had expected a quick and easy war, no more than a mopping-up operation, and they began with a confident, light-hearted holiday spirit. At the Hyde Park Barracks in London, a send-off supper was given, with a special menu showing a British soldier holding up the head of a boar on a tray. The menu read:

SEND-OFF SUPPER

To the CAPE SQUADRON,
November 27, 1899

MENU

Oysters—Blue Points
Compo Soup
Toady in the Hole
Sandy Sole
Mafeking Mutton
Transvaal Turnips. Cape Sauce
Pretoria Pheasants
White Sauce
Tinker Taters
Peace Pudding. Massa Ices
Dutch Cheese
Dessert

(You are requested not to throw
shells under the tables)

Boer Whines—Long Tom
Hollands-in-Skin
Orange Wine

The British were in for a surprise. The Boers were on their own home territory, and they were tough and determined. The first battle of the war took place in Mafeking, hardly more than a village, and for the first time, the British began to realize what they were up against. More troops were quickly sent over from England. They laid siege to Kimberley, and it was only after a fierce and bloody fight that they went on to take Ladysmith. The cannons of the Boers had a longer range than those of the British, so long-range guns were removed from British warships, moved inland and manned by sailors hundreds of miles from their ships.

In Klipdrift, Margaret listened eagerly for news of each battle, and she and those around her lived on rumors, their moods varying from elation to despair, depending on the news. And then one morning one of Margaret's employees came running into her office and said, "I just heard a report that the British are advancing on Klipdrift. They're going to kill us all!"

"Nonsense. They wouldn't dare touch us."

Five hours later, Margaret McGregor was a prisoner of war.

Margaret and Kate were taken to Paardeberg, one of the hundreds of prison camps that had sprung up all over South Africa. The prisoners were kept inside an enormous open field, ringed by barbed wire and guarded by armed British soldiers. The conditions were deplorable.

Margaret took Kate in her arms and said, "Don't worry, darling, nothing's going to happen to you."

But neither of them believed it. Each day became a calendar of horrors. They watched those around them die by the tens and the hundreds and then by the thousands as fever swept through the camp. There were no doctors or medication for the wounded, and food was scarce. It was a constant nightmare that went on for almost three harrowing years. The worst of it was the feeling of utter helplessness. Margaret and Kate were at the complete mercy of their captors. They were dependent upon them for meals and shelter, for their very lives. Kate lived in terror. She watched the children around her die, and she was afraid that she would be next. She was powerless to protect her mother or herself, and it was a lesson she was never to forget. *Power.* If you had power, you had food. You had medicine. You had freedom. She saw those around her fall ill and die, and she equated power with life. *One day,* Kate thought, *I'll have power. No one will be able to do this to me again.*

The violent battles went on—Belmont and Graspan and Stormberg and Spioenkop—but in the end, the brave Boers were no match for the might of the British Empire. In 1902, after nearly three years of bloody war, the Boers surrendered. Fifty-five thousand Boers fought, and thirty-four thousand of their soldiers, women and children died. But what filled the survivors with a deep savage bitterness was the knowledge that twenty-eight thousand of those died in British concentration camps.

On the day the gates of the camp were flung open, Margaret and Kate returned to Klipdrift. A few weeks later, on a quiet Sunday, David Blackwell arrived. The war had matured him, but he was still the same grave, thoughtful David Margaret had learned to rely upon. David had spent these hellish years fighting and worrying about whether Margaret and Kate were dead or alive. When he found them safe at home, he was filled with joy.

"I wish I could have protected you both," David told Margaret.

"That's all past, David. We must think only of the future." And the future was Kruger-Brent, Ltd.

For the world, the year 1900 was a clean slate on which history was going to be written, a new era that promised peace and limitless hope for everyone. A new century had begun, and it brought with it a series of astonishing inventions that reshaped life around the globe. Steam and electric automobiles were replaced by the combustion engine. There were submarines and airplanes. The world population exploded to a billion and a half people. It was a time to grow and expand, and during the next six years, Margaret and David took full advantage of every opportunity.

During those years, Kate grew up with almost no supervision. Her mother was too busy running the company with David to pay much attention to her. She was a wild child, stubborn and opinionated and intractable. One afternoon when Margaret came home from a business meeting, she saw her fourteen-year-old daughter in the muddy yard in a fistfight with two boys. Margaret stared in horrified disbelief.

"Bloody hell!" she said under her breath. "That's the girl who one day is going to run Kruger-Brent, Limited! God help us all!"

BOOK TWO

Kate and David
1906–1914

12

On a hot summer night in 1914, Kate McGregor was working alone in her office at the new Kruger-Brent, Ltd., headquarters building in Johannesburg when she heard the sound of approaching automobiles. She put down the papers she had been studying, walked over to the window and looked out. Two cars of police and a paddy wagon had come to a stop in front of the building. Kate watched, frowning, as half a dozen uniformed policemen leaped from the cars and hurried to cover the two entrances and exits to the building. It was late, and the streets were deserted. Kate caught a wavy reflection of herself in the window. She was a beautiful woman, with her father's light-gray eyes and her mother's full figure.

There was a knock at the office door and Kate called, "Come in."

The door opened and two uniformed men entered. One wore the bars of a superintendent of police.

"What on earth is going on?" Kate demanded.

"I apologize for disturbing you at this late hour, Miss McGregor. I'm Superintendent Cominsky."

"What's the problem, Superintendent?"

"We've had a report that an escaped killer was seen entering this building a short time ago."

There was a shocked look on Kate's face. "Entering *this* building?"

"Yes, ma'am. He's armed and dangerous."

Kate said nervously, "Then I would very much appreciate it, Superintendent, if you would find him and get him out of here."

"That's exactly what we intend to do, Miss McGregor. You haven't seen or heard anything suspicious, have you?"

"No. But I'm alone here, and there are a lot of places a person could hide. I'd like you to have your men search this place thoroughly."

"We'll get started immediately, ma'am."

The superintendent turned and called to the men in the hallway, "Spread out. Start at the basement and work your way up to the roof." He turned to Kate. "Are any of the offices locked?"

"I don't believe so," Kate said, "but if they are, I'll open them for you."

Superintendent Cominsky could see how nervous she was, and he did not blame her. She would be even more nervous if she knew how desperate the man was for whom they were looking. "We'll find him," the superintendent assured Kate.

Kate picked up the report she had been working on, but she was unable to concentrate. She could hear the police moving through the building, going from office to office. *Would they find him?* She shivered.

The policemen moved slowly, methodically searching every possible hiding place from the basement to the roof. Forty-five minutes later, Superintendent Cominsky returned to Kate's office.

She looked at his face. "You didn't find him."

"Not yet, ma'am, but don't worry—"

"I *am* worried, Superintendent. If there is an escaped killer in this building, I want you to find him."

"We will, Miss McGregor. We have tracking dogs."

From the corridor came the sound of barking and a moment later a handler came into the office with two large German shepherds on leashes.

"The dogs have been all over the building, sir. They've searched everyplace but this office."

The superintendent turned to Kate. "Have you been out of this office anytime in the past hour or so?"

"Yes. I went to look up some records in the file room. Do you think he could have—?" She shuddered. "I'd like you to check this office, please."

The superintendent gave a signal and the handler slipped the leashes off the dogs and gave the command, "Track."

The dogs went crazy. They raced to a closed door and began barking wildly.

"Oh, my God!" Kate cried. "He's in there!"

The superintendent pulled out his gun. "Open it," he ordered.

The two policemen moved to the closet door with drawn guns and pulled the door open. The closet was empty. One of the dogs raced to another door and pawed excitedly at it.

"Where does that door lead?" Superintendent Cominsky asked.

"To a washroom."

The two policemen took up places on either side of the door and yanked it open. There was no one inside.

The handler was baffled. "They've never behaved this way before." The dogs were racing around the room frantically. "They've got the scent," the handler said. "But where is he?"

Both dogs ran to the drawer of Kate's desk and continued their barking.

"There's your answer," Kate tried to laugh. "He's in the drawer."

Superintendent Cominsky was embarrassed. "I'm sorry to have troubled you, Miss McGregor." He turned to the handler and snapped, "Take these dogs out of here."

"You're not leaving?" There was concern in Kate's voice.

"Miss McGregor, I can assure you you're perfectly safe. My

men have covered every inch of this building. You have my personal guarantee that he's not here. I'm afraid it was a false alarm. My apologies."

Kate swallowed. "You certainly know how to bring excitement to a woman's evening."

Kate stood looking out the window, watching the last of the police vehicles drive away. When they were out of sight, she opened her desk drawer and pulled out a blood-stained pair of canvas shoes. She carried them down the corridor to a door marked *Private, Authorized Personnel Only,* and entered. The room was bare except for a large, locked, walk-in safe built into the wall, the vault where Kruger-Brent, Ltd., stored its diamonds before shipping. Quickly, Kate dialed the combination on the safe and pulled open the giant door. Dozens of metal safe-deposit boxes were built into the sides of the vault, all crammed with diamonds. In the center of the room, lying on the floor half-conscious, was Banda.

Kate knelt beside him. "They've gone."

Banda slowly opened his eyes and managed a weak grin. "If I had a way out of this vault, do you know how rich I'd be, Kate?"

Kate carefully helped him to his feet. He winced with pain as she touched his arm. She had wrapped a bandage around it, but blood was seeping through.

"Can you put your shoes on?" She had taken them from him earlier, and, to confuse the tracking dogs she knew would be brought in, she had walked around her office in them and then hidden them in her drawer.

Now Kate said, "Come on. We have to get you out of here."

Banda shook his head. "I'll make it on my own. If they catch you helping me, you'll be in more trouble than you can handle."

"Let me worry about that."

Banda took a last look around the vault.

"Do you want any samples?" Kate asked. "You can help yourself."

Banda looked at her and saw that she was serious. "Your daddy made me that offer once, a long time ago."

Kate smiled wryly. "I know."

"I don't need money. I just have to leave town for a while."

"How do you think you're going to get out of Johannesburg?"

"I'll find a way."

"Listen to me. The police have roadblocks out by now. Every exit from the city will be watched. You won't have a chance by yourself."

He said stubbornly, "You've done enough." He had managed to put his shoes on. He was a forlorn looking figure, standing there in a torn, bloodied shirt and jacket. His face was seamed and his hair was gray, but when Kate looked at him she saw the tall, handsome figure she had first met as a child.

"Banda, if they catch you, they'll kill you," Kate said quietly. "You're coming with me."

She knew she was right about the roadblocks. Every exit from Johannesburg would be guarded by police patrols. Banda's capture was a top priority and the authorities had orders to bring him in dead or alive. The railroad stations and roads would be watched.

"I hope you have a better plan than your daddy had," Banda said. His voice was weak. Kate wondered how much blood he had lost.

"Don't talk. Save your strength. Just leave everything to me." Kate sounded more confident than she felt. Banda's life was in her hands, and she could not bear it if anything happened to him. She wished again, for the hundredth time, that David was not away. Well, she would simply have to manage without him.

"I'm going to bring my automobile around to the alley," Kate said. "Give me ten minutes, then come outside. I'll have the back door of the car open. Get in and lie on the floor. There will be a blanket to cover yourself with."

"Kate, they're going to search every automobile leaving the city. If—"

"We're not going by automobile. There's a train leaving for Cape Town at eight A.M. I ordered my private car connected to it."

"You're getting me out of here in your private railroad car?"

"That's right."

Banda managed a grin. "You McGregors really like excitement."

Thirty minutes later, Kate drove into the railroad yards. Banda was on the floor of the backseat, concealed by a blanket. They had had no trouble passing the roadblocks in the city, but now as Kate's car turned into the train yards, a light suddenly flashed on, and Kate saw that her way was blocked by several policemen. A familiar figure walked toward Kate's car.

"Superintendent Cominsky!"

He registered surprise. "Miss McGregor, what are you doing here?"

Kate gave him a quick, apprehensive smile. "You'll think I'm just a silly, weak female, Superintendent, but to tell you the truth, what happened back at the office scared the wits out of me. I decided to leave town until you catch this killer you're looking for. Or have you found him?"

"Not yet, ma'am, but we will. I have a feeling he'll make for these railroad yards. Wherever he runs, we'll catch him."

"I certainly hope so!"

"Where are you headed?"

"My railway car is on a siding up ahead. I'm taking it to Cape Town."

"Would you like one of my men to escort you?"

"Oh, thank you, Superintendent, but that won't be necessary. Now that I know where you and your men are, I'll breathe a lot easier, believe me."

Five minutes later, Kate and Banda were safely inside the private railway car. It was pitch black.

"Sorry about the dark," Kate said. "I don't want to light any lamps."

She helped Banda onto a bed. "You'll be fine here until morning. When we start to pull out, you'll hide out in the washroom."

Banda nodded. "Thank you."

Kate drew the shades. "Have you a doctor who will take care of you when we get to Cape Town?"

He looked up into her eyes. *"We?"*

"You didn't think I was going to let you travel alone while I missed all the fun?"

Banda threw back his head and laughed. *She's her father's daughter, all right.*

As dawn was breaking, an engine pulled up to the private railroad car and shunted it onto the main track in back of the train that was leaving for Cape Town. The car rocked back and forth as the connection was made.

At exactly eight o'clock, the train pulled out of the station. Kate had left word that she did not wish to be disturbed. Banda's wound was bleeding again, and Kate attended to it. She had not had a chance to talk to Banda since earlier that evening, when he had stumbled half-dead into her office. Now she said, "Tell me what happened, Banda."

Banda looked at her and thought, *Where can I begin?* How could he explain to her the *trekboers* who pushed the Bantus from their ancestral land? Had it started with them? Or had it started with the giant Oom Paul Kruger, President of the Transvaal, who said in a speech to the South African Parliament, "We must be the lords over the blacks and let them be a subject race . . ." Or had it begun with the great empire-builder Cecil Rhodes, whose motto was, "Africa for the whites?" How could he sum up the history of his people in a sentence? He thought of a way. "The police murdered my son," Banda said.

The story came pouring out. Banda's older son, Ntombenthle, was attending a political rally when the police charged in to break it up. Some shots were fired, and a riot began. Ntombenthle was arrested, and the next morning he was found hanged in his cell. "They said it was suicide," Banda told Kate. "But I know my son. It was murder."

"My God, he was so young," Kate breathed. She thought of all the times they had played together, laughed together. Ntombenthle had been such a handsome boy. "I'm sorry, Banda. I'm so sorry. But why are they after you?"

"After they killed him I began to rally the blacks. I had to fight back, Kate. I couldn't just sit and do nothing. The police called me an enemy of the state. They arrested me for a robbery I did not commit and sentenced me to prison for twenty years. Four of us made a break. A guard was shot and killed, and they're blaming me. I've never carried a gun in my life."

"I believe you," Kate said. "The first thing we have to do is get you somewhere where you'll be safe."

"I'm sorry to involve you in all this."

"You didn't involve me in anything. You're my friend."

He smiled. "You know the first white man I ever heard call me friend? Your daddy." He sighed. "How do you think you're going to sneak me off the train at Cape Town?"

"We're not going to Cape Town."

"But you said—"

"I'm a woman. I have a right to change my mind."

In the middle of the night when the train stopped at the station at Worcester, Kate arranged to have her private railroad car disconnected and shunted to a siding. When Kate woke up in the morning, she went over to Banda's cot. It was empty. Banda was gone. He had refused to compromise her any further. Kate was sorry, but she was sure he would be safe. He had many friends to take care of him. *David will be proud of me*, Kate thought.

"I can't believe you could be so stupid!" David roared, when Kate returned to Johannesburg and told him the news. "You not only jeopardized your own safety, but you put the company in danger. If the police had found Banda here, do you know what they would have done?"

Kate said defiantly, "Yes. They would have killed him."

David rubbed his forehead in frustration. "Don't you understand anything?"

"You're bloody right, I do! I understand that you're cold and unfeeling." Her eyes were ablaze with fury.

"You're still a child."

She raised her hand to strike him, and David grabbed her arms. "Kate, you've got to control your temper."

The words reverberated in Kate's head. *Kate, you've got to learn to control your temper* . . .

It was so long ago. She was four years old, in the middle of a fistfight with a boy who had dared tease her. When David appeared, the boy ran away. Kate started to chase him, and David grabbed her. "Hold it, Kate. You've got to learn to control your temper. Young ladies don't get into fistfights."

"I'm not a young lady," Kate snapped. "Let go of me." David released her.

The pink frock she was wearing was muddied and torn, and her cheek was bruised.

"We'd better get you cleaned up before your mother sees you," David told her.

Kate looked after the retreating boy with regret. "I could have licked him if you had left me alone."

David looked down into the passionate little face and laughed. "You probably could have."

Mollified, Kate allowed him to pick her up and carry her into her house. She liked being in David's arms. She liked everything about David. He was the only grown-up who understood her. Whenever he was in town, he spent time with her. In relaxed moments, Jamie had told young David about his adventures with Banda, and now David told the stories to Kate. She could not get enough of them.

"Tell me again about the raft they built."

And David would tell her.

"Tell me about the sharks . . . Tell me about the sea *mis* . . . Tell me about the day . . ."

Kate did not see very much of her mother. Margaret was too involved in running the affairs of Kruger-Brent, Ltd. She did it for Jamie.

Margaret talked to Jamie every night, just as she had during the year before he died. "David is such a great help, Jamie, and he'll be around when Kate's running the company. I don't want to worry you, but I don't know what to do with that child . . ."

Kate was stubborn and willful and impossible. She refused to obey her mother or Mrs. Talley. If they chose a dress for her to wear, Kate would discard it for another. She would not eat properly. She ate what she wanted to, when she wanted to, and no threat or bribe could sway her. When Kate was forced to go to a birthday party, she found ways to disrupt it. She had no girl friends. She refused to go to dancing class and instead spent her time playing rugby with teen-age boys. When Kate finally started school, she set a record for mischief. Margaret found herself going to see the headmistress at least once a month to persuade her to forgive Kate and let her remain in school.

"I don't understand her, Mrs. McGregor," the headmistress sighed. "She's extremely bright, but she rebels against simply everything. I don't know what to do with her."

Neither did Margaret.

The only one who could handle Kate was David. "I understand you're invited to a birthday party this afternoon," David said.

"I hate birthday parties."

David stooped down until he was at her eye level. "I know you do, Kate. But the father of the little girl who's having the birthday party is a friend of mine. It will make me look bad if you don't attend and behave like a lady."

Kate stared at him. "Is he a *good* friend of yours?"

"Yes."

"I'll go."

Her manners that afternoon were impeccable.

"I don't know how you do it," Margaret told David. "It's magic."

"She's just high-spirited," David laughed. "She'll grow out of it. The important thing is to be careful not to break that spirit."

"I'll tell you a secret," Margaret said grimly, "half the time I'd like to break her neck."

*   *   *

When Kate was ten, she said to David, "I want to meet Banda."

David looked at her in surprise. "I'm afraid that's not possible, Kate. Banda's farm is a long way from here."

"Are you going to take me there, David, or do you want me to go by myself?"

The following week David took Kate to Banda's farm. It was a good-sized piece of land, two morgens, and on it Banda raised wheat, sheep and ostriches. The living accommodations were circular huts with walls made of dried mud. Poles supported a cone-shaped roof covered with thatches. Banda stood in front, watching as Kate and David drove up and got out of the carriage. Banda looked at the gangling, serious-faced girl at David's side and said, "I'd have known you were Jamie McGregor's daughter."

"And I'd have known you were Banda," Kate said gravely. "I came to thank you for saving my father's life."

Banda laughed. "Someone's been telling you stories. Come in and meet my family."

Banda's wife was a beautiful Bantu woman named Ntame. Banda had two sons, Ntombenthle, seven years older than Kate, and Magena, six years older. Ntombenthle was a miniature of his father. He had the same handsome features and proud bearing and an inner dignity.

Kate spent the entire afternoon playing with the two boys. They had dinner in the kitchen of the small, neat farmhouse. David felt uncomfortable eating with a black family. He respected Banda, but it was traditional that there was no socializing between the two races. In addition to that, David was concerned about Banda's political activities. There were reports that he was a disciple of John Tengo Javabu, who was fighting for drastic social changes. Because mine owners could not get enough natives to work for them, the government had imposed a tax of ten shillings on all natives who did not work as mine laborers, and there were riots all over South Africa.

In the late afternoon, David said, "We'd better get started home, Kate. We have a long ride."

"Not yet." Kate turned to Banda. "Tell me about the sharks . . ."

From that time on, whenever David was in town, Kate made him take her to visit Banda and his family.

David's assurance that Kate would grow out of her high-spiritedness showed no signs of coming to pass. If anything, she grew more willful every day. She flatly refused to take part in any of the activities that other girls her age participated in. She insisted on going into the mines with David, and he took her hunting and fishing and camping. Kate adored it. One day when Kate and David were fishing the Vaal, and Kate gleefully pulled in a trout larger than anything David had caught, he said, "You should have been born a boy."

She turned to him in annoyance. "Don't be silly, David. Then I couldn't marry you."

David laughed.

"We *are* going to be married, you know."

"I'm afraid not, Kate. I'm twenty-two years older than you. Old enough to be your father. You'll meet a boy one day, a nice young man—"

"I don't want a nice young man," she said wickedly. "I want you."

"If you're really serious," David said, "then I'll tell you the secret to a man's heart."

"Tell me!" Kate said eagerly.

"Through his stomach. Clean that trout and let's have lunch."

There was not the slightest doubt in Kate's mind that she was going to marry David Blackwell. He was the only man in the world for her.

Once a week Margaret invited David to dinner at the big house. As a rule, Kate preferred to eat dinner in the kitchen with the servants, where she did not have to mind her manners. But on Friday nights when David came, Kate sat in the big dining room. David usually came alone, but occasionally he would bring a female guest and Kate would hate her instantly.

Kate would get David alone for a moment and say, with sweet innocence, "I've never seen hair that shade of blond," or, "She certainly has peculiar taste in dresses, hasn't she?" or, "Did she use to be one of Madam Agnes's girls?"

When Kate was fourteen, her headmistress sent for Margaret. "I run a respectable school, Mrs. McGregor. I'm afraid your Kate is a bad influence."

Margaret sighed. "What's she done now?"

"She's teaching the other children words they've never heard before." Her face was grim. "I might add, Mrs. McGregor, that *I've* never heard some of the words before. I can't imagine where the child picked them up."

Margaret could. Kate picked them up from her street friends. *Well,* Margaret decided, *it is time to end all that.*

The headmistress was saying, "I do wish you would speak to her. We'll give her another chance, but—"

"No. I have a better idea. I'm going to send Kate away to school."

When Margaret told David her idea, he grinned. "She's not going to like that."

"I can't help it. Now the headmistress is complaining about the language Kate uses. She gets it from those prospectors she's always following around. My daughter's starting to sound like them, look like them and smell like them. Frankly, David, I don't understand her at all. I don't know why she behaves as she does. She's pretty, she's bright, she's—"

"Maybe she's too bright."

"Well, too bright or not, she's going away to school."

When Kate arrived home that afternoon, Margaret broke the news to her.

Kate was furious. "You're trying to get rid of me!"

"Of course I'm not, darling. I just think you'd be better off—"

"I'm better off *here*. All my friends are here. You're trying to separate me from my friends."

"If you're talking about that riffraff you—"

"They're *not* riffraff. They're as good as anybody."

"Kate, I'm not going to argue with you. You're going away to a boarding school for young ladies, and that's that."

"I'll kill myself," Kate promised.

"All right, darling. There's a razor upstairs, and if you look around, I'm sure you'll find various poisons in the house."

Kate burst into tears. "Please don't do this to me, Mother."

Margaret took her in her arms. "It's for your own good, Kate. You'll be a young woman soon. You'll be ready for marriage. No man is going to marry a girl who talks and dresses and behaves the way you do."

"That's not true," Kate sniffled. "David doesn't mind."

"What does David have to do with this?"

"We're going to be married."

Margaret sighed. "I'll have Mrs. Talley pack your things."

There were half a dozen good English boarding schools for young girls. Margaret decided that Cheltenham, in Gloucestershire, was best suited for Kate. It was a school noted for its rigid discipline. It was set on acres of land surrounded by high battlements and, according to its charter, was founded for the daughters of noblemen and gentlemen. David did business with the husband of the headmistress, Mrs. Keaton, and he had no trouble arranging for Kate to be enrolled there.

When Kate heard where she was going, she exploded anew. "I've heard about that school! It's awful. I'll come back like one of those stuffed English dolls. Is that what you'd like?"

"What I would like is for you to learn some manners," Margaret told her.

"I don't need manners. I've got brains."

"That's not the first thing a man looks for in a woman," Margaret said dryly, "and you're becoming a woman."

"I don't want to become a woman," Kate screamed. "Why the bloody hell can't you just leave me alone?"

"I will not have you using that language."

And so it went until the morning arrived when Kate was to leave. Since David was going to London on a business trip, Margaret asked, "Would you mind seeing that Kate gets to school safely? The Lord only knows where she'll end up if she goes on her own."

"I'll be happy to," David said.

"You! You're as bad as my mother! You can't wait to get rid of me."

David grinned. "You're wrong. I can wait."

They traveled by private railway car from Klipdrift to Cape Town and from there by ship to Southampton. The journey took four weeks. Kate's pride would not let her admit it, but she was thrilled to be traveling with David. *It's like a honeymoon,* she thought, *except that we're not married. Not yet.*

Aboard ship, David spent a great deal of time working in his stateroom. Kate curled up on the couch, silently watching him, content to be near him.

Once she asked, "Don't you get bored working on all those figures, David?"

He put down his pen and looked at her. "They're not just figures, Kate. They're stories."

"What kind of stories?"

"If you know how to read them, they're stories about companies we're buying or selling, people who work for us. Thousands of people all over the world earn a living because of the company your father founded."

"Am I anything like my father?"

"In many ways, yes. He was a stubborn, independent man."

"Am I a stubborn, independent woman?"

"You're a spoiled brat. The man who marries you is going to have one hell of a life."

Kate smiled dreamily. *Poor David.*

In the dining room, on their last night at sea, David asked, "Why are you so difficult, Kate?"

"Am I?"

"You know you are. You drive your poor mother crazy."

Kate put her hand over his. "Do I drive you crazy?"

David's face reddened. "Stop that. I don't understand you."

"Yes, you do."

"Why can't you be like other girls your age?"

"I'd rather die first. I don't want to be like anybody else."

"God knows you're not!"

"You won't marry anyone else until I'm grown up enough for you, will you, David? I'll get older as fast as I can. I promise. Just don't meet anybody you love, please."

He was touched by her earnestness. He took her hand in his and said, "Kate, when I get married, I'd like my daughter to be exactly like you."

Kate rose to her feet and said in a voice that rang through the dining salon, "You can bloody well go to hell, David Blackwell!" And she stormed out of the room, as everyone stared.

They had three days together in London, and Kate loved every minute of it.

"I have a treat for you," David told her. "I got two tickets for *Mrs. Wiggs of the Cabbage Patch.*"

"Thank you, David. I want to go to the Gaiety."

"You can't. That's a—a music-hall revue. That's not for you."

"I won't know until I see it, will I?" she said stubbornly.

They went to the Gaiety.

Kate loved the look of London. The mixture of motorcars and carriages, the ladies beautifully dressed in lace and tulle and light satins and glittering jewelry, and the men in dinner clothes with piqué waistcoats and white shirtfronts. They had dinner at the Ritz, and a late supper at the Savoy. And when it was time to leave, Kate thought, *We'll come back here. David and I will come back here.*

When they arrived at Cheltenham, they were ushered into the office of Mrs. Keaton.

"I want to thank you for enrolling Kate," David said.

"I'm sure we'll enjoy having her. And it's a pleasure to accommodate a friend of my husband."

At that moment, Kate knew she had been deceived. It was *David* who had wanted her sent away and had arranged for her to come here.

She was so furious and hurt she refused to say good-bye to him.

13

Cheltenham School was unbearable. There were rules and regulations for everything. The girls had to wear identical uniforms, down to their knickers. The school day was ten hours long, and every minute was rigidly structured. Mrs. Keaton ruled the pupils and her staff with a rod of iron. The girls were there to learn manners and discipline, etiquette and decorum, so that they could one day attract desirable husbands.

Kate wrote her mother, "It's a bloody prison. The girls here are awful. All they ever talk about are bloody clothes and bloody boys. The bloody teachers are monsters. They'll never keep me here. I'm going to escape."

Kate managed to run away from the school three times, and each time she was caught and brought back, unrepentant.

At a weekly staff meeting, when Kate's name was brought up, one of the teachers said, "The child is uncontrollable. I think we should send her back to South Africa."

Mrs. Keaton replied, "I'm inclined to agree with you, but let's look upon it as a challenge. If we can succeed in disciplining Kate McGregor, we can succeed in disciplining anyone."

Kate remained in school.

* * *

To the amazement of her teachers, Kate became interested in the farm that the school maintained. The farm had vegetable gardens, chickens, cows, pigs and horses. Kate spent as much time as possible there, and when Mrs. Keaton learned of this, she was immensely pleased.

"You see," the headmistress told her staff, "it was simply a question of patience. Kate has finally found her interest in life. One day she will marry a landowner and be of enormous assistance to him."

The following morning, Oscar Denker, the man in charge of running the farm, came to see the headmistress. "One of your students," he said, "that Kate McGregor—I wish you'd keep her away from my farm."

"Whatever are you talking about?" Mrs. Keaton asked. "I happen to know she's very interested."

"Sure she is, but do you know what she's interested in? The animals fornicating, if you'll excuse my language."

"*What?*"

"That's right. She stands around all day, just watching the animals do it to each other."

"Bloody hell!" Mrs. Keaton said.

Kate still had not forgiven David for sending her into exile, but she missed him terribly. *It's my fate,* she thought gloomily, *to be in love with a man I hate.* She counted the days she was away from him, like a prisoner marking time until the day of release. Kate was afraid he would do something dreadful, like marry another woman while she was trapped in the bloody school. *If he does,* Kate thought, *I'll kill them both. No. I'll just kill her. They'll arrest me and hang me, and when I'm on the gallows, he'll realize that he loves me. But it will be too late. He'll beg me to forgive him. "Yes, David, my darling, I forgive you. You were too foolish to know when you held a great love in the palm of your hand. You let it fly away like a little bird. Now that little bird is about to be hanged. Good-bye, David." But at the last minute she would be reprieved and David would take her in his arms and carry her off to some exotic country where the food was better than the bloody slop they served at bloody Cheltenham.*

Kate received a note from David saying he was going to be in London and would come to visit her. Kate's imagination was inflamed. She found a dozen hidden meanings in his note. *Why was he going to be in England? To be near her, of course. Why was he coming to visit her? Because he finally knew he loved her and could not bear to be away from her any longer. He was going to sweep her off her feet and take her out of this terrible place.* She could scarcely contain her happiness. Kate's fantasy was so real that the day David arrived, Kate went around saying good-bye to her classmates. "My lover is coming to take me out of here," she told them.

The girls looked at her in silent disbelief. All except Georgina Christy, who scoffed, "You're lying again, Kate McGregor."

"Just wait and see. He's tall and handsome, and he's mad about me."

When David arrived, he was puzzled by the fact that all the girls in the school seemed to be staring at him. They looked at him and whispered and giggled, and the minute they caught his eye, they blushed and turned away.

"They act as though they've never seen a man before," David told Kate. He looked at her suspiciously. "Have you been saying anything about me?"

"Of course not," Kate said haughtily. "Why would I do that?"

They ate in the school's large dining room, and David brought Kate up to date on everything that was happening at home. "Your mother sends her love. She's expecting you home for the summer holiday."

"How is mother?"

"She's fine. She's working hard."

"Is the company doing well, David?"

He was surprised by her sudden interest. "It's doing very well. Why?"

Because, Kate thought, *someday it will belong to me, and you and I will share it.* "I was just curious."

He looked at her untouched plate. "You're not eating."

Kate was not interested in food. She was waiting for the magic moment, the moment when David would say, *"Come away with me, Kate. You're a woman now, and I want you. We're going to be married."*

The dessert came and went. Coffee came and went, and still no magic words from David.

It was not until he looked at his watch and said, "Well, I'd better be going or I'll miss my train," that Kate realized with a feeling of horror that he had not come to take her away at all. The bastard was going to leave her there to rot!

David had enjoyed his visit with Kate. She was a bright and amusing child, and the waywardness she had once shown was now under control. David patted Kate's hand fondly and asked, "Is there anything I can do for you before I leave, Kate?"

She looked him in the eye and said sweetly, "Yes, David, there is. You can do me an enormous favor. *Get out of my bloody life!*" And she walked out of the room with great dignity, her head held high, leaving him sitting there, mouth agape.

Margaret found that she missed Kate. The girl was unruly and contrary, but Margaret realized that she was the only living person she loved. *She's going to be a great woman,* Margaret thought with pride. *But I want her to have the manners of a lady.*

Kate came home for summer vacation. "How are you getting along in school?" Margaret asked.

"I hate it! It's like being surrounded by a hundred nannies."

Margaret studied her daughter. "Do the other girls feel the same way, Kate?"

"What do *they* know?" she said contemptuously. "You should *see* the girls at that school! They've been sheltered all their lives. They don't know a damn thing about life."

"Oh, dear," Margaret said. "That must be awful for you."

"Don't laugh at me, please. The've never even been to South Africa. The only animals they've seen have been in zoos. None of them has ever seen a diamond mine or a gold mine."

"Underprivileged."

Kate said, "All right. But when I turn out like them, you're going to be bloody sorry."

"Do you think you'll turn out like them?"

Kate grinned wickedly. "Of course not! Are you mad?"

An hour after Kate arrived home, she was outside playing rugby with the children of the servants. Margaret watched her through the window and thought, *I'm wasting my money. She's never going to change.*

That evening, at dinner, Kate asked casually, "Is David in town?"

"He's been in Australia. He'll be back tomorrow, I think."

"Is he coming to dinner Friday night?"

"Probably." She studied Kate and said, "You like David, don't you?"

She shrugged. "He's all right, I suppose."

"I see," Margaret said. She smiled to herself as she remembered Kate's vow to marry David.

"I don't *dislike* him, Mother. I mean, I like him as a human being. I just can't stand him as a *man*."

When David arrived for dinner Friday night, Kate flew to the door to greet him. She hugged him and whispered in his ear, "I forgive you. Oh, I've missed you so much, David! Have you missed me?"

Automatically he said, "Yes." And then he thought with astonishment, *By God, I have missed her.* He had never known anyone like this child. He had watched her grow up, and each time he encountered her she was a revelation to him. She was almost sixteen years old and she had started to fill out. She had let her black hair grow long, and it fell softly over her shoulders. Her features had matured, and there was a sensuality about her that he had not noticed before. She was a beauty, with a quick intelligence and a strong will. *She's going to be a handful for some man,* David thought.

At dinner David asked, "How are you getting along in school, Kate?"

"Oh, I just love it," she gushed. "I'm really learning a lot. The teachers are wonderful, and I've made a lot of great friends."

Margaret sat in stunned silence.

"David, will you take me to the mines with you?"

"Is that how you want to waste your vacation?"

"Yes, please."

A trip down into the mines took a full day, and that meant she would be with David all that time.

"If your mother says it's all right—"

"Please, mother!"

"All right, darling. As long as you're with David, I know you'll be safe." Margaret hoped David would be safe.

The Kruger-Brent Diamond Mine near Bloemfontein was a gigantic operation, with hundreds of workers engaged in digging, engineering, washing or sorting.

"This is one of the company's most profitable mines," David told Kate. They were above ground in the manager's office, waiting for an escort to take them down into the mine. Against one wall was a showcase filled with diamonds of all colors and sizes.

"Each diamond has a distinct characteristic," David explained. "The original diamonds from the banks of the Vaal are alluvial, and their sides are worn down from the abrasion of centuries."

He's more handsome than ever, Kate thought. *I love his eyebrows.*

"These stones all come from different mines, but they can be easily identified by their appearance. See this one? You can tell by the size and yellow cast that it comes from Paardspan. De Beers's diamonds have an oily-looking surface and are dodecahedral in shape."

He's brilliant. He knows everything.

"You can tell this one is from the mine at Kimberley because it's an octahedron. Their diamonds range from smoky-glassy to pure white."

I wonder if the manager thinks David is my lover. I hope so.

"The color of a diamond helps determine its value. The colors are named on a scale of one to ten. At the top is the tone blue-white, and at the bottom is the draw, which is a brown color."

He smells so wonderful. It's such a—such a male smell. I love his arms and shoulders. I wish—

"Kate!"

She said guiltily, "Yes, David?"

"Are you listening to me?"

"Of course I am." There was indignation in her voice. "I've heard every word."

They spent the next two hours in the bowels of the mine, and then had lunch. It was Kate's idea of a heavenly day.

When Kate returned home late in the afternoon, Margaret said, "Did you enjoy yourself?"

"It was wonderful. Mining is really fascinating."

Half an hour later, Margaret happened to glance out the window. Kate was on the ground wrestling with the son of one of the gardeners.

The following year, Kate's letters from school were cautiously optimistic. She had been made captain of the hockey and lacrosse teams, and was at the head of her class scholastically. The school was not really all *that* bad, she wrote, and there were even a few girls in her classes who were reasonably nice. She asked permission to bring two of her friends home for the summer vacation, and Margaret was delighted. The house would be alive again with the sound of youthful laughter. She could not wait for her daughter to come home. Her dreams were all for Kate now. *Jamie and I are the past,* Maggie thought. *Kate is the future. And what a wonderful, bright future it will be!*

When Kate was home during her vacation, all the eligible young men of Klipdrift flocked around besieging her for dates, but Kate was not interested in any of them. David was in America, and she impatiently awaited his return. When he came to the house, Kate greeted him at the door. She wore a white dress circled in by a black velvet belt that accentuated her lovely bosom. When David embraced her, he was astonished by the warmth of her response. He drew back and looked at her. There was something different about her, something knowing. There was an expression in her eyes he could not define, and it made him vaguely uneasy.

The few times David saw Kate during that vacation she was surrounded by boys, and he found himself wondering which would be the lucky one. David was called back to Australia on business, and when he returned to Klipdrift, Kate was on her way to England.

In Kate's last year of school, David appeared unexpectedly one evening. Usually his visits were preceded by a letter or a telephone call. This time there had been no warning.

"David! What a wonderful surprise!" Kate hugged him. "You should have told me you were coming. I would have—"

"Kate, I've come to take you home."

She pulled back and looked up at him. "Is something wrong?"

"I'm afraid your mother is very ill."

Kate stood stark still for a moment. "I'll get ready."

Kate was shocked by her mother's appearance. She had seen her only a few months earlier, and Margaret had seemed to be in robust health. Now she was pale and emaciated, and the bright spirit had gone out of her eyes. It was as though the cancer that was eating at her flesh had also eaten at her soul.

Kate sat at the side of the bed and held her mother's hand in hers. "Oh, Mother," she said. "I'm so bloody sorry."

Margaret squeezed her daughter's hand. "I'm ready, darling. I suppose I've been ready ever since your father died." She looked up at Kate. "Do you want to hear something silly? I've never told this to a living soul before." She hesitated, then went on. "I've always been worried that there was no one to take proper care of your father. Now I can do it."

Margaret was buried three days later. Her mother's death shook Kate deeply. She had lost her father and a brother, but she had never known them; they were only storied figments of the past. Her mother's death was real and painful. Kate was eighteen years old and suddenly alone in the world, and the thought of that was frightening.

David watched her standing at her mother's graveside, bravely fighting not to cry. But when they returned to the house, Kate broke down, unable to stop sobbing. "She was always so w-wonderful to me, David, and I was such a r-rotten daughter."

David tried to console her. "You've been a wonderful daughter, Kate."

"I was n-nothing b-but trouble. I'd give anything if I could m-make it up to her. I didn't want her to die, David! Why did God do this to her?"

He waited, letting Kate cry herself out. When she was calmer, David said, "I know it's hard to believe now, but one day this pain will go away. And you know what you'll be left with, Kate? Happy memories. You'll remember all the good things you and your mother had."

"I suppose so. Only right now it hurts so b-bloody much."

The following morning they discussed Kate's future.

"You have family in Scotland," David reminded her.

"No!" Kate replied sharply. "They're not family. They're relatives." Her voice was bitter. "When Father wanted to come to this country, they laughed at him. No one would help him except his mother, and she's dead. No. I won't have anything to do with them."

David sat there thinking. "Do you plan to finish out the school term?" Before Kate could answer, David went on. "I think your mother would have wanted you to."

"Then I'll do it." She looked down at the floor, her eyes unseeing. "Bloody hell," Kate said.

"I know," David said gently. "I know."

Kate finished the school term as class valedictorian, and David was there for the graduation.

* * *

Riding from Johannesburg to Klipdrift in the private railway car, David said, "You know, all this will belong to you in a few years. This car, the mines, the company—it's yours. You're a very rich young woman. You can sell the company for many millions of pounds." He looked at her and added, "Or you can keep it. You'll have to think about it."

"I have thought about it," Kate told him. She looked at him and smiled. "My father was a pirate, David. A wonderful old pirate. I wish I could have known him. I'm not going to sell this company. Do you know why? Because the pirate named it after two guards who were trying to kill him. Wasn't that a lovely thing to do? Sometimes at night when I can't sleep, I think about my father and Banda crawling through the sea *mis,* and I can hear the voices of the guards: *Kruger . . . Brent . . .*" She looked up at David. "No, I'll never sell my father's company. Not as long as you'll stay on and run it."

David said quietly, "I'll stay as long as you need me."

"I've decided to enroll in a business school."

"A business school?" There was surprise in his voice.

"This is 1910," Kate reminded him. "They have business schools in Johannesburg where women are allowed to attend."

"But—"

"You asked me what I wanted to do with my money." She looked him in the eye and said, "I want to earn it."

14

Business school was an exciting new adventure. When Kate had gone to Cheltenham, it had been a chore, a necessary evil. This was different. Every class taught her something useful, something that would help her when she ran the company. The courses included accounting, management, international trade and business administration. Once a week David telephoned to see how she was getting along.

"I love it," Kate told him. "It's really exciting, David."

One day she and David would be working together, side by side, late at night, all by themselves. *And one of those nights, David would turn to her and say, "Kate, darling, I've been such a blind fool. Will you marry me?" And an instant later, she would be in his arms* . . .

But that would have to wait. In the meantime, she had a lot to learn. Resolutely, Kate turned to her homework.

The business course lasted two years, and Kate returned to Klipdrift in time to celebrate her twentieth birthday. David met her at the station. Impulsively, Kate flung her arms around him and hugged him. "Oh, David, I'm so happy to see you."

He pulled away and said awkwardly, "It's nice to see you, Kate." There was an uncomfortable stiffness in his manner.

"Is something wrong?"

"No. It's—it's just that young ladies don't go around hugging men in public."

She looked at him a moment. "I see. I promise not to embarrass you again."

As they drove to the house, David covertly studied Kate. She was a hauntingly beautiful girl, innocent and vulnerable, and David was determined that he would never take advantage of that.

On Monday morning Kate moved into her new office at Kruger-Brent, Ltd. It was like suddenly being plunged into some exotic and bizarre universe that had its own customs and its own language. There was a bewildering array of divisions, subsidiaries, regional departments, franchises and foreign branches. The products that the company manufactured or owned seemed endless. There were steel mills, cattle ranches, a railroad, a shipping line and, of course, the foundation of the family fortune: diamonds and gold, zinc and platinum and magnesium, mined each hour around the clock, pouring into the coffers of the company.

Power.

It was almost too much to take in. Kate sat in David's office listening to him make decisions that affected thousands of people around the world. The general managers of the various divisions made recommendations, but as often as not, David overruled them.

"Why do you do that? Don't they know their jobs?" Kate asked.

"Of course they do, but that's not the point," David explained. "Each manager sees his own division as the center of the world, and that's as it should be. But someone has to have an overall view and decide what's best for the company. Come on. We're having lunch with someone I want you to meet."

David took Kate into the large, private dining room adjoining Kate's office. A young, raw-boned man with a lean face and inquisitive brown eyes was waiting for them.

"This is Brad Rogers," David said. "Brad, meet your new boss, Kate McGregor."

Brad Rogers held out his hand. "I'm pleased to meet you, Miss McGregor."

"Brad is our secret weapon," David said. "He knows as much about Kruger-Brent, Limited, as I do. If I ever leave, you don't have to worry. Brad will be here."

If I ever leave. The thought of it sent a wave of panic through Kate. *Of course, David would never leave the company.* Kate could think of nothing else through lunch, and when it was over she had no idea what she had eaten.

After lunch, they discussed South Africa.

"We're going to run into trouble soon," David warned. "The government has just imposed poll taxes."

"Exactly what does that mean?" Kate asked.

"It means that blacks, coloreds and Indians have to pay two pounds each for every member of their family. That's more than a month's wages for them."

Kate thought about Banda and was filled with a sense of apprehension. The discussion moved on to other topics.

Kate enjoyed her new life tremendously. Every decision involved a gamble of millions of pounds. Big business was a matching of wits, the courage to gamble and the instinct to know when to quit and when to press ahead.

"Business is a game," David told Kate, "played for fantastic stakes, and you're in competition with experts. If you want to win, you have to learn to be a master of the game."

And that was what Kate was determined to do. Learn.

Kate lived alone in the big house, except for the servants. She and David continued their ritual Friday-night dinners, but when Kate invited him over on any other night, he invariably found an excuse not to come. During business hours they were together constantly, but even then David seemed to have erected a barrier between them, a wall that Kate was unable to penetrate.

On her twenty-first birthday, all the shares in Kruger-Brent, Ltd., were turned over to Kate. She now officially had control of the company. "Let's have dinner tonight to celebrate," she suggested to David.

"I'm sorry, Kate, I have a lot of work to catch up on."

Kate dined alone that night, wondering why. *Was it she, or was it David?* He would have to be deaf, dumb and blind not to know how she felt about him, how she had always felt about him. She would have to do something about it.

The company was negotiating for a shipping line in the United States.

"Why don't you and Brad go to New York and close the deal?" David suggested to Kate. "It will be good experience for you."

Kate would have liked for David to have gone with her, but she was too proud to say so. She would handle this without him. Besides, she had never been to America. She looked forward to the experience.

The closing of the shipping-line deal went smoothly. "While you're over there," David had told her, "you should see something of the country."

Kate and Brad visited company subsidiaries in Detroit, Chicago, Pittsburgh and New York, and Kate was amazed by the size and energy of the United States. The highlight of Kate's trip was a visit to Dark Harbor, Maine, on an enchanting little island called Islesboro, in Penobscot Bay. She had been invited to dinner at the home of Charles Dana Gibson, the artist. There were twelve people at dinner and, except for Kate, they all had homes on the island.

"This place has an interesting history," Gibson told Kate.

"Years ago, residents used to get here by small coasting vessels from Boston. When the boat landed, they'd be met by a buggy and taken to their houses."

"How many people live on this island?" Kate asked.

"About fifty families. Did you see the lighthouse when the ferry docked?"

"Yes."

"It's run by a lighthouse keeper and his dog. When a boat goes by the dog goes out and rings the bell."

Kate laughed. "You're joking."

"No, ma'am. The funny thing is the dog is deaf as a stone. He puts his ear against the bell to feel if there's any vibration."

Kate smiled. "It sounds as if you have a fascinating island here."

"It might be worth your while staying over and taking a look around in the morning."

On an impulse, Kate said, "Why not?"

She spent the night at the island's only hotel, the Islesboro Inn. In the morning she hired a horse and carriage, driven by one of the islanders. They left the center of Dark Harbor, which consisted of a general store, a hardware store and a small restaurant, and a few minutes later they were driving through a beautiful wooded area. Kate noticed that none of the little winding roads had names, nor were there any names on the mailboxes. She turned to her guide. "Don't people get lost here without any signs?"

"Nope. The islanders know where everythin' is."

Kate gave him a sidelong look. "I see."

At the lower end of the island, they passed a burial ground. "Would you stop, please?" Kate asked.

She stepped out of the carriage and walked over to the old cemetery and wandered around looking at the tombstones.

JOB PENDLETON, DIED JANUARY 25, 1794, AGE 47. The epitaph read: *Beneath this stone, I rest my head in slumber sweet; Christ blessed the bed.*

JANE, WIFE OF THOMAS PENDLETON, DIED FEBRUARY 25, 1802, AGE 47.

There were spirits here from another century, from an era long gone. CAPTAIN WILLIAM HATCH DROWNED IN LONG ISLAND SOUND, OCTOBER 1866, AGE 30 YEARS. The epitaph on his stone read: *Storms all weathered and life's seas crossed.*

Kate stayed there a long time, enjoying the quiet and peace. Finally, she returned to the carriage and they drove on.

"What is it like here in the winter?" Kate asked.

"Cold. The bay used to freeze solid, and they'd come from the mainland by sleigh. Now a' course, we got the ferry."

They rounded a curve, and there, next to the water below, was a beautiful white-shingled, two-story house surrounded by delphinium, wild roses and poppies. The shutters on the eight front windows were painted green, and next to the double doors were white benches and six pots of red geraniums. It looked like something out of a fairy tale.

"Who owns that house?"

"That's the old Dreben house. Mrs. Dreben died a few months back."

"Who lives there now?"

"Nobody, I reckon."

"Do you know if it's for sale?"

The guide looked at Kate and said, "If it is, it'll probably be bought by the son of one of the families already livin' here. The islanders don't take kindly to strangers."

It was the wrong thing to say to Kate.

One hour later, she was speaking to a lawyer for the estate. "It's about the Dreben house," Kate said. "Is it for sale?"

The lawyer pursed his lips. "Well, yes, and no."

"What does that mean?"

"It's for sale, but a few people are already interested in buying it."

The old families on the island, Kate thought. "Have they made an offer?"

"Not yet, but—"

"I'm making one," Kate said.

He said condescendingly, "That's an expensive house."

"Name your price."

"Fifty thousand dollars."

"Let's go look at it."

The inside of the house was even more enchanting than Kate had anticipated. The large, lovely hall faced the sea through a wall of glass. On one side of the hall was a large ballroom, and on the other side, a living room with fruitwood paneling stained by time and an enormous fireplace. There was a library, and a huge kitchen with an iron stove and a large pine worktable, and off of that was a butler's pantry and laundry room. Downstairs, the house had six bedrooms for the servants and one bathroom. Upstairs was a master bedroom suite and four smaller bedrooms. It was a much larger house than Kate had expected. *But when David and I have our children,* she thought, *we'll need all these rooms.* The grounds ran all the way down to the bay, where there was a private dock.

Kate turned to the lawyer. "I'll take it."

She decided to name it Cedar Hill House.

She could not wait to get back to Klipdrift to break the news to David.

On the way back to South Africa, Kate was filled with a wild excitement. The house in Dark Harbor was a sign, a symbol that she and David would be married. She knew he would love the house as much as she did.

On the afternoon Kate and Brad arrived back in Klipdrift, Kate hurried to David's office. He was seated at his desk, working, and the sight of him set Kate's heart pounding. She had not realized how much she had missed him.

David rose to his feet. "Kate! Welcome home!" And before she could speak, he said, "I wanted you to be the first to know. I'm getting married."

15

It had begun casually six weeks earlier. In the middle of a hectic day, David received a message that Tim O'Neil, the friend of an important American diamond buyer, was in Klipdrift and asking if David would be good enough to welcome him and perhaps take him to dinner. David had no time to waste on tourists, but he did not want to offend his customer. He would have asked Kate to entertain the visitor, but she was on a tour of the company's plants in North America with Brad Rogers. *I'm stuck*, David decided. He called the hotel where O'Neil was staying and invited him to dinner that evening.

"My daughter is with me," O'Neil told him. "I hope you don't mind if I bring her along?"

David was in no mood to spend the evening with a child. "Not at all," he said politely. He would make sure the evening was a short one.

They met at the Grand Hotel, in the dining room. When David arrived, O'Neil and his daughter were already seated at the table. O'Neil was a handsome, gray-haired Irish-American in his early fifties. His daughter, Josephine, was the most beautiful woman David had ever seen. She was in her early thirties, with a stunning figure, soft blond hair and clear blue eyes. The breath went out of David at the sight of her.

"I—I'm sorry I'm late," he said. "Some last-minute business."

Josephine watched his reaction to her with amusement. "Sometimes that's the most exciting kind," she said innocently. "My father tells me you're a very important man, Mr. Blackwell."

"Not really—and it's David."

She nodded. "That's a good name. It suggests great strength."

Before the dinner was over, David decided that Josephine O'Neil was much more than just a beautiful woman. She was intelligent, had a sense of humor and was skillful at making him feel at ease. David felt she was genuinely interested in him. She asked him questions about himself that no one had ever asked before. By the time the evening ended, he was already half in love with her.

"Where's your home?" David asked Tim O'Neil.

"San Francisco."

"Will you be going back soon?" He made it sound as casual as he could.

"Next week."

Josephine smiled at David. "If Klipdrift is as interesting as it promises to be, I might persuade Father to stay a little longer."

"I intend to make it as interesting as possible," David assured her. "How would you like to go down into a diamond mine?"

"We'd love it," Josephine answered. "Thank you."

At one time David had personally escorted important visitors down into the mines, but he had long since delegated that task to subordinates. Now he heard himself saying, "Would tomorrow morning be convenient?" He had half a dozen meetings scheduled for the morning, but they suddenly seemed unimportant.

He took the O'Neils down a rockshaft, twelve hundred feet below ground. The shaft was six feet wide and twenty feet long, divided into four compartments, one for pumping, two for hoisting the blue diamondiferous earth and one with a double-decked cage to carry the miners to and from work.

"I've always been curious about something," Josephine said. "Why are diamonds measured in carats?"

"The carat was named for the carob seed," David explained, "because of its consistency in weight. One carat equals two hundred milligrams, or one one-hundred-forty-second of an ounce."

Josephine said, "I'm absolutely fascinated, David."

And he wondered if she was referring only to the diamonds. Her nearness was intoxicating. Every time he looked at Josephine, David felt a fresh sense of excitement.

"You really should see something of the countryside," David told the O'Neils. "If you're free tomorrow, I'd be happy to take you around."

Before her father could say anything, Josephine replied, "That would be lovely."

David was with Josephine and her father every day after that, and each day David fell more deeply in love. He had never known anyone as bewitching.

When David arrived to pick up the O'Neils for dinner one evening and Tim O'Neil said, "I'm a bit tired tonight, David. Would you mind if I didn't go along?" David tried to hide his pleasure.

"No, sir. I understand."

Josephine gave David a mischievous smile. "I'll try to keep you entertained," she promised.

David took her to a restaurant in a hotel that had just opened. The room was crowded, but David was recognized and given a table immediately. A three-piece ensemble was playing American music.

David asked, "Would you like to dance?"

"I'd love to."

A moment later, Josephine was in his arms on the dance floor, and it was magic. David held her lovely body close to his, and he could feel her respond.

"Josephine, I'm in love with you."

She put a finger to his lips. "Please, David . . . don't . . ."

"Why?"

"Because I couldn't marry you."

"Do you love me?"

She smiled up at him, her blue eyes sparkling. "I'm crazy about you, my darling. Can't you tell?"

"Then why?"

"Because I could never live in Klipdrift. I'd go mad."

"You could give it a try."

"David, I'm tempted, but I know what would happen. If I married you and had to live here, I'd turn into a screaming shrew and we'd end up hating each other. I'd rather we said good-bye this way."

"I don't want to say good-bye."

She looked up into his face, and David felt her body melt into his. "David, is there any chance that you could live in San Francisco?"

It was an impossible idea. "What would I do there?"

"Let's have breakfast in the morning. I want you to talk to Father."

Tim O'Neil said, "Josephine has told me about your conversation last night. Looks like you two have a problem. But I might have a solution, if you're interested."

"I'm very interested, sir."

O'Neil picked up a brown-leather briefcase and removed some blueprints. "Do you know anything about frozen foods?"

"I'm afraid I don't."

"They first started freezing food in the United States in 1865. The problem was transporting it long distances without the food thawing out. We've got refrigerated railway cars, but no one's been able to come up with a way to refrigerate trucks." O'Neil tapped the blueprints. "Until now. I just received a patent on it. This is going to revolutionize the entire food industry, David."

David glanced at the blueprints. "I'm afraid these don't mean much to me, Mr. O'Neil."

"That doesn't matter. I'm not looking for a technical expert. I have plenty of those. What I'm looking for is financing and someone to run the business. This isn't some wild pipe dream. I've talked to the top food processors in the business. This is going to be big—bigger than you can imagine. I need someone like you."

"The company headquarters will be in San Francisco," Josephine added.

David sat there silent, digesting what he had just heard. "You say you've been given a patent on this?"

"That's right. I'm all set to move."

"Would you mind if I borrowed these blueprints and showed them to someone?"

"I have no objection at all."

The first thing David did was to check on Tim O'Neil. He learned that O'Neil had a solid reputation in San Francisco. He had been head of the science department at a Berkeley College there and was highly regarded. David knew nothing about the freezing of food, but he intended to find out.

"I'll be back in five days, darling. I want you and your father to wait for me."

"As long as you like. I'll miss you," Josephine said.

"I'll miss you, too." And he meant it more than she knew.

David took the train to Johannesburg and made an appointment to see Edward Broderick, the owner of the largest meat-packing plant in South Africa.

"I want your opinion on something." David handed him the blueprints. "I need to know if this can work."

"I don't know a damned thing about frozen foods or trucks, but I know people who do. If you come back this afternoon, I'll have a couple of experts here for you, David."

At four o'clock that afternoon David returned to the packing plant. He found that he was nervous, in a state of uncertainty, because he was not sure how he wanted the meeting to go. Two weeks earlier, he would have laughed if anyone had even suggested he would ever leave Kruger-Brent, Ltd. It was a part of him. He would have laughed even harder if they had told him he would have considered heading a little food company in San Francisco. It was insane, except for one thing: Josephine O'Neil.

There were two men in the room with Edward Broderick. "This is Dr. Crawford and Mr. Kaufman. David Blackwell."

They exchanged greetings. David asked, "Have you gentlemen had a chance to look at the blueprints?"

Dr. Crawford replied, "We certainly have, Mr. Blackwell. We've been over them thoroughly."

David took a deep breath. "And?"

"I understand that the United States Patent Office has granted a patent on this?"

"That's right."

"Well, Mr. Blackwell, whoever got that patent is going to be one very rich man."

David nodded slowly, filled with conflicting emotions.

"It's like all great inventions—it's so simple you wonder why someone didn't think of it sooner. This one can't miss."

David did not know how to react. He had half-hoped that the decision would be taken out of his hands. If Tim O'Neil's invention was useless, there was a chance of persuading Josephine to stay in South Africa. But what O'Neil had told him was true. It *did* work. Now David had to make his decision.

He thought of nothing else on the journey back to Klipdrift. If he accepted, it would mean leaving the company, starting up a new, untried business. He was an American, but America was a foreign country to him. He held an important position in one of the most powerful companies in the world. He loved his job. Jamie and Margaret McGregor had been very good to him. And then there was Kate. He had cared for her since she was a baby. He had watched her grow up from a stubborn, dirty-faced tomboy to a lovely young woman. Her life was a photo album in his mind. He turned the pages and there was Kate at four, eight, ten, fourteen, twenty-one—vulnerable, unpredictable . . .

By the time the train arrived at Klipdrift, David had made up his mind. He was not going to leave Kruger-Brent, Ltd.

He drove directly to the Grand Hotel and went up to the O'Neils' suite. Josephine opened the door for him.

"David!"

He took her in his arms and kissed her hungrily, feeling her warm body pressing against his.

"Oh, David, I've missed you so much. I don't ever want to be away from you again."

"You won't have to," David said slowly. "I'm going to San Francisco . . ."

David had waited with growing anxiety for Kate to return from the United States. Now that he had made his decision, he was eager to get started on his new life, impatient to marry Josephine.

And now Kate was back, and he was standing in front of her saying, "I'm getting married."

Kate heard the words through a roaring in her ears. She felt suddenly faint, and she gripped the edge of the desk for support. *I want to die,* she thought. *Please let me die.*

Somehow, from some deep wellspring of will, she managed a smile. "Tell me about her, David." She was proud of how calm her voice sounded. "Who is she?"

"Her name is Josephine O'Neil. She's been visiting here with her father. I know you two will be good friends, Kate. She's a fine woman."

"She must be, if you love her, David."

He hesitated. "There's one more thing, Kate. I'm going to be leaving the company."

The world was falling in on her. "Just because you're getting married, doesn't mean you have to—"

"It isn't that. Josephine's father is starting a new business in San Francisco. They need me."

"So—so you'll be living in San Francisco."

"Yes. Brad Rogers can handle my job easily, and we'll pick a top management team to back him up. Kate, I—I can't tell you what a difficult decision this was for me."

"Of course, David. You—you must love her very much. When do I get to meet the bride?"

David smiled, pleased at how well Kate was taking the news. "Tonight, if you're free for dinner."

"Yes, I'm free."

She would not let the tears come until she was alone.

The four of them had dinner at the McGregor mansion. The moment Kate saw Josephine, she blanched, *Oh God! No wonder he's in love with her!* She was dazzling. Just being in her presence made Kate feel awkward and ugly. And to make matters worse, Josephine was gracious and charming. And obviously very much in love with David. *Bloody hell!*

During dinner Tim O'Neil told Kate about the new company.

"It sounds very interesting," Kate said.

"I'm afraid it's no Kruger-Brent, Limited, Miss McGregor. We'll have to start small, but with David running it, we'll do all right."

"With David running it, you can't miss," Kate assured him.

The evening was an agony. In the same cataclysmic moment, she had lost the man she loved and the one person who was indispensable to Kruger-Brent, Ltd. She carried on a conversation and managed to get through the evening, but afterward she had no recollection of what she said or did. She only knew that every time David and Josephine looked at each other or touched, she wanted to kill herself.

On the way back to the hotel, Josephine said, "She's in love with you, David."

He smiled. "Kate? No. We're friends. We have been since she was a baby. She liked you a lot."

Josephine smiled. *Men are so naïve.*

In David's office the following morning, Tim O'Neil and David sat facing each other. "I'll need about two months to get my affairs in order here," David said. "I've been thinking about the financing we'll need to begin with. If we go to one of the big companies, they'll swallow us up and give us a small share. It

won't belong to us anymore. I think we should finance it ourselves. I figure it will cost eighty thousand dollars to get started.
I've saved the equivalent of about forty thousand dollars. We'll
need forty thousand more."

"I have ten thousand dollars," Tim O'Neil said. "And I have
a brother who will loan me another five thousand."

"So, we're twenty-five thousand dollars short," David said.
"We'll try to borrow that from a bank."

"We'll leave for San Francisco right away," O'Neil told
David, "and get everything set up for you."

Josephine and her father left for the United States two days
later. "Send them to Cape Town in the private railway car,
David," Kate offered.

"That's very generous of you, Kate."

The morning Josephine left, David felt as though a piece of
his life had been taken away. He could not wait to join her in
San Francisco.

The next few weeks were taken up with a search for a management team to back up Brad Rogers. A list of possible candidates was carefully drawn up, and Kate and David and Brad
spent hours discussing each one.

"... Taylor is a good technician, but he's weak on management."

"What about Simmons?"

"He's good, but he's not ready yet," Brad decided. "Give him
another five years."

"Babcock?"

"Not a bad choice. Let's discuss him."

"What about Peterson?"

"Not enough of a company man," David said. "He's too concerned with himself." And even as he said it, he felt a pang of
guilt because he was deserting Kate.

They continued on with the list of names. By the end of the
month, they had narrowed the choice to four men to work with
Brad Rogers. All of them were working abroad, and they were

sent for so that they could be interviewed. The first two interviews went well. "I'd be satisfied with either one of them," Kate assured David and Brad.

On the morning the third interview was to take place, David walked into Kate's office, his face pale. "Is my job still open?"

Kate looked at his expression and stood up in alarm. "What is it, David?"

"I—I—" He sank into a chair. "Something has happened."

Kate was out from behind the desk and by his side in an instant. "Tell me!"

"I just got a letter from Tim O'Neil. He's sold the business."

"What do you mean?"

"Exactly what I said. He accepted an offer of two hundred thousand dollars and a royalty for his patent from the Three Star Meat Packing Company in Chicago." David's voice was filled with bitterness. "The company would like to hire me to manage it for them. He regrets any inconvenience to me, but he couldn't turn down that kind of money."

Kate looked at him intently. "And Josephine? What does she say? She must be furious with her father."

"There was a letter from her, too. We'll marry as soon as I come to San Francisco."

"And you're not going?"

"Of course I'm not going!" David exploded. "Before, I had something to offer. I could have built it into a great company. But they were in too much of a damned hurry for the money."

"David, you're not being fair when you say 'they.' Just be—"

"O'Neil would never have made that deal without Josephine's approval."

"I—I don't know what to say, David."

"There is nothing to say. Except that I almost made the biggest mistake of my life."

Kate walked over to the desk and picked up the list of candidates. Slowly, she began to tear it up.

In the weeks that followed, David plunged himself deeply into his work, trying to forget his bitterness and hurt. He received several letters from Josephine O'Neil, and he threw them all away, unread. But he could not get her out of his mind. Kate, deeply aware of David's pain, let him know she was there if he needed her.

Six months had passed since David received the letter from Tim O'Neil. During that time, Kate and David continued to work closely together, travel together and be alone together much of the time. Kate tried to please him in every way she could. She dressed for him, planned things he would enjoy and went out of her way to make his life as happy as possible. As far as she could tell, it was having no effect at all. And finally she lost her patience.

She and David were in Rio de Janeiro, checking on a new mineral find. They had had dinner at their hotel and were in Kate's room going over some figures late at night. Kate had changed to a comfortable kimono and slippers. When they finished, David stretched and said, "Well, that's it for tonight. I guess I'll go on to bed."

Kate said quietly, "Isn't it time you came out of mourning, David?"

He looked at her in surprise. "Mourning?"

"For Josephine O'Neil."

"She's out of my life."

"Then act like it."

"Just what would you like me to do, Kate?" he asked curtly.

Kate was angry now. Angry at David's blindness, angry about all the wasted time. "I'll tell you what I'd like you to do—kiss me."

"What?"

"Bloody hell, David! I'm your boss, damn it!" She moved close to him. "Kiss me." And she pressed her lips against his and put her arms around him. She felt him resist and start to draw back. And then slowly his arms circled her body, and he kissed her.

"Kate . . ."

She whispered against his lips. "I thought you'd never ask . . ."

They were married six weeks later. It was the biggest wedding Klipdrift had ever seen or would see again. It was held in the town's largest church and afterward there was a reception in the town hall and everyone was invited. There were mountains of food and uncounted cases of beer and whiskey and champagne, and musicians played and the festivities lasted until dawn. When the sun came up, Kate and David slipped away.

"I'll go home and finish packing," Kate said. "Pick me up in an hour."

In the pale dawn light, Kate entered the huge house alone and went upstairs to her bedroom. She walked over to a painting on the wall and pressed against the frame. The painting flew back, revealing a wall safe. She opened it and brought out a contract. It was for the purchase of the Three Star Meat Packing Company of Chicago by Kate McGregor. Next to it was a contract from the Three Star Meat Packing Company purchasing the rights to Tim O'Neil's freezing process for two hundred thousand dollars. Kate hesitated a moment, then returned the papers to the safe and locked it. David belonged to her now. He had always belonged to her. And to Kruger-Brent, Ltd. Together, they would build it into the biggest, most powerful company in the world.

Just as Jamie and Margaret McGregor would have wanted it.

BOOK THREE

Kruger-Brent, Ltd.
1914–1945

16

They were in the library, where Jamie had once liked to sit with his brandy glass in front of him. David was arguing that there was no time for a real honeymoon. "Someone has to mind the store, Kate."

"Yes, Mr. Blackwell. But who's going to mind me?" She curled up in David's lap, and he felt the warmth of her through her thin dress. The documents he had been reading fell to the floor. Her arms were around him, and he felt her hands sliding down his body. She pressed her hips against him, making slow, small circles, and the papers on the floor were forgotten. She felt him respond, and she rose and slipped out of her dress. David watched her, marveling at her loveliness. How could he have been so blind for so long? She was undressing him now, and there was a sudden urgency in him. They were both naked, and their bodies were pressed together. He stroked her, his fingers lightly touching her face and her neck, down to the swell of her breasts. She was moaning, and his hands moved down until he felt the velvety softness between her legs. His fingers stroked her and she whispered, "Take me, David," and they were on the deep, soft rug and she felt the strength of his body on top of her.

There was a long, sweet thrust and he was inside her, filling her, and she moved to his rhythm. It became a great tidal wave, sweeping her up higher and higher until she thought she could not bear the ecstasy of it. There was a sudden, glorious explosion deep inside her and another and another, and she thought, *I've died and gone to heaven.*

They traveled all over the world, to Paris and Zurich and Sydney and New York, taking care of company business, but wherever they went they carved out moments of time for themselves. They talked late into the night and made love and explored each other's minds and bodies. Kate was an inexhaustible delight to David. She would awaken him in the morning to make wild and pagan love to him, and a few hours later she would be at his side at a business conference, making more sense than anyone else there. She had a natural flair for business that was as rare as it was unexpected. Women were few in the top echelons of the business world. In the beginning Kate was treated with a tolerant condescension, but the attitude quickly changed to a wary respect. Kate took a delight in the maneuvering and machinations of the game. David watched her outwit men with much greater experience. She had the instincts of a winner. She knew what she wanted and how to get it. *Power.*

They ended their honeymoon with a glorious week in Cedar Hill House at Dark Harbor.

It was on June 28, 1914, that the first talk of war was heard. Kate and David were guests at a country estate in Sussex. It was the age of country-house living and weekend guests were expected to conform to a ritual. Men dressed for breakfast, changed for midmorning lounging, changed for lunch, changed for tea—to a velvet jacket with satin piping—and changed to a formal jacket for dinner.

"For God's sake," David protested to Kate. "I feel like a damned peacock."

"You're a very handsome peacock, my darling," Kate assured him. "When you get home, you can walk around naked."

He took her in his arms. "I can't wait."

At dinner, the news came that Francis Ferdinand, heir to the Austrian-Hungarian throne, and his wife, Sophie, had been slain by an assassin.

Their host, Lord Maney, said, "Nasty business, shooting a woman, what? But no one is going to war over some little Balkan country."

And the conversation moved on to cricket.

Later in bed, Kate said, "Do you think there's going to be a war, David?"

"Over some minor archduke being assassinated? No."

It proved to be a bad guess. Austria-Hungary, suspecting that its neighbor, Serbia, had instigated the plot to assassinate Ferdinand, declared war on Serbia, and by October, most of the world's major powers were at war. It was a new kind of warfare. For the first time, mechanized vehicles were used—airplanes, airships and submarines.

The day Germany declared war, Kate said, "This can be a wonderful opportunity for us, David."

David frowned. "What are you talking about?"

"Nations are going to need guns and ammunition and—"

"They're not getting them from us," David interrupted firmly. "We have enough business, Kate. We don't have to make profits from anyone's blood."

"Aren't you being a bit dramatic? Someone has to make guns."

"As long as I'm with this company, it won't be us. We won't discuss it again, Kate. The subject is closed."

And Kate thought, *The bloody hell it is.* For the first time in their marriage, they slept apart. Kate thought, *How can David be such an idealistic ninny?*

And David thought, *How can she be so cold-blooded? The business has changed her.* The days that followed were miserable for both of them. David regretted the emotional chasm between them, but he did not know how to bridge it. Kate was too proud and headstrong to give in to him because she knew she was right.

President Woodrow Wilson had promised to keep the United States out of the war, but as German submarines began torpedoing unarmed passenger ships, and stories of German atrocities spread, pressure began to build up for America to help the Allies. "Make the world safe for democracy," was the slogan.

David had learned to fly in the bush country of South Africa, and when the Lafayette Escadrille was formed in France with American pilots, David went to Kate. "I've got to enlist."

She was appalled. "No! It's not your war!"

"It's going to be," David said quietly. "The United States can't stay out. I'm an American. I want to help now."

"You're forty-six years old!"

"I can still fly a plane, Kate. And they need all the help they can get."

There was no way Kate could dissuade him. They spent the last few days together quietly, their differences forgotten. They loved each other, and that was all that mattered.

The night before David was to leave for France, he said, "You and Brad Rogers can run the business as well as I can, maybe better."

"What if something happens to you? I couldn't bear it."

He held her close. "Nothing will happen to me, Kate. I'll come back to you with all kinds of medals."

He left the following morning.

David's absence was death for Kate. It had taken her so long to win him, and now every second of her day there was the ugly, creeping fear of losing him. He was always with her. She found him in the cadence of a stranger's voice, the sudden laughter on a quiet street, a phrase, a scent, a song. He was everywhere. She wrote him long letters every day. Whenever she received a letter from him, she reread it until it was in tatters. He was well, he wrote. The Germans had air superiority, but that would change.

There were rumors that America would be helping soon. He would write again when he could. He loved her.

Don't let anything happen to you, my darling. I'll hate you forever if you do.

She tried to forget her loneliness and misery by plunging into work. At the beginning of the war, France and Germany had the best-equipped fighting forces in Europe, but the Allies had far greater manpower, resources and materials. Russia, with the largest army, was badly equipped and poorly commanded.

"They all need help," Kate told Brad Rogers. "They need tanks and guns and ammunition."

Brad Rogers was uncomfortable. "Kate, David doesn't think—"

"David isn't here, Brad. It's up to you and me."

But Brad Rogers knew that what Kate meant was, *It's up to me.*

Kate could not understand David's attitude about manufacturing armaments. The Allies needed weapons, and Kate felt it was her patriotic duty to supply them. She conferred with the heads of half a dozen friendly nations, and within a year Kruger-Brent, Ltd., was manufacturing guns and tanks, bombs and ammunition. The company supplied trains and tanks and uniforms and guns. Kruger-Brent was rapidly becoming one of the fastest-growing conglomerates in the world. When Kate saw the most recent revenue figures, she said to Brad Rogers, "Have you seen these? David will have to admit he was mistaken."

South Africa, meanwhile, was in turmoil. The party leaders had pledged their support to the Allies and accepted responsibility for defending South Africa against Germany, but the majority of Afrikaners opposed the country's support of Great Britain. They could not forget the past so quickly.

In Europe the war was going badly for the Allies. Fighting on the western front reached a standstill. Both sides dug in, protected by trenches that stretched across France and Belgium, and the soldiers were miserable. Rain filled the dugouts with water and mud, and rats swarmed through the vermin-infested trenches. Kate was grateful that David was fighting his war in the air.

On April 6, 1917, President Wilson declared war, and David's prediction came true. America began to mobilize.

The first American Expeditionary Force under General John J. Pershing began landing in France on June 26, 1917. New place names became a part of everyone's vocabulary: Saint-Mihiel . . . Château-Thierry . . . the Meuse-Argonne . . . Belleau Wood . . . Verdun . . . The Allies had become an irresistible force, and on November 11, 1918, the war was finally over. The world was safe for democracy.

David was on his way home.

When David disembarked from the troop ship in New York, Kate was there to meet him. They stood staring at each other for one eternal moment, ignoring the noise and the crowds around them, then Kate was in David's arms. He was thinner and tired-looking, and Kate thought, *Oh, God. I've missed him so.* She had a thousand questions to ask him, but they could wait. "I'm taking you to Cedar Hill House," Kate told him. "It's a perfect place for you to rest."

Kate had done a great deal with the house in anticipation of David's arrival home. The large, airy living room had been furnished with twin sofas covered in old rose-and-green floral chintz. Matching down-filled armchairs were grouped around the fireplace. Over the fireplace was a Vlaminck floral canvas, and, on each side of it, doré sconces. Two sets of French doors opened out onto the veranda, which ran the entire length of the house on three sides, covered with a striped awning. The rooms were bright and airy, and the view of the harbor spectacular.

Kate led David through the house, chattering away happily. He seemed strangely quiet. When they had completed the tour, Kate asked, "Do you like what I've done with it, darling?"

"It's beautiful, Kate. Now, sit down. I want to talk to you."

She had a sudden sinking feeling. "Is anything wrong?"

"We seem to have become a munitions supplier for half the world."

"Wait until you look at the books," Kate began. "Our profit has—"

"I'm talking about something else. As I recall, our profit was pretty good before I left. I thought we agreed we wouldn't get involved in manufacturing war supplies."

Kate felt an anger rising in her. "You agreed. I didn't." She fought to control it. "Times change, David. We have to change with them."

He looked at her and asked quietly, "Have you changed?"

Lying in bed that night, Kate asked herself whether it was she who had changed, or David. Had she become stronger, or had David become weaker? She thought about his argument against manufacturing armaments. It was a weak argument. After all, *someone* was going to supply the merchandise to the Allies, and there was an enormous profit in it. What had happened to David's business sense? She had always looked up to him as one of the cleverest men she knew. But now, she felt that she was more capable of running the business than David. She spent a sleepless night.

In the morning Kate and David had breakfast and walked around the grounds.

"It's really lovely," David told her. "I'm glad to be here."

Kate said, "About our conversation last night—"

"It's done. I was away, and you did what you thought was right."

Would I have done the same thing if you had been here? Kate wondered. But she did not say the words aloud. She had done what she had for the sake of the company. *Does the company mean more to me than my marriage?* She was afraid to answer the question.

17

The next five years witnessed a period of incredible world-wide growth. Kruger-Brent, Ltd., had been founded on diamonds and gold, but it had diversified and expanded all over the world, so that its center was no longer South Africa. The company recently had acquired a publishing empire, an insurance company and half a million acres of timberland.

One night Kate nudged David awake. "Darling, let's move the company headquarters."

David sat up groggily. "W—what?"

"The business center of the world today is New York. That's where our headquarters should be. South Africa's too far away from everything. Besides, now that we have the telephone and cable, we can communicate with any of our offices in minutes."

"Now why didn't I think of that?" David mumbled. And he went back to sleep.

New York was an exciting new world. On her previous visits there, Kate had felt the quick pulse of the city, but living there was like being caught up at the center of a matrix. The earth seemed to spin faster, everything moved at a more rapid pace.

Kate and David selected a site for the new company head-quarters on Wall Street, and the architects went to work. Kate chose another architect to design a sixteenth-century French Renaissance mansion on Fifth Avenue.

"This city is so damned *noisy,*" David complained.

And it was true. The chatter of riveters filled the air in every part of the city as skyscrapers began to soar into the heavens. New York had become the mecca for trade from all over the world, the headquarters for shipping, insurance, communications and transportation. It was a city bursting with a unique vitality. Kate loved it, but she sensed David's unhappiness.

"David, this is the future. This place is growing, and we'll grow with it."

"My God, Kate, how much more do you want?"

And without thinking, she replied, "All there is."

She could not understand why David had even asked the question. The name of the game was to win, and you won by beating everyone else. It seemed so obvious to her. Why couldn't David see it? David was a good businessman, but there was something missing in him, a hunger, a compulsion to conquer, to be the biggest and the best. Her father had had that spirit, and she had it. Kate was not sure exactly when it had happened, but at some point in her life, the company had become the master, and she the slave. It owned her more than she owned it.

When she tried to explain her feelings to David, he laughed and said, "You're working too hard." *She's so much like her father,* David thought. And he was not sure why he found that vaguely disturbing.

How could one work too hard? Kate wondered. There was no greater joy in life. It was when she felt most alive. Each day brought a new set of problems, and each problem was a challenge, a puzzle to be solved, a new game to be won. And she was wonderful at it. She was caught up in something beyond imagination. It had nothing to do with money or achievement; it had to do with *power*. A power that controlled the lives of thousands of people in every corner of the earth. Just as her life had once been controlled. As long as she had power, she would never truly need anyone. It was a weapon that was awesome beyond belief.

Kate was invited to dine with kings and queens and presidents, all seeking her favor, her goodwill. A new Kruger-Brent factory could mean the difference between poverty and riches. *Power*. The company was alive, a growing giant that had to be fed, and sometimes sacrifices were necessary, for the giant could not be shackled. Kate understood that now. It had a rhythm, a pulse, and it had become her own.

In March, a year after they had moved to New York, Kate felt unwell. David persuaded her to see a doctor.

"His name is John Harley. He's a young doctor with a good reputation."

Reluctantly, Kate went to see him. John Harley was a thin, serious-looking young Bostonian about twenty-six, five years younger than Kate.

"I warn you," Kate informed him, "I don't have time to be sick."

"I'll bear that in mind, Mrs. Blackwell. Meanwhile, let's have a look at you."

Dr. Harley examined her, made some tests and said, "I'm sure it's nothing serious. I'll have the results in a day or two. Give me a call on Wednesday."

Early Wednesday morning Kate telephoned Dr. Harley. "I have good news for you, Mrs. Blackwell," he said cheerfully. "You're going to have a baby."

It was one of the most exciting moments of Kate's life. She could not wait to tell David.

She had never seen David so thrilled. He scooped her up in his strong arms and said, "It's going to be a girl, and she'll look exactly like you." He was thinking, *This is exactly what Kate needs. Now she'll stay home more. She'll be more of a wife.*

And Kate was thinking, *It will be a boy. One day he'll take over Kruger-Brent.*

As the time for the birth of the baby drew nearer, Kate worked shorter hours, but she still went to the office every day.

"Forget about the business and relax," David advised her.

What he did not understand was that the business *was* Kate's relaxation.

The baby was due in December. "I'll try for the twenty-fifth," Kate promised David. "He'll be our Christmas present."

It's going to be a perfect Christmas, Kate thought. She was head of a great conglomerate, she was married to the man she loved and she was going to have his baby. If there was irony in the order of her priorities, Kate was not aware of it.

Her body had grown large and clumsy, and it was getting more and more difficult for Kate to go to the office, but whenever David or Brad Rogers suggested she stay home, her answer was, "My brain is still working." Two months before the baby was due, David was in South Africa on an inspection tour of the mine at Pniel. He was scheduled to return to New York the following week.

Kate was at her desk when Brad Rogers walked in unannounced. She looked at the grim expression on his face and said, "We lost the Shannon deal!"

"No. I— Kate, I just got word. There's been an accident. A mine explosion."

She felt a sharp pang. "Where? Was it bad? Was anyone killed?"

Brad took a deep breath. "Half a dozen. Kate— David was with them."

The words seemed to fill the room and reverberate against the paneled walls, growing louder and louder, until it was a screaming in her ears, a Niagara of sound that was drowning her, and she felt herself being sucked into its center, deeper and deeper, until she could no longer breathe.

And everything became dark and silent.

* * *

The baby was born one hour later, two months premature. Kate named him Anthony James Blackwell, after David's father. *I'll love you, my son, for me, and I'll love you for your father.*

One month later the new Fifth Avenue mansion was ready, and Kate and the baby and a staff of servants moved into it. Two castles in Italy had been stripped to furnish the house. It was a showplace, with elaborately carved sixteenth-century Italian walnut furniture and rose-marble floors bordered with sienna-red marble. The paneled library boasted a magnificent eighteenth-century fireplace over which hung a rare Holbein. There was a trophy room with David's gun collection, and an art gallery that Kate filled with Rembrandts and Vermeers and Velázquezes and Bellinis. There was a ballroom and a sun room and a formal dining room and a nursery next to Kate's room, and uncounted bedrooms. In the large formal gardens were statues by Rodin, Augustus Saint-Gaudens and Maillol. It was a palace fit for a king. *And the king is growing up in it,* Kate thought happily.

In 1928, when Tony was four, Kate sent him to nursery school. He was a handsome, solemn little boy, with his mother's gray eyes and stubborn chin. He was given music lessons, and when he was five he attended dancing school. Some of the best times the two of them spent together were at Cedar Hill House in Dark Harbor. Kate bought a yacht, an eighty-foot motor sailer she named the *Corsair,* and she and Tony cruised the waters along the coast of Maine. Tony adored it. But it was the work that gave Kate her greatest pleasure.

There was something mystic about the company Jamie McGregor had founded. It was alive, consuming. It was her lover, and it would never die on a winter day and leave her alone. It would live forever. She would see to it. And one day she would give it to her son.

The only disturbing factor in Kate's life was her homeland. She cared deeply about South Africa. The racial problems there were growing, and Kate was troubled. There were two political camps: the *verkramptes*—the narrow ones, the pro-segregation-ists—and the *verligtes*—the enlightened ones, who wanted to improve the position of the blacks. Prime Minister James Hert-zog and Jan Smuts had formed a coalition and combined their power to have the New Land Act passed. Blacks were removed from the rolls and were no longer able to vote or own land. Mil-lions of people belonging to different minority groups were disrupted by the new law. The areas that had no minerals, in-dustrial centers or ports were assigned to coloreds, blacks and Indians.

Kate arranged a meeting in South Africa with several high government officials. "This is a time bomb," Kate told them. "What you're doing is trying to keep eight million people in slavery."

"It's not slavery, Mrs. Blackwell. We're doing this for their own good."

"Really? How would you explain that?"

"Each race has something to contribute. If the blacks mingle with the whites, they'll lose their individuality. We're trying to protect them."

"That's bloody nonsense," Kate retorted. "South Africa has become a racist hell."

"That's not true. Blacks from other countries come thousands of miles in order to enter this country. They pay as much as fifty-six pounds for a forged pass. The black is better off here than anywhere else on earth."

"Then I pity them," Kate retorted.

"They're primitive children, Mrs. Blackwell. It's for their own good."

Kate left the meeting frustrated and deeply fearful for her country.

Kate was also concerned about Banda. He was in the news a good deal. The South African newspapers were calling him the *scarlet pimpernel,* and there was a grudging admiration in their stories. He escaped the police by disguising himself as a laborer, a chauffeur, a janitor. He had organized a guerrilla army and he headed the police's most-wanted list. One article in the *Cape*

Times told of his being carried triumphantly through the streets of a black village on the shoulders of demonstrators. He went from village to village addressing crowds of students, but every time the police got wind of his presence, Banda disappeared. He was said to have a personal bodyguard of hundreds of friends and followers, and he slept at a different house every night. Kate knew that nothing would stop him but death.

She had to get in touch with him. She summoned one of her veteran black foremen, a man she trusted. "William, do you think you can find Banda?"

"Only if he wishes to be found."

"Try. I want to meet with him."

"I'll see what I can do."

The following morning the foreman said, "If you are free this evening, a car will be waiting to take you out to the country."

Kate was driven to a small village seventy miles north of Johannesburg. The driver stopped in front of a small frame house, and Kate went inside. Banda was waiting for her. He looked exactly the same as when Kate had last seen him. *And he must be sixty years old,* Kate thought. He had been on the run from the police for years, and yet he appeared serene and calm.

He hugged Kate and said, "You look more beautiful every time I see you."

She laughed. "I'm getting old. I'm going to be forty in a few years."

"The years sit lightly on you, Kate."

They went into the kitchen, and while Banda fixed coffee, Kate said, "I don't like what's happening, Banda. Where is it going to lead?"

"It will get worse," Banda said simply. "The government will not allow us to speak with them. The whites have destroyed the bridges between us and them, and one day they will find they need those bridges to reach us. We have our heroes now, Kate. Nehemiah Tile, Mokone, Richard Msimang. The whites goad us and move us around like cattle to pasture."

"Not all whites think like that," Kate assured him. "You have friends who are fighting to change things. It will happen one day, Banda, but it will take time."

"Time is like sand in an hourglass. It runs out."

"Banda, what's happened to Ntame and to Magena?"

"My wife and son are in hiding," Banda said sadly. "The police are still very busy looking for me."

"What can I do to help? I can't just sit by and do nothing. Will money help?"

"Money always helps."

"I will arrange it. What else?"

"Pray. Pray for all of us."

The following morning, Kate returned to New York.

When Tony was old enough to travel, Kate took him on business trips during his school holidays. He was fond of museums, and he could stand for hours looking at the paintings and statues of the great masters. At home, Tony sketched copies of the paintings on the wall, but he was too self-conscious to let his mother see his work.

He was sweet and bright and fun to be with, and there was a shyness about him that people found appealing. Kate was proud of her son. He was always first in his class. "You beat all of them, didn't you, darling?" And she would laugh and hold him fiercely in her arms.

And young Tony would try even harder to live up to his mother's expectations.

In 1936, on Tony's twelfth birthday, Kate returned from a trip to the Middle East. She had missed Tony and was eager to see him. He was at home waiting for her. She took him in her arms and hugged him. "Happy birthday, darling! Has it been a good day?"

"Y-yes, m-ma'am. It's b-b-been wonderful."

Kate pulled back and looked at him. She had never noticed him stutter before. "Are you all right, Tony?"

"F-fine, thank you, M-mother."

"You mustn't stammer," she told him. "Speak more slowly."

"Yes, M-mother."

Over the next few weeks, it got worse. Kate decided to talk to Dr. Harley. When he finished the examination, John Harley said, "Physically, there's nothing wrong with the boy, Kate. Is he under any kind of pressure?"

"My son? Of course not. How can you ask that?"

"Tony's a sensitive boy. Stuttering is very often a physical manifestation of frustration, an inability to cope."

"You're wrong, John. Tony is at the very top of all the achievement tests in school. Last term he won three awards. Best all-around athlete, best all-around scholar and best student in the arts. I'd hardly call that unable to cope."

"I see." He studied her. "What do you do when Tony stammers, Kate?"

"I correct him, of course."

"I would suggest that you don't. That will only make him more tense."

Kate was stung to anger. "If Tony has any psychological problems, as you seem to think, I can assure you it's not because of his mother. I adore him. And he's aware that I think he's the most fantastic child on earth."

And that was the core of the problem. No child could live up to that. Dr. Harley glanced down at his chart. "Let's see now. Tony is twelve?"

"Yes."

"Perhaps it might be good for him if he went away for a while. Maybe a private school somewhere."

Kate just stared at him.

"Let him be on his own a bit. Just until he finishes high school. They have some excellent schools in Switzerland."

Switzerland! The idea of Tony being so far away from her was appalling. He was too young, he was not ready yet, he— Dr. Harley was watching her. "I'll think about it," Kate told him.

That afternoon she canceled a board meeting and went home early. Tony was in his room, doing homework.

Tony said, "I g-g-got all A's t-today, M-mother."

"What would you think of going to school in Switzerland, darling?"

And his eyes lit up and he said, "M-m-may I?"

Six weeks later, Kate put Tony aboard a ship. He was on his way to the Institute Le Rosey in Rolle, a small town on the shore of Lake Geneva. Kate stood at the New York pier and watched until the huge liner cut loose from the tugboats. *Bloody hell! I'm going to miss him.* Then she turned and walked back to the limousine waiting to take her to the office.

Kate enjoyed working with Brad Rogers. He was forty-six, two years older than Kate. They had become good friends through the years, and she loved him for his devotion to Kruger-Brent. Brad was unmarried and had a variety of attractive girl friends, but gradually Kate became aware that he was half in love with her. More than once he made studiously ambiguous remarks, but she chose to keep their relationship on an impersonal, business level. She broke that pattern only once.

Brad had started seeing someone regularly. He stayed out late every night and came into morning meetings tired and distracted, his mind elsewhere. It was bad for the company. When a month went by and his behavior was becoming more flagrant, Kate decided that something had to be done. She remembered how close David had come to quitting the company because of a woman. She would not let that happen with Brad.

Kate had planned to travel to Paris alone to acquire an import-export company, but at the last minute she asked Brad to accompany her. They spent the day of their arrival in meetings and that evening had dinner at the Grand Véfour. Afterward, Kate suggested that Brad join her in her suite at the George V to go over the reports on the new company. When he arrived, Kate was waiting for him in a filmy negligee.

"I brought the revised offer with me," Brad began, "so we—"

"That can wait," Kate said softly. There was an invitation in her voice that made him look at her again. "I wanted us to be alone, Brad."

"Kate—"

She moved into his arms and held him close.

"My God!" he said. "I've wanted you for so long."

"And I you, Brad."

And they moved into the bedroom.

Kate was a sensual woman, but all of her sexual energy had long since been harnessed into other channels. She was completely fulfilled by her work. She needed Brad for other reasons.

He was on top of her, and she moved her legs apart and felt his hardness in her, and it was neither pleasant nor unpleasant.

"Kate, I've loved you for so long . . ."

He was pressing into her, moving in and out in an ancient, timeless rhythm, and she thought, *They're asking too bloody much for the company. They're going to hold out because they know I really want it.*

Brad was whispering words of endearment in her ear.

I could call off the negotiations and wait for them to come back to me. But what if they don't? Do I dare risk losing the deal?

His rhythm was faster now, and Kate moved her hips, thrusting against his body.

No. They could easily find another buyer. Better to pay them what they want. I'll make up for it by selling off one of their subsidiaries.

Brad was moaning, in a frenzy of delight, and Kate moved faster, bringing him to a climax.

I'll tell them I've decided to meet their terms.

There was a long, shuddering gasp, and Brad said, "Oh, God, Kate, it was wonderful. Was it good for you, darling?"

"It was heaven."

She lay in Brad's arms all night, thinking and planning, while he slept. In the morning when he woke up, she said, "Brad, that woman you've been seeing—"

"My God! You're jealous!" He laughed happily. "Forget about her. I'll never see her again, I promise."

Kate never went to bed with Brad again. When he could not understand why she refused him, all she said was, "You don't know how much I want to, Brad, but I'm afraid we wouldn't be able to work together any longer. We must both make a sacrifice."

And he was forced to live with that.

As the company kept expanding, Kate set up charitable foundations that contributed to colleges, churches and schools. She kept adding to her art collection. She acquired the great Renaissance and post-Renaissance artists Raphael and Titian, Tintoretto and El Greco; and the baroque painters Rubens, Caravaggio and Vandyck.

The Blackwell collection was reputed to be the most valuable private collection in the world. *Reputed,* because no one outside of invited guests was permitted to see it. Kate would not allow it to be photographed, nor would she discuss it with the press. She had strict, inflexible rules about the press. The personal life of the Blackwell family was off limits. Neither servants nor employees of the company were permitted to discuss the Blackwell family. It was impossible, of course, to stop rumors and speculation, for Kate Blackwell was an intriguing enigma—one of the richest, most powerful women in the world. There were a thousand questions about her, but few answers.

Kate telephoned the headmistress at Le Rosey. "I'm calling to find out how Tony is."

"Ah, he is doing very well, Mrs. Blackwell. Your son is a superb student. He—"

"I wasn't referring to that. I meant—" She hesitated, as though reluctant to admit there could be a weakness in the Blackwell family. "I meant his stammering."

"Madame, there is no sign of any stammering. He is perfectly fine."

Kate heaved an inward sigh of relief. She had known all along that it was only temporary, a passing phase of some kind. So much for doctors!

Tony arrived home four weeks later, and Kate was at the airport to meet him. He looked fit and handsome, and Kate felt a surge of pride. "Hello, my love. How are you?"

"I'm f-f-fine, M-m-mother. How are y-y-you?"

On his vacations at home, Tony eagerly looked forward to examining the new paintings his mother had acquired while he was away. He was awed by the masters, and enchanted by the French Impressionists: Monet, Renoir, Manet and Morisot. They evoked a magic world for Tony. He bought a set of paints and an easel and went to work. He thought his paintings were terrible, and he still refused to show them to anyone. How could they compare with the exquisite masterpieces?

Kate told him, "One day all these paintings will belong to you, darling."

The thought of it filled the thirteen-year-old boy with a sense of unease. His mother did not understand. They could never be truly his, because he had done nothing to earn them. He had a fierce determination somehow to earn his own way. He had ambivalent feelings about being away from his mother, for everything around her was always exciting. She was at the center of a whirlwind, giving orders, making incredible deals, taking him to exotic places, introducing him to interesting people. She was an awesome figure, and Tony was inordinately proud of her. He thought she was the most fascinating woman in the world. He felt guilty because it was only in her presence that he stuttered.

Kate had no idea how deeply her son was in awe of her until one day when he was home on vacation he asked, "M-m-mother, do you r-r-run the world?"

And she had laughed and said, "Of course not. What made you ask such a silly question?"

"All my f-friends at school talk about you. Boy, you're really s-something."

"I am something," Kate said. "I'm your mother."

Tony wanted more than anything in the world to please Kate. He knew how much the company meant to her, how much she planned on his running it one day, and he was filled with regret, because he knew he could not. That was not what he intended to do with his life.

When he tried to explain this to his mother, she would laugh, "Nonsense, Tony. You're much too young to know what you want to do with your future."

And he would begin to stammer.

The idea of being a painter excited Tony. To be able to capture beauty and freeze it for all eternity; that was something worthwhile. He wanted to go abroad and study in Paris, but he knew he would have to broach the subject to his mother very carefully.

They had wonderful times together. Kate was the chatelaine of vast estates. She had acquired homes in Palm Beach and South Carolina, and a stud farm in Kentucky, and she and Tony visited all of them during his vacations. They watched the America's Cup races in Newport, and when they were in New York, they had lunch at Delmonico's and tea at the Plaza and Sunday dinner at Lüchow's. Kate was interested in horse racing, and her stable became one of the finest in the world. When one of Kate's horses was running and Tony was home from school, Kate would take him to the track with her. They would sit in her box and Tony would watch in wonder as his mother cheered until she was hoarse. He knew her excitement had nothing to do with money.

"It's winning, Tony. Remember that. Winning is what's important."

They had quiet, lazy times at Dark Harbor. They shopped at Pendleton and Coffin, and had ice-cream sodas at the Dark Harbor Shop. In summer they went sailing and hiking and visited art galleries. In the winter there was skiing and skating and sleigh riding. They would sit in front of a fire in the large fireplace in the library, and Kate would tell her son all the old family stories about his grandfather and Banda, and about the baby shower Madam Agnes and her girls gave for Tony's grandmother. It was a colorful family, a family to be proud of, to cherish.

"Kruger-Brent, Limited, will be yours one day, Tony. You'll run it and—"

"I d-don't want to r-run it, Mother. I'm not interested in big business or p-power."

And Kate exploded. "You bloody fool! What do you know about big business or power? Do you think I go around the world spreading evil? Hurting people? Do you think Kruger-Brent is some kind of ruthless money machine crushing anything that gets in its way? Well, let me tell you something, Son. It's the next best thing to Jesus Christ. We're the resurrection, Tony. We save lives by the hundreds of thousands. When we open a factory in a depressed community or country, those people can afford to build schools and libraries and churches, and give their children decent food and clothing and recreation facilities." She was breathing hard, carried away by her anger. "We build factories where people are hungry and out of work, and because of us they're able to live decent lives and hold up their heads. We become their saviors. Don't ever again let me hear you sneer at big business and power."

All Tony could say was, "I'm s-s-sorry, M-m-mother."

And he thought stubbornly: *I'm going to be an artist.*

When Tony was fifteen, Kate suggested he spend his summer vacation in South Africa. He had never been there. "I can't get away just now, Tony, but you'll find it a fascinating place. I'll make all the arrangements for you."

"I was s-sort of h-hoping to spend my vacation at Dark Harbor, M-mother."

"Next summer," Kate said firmly. "This summer I would like you to go to Johannesburg."

Kate carefully briefed the company superintendent in Johannesburg, and together they laid out an itinerary for Tony. Each day was planned with one objective in view: to make this trip as exciting as possible for Tony, to make him realize his future lay with the company.

Kate received a daily report about her son. He had been taken into one of the gold mines. He had spent two days in the diamond fields. He had been on a guided tour of the Kruger-Brent plants, and had gone on a safari in Kenya.

A few days before Tony's vacation ended, Kate telephoned the company manager in Johannesburg. "How is Tony getting along?"

"Oh, he's having a great time, Mrs. Blackwell. In fact, this morning he asked if he couldn't stay on a little longer."

Kate felt a surge of pleasure. "That's wonderful! Thank you."

When Tony's vacation was over, he went to Southampton, England, where he boarded a Pan American Airways System plane for the United States. Kate flew Pan American whenever possible. It spoiled her for other airlines.

Kate left an important meeting to greet her son when he arrived at the Pan American terminal at the newly built La Guardia Airport in New York. His handsome face was filled with enthusiasm.

"Did you have a good time, darling?"

"South Africa's a f-fantastic country, M-mother. Did you know they f-flew me to the Namib Desert where grandfather s-stole those diamonds from Great-grandfather v-van der Merwe?"

"He didn't steal them, Tony," Kate corrected him. "He merely took what was his."

"Sure," Tony scoffed. "Anyway, I was th-there. There was no sea *mis,* but they s-still have the guards and dogs and everything." He grinned. "They wouldn't give me any s-samples."

Kate laughed happily. "They don't have to give you any samples, darling. One day they will all be yours."

"*You* t-tell them. They wouldn't l-listen to me."

She hugged him. "You *did* enjoy it, didn't you?" She was enormously pleased that at last Tony was excited about his heritage.

"You know what I loved m-most?"

Kate smiled lovingly. "What?"

"The colors. I p-painted a lot of landscapes th-there. I hated to leave. I want to go back there and p-paint."

"Paint?" Kate tried to sound enthusiastic. "That sounds like a wonderful hobby, Tony."

"No. I don't m-mean as a hobby, Mother. I want to be a

p-painter. I've been thinking a lot about it. I'm going to P-paris to study. I really think I might have some talent."

Kate felt herself tensing. "You don't want to spend the rest of your life painting."

"Yes, I do, M-mother. It's the only thing I really c-care about."

And Kate knew she had lost.

He has a right to live his own life, Kate thought. *But how can I let him make such a terrible mistake?*

In September, the decision was taken out of both their hands. Europe went to war.

"I want you to enroll in the Wharton School of Finance and Commerce," Kate informed Tony. "In two years if you still want to be an artist, you'll have my blessing." Kate was certain that by then Tony would change his mind. It was inconceivable that her son would choose to spend his life slapping daubs of color on bits of canvas when he could head the most exciting conglomerate in the world. He was, after all, her son.

To Kate Blackwell, World War II was another great opportunity. There were worldwide shortages of military supplies and materials, and Kruger-Brent was able to furnish them. One division of the company provided equipment for the armed forces, while another division took care of civilian needs. The company factories were working twenty-four hours a day.

Kate was certain the United States was not going to be able to remain neutral. President Franklin D. Roosevelt called upon the country to be the great arsenal of democracy, and on March 11, 1941, the Lend-Lease Bill was pushed through Congress. Allied shipping across the Atlantic was menaced by the German blockade. U-boats, the German submarines, attacked and sank scores of Allied ships, fighting in wolf packs of eight.

Germany was a juggernaut that seemingly could not be stopped. In defiance of the Versailles Treaty, Adolf Hitler had built up one of the greatest war machines in history. In a new *blitzkrieg* technique, Germany attacked Poland, Belgium and the Netherlands, and in rapid succession, the German machine crushed Denmark, Norway, Luxembourg and France.

Kate went into action when she received word that Jews working in the Nazi-confiscated Kruger-Brent, Ltd., factories were being arrested and deported to concentration camps. She made two telephone calls, and the following week she was on her way to Switzerland. When she arrived at the Baur au Lac Hotel in Zurich, there was a message that Colonel Brinkmann wished to see her. Brinkmann had been a manager of the Berlin branch of Kruger-Brent, Ltd. When the factory had been taken over by the Nazi government, Brinkmann was given the rank of colonel and kept in charge.

He came to see Kate at the hotel. He was a thin, precise man with blond hair combed carefully over his balding skull. "I am delighted to see you, Frau Blackwell. I have a message for you from my government. I am authorized to assure you that as soon as we have won the war, your factories will be returned to you. Germany is going to be the greatest industrial power the world has ever known, and we welcome the collaboration of people such as yourself."

"What if Germany loses?"

Colonel Brinkmann allowed a small smile to play on his lips. "We both know that cannot happen, Frau Blackwell. The United States is wise to stay out of Europe's business. I hope it continues to do so."

"I'm sure you do, Colonel." She leaned forward. "I've heard rumors about Jews being sent to concentration camps and being exterminated. Is that true?"

"British propaganda, I assure you. It is true that *die Juden* are sent to work camps, but I give you my word as an officer that they are being treated as they should be."

Kate wondered exactly what those words meant. She intended to find out.

The following day Kate made an appointment with a prominent German merchant named Otto Bueller. Bueller was in his fifties, a distinguished-looking man with a compassionate face and eyes that had known deep suffering. They met at a small café near the *bahnhof*. Herr Bueller selected a table in a deserted corner.

"I've been told," Kate said softly, "that you've started an underground to help smuggle Jews into neutral countries. Is that true?"

"It's not true, Mrs. Blackwell. Such an act would be treason against the Third Reich."

"I have also heard that you're in need of funds to run it."

Herr Bueller shrugged. "Since there is no underground, I have no need of funds to run it, is that not so?"

His eyes kept nervously darting around the café. This was a man who breathed and slept with danger each day of his life.

"I was hoping I might be of some help," Kate said carefully. "Kruger-Brent, Limited, has factories in many neutral and Allied countries. If someone could get the refugees there, I would arrange for them to have employment."

Herr Bueller sat there sipping a bitter coffee. Finally, he said, "I know nothing about these things. Politics are dangerous these days. But if you are interested in helping someone in distress, I have an uncle in England who suffers from a terrible, debilitating disease. His doctor bills are very high."

"How high?"

"Fifty thousand dollars a month. Arrangements would have to be made to deposit the money for his medical expenses in London and transfer the deposits to a Swiss bank."

"That can be arranged."

"My uncle would be very pleased."

Some eight weeks later, a small but steady stream of Jewish refugees began to arrive in Allied countries to go to work in Kruger-Brent factories.

Tony quit school at the end of two years. He went up to Kate's office to tell her the news. "I t-tried, M-mother. I really d-did. But I've m-made up m-my mind. I want to s-study p-painting. When the w-war is over, I'm g-going to P-paris."

Each word was like a hammerblow.

"I kn-know you're d-disappointed, but I have to l-live my own life. I think I can be good—*really* good." He saw the look on Kate's face. "I've done what you've asked me to do. Now you've got to g-give me my chance. They've accepted me at the Art I-institute in Chicago."

Kate's mind was in a turmoil. What Tony wanted to do was such a bloody *waste*. All she could say was, "When do you plan to leave?"

"Enrollment starts on the fifteenth."

"What's the date today?"

"D-december sixth."

On Sunday, December 7, 1941, squadrons of Nakajima bombers and Zero fighter planes from the Imperial Japanese Navy attacked Pearl Harbor, and the following day, the United States was at war. That afternoon Tony enlisted in the United States Marine Corps. He was sent to Quantico, Virginia, where he was graduated from Officers' Training School and from there to the South Pacific.

Kate felt as though she were living on the edge of an abyss. Her working day was filled with the pressures of running the company, but every moment at the back of her mind was the fear that she would receive some dreaded news about Tony—that he had been wounded or killed.

The war with Japan was going badly. Japanese bombers struck at American bases on Guam, Midway and Wake islands. They took Singapore in February 1942, and quickly overran New Britain, New Ireland and the Admiralty and Solomon islands. General Douglas MacArthur was forced to withdraw from the Philippines. The powerful forces of the Axis were slowly conquering the world, and the shadows were darkening everywhere. Kate was afraid that Tony might be taken prisoner of war and tortured. With all her power and influence, there was nothing she could do except pray. Every letter from Tony was a beacon of hope, a sign that, a few short weeks before, he had been alive. "They keep us in the dark here," Tony wrote. "Are the Russians still holding on? The Japanese soldier is brutal, but you have to respect him. He's not afraid to die . . ."

"What's happening in the States? Are factory workers really striking for more money? . . ."

"The PT boats are doing a wonderful job here. Those boys are all heroes . . ."

"You have great connections, Mother. Send us a few hundred F4U's, the new Navy fighters. Miss you. . . ."

On August 7, 1942, the Allies began their first offensive action in the Pacific. United States Marines landed on Guadalcanal in the Solomon Islands, and from then on they kept moving to take back the islands the Japanese had conquered.

In Europe, the Allies were enjoying an almost unbroken string of victories. On June 6, 1944, the Allied invasion of Western Europe was launched with landings by American, British and Canadian troops on the Normandy beaches, and a year later, on May 7, 1945, Germany surrendered unconditionally.

In Japan, on August 6, 1945, an atomic bomb with a destructive force of more than twenty thousand tons of TNT was dropped on Hiroshima. Three days later, another atomic bomb destroyed the city of Nagasaki. On August 14, the Japanese surrendered. The long and bloody war was finally over.

Three months later, Tony returned home. He and Kate were at Dark Harbor, sitting on the terrace looking over the bay dotted with graceful white sails.

The war has changed him, Kate thought. There was a new maturity about Tony. He had grown a small mustache, and looked tanned and fit and handsome. There were lines about his eyes that had not been there before. Kate was sure the years overseas had given him time to reconsider his decision about not going into the company.

"What are your plans now, Son?" Kate asked.

Tony smiled. "As I was saying before we were so rudely interrupted, Mother—I'm going to P-paris."

BOOK FOUR

Tony
1946–1950

18

Tony had been to Paris before, but this time the circumstances were different. The City of Light had been dimmed by the German occupation, but had been saved from destruction when it was declared an open city. The people had suffered a great deal, and though the Nazis had looted the Louvre, Tony found Paris relatively untouched. Besides, this time he was going to live there, to be a part of the city, rather than be a tourist. He could have stayed at Kate's penthouse on Avenue du Maréchal Foch, which had not been damaged during the occupation. Instead, he rented an unfurnished flat in an old converted house behind Grand Montparnasse. The apartment consisted of a living room with a fireplace, a small bedroom and a tiny kitchen that had no refrigerator. Between the bedroom and the kitchen crouched a bathroom with a claw-footed tub and small stained bidet and a temperamental toilet with a broken seat.

When the landlady started to make apologies, Tony stopped her. "It's perfect."

He spent all day Saturday at the flea market. Monday and Tuesday he toured the secondhand shops along the Left Bank, and by Wednesday he had the basic furniture he needed. A sofa bed, a scarred table, two overstuffed chairs, an old, ornately carved wardrobe, lamps and a rickety kitchen table and two straight chairs. *Mother would be horrified,* Tony thought. He could have had his apartment crammed with priceless antiques, but that would have been *playing* the part of a young American artist in Paris. He intended to *live* it.

The next step was getting into a good art school. The most prestigious art school in all of France was the École des Beaux-Arts of Paris. Its standards were high, and few Americans were admitted. Tony applied for a place there. *They'll never accept me,* he thought. *But if they do!* Somehow, he had to show his mother he had made the right decision. He submitted three of his paintings and waited four weeks to hear whether he had been accepted. At the end of the fourth week, his concierge handed him a letter from the school. He was to report the following Monday.

The École des Beaux-Arts was a large stone building, two stories high, with a dozen classrooms filled with students. Tony reported to the head of the school, Maître Gessand, a towering, bitter-looking man with no neck and the thinnest lips Tony had ever seen.

"Your paintings are amateurish," he told Tony. "But they show promise. Our committee selected you more for what was *not* in the paintings than for what *was* in them. Do you understand?"

"Not exactly, maître."

"You will, in time. I am assigning you to Maître Cantal. He will be your teacher for the next five years—if you last that long."

I'll last that long, Tony promised himself.

Maître Cantal was a very short man, with a totally bald head which he covered with a purple beret. He had dark-brown eyes, a large, bulbous nose and lips like sausages. He greeted Tony with, "Americans are dilettantes, barbarians. Why are you here?"

"To learn, maître."

Maître Cantal grunted.

There were twenty-five pupils in the class, most of them French. Easels had been set up around the room, and Tony selected one near the window that overlooked a workingman's bistro. Scattered around the room were plaster casts of various parts of the human anatomy taken from Greek statues. Tony looked around for the model. He could see no one.

"You will begin," Maître Cantal told the class.

"Excuse me," Tony said. "I—I didn't bring my paints with me."

"You will not need paints. You will spend the first year learning to draw properly."

The maître pointed to the Greek statuary. "You will draw those. If it seems too simple for you, let me warn you: Before the year is over, more than half of you will be eliminated." He warmed to his speech. "You will spend the first year learning anatomy. The second year—for those of you who pass the course—you will draw from live models, working with oils. The third year—and I assure you there will be fewer of you—you will paint with me, in my style, greatly improving on it, naturally. In the fourth and fifth years, you will find your own style, your own voice. Now let us get to work."

The class went to work.

The maître went around the room, stopping at each easel to make criticisms or comments. When he came to the drawing Tony was working on, he said curtly, "No! That will not do. What I see is the *outside* of an arm. I want to see the *inside*. Muscles, bones, ligaments. I want to know there is *blood* flowing underneath. Do you know how to do that?"

"Yes, maître. You think it, see it, feel it, and then you draw it."

When Tony was not in class, he was usually in his apartment sketching. He could have painted from dawn to dawn. Painting gave him a sense of freedom he had never known before. The simple act of sitting in front of an easel with a paintbrush in his hand made him feel godlike. He could create whole worlds with one hand. He could make a tree, a flower, a human, a universe. It was a heady experience. He had been born for this. When he was not painting, he was out on the streets of Paris exploring the fabulous city. Now it was *his* city, the place where his art was being born. There were two Parises, divided by the Seine into the Left Bank and the Right Bank, and they were worlds apart. The Right Bank was for the wealthy, the established. The Left Bank belonged to the students, the artists, the struggling. It was Montparnasse and the Boulevard Raspail and Saint-Germain-des-Prés. It was the Café Flore and Henry Miller and Elliot Paul. For Tony, it was home. He would sit for hours at the Boule Blanche or La Coupole with fellow students, discussing their arcane world.

"I understand the art director of the Guggenheim Museum is in Paris, buying up everything in sight."

"Tell him to wait for me!"

They all read the same magazines and shared them because they were expensive: *Studio* and *Cahiers d'Art, Formes et Couleurs* and *Gazette des Beaux-Arts*.

Tony had learned French at Le Rosey, and he found it easy to make friends with the other students in his class, for they all shared a common passion. They had no idea who Tony's family was, and they accepted him as one of them. Poor and struggling artists gathered at Café Flore and Les Deux Magots on Boulevard Saint-Germain, and ate at Le Pot d'Etian on the Rue des Canettes or at the Rue de l'Université. None of the others had ever seen the inside of Lasserre or Maxim's.

In 1946, giants were practicing their art in Paris. From time to time, Tony caught glimpses of Pablo Picasso, and one day Tony and a friend saw Marc Chagall, a large, flamboyant man in his fifties, with a wild mop of hair just beginning to turn gray. Chagall was seated at a table across the café, in earnest conversation with a group of people.

"We're lucky to see him," Tony's friend whispered. "He comes to Paris very seldom. His home is at Vence, near the Mediterranean coast."

There was Max Ernst sipping an aperitif at a sidewalk café,

and the great Alberto Giacometti walking down the Rue de Ri-
voli, looking like one of his own sculptures, tall and thin and
gnarled. Tony was surprised to note he was clubfooted. Tony
met Hans Belmer, who was making a name for himself with
erotic paintings of young girls turning into dismembered dolls.
But perhaps Tony's most exciting moment came when he was
introduced to Braque. The artist was cordial, but Tony was
tongue-tied.

The future geniuses haunted the new art galleries, studying
their competition. The Drouant-David Gallery was exhibiting
an unknown young artist named Bernard Buffet, who had studied at the École des Beaux-Arts, and Soutine, Utrillo and Dufy.
The students congregated at the Salon d'Automne and the
Charpentier Gallery and Mlle. Roussa's Gallery on the Rue de
Seine, and spent their spare time gossiping about their successful rivals.

The first time Kate saw Tony's apartment, she was stunned.
She wisely made no comment, but she thought, *Bloody hell!
How can a son of mine live in this dreary closet?* Aloud she said,
"It has great charm, Tony. I don't see a refrigerator. Where do
you keep your food?"

"Out on the w-windowsill."

Kate walked over to the window, opened it and selected an
apple from the sill outside. "I'm not eating one of your subjects,
am I?"

Tony laughed. "N-no, Mother."

Kate took a bite. "Now," she demanded, "tell me about your
painting."

"There's n-not much to t-tell yet," Tony confessed. "We're
just doing d-drawings this year."

"Do you like this Maître Cantal?"

"He's m-marvelous. The important question is whether he
l-likes *me*. Only about one-third of the class is going to m-make
it to next year."

Not once did Kate mention Tony's joining the company.

* * *

Maître Cantal was not a man to lavish praise. The biggest
compliment Tony would get would be a grudging, "I suppose
I've seen worse," or, "I'm almost beginning to see *underneath*."

At the end of the school term, Tony was among the eight advanced to the second-year class. To celebrate, Tony and the
other relieved students went to a nightclub in Montmartre, got
drunk and spent the night with some young English women who
were on a tour of France.

When school started again, Tony began to work with oils and
live models. It was like being released from kindergarten. After
one year of sketching parts of anatomy, Tony felt he knew every
muscle, nerve and gland in the human body. That wasn't drawing—it was *copying*. Now, with a paintbrush in his hand and a
live model in front of him, Tony began to create. Even Maître
Cantal was impressed.

"You have the *feel*," he said grudgingly. "Now we must work
on the technique."

There were about a dozen models who sat for classes at the
school. The ones Maître Cantal used most frequently were
Carlos, a young man working his way through medical school;
Annette, a short, buxom brunette with a clump of red pubic hair
and an acne-scarred back; and Dominique Masson, a beautiful,
young, willowy blonde with delicate cheekbones and deep-green
eyes. Dominique also posed for several well-known painters.
She was everyone's favorite. Every day after class the male students would gather around her, trying to make a date.

"I never mix pleasure with business," she told them. "Anyway," she teased, "it would not be fair. You have all seen what I
have to offer. How do I know what you have to offer?"

And the ribald conversation would go on. But Dominique
never went out with anyone at the school.

Late one afternoon when all the other students had left and
Tony was finishing a painting of Dominique, she came up behind him unexpectedly. "My nose is too long."

Tony was flustered. "Oh. I'm sorry, I'll change it."

"No, no. The nose in the painting is fine. It is *my* nose that is too long."

Tony smiled. "I'm afraid I can't do much about that."

"A Frenchman would have said, 'Your nose is perfect, *chérie.*'"

"I like your nose, and I'm not French."

"Obviously. You have never asked me out. I wonder why."

Tony was taken aback. "I—I don't know. I guess it's because everyone else has, and you never go out with anybody."

Dominique smiled. *"Everybody* goes out with somebody. Good night."

And she was gone.

Tony noticed that whenever he stayed late, Dominique dressed and then returned to stand behind him and watched him paint.

"You are very good," she announced one afternoon. "You are going to be an important painter."

"Thank you, Dominique. I hope you're right."

"Painting is very serious to you, *oui?"*

"Oui."

"Would a man who is going to be an important painter like to buy me dinner?" She saw the look of surprise on his face. "I do not eat much. I must keep my figure."

Tony laughed. "Certainly. It would be a pleasure."

They ate at a bistro near Sacré-Coeur, and they discussed painters and painting. Tony was fascinated with her stories of the well-known artists for whom she posed. As they were having *café au lait,* Dominique said, "I must tell you, you are as good as any of them."

Tony was inordinately pleased, but all he said was, "I have a long way to go."

Outside the café, Dominique asked, "Are you going to invite me to see your apartment?"

"If you'd like to. I'm afraid it isn't much."

When they arrived, Dominique looked around the tiny, messy apartment and shook her head. "You were right. It is not much. Who takes care of you?"

"A cleaning lady comes in once a week."

"Fire her. This place is filthy. Don't you have a girl friend?"

"No."

She studied him a moment. "You're not queer?"

"No."

"Good. It would be a terrible waste. Find me a pail of water and some soap."

Dominique went to work on the apartment, cleaning and scrubbing and finally tidying up. When she had finished, she said, "That will have to do for now. My God, I need a bath."

She went into the tiny bathroom and ran water in the tub. "How do you fit yourself in this?" she called out.

"I pull up my legs."

She laughed. "I would like to see that."

Fifteen minutes later, she came out of the bathroom with only a towel around her waist, her blond hair damp and curling. She had a beautiful figure, full breasts, a narrow waist and long, tapering legs. Tony had been unaware of her as a woman before. She had been merely a nude figure to be portrayed on canvas. Oddly enough, the towel changed everything. He felt a sudden rush of blood to his loins.

Dominique was watching him. "Would you like to make love to me?"

"Very much."

She slowly removed the towel. "Show me."

Tony had never known a woman like Dominique. She gave him everything and asked for nothing. She came over almost every evening to cook for Tony. When they went out to dinner, Dominique insisted on going to inexpensive bistros or sandwich bars. "You must save your money," she scolded him. "It is very difficult even for a good artist to get started. And you are good, chéri."

They went to Les Halles in the small hours of the morning and had onion soup at Pied de Cochon. They went to the Musée Carnavalet and out-of-the-way places where tourists did not go, like Cimetière Père-Lachaise—the final resting place of Oscar Wilde, Frédéric Chopin, Honoré de Balzac and Marcel Proust. They visited the catacombs and spent a lazy holiday week going down the Seine on a barge owned by a friend of Dominique's.

Dominique was a delight to be with. She had a quixotic sense of humor, and whenever Tony was depressed, she would laugh him out of it. She seemed to know everyone in Paris, and she took Tony to interesting parties where he met some of the most prominent figures of the day, like the poet Paul Éluard, and André Breton, in charge of the prestigious Galerie Maeght.

Dominique was a source of constant encouragement. "You are going to be better than all of them, *chéri*. Believe me. I know."

If Tony was in the mood to paint at night, Dominique would cheerfully pose for him, even though she had been working all day. *God, I'm lucky,* Tony thought. This was the first time he had been sure someone loved him for what he was, not who he was, and it was a feeling he cherished. Tony was afraid to tell Dominique he was the heir to one of the world's largest fortunes, afraid she would change, afraid they would lose what they had. But for her birthday Tony could not resist buying her a Russian lynx coat.

"It's the most beautiful thing I've ever seen in my life!" Dominique swirled the coat around her and danced around the room. She stopped in the middle of a spin. "Where did it come from? Tony, where did you get the money to buy this coat?"

He was ready for her. "It's hot—stolen. I bought it from a little man outside the Rodin Museum. He was anxious to get rid of it. It didn't cost me much more than a good cloth coat would cost at Au Printemps."

Dominique stared at him a moment, then burst out laughing. "I'll wear it even if we both go to prison!"

Then she threw her arms around Tony and started to cry. "Oh, Tony, you idiot. You darling, fantastic idiot."

It was well worth the lie, Tony decided.

One night Dominique suggested to Tony that he move in with her. Between working at the École des Beaux-Arts and modeling for some of the better-known artists in Paris, Dominique was able to rent a large, modern apartment on Rue Prêtres-Saint Severin. "You should not be living in a place like this, Tony. It is dreadful. Live with me, and you will not have to pay any rent. I can do your laundry, cook for you and—"

"No, Dominique. Thank you."

"But why?"

How could he explain? In the beginning he might have told her he was rich, but now it was too late. She would feel he had been making a fool of her. So he said, "It would be like living off you. You've already given me too much."

"Then I'm giving up my apartment and moving in here. I want to be with you."

She moved in the following day.

There was a wonderful, easy intimacy between them. They spent weekends in the country and stopped at little hostels where Tony would set up his easel and paint landscapes, and when they got hungry Dominique would spread out a picnic lunch she had prepared and they would eat in a meadow. Afterward, they made long, sweet love. Tony had never been so completely happy.

His work was progressing beautifully. One morning Maître Cantal held up one of Tony's paintings and said to the class, "Look at that body. You can see it *breathing.*"

Tony could hardly wait to tell Dominique that night. "You know how I got the breathing just right? I hold the model in my arms every night."

Dominique laughed in excitement and then grew serious. "Tony, I do not think you need three more years of school. You are ready now. Everyone at the school sees that, even Cantal."

Tony's fear was that he was not good enough, that he was just another painter, that his work would be lost in the flood of pictures turned out by thousands of artists all over the world every day. He could not bear the thought of it. *Winning is what's important, Tony. Remember that.*

Sometimes when Tony finished a painting he would be filled with a sense of elation and think, *I have talent. I really have tal-*

ent. At other times he would look at his work and think, *I'm a bloody amateur.*

With Dominique's encouragement, Tony was gaining more and more confidence in his work. He had finished almost two dozen paintings on his own. Landscapes, still lifes. There was a painting of Dominique lying nude under a tree, the sun dappling her body. A man's jacket and shirt were in the foreground, and the viewer knew the woman awaited her lover.

When Dominique saw the painting, she cried, "You must have an exhibition!"

"You're mad, Dominique! I'm not ready."

"You're wrong, *mon cher.*"

Tony arrived home late the next afternoon to find that Dominique was not alone. Anton Goerg, a thin man with an enormous potbelly and protuberant hazel eyes, was with her. He was the owner and proprietor of the Goerg Gallery, a modest gallery on the Rue Dauphine. Tony's paintings were spread around the room.

"What's going on?" Tony asked.

"What's going on, monsieur," Anton Goerg exclaimed, "is that I think your work is brilliant." He clapped Tony on the back. "I would be honored to give you a showing in my gallery."

Tony looked over at Dominique, and she was beaming at him.

"I—I don't know what to say."

"You have already said it," Goerg replied. "On these canvases."

Tony and Dominique stayed up half the night discussing it.

"I don't feel I'm ready. The critics will crucify me."

"You're wrong, *chéri.* This is perfect for you. It is a small gallery. Only the local people will come and judge you. There is no way you can get hurt. Monsieur Goerg would never offer to give you an exhibition if he did not believe in you. He agrees with me that you are going to be a very important artist."

"All right," Tony finally said. "Who knows? I might even sell a painting."

* * *

The cable read: ARRIVING PARIS SATURDAY. PLEASE JOIN ME FOR DINNER. LOVE, MOTHER.

Tony's first thought as he watched his mother walk into the studio was, *What a handsome woman she is.* She was in her mid-fifties, hair untinted, with white strands laced through the black. There was a charged vitality about her. Tony had once asked her why she had not remarried. She had answered quietly, "Only two men were ever important in my life. Your father and you."

Now, standing in the little apartment in Paris, facing his mother, Tony said, "It's g-good to see you, M-mother."

"Tony, you look absolutely wonderful! The beard is new." She laughed and ran her fingers through it. "You look like a young Abe Lincoln." Her eyes swept the small apartment. "Thank God, you've gotten a good cleaning woman. It looks like a different place."

Kate walked over to the easel, where Tony had been working on a painting, and she stopped and stared at it for a long time. He stood there, nervously awaiting his mother's reaction.

When Kate spoke, her voice was very soft. "It's brilliant, Tony. Really brilliant." There was no effort to conceal the pride she felt. She could not be deceived about art, and there was a fierce exultation in her that her son was so talented.

She turned to face him. "Let me see more!"

They spent the next two hours going through his stack of paintings. Kate discussed each one in great detail. There was no condescension in her voice. She had failed in her attempt to control his life, and Tony admired her for taking her defeat so gracefully.

Kate said, "I'll arrange for a showing. I know a few dealers who—"

"Thanks, M-mother, but you d-don't have to. I'm having a showing next F-friday. A g-gallery is giving me an exhibition."

Kate threw her arms around Tony. "That's wonderful! Which gallery?"

"The G-goerg Gallery."

"I don't believe I know it."

"It's s-small, but I'm not ready for Hammer or W-wildenstein yet."

She pointed to the painting of Dominique under the tree. "You're wrong, Tony. I think this—"

There was the sound of the front door opening. "I'm horny, *chéri*. Take off your—" Dominique saw Kate. "Oh, *merde!* I'm sorry. I—I didn't know you had company, Tony."

There was a moment of frozen silence.

"Dominique, this is my m-mother. M-mother, may I present D-dominique Masson."

The two women stood there, studying each other.

"How do you do, Mrs. Blackwell."

Kate said, "I've been admiring my son's portrait of you." The rest was left unspoken.

There was another awkward silence.

"Did Tony tell you he's going to have an exhibition, Mrs. Blackwell?"

"Yes, he did. It's wonderful news."

"Can you s-stay for it, Mother?"

"I'd give anything to be able to be there, but I have a board meeting the day after tomorrow in Johannesburg and there's no way I can miss it. I wish I'd known about it sooner, I'd have rearranged my schedule."

"It's all r-right," Tony said. "I understand." Tony was nervous that his mother might say more about the company in front of Dominique, but Kate's mind was on the paintings.

"It's important for the right people to see your exhibition."

"Who are the right people, Mrs. Blackwell?"

Kate turned to Dominique. "Opinion-makers, critics. Someone like Andre d'Usseau—he should be there."

Andre d'Usseau was the most respected art critic in France. He was a ferocious lion guarding the temple of art, and a single review from him could make or break an artist overnight. D'Usseau was invited to the opening of every exhibition, but he attended only the major ones. Gallery owners and artists trembled, waiting for his reviews to appear. He was a master of the *bon mot,* and his quips flew around Paris on poisoned wings. Andre d'Usseau was the most hated man in Parisian art circles, and the most respected. His mordant wit and savage criticism were tolerated because of his expertise.

Tony turned to Dominique. "That's a m-mother for you." Then to Kate, "Andre d'Usseau doesn't g-go to little galleries."

"Oh, Tony, he *must* come. He can make you famous over-night."

"Or b-break me."

"Don't you believe in yourself?" Kate was watching her son.

"Of course he does," Dominique said. "But we couldn't dare hope that Monsieur d'Usseau would come."

"I could probably find some friends who know him."

Dominique's face lighted up. "That would be fantastic!" She turned to Tony. *"Chéri,* do you know what it would mean if he came to your opening?"

"Oblivion?"

"Be serious. I know his taste, Tony. I know what he likes. He will adore your paintings."

Kate said, "I won't try to arrange for him to come unless you want me to, Tony."

"Of course he wants it, Mrs. Blackwell."

Tony took a deep breath. "I'm s-scared, but what the hell! L-let's try."

"I'll see what I can do." Kate looked at the painting on the easel for a long, long time, then turned back to Tony. There was a sadness in her eyes. "Son, I must leave Paris tomorrow. Can we have dinner tonight?"

Tony replied, "Yes, of course, Mother. *We're* f-free."

Kate turned to Dominique and said graciously, "Would you like to have dinner at Maxim's or—"

Tony said quickly, "Dominique and I know a w-wonderful little café not f-far from here."

They went to a bistro at the Place Victoire. The food was good and the wine was excellent. The two women seemed to get along well, and Tony was terribly proud of both of them. *It's one of the best nights of my life,* he thought. *I'm with my mother and the woman I'm going to marry.*

The next morning Kate telephoned from the airport. "I've made a half a dozen phone calls," she told Tony. "No one could give me a definite answer about Andre d'Usseau. But whichever way it goes, darling, I'm proud of you. The paintings are wonderful. Tony, I love you."

"I l-love you, too, M-mother."

The Goerg Gallery was just large enough to escape being called *intime.* Two dozen of Tony's paintings were being hung on the walls in frantic, last-minute preparation for the opening. On a marble sideboard were slabs of cheese and biscuits and bottles of Chablis. The gallery was empty except for Anton Goerg, Tony, Dominique and a young female assistant who was hanging the last of the paintings.

Anton Goerg looked at his watch. "The invitations said 'seven o'clock.' People should start to arrive at any moment now."

Tony had not expected to be nervous. *And I'm not nervous,* he told himself. *I'm panicky!*

"What if no one shows up?" he asked. "I mean, what if not one single, bloody person shows up?"

Dominique smiled and stroked his cheek. "Then we'll have all this cheese and wine for ourselves."

People began to arrive. Slowly at first, and then in larger numbers. Monsieur Goerg was at the door, effusively greeting them. *They don't look like art buyers to me,* Tony thought grimly. His discerning eye divided them into three categories: There were the artists and art students who attended each exhibition to evaluate the competition; the art dealers who came to every exhibition so they could spread derogatory news about aspiring painters; and the *arty* crowd, consisting to a large extent of homosexuals and lesbians who seemed to spend their lives around the fringes of the art world. *I'm not going to sell a single, goddamned picture,* Tony decided.

Monsieur Goerg was beckoning to Tony from across the room.

"I don't think I want to meet any of these people," Tony whispered to Dominique. "They're here to rip me apart."

"Nonsense. They came here to meet you. Now be charming, Tony."

And so, he was charming. He met everybody, smiled a lot and uttered all the appropriate phrases in response to the compliments that were paid him. *But were they really compliments?* Tony wondered. Over the years a vocabulary had developed in art circles to cover exhibitions of unknown painters. Phrases that said everything and nothing.

"You really feel you're there . . ."

"I've never seen a style quite like yours . . ."

"Now, that's a painting! . . ."

"It speaks to me . . ."

"You couldn't have done it any better . . ."

People kept arriving, and Tony wondered whether the attraction was curiosity about his paintings or the free wine and cheese. So far, not one of his paintings had sold, but the wine and cheese were being consumed rapaciously.

"Be patient," Monsieur Goerg whispered to Tony. "They are interested. First they must get a smell of the paintings. They see one they like, they keep wandering back to it. Pretty soon they ask the price, and when they nibble, *voilà!* The hook is set!"

"Jesus! I feel like I'm on a fishing cruise," Tony told Dominique.

Monsieur Goerg bustled up to Tony. "We've sold one!" he exclaimed. "The Normandy landscape. Five hundred francs."

It was a moment that Tony would remember as long as he lived. Someone had bought a painting of his! Someone had thought enough of his work to pay money for it, to hang it in his home or office, to look at it, live with it, show it to friends. It was a small piece of immortality. It was a way of living more than one life, of being in more than one place at the same time. A successful artist was in hundreds of homes and offices and museums all over the world, bringing pleasure to thousands—sometimes millions of people. Tony felt as though he had stepped into the pantheon of Da Vinci and Michelangelo and Rembrandt. He was no longer an amateur painter, he was a professional. Someone had paid money for his work.

Dominique hurried up to him, her eyes bright with excitement. "You've just sold another one, Tony."

"Which one?" he asked eagerly.

"The floral."

The small gallery was filled now with people and loud chatter and the clink of glasses; and suddenly a stillness came over the room. There was an undercurrent of whispers and all eyes turned to the door.

Andre d'Usseau was entering the gallery. He was in his middle fifties, taller than the average Frenchman, with a strong, leonine face and a mane of white hair. He wore a flowing inverness cape and Borsalino hat, and behind him came an entourage of hangers-on. Automatically, everyone in the room began to make way for d'Usseau. There was not one person present who did not know who he was.

Dominique squeezed Tony's hand. "He's come!" she said. "He's here!"

Such an honor had never befallen Monsieur Goerg before, and he was beside himself, bowing and scraping before the great man, doing everything but tugging at his forelock.

"Monsieur d'Usseau," he babbled. "What a great pleasure this is! What an honor! May I offer you some wine, some cheese?" He cursed himself for not having bought a decent wine.

"Thank you," the great man replied. "I have come to feast only my eyes. I would like to meet the artist."

Tony was too stunned to move. Dominique pushed him forward.

"Here he is," Monsieur Goerg said. "Mr. Andre d'Usseau, this is Tony Blackwell."

Tony found his voice. "How do you do, sir? I—thank you for coming."

Andre d'Usseau bowed slightly and moved toward the paintings on the walls. Everyone pushed back to give him room. He made his way slowly, looking at each painting long and carefully, then moving on to the next one. Tony tried to read his face, but he could tell nothing. D'Usseau neither frowned nor smiled. He stopped for a long time at one particular painting, a nude of Dominique, then moved on. He made a complete circle of the room, missing nothing. Tony was perspiring profusely.

When Andre d'Usseau had finished, he walked over to Tony. "I am glad I came," was all he said.

Within minutes after the famous critic had left, every painting in the gallery was sold. A great new artist was being born, and everyone wanted to be in at the birth.

"I have never seen anything like it," Monsieur Goerg exclaimed. "Andre d'Usseau came to my gallery. *My* gallery! All Paris will read about it tomorrow. 'I am glad I came.' Andre d'Usseau is not a man to waste words. This calls for champagne. Let us celebrate."

Later that night, Tony and Dominique had their own private celebration. Dominique snuggled in his arms. "I've slept with painters before," she said, "but never anyone as famous as you're going to be. Tomorrow everyone in Paris will know who you are."

And Dominique was right.

At five o'clock the following morning, Tony and Dominique hurriedly got dressed and went out to get the first edition of the morning paper. It had just arrived at the kiosk. Tony snatched up the paper and turned to the art section. His review was the headline article under the by-line of Andre d'Usseau. Tony read it aloud:

> "An exhibition by a young American painter, Anthony Blackwell, opened last night at the Goerg Gallery. It was a great learning experience for this critic. I have attended so many exhibitions of talented painters that I had forgotten what truly bad paintings looked like. I was forcibly reminded last night ..."

Tony's face turned ashen.

"Please don't read any more," Dominique begged. She tried to take the paper from Tony.

"Let go!" he commanded.

He read on.

"At first I thought a joke was being perpetrated. I could not seriously believe that anyone would have the nerve to hang such amateurish paintings and dare to call them art. I searched for the tiniest glimmering of talent. Alas, there was none. They should have hung the painter instead of his paintings. I would earnestly advise that the confused Mr. Blackwell return to his real profession, which I can only assume is that of house painter."

"I can't believe it," Dominique whispered. "I can't believe he couldn't see it. Oh, that bastard!" Dominique began to cry helplessly.

Tony felt as though his chest were filled with lead. He had difficulty breathing. "He saw it," he said. "And he does know, Dominique. He does know." His voice was filled with pain. "That's what hurts so much. Christ! What a fool I was!" He started to move away.

"Where are you going, Tony?"

"I don't know."

He wandered around the cold, dawn streets, unaware of the tears running down his face. Within a few hours, everyone in Paris would have read that review. He would be an object of ridicule. But what hurt more was that he had deluded himself. He had really believed he had a career ahead of him as a painter. At least Andre d'Usseau had saved him from that mistake. *Pieces of posterity,* Tony thought grimly. *Pieces of shit!* He walked into the first open bar and proceeded to get mindlessly drunk.

When Tony finally returned to his apartment, it was five o'clock the following morning.

Dominique was waiting for him, frantic. "Where have you been, Tony? Your mother has been trying to get in touch with you. She's sick with worry."

"Did you read it to her?"

"Yes, she insisted. I—"

The telephone rang. Dominique looked at Tony, and picked up the receiver. "Hello? Yes, Mrs. Blackwell. He just walked in." She held the receiver out to Tony. He hesitated, then took it.

"Hello, M-mother."

Kate's voice was filled with distress. "Tony, darling, listen to me. I can make him print a retraction. I—"

"Mother," Tony said wearily, "this isn't a b-business transaction. This is a c-critic expressing an opinion. His opinion is that I should be h-hanged."

"Darling, I hate to have you hurt like this. I don't think I can stand—" She broke off, unable to continue.

"It's all right, M-mother. I've had my little f-fling. I tried it and it didn't w-work. I don't have what it t-takes. It's as simple as that. I h-hate d'Usseau's guts, but he's the best g-goddamned art critic in the world, I have to g-give him that. He saved me from making a t-terrible mistake."

"Tony, I wish there was something I could say . . ."

"D'Usseau s-said it all. It's b-better that I f-found it out now instead of t-ten years from now, isn't it? I've got to g-get out of this town."

"Wait there for me, darling. I'll leave Johannesburg tomorrow and we'll go back to New York together."

"All right," Tony said. He replaced the receiver and turned toward Dominique. "I'm sorry, Dominique. You picked the wrong fellow."

Dominique said nothing. She just looked at him with eyes filled with an unspeakable sorrow.

The following afternoon at Kruger-Brent's office on Rue Matignon, Kate Blackwell was writing out a check. The man seated across the desk from her sighed. "It is a pity. Your son has talent, Mrs. Blackwell. He could have become an important painter."

Kate stared at him coldly. "Mr. d'Usseau, there are tens of thousands of painters in the world. My son was not meant to be one of the crowd." She passed the check across the desk. "You fulfilled your part of the bargain, I'm prepared to fulfill mine.

Kruger-Brent, Limited, will sponsor art museums in Johannesburg, London and New York. You will be in charge of selecting
the paintings—with a handsome commission, of course."

But long after d'Usseau had gone, Kate sat at her desk, filled
with a deep sadness. She loved her son so much. If he ever found
out . . . She knew the risk she had taken. But she could not stand
by and let Tony throw away his inheritance. No matter what it
might cost her, he had to be protected. The company had to be
protected. Kate rose, feeling suddenly very tired. It was time to
pick up Tony and take him home. She would help him get over
this, so he could get on with what he had been born to do.

Run the company.

19

For the next two years, Tony Blackwell felt he was on a giant treadmill that was taking him nowhere. He was the heir apparent to an awesome conglomerate. Kruger-Brent's empire had expanded to include paper mills, an airline, banks and a chain of hospitals. Tony learned that a name is a key that opens all doors. There are clubs and organizations and social cliques where the coin of the realm is not money or influence, but the proper name. Tony was accepted for membership in the Union Club, The Brook and The Links Club. He was catered to everywhere he went, but he felt like an imposter. He had done nothing to deserve any of it. He was in the giant shadow of his grandfather, and he felt he was constantly being measured against him. It was unfair, for there were no more mine fields to crawl over, no guards shooting at him, no sharks threatening him. The ancient tales of derring-do had nothing to do with Tony. They belonged to a past century, another time, another place, heroic acts committed by a stranger.

Tony worked twice as hard as anyone else at Kruger-Brent, Ltd. He drove himself mercilessly, trying to rid himself of memories too searing to bear. He wrote to Dominique, but his letters were returned unopened. He telephoned Maître Cantal, but Dominique no longer modeled at the school. She had disappeared.

Tony handled his job expertly and methodically, with neither passion nor love, and if he felt a deep emptiness inside himself, no one suspected it. Not even Kate. She received weekly reports on Tony, and she was pleased with them.

"He has a natural aptitude for business," she told Brad Rogers.

To Kate, the long hours her son worked were proof of how much he loved what he was doing. When Kate thought of how Tony had almost thrown his future away, she shuddered and was grateful she had saved him.

In 1948 the Nationalist Party was in full power in South Africa, with segregation in all public places. Migration was strictly controlled, and families were split up to suit the convenience of the government. Every black man had to carry a *bewyshoek,* and it was more than a pass, it was a lifeline, his birth certificate, his work permit, his tax receipt. It regulated his movements and his life. There were increasing riots in South Africa, and they were ruthlessly put down by the police. From time to time, Kate read newspaper stories about sabotage and unrest, and Banda's name was always prominently mentioned. He was still a leader in the underground, despite his age. *Of course he would fight for his people,* Kate thought. *He's Banda.*

Kate celebrated her fifty-sixth birthday alone with Tony at the house on Fifth Avenue. She thought, *This handsome twenty-four-year-old man across the table can't be my son. I'm too young.* And he was toasting her, "To m-my f-fantastic m-mother. Happy b-birthday!"

"You should make that to my fantastic *old* mother." *Soon I'll be retiring,* Kate thought, *but my son will take my place. My son!*

At Kate's insistence, Tony had moved into the mansion on Fifth Avenue.

"The place is too bloody large for me to rattle around in alone," Kate told him. "You'll have the whole east wing to yourself and all the privacy you need." It was easier for Tony to give in than to argue.

Tony and Kate had breakfast together every morning, and the topic of conversation was always Kruger-Brent, Ltd. Tony marveled that his mother could care so passionately for a faceless, soulless entity, an amorphous collection of buildings and machines and bookkeeping figures. *Where did the magic lie?* With all the myriad mysteries of the world to explore, why would anyone want to waste a lifetime accumulating wealth to pile on more wealth, gathering power that was beyond power? Tony did not understand his mother. But he loved her. And he tried to live up to what she expected of him.

The Pan American flight from Rome to New York had been uneventful. Tony liked the airline. It was pleasant and efficient. He worked on his overseas acquisitions reports from the time the plane took off, skipping dinner and ignoring the stewardesses who kept offering him drinks, pillows or whatever else might appeal to their attractive passenger.

"Thank you, miss. I'm fine."

"If there's *anything* at all, Mr. Blackwell . . ."

"Thank you."

A middle-aged woman in the seat next to Tony was reading a fashion magazine. As she turned a page, Tony happened to glance over, and he froze. There was a picture of a model wearing a ball gown. It was Dominique. There was no question about it. There were the high, delicate cheekbones and the deep-green eyes, the luxuriant blond hair. Tony's pulse began to race.

"Excuse me," Tony said to his seat companion. "May I borrow that page?"

Early the following morning, Tony called the dress shop and got the name of their advertising agency. He telephoned them. "I'm trying to locate one of your models," he told the switchboard operator. "Could you—"

"One moment, please."

A man's voice came on. "May I help you?"

"I saw a photograph in this month's issue of *Vogue*. A model advertising a ball gown for the Rothman stores. Is that your account?"

"Yes."

"Can you give me the name of your model agency?"

"That would be the Carleton Blessing Agency." He gave Tony the telephone number.

A minute later, Tony was talking to a woman at the Blessing Agency. "I'm trying to locate one of your models," he said. "Dominique Masson."

"I'm sorry. It is our policy not to give out personal information." And the line went dead.

Tony sat there, staring at the receiver. There *had* to be a way to get in touch with Dominique. He went into Brad Rogers's office.

"Morning, Tony. Coffee?"

"No, thanks. Brad, have you heard of the Carleton Blessing Model Agency?"

"I should think so. We own it."

"*What?*"

"It's under the umbrella of one of our subsidiaries."

"When did we acquire it?"

"A couple of years ago. Just about the time you joined the company. What's your interest in it?"

"I'm trying to locate one of their models. She's an old friend."

"No problem. I'll call and—"

"Never mind. I'll do it. Thanks, Brad."

A feeling of warm anticipation was building up inside Tony.

Late that afternoon, Tony went uptown to the offices of the Carleton Blessing Agency and gave his name. Sixty seconds later, he was seated in the office of the president, a Mr. Tilton.

"This is certainly an honor, Mr. Blackwell. I hope there's no problem. Our profits for the last quarter—"

"No problem. I'm interested in one of your models. Dominique Masson."

Tilton's face lighted up. "She's turned out to be one of our very best. Your mother has a good eye."

Tony thought he had misunderstood him. "I beg your pardon?"

"Your mother personally requested that we engage Dominique. It was part of our deal when Kruger-Brent, Limited, took us over. It's all in our file, if you'd care to—"

"No." Tony could make no sense of what he was hearing. *Why would his mother*—? "May I have Dominique's address, please?"

"Certainly, Mr. Blackwell. She's doing a layout in Vermont today, but she should be back"—he glanced at a schedule on his desk—"tomorrow afternoon."

Tony was waiting outside Dominique's apartment building when a black sedan pulled up and Dominique stepped out. With her was a large, athletic-looking man carrying Dominique's suitcase. Dominique stopped dead when she saw Tony.

"Tony! My God! What—what are you doing here?"

"I need to talk to you."

"Some other time, buddy," the athlete said. "We have a busy afternoon."

Tony did not even look at him. "Tell your friend to go away."

"Hey! Who the hell do you think—?"

Dominique turned to the man. "Please go, Ben. I'll call you this evening."

He hesitated a moment, then shrugged. "Okay." He glared at Tony, got back in the car and roared off.

Dominique turned to Tony. "You'd better come inside."

The apartment was a large duplex with white rugs and drapes and modern furniture. It must have cost a fortune.

"You're doing well," Tony said.

"Yes. I've been lucky." Dominique's fingers were picking nervously at her blouse. "Would you like a drink?"

"No, thanks. I tried to get in touch with you after I left Paris."

"I moved."

"To America?"

"Yes."

"How did you get a job with the Carleton Blessing Agency?"

"I—I answered a newspaper advertisement," she said lamely.

"When did you first meet my mother, Dominique?"

"I—at your apartment in Paris. Remember? We—"

"No more games," Tony said. He felt a wild rage building in him. "It's over. I've never hit a woman in my life, but if you tell me one more lie, I promise you your face won't be fit to photograph."

Dominique started to speak, but the fury in Tony's eyes stopped her.

"I'll ask you once more. When did you first meet my mother?"

This time there was no hesitation. "When you were accepted at École des Beaux-Arts. Your mother arranged for me to model there."

He felt sick to his stomach. He forced himself to go on. "So I could meet you?"

"Yes, I—"

"And she paid you to become my mistress, to pretend to love me?"

"Yes. It was just after the war—it was terrible. I had no money. Don't you see? But Tony, believe me, I cared. I really cared—"

"Just answer my questions." The savagery in his voice frightened her. This was a stranger before her, a man capable of untold violence.

"What was the point of it?"

"Your mother wanted me to keep an eye on you."

He thought of Dominique's tenderness and her lovemaking—bought and paid for, courtesy of his mother—and he was sick with shame. All along, he had been his mother's puppet, controlled, manipulated. His mother had never given a damn about him. He was not her son. He was her crown prince, her heir apparent. All that mattered to her was the company. He took one last look at Dominique, then turned and stumbled out. She looked after him, her eyes blinded by tears, and she thought, *I didn't lie about loving you, Tony. I didn't lie about that.*

Kate was in the library when Tony walked in, very drunk.

"I t-talked to D-dominique," he said. "You t-two m-must have had a w-wonderful time l-laughing at me behind my back."

Kate felt a quick sense of alarm. "Tony—"

"From now on I want you to s-stay out of my p-personal l-life. Do you hear me?" And he turned and staggered out of the room.

Kate watched him go, and she was suddenly filled with a terrible sense of foreboding.

20

The following day, Tony took an apartment in Greenwich Village. There were no more sociable dinners with his mother. He kept his relationship with Kate on an impersonal, business-like basis. From time to time Kate made conciliatory overtures, which Tony ignored.

Kate's heart ached. But she had done what was right for Tony. Just as she had once done what was right for David. She could not have let either of them leave the company. Tony was the one human being in the world Kate loved, and she watched as he became more and more insular, drawing deep within himself, rejecting everyone. He had no friends. Where once he had been warm and outgoing, he was now cool and reserved. He had built a wall around himself that no one was able to breach. *He needs a wife to care for him,* Kate thought. *And a son to carry on. I must help him. I must.*

Brad Rogers came into Kate's office and said, "I'm afraid we're in for some more trouble, Kate."

"What's happened?"

He put a cable on her desk. "The South African Parliament has outlawed the Natives' Representative Council and passed the Communist Act."

Kate said, "My God!" The act had nothing to do with communism. It stated that anyone who disagreed with any government policy and tried to change it in any way was guilty under the Communist Act and could be imprisoned.

"It's their way of breaking the black resistance movement," she said. "If—" She was interrupted by her secretary.

"There's an overseas call for you. It's Mr. Pierce in Johannesburg."

Jonathan Pierce was the manager of the Johannesburg branch office. Kate picked up the phone. "Hello, Johnny. How are you?"

"Fine, Kate. I have some news I thought you'd better be aware of."

"What's that?"

"I've just received a report that the police have captured Banda."

Kate was on the next flight to Johannesburg. She had alerted the company lawyers to see what could be done for Banda. Even the power and prestige of Kruger-Brent, Ltd., might not be able to help him. He had been designated an enemy of the state, and she dreaded to think what his punishment would be. At least she must see him and talk to him and offer what support she could.

When the plane landed in Johannesburg, Kate went to her office and telephoned the director of prisons.

"He's in an isolation block, Mrs. Blackwell, and he's allowed no visitors. However, in your case, I will see what can be done . . ."

The following morning, Kate was at the Johannesburg prison, face to face with Banda. He was manacled and shackled, and there was a glass partition between them. His hair was completely white. Kate had not known what to expect—despair, defiance—but Banda grinned when he saw her and said, "I knew you'd come. You're just like your daddy. You can't stay away from trouble, can you?"

"Look who's talking," Kate retorted. "Bloody hell! How do we get you out of here?"

"In a box. That's the only way they're going to let me go."

"I have a lot of fancy lawyers who—"

"Forget it, Kate. They caught me fair and square. Now I've got to get away fair and square."

"What are you talking about?"

"I don't like cages, I never did. And they haven't built one yet that can keep me."

Kate said, "Banda, don't try it. Please. They'll kill you."

"Nothing can kill me," Banda said. "You're talking to a man who lived through sharks and land mines and guard dogs." A soft gleam came into his eyes. "You know something, Kate? I think maybe that was the best time of my life."

When Kate went to visit Banda the next day, the superintendent said, "I'm sorry, Mrs. Blackwell. We've had to move him for security reasons."

"Where is he?"

"I'm not at liberty to say."

When Kate woke up the following morning, she saw the headline in the newspaper carried in with her breakfast tray. It read: REBEL LEADER KILLED WHILE TRYING TO ESCAPE PRISON. She was at the prison an hour later, in the superintendent's office.

"He was shot during an attempted prison break, Mrs. Blackwell. That's all there is to it."

You're wrong, thought Kate, *there's more. Much more.* Banda was dead, but was his dream of freedom for his people dead?

Two days later, after making the funeral arrangements, Kate was on the plane to New York. She looked out the window to take one last look at her beloved land. The soil was red and rich and fertile, and in the bowels of its earth were treasures beyond man's dreams. This was God's chosen land, and He had been lavish in his generosity. But there was a curse upon the country. *I'll never come back here again,* Kate thought sadly. *Never.*

One of Brad Rogers's responsibilities was to oversee the Long-Range Planning Department of Kruger-Brent, Ltd. He was brilliant at finding businesses that would make profitable acquisitions.

One day in early May, he walked into Kate Blackwell's office. "I've come across something interesting, Kate." He placed two folders on her desk. "Two companies. If we could pick up either one of them, it would be a coup."

"Thanks, Brad. I'll look them over tonight."

That evening, Kate dined alone and studied Brad Rogers's confidential reports on the two companies—Wyatt Oil & Tool and International Technology. The reports were long and detailed, and both ended with the letters NIS, the company code for *Not Interested in Selling,* which meant that if the companies were to be acquired, it would take more than a straightforward business transaction to accomplish it. *And,* Kate thought, *they're well worth taking over.* Each company was privately controlled by a wealthy and strong-minded individual, which eliminated any possibility of a takeover attempt. It was a challenge, and it had been a long time since Kate had faced a challenge. The more she thought about it, the more the possibilities began to excite her. She studied again the confidential balance sheets. Wyatt Oil & Tool was owned by a Texan, Charlie Wyatt, and the company's assets included producing oil wells, a utility company and dozens of potentially profitable oil leases. There was no question about it, Wyatt Oil & Tool would make a handsome acquisition for Kruger-Brent, Ltd.

Kate turned her attention to the second company. International Technology was owned by a German, Count Frederick Hoffman. The company had started with a small steel mill in Essen, and over the years had expanded into a huge conglomerate, with shipyards, petrochemical plants, a fleet of oil tankers and a computer division.

As large as Kruger-Brent, Ltd., was, it could digest only one of these giants. She knew which company she was going after. NIS, the sheet read.

We'll see about that, Kate thought.

Early the following morning, she sent for Brad Rogers. "I'd love to know how you got hold of those confidential balance sheets," Kate grinned. "Tell me about Charlie Wyatt and Frederick Hoffman."

Brad had done his homework. "Charlie Wyatt was born in Dallas. Flamboyant, loud, runs his own empire, smart as hell. He started with nothing, got lucky in oil wildcatting, kept expanding and now he owns about half of Texas."

"How old is he?"

"Forty-seven."

"Children?"

"One daughter, twenty-five. From what I hear, she's a raving beauty."

"Is she married?"

"Divorced."

"Frederick Hoffman."

"Hoffman's a couple of years younger than Charlie Wyatt. He's a count, comes from a distinguished German family going back to the Middle Ages. He's a widower. His grandfather started with a small steel mill. Frederick Hoffman inherited it from his father and built it into a conglomerate. He was one of the first to get into the computer field. He holds a lot of patents on microprocessors. Every time we use a computer, Count Hoffman gets a royalty."

"Children?"

"A daughter, twenty-three."

"What is she like?"

"I couldn't find out," Brad Rogers apologized. "It's a very buttoned-up family. They travel in their own little circles." He hesitated. "We're probably wasting our time on this, Kate. I had a few drinks with a couple of top executives in both companies.

Neither Wyatt nor Hoffman has the slightest interest in a sale, merger or joint venture. As you can see from their financials, they'd be crazy even to think about it."

That feeling of challenge was there in Kate again, tugging at her.

Ten days later Kate was invited by the President of the United States to a Washington conference of leading international industrialists to discuss assistance to underdeveloped countries. Kate made a telephone call, and shortly afterward Charlie Wyatt and Count Frederick Hoffman received invitations to attend the conference.

Kate had formed a mental impression of both the Texan and the German, and they fitted her preconceived notions almost precisely. She had never met a shy Texan, and Charlie Wyatt was no exception. He was a huge man—almost six feet four inches—with enormous shoulders and a football player's body that had gone to fat. His face was large and ruddy, and his voice loud and booming. He came off as a good ol' boy—or would have if Kate had not known better. Charlie Wyatt had not built his empire by luck. He was a business genius. Kate had talked to him for less than ten minutes when she knew that there was no way this man could be persuaded to do anything he did not want to do. He was opinionated, and he had a deep stubborn streak. No one was going to cajole him, threaten him or con him out of his company. But Kate had found his Achilles' heel, and that was enough.

Frederick Hoffman was Charlie Wyatt's opposite. He was a handsome man, with an aristocratic face and soft brown hair tinged with gray at the temples. He was punctiliously correct and filled with a sense of old-fashioned courtesy. On the surface, Frederick Hoffman was pleasant and debonair; on the inside Kate sensed a core of steel.

The conference in Washington lasted three days, and it went well. The meetings were chaired by the Vice-President, and the President made a brief appearance. Everyone there was impressed with Kate Blackwell. She was an attractive, charismatic woman, head of a corporate empire she had helped build, and they were fascinated, as Kate meant them to be.

When Kate got Charlie Wyatt alone for a moment, she asked innocently, "Is your family with you, Mr. Wyatt?"

"I brought my daughter along. She has a little shoppin' to do,"

"Oh, really? How nice." No one would have suspected that Kate not only knew his daughter was with him, but what kind of dress she had bought at Garfinckel's that morning. "I'm giving a little dinner party at Dark Harbor Friday. I'd be pleased if you and your daughter would join us for the weekend."

Wyatt did not hesitate. "I've heard a lot about your spread, Mrs. Blackwell. I'd sure like to see it."

Kate smiled. "Good. I'll make arrangements for you to be flown up there tomorrow night."

Ten minutes later, Kate was speaking to Frederick Hoffman. "Are you alone in Washington, Mr. Hoffman?" she asked. "Or is your wife with you?"

"My wife died a few years ago," Frederick Hoffman told her. "I'm here with my daughter."

Kate knew they were staying at the Hay-Adams Hotel in Suite 418. "I'm giving a little dinner party at Dark Harbor. I would be delighted if your daughter could join us tomorrow for the weekend."

"I should be getting back to Germany," Hoffman replied. He studied her a moment, and smiled. "I suppose another day or two won't make much difference."

"Wonderful. I'll arrange transportation for you."

It was Kate's custom to give a party at the Dark Harbor estate once every two months. Some of the most interesting and powerful people in the world came to these gatherings, and the get-togethers were always fruitful. Kate intended to see to it that this one was a very special party. Her problem was to make sure Tony attended. During the past year, he had seldom bothered to show up, and when he did he had made a perfunctory appearance and left. This time it was imperative that he come and that he stay.

When Kate mentioned the weekend to Tony, he said curtly, "I c-can't make it. I'm leaving for C-canada Monday and I have a lot of w-work to clean up before I go."

"This is important," Kate told him. "Charlie Wyatt and Count Hoffman are going to be there and they're—"

"I know who they are," he interrupted. "I t-talked to Brad Rogers. We haven't got a p-prayer of acquiring either one of those companies."

"I want to give it a try."

He looked at her and asked, "W-which one are you after?"

"Wyatt Oil and Tool. It could increase our profits as much as fifteen percent, perhaps more. When the Arab countries realize they have the world by the throat, they're going to form a cartel, and oil prices will skyrocket. Oil is going to turn into liquid gold."

"What about International T-t-technology?"

Kate shrugged. "It's a good company, but the plum is Wyatt Oil and Tool. It's a perfect acquisition for us. I need you there, Tony. Canada can wait a few days."

Tony loathed parties. He hated the endless, boring conversations, the boastful men and the predatory women. But this was business. "All right."

All the pieces were in place.

The Wyatts were flown to Maine in a company Cessna, and from the ferry were driven to Cedar Hill House in a limousine. Kate was at the door to greet them. Brad Rogers had been right about Charlie Wyatt's daughter, Lucy. She was strikingly beautiful. She was tall, with black hair and gold-flecked brown eyes, set in almost perfect features. Her sleek Galanos dress outlined a firm, stunning figure. She had, Brad informed Kate, been divorced from a wealthy Italian playboy two years earlier. Kate introduced Lucy to Tony and watched for her son's reaction. There was none. He greeted both the Wyatts with equal courtesy and led them into the bar, where a bartender was waiting to mix drinks.

"What a lovely room," Lucy exclaimed. Her voice was unexpectedly soft and mellow, with no trace of a Texas accent. "Do you spend much time here?" she asked Tony.

"No."

She waited for him to go on. Then, "Did you grow up here?"

"Partly."

Kate picked up the conversation, adroitly smoothing over Tony's silence. "Some of Tony's happiest memories are of this house. The poor man is so busy he doesn't get much chance to come back here and enjoy it, do you, Tony?"

He gave his mother a cool look and said, "No. As a matter of fact, I should be in C-canada—"

"But he postponed it so he could meet both of you," Kate finished for him.

"Well, I'm mighty pleased," Charlie Wyatt said. "I've heard a lot about you, son." He grinned. "You wouldn't want to come to work for me, would you?"

"I don't think that's q-quite what my mother had in mind, Mr. Wyatt."

Charlie Wyatt grinned again. "I know." He turned to look at Kate. "Your mother's quite a lady. You should have seen her rope and hog-tie everybody at that White House meetin'. She—" He stopped as Frederick Hoffman and his daughter, Marianne, entered the room. Marianne Hoffman was a pale version of her father. She had the same aristocratic features and she had long, blond hair. She wore an off-white chiffon dress. Next to Lucy Wyatt she looked washed out.

"May I present my daughter, Marianne?" Count Hoffman said. "I'm sorry we're late," He apologized. "The plane was delayed at La Guardia."

"Oh, what a shame," Kate said. Tony was aware that Kate had arranged the delay. She had had the Wyatts and the Hoffmans flown up to Maine in separate planes, so that the Wyatts would arrive early and the Hoffmans late. "We were just having a drink. What would you like?"

"A Scotch, please," Count Hoffman said.

Kate turned to Marianne. "And you, my dear?"

"Nothing, thank you."

A few minutes later, the other guests began to arrive, and Tony circulated among them, playing the part of the gracious host. No one except Kate could have guessed how little the festivities meant to him. It was not, Kate knew, that Tony was bored. It was simply that he was completely removed from what was happening around him. He had lost his pleasure in people. It worried Kate.

Two tables had been set in the large dining room. Kate seated Marianne Hoffman between a Supreme Court justice and a senator at one table, and she seated Lucy Wyatt on Tony's right at the other table. All the men in the room—married and unmarried—were eyeing Lucy. Kate listened to Lucy trying to draw Tony into conversation. It was obvious that she liked him. Kate smiled to herself. It was a good beginning.

The following morning, Saturday, at breakfast, Charlie Wyatt said to Kate, "That's a mighty pretty yacht you've got sittin' out there, Mrs. Blackwell. How big is it?"

"I'm really not quite sure." Kate turned to her son. "Tony, how large is the *Corsair?*"

His mother knew exactly how large it was, but Tony said politely, "Eighty f-feet."

"We don't go in much for boats in Texas. We're in too much of a hurry. We do most of our travelin' in planes." Wyatt gave a booming laugh. "Guess maybe I'll try it and get my feet wet."

Kate smiled. "I was hoping you would let me show you around the island. We could go out on the boat tomorrow."

Charlie Wyatt looked at her thoughtfully and said, "That's mighty kind of you, Mrs. Blackwell."

Tony quietly watched the two of them and said nothing. The first move had just been made, and he wondered whether Charlie Wyatt was aware of it. Probably not. He was a clever businessman, but he had never come up against anyone like Kate Blackwell.

Kate turned to Tony and Lucy. "It's such a beautiful day. Why don't you two go for a sail in the catboat?"

Before Tony could refuse, Lucy said, "Oh, I'd love that."

"I'm s-sorry," Tony said curtly. "I'm expecting s-some overseas calls." Tony could feel his mother's disapproving eyes on him.

Kate turned to Marianne Hoffman. "I haven't seen your father this morning."

"He's out exploring the island. He's an early riser."

"I understand you like to ride. We have a fine stable here."

"Thank you, Mrs. Blackwell. I'll just wander around, if you don't mind."

"Of course not." Kate turned back to Tony. "Are you sure you won't change your mind about taking Miss Wyatt for a sail?" There was steel in her voice.

"I'm s-sure."

It was a small victory, but it was a victory nevertheless. The battle was joined, and Tony had no intention of losing it. Not this time. His mother no longer had the power to deceive him. She had used him as a pawn once, and he was fully aware she was planning to try it again; but this time she would fail. She wanted the Wyatt Oil & Tool Company. Charlie Wyatt had no intention of merging or selling his company. But every man has a weakness, and Kate had found his: his daughter. If Lucy were to marry into the Blackwell family, a merger of some kind would become inevitable. Tony looked across the breakfast table at his mother, despising her. She had baited the trap well. Lucy was not only beautiful, she was intelligent and charming. But she was as much of a pawn in this sick game as Tony was, and nothing in the world could induce him to touch her. This was a battle between his mother and himself.

When breakfast was over, Kate rose. "Tony, before your phone call comes in, why don't you show Miss Wyatt the gardens?"

There was no way Tony could refuse graciously. "All right." He would make it short.

Kate turned to Charlie Wyatt. "Are you interested in rare books? We have quite a collection in the library."

"I'm interested in anything you want to show me," the Texan said.

Almost as an afterthought, Kate turned back to Marianne Hoffman. "Will you be all right, dear?"

"I'll be fine, thank you, Mrs. Blackwell. Please don't worry about me."

"I won't," Kate said.

And Tony knew she meant it. Miss Hoffman was of no use to Kate, and so she dismissed her. It was done with a light charm and a smile, but beneath it was a single-minded ruthlessness that Tony detested.

Lucy was watching him. "Are you ready, Tony?"

"Yes."

Tony and Lucy moved toward the door. They were not quite out of earshot when Tony heard his mother say, "Don't they make a lovely couple?"

The two of them walked through the large, formal gardens toward the dock where the *Corsair* was tied up. There were acres and acres of wildly colored flowers staining the summer air with their scent.

"This is a heavenly place," Lucy said.

"Yes."

"We don't have flowers like these in Texas."

"No?"

"It's so quiet and peaceful here."

"Yes."

Lucy stopped abruptly and turned to face Tony.

He saw the anger in her face. "Have I said something to offend you?" he asked.

"You haven't said anything. That's what I find offensive. All I can get out of you is a yes or a no. You make me feel as though I'm—I'm chasing you."

"Are you?"

She laughed. "Yes. If I could only teach you to talk, I think we might have something."

Tony grinned.

"What are you thinking?" Lucy asked.

"Nothing."

He was thinking of his mother, and how much she hated losing.

Kate was showing Charlie Wyatt the large, oak-paneled library. On the shelves were first editions of Oliver Goldsmith, Laurence Sterne, Tobias Smollett and John Donne, along with a Ben Jonson first folio. There was Samuel Butler and John Bunyan, and the rare 1813 privately printed edition of *Queen Mab*. Wyatt walked along the shelves of treasures, his eyes gleaming. He paused in front of a beautifully bound edition of John Keats's *Endymion*.

"This is a Roseberg copy," Charlie Wyatt said.

Kate looked at him in surprise. "Yes. There are only two known copies."

"I have the other one," Wyatt told her.

"I should have known," Kate laughed. "That 'good ol' Texas boy' act you put on had me fooled."

Wyatt grinned. "Did it? It's good camouflage."

"Where did you go to school?"

"Colorado School of Mining, then Oxford on a Rhodes Scholarship." He studied Kate a moment. "I'm told it was you who got me invited to that White House conference."

She shrugged. "I merely mentioned your name. They were delighted to have you."

"That was mighty kind of you, Kate. Now, as long as you and I are alone, why don't you tell me exactly what's on your mind?"

Tony was at work in his private study, a small room off the main downstairs hallway. He was seated in a deep armchair when he heard the door open and someone come in. He turned to look. It was Marianne Hoffman. Before Tony could open his mouth to make his presence known, he heard her gasp.

She was looking at the paintings on the wall. They were Tony's paintings—the few he had brought back from his apartment in Paris, and this was the only room in the house where he would allow them to be hung. He watched her walk around the room, going from painting to painting, and it was too late to say anything.

"I don't believe it," she murmured.

And Tony felt a sudden anger within him. He knew they were not *that* bad. As he moved, the leather of his chair creaked, and Marianne turned and saw him.

"Oh! I'm sorry," she apologized. "I didn't know anyone was in here."

Tony rose. "That's quite all right." His tone was rude. He disliked having his sanctuary invaded. "Were you looking for something?"

"No. I—I was just wandering around. Your collection of paintings belongs in a museum."

"Except for these," Tony heard himself saying.

She was puzzled by the hostility in his voice. She turned to look at the paintings again. She saw the signature. "*You* painted these?"

"I'm sorry if they don't appeal to you."

"They're fantastic!" She moved toward him. "I don't understand. If you can do this, why would you ever want to do anything else? You're wonderful. I don't mean you're good. I mean you're *wonderful.*"

Tony stood there, not listening, just wanting her to get out.

"I wanted to be a painter," Marianne said. "I studied with Oskar Kokoschka for a year. I finally quit because I knew I never could be as good as I wanted to be. But you!" She turned to the paintings again. "Did you study in Paris?"

He wished she would leave him alone. "Yes."

"And you quit—just like that?"

"Yes."

"What a pity. You—"

"*There* you are!"

They both turned. Kate was standing in the doorway. She eyed the two of them a moment, then walked over to Marianne. "I've been looking everywhere for you, Marianne. Your father mentioned that you like orchids. You must see our greenhouse."

"Thank you," Marianne murmured. "I'm really—"

Kate turned to Tony. "Tony, perhaps you should see to your other guests." There was a note of sharp displeasure in her voice.

She took Marianne's arm, and they were gone.

There was a fascination to watching his mother maneuver people. It was done so smoothly. Not a move was wasted. It had started with the Wyatts arriving early and the Hoffmans arriving late. Lucy being placed next to him at every meal. The private conferences with Charlie Wyatt. It was so damned obvious, and yet Tony had to admit to himself that it was obvious only because he had the key. He knew his mother and the way her mind worked. Lucy Wyatt was a lovely girl. She would make a wonderful wife for someone, but not for him. Not with Kate Blackwell as her sponsor. His mother was a ruthless, calculating bitch, and as long as Tony remembered that, he was safe from her machinations. He wondered what her next move would be.

He did not have to wait long to find out.

They were on the terrace having cocktails. "Mr. Wyatt has been kind enough to invite us to his ranch next weekend," Kate told Tony. "Isn't that lovely?" Her face radiated her pleasure. "I've never seen a Texas ranch."

Kruger-Brent *owned* a ranch in Texas, and it was probably twice as big as the Wyatt spread.

"You will come, won't you, Tony?" Charlie Wyatt asked.

Lucy said, "Please do."

They were ganging up on him. It was a challenge. He decided to accept it. "I'd be d-delighted."

"Good." There was real pleasure on Lucy's face. And on Kate's.

If Lucy is planning to seduce me, Tony thought, *she is wasting her time.* The hurt done to Tony by his mother and Dominique had implanted in him such a deep distrust of females that his only association with them now was with high-priced call girls. Of all the female species, they were the most honest. All they wanted was money and told you how much up front. You paid for what you got, and you got what you paid for. No complications, no tears, no deceit.

Lucy Wyatt was in for a surprise.

Early Sunday morning, Tony went down to the pool for a swim. Marianne Hoffman was already in the water, wearing a white maillot. She had a lovely figure, tall and slender and graceful. Tony stood there watching her cutting cleanly through the water, her arms flashing up and down in a regular, graceful rhythm. She saw Tony and swam over to him.

"Good morning."

"Morning. You're good," Tony said.

Marianne smiled. "I love sports. I get that from my father." She pulled herself up to the edge of the pool, and Tony handed her a towel. He watched as she unselfconsciously dried her hair.

"Have you had breakfast?" Tony asked.

"No. I wasn't sure the cook would be up this early."

"This is a hotel. There's twenty-four-hour service."

She smiled up at him. "Nice."

"Where is your home?"

"Mostly in Munich. We live in an old *schloss*—a castle—outside the city."

"Where were you brought up?"

Marianne sighed. "That's a long story. During the war, I was sent away to school in Switzerland. After that, I went to Oxford, studied at the Sorbonne and lived in London for a few years." She looked directly into his eyes. "That's where I've been. Where have you been?"

"Oh, New York, Maine, Switzerland, South Africa, a few years in the South Pacific during the war, Paris . . ." He broke off abruptly, as though he were saying too much.

"Forgive me if I seem to pry, but I can't imagine why you stopped painting."

"It's not important," Tony said curtly. "Let's have breakfast."

They ate alone on the terrace overlooking the sparkling sweep of the bay. She was easy to talk to. There was a dignity about her, a gentleness that Tony found appealing. She did not flirt, she did not chatter. She seemed genuinely interested in him. Tony found himself attracted to this quiet, sensitive woman. He could not help wondering how much of that attraction was due to the thought that it would spite his mother.

"When do you go back to Germany?"

"Next week," Marianne replied. "I'm getting married."

Her words caught him off guard. "Oh," Tony said lamely. "That's great. Who is he?"

"He's a doctor. I've known him all my life." *Why had she added that? Did it have some significance?*

On an impulse, Tony asked, "Will you have dinner with me in New York?"

She studied him, weighing her answer. "I would enjoy that." Tony smiled, pleased. "It's a date."

They had dinner at a little seashore restaurant on Long Island. Tony wanted Marianne to himself, away from the eyes of his mother. It was an innocent evening, but Tony knew that if his mother learned about it, she would find some way to poison it. This was a private thing between him and Marianne, and for the brief time it existed, Tony wanted nothing to spoil it. Tony enjoyed Marianne's company even more than he had anticipated. She had a quick, sly sense of humor, and Tony found himself laughing more than he had laughed since he left Paris. She made him feel lighthearted and carefree.

When do you go back to Germany?
Next week . . . I'm getting married.

During the next five days, Tony saw a great deal of Marianne. He canceled his trip to Canada, and he was not certain why. He had thought it might be a form of rebellion against his mother's plan, a petty vengeance, but if that had been true in the beginning, it was no longer true. He found himself drawn to Marianne more and more strongly. He loved her honesty. It was a quality he had despaired of ever finding.

Since Marianne was a tourist in New York, Tony took her

everywhere. They climbed the Statue of Liberty and rode the ferry to Staten Island, went to the top of the Empire State Building, and ate in Chinatown. They spent an entire day at the Metropolitan Museum of Art, and an afternoon at the Frick Collection. They shared the same tastes. They carefully avoided speaking of any personal things, and yet both were conscious of the powerful sexual undercurrent between them. The days spilled into one another, and it was Friday, the day Tony was to leave for the Wyatt Ranch.

"When do you fly back to Germany?"

"Monday morning." There was no joy in her voice.

Tony left for Houston that afternoon. He could have gone with his mother in one of the company planes, but he preferred to avoid any situation where he and Kate would be alone together. As far as he was concerned, his mother was solely a business partner: brilliant and powerful, devious and dangerous.

There was a Rolls-Royce to pick up Tony at the William P. Hobby Airport in Houston, and he was driven to the ranch by a chauffeur dressed in Levi's and a colorful sport shirt.

"Most folks like to fly direct to the ranch," the driver told Tony. "Mr. Wyatt's got a big landin' strip there. From here, it's 'bout an hour's drive to the gate, then another half hour before we git to the main house."

Tony thought he was exaggerating, but he was wrong. The Wyatt Ranch turned out to be more of a town than a ranch. They drove through the main gate onto a private road, and after thirty minutes they began to pass generator buildings and barns and corrals and guest houses and servants' bungalows. The main house was an enormous one-story ranch house that seemed to go on forever. Tony thought it was depressingly ugly.

Kate had already arrived. She and Charlie Wyatt were seated on the terrace overlooking a swimming pool the size of a small lake. They were in the midst of an intense conversation when Tony appeared. When Wyatt saw him, he broke off abruptly in the middle of a sentence. Tony sensed that he had been the subject of their discussion.

"Here's our boy! Have a good trip, Tony?"

"Yes, th-thank you."

"Lucy was hopin' you'd be able to catch an earlier plane," Kate said.

Tony turned to look at his mother. "Was sh-she?"

Charlie Wyatt clapped Tony on the shoulder. "We're puttin' on a whoppin' barbecue in honor of you and Kate. *Everybody's flyin' in for it.*"

"That's very k-kind of you," Tony said. *If they're planning to serve fatted calf,* he thought, *they're going to go hungry.*

Lucy appeared, wearing a white shirt and tight-fitting, well-worn jeans, and Tony had to admit she was breathtakingly lovely.

She went up to him and took his arm. "Tony! I was wondering if you were coming."

"S-sorry I'm late," Tony said. "I had some b-business to finish up."

Lucy gave him a warm smile. "It doesn't matter, as long as you're here. What would you like to do this afternoon?"

"What do you have to offer?"

Lucy looked him in the eye. "Anything you want," she said softly.

Kate Blackwell and Charlie Wyatt beamed.

The barbecue was spectacular, even by Texas standards. Approximately two hundred guests had arrived by private plane, Mercedes or Rolls-Royce. Two bands were playing simultaneously in different areas of the grounds. Half a dozen bartenders dispensed champagne, whiskey, soft drinks and beer, while four chefs busily prepared food over outdoor fires. There was barbecued beef, lamb, steaks, chicken and duck. There were bubbling earthen pots of chili, and whole lobsters; crabs and corn on the cob were cooking in the ground. There were baked potatoes and yams and fresh peas in the pod, six kinds of salads, homemade hot biscuits, and corn bread with honey and jam. Four dessert tables were laden with freshly baked pies, cakes and puddings, and a dozen flavors of homemade ice cream. It was the most conspicuous waste Tony had ever seen. It was, he supposed, the difference between new money and old money. Old money's motto was, *If you have it, hide it.* New money's motto was, *If you have it, flaunt it.*

This was flaunting on a scale that was unbelievable. The women were dressed in daring gowns, and the display of jewelry was blinding. Tony stood to one side watching the guests gorging themselves, calling out noisily to old friends. He felt as though he were attending some mindless, decadent rite. Every time he turned around, Tony found himself confronted with a waiter carrying a tray containing large crocks of beluga caviar or pâté or champagne. It seemed to Tony that there were almost as many servants as guests. He listened to conversations around him.

"He came out here from New York to sell me a bill of goods, and I said, 'You're wastin' your time, mister. No good oil deal gets east of Houston . . .' "

"You gotta watch out for the smooth talkers. They're all hat and no cattle . . ."

Lucy appeared at Tony's side. "You're not eating." She was watching him intently. "Is anything wrong, Tony?"

"No, everything's fine. It's quite a party."

She grinned. "You ain't seen nothin' yet, pardner. Wait until you see the fireworks display."

"The fireworks display?"

"Uh-huh." She touched Tony's arm. "Sorry about the mob scene. It's not always like this. Daddy wanted to impress your mother." She smiled. "Tomorrow they'll all be gone."

So will I, Tony thought grimly. It had been a mistake for him to come here. If his mother wanted the Wyatt Oil & Tool Company so badly, she would have to figure out some other way to get it. His eyes searched the crowd for his mother, and he saw her in the middle of an admiring group. She was beautiful. She was almost sixty years old, but she looked ten years younger. Her face was unlined, and her body was firm and trim, thanks to exercise and daily massage. She was as disciplined with herself as with everyone around her, and in a perverse way, Tony admired her. To a casual onlooker, Kate Blackwell seemed to be having a marvelous time. She was chatting with the guests, beaming, laughing. *She's loathing every moment of this,* Tony thought. *There isn't anything she won't suffer to get what she wants.* He thought of Marianne and of how much she would have hated this kind of senseless orgy. The thought of her was a sudden ache in him.

I'm marrying a doctor. I've known him all my life.

Half an hour later when Lucy came looking for Tony, he was on his way back to New York.

He called Marianne from a telephone booth at the airport. "I want to see you."

There was no hesitation. "Yes."

Tony had not been able to get Marianne Hoffman out of his thoughts. He had been alone for a long time, but he had not felt lonely. Being away from Marianne was a loneliness, a feeling that a part of him was missing. Being with her was a warmth, a celebration of life, a chasing away of the ugly dark shadows that had been haunting him. He had the terrifying feeling that if he let Marianne go, he would be lost. He needed her as he had never needed anyone in his life.

Marianne met him at his apartment, and as she walked in the door, there was a hunger in Tony that he had thought forever dead. And looking at her, he knew the hunger was hers, too, and there were no words for the miracle of it.

She went into his arms, and their emotion was an irresistible riptide that caught them both up and swept them away in a glorious explosion, an eruption, and a contentment beyond words. They were floating together in a velvety softness that knew no time or place, lost in the wondrous glory and magic of each other. Later they lay spent, holding each other, her hair soft against his face.

"I'm going to marry you, Marianne."

She took his face in her hands and looked searchingly into his eyes. "Are you sure, Tony?" Her voice was gentle. "There's a problem, darling."

"Your engagement?"

"No. I'll break it off. I'm concerned about your mother."

"She has nothing to do with—"

"No. Let me finish, Tony. She's planning for you to marry Lucy Wyatt."

"That's *her* plan." He took her in his arms again. "*My* plans are right here."

"She'll hate me, Tony. I don't want that."

"Do you know what I want?" Tony whispered.

And the miracle started all over again.

It was another forty-eight hours before Kate Blackwell heard from Tony. He had disappeared from the Wyatt Ranch without an explanation or good-bye and had flown back to New York. Charlie Wyatt was baffled, and Lucy Wyatt was furious. Kate had made awkward apologies and had taken the company plane back to New York that night. When she reached home, she telephoned Tony at his apartment. There was no answer. Nor was there any answer the following day.

Kate was in her office when the private phone on her desk rang. She knew who it was before she picked it up.

"Tony, are you all right?"

"I'm f-fine, Mother."

"Where are you?"

"On my h-honeymoon. Marianne Hoffman and I were m-married yesterday." There was a long, long silence. "Are you there, M-mother?"

"Yes. I'm here."

"You might s-say congratulations, or m-much happiness or one of those c-customary phrases." There was a mocking bitterness in his voice.

Kate said, "Yes. Yes, of course, I wish you much happiness, Son."

"Thank you, M-mother." And the line went dead.

Kate replaced the receiver and pressed down an intercom button. "Would you please come in, Brad?"

When Brad Rogers walked into the office, Kate said, "Tony just called."

Brad took one look at Kate's face and said, "Jesus! Don't tell me you did it!"

"*Tony* did it," Kate smiled. "We've got the Hoffman empire in our lap."

Brad Rogers sank into a chair. "I can't believe it! I know how stubborn Tony can be. How did you ever get him to marry Marianne Hoffman?"

"It was really very simple," Kate sighed. "I pushed him in the wrong direction."

But she knew it was really the right direction. Marianne would be a wonderful wife for Tony. She would dispel the darkness in him.

Lucy had had a hysterectomy.

Marianne would give him a son.

21

Six months from the day Tony and Marianne were married, the Hoffman company was absorbed into Kruger-Brent, Ltd. The formal signing of the contracts took place in Munich as a gesture to Frederick Hoffman, who would run the subsidiary from Germany. Tony had been surprised by the meekness with which his mother accepted his marriage. It was not like her to lose gracefully, yet she had been cordial to Marianne when Tony and his bride returned from their honeymoon in the Bahamas, and had told Tony how pleased she was with the marriage. What puzzled Tony was that her sentiments seemed genuine. It was too quick a turnaround, out of character for her. Perhaps, Tony decided, he did not understand his mother as well as he thought he did.

The marriage was a brilliant success from the beginning. Marianne filled a long-felt need in Tony, and everyone around him noticed the change in him—especially Kate.

When Tony took business trips, Marianne accompanied him. They played together, they laughed together, they truly enjoyed each other. Watching them, Kate thought happily, *I have done well for my son.*

It was Marianne who succeeded in healing the breach between Tony and his mother. When t'   returned from their honeymoon, Marianne said, "I want to ir vite your mother to dinner."

"No. You don't know her, Marianne. She—"

"I want to get to know her. Please, Tony."

He hated the idea, but in the end he gave in. Tony had been prepared for a grim evening, but he had been surprised. Kate had been touchingly happy to be with them. The following week Kate invited them to the house for dinner, and after that it became a weekly ritual.

Kate and Marianne became friends. They spoke to each other over the telephone several times a week, and lunched together at least once a week.

They were meeting for lunch at Lutèce, and the moment Marianne walked in, Kate knew something was wrong.

"I'd like a double whiskey, please," Marianne told the captain. "Over ice."

As a rule, Marianne drank only wine.

"What's happened, Marianne?"

"I've been to see Dr. Harley."

Kate felt a sudden stab of alarm. "You're not ill, are you?"

"No. I'm just fine. Only ..." The whole story came tumbling out.

It had begun a few days earlier. Marianne had not been feeling well, and she had made an appointment with John Harley. . . .

"You look healthy enough," Dr. Harley smiled. "How old are you, Mrs. Blackwell?"

"Twenty-three."

"Any history of heart disease in your family?"

"No."

He was making notes. "Cancer?"

"No."

"Are your parents alive?"

"My father is. My mother died in an accident."

"Have you ever had mumps?"

"No."

"Measles?"

"Yes. When I was ten."

"Whooping cough?"

"No."

"Any surgery?"

"Tonsils. I was nine."

"Other than that, you've never been hospitalized for anything?"

"No. Well, yes—that is, once. Briefly."

"What was that for?"

"I was on the girls' hockey team at school and during a game I blacked out. I woke up in a hospital. I was only there two days. It was really nothing."

"Did you suffer an injury during the game?"

"No. I—I just blacked out."

"How old were you then?"

"Sixteen. The doctor said it was probably some kind of adolescent glandular upset."

John Harley sat forward in his chair. "When you woke up, do you remember if you felt any weakness on either side of your body?"

Marianne thought a moment. "As a matter of fact, yes. My right side. But it went away in a few days. I haven't had anything like it since."

"Did you have headaches? Blurred vision?"

"Yes. But they went away, too." She was beginning to be alarmed. "Do you think there's something wrong with me, Dr. Harley?"

"I'm not sure. I'd like to make a few tests—just to be on the safe side."

"What kind of tests?"

"I'd like to do a cerebral angiogram. Nothing to be concerned about. We can have it done right away."

Three days later, Marianne received a call from Dr. Harley's nurse asking her to come in. John Harley was waiting for her in his office. "Well, we've solved the mystery."

"Is it something bad?"

"Not really. The angiogram showed that what you had, Mrs. Blackwell, was a small stroke. Medically, it's called a berry aneurysm, and it's very common in women—particularly in teenage girls. A small blood vessel in the brain broke and leaked small amounts of blood. The pressure is what caused the headaches and blurred vision. Fortunately, those things are self-healing."

Marianne sat there listening, her mind fighting panic. "What—what does all this mean, exactly? Could it happen again?"

"It's very unlikely." He smiled. "Unless you're planning to go out for the hockey team again, you can live an absolutely normal life."

"Tony and I like to ride and play tennis. Is that—?"

"As long as you don't overdo, everything goes. From tennis to sex. No problem."

She smiled in relief. "Thank God."

As Marianne rose, John Harley said, "There is one thing, Mrs. Blackwell. If you and Tony are planning to have children, I would advise adopting them."

Marianne froze. "You said I was perfectly normal."

"You are. Unfortunately, pregnancy increases the vascular volume enormously. And during the last six to eight weeks of pregnancy, there's an additional increase in blood pressure. With the history of that aneurysm, the risk factor would be unacceptably high. It would not only be dangerous—it could be fatal. Adoptions are really quite easy these days. I can arrange—"

But Marianne was no longer listening. She was hearing Tony's voice: *I want us to have a baby. A little girl who looks exactly like you.*

"... I couldn't bear to hear any more," Marianne told Kate. "I ran out of his office and came straight here."

Kate made a tremendous effort not to let her feelings show. It was a stunning blow. But there had to be a way. There was always a way.

She managed a smile and said, "Well! I was afraid it was going to be something much worse."

"But, Kate, Tony and I want so much to have a baby."

"Marianne, Dr. Harley is an alarmist. You had a minor problem years ago, and Harley's trying to turn it into something important. You know how doctors are." She took Marianne's hand. "You feel well, don't you, darling?"

"I felt wonderful until—"

"Well, there you are. You aren't going around having any fainting spells?"

"No."

"Because it's all over. He said himself that those things are self-healing."

"He said the risks—"

Kate sighed. "Marianne, every time a woman gets pregnant, there's always a risk. Life is full of risks. The important thing in life is to decide which risks are the ones worth taking, don't you agree?"

"Yes." Marianne sat there thinking. She made her decision. "You're right. Let's not say anything to Tony. It would only worry him. We'll keep it our secret."

Kate thought, *I could bloody well kill John Harley for scaring her to death.* "It will be our secret," Kate agreed.

Three months later, Marianne became pregnant. Tony was thrilled. Kate was quietly triumphant. Dr. John Harley was horrified.

"I'll arrange for an immediate abortion," he told Marianne.

"No, Dr. Harley. I feel fine. I'm going to have the baby."

When Marianne told Kate about her visit, Kate stormed into John Harley's office. "How dare you suggest my daughter-in-law have an abortion?"

"Kate, I told her that if she carries that baby to term, there's a chance it might kill her."

"You don't *know* that. She's going to be fine. Stop alarming her."

Eight months later, at four A.M. in early February, Marianne's labor pains began prematurely. Her moans awakened Tony.

He began hurriedly dressing. "Don't worry, darling. I'll have you at the hospital in no time."

The pains were agonizing. "Please hurry."

She wondered whether she should have told Tony about her conversations with Dr. Harley. No, Kate had been right. It was her decision to make. Life was so wonderful that God would not let anything bad happen to her.

When Marianne and Tony arrived at the hospital, everything was in readiness. Tony was escorted to a waiting room. Marianne was taken into an examining room. The obstetrician, Dr. Mattson, took Marianne's blood pressure. He frowned and took it again. He looked up and said to his nurse, "Get her into the operating room—fast!"

Tony was at the cigarette machine in the hospital corridor when a voice behind him said, "Well, well, if it isn't Rembrandt." Tony turned. He recognized the man who had been with Dominique in front of her apartment building. What had she called him? Ben. The man was staring at Tony, an antagonistic expression on his face. Jealousy? What had Dominique told him? At that moment, Dominique appeared. She said to Ben, "The nurse said Michelline is in intensive care. We'll come—" She saw Tony, and stopped.

"Tony! What are you doing here?"

"My wife is having a baby."

"Did your mother arrange it?" Ben asked.

"What's that supposed to mean?"

"Dominique told me your mother arranges everything for you, sonny."

"Ben! Stop it!"

"Why? It's the truth, isn't it, baby? Isn't that what you said?"

Tony turned to Dominique. "What is he talking about?"

"Nothing," she said quickly. "Ben, let's get out of here."

But Ben was enjoying himself. "I wish I had a mother like yours, buddy boy. You want a beautiful model to sleep with, she buys you one. You want to have an art exhibition in Paris, she arranges it for you. You—"

"You're crazy."

"Am I?" Ben turned to Dominique. "Doesn't he know?"

"Don't I know what?" Tony demanded.

"Nothing, Tony."

"He said my mother arranged the exhibition in Paris. That's a lie, isn't it?" He saw the expression on Dominique's face. *"Isn't* it?"

"No," Dominique said reluctantly.

"You mean she had to pay Goerg to—to show my paintings?"

"Tony, he really liked your paintings."

"Tell him about the art critic," Ben urged.

"That's enough, Ben!" Dominique turned to go. Tony grabbed her arm. "Wait! What about him? Did my mother arrange for him to be at the exhibit?"

"Yes." Dominique's voice had dropped to a whisper.

"But he *hated* my paintings."

She could hear the pain in his voice. "No, Tony. He didn't. Andre d'Usseau told your mother you could have become a great artist."

And he was face to face with the unbelievable. "My mother paid d'Usseau to destroy me?"

"Not to destroy you. She believed she was doing it for your own good."

The enormity of what his mother had done was staggering. *Everything she had told him was a lie. She had never intended to let him live his own life.* And Andre d'Usseau! How could a man like that be bought? But of course Kate would know the price of any man. Wilde could have been referring to Kate when he talked of someone who knew the price of everything, the value of nothing. Everything had always been for the company. And the company was Kate Blackwell. Tony turned and walked blindly down the corridor.

* * *

In the operating room, the doctors were fighting desperately to save Marianne's life. Her blood pressure was alarmingly low, and her heartbeat was erratic. She was given oxygen and a blood transfusion, but it was useless. Marianne was unconscious from a cerebral hemorrhage when the first baby was delivered, and dead three minutes later when the second twin was taken.

Tony heard a voice calling, "Mr. Blackwell." He turned. Dr. Mattson was at his side.

"You have two beautiful, healthy twin daughters, Mr. Blackwell."

Tony saw the look in his eyes. "Marianne—she's all right, isn't she?"

Dr. Mattson took a deep breath. "I'm so sorry. We did everything we could. She died on the—"

"She *what?*" It was a scream. Tony grabbed Dr. Mattson's lapels and shook him. "You're lying! She's *not* dead."

"Mr. Blackwell—"

"Where is she? I want to see her."

"You can't go in just now. They're preparing her—"

Tony cried out, "You killed her, you bastard! You killed her." He began attacking the doctor. Two interns hurried in and grabbed Tony's arms.

"Now take it easy, Mr. Blackwell."

Tony fought like a madman. "I want to see my wife!"

Dr. John Harley hurried up to the group. "Let him go," he commanded. "Leave us alone."

Dr. Mattson and the interns left. Tony was weeping brokenly. "John, they k-killed Marianne. They m-murdered her."

"She's dead, Tony, and I'm sorry. But no one murdered her. I told her months ago if she went ahead with this pregnancy it could kill her."

It took a long moment for the words to sink in. "What are you talking about?"

"Marianne didn't tell you? Your mother didn't say anything?"

Tony was staring at him, his eyes uncomprehending. "My mother?"

"She thought I was being an alarmist. She advised Marianne to go ahead with it. I'm so sorry, Tony. I've seen the twins. They're beautiful. Wouldn't you like to—?"

Tony was gone.

Kate's butler opened the door for Tony.

"Good morning, Mr. Blackwell."

"Good morning, Lester."

The butler took in Tony's disheveled appearance. "Is everything all right, sir?"

"Everything is fine. Would you make me a cup of coffee, Lester?"

"Certainly, sir."

Tony watched the butler move toward the kitchen. *Now, Tony,* the voice in his head commanded.

Yes. Now. Tony turned and walked into the trophy room. He went to the cabinet that held the gun collection, and he stared at the gleaming array of instruments of death.

Open the cabinet, Tony.

He opened it. He selected a revolver from the gun rack and checked the barrel to make sure it was loaded.

She'll be upstairs, Tony.

Tony turned and started up the stairs. He knew now that it was not his mother's fault that she was evil. She was possessed, and he was going to cure her. The company had taken her soul, and Kate was not responsible for what she did. His mother and the company had become one, and when he killed her, the company would die.

He was outside Kate's bedroom door.

Open the door, the voice commanded.

Tony opened the door. Kate was dressing in front of a mirror when she heard the door open.

"Tony! What on earth—"

He carefully aimed the gun at her and began squeezing the trigger.

22

The right of primogeniture—the claim of the first-born to a family title or estate—is deeply rooted in history. Among royal families in Europe a high official is present at every birth of a possible heir to a queen or princess so that should twins be born, the right of succession will not be in dispute. Dr. Mattson was careful to note which twin had been delivered first.

Everyone agreed that the Blackwell twins were the most beautiful babies they had ever seen. They were healthy and unusually lively, and the nurses at the hospital kept finding excuses to go in and look at them. Part of the fascination, although none of the nurses would have admitted it, was the mysterious stories that were circulating about the twins' family. Their mother had died during childbirth. The twins' father had disappeared, and there were rumors he had murdered his mother, but no one was able to substantiate the reports. There was nothing about it in the newspapers, save for a brief item that Tony Blackwell had suffered a nervous breakdown over the death of his wife and was in seclusion. When the press tried to question Dr. Harley, he gave them a brusque, "No comment."

The past few days had been hell for John Harley. As long as

he lived, he would remember the scene when he reached Kate Blackwell's bedroom after a frantic phone call from the butler. Kate was lying on the floor in a coma, bullet wounds in her neck and chest, her blood spilling onto the white rug. Tony was going through her closets, slashing his mother's clothes to shreds with a pair of scissors.

Dr. Harley took one quick look at Kate and hurriedly telephoned for an ambulance. He knelt at Kate's side and felt her pulse. It was weak and thready, and her face was turning blue. She was going into shock. He swiftly gave her an injection of adrenaline and sodium bicarbonate.

"What happened?" Dr. Harley asked.

The butler was soaked in perspiration. "I—I don't know. Mr. Blackwell asked me to make him some coffee. I was in the kitchen when I heard the sound of gunfire. I ran upstairs and found Mrs. Blackwell on the floor, like this. Mr. Blackwell was standing over her, saying, 'It can't hurt you anymore, Mother. I killed it.' And he went into the closet and started cutting her dresses."

Dr. Harley turned to Tony. "What are you doing, Tony?"

A savage slash. "I'm helping Mother. I'm destroying the company. It killed Marianne, you know." He continued slashing at the dresses in Kate's closet.

Kate was rushed to the emergency ward of a midtown private hospital owned by Kruger-Brent, Ltd. She was given four blood transfusions during the operation to remove the bullets.

It took three male nurses to force Tony into an ambulance, and it was only after Dr. Harley gave him an injection that Tony was quiet. A police unit had responded to the ambulance call, and Dr. Harley summoned Brad Rogers to deal with them. Through means that Dr. Harley did not understand, there was no mention in the media of the shooting.

Dr. Harley went to the hospital to visit Kate in intensive care. Her first words were a whispered, "Where's my son?"

"He's being taken care of, Kate. He's all right."

Tony had been taken to a private sanitarium in Connecticut.

"John, why did he try to kill me? Why?" The anguish in her voice was unbearable.

"He blames you for Marianne's death."

"That's insane!"

John Harley made no comment.

He blames you for Marianne's death.

Long after Dr. Harley had left, Kate lay there, refusing to accept those words. She had loved Marianne because she made Tony happy. *Everything I have done has been for you, my son. All my dreams were for you. How could you not know that?* And he hated her so much he had tried to kill her. She was filled with such a deep agony that she wanted to die. But she would not let herself die. She had done what was right. They were wrong. Tony was a weakling. They had all been weaklings. Her father had been too weak to face his son's death. Her mother had been too weak to face life alone. *But I am not weak,* Kate thought. *I can face this. I can face anything. I'm going to live. I'll survive. The company will survive.*

BOOK FIVE

Eve and Alexandra
1950–1975

23

Kate recuperated at Dark Harbor, letting the sun and the sea heal her.

Tony was in a private asylum, where he could get the best care possible. Kate had psychiatrists flown in from Paris, Vienna and Berlin, but when all the examinations and tests had been completed, the diagnosis was the same: Her son was a homicidal schizophrenic and paranoiac.

"He doesn't respond to drugs or psychiatric treatment, and he's violent. We have to keep him under restraint."

"What kind of restraint?" Kate asked.

"He's in a padded cell. Most of the time we have to keep him in a straitjacket."

"Is that necessary?"

"Without it, Mrs. Blackwell, he would kill anyone who got near him."

She closed her eyes in pain. This was not her sweet, gentle Tony they were talking about. It was a stranger, someone possessed. She opened her eyes. "Is there nothing that can be done?"

"Not if we can't reach his mind. We're keeping him on drugs, but the moment they wear off, he gets manic again. We can't continue this treatment indefinitely."

Kate stood very straight. "What do you suggest, Doctor?"

"In similar cases, we've found that removing a small portion of the brain has produced remarkable results."

Kate swallowed. "A lobotomy?"

"That is correct. Your son will still be able to function in every way, except that he will no longer have any strong dysfunctional emotions."

Kate sat there, her mind and body chilled. Dr. Morris, a young doctor from the Menninger Clinic, broke the silence. "I know how difficult this must be for you, Mrs. Blackwell. If you'd like to think about—"

"If that's the only thing that will stop his torment," Kate said, "do it."

Frederick Hoffman wanted his granddaughters. "I will take them back to Germany with me."

It seemed to Kate that he had aged twenty years since Marianne's death. Kate felt sorry for him, but she had no intention of giving up Tony's children. "They need a woman's care, Frederick. Marianne would have wanted them brought up here. You'll come and visit them often."

And he was finally persuaded.

The twins were moved into Kate's home, and a nursery suite was set up for them. Kate interviewed governesses, and finally hired a young French woman named Solange Dunas.

Kate named the first-born Eve, and her twin, Alexandra. They were identical—impossible to tell apart. Seeing them together was like looking at an image in a mirror, and Kate marveled at the double miracle that her son and Marianne had created. They were both bright babies, quick and responsive, but even after a few weeks, Eve seemed more mature than Alexandra. Eve was the first to crawl and talk and walk. Alexandra followed quickly, but from the beginning it was Eve who was the leader. Alexandra adored her sister and tried to imitate everything she did. Kate spent as much time with her granddaughters as possible. They made her feel young. And Kate began to dream again. *One day, when I'm old and ready to retire . . .*

On the twins' first birthday, Kate gave them a party. They each had an identical birthday cake, and there were dozens of presents from friends, company employees and the household staff. Their second birthday party seemed to follow almost immediately. Kate could not believe how rapidly the time went by and how quickly the twins were growing. She was able to discern even more clearly the differences in their personalities: Eve, the stronger, was more daring, Alexandra was softer, content to follow her sister's lead. *With no mother or father,* Kate thought repeatedly, *it's a blessing that they have each other and love each other so much.*

The night before their fifth birthday, Eve tried to murder Alexandra.

It is written in Genesis 25: 22–23:

And the children struggled together within her . . .
And the Lord said unto her, Two [nations] are in thy womb, and two manner of people shall be separated from thy bowels; and the one [people] shall be stronger than the other [people]; and the elder shall serve the younger.

In the case of Eve and Alexandra, Eve had no intention of serving her younger sister.

Eve had hated her sister for as long as she could remember. She went into a silent rage when someone picked up Alexandra, or petted her or gave her a present. Eve felt she was being cheated. She wanted it all for herself—all the love and the beautiful things that surrounded the two of them. She could not have even a birthday of her own. She hated Alexandra for looking like her, dressing like her, stealing the part of her grandmother's love that belonged to her. Alexandra adored Eve, and Eve despised her for that. Alexandra was generous, eager to give up her toys and dolls, and that filled Eve with still more contempt. Eve shared nothing. What was hers belonged to her; but it was not enough. She wanted everything Alexandra had. At night, under the watchful eye of Solange Dunas, both girls would say their prayers aloud, but Eve always added a silent prayer begging God to strike Alexandra dead. When the prayer went unanswered, Eve decided she would have to take care of it herself. Their fifth birthday was only a few days away, and Eve could not bear the thought of sharing another party with Alexandra. They were *her* friends, and *her* gifts that her sister was stealing from her. She had to kill Alexandra soon.

On the night before their birthday, Eve lay in her bed, wide awake. When she was sure the household was asleep, she went over to Alexandra's bed and awakened her. "Alex," she whispered, "let's go down to the kitchen and see our birthday cakes."

Alexandra said sleepily, "Everybody's sleeping."

"We won't wake anyone up."

"Mademoiselle Dunas won't like it. Why don't we look at the cakes in the morning?"

"Because I want to look at them now. Are you coming or not?"

Alexandra rubbed the sleep out of her eyes. She had no interest in seeing the birthday cakes, but she did not want to hurt her sister's feelings. "I'm coming," she said.

Alexandra got out of bed and put on a pair of slippers. Both girls wore pink nylon nightgowns.

"Come on," Eve said. "And don't make any noise."

"I won't," Alexandra promised.

They tiptoed out of their bedroom, into the long corridor, past the closed door of Mademoiselle Dunas's bedroom, down the steep back stairs that led to the kitchen. It was an enormous kitchen, with two large gas stoves, six ovens, three refrigerators and a walk-in freezer.

In the refrigerator Eve found the birthday cakes that the cook,

Mrs. Tyler, had made. One of them said Happy Birthday, Alexandra. The other said Happy Birthday, Eve.

Next year, Eve thought happily, *there will only be one.*

Eve took Alexandra's cake out of the refrigerator and placed it on the wooden chopping block in the middle of the kitchen. She opened a drawer and took out a package of brightly colored candles.

"What are you doing?" Alexandra asked.

"I want to see how it looks with the candles all lighted." Eve began pressing the candles into the icing of the cake.

"I don't think you should do that, Eve. You'll ruin the cake. Mrs. Tyler is going to be angry."

"She won't mind." Eve opened another drawer and took out two large boxes of kitchen matches. "Come on, help me."

"I want to go back to bed."

Eve turned on her angrily. "All right. Go back to bed, scaredy cat. I'll do it alone."

Alexandra hesitated. "What do you want me to do?"

Eve handed her one of the boxes of matches. "Start lighting the candles."

Alexandra was afraid of fire. Both girls had been warned again and again about the danger of playing with matches. They knew the horror stories about children who had disobeyed that rule. But Alexandra did not want to disappoint Eve, and so she obediently began lighting the candles.

Eve watched her a moment. "You're leaving out the ones on the other side, silly," she said.

Alexandra leaned over to reach the candles at the far side of the cake, her back to Eve. Quickly, Eve struck a match and touched it to the matches in the box she was holding. As they burst into flames, Eve dropped the box at Alexandra's feet, so that the bottom of Alexandra's nightgown caught fire. It was an instant before Alexandra was aware of what was happening. When she felt the first agonizing pain against her legs, she looked down and screamed, "Help! Help me!"

Eve stared at the flaming nightgown a moment, awed by the

extent of her success. Alexandra was standing there, petrified, frozen with fear.

"Don't move!" Eve said. "I'll get a bucket of water." She hurried off to the butler's pantry, her heart pounding with a fearful joy.

It was a horror movie that saved Alexandra's life. Mrs. Tyler, the Blackwells' cook, had been escorted to the cinema by a police sergeant whose bed she shared from time to time. On this particular evening, the motion-picture screen was so filled with dead and mutilated bodies that finally Mrs. Tyler could bear it no longer. In the middle of a beheading, she said, "This may all be in a day's work for you, Richard, but I've had enough."

Sergeant Richard Dougherty reluctantly followed her out of the theater.

They arrived back at the Blackwell mansion an hour earlier than they had expected to, and as Mrs. Tyler opened the back door, she heard Alexandra's screams coming from the kitchen. Mrs. Tyler and Sergeant Dougherty rushed in, took one horrified look at the scene before them and went into action. The sergeant leaped at Alexandra and ripped off her flaming nightgown. Her legs and hips were blistered, but the flames had not reached her hair or the front of her body. Alexandra fell to the floor, unconscious. Mrs. Tyler filled a large pot with water and poured it over the flames licking at the floor.

"Call an ambulance," Sergeant Dougherty ordered. "Is Mrs. Blackwell home?"

"She should be upstairs asleep."

"Wake her up."

As Mrs. Tyler finished phoning for an ambulance, there was a cry from the butler's pantry, and Eve ran in carrying a pan of water, sobbing hysterically.

"Is Alexandra dead?" Eve screamed. "Is she dead?"

Mrs. Tyler took Eve in her arms to soothe her. "No, darling, she's all right. She's going to be just fine."

"It was my fault," Eve sobbed. "She wanted to light the candles on her birthday cake. I shouldn't have let her do it."

Mrs. Tyler stroked Eve's back. "It's all right. You mustn't blame yourself."

"The m-matches fell out of my hand, and Alex caught on fire. It was t-terrible."

Sergeant Dougherty looked at Eve and said sympathetically, "Poor child."

"Alexandra has second-degree burns on her legs and back," Dr. Harley told Kate, "but she's going to be fine. We can do amazing things with burns these days. Believe me, this could have been a terrible tragedy."

"I know," Kate said. She had seen Alexandra's burns, and they had filled her with horror. She hesitated a moment. "John, I think I'm even more concerned about Eve."

"Was Eve hurt?"

"Not physically, but the poor child blames herself for the accident. She's having terrible nightmares. The last three nights I've had to go in and hold her in my arms before she could go back to sleep. I don't want this to become more traumatic. Eve is very sensitive."

"Kids get over things pretty quickly, Kate. If there's any problem, let me know, and I'll recommend a child therapist."

"Thank you," Kate said gratefully.

Eve *was* terribly upset. The birthday party had been canceled. *Alexandra cheated me out of that,* Eve thought bitterly.

Alexandra healed perfectly, with no signs of scars. Eve got over her feelings of guilt with remarkable ease. As Kate assured her, "Accidents can happen to anybody, darling. You mustn't blame yourself."

Eve didn't. She blamed Mrs. Tyler. Why did she have to come home and spoil everything? It had been a perfect plan.

The sanitarium where Tony was confined was in a peaceful, wooded area in Connecticut. Kate was driven out to see him once a month. The lobotomy had been successful. There was no longer the slightest sign of aggression in Tony. He recognized

Kate and he always politely asked about Eve and Alexandra, but he showed no interest in seeing them. He showed very little interest in anything. He seemed happy. *No, not happy,* Kate corrected herself. *Content. But content—to do what?*

Kate asked Mr. Burger, the superintendent of the asylum, "Doesn't my son *do* anything all day?"

"Oh, yes, Mrs. Blackwell. He sits by the hour and paints."

Her son, who could have owned the world, sat and painted all day. Kate tried not to think of the waste, that brilliant mind gone forever. "What does he paint?"

The man was embarrassed. "No one can quite figure it out."

24

During the next two years, Kate became seriously concerned about Alexandra. The child was definitely accident-prone. During Eve and Alexandra's summer vacation at the Blackwell estate in the Bahamas, Alexandra almost drowned while playing with Eve in the pool, and it was only the prompt intervention of a gardener that saved her. The following year when the two girls were on a picnic in the Palisades, Alexandra somehow slipped off the edge of a cliff and saved herself by clinging to a shrub growing out of the steep mountainside.

"I wish you would keep a closer eye on your sister," Kate told Eve. "She can't seem to take care of herself the way you can."

"I know," Eve said solemnly. "I'll watch her, Gran."

Kate loved both her granddaughters, but in different ways. They were seven years old now, and identically beautiful, with long, soft blond hair, exquisite features and the McGregor eyes. They looked alike, but their personalities were quite different. Alexandra's gentleness reminded Kate of Tony, while Eve was more like her, headstrong and self-sufficient.

A chauffeur drove them to school in the family Rolls-Royce. Alexandra was embarrassed to have her classmates see her with the car and chauffeur; Eve reveled in it. Kate gave each girl a weekly allowance, and ordered them to keep a record of how they spent it. Eve invariably ran short of money before the week was out and borrowed from Alexandra. Eve learned to adjust the books so that Gran would not know. But Kate knew, and she could hardly hold back her smile. Seven years old and already a creative accountant!

In the beginning, Kate had nurtured a secret dream that one day Tony would be well again, that he would leave the asylum and return to Kruger-Brent. But as time passed, the dream slowly faded. It was tacitly understood that while Tony might leave the asylum for short visits, accompanied by a male nurse, he would never again be able to participate in the outside world.

It was 1962, and as Kruger-Brent, Ltd., prospered and expanded, the demands for new leadership grew more urgent. Kate celebrated her seventieth birthday. Her hair was white now, and she was a remarkable figure of a woman, strong and erect and vital. She was aware that the attrition of time would overtake her. She had to be prepared. The company had to be safeguarded for the family. Brad Rogers was a good manager, but he was not a Blackwell. *I have to last until the twins can take over.* She thought of Cecil Rhodes's last words: "So little done—so much to do."

The twins were twelve years old, on the verge of becoming young ladies. Kate had spent as much time with them as she possibly could, but now she turned even more of her attention to them. It was time to make an important decision.

During Easter week, Kate and the twins flew to Dark Harbor in a company plane. The girls had visited all the family estates except the one in Johannesburg, and of them all, Dark Harbor was their favorite. They enjoyed the wild freedom and the seclusion of the island. They loved to sail and swim and water-ski, and Dark Harbor held all these things for them. Eve asked if she could bring some schoolmates along, as she had in the past, but this time her grandmother refused. Grandmother, that powerful, imposing figure who swept in and out, dropping off a present here, a kiss on the cheek there, with occasional admonitions about how young ladies behaved, wanted to be alone with them. This time the girls sensed that something different was happening. Their grandmother was with them at every meal. She took them boating and swimming and even riding. Kate handled her horse with the sureness of an expert.

The girls still looked amazingly alike, two golden beauties, but Kate was interested less in their similarities than in their differences. Sitting on the veranda watching them as they finished a tennis game, Kate summed them up in her mind. Eve was the leader, Alexandra the follower. Eve had a stubborn streak. Alexandra was flexible. Eve was a natural athlete. Alexandra was still having accidents. Only a few days before, when the two girls were out alone in a small sailboat with Eve at the rudder, the wind had come behind the sail and the sail had luffed, swinging it crashing toward Alexandra's head. She had not gotten out of the way in time and had been swept overboard and nearly drowned. Another boat nearby had assisted Eve in rescuing her sister. Kate wondered whether all these things could have anything to do with Alexandra having been born three minutes later than Eve, but the reasons did not matter. Kate had made her decision. There was no longer any question in her mind. She was putting her money on Eve, and it was a ten-billion-dollar bet. She would find a perfect consort for Eve, and when Kate retired, Eve would run Kruger-Brent. As for Alexandra, she would have a life of wealth and comfort. She might be very good working on the charitable grants Kate had set up. Yes, that would be perfect for Alexandra. She was such a sweet and compassionate child.

The first step toward implementing Kate's plan was to see that Eve got into the proper school. Kate chose Briarcrest, an excellent school in South Carolina. "Both my granddaughters are delightful," Kate informed Mrs. Chandler, the headmistress. "But you'll find that Eve is the clever one. She's an extraordinary girl, and I'm sure you'll see to it that she has every advantage here."

"All our students have every advantage here, Mrs. Blackwell. You spoke of Eve. What about her sister?"

"Alexandra? A lovely girl." It was a pejorative. Kate stood up. "I shall be checking their progress regularly."

In some odd way, the headmistress felt the words were a warning.

Eve and Alexandra adored the new school, particularly Eve. She enjoyed the freedom of being away from home, of not having to account to her grandmother and Solange Dunas. The rules at Briarcrest were strict, but that did not bother Eve, for she was adept at getting around rules. The only thing that disturbed her was that Alexandra was there with her. When Eve first heard the news about Briarcrest, she begged, "May I go alone? Please, Gran?"

And Kate said, "No, darling. I think it's better if Alexandra goes with you."

Eve concealed her resentment. "Whatever you say, Gran."

She was always very polite and affectionate around her grandmother. Eve knew where the power lay. Their father was a crazy man, locked up in an insane asylum. Their mother was dead. It was their grandmother who controlled the money. Eve knew they were rich. She had no idea how much money there was, but it was a lot—enough to buy all the beautiful things she wanted. Eve loved beautiful things. There was only one problem: Alexandra.

One of the twins' favorite activities at Briarcrest School was the morning riding class. Most of the girls owned their own jumpers, and Kate had given each twin one for her twelfth birthday. Jerome Davis, the riding instructor, watched as his pupils went through their paces in the ring, jumping over a one-foot stile, then a two-foot stile and finally a four-foot stile. Davis was one of the best riding teachers in the country. Several of his former pupils had gone on to win gold medals, and he was adept at spotting a natural-born rider. The new girl, Eve Blackwell, was a natural. She did not have to think about what she was doing, how to hold the reins or post in the saddle. She and her horse were one, and as they sailed over the hurdles, Eve's golden hair flying in the wind, it was a beautiful sight to behold. *Nothing's going to stop that one*, Mr. Davis thought.

Tommy, the young groom, favored Alexandra. Mr. Davis watched Alexandra saddle up her horse, preparing for her turn. Alexandra and Eve wore different-colored ribbons on their sleeves so he could tell them apart. Eve was helping Alexandra saddle her horse while Tommy was busy with another student. Davis was summoned to the main building for a telephone call, and what happened after that was a matter of great confusion.

From what Jerome Davis was able to piece together later, Alexandra mounted her horse, circled the ring and started toward the first low jump. Her horse inexplicably began rearing and bucking, and threw Alexandra into a wall. She was knocked unconscious, and it was only by inches that the wild horse's hooves missed her face. Tommy carried Alexandra to the infirmary, where the school doctor diagnosed a mild concussion.

"Nothing broken, nothing serious," he said. "By tomorrow morning, she'll be right as rain, ready to get up on her horse again."

"But she could have been killed!" Eve screamed.

Eve refused to leave Alexandra's side. Mrs. Chandler thought she had never seen such devotion in a sister. It was truly touching.

When Mr. Davis was finally able to corral Alexandra's horse to unsaddle it, he found the saddle blanket stained with blood. He lifted it off and discovered a large piece of jagged metal from a beer can still protruding from the horse's back, where it had been pressed down by the saddle. When he reported this to Mrs. Chandler, she started an immediate investigation. All the girls who had been in the vicinity of the stable were questioned.

"I'm sure," Mrs. Chandler said, "that whoever put that piece of metal there thought she was playing a harmless prank, but it could have led to very serious consequences. I want the name of the girl who did it."

When no one volunteered, Mrs. Chandler talked to them in her office, one by one. Each girl denied any knowledge of what had happened. When it was Eve's turn to be questioned, she seemed oddly ill at ease.

"Do you have any idea who could have done this to your sister?" Mrs. Chandler asked.

Eve looked down at the rug. "I'd rather not say," she mumbled.

"Then you *did* see something?"

"Please, Mrs. Chandler . . ."

"Eve, Alexandra could have been seriously hurt. The girl who did this must be punished so that it does not happen again."

"It wasn't one of the girls."

"What do you mean?"

"It was Tommy."

"The *groom?*"

"Yes, ma'am. I saw him. I thought he was just tightening the cinch. I'm sure he didn't mean any harm. Alexandra orders him around a lot, and I guess he wanted to teach her a lesson. Oh, Mrs. Chandler, I wish you hadn't made me tell you. I don't want to get anyone in trouble." The poor child was on the verge of hysteria.

Mrs. Chandler walked around the desk and put her arm around her. "It's all right, Eve. You did right to tell me. Now you just forget about everything. I'll take care of it."

The following morning when the girls went out to the stables, there was a new groom.

A few months later, there was another unpleasant incident at the school. Several of the girls had been caught smoking marijuana and one of them accused Eve of supplying it and selling it. Eve angrily denied it. A search by Mrs. Chandler revealed marijuana hidden in Alexandra's locker.

"I don't believe she did it," Eve said stoutly. "Someone put it there. I know it."

An account of the incident was sent to Kate by the headmistress, and Kate admired Eve's loyalty in shielding her sister. She was a McGregor, all right.

On the twins' fifteenth birthday, Kate took them to the estate in South Carolina, where she gave a large party for them. It was not too early to see to it that Eve was exposed to the proper young men, and every eligible young man around was invited to the girls' party.

The boys were at the awkward age where they were not yet seriously interested in girls, but Kate made it her business to see that acquaintances were made and friendships formed. Somewhere among these young boys could be the man in Eve's future, the future of Kruger-Brent, Ltd.

Alexandra did not enjoy parties, but she always pretended she was having a good time in order not to disappoint her grandmother. Eve adored parties. She loved dressing up, being admired. Alexandra preferred reading and painting. She spent hours looking at her father's paintings at Dark Harbor, and she wished she could have known him before he became ill. He appeared at the house on holidays with his male companion, but Alexandra found it impossible to reach her father. He was a pleasant, amiable stranger who wanted to please, but had nothing to say. Their grandfather, Frederick Hoffman, lived in Germany, but was ill. The twins seldom saw him.

In her second year at school, Eve became pregnant. For several weeks she had been pale and listless and had missed some morning classes. When she began to have frequent periods of nausea, she was sent to the infirmary and examined. Mrs. Chandler had been hastily summoned.

"Eve is pregnant," the doctor told her.

"But—that's impossible! How could it have happened?"

The doctor replied mildly, "In the usual fashion, I would presume."

"But she's just a child."

"Well, this child is going to be a mother."

Eve bravely refused to talk. "I don't want to get anyone in trouble," she kept saying.

It was the kind of answer Mrs. Chandler expected from Eve.

"Eve, dear, you must tell me what happened."

And so at last Eve broke down. "I was raped," she said, and burst into tears.

Mrs. Chandler was shocked. She held Eve's trembling body close to her and demanded, "Who was it?"

"Mr. Parkinson."

Her English teacher.

If it had been anyone else but Eve, Mrs. Chandler would not have believed it. Joseph Parkinson was a quiet man with a wife and three children. He had taught at Briarcrest School for eight years, and he was the last one Mrs. Chandler would have ever suspected. She called him into her office, and she knew instantly that Eve had told the truth. He sat facing her, his face twitching with nervousness.

"You know why I've sent for you, Mr. Parkinson?"

"I—I think so."

"It concerns Eve."

"Yes. I—I guessed that."

"She says you raped her."

Parkinson looked at her in disbelief. "*Raped* her? My God! If anyone was raped, it was me." In his excitement he lapsed into the ungrammatical.

Mrs. Chandler said contemptuously, "Do you know what you're saying? That child is—"

"She's *not* a child." His voice was venomous. "She's a devil." He wiped the perspiration from his brow. "All semester she sat in the front row of my class, with her dress hiked up. After class she would come up and ask a lot of meaningless questions while she rubbed herself against me. I didn't take her seriously. Then one afternoon about six weeks ago she came over to my house when my wife and children were away and—" His voice broke. "Oh, Jesus! I couldn't help it." He burst into tears.

They brought Eve into the office. Her manner was composed. She looked into Mr. Parkinson's eyes, and it was he who turned away first. In the office were Mrs. Chandler, the assistant principal and the chief of police of the small town where the school was located.

The chief of police said gently, "Do you want to tell us what happened, Eve?"

"Yes, sir." Eve's voice was calm. "Mr. Parkinson said he wanted to discuss my English work with me. He asked me to come to his house on a Sunday afternoon. He was alone in the house. He said he wanted to show me something in the bedroom, so I followed him upstairs. He forced me onto the bed, and he—"

"It's a lie!" Parkinson yelled. "That's not the way it happened. That's not the way it happened . . ."

Kate was sent for, and the situation was explained to her. It was decided that it was in everyone's interest to keep the incident quiet. Mr. Parkinson was dismissed from the school and given forty-eight hours to leave the state. An abortion was discreetly arranged for Eve.

Kate quietly bought up the school mortgage, carried by a local bank, and foreclosed.

When Eve heard the news, she sighed, "I'm so sorry, Gran. I really liked that school."

A few weeks later when Eve had recovered from her operation, she and Alexandra were registered at L'Institut Fernwood, a Swiss finishing school near Lausanne.

25

There was a fire burning in Eve that was so fierce she could not put it out. It was not sex alone: That was only a small part of it. It was a rage to live, a need to do everything, be everything. Life was a lover, and Eve was desperate to possess it with all she had in her. She was jealous of everyone. She went to the ballet and hated the ballerina because she herself was not up there dancing and winning the cheers of the audience. She wanted to be a scientist, a singer, a surgeon, a pilot, an actress. She wanted to do everything, and do it better than anyone else had ever done it. She wanted it all, and she could not wait.

Across the valley from L'Institut Fernwood was a boys' military school. By the time Eve was seventeen, nearly every student and almost half the instructors were involved with her. She flirted outrageously and had affairs indiscriminately, but this time she took proper precautions, for she had no intention of ever getting pregnant again. She enjoyed sex, but it was not the act itself Eve loved, it was the power it gave her. She was the one in control. She gloated over the pleading looks of the boys and men who wanted to take her to bed and make love to her. She enjoyed teasing them and watching their hunger grow. She enjoyed the lying promises they made in order to possess her. But most of all, Eve enjoyed the power she had over their bodies. She could bring them to an erection with a kiss, and wither them with a word. She did not need them, they needed her. She controlled them totally, and it was a tremendous feeling. Within minutes she could measure a man's strengths and weaknesses. She decided men were fools, all of them.

Eve was beautiful and intelligent and an heiress to one of the world's great fortunes, and she had had more than a dozen serious proposals of marriage. She was not interested. The only boys who attracted her were the ones Alexandra liked.

At a Saturday-night school dance, Alexandra met an attentive young French student named Rene Mallot. He was not handsome, but he was intelligent and sensitive, and Alexandra thought he was wonderful. They arranged to meet in town the following Saturday.

"Seven o'clock," Rene said.

"I'll be waiting."

In their room that night, Alexandra told Eve about her new friend. "He's not like the other boys. He's rather shy and sweet. We're going to the theater Saturday."

"You like him a lot, don't you, little sister?" Eve teased.

Alexandra blushed. "I just met him, but he seems— Well, you know."

Eve lay back on her bed, hands clasped behind her head. "No, I don't know. Tell me. Did he try to take you to bed?"

"Eve! He's not that kind of boy at all. I told you . . . he's—he's shy."

"Well, well. My little sister's in love."

"Of course I'm not! Now I wish I hadn't told you."

"I'm glad you did," Eve said sincerely.

When Alexandra arrived in front of the theater the following Saturday, Rene was nowhere in sight. Alexandra waited on the street corner for more than an hour, ignoring the stares of passers-by, feeling like a fool. Finally she had a bad dinner alone in a small café and returned to school, miserable. Eve was not in their room. Alexandra read until curfew and then turned out the lights. It was almost two A.M. when Alexandra heard Eve sneak into the room.

"I was getting worried about you," Alexandra whispered.

"I ran into some old friends. How was your evening—divine?"

"It was dreadful. He never even bothered to show up."

"That's a shame," Eve said sympathetically. "But you must learn never to trust a man."

"You don't think anything could have happened to him?"

"No, Alex. I think he probably found somebody he liked better."

Of course he did, Alexandra thought. She was not really surprised. She had no idea how beautiful she was, or how admirable. She had lived all her life in the shadow of her twin sister. She adored her, and it seemed only right to Alexandra that everyone should be attracted to Eve. She felt inferior to Eve, but it never occurred to her that her sister had been carefully nourishing that feeling since they were children.

There were other broken dates. Boys Alexandra liked would seem to respond to her, and then she would never see them again. One weekend she ran into Rene unexpectedly on the streets of Lausanne. He hurried up to her and said, "What happened? You promised you would call me."

"Call you? What are you talking about?"

He stepped back, suddenly wary. "Eve . . . ?"

"No, Alexandra."

His face flushed. "I—I'm sorry. I have to go." And he hurried away, leaving her staring after him in confusion.

That evening when Alexandra told Eve about the incident, Eve shrugged and said, "He's obviously *fou.* You're much better off without him, Alex."

In spite of her feeling of expertise about men, there was one male weakness of which Eve was unaware, and it almost proved to be her undoing. From the beginning of time, men have boasted of their conquests, and the students at the military school were no different. They discussed Eve Blackwell with admiration and awe.

"When she was through with me, I couldn't move . . ."

"I never thought I'd have a piece of ass like that . . ."

"She's got a pussy that *talks* to you . . ."

"God, she's like a tigress in bed!"

Since at least two dozen boys and half a dozen teachers were praising Eve's libidinous talents, it soon became the school's worst-kept secret. One of the instructors at the military school mentioned the gossip to a teacher at L'Institut Fernwood, and she in turn reported it to Mrs. Collins, the headmistress. A discreet investigation was begun, and the result was a meeting between the headmistress and Eve.

"I think it would be better for the reputation of this school if you left immediately."

Eve stared at Mrs. Collins as though the lady were demented. "What on earth are you talking about?"

"I'm talking about the fact that you have been servicing half the military academy. The other half seems to be lined up, eagerly waiting."

"I've never heard such terrible lies in my whole life." Eve's voice was quivering with indignation. "Don't think I'm not going to report this to my grandmother. When she hears—"

"I will spare you the trouble," the headmistress interrupted. "I would prefer to avoid embarrassment to L'Institut Fernwood, but if you do not leave quietly, I have a list of names I intend to send to your grandmother."

"I'd like to see that list!"

Mrs. Collins handed it to Eve without a word. It was a long list. Eve studied it and noted that at least seven names were missing. She sat there, quietly thinking.

Finally she looked up and said imperiously, "This is obviously some kind of plot against my family. Someone is trying to embarrass my grandmother through me. Rather than let that happen, I will leave."

"A very wise decision," Mrs. Collins said dryly. "A car will drive you to the airport in the morning. I'll cable your grandmother that you're coming home. You're dismissed."

Eve turned and started for the door, then suddenly thought of something. "What about my sister?"

"Alexandra may remain here."

When Alexandra returned to the dormitory after her last class, she found Eve packing. "What are you doing?"

"I'm going home."

"Home? In the middle of the term?"

Eve turned to face her sister. "Alex, don't you really have any idea what a waste this school is? We're not learning anything here. We're just killing time."

Alexandra was listening in surprise. "I had no idea you felt that way, Eve."

"I've felt like this every damn day for the whole bloody year. The only reason I stuck it out was because of you. You seemed to be enjoying it so much."

"I am, but—"

"I'm sorry, Alex. I just can't take it any longer. I want to get back to New York. I want to go home where *we* belong."

"Have you told Mrs. Collins?"

"A few minutes ago."

"How did she take it?"

"How did you expect her to take it? She was miserable—afraid it would make her school look bad. She begged me to stay."

Alexandra sat down on the edge of the bed. "I don't know what to say."

"You don't have to say anything. This has nothing to do with you."

"Of course it has. If you're that unhappy here—" She stopped. "You're probably right. It is a bloody waste of time. Who needs to conjugate Latin verbs?"

"Right. Or who gives a fig about Hannibal or his bloody brother, Hasdrubal?"

Alexandra walked over to the closet, took out her suitcase and put it on the bed.

Eve smiled. "I wasn't going to ask you to leave here, Alex, but I'm really glad we're going home together."

Alexandra pressed her sister's hand. "So am I."

Eve said casually, "Tell you what. While I finish packing, call Gran and tell her we'll be on the plane home tomorrow. Tell her we can't stand this place. Will you do that?"

"Yes." Alexandra hesitated. "I don't think she's going to like it."

"Don't worry about the old lady," Eve said confidently. "I can handle her."

And Alexandra had no reason to doubt it. Eve was able to make Gran do pretty much what she wanted. *But then,* Alexandra thought, *how could anyone refuse Eve anything?*

She went to make the phone call.

Kate Blackwell had friends and enemies and business associates in high places, and for the last few months disturbing rumors had been coming to her ears. In the beginning she had ignored them as petty jealousies. But they persisted. Eve was seeing too much of the boys at a military school in Switzerland. Eve had an abortion. Eve was being treated for a social disease.

Thus, it was with a degree of relief that Kate learned that her granddaughters were coming home. She intended to get to the bottom of the vile rumors.

The day the girls arrived, Kate was at home waiting for them. She took Eve into the sitting room off her bedroom. "I've been hearing some distressing stories," she said. "I want to know why you were thrown out of school." Her eyes bored into those of her granddaughter.

"We weren't thrown out," Eve replied. "Alex and I decided to leave."

"Because of some incidents with boys?"

Eve said, "Please, Grandmother. I'd rather not talk about it."

"I'm afraid you're going to have to. What have you been doing?"

"I haven't been doing anything. It is Alex who—" She broke off.

"Alex who what?" Kate was relentless.

"Please don't blame her," Eve said quickly. "I'm sure she couldn't help it. She likes to play this childish game of pretending to be me. I had no idea what she was up to until the girls started gossiping about it. It seems she was seeing a lot of—of boys—" Eve broke off in embarrassment.

"Pretending to be you?" Kate was stunned. "Why didn't you put a stop to it?"

"I tried," Eve said miserably. "She threatened to kill herself. Oh, Gran, I think Alexandra is a bit"—she forced herself to say the word—"unstable. If you even discuss any of this with her, I'm afraid of what she might do." There was naked agony in the child's tear-filled eyes.

Kate's heart felt heavy at Eve's deep unhappiness. "Eve, don't. Don't cry, darling. I won't say anything to Alexandra. This will be just between the two of us."

"I—I didn't want you to know. Oh, Gran," she sobbed, "I knew how much it would hurt you."

Later, over tea, Kate studied Alexandra. *She's beautiful outside and rotten inside,* Kate thought. It was bad enough that Alexandra was involved in a series of sordid affairs, but to try to put the blame on her sister! Kate was appalled.

During the next two years, while Eve and Alexandra finished school at Miss Porter's, Eve was very discreet. She had been frightened by the close call. Nothing must jeopardize the relationship with her grandmother. The old lady could not last much longer—she was seventy-nine!—and Eve intended to make sure that she was Gran's heiress.

For the girls' twenty-first birthday, Kate took her granddaughters to Paris and bought them new wardrobes at Coco Chanel.

At a small dinner party at Le Petit Bedouin, Eve and

Alexandra met Count Alfred Maurier and his wife, the Countess Vivien. The count was a distinguished-looking man in his fifties, with iron-gray hair and the disciplined body of an athlete. His wife was a pleasant-looking woman with a reputation as an international hostess.

Eve would have paid no particular attention to either of them, except for a remark she overheard someone make to the countess. "I envy you and Alfred. You're the happiest married couple I know. How many years have you been married? Twenty-five?"

"It will be twenty-six next month," Alfred replied for her. "And I may be the only Frenchman in history who has never been unfaithful to his wife."

Everyone laughed except Eve. During the rest of the dinner, she studied Count Maurier and his wife. Eve could not imagine what the count saw in that flabby, middle-aged woman with her crepey neck. Count Maurier had probably never known what real lovemaking was. That boast of his was stupid. Count Alfred Maurier was a challenge.

The following day, Eve telephoned Maurier at his office. "This is Eve Blackwell. You probably don't remember me, but—"

"How could I forget you, child? You are one of the beautiful granddaughters of my friend Kate."

"I'm flattered that you remember, Count. Forgive me for disturbing you, but I was told you're an expert on wines. I'm planning a surprise dinner party for Grandmother." She gave a rueful little laugh. "I know what I want to serve, but I don't know a thing about wines. I wondered whether you'd be kind enough to advise me."

"I would be delighted," he said, flattered. "It depends on what you are serving. If you are starting with a fish, a nice, light Chablis would be—"

"Oh, I'm afraid I could never remember all this. Would it be possible for me to see you so that we could discuss it? If you're free for lunch today. . . ?"

"For an old friend, I can arrange that."

"Oh, good." Eve replaced the receiver slowly. It would be a lunch the count would remember the rest of his life.

They met at Lasserre. The discussion on wines was brief. Eve listened to Maurier's boring discourse impatiently, and then interrupted. "I'm in love with you, Alfred."

The count stopped dead in the middle of a sentence. "I beg your pardon?"

"I said I'm in love with you."

He took a sip of wine. "A vintage year." He patted Eve's hand and smiled. "All good friends should love one another."

"I'm not talking about that kind of love, Alfred."

And the count looked into Eve's eyes and knew exactly what kind of love she was talking about. It made him decidedly nervous. This girl was twenty-one years old, and he was past middle age, a happily married man. He simply could not understand what got into young girls these days. He felt uneasy sitting across from her, listening to what she was saying, and he felt even uneasier because she was probably the most beautiful, desirable young woman he had ever seen. She was wearing a beige pleated skirt and a soft green sweater that revealed the outline of a full, rich bosom. She was not wearing a brassiere, and he could see the thrust of her nipples. He looked at her innocent young face, and he was at a loss for words. "You—you don't even know me."

"I've dreamed about you from the time I was a little girl. I imagined a man in shining armor who was tall and handsome and—"

"I'm afraid my armor's a little rusty. I—"

"Please don't make fun of me," Eve begged. "When I saw you at dinner last night, I couldn't take my eyes off you. I haven't been able to think of anything else. I haven't slept. I haven't been able to get you out of my mind for a moment." Which was almost true.

"I—I don't know what to say to you, Eve. I am a happily married man. I—"

"Oh, I can't tell you how I envy your wife! She's the luckiest woman in the world. I wonder if she realizes that, Alfred."

"Of course she does. I tell her all the time." He smiled nervously, and wondered how to change the subject.

"Does she *really* appreciate you? Does she know how sensitive you are? Does she worry about your happiness? I would."

The count was becoming increasingly uncomfortable. "You're a beautiful young woman," he said. "And one day you're going to find your knight in shining, *unrusted* armor, and then—"

"I've found him and I want to go to bed with him."

He looked around, afraid that someone might have overheard. "Eve! Please!"

She leaned forward. "That's all I ask. The memory will last me for the rest of my life."

The count said firmly, "This is impossible. You are placing me in a most embarrassing position. Young women should not go around propositioning strangers."

Slowly, Eve's eyes filled with tears. "Is *that* what you think of me? That I go around—I've known only one man in my life. We were engaged to be married." She did not bother to brush the tears away. "He was kind and loving and gentle. He was killed in a mountain-climbing accident. I saw it happen. It was awful."

Count Maurier put his hand over hers. "I am so sorry."

"You remind me so much of him. When I saw you, it was as though Bill had returned to me. If you would give me just one hour, I would never bother you again. You'd never even have to see me again. Please, Alfred!"

The count looked at Eve for a long time, weighing his decision.

After all, he was French.

They spent the afternoon in a small hotel on Rue Sainte-Anne. In all his experience before his marriage, Count Maurier had never bedded anyone like Eve. She was a hurricane, a nymphet, a devil. She knew too much. By the end of the afternoon, Count Maurier was completely exhausted.

As they were getting dressed, Eve said, "When will I see you again, darling?"

"I'll telephone you," Maurier said.

He did not plan ever to see this woman again. There was something about her that was frightening—almost evil. She was what the Americans so appropriately called *bad news,* and he had no intention of becoming involved further with her.

The matter would have ended there, had they not been seen coming out of the hotel together by Alicia Vanderlake, who had served on a charity committee with Kate Blackwell the previous year. Mrs. Vanderlake was a social climber, and this was a heaven-sent ladder. She had seen newspaper photographs of Count Maurier and his wife, and she had seen photographs of the Blackwell twins. She was not sure which twin this was, but that was not important. Mrs. Vanderlake knew where her duty lay. She looked in her private telephone book and found Kate Blackwell's number.

The butler answered the telephone. *"Bonjour."*

"I would like to speak with Mrs. Blackwell, please."

"May I tell her who is calling?"

"Mrs. Vanderlake. It's a personal matter."

A minute later, Kate Blackwell was on the phone. "Who is this?"

"This is Alicia Vanderlake, Mrs. Blackwell. I'm sure you'll remember me. We served on a committee together last year and—"

"If it's for a donation, call my—"

"No, no," Mrs. Vanderlake said hastily. "It's personal. It's about your granddaughter."

Kate Blackwell would invite her over to tea, and they would discuss it, woman to woman. It would be the beginning of a warm friendship.

Kate Blackwell said, "What about her?"

Mrs. Vanderlake had had no intention of discussing the matter over the telephone, but Kate Blackwell's unfriendly tone left her no choice. "Well, I thought it my duty to tell you that a few minutes ago I saw her sneaking out of a hotel with Count Alfred Maurier. It was an obvious assignation."

Kate's voice was icy. "I find this difficult to believe. Which one of my granddaughters?"

Mrs. Vanderlake gave an uncertain laugh. "I—I don't know. I can't tell them apart. But then, no one can, can they? It—"

"Thank you for the information." And Kate hung up.

She stood there digesting the information she had just heard. Only the evening before they had dined together. Kate had known Alfred Maurier for fifteen years, and what she had just been told was entirely out of character for him, unthinkable. And yet, men were susceptible. If Alexandra had set out to lure Alfred into bed . . .

Kate picked up the telephone and said to the operator, "I wish to place a call to Switzerland. L'Institut Fernwood at Lausanne."

When Eve returned home late that afternoon, she was flushed with satisfaction, not because she ¹ enjoyed sex with Count Maurier, but because of her victc   r him. *If I can have him so easily,* Eve thought, *I can have ... one. I can own the world.* She walked into the library and found Kate there.

"Hello, Gran. Did you have a lovely day?"

Kate stood there studying her lovely young granddaughter. "Not a very good one, I'm afraid. What about you?"

"Oh, I did a little shopping. I didn't see anything more I really wanted. You bought me everything. You always—"

"Close the door, Eve."

Something in Kate's voice sent out a warning signal. Eve closed the large oak door.

"Sit down."

"Is something wrong, Gran?"

"That's what you're going to tell me. I was going to invite Alfred Maurier here, but I decided to spare us all that humiliation."

Eve's brain began to spin. *This was impossible! There was no*

way anyone could have found out about her and Alfred Maurier.
She had left him only an hour earlier. "I—I don't understand
what you're talking about."

"Then let me put it bluntly. You were in bed this afternoon
with Count Maurier."

Tears sprang to Eve's eyes. "I—I was hoping you'd never find
out what he did to me, because he's your friend." She fought to
keep her voice steady. "It was terrible. He telephoned and invited me to lunch and got me drunk and—"

"Shut up!" Kate's voice was like a whiplash. Her eyes were
filled with loathing. "You're despicable."

Kate had spent the most painful hour of her life, coming to a
realization of the truth about her granddaughter. She could hear
again the voice of the headmistress saying, *Mrs. Blackwell,
young women will be young women, and if one of them has a discreet affair, it is none of my business. But Eve was so blatantly pro-
miscuous that for the good of the school . . .*

And Eve had blamed Alexandra.

Kate started to remember the accidents. The fire, when
Alexandra almost burned to death. Alexandra's fall from the
cliff. Alexandra being knocked out of the boat Eve was sailing,
and almost drowning. Kate could hear Eve's voice recounting
the details of her "rape" by her English teacher: *Mr. Parkinson
said he wanted to discuss my English work with me. He asked me
to come to his house on a Sunday afternoon. When I got there, he
was alone in the house. He said he wanted to show me something
in the bedroom. I followed him upstairs. He forced me onto the
bed, and he . . .*

Kate remembered the incident at Briarcrest when Eve was
accused of selling marijuana and the blame had been put on
Alexandra. Eve had not *blamed* Alexandra, she had *defended*
her. That was Eve's technique—to be the villain and play the
heroine. Oh, she was clever.

Now Kate studied the beautiful, angel-faced monster in front
of her. *I built all my future plans around you. It was you who was
going to take control of Kruger-Brent one day. It was you I loved*

and cherished. Kate said, "I want you to leave this house. I never want to see you again."

Eve had gone very pale.

"You're a whore. I think I could live with that. But you're also deceitful and cunning and a psychopathic liar. I cannot live with that."

It was all happening too fast. Eve said desperately, "Gran, if Alexandra has been telling you lies about me—"

"Alexandra doesn't know anything about this. I just had a long talk with Mrs. Collins."

"Is *that* all?" Eve forced a note of relief in her voice. "Mrs. Collins hates me because—"

Kate was filled with a sudden weariness. "It won't work, Eve. Not anymore. It's over. I've sent for my lawyer. I'm disinheriting you."

Eve felt her world crumbling around her. "You can't. How— how will I live?"

"You will be given a small allowance. From now on, you will live your own life. Do anything you please." Kate's voice hardened. "But if I ever hear or read one word of scandal about you, if you ever disgrace the Blackwell name in any way, your allowance will stop forever. Is that clear?"

Eve looked into her grandmother's eyes and knew this time there would be no reprieve. A dozen excuses sprang to her lips, but they died there.

Kate rose to her feet and said in an unsteady voice, "I don't suppose this will mean anything to you, but this is—this is the most difficult thing I've ever had to do in my life."

And Kate turned and walked out of the room, her back stiff and straight.

Kate sat in her darkened bedroom alone, wondering why everything had gone wrong.

If David had not been killed, and Tony could have known his father . . .

If Tony had not wanted to be an artist . . .

If Marianne had lived . . .

If. A two-letter word for futility.

The future was clay, to be molded day by day, but the past was bedrock, immutable. *Everyone I've loved has betrayed me,* Kate thought. *Tony. Marianne. Eve. Sartre said it well: "Hell is other people."* She wondered when the pain would go away.

If Kate was filled with pain, Eve was filled with fury. All she had done was to enjoy herself in bed for an hour or two, and her grandmother acted as though Eve had committed some unspeakable crime. *The old-fashioned bitch!* No, not old-fashioned: *senile.* That was it. She was senile. Eve would find a good attorney and have the new will laughed out of court. Her father and grandmother were both insane. No one was going to disinherit her. Kruger-Brent was *her* company. How many times had her grandmother told her that one day it would belong to her. And Alexandra! All this time Alexandra had been undermining her, whispering God-knows-what poison into their grandmother's ears. Alexandra wanted the company for herself. The terrible part was that now she would probably get it. What had happened this afternoon was bad enough, but the thought of Alexandra gaining control was unbearable. *I can't let that happen,* Eve thought. *I'll find a way to stop her.* She closed the snaps on her suitcase and went to find her sister.

Alexandra was in the garden reading. She looked up as Eve approached.

"Alex, I've decided to go back to New York."

Alexandra looked at her sister in surprise. *"Now?* Gran's planning a cruise to the Dalmatian coast next week. You—"

"Who cares about the Dalmatian coast? I've been thinking a lot about this. It's time I had my own apartment." She smiled. "I'm a big girl now. So I'm going to find the most divine little apartment, and if you're good, I'll let you spend the night once in a while." *That's just the right note,* Eve thought. *Friendly, but not gushy. Don't let her know you're on to her.*

Alexandra was studying her sister with concern. "Does Gran know?"

"I told her this afternoon. She hates the idea, of course, but she understands. I wanted to get a job, but she insisted on giving me an allowance."

Alexandra asked, "Would you like me to come with you?"

The goddamned, two-faced bitch! First she forced her out of the house, and now she was pretending she wanted to go with her. *Well, they're not going to dispose of little Eve so easily. I'll show them all.* She would have her own apartment—she would find some fabulous decorator to do it—and she would have complete freedom to come and go as she pleased. She could invite men up to her place and have them spend the night. She would be truly free for the first time in her life. It was an exhilarating thought.

Now she said, "You're sweet, Alex, but I'd like to be on my own for a while."

Alexandra looked at her sister and felt a deep sense of loss. It would be the first time they had ever been parted. "We'll see each other often, won't we?"

"Of course we will," Eve promised. "More than you imagine."

26

When Eve returned to New York, she checked into a midtown hotel, as she had been instructed. An hour later, Brad Rogers telephoned.

"Your grandmother called from Paris, Eve. Apparently there's some problem between you two."

"Not really," Eve laughed. "It's just a little family—" She was about to launch into an elaborate defense when she suddenly realized the danger that lay in that direction. From now on, she would have to be very careful. She had never had to think about money. It had always been there. Now it loomed large in her thoughts. She had no idea how large her allowance was going to be and for the first time in her life Eve felt fear.

"She told you she's having a new will drawn up?" Brad asked.

"Yes, she mentioned something about it." She was determined to play it cool.

"I think we had better discuss this in person. How's Monday at three?"

"That will be fine, Brad."

"My office. All right?"

"I'll be there."

* * *

At five minutes before three, Eve entered the Kruger-Brent, Ltd., Building. She was greeted deferentially by the security guard, the elevator starter and even the elevator operator. *Everyone knows me,* Eve thought. *I'm a Blackwell.* The elevator took her to the executive floor, and a few moments later Eve was seated in Brad Rogers's office.

Brad had been surprised when Kate telephoned him to say she was going to disinherit Eve, for he knew how much Kate cared about this particular granddaughter and what plans she had for her. Brad could not imagine what had happened. Well, it was none of his business. If Kate wanted to discuss it with him, she would. His job was to carry out her orders. He felt a momentary flash of pity for the lovely young woman before him. Kate had not been much older when he had first met her. Neither had he. And now he was a gray-haired old fool, still hoping that one day Kate Blackwell would realize there was someone who loved her very deeply.

He said to Eve, "I have some papers for you to sign. If you'll just read them over and—"

"That won't be necessary."

"Eve, it's important that you understand." He began to explain. "Under your grandmother's will, you're the beneficiary of an irrevocable trust fund currently in excess of five million dollars. Your grandmother is the executor. At her discretion, the money can be paid to you at any time from the age of twenty-one to thirty-five." He cleared his throat. "She has elected to give it to you when you reach age thirty-five."

It was a slap in the face.

"Beginning today, you will receive a weekly allowance of two hundred fifty dollars."

It was impossible! One decent dress cost more than that. There was no way she could live on $250 a week. This was being done to humiliate her. This bastard was probably in on it with her grandmother. He was sitting behind his big desk, enjoying himself, laughing. She wanted to pick up the large bronze paperweight in front of him and smash his head in.

She could almost feel the crunch of bone under her hand.

Brad droned on. "You are not to have any charge accounts, private or otherwise, and you are not to use the Blackwell name at any stores. Anything you purchase must be paid for in cash."

The nightmare was getting worse and worse.

"Next. If there is any gossip connected with your name in any newspaper or magazine—local or foreign—your weekly income will be stopped. Is that clear?"

"Yes." Her voice was a whisper.

"You and your sister Alexandra were issued insurance policies on your grandmother's life for five million dollars apiece. The policy you hold was canceled as of this morning. At the end of one year," Brad went on, "if your grandmother is satisfied with your behavior, your weekly allowance will be doubled." He hesitated. "There is one final stipulation."

She wants to hang me in public by my thumbs. "Yes?"

Brad Rogers looked uncomfortable. "Your grandmother does not wish ever to see you again, Eve."

Well, I want to see you one more time, old woman. I want to see you dying in agony.

Brad's voice trickled through to the cauldron of Eve's mind. "If you have any problems, you are to telephone me. She does not want you to come to this building again, or to visit any of the family estates."

He had tried to argue with Kate about that. "My God, Kate, she's your granddaughter, your flesh and blood. You're treating her like a leper."

"She *is* a leper."

And the discussion had ended.

Now Brad said awkwardly, "Well, I think that covers everything. Are there any questions, Eve?"

"No." She was in shock.

"Then if you'll just sign these papers . . ."

Ten minutes later, Eve was on the street again. There was a check for $250 in her purse.

* * *

The following morning Eve called on a real-estate agent and began looking for an apartment. In her fantasies, she had envisioned a beautiful penthouse overlooking Central Park, the rooms done in white with modern furniture, and a terrace where she could entertain guests. Reality came as a stunning blow. It seemed there were no Park Avenue penthouses available for someone with an income of $250 a week. What *was* available was a one-room studio apartment in Little Italy with a couch that became a bed, a nook that the real-estate agent euphemistically referred to as the "library," a small kitchenette and a tiny bathroom with stained tile.

"Is—is this the best you have?" Eve asked.

"No," the agent informed her. "I've got a twenty-room townhouse on Sutton Place for a half a million dollars, plus maintenance."

You bastard! Eve thought.

Real despair did not hit Eve until the following afternoon when she moved in. It was a prison. Her dressing room at home had been as large as this entire apartment. She thought of Alexandra enjoying herself in the huge house on Fifth Avenue. *My God, why couldn't Alexandra have burned to death? It had been so close!* If she had died and Eve had been the only heiress, things would have been different. Her grandmother would not have dared disinherit her.

But if Kate Blackwell thought that Eve intended to give up her heritage that easily, she did not know her granddaughter. Eve had no intention of trying to live on $250 a week. There was five million dollars that belonged to her, sitting in a bank, and that vicious old woman was keeping it from her. *There has to be a way to get my hands on that money. I will find it.*

The solution came the following day.

"And what can I do for you, Miss Blackwell?" Alvin Seagram asked deferentially. He was vice-president of the National Union Bank, and he was, in fact, prepared to do almost anything. What kind Fates had brought this young woman to him? If he could secure the Kruger-Brent account, or any part of it, his career would rise like a rocket.

"There's some money in trust for me," Eve explained. "Five million dollars. Because of the rules of the trust, it won't come to me until I'm thirty-five years old." She smiled ingenuously. "That seems so long from now."

"At your age, I'm sure it does," the banker smiled. "You're— nineteen?"

"Twenty-one."

"And beautiful, if you'll permit me to say so, Miss Blackwell."

Eve smiled demurely. "Thank you, Mr. Seagram." It was going to be simpler than she thought. *The man's an idiot.*

He could feel the rapport between them. *She likes me.* "How exactly may we help you?"

"Well, I was wondering if it would be possible to borrow an advance on my trust fund. You see, I need the money now more than I'll need it later. I'm engaged to be married. My fiancé is a construction engineer working in Israel, and he won't be back in this country for another three years."

Alvin Seagram was all sympathy. "I understand perfectly." His heart was pounding wildly. *Of course, he could grant her request.* Money was advanced against trust funds all the time. And when he had satisfied her, she would sent him other members of the Blackwell family, and he would satisfy them. Oh, how he would satisfy them! After that, there would be no stopping him. He would be made a member of the executive board of National Union. Perhaps one day its chairman. And he owed all this to the delicious little blonde seated across the desk.

"No problem at all," Alvin Seagram assured Eve. "It's a very simple transaction. You understand that we could not loan you the entire amount, but we could certainly let you have, say, a million immediately. Would that be satisfactory?"

"Perfectly," Eve said, trying not to show her exhilaration.

"Fine. If you'll just give me the details of the trust . . ." He picked up a pen.

"You can get in touch with Brad Rogers at Kruger-Brent. He'll give you all the information you need."

"I'll give him a call right away."

Eve rose. "How long will it take?"

"No more than a day or two. I'll rush it through personally."

She held out a lovely, delicate hand. "You're very kind."

The moment Eve was out of the office, Alvin Seagram picked up the telephone. "Get me Mr. Brad Rogers at Kruger-Brent, Limited." The very name sent a delicious shiver up his spine.

Two days later Eve returned to the bank and was ushered into Alvin Seagram's office. His first words were, "I'm afraid I can't help you, Miss Blackwell."

Eve could not believe wl   .e was hearing. "I don't understand. You said it was simple. You said—"

"I'm sorry. I was not in possession of all the facts."

How vividly he recalled the conversation with Brad Rogers. "Yes, there is a five-million-dollar trust fund in Eve Blackwell's name. Your bank is perfectly free to advance any amount of money you wish against it. However, I think it only fair to caution you that Kate Blackwell would consider it an unfriendly act."

There was no need for Brad Rogers to spell out what the consequences could be. Kruger-Brent had powerful friends everywhere. And if those friends started pulling money out of National Union, Alvin Seagram did not have to guess what it would do to his career.

"I'm sorry," he repeated to Eve. "There's nothing I can do."

Eve looked at him, frustrated. But she would not let this man know what a blow he had dealt her. "Thank you for your trouble. There are other banks in New York. Good day."

"Miss Blackwell," Alvin Seagram told her, "there isn't a bank in the world that will loan you one penny against that trust."

Alexandra was puzzled. In the past, her grandmother had made it obvious in a hundred ways that she favored Eve. Now, overnight everything had changed. She knew something terrible had happened between Kate and Eve, but she had no idea what it could have been.

Whenever Alexandra tried to bring up the subject, her grandmother would say, "There is nothing to discuss. Eve chose her own life."

Nor could Alexandra get anything out of Eve.

Kate Blackwell began spending a great deal of time with Alexandra. Alexandra was intrigued. She was not merely in her grandmother's presence, she was becoming an actual part of her life. It was as though her grandmother were seeing her for the first time. Alexandra had an odd feeling she was being evaluated.

Kate *was* seeing her granddaughter for the first time, and because she had been bitterly deceived once, she was doubly careful in forming an opinion about Eve's twin. She spent every possible moment with Alexandra, and she probed and questioned and listened. And in the end she was satisfied.

It was not easy to know Alexandra. She was a private person, more reserved than Eve. Alexandra had a quick, lively intelligence, and her innocence, combined with her beauty, made her all the more endearing. She had always received countless invitations to parties and dinners and the theater, but now it was Kate who decided which invitations Alexandra should accept and which ones she should refuse. The fact that a suitor was eligible was not enough—not nearly enough. What Kate was looking for was a man capable of helping Alexandra run Kate's dynasty. She said nothing of this to Alexandra. There would be time enough for that when Kate found the right man for her granddaughter. Sometimes, in the lonely early-morning hours when Kate had trouble sleeping, she thought about Eve.

Eve was doing beautifully. The episode with her grandmother had bruised her ego so badly that for a short time she had forgotten something very important: She had forgotten how attractive she was to men. At the first party she was invited to after she moved into her own apartment, she gave her telephone number to six men—four of them married—and within twenty-four hours she had heard from all six of them. From that day on, Eve knew she would no longer have to worry about money. She was showered with gifts: expensive jewelry, paintings and, more often, cash.

"I've just ordered a new credenza, and my allowance check hasn't come. Would you mind, darling?"

And they never minded.

When Eve went out in public, she made sure she was escorted by men who were single. Married men she saw afternoons at her apartment. Eve was very discreet. She was careful to see that her name was kept out of gossip columns, not because she was any longer concerned about her allowance being stopped, but because she was determined that one day her grandmother was going to come crawling to her. Kate Blackwell needed an heir to take over Kruger-Brent. *Alexandra is not equipped to be anything but a stupid housewife,* Eve gloated.

One afternoon, leafing through a new issue of *Town and Country,* Eve came across a photograph of Alexandra dancing with an attractive man. Eve was not looking at Alexandra, she was looking at the man. And realizing that if Alexandra married and had a son, it would be a disaster for Eve and her plans.

She stared at the picture a long time.

Over a period of a year, Alexandra had called Eve regularly, for lunch or dinner, and Eve had always put her off with excuses. Now Eve decided it was time to have a talk with her sister. She invited Alexandra to her apartment.

Alexandra had not seen the apartment before, and Eve braced herself for pity. But all Alexandra said was, "It's charming, Eve. It's very cozy, isn't it?"

Eve smiled. "It suits me. I wanted something *intime.*" She had pawned enough jewelry and paintings so that she could have moved into a beautiful apartment, but Kate would have learned of it and would have demanded to know where the money had come from. For the moment, the watchword was *discretion.*

"How is Gran?" Eve asked.

"She's fine." Alexandra hesitated. "Eve, I don't know what

happened between you two, but you know if there's anything I can do to help, I'll—"

Eve sighed. "She didn't tell you?"

"No. She won't discuss it."

"I don't blame her. The poor dear probably feels as guilty as hell. I met a wonderful young doctor. We were going to be married. We went to bed together. Gran found out about it. She told me to get out of the house, that she never wanted to see me again. I'm afraid our grandmother is very old-fashioned, Alex."

She watched the look of dismay on Alexandra's face. "That's terrible! The two of you must go to Gran. I'm sure she would—"

"He was killed in an airplane accident."

"Oh, Eve! Why didn't you tell me this before?"

"I was too ashamed to tell anyone, even you." She squeezed her sister's hand. "And you know I tell you everything."

"Let me talk to Gran. I'll explain—"

"No! I have too much pride. Promise me you'll never discuss this with her. Ever!"

"But I'm sure she would—"

"Promise!"

Alexandra sighed. "All right."

"Believe me, I'm very happy here. I come and go as I please. It's great!"

Alexandra looked at her sister and thought how much she had missed Eve.

Eve put her arm around Alexandra and began to tease. "Now, enough about me. Tell me what's going on in your life. Have you met Prince Charming yet? I'll bet you have!"

"No."

Eve studied her sister. It was a mirror image of herself, and she was determined to destroy it. "You will, darling."

"I'm in no hurry. I decided it's time I started earning a living. I talked to Gran about it. Next week I'm going to meet with the head of an advertising agency about a job."

They had lunch at a little bistro near Eve's apartment, and Eve insisted on paying. She wanted nothing from her sister.

When they were bidding each other good-bye, Alexandra said, "Eve, if you need any money—"

"Don't be silly, darling. I have more than enough."

Alexandra persisted. "Still, if you run short, you can have anything I've got."

Eve looked into Alexandra's eyes and said, "I'm counting on that." She smiled. "But I really don't need a thing, Alex." She did not need crumbs. She intended to have the whole cake. The question was: How was she going to get it?

There was a weekend party in Nassau.

"It wouldn't be the same without you, Eve. All your friends will be here."

The caller was Nita Ludwig, a girl whom Eve had known at school in Switzerland.

She would meet some new men. The present crop was tiresome.

"It sounds like fun," Eve said. "I'll be there."

That afternoon she pawned an emerald bracelet she had been given a week earlier by an infatuated insurance executive with a wife and three children, and bought some new summer outfits at Lord & Taylor and a round-trip ticket to Nassau. She was on the plane the following morning.

The Ludwig estate was a large, sprawling mansion on the beach. The main house had thirty rooms, and the smallest was larger than Eve's entire apartment. Eve was escorted to her room by a uniformed maid, who unpacked for her while Eve freshened up. Then she went down to meet her fellow guests.

There were sixteen people in the drawing room, and they had one thing in common: They were wealthy. Nita Ludwig was a firm believer in the "birds of a feather" philosophy. These people felt the same way about the same things; they were comfortable with one another because they spoke the same language. They shared the commonality of the best boarding schools and colleges, luxurious estates, yachts, private jets and tax problems.

A columnist had dubbed them the "jet set," an appellation they derided publicly and enjoyed privately. They were the privileged, the chosen few, set apart from all others by a discriminating god. Let the rest of the world believe that money could not buy everything. These people knew better. Money bought them beauty and love and luxury and a place in heaven. And it was from all this that Eve had been excluded by the whim of a narrow-minded old lady. *But not for long,* Eve thought.

She entered the drawing room and the conversation dropped as Eve walked in. In a room full of beautiful women, she was the most beautiful of all. Nita took Eve around to greet her friends, and to introduce her to the people she did not know. Eve was charming and pleasant, and she studied each man with a knowing eye, expertly selecting her targets. Most of the older men were married, but that only made it easier.

A bald-headed man dressed in plaid slacks and Hawaiian sport shirt came up to her. "I'll bet you get tired of people telling you you're beautiful, honey."

Eve rewarded him with a warm smile. "I never get tired of that, Mr.—?"

"Peterson. Call me Dan. You should be a Hollywood star."

"I'm afraid I have no talent for acting."

"I'll bet you've got a lot of other talents, though."

Eve smiled enigmatically. "You never know until you try, do you, Dan?"

He wet his lips. "You down here alone?"

"Yes."

"I've got my yacht anchored in the bay. Maybe you and I could take a little cruise tomorrow?"

"That sounds lovely," Eve said.

He grinned. "I don't know why we've never met before. I've known your grandmother, Kate, for years."

The smile stayed on Eve's face, but it took a great effort. "Gran's a darling," Eve said. "I think we'd better join the others."

"Sure, honey." He winked. "Remember tomorrow."

* * *

From that moment on, he was unable to get Eve alone again. She avoided him at lunch, and after lunch she borrowed one of the automobiles kept in the garage for guests and drove into town. She drove past Blackbeard's Tower and the lovely Ardastra Gardens where the colorful flamingos were on parade. She stopped at the waterfront to watch the fishing boats unload their catch of giant turtles, enormous lobsters, tropical fish and a brilliantly colored variety of conch shells, which would be polished and sold to the tourists.

The bay was smooth, and the sea sparkled like diamonds. Across the water Eve could see the crescent curve of Paradise Island Beach. A motorboat was leaving the dock at the beach, and as it picked up speed, the figure of a man suddenly rose into the sky, trailing behind the boat. It was a startling sight. He appeared to be hanging on to a metal bar fastened to a blue sail, his long, lean body stretched against the wind. *Para-sailing.* Eve watched, fascinated, as the motorboat roared toward the harbor, and the airborne figure swept closer. The boat approached the dock and made a sharp turn, and for an instant Eve caught a glimpse of the dark, handsome face of the man in the air, and then he was gone.

He walked into Nita Ludwig's drawing room five hours later, and Eve felt as though she had willed him there. She had known he would appear. Up close he was even more handsome. He was six foot three, with perfectly sculptured, tanned features, black eyes and a trim, athletic body. When he smiled, he revealed white, even teeth. He smiled down at Eve as Nita introduced him.

"This is George Mellis. Eve Blackwell."

"My God, you belong in the Louvre," George Mellis said. His voice was deep and husky, with the trace of an indefinable accent.

"Come along, darling," Nita commanded. "I'll introduce you to the other guests."

He waved her away. "Don't bother. I just met everybody."

Nita looked at the two of them thoughtfully. "I see. Well,

if I can do anything, call me." She walked away.

"Weren't you a little rude to her?" Eve asked.

He grinned. "I'm not responsible for what I say or do. I'm in love."

Eve laughed.

"I mean it. You're the most beautiful thing I've ever seen in my life."

"I was thinking the same about you."

Eve did not care whether this man had money or not. She was fascinated by him. It was more than his looks. There was a magnetism, a sense of power that excited her. No man had ever affected her this way before. "Who are you?" Eve asked.

"Nita told you. George Mellis."

"Who are you?" she repeated.

"Ah, you mean in the philosophical sense. The *real* me. Nothing colorful to tell, I'm afraid. I'm Greek. My family grows olives and other things."

That Mellis! The Mellis food brands could be found in every corner grocery store and supermarket in America.

"Are you married?" Eve asked.

He grinned. "Are you always this direct?"

"No."

"I'm not married."

The answer gave her an unexpected feeling of pleasure. Just looking at him made Eve want to possess him, to be possessed. "Why did you miss dinner?"

"The truth?"

"Yes."

"It's very personal."

She waited.

"I was busy persuading a young lady not to commit suicide." He said it matter-of-factly, as though it were a common occurrence.

"I hope you succeeded."

"For now. I hope you're not the suicidal type."

"No. I hope *you're* not."

George Mellis laughed aloud. "I love you," he said. "I really love you." He took Eve's arm, and his touch made her shiver.

He stayed at Eve's side all evening, and he was totally attentive to her, oblivious to everyone else. He had long, delicate hands, and they were constantly doing things for Eve: bringing her a drink, lighting her cigarette, touching her discreetly. His nearness set her body afire, and she could not wait to be alone with him.

Just after midnight when the guests began to retire to their rooms, George Mellis asked, "Which is your bedroom?"

"At the end of the north hall."

He nodded, his long-lashed eyes boring into hers.

Eve undressed and bathed and put on a new sheer, black negligee that clung to her figure. At one A.M. there was a discreet tap on the door. She hurried to open it, and George Mellis stepped in.

He stood there, his eyes filled with admiration. *"Matia mou,* you make the *Venus de Milo* look like a hag."

"I have an advantage over her," Eve whispered. "I have two arms."

And she put both arms around George Mellis and drew him to her. His kiss made something explode inside her. His lips pressed hard against hers, and she felt his tongue exploring her mouth.

"Oh, my God!" Eve moaned.

He started to strip off his jacket, and she helped him. In a moment he was free of his trousers and French shorts, and he was naked before her. He had the most glorious physique Eve had ever seen. He was hard and erect.

"Quick," Eve said. "Make love to me." She moved onto the bed, her body on fire.

He commanded, "Turn over. Give me your ass."

She looked up at him. "I—I don't—"

And he hit her on the mouth. She stared up at him in shock.

"Turn over."

"No."

He hit her again, harder, and the room began to swim in front of her.

"Please, no."

He hit her again, savagely. She felt his powerful hands turning her over, pulling her up on her knees.

"For God's sake," she gasped, "stop it! I'll scream."

He smashed his arm across the back of her neck, and Eve started to lose consciousness. Dimly, she felt him raise her hips higher into the air. He pulled her cheeks apart, and his body pressed against hers. There was a sudden, excruciating pain as he plunged deep inside her. She opened her mouth to scream, but she stopped in terror of what he might do to her.

She begged, "Oh, please, you're hurting me . . ."

She tried to pull away from him, but he was holding her hips tightly, plunging into her again and again, tearing her apart with his enormous penis. The pain was unbearable.

"Oh, God, no!" she whispered. "Stop it! Please stop it!"

He kept moving in, deeper and faster, and the last thing Eve remembered was a wild groan that came from deep inside him and seemed to explode in her ears.

When she regained consciousness and opened her eyes, George Mellis was sitting in a chair, fully dressed, smoking a cigarette. He moved over to the bed and stroked her forehead. She cringed from his touch.

"How do you feel, darling?"

Eve tried to sit up, but the pain was too great. She felt as though she had been ripped apart. "You goddamned animal . . ." Her voice was a ragged whisper.

He laughed. "I was gentle with you."

She looked at him in disbelief.

He smiled. "I can sometimes be very rough." He stroked her hair again. "But I love you, so I was kind. You'll get used to it, *Hree-se'e-moo*. I promise you."

If she had had a weapon at that moment, Eve would have killed him. "You're insane!"

She saw the gleam that came into his eyes, and she saw his hand clench into a fist, and in that instant she knew stark terror. He *was* insane.

She said quickly, "I didn't mean it. It's just that I—I've never experienced anything like that before. Please, I'd like to go to sleep now. Please."

George Mellis stared at her for a long moment, and then relaxed. He rose and walked over to the dressing table where Eve had put her jewelry. There was a platinum bracelet and an expensive diamond necklace lying there. He scooped up the necklace, examined it and slipped it into his pocket. "I'll keep this as a little souvenir."

She was afraid to open her mouth to protest.

"Good night, darling." And he walked back to the bed, leaned over and gently kissed Eve's lips.

She waited until he had gone, and then crawled out of bed, her body burning with pain. Every step was an agony. It was not until she had locked the bedroom door that she felt safe again. She was not sure she would be able to make it to the bathroom, and she fell back onto the bed, waiting for the pain to recede. She couldn't believe the enormity of the rage she felt. He had sodomized her—horribly and brutally. She wondered what he had done to that other girl who had wanted to commit suicide.

When Eve finally dragged herself into the bathroom and looked in the mirror, she was aghast. Her face was bruised and discolored where he had hit her, and one eye was almost swollen shut. She ran a hot bath and crawled into it like a wounded animal, letting the soothing water wash away the pain. Eve lay there for a long time, and, finally, when the water was starting to cool, she got out of the tub and took a few tentative steps. The pain had lessened, but it was still agonizing. She lay awake for the rest of the night, terrified that he might return.

When Eve arose at dawn, she saw that the sheets were stained with her blood. She was going to make him pay for that. She walked into the bathroom, moving carefully, and ran another hot bath. Her face was even more swollen and the bruises were livid. She dipped a washcloth into cold water and applied it to her cheek and eye. Then she lay in the tub, thinking about George Mellis. There was something puzzling about his behavior that had nothing to do with his sadism. And she suddenly realized what it was. The necklace. Why had he taken it?

Two hours later, Eve went downstairs to join the other guests for breakfast, even though she had no appetite. She badly needed to talk to Nita Ludwig.

"My God! What happened to your face?" Nita asked.

Eve smiled ruefully. "The silliest thing. I got up in the middle of the night to go to the loo, and I didn't bother turning on the light. I walked right into one of your fancy doors."

"Would you like to have a doctor look at that?"

"It's nothing," Eve assured her. "It's just a little bruise." Eve looked around. "Where's George Mellis?"

"He's out playing tennis. He's one of the top-seeded players. He said to tell you he'd see you at lunch. I think he really likes you, darling."

"Tell me about him," Eve said casually. "What's his background?"

"George? He comes from a long line of wealthy Greeks. He's the oldest son, and he's filthy rich. He works at a New York brokerage firm, Hanson and Hanson."

"He's not in the family business?"

"No. He probably hates olives. Anyway, with the Mellis fortune, he doesn't have to work. I suppose he does it just to occupy his days." She grinned and said, "His nights are full enough."

"Are they?"

"Darling, George Mellis is the most eligible bachelor around. The girls can't wait to pull their little panties down for him. They all see themselves as the future Mrs. Mellis. Frankly, if my husband weren't so damned jealous, I'd go for George myself. Isn't he a gorgeous hunk of animal?"

"Gorgeous," Eve said.

* * *

George Mellis walked onto the terrace where Eve was seated alone, and in spite of herself, she felt a stab of fear.

He walked up to her and said, "Good morning, Eve. Are you all right?" His face was filled with genuine concern. He touched her bruised cheek gently. "My darling, you are so beautiful." He pulled up a chair and straddled it, sitting across from her, and gestured toward the sparkling sea. "Have you ever seen anything so lovely?"

It was as though the previous night had never happened. She listened to George Mellis as he went on talking, and she felt once again the powerful magnetism of the man. Even after the nightmare she had experienced, she could still feel *that*. It was incredible. *He looks like a Greek god. He belongs in a museum. He belongs in an insane asylum.*

"I have to return to New York tonight," George Mellis was saying. "Where can I call you?"

"I just moved," Eve said quickly. "I don't have a telephone yet. Let me call you."

"All right, my darling." He grinned. "You really enjoyed last night, didn't you?"

Eve could not believe her ears.

"I have many things to teach you, Eve," he whispered.

And I have something to teach you, Mr. Mellis, Eve promised herself.

The moment she returned home, Eve telephoned Dorothy Hollister. In New York, where an insatiable segment of the media covered the comings and goings of the so-called beautiful people, Dorothy was the fountainhead of information. She had been married to a socialite, and when he divorced her for his twenty-one-year-old secretary, Dorothy Hollister was forced to go to work. She took a job that suited her talents well: She became a gossip columnist. Because she knew everyone in the milieu she was writing about, and because they believed she could be trusted, few people kept any secrets from her.

If anyone could tell Eve about George Mellis, it would be Dorothy Hollister. Eve invited her to lunch at La Pyramide.

Hollister was a heavyset woman with a fleshy face, dyed red hair, a loud, raucous voice and a braying laugh. She was loaded down with jewelry—all fake.

When they had ordered, Eve said casually, "I was in the Bahamas last week. It was lovely there."

"I know you were," Dorothy Hollister said. "I have Nita Ludwig's guest list. Was it a fun party?"

Eve shrugged. "I saw a lot of old friends. I met an interesting man named"—she paused, her brow wrinkled in thought—"George somebody. Miller, I think. A Greek."

Dorothy Hollister laughed, a loud, booming laugh that could be heard across the room. "Mellis, dear. George Mellis."

"That's right. Mellis. Do you know him?"

"I've seen him. I thought I was going to turn into a pillar of salt. My God, he's fantastic looking."

"What's his background, Dorothy?"

Dorothy Hollister looked around, then leaned forward confidentially. "No one knows this, but you'll keep it to yourself, won't you? George is the black sheep of the family. His family is in the wholesale food business, and they're too rich for words, my dear. George was supposed to take over the business, but he got in so many scrapes over there with girls and boys and goats, for all I know, that his father and his brothers finally got fed up and shipped him out of the country."

Eve was absorbing every word.

"They cut the poor boy off without a drachma, so he had to go to work to support himself."

So that explained the necklace!

"Of course, he doesn't have to worry. One of these days George will marry rich." She looked over at Eve and asked, "Are you interested, sweetie?"

"Not really."

Eve was more than interested. George Mellis might be the key she had been looking for. The key to her fortune.

Early the next morning, she telephoned him at the brokerage firm where he worked. He recognized her voice immediately.

"I've been going mad waiting for your call, Eve. We'll have dinner tonight and—"

"No. Lunch, tomorrow."

He hesitated, surprised. "All right. I was supposed to have lunch with a customer, but I'll put him off."

Eve did not believe it was a *him*. "Come to my apartment," Eve said. She gave him the address. "I'll see you at twelve-thirty."

"I'll be there." She could hear the smug satisfaction in his voice.

George Mellis was due for a surprise.

He arrived thirty minutes late, and Eve realized it was a pattern with him. It was not a deliberate rudeness, it was an indifference, the knowledge that people would always wait for him. His pleasures would be there for him whenever he bothered to reach out and take them. With his incredible looks and charm, the world belonged to him. Except for one thing: He was poor. That was his vulnerable point.

George looked around the little apartment, expertly appraising the value of its contents. "Very pleasant."

He moved toward Eve, his arms outstretched. "I've thought about you every minute."

She evaded his embrace. "Wait. I have something to tell you, George."

His black eyes bored into hers. "We'll talk later."

"We'll talk now." She spoke slowly and distinctly. "If you ever touch me like that again, I'm going to kill you."

He looked at her, his lips curved in a half smile. "What kind of joke is that?"

"It's not a joke. I mean it. I have a business proposition for you."

There was a puzzled expression on his face. "You called me here to discuss business?"

"Yes. I don't know how much you make conning silly old ladies into buying stocks and bonds, but I'm sure it's not enough."

His face went dark with anger. "Are you crazy? My family—"

"Your family is rich—you're not. My family is rich—*I'm* not. We're both in the same leaky rowboat, darling. I know a way we can turn it into a yacht." She stood there, watching his curiosity get the better of his anger.

"You'd better tell me what you're talking about."

"It's quite simple. I've been disinherited from a very large fortune. My sister Alexandra hasn't."

"What does that have to do with me?"

"If you married Alexandra, that fortune would be yours—ours."

"Sorry. I could never stand the idea of being tied down to anyone."

"As it happens," Eve assured him, "that's no problem. My sister has always been accident-prone."

27

Berkley and Mathews Advertising Agency was the diadem in Madison Avenue's roster of agencies. Its annual billings exceeded the combined billings of its two nearest competitors, chiefly because its major account was Kruger-Brent, Ltd., and its dozens of worldwide subsidiaries. More than seventy-five account executives, copywriters, creative directors, photographers, engravers, artists and media experts were employed on the Kruger-Brent account alone. It came as no surprise, therefore, that when Kate Blackwell telephoned Aaron Berkley to ask him if he could find a position in his agency for Alexandra, a place was found for her instantly. If Kate Blackwell had desired it, they would probably have made Alexandra president of the agency.

"I believe my granddaughter is interested in being a copywriter," Kate informed Aaron Berkley.

Berkley assured Kate that there just happened to be a copywriter vacancy, and that Alexandra could start any time she wished.

She went to work the following Monday.

* * *

Few Madison Avenue advertising agencies are actually located on Madison Avenue, but Berkley and Mathews was an exception. The agency owned a large, modern building at the corner of Madison and Fifty-seventh Street. The agency occupied eight floors of the building and leased the other floors. In order to save a salary, Aaron Berkley and his partner, Norman Mathews, decided Alexandra Blackwell would replace a young copywriter hired six months earlier. The word spread rapidly. When the staff learned the young woman who was fired was being replaced by the granddaughter of the agency's biggest client, there was general indignation. Without even having met Alexandra, the consensus was that she was a spoiled bitch who had probably been sent there to spy on them.

When Alexandra reported for work, she was escorted to the huge, modern office of Aaron Berkley, where both Berkley and Mathews waited to greet her. The two partners looked nothing alike. Berkley was tall and thin, with a full head of white hair, and Mathews was short, tubby and completely bald. They had two things in common: They were brilliant advertising men who had created some of the most famous slogans of the past decade; and they were absolute tyrants. They treated their employees like chattels, and the only reason the employees stood for such treatment was that anyone who had worked for Berkley and Mathews could work at any advertising agency in the world. It was *the* training ground.

Also present in the office when Alexandra arrived was Lucas Pinkerton, a vice-president of the firm, a smiling man with an obsequious manner and cold eyes. Pinkerton was younger than the senior partners, but what he lacked in age, he made up for in vindictiveness toward the men and women who worked under him.

Aaron Berkley ushered Alexandra to a comfortable armchair. "What can I get you, Miss Blackwell? Would you like some coffee, tea?"

"Nothing, thank you."

"So. You're going to work with us here as a copywriter."

"I really appreciate your giving me this opportunity, Mr. Berkley. I know I have a great deal to learn, but I'll work very hard."

"No need for that," Norman Mathews said quickly. He caught himself. "I mean—you can't rush a learning experience like this. You take all the time you want."

"I'm sure you'll be very happy here," Aaron Berkley added. "You'll be working with the best people in the business."

One hour later, Alexandra was thinking, *They may be the best, but they're certainly not the friendliest.* Lucas Pinkerton had taken Alexandra around to introduce her to the staff, and the reception everywhere had been icy. They acknowledged her presence and then quickly found other things to do. Alexandra sensed their resentment, but she had no idea what had caused it. Pinkerton led her into a smoke-filled conference room. Against one wall was a cabinet filled with Clios and Art Directors' awards. Seated around a table were a woman and two men, all of them chain-smoking. The woman was short and dumpy, with rust-colored hair. The men were in their middle thirties, pale and harassed-looking.

Pinkerton said, "This is the creative team you'll be working with. Alice Koppel, Vince Barnes and Marty Bergheimer. This is Miss Blackwell."

The three of them stared at Alexandra.

"Well, I'll leave you to get acquainted with one another," Pinkerton said. He turned to Vince Barnes. "I'll expect the new perfume copy on my desk by tomorrow morning. See that Miss Blackwell has everything she needs." And he left.

"What do you need?" Vince Barnes asked.

The question caught Alexandra off guard. "I—I guess I just need to learn the advertising business."

Alice Koppel said sweetly, "You've come to the right place, Miss Blackwell. We're dying to play teacher."

"Lay off," Marty Bergheimer told her.

Alexandra was puzzled. "Have I done something to offend any of you?"

Marty Bergheimer replied, "No, Miss Blackwell. We're just under a lot of pressure here. We're working on a perfume campaign, and so far Mr. Berkley and Mr. Mathews are underwhelmed by what we've delivered."

"I'll try not to be a bother," Alexandra promised.

"That would be peachy," Alice Koppel said.

The rest of the day went no better. There was not a smile in the place. One of their co-workers had been summarily fired because of this rich bitch, and they were going to make her pay.

At the end of Alexandra's first day, Aaron Berkley and Norman Mathews came into the little office Alexandra had been assigned, to make sure she was comfortable. The gesture was not lost on Alexandra's fellow workers.

Everyone in the agency was on a first-name basis—except for Alexandra. She was Miss Blackwell to everyone.

"Alexandra," she said.

"Right."

And the next time they addressed her, it was "Miss Blackwell."

Alexandra was eager to learn and to make a contribution. She attended think-tank meetings where the copywriters brainstormed ideas. She watched art editors draw up their designs. She listened to Lucas Pinkerton tear apart the copy that was brought to him for approval. He was a nasty, mean-spirited man, and Alexandra felt sorry for the copywriters who suffered under him. Alexandra found herself shuttling from floor to floor for meetings with department heads, meetings with clients, photographic sessions, strategy discussion meetings. She kept her mouth shut, listened and learned. At the end of her first week, she felt as though she had been there a month. She came home exhausted, not from the work but from the tension that her presence seemed to create.

When Kate asked how the job was going, Alexandra replied, "Fine, Gran. It's very interesting."

"I'm sure you'll do well, Alex. If you have any problems, just see Mr. Berkley or Mr. Mathews."

That was the last thing Alexandra intended to do.

On the following Monday Alexandra went to work determined to find a way to solve her problem. There were daily morning and afternoon coffee breaks, and the conversation was easy and casual.

"Did you hear what happened over at National Media? Some genius there wanted to call attention to the great year they had, so he printed their financial report in *The New York Times* in red ink!"

"Remember that airline promotion: *Fly Your Wife Free*? It was a smash until the airline sent letters of appreciation to the wives and got back a flood of mail demanding to know who their husbands had flown with. They—"

Alexandra walked in, and the conversation stopped dead.

"Can I get you some coffee, Miss Blackwell?"

"Thank you. I can get it."

There was silence while Alexandra fed a quarter into the coffee machine. When she left, the conversation started again.

"Did you hear about the Pure Soap foul-up? The angelic-looking model they used turned out to be a porno star . . ."

At noon Alexandra said to Alice Koppel, "If you're free for lunch, I thought we might—"

"Sorry. I have a date."

Alexandra looked at Vince Barnes. "Me, too," he said.

She looked at Marty Bergheimer. "I'm all booked up."

Alexandra was too upset to eat lunch. They were making her feel as though she were a pariah, and she found herself getting angry. She did not intend to give up. She was going to find a way to reach them, to let them know that deep down under the Blackwell name she was one of *them*. She sat at meetings and listened to Aaron Berkley and Norman Mathews and Lucas Pinkerton tongue-lash the creators who were merely trying to do their jobs as well as they could. Alexandra sympathized, but they did not want her sympathy. Or her.

Alexandra waited three days before trying again. She said to Alice Koppel, "I heard of a wonderful little Italian restaurant near here—"

"I don't eat Italian food."

She turned to Vince Barnes. "I'm on a diet."

Alexandra looked at Marty Bergheimer. "I'm going to eat Chinese."

Alexandra's face was flushed. They did not want to be seen with her. *Well, to hell with them. To hell with all of them.* She had had enough. She had gone out of her way to try to make friends, and each time she had been slapped down. Working there was a mistake. She would find another job somewhere with a company that her grandmother had nothing to do with. She would quit at the end of the week. *But I'm going to make you all remember I was here,* Alexandra thought grimly.

At 1:00 P.M. on Thursday, everyone except the receptionist at the switchboard was out to lunch. Alexandra stayed behind. She had observed that in the executive offices there were intercoms connecting the various departments, so that if an executive wanted to talk to an underling, all he had to do was press a button on the talk box where the employee's name was written on a card. Alexandra slipped into the deserted offices of Aaron Berkley and Norman Mathews and Lucas Pinkerton and spent the next hour changing all the cards around. Thus it was that early that afternoon Lucas Pinkerton pressed down the key that connected him to his chief copywriter and said, "Get your ass in here. Now!"

There was a moment of stunned silence, then Norman Mathews's voice bellowed, "What did you say?"

Pinkerton stared at the machine, transfixed. "Mr. Mathews, is that you?"

"You're damned right it is. Get *your* fucking ass in *here.* Now!"

A minute later, a copywriter pressed down a button on the machine on his desk and said, "I've got some copy for you to run downstairs."

Aaron Berkley's voice roared back at him. "You *what?*"

It was the beginning of pandemonium. It took four hours to straighten out the mess that Alexandra had created, and it was the best four hours that the employees of Berkley and Mathews had ever known. Each time a fresh incident occurred, they whooped with joy. The executives were being buzzed to run errands, fetch cigarettes and repair a broken toilet. Aaron Berkley and Norman Mathews and Lucas Pinkerton turned the place upside down trying to find out who the culprit was, but no one knew anything.

The only one who had seen Alexandra go into the various offices was Fran, the woman on the switchboard, but she hated her bosses more than she hated Alexandra, so all she would say was, "I didn't see a soul."

That night when Fran was in bed with Vince Barnes, she related what had happened.

He sat up in bed. "The *Blackwell* girl did it? I'll be a sonofabitch!"

The following morning when Alexandra walked into her office, Vince Barnes, Alice Koppel and Marty Bergheimer were there, waiting. They stared at her in silence. "Is something wrong?" Alexandra asked.

"Not a thing, Alex," Alice Koppel said. "The boys and I were just wondering if you'd like to join us for lunch. We know this great little Italian joint near here . . ."

28

From the time she was a little girl, Eve Blackwell had been aware of her ability to manipulate people. Before, it had always been a game with her, but now it was deadly serious. She had been treated shabbily, deprived of a vast fortune that was rightfully hers, by her scheming sister and her vindictive old grandmother. They were going to pay in full for what they had done to her, and the thought of it gave Eve such intense pleasure that it almost brought her to orgasm. Their lives were now in her hands.

Eve worked out her plan carefully and meticulously, orchestrating every move. In the beginning, George Mellis had been a reluctant conspirator.

"Christ, it's too dangerous. I don't need to get involved in anything like this," he argued. "I can get all the money I need."

"How?" Eve asked contemptuously. "By laying a lot of fat women with blue hair? Is that how you want to spend the rest of your life? What happens when you put on a little weight and start to get a few wrinkles around your eyes? No, George, you'll never have another opportunity like this. If you listen to me, you and I can own one of the largest conglomerates in the world. You hear me? *Own* it."

"How do you know this plan will work?"

"Because I'm the greatest living expert on my grandmother and my sister. Believe me, it will work."

Eve sounded confident, but she had reservations and they concerned George Mellis. Eve knew she could do her part, but she was not sure George would be able to do his. He was unstable, and there was no room for error. One mistake, and the whole plan would fall apart.

She said to him now, "Make up your mind. Are you in or out?"

He studied her for a long time. "I'm in." He moved close to her and stroked her shoulders. His voice was husky. "I want to be all the way in."

Eve felt a sexual thrill go through her. "All right," she whispered, "but we do it my way."

They were in bed. Naked, he was the most magnificent animal Eve had ever seen. And the most dangerous, but that only added to her excitement. She had the weapon now to control him. She nibbled at his body, slowly moving down toward his groin, tiny, teasing bites that made his penis grow stiff and hard.

"Fuck me, George," Eve said.

"Turn over."

"No. My way."

"I don't enjoy that."

"I know. You'd like me to be a tight-assed little boy, wouldn't you, darling? I'm not. I'm a woman. Get on top of me."

He mounted her and put his tumescent penis inside her. "I can't be satisfied this way, Eve."

She laughed. "I don't care, sweetheart. *I* can."

She began to move her hips, thrusting against him, feeling him going deeper and deeper inside her. She had orgasm after orgasm, and watched his frustration grow. He wanted to hurt her, to make her scream with pain, but he dared not.

"Again!" Eve commanded. And he pounded his body into her

until she moaned aloud with pleasure. "Ahh-h-h ... that's enough for now."

He withdrew and lay at her side. He reached for her breasts. "Now it's my—"

And she said curtly, "Get dressed."

He rose from the bed, trembling with frustration and rage. Eve lay in bed watching him put on his clothes, a tight smile on her face. "You've been a good boy, George. It's time you got your reward. I'm going to turn Alexandra over to you."

Overnight, everything had changed for Alexandra. What was to have been her last day at Berkley and Mathews had turned into a triumph for her. She had gone from outcast to heroine. News of her caper spread all over Madison Avenue.

"You're a legend in your own time," Vince Barnes grinned. Now she was one of them.

Alexandra enjoyed her work, particularly the creative sessions that went on every morning. She knew this was not what she wanted to do for the rest of her life, but she was not sure what she wanted. She had had at least a dozen proposals of marriage, and she had been tempted by one or two of them, but something had been lacking. She simply had not found the right man.

On Friday morning, Eve telephoned to invite Alexandra to lunch. "There's a new French restaurant that just opened. I hear the food is marvelous."

Alexandra was delighted to hear from her sister. She was concerned about Eve. Alexandra telephoned her two or three times a week, but Eve was either out or too busy to see her. So now, even though Alexandra had an engagement, she said, "I'd love to have lunch with you."

The restaurant was chic and expensive, and the bar was filled with patrons waiting for tables. Eve had had to use her grandmother's name in order to get a reservation. It galled her, and she thought, *Just wait. One day you'll be begging me to eat at your crummy restaurant.* Eve was already seated when

Alexandra arrived. She watched Alexandra as the maître d' escorted her to the table, and she had the odd sensation she was watching herself approach the table.

Eve greeted her sister with a kiss on the cheek. "You look absolutely marvelous, Alex. Work must agree with you."

They ordered, and then caught up with each other's lives.

"How's the job going?" Eve asked.

Alexandra told Eve everything that was happening to her, and Eve gave Alexandra a carefully edited version of her own life. In the midst of their conversation, Eve glanced up. George Mellis was standing there. He was looking at the two of them, momentarily confused. *My God,* Eve realized, *he doesn't know which one I am!*

"George!" she said.

He turned to her in relief. "Eve!"

Eve said, "What a pleasant surprise." She nodded toward Alexandra. "I don't believe you've met my sister. Alex, may I present George Mellis."

George took Alexandra's hand and said, "Enchanted." Eve had mentioned that her sister was a twin, but it had not occurred to him that they would be identical twins.

Alexandra was staring at George, fascinated.

Eve said, "Won't you join us?"

"I wish I could. I'm afraid I'm late for an appointment. Another time, perhaps." He looked at Alexandra. "And soon, I hope."

They watched him leave. "Good heavens!" Alexandra said. "Who was *that?*"

"Oh, he's a friend of Nita Ludwig. I met him at her house party."

"Am I crazy, or is he as stunning as I think he is?"

Eve laughed. "He's not my type, but women seem to find him attractive."

"I would think so! Is he married?"

"No. But it's not because they aren't out there trying, darling. George is very rich. You might say he has everything: looks, money, social background." And Eve skillfully changed the subject.

When Eve asked for the check, the captain told her it had been taken care of by Mr. Mellis.

Alexandra was unable to stop thinking about George Mellis. On Monday afternoon, Eve called Alexandra and said, "Well, it looks like you made a hit, darling. George Mellis called me and asked for your telephone number. Is it all right to give it to him?"

Alexandra was surprised to find that she was smiling. "If you're sure *you're* not interested in—"

"I told you, Alex, he's not my type."

"Then I don't mind if you give him my number."

They chatted a few minutes more, and Eve hung up. She replaced the receiver and looked up at George, who was lying next to her on the bed, naked. "The lady said yes."

"How soon?"

"When I tell you."

Alexandra tried to forget that George Mellis was going to telephone her, but the more she tried to put him out of her mind, the more she thought about him. She had never been particularly attracted to handsome men, for she had found that most of them were self-centered. But George Mellis, Alexandra thought, seemed different. There was an overpowering quality about him. The mere touch of his hand had stirred her. *You're crazy,* she told herself. *You've only seen the man for two minutes.*

He did not call all that week, and Alexandra's emotions went from impatience to frustration to anger. *To hell with him,* she thought. *He's found someone else. Good!*

When the phone rang at the end of the following week and Alexandra heard his deep, husky voice, her anger dissipated as if by magic.

"This is George Mellis," he said. "We met briefly when you and your sister were having lunch. Eve said you wouldn't mind if I telephoned you."

"She did mention that you might call," Alexandra said casually. "By the way, thank you for the lunch."

"You deserve a feast. You deserve a monument."

Alexandra laughed, enjoying his extravagance.

"I wonder if you would care to have dinner with me one evening?"

"Why—I—yes. That would be nice."

"Wonderful. If you had said no, I should have killed myself."

"Please don't," Alexandra said. "I hate eating alone."

"So do I. I know a little restaurant on Mulberry Street: Matoon's. It's very obscure, but the food is—"

"*Matoon's!* I love it!" Alexandra exclaimed. "It's my favorite."

"You know it?" There was surprise in his voice.

"Oh, yes."

George looked over at Eve and grinned. He had to admire her ingenuity. She had briefed him on all of Alexandra's likes and dislikes. George Mellis knew everything there was to know about Eve's sister.

When George finally replaced the receiver, Eve thought, *It's started.*

It was the most enchanting evening of Alexandra's life. One hour before George Mellis was due, a dozen pink balloons arrived, with an orchid attached. Alexandra had been filled with a fear that her imagination might have led her to expect too much, but the moment she saw George Mellis again, all her doubts were swept away. She felt once again his overpowering magnetism.

They had a drink at the house and then went on to the restaurant.

"Would you like to look at the menu?" George asked. "Or shall I order for you?"

Alexandra had her favorite dishes here, but she wanted to please George. "Why don't you order?"

He chose every one of Alexandra's favorites, and she had the heady feeling he was reading her mind. They dined on stuffed artichokes, veal Matoon, a specialty of the house, and angel hair, a delicate pasta. They had a salad that George mixed at the table with a deft skill.

"Do you cook?" Alexandra asked.

"Ah, it's one of the passions of my life. My mother taught me. She was a brilliant cook."

"Are you close to your family, George?"

He smiled, and Alexandra thought it was the most attractive smile she had ever seen.

"I'm Greek," he said simply. "I'm the oldest of three brothers and two sisters, and we are like one." A look of sadness came into his eyes. "Leaving them was the most difficult thing I ever had to do. My father and my brothers begged me to stay. We have a large business, and they felt I was needed there."

"Why didn't you stay?"

"I will probably seem a fool to you, but I prefer to make my own way. It has always been difficult for me to accept gifts from anyone, and the business was a gift handed down from my grandfather to my father. No, I will take nothing from my father. Let my brothers have my share."

How Alexandra admired him.

"Besides," George added softly, "if I had stayed in Greece, I never would have met you."

Alexandra felt herself blushing. "You've never been married?"

"No. I used to get engaged once a day," he teased, "but at the last moment I always felt there was something wrong." He leaned forward, and his voice was earnest. "Beautiful Alexandra, you are going to think me very old-fashioned, but when I get married, it will be forever. One woman is enough for me, but it must be the right woman."

"I think that's lovely," she murmured.

"And you?" George Mellis asked. "Have you ever been in love?"

"No."

"How unlucky for someone," he said. "But how lucky for—"

At that moment, the waiter appeared with dessert. Alexandra

was dying to ask George to finish the sentence, but she was afraid to.

Alexandra had never felt so completely at ease with anyone. George Mellis seemed so genuinely interested in her that she found herself telling him about her childhood, her life, the experiences she had stored up and treasured.

George Mellis prided himself on being an expert on women. He knew that beautiful women were usually the most insecure, for men concentrated on that beauty, leaving the women feeling like objects rather than human beings. When George was with a beautiful woman, he never mentioned her looks. He made the woman feel that he was interested in her mind, her feelings, that he was a soul mate sharing her dreams. It was an extraordinary experience for Alexandra. She told George about Kate, and about Eve.

"Your sister does not live with you and your grandmother?"

"No. She—Eve wanted an apartment of her own."

Alexandra could not imagine why George Mellis had not been attracted to her sister. Whatever the reason, Alexandra was grateful. During the course of the dinner, Alexandra noted that every woman in the place was aware of George, but not once did he look around or take his eyes from her.

Over coffee, George said, "I don't know if you like jazz, but there's a club on St. Marks Place called the Five Spot . . ."

"Where Cecil Taylor plays!"

He looked at Alexandra in astonishment. "You've been there?"

"Often!" Alexandra laughed. "I love him! It's incredible how we share the same tastes."

George replied quietly, "It's like some kind of miracle."

They listened to Cecil Taylor's spellbinding piano playing, long solos that rocked the room with arpeggios and rippling glissandi. From there they went to a bar on Bleecker Street, where the customers drank, ate popcorn, threw darts and listened to good piano music. Alexandra watched as George got into a dart contest with one of the regular patrons. The man was good, but he never had a chance. George played with a grim intensity that was almost frightening. It was only a game, but he played it as though it meant life or death. *He's a man who has to win,* Alexandra thought.

It was 2:00 A.M. when they left the bar, and Alexandra hated for the evening to end.

George sat beside Alexandra in the chauffeur-driven Rolls-Royce he had rented. He did not speak. He just looked at her. The resemblance between the two sisters was startling. *I wonder if their bodies are alike.* He visualized Alexandra in bed with him, writhing and screaming with pain.

"What are you thinking?" Alexandra asked.

He looked away from her so she could not read his eyes. "You'll laugh at me."

"I won't. I promise."

"I wouldn't blame you if you did. I suppose I'm considered something of a playboy. You know the life—yachting trips and parties, and all the rest of it."

"Yes . . ."

He fixed his dark eyes on Alexandra. "I think you are the one woman who could change all that. Forever."

Alexandra felt her pulse quicken. "I—I don't know what to say."

"Please. Don't say anything." His lips were very close to hers, and Alexandra was ready. But he made no move. *Don't make any advances,* Eve had warned. *Not on the first night. If you do, you become one of a long line of Romeos dying to get their hands on her and her fortune. She has to make the first move.*

And so, George Mellis merely held Alexandra's hand in his until the car glided to a smooth stop in front of the Blackwell mansion. George escorted Alexandra to her front door. She turned to him and said, "I can't tell you how much I've enjoyed this evening."

"It was magic for me."

Alexandra's smile was bright enough to light up the street. "Good night, George," she whispered. And she disappeared inside.

*　*　*

Fifteen minutes later, Alexandra's phone rang. "Do you know what I just did? I telephoned my family. I told them about the wonderful woman I was with tonight. Sleep well, lovely Alexandra."

When he hung up, George Mellis thought, *After we're married, I will call my family. And I'll tell them all to go fuck themselves.*

29

Alexandra did not hear from George Mellis again. Not that day, or the next, or the rest of that week. Every time the phone rang, she rushed to pick it up, but she was always disappointed. She could not imagine what had gone wrong. She kept replaying the evening in her mind: *I think you are the one woman who could change all that forever,* and *I telephoned my mother and father and brothers and told them about the wonderful woman I was with tonight.* Alexandra went through a litany of reasons why he had not telephoned her.

She had offended him in some way without realizing it.

He liked her too much, was afraid of falling in love with her and had made up his mind never to see her again.

He had decided she was not his type.

He had been in a terrible accident and was lying helpless in a hospital somewhere.

He was dead.

When Alexandra could stand it no longer, she telephoned Eve. Alexandra forced herself to make small talk for a full minute before she blurted out, "Eve, you haven't heard from George Mellis lately, by any chance, have you?"

"Why, no. I thought he was going to call you about dinner."

"We did have dinner—last week."

"And you haven't heard from him since?"

"No."

"He's probably busy."

No one is that busy, Alexandra thought. Aloud she said, "Probably."

"Forget about George Mellis, darling. There's a very attractive Canadian I'd like you to meet. He owns an airline and . . ."

When Eve had hung up, she sat back, smiling. She wished her grandmother could have known how beautifully she had planned everything.

"Hey, what's eating you?" Alice Koppel asked.

"I'm sorry," Alexandra replied.

She had been snapping at everyone all morning. It had been two full weeks since she had heard from George Mellis, and Alexandra was angry—not with him, but with herself for not being able to forget him. He owed her nothing. They were strangers who had shared an evening together, and she was acting as though she expected him to marry her, for God's sake. George Mellis could have any woman in the world. Why on earth would he want her?

Even her grandmother had noticed how irritable she had become. "What's the matter with you, child? Are they working you too hard at that agency?"

"No, Gran. It's just that I—I haven't been sleeping well lately."

When she did sleep, she had erotic dreams about George Mellis. *Damn him!* She wished Eve had never introduced him to her.

The call came at the office the following afternoon. "Alex? George Mellis." As though she didn't hear that deep voice in her dreams.

"Alex? Are you there?"

"Yes, I'm here." She was filled with mixed emotions. She

did not know whether to laugh or cry. He was a thoughtless, selfish egotist, and she did not care whether she ever saw him again.

"I wanted to call you sooner," George apologized, "but I just returned from Athens a few minutes ago."

Alexandra's heart melted. "You've been in Athens?"

"Yes. Remember the evening we had dinner together?"

Alexandra remembered.

"The next morning Steve, my brother, telephoned me— My father had a heart attack."

"Oh, George!" She felt so guilty for having thought such terrible things about him. "How is he?"

"He's going to be all right, thank God. But I felt as though I was being torn in pieces. He begged me to come back to Greece and take over the family business."

"Are you going to?" She was holding her breath.

"No."

She exhaled.

"I know now that my place is here. There isn't one day or one hour that's gone by that I haven't thought about you. When can I see you?"

Now! "I'm free for dinner this evening."

He was almost tempted to name another of Alexandra's favorite restaurants. Instead he said, "Wonderful. Where would you like to dine?"

"Anywhere. I don't care. Would you like to have dinner at the house?"

"No." He was not ready to meet Kate yet. *Whatever you do, stay away from Kate Blackwell for now. She's your biggest obstacle.* "I'll pick you up at eight o'clock," George told her.

Alexandra hung up, kissed Alice Koppel, Vince Barnes and Marty Bergheimer and said, "I'm off to the hairdresser. I'll see you all tomorrow."

They watched her race out of the office.

"It's a man," Alice Koppel said.

* * *

They had dinner at Maxwell's Plum. A captain led them past the crowded horseshoe bar near the front door and up the stairs to the dining room. They ordered.

"Did you think about me while I was away?" George asked.

"Yes." She felt she had to be completely honest with this man—this man who was so open, so vulnerable. "When I didn't hear from you, I thought something terrible might have happened. I—I got panicky. I don't think I could have stood it another day."

Full marks for Eve, George thought. *Sit tight,* Eve had said. *I'll tell you when to call her.* For the first time George had the feeling the plan really was going to work. Until now he had let it nibble at the edges of his mind, toying with the idea of controlling the incredible Blackwell fortune, but he had not really dared believe it. It had been merely a game that he and Eve had been playing. Looking at Alexandra now, seated across from him, her eyes filled with naked adoration, George Mellis knew it was no longer just a game. Alexandra was his. That was the first step in the plan. The other steps might be dangerous, but with Eve's help, he would handle them.

We're in this together all the way, George, and we'll share everything right down the middle.

George Mellis did not believe in partners. When he had what he wanted, when he had disposed of Alexandra, then he would take care of Eve. That thought gave him enormous pleasure.

"You're smiling," Alexandra said.

He put his hand over hers, and his touch warmed her. "I was thinking how nice it was our being here together. About our being *anywhere* together." He reached into his pocket and pulled out a jewel box. "I brought something for you from Greece."

"Oh, George . . ."

"Open it, Alex."

Inside the box was an exquisite diamond necklace.

"It's beautiful."

It was the one he had taken from Eve. *It's safe to give it to her,* Eve had told him. *She's never seen it.*

"It's too much. Really."

"It's not nearly enough. I'll enjoy watching you wear it."

"I—" Alexandra was trembling. "Thank you."

He looked at her plate. "You haven't eaten anything."

"I'm not hungry."

He saw the look in her eyes again and felt the familiar soaring sense of power. He had seen that look in the eyes of so many women: beautiful women, ugly women, rich women, poor women. He had used them. In one way or another, they had all given him something. But this one was going to give him more than all of them put together.

"What would you like to do?" His husky voice was an invitation.

She accepted it, simply and openly. "I want to be with you."

George Mellis had every right to be proud of his apartment. It was a tasteful jewel of a place, furnished by grateful lovers—men and women—who had tried to buy his affection with expensive gifts, and had succeeded, always temporarily.

"It's a lovely apartment," Alexandra exclaimed.

He went over to her and slowly turned her around so that the diamond necklace twinkled in the subdued lighting of the room. "It becomes you, darling."

And he kissed her gently, and then more urgently, and Alexandra was hardly aware when he led her into the bedroom. The room was done in tones of blue, with tasteful, masculine furniture. In the center of the room stood a large, king-size bed. George took Alexandra in his arms again and found that she was shaking. "Are you all right, *kale' mou*?"

"I—I'm a little nervous." She was terrified that she would disappoint this man. She took a deep breath and started to unbutton her dress.

George whispered, "Let me." He began to undress the exquisite blonde standing before him, and he remembered Eve's words: *Control yourself. If you hurt Alexandra, if she finds out what a pig you really are, you'll never see her again. Do you un-*

derstand that? Save your fists for your whores and your pretty little boys.

And so George tenderly undressed Alexandra and studied her nakedness. Her body was exactly the same as Eve's: beautiful and ripe and full. He had an overwhelming desire to bruise the white, delicate skin; to hit her, choke her, make her scream. *If you hurt her, you'll never see her again.*

He undressed and drew Alexandra close to his body. They stood there together, looking into each other's eyes, and then George gently led Alexandra to the bed and began to kiss her, slowly and lovingly, his tongue and fingers expertly exploring every crevice of her body until she was unable to wait another moment.

"Oh, please," she said. "Now. Now!"

He mounted her then, and she was plunged into an ecstasy that was almost unbearable. When finally Alexandra lay still in his arms and sighed, "Oh, my darling. I hope it was as wonderful for you," he lied and said, "It was."

She held him close and wept, and she did not know why she was weeping, only that she was grateful for the glory and the joy of it.

"There, there," George said soothingly. "Everything is marvelous."

And it was.

Eve would have been so proud of him.

In every love affair, there are misunderstandings, jealousies, small hurts, but not in the romance between George and Alexandra. With Eve's careful coaching, George was able to play skillfully on Alexandra's every emotion. George knew Alexandra's fears, her fantasies, her passions and aversions, and he was always there, ready to give her exactly what she needed. He knew what made her laugh, and what made her cry. Alexandra was thrilled by his lovemaking, but George found it frustrating. When he was in bed with Alexandra, listening to her animal cries, her excitement aroused him to a fever pitch. He wanted to savage her, make her scream for mercy so he could have his own relief. But he knew if he did that he would destroy everything. His frustration kept growing. The more they made love, the more he grew to despise Alexandra.

There were certain places where George Mellis could find satisfaction, but he knew he had to be cautious. Late at night he haunted anonymous singles' bars and gay discos, and he picked up lonely widows looking for an evening's comfort, gay boys hungry for love, prostitutes hungry for money. George took them to a series of seedy hotels on the West Side, in the Bowery and in Greenwich Village. He never returned to the same hotel twice, nor would he have been welcomed back. His sexual partners usually were found either unconscious or semiconscious, their bodies battered and sometimes covered with cigarette burns.

George avoided masochists. They enjoyed the pain he inflicted, and that took away his pleasure. No, he had to hear them scream and beg for mercy, as his father had made him scream and beg for mercy when George was a small boy. His punishments for the smallest infractions were beatings that often left him unconscious. When George was eight years old and his father caught him and a neighbor's son naked together, George's father beat him until the blood ran from his ears and nose, and to make sure the boy never sinned again, his father pressed a lighted cigar to George's penis. The scar healed, but the deeper scar inside festered.

George Mellis had the wild, passionate nature of his Hellenic ancestors. He could not bear the thought of being controlled by anyone. He put up with the taunting humiliation Eve Blackwell inflicted upon him only because he needed her. When he had the Blackwell fortune in his hands, he intended to punish her until she begged him to kill her. Meeting Eve was the luckiest thing that had ever happened to him. *Lucky for me,* George mused. *Unlucky for her.*

Alexandra continually marveled at how George always knew just what flowers to send her, what records to buy, what books would please her. When he took her to a museum, he was excited about the same paintings she loved. It was incredible to Alexandra how identical their tastes were. She looked for a single flaw in George Mellis, and she could find none. He was perfect. She grew more and more eager for Kate to meet him.

But George always found an excuse to avoid meeting Kate Blackwell.

"Why, darling? You'll love her. Besides, I want to show you off."

"I'm sure she's wonderful," George said boyishly. "I'm terrified she'll think I'm not good enough for you."

"That's ridiculous!" His modesty touched her. "Gran will adore you."

"Soon," he told Alexandra. "As soon as I get up my courage."

He discussed it with Eve one night.

She thought about it. "All right. You'll have to get it over with sooner or later. But you'll have to watch yourself every second. She's a bitch, but she's a smart bitch. Don't underestimate her for a second. If she suspects you're after anything, she'll cut your heart out and feed it to her dogs."

"Why do we need her?" George asked.

"Because if you do anything to make Alexandra antagonize her, we'll all be out in the cold."

Alexandra had never been so nervous. They were going to dine together for the first time, George and Kate and Alexandra, and Alexandra prayed that nothing would go wrong. She wanted more than anything in the world for her grandmother and George to like each other, for her grandmother to see what a wonderful person George was and for George to appreciate Kate Blackwell.

Kate had never seen her granddaughter so happy. Alexandra had met some of the most eligible young men in the world, and none of them had interested her. Kate intended to take a very close look at the man who had captivated her granddaughter. Kate had had long years of experience with fortune hunters, and she had no intention of allowing Alexandra to be taken in by one.

She was eagerly looking forward to meeting Mr. George Mellis. She had a feeling he had been reluctant to meet her, and she wondered why.

Kate heard the front doorbell ring, and a minute later Alexandra came into the drawing room leading a tall, classically handsome stranger by the hand.

"Gran, this is George Mellis."

"At last," Kate said. "I was beginning to think you were avoiding me, Mr. Mellis."

"On the contrary, Mrs. Blackwell, you have no idea how much I've been looking forward to this moment." He was about to say, "You're even more beautiful than Alex told me," but he stopped himself.

Be careful. No flattery, George. It's like a red flag to the old lady.

A butler came in, fixed drinks and discreetly withdrew.

"Please sit down, Mr. Mellis."

"Thank you."

Alexandra sat beside him on the couch, facing her grandmother.

"I understand you've been seeing quite a bit of my granddaughter."

"That's been my pleasure, yes."

Kate was studying him with her pale-gray eyes. "Alexandra tells me you're employed by a brokerage firm."

"Yes."

"Frankly, I find it strange, Mr. Mellis, that you should choose to work as a salaried employee when you could be heading a very profitable family business."

"Gran, I explained that—"

"I would like to hear it from Mr. Mellis, Alexandra."

Be polite, but for Christ's sake, don't kowtow to her. If you show the slightest sign of weakness, she'll tear you apart.

"Mrs. Blackwell, I'm not in the habit of discussing my personal life." He hesitated, as though making a decision. "However, under the circumstances, I suppose . . ." He looked Kate Blackwell in the eye and said, "I'm a very independent man. I don't accept charity. If I had founded Mellis and Company, I would be running it today. But it was founded by my grandfather and built into a very profitable business by my father. It does not need me. I have three brothers who are perfectly capable of running it. I prefer being a salaried employee, as you call it, until I find something that I can build up myself and take pride in."

Kate nodded slowly. This man was not what she had expected at all. She had been prepared for a playboy, a fortune hunter, the kind who had been pursuing her granddaughters ever since Kate could remember. This one appeared to be different. And yet, there was something disturbing about him that Kate could not define. He seemed almost *too* perfect.

"I understand your family is wealthy."

All she has to believe is that you're filthy rich, and madly in love with Alex. Be charming. Keep your temper under control, and you've got it made.

"Money is a necessity, of course, Mrs. Blackwell. But there are a hundred things that interest me more."

Kate had checked on the net worth of Mellis and Company. According to the Dun & Bradstreet report, it was in excess of thirty million dollars.

"Are you close to your family, Mr. Mellis?"

George's face lighted up. "Perhaps too close." He allowed a smile to play on his lips. "We have a saying in our family, Mrs. Blackwell. When one of us cuts his finger, the rest of us bleed. We are in touch with each other constantly." He had not spoken to any member of his family for more than three years.

Kate nodded approvingly. "I believe in closely knit families."

Kate glanced at her granddaughter. There was a look of adoration on Alexandra's face. For one fleeting instant, it reminded Kate of herself and David in those long-ago days when they were so much in love. The years had not dimmed the memory of how she had felt.

Lester came into the room. "Dinner is served, madame."

* * *

The conversation at dinner seemed more casual, but Kate's questions were pointed. George was prepared for the most important question when it came.

"Do you like children, Mr. Mellis?"

She's desperate for a great-grandson. . . . She wants that more than anything in the world.

George turned toward Kate in surprise. "Like children? What is a man without sons and daughters? I am afraid that when I marry, my poor wife will be kept very busy. In Greece, a man's worth is measured by the number of children he has sired."

He seems genuine, Kate thought. *But, one can't be too careful. Tomorrow I'll have Brad Rogers run a check on his personal finances.*

Before Alexandra went to bed, she telephoned Eve. She had told Eve that George Mellis was coming to dinner.

"I can't wait to hear all about it, darling," Eve had said. "You must call me the moment he leaves. I want a full report."

And now Alexandra was reporting. "I think Gran liked him a lot."

Eve felt a small *frisson* of satisfaction. "What did she say?"

"She asked George a hundred personal questions. He handled himself beautifully."

So he had behaved.

"Ah! Are you two lovebirds going to get married?"

"I— He hasn't asked me yet, Eve, but I think he's going to."

She could hear the happiness in Alexandra's voice. "And Gran will approve?"

"Oh, I'm sure she will. She's going to check on George's personal finances, but of course that will be no problem."

Eve felt her heart lurch.

Alexandra was saying, "You know how cautious Gran is."

"Yes," Eve said slowly. "I know."

They were finished. Unless she could think of something quickly.

"Keep me posted," Eve said.

"I will. Good night."

The moment Eve replaced the receiver, she dialed George Mellis's number. He had not reached home yet. She called him every ten minutes, and when he finally answered Eve said, "Can you get your hands on a million dollars in a hurry?"

"What the hell are you talking about?"

"Kate is checking out your finances."

"She knows what my family is worth. She—"

"I'm not talking about your family. I'm talking about you. I told you she's no fool."

There was a silence. "Where would I get hold of a million dollars?"

"I have an idea," Eve told him.

When Kate arrived at her office the following morning, she said to her assistant, "Ask Brad Rogers to run a personal financial check on George Mellis. He's employed by Hanson and Hanson."

"Mr. Rogers is out of town until tomorrow, Mrs. Blackwell. Can it wait until then or—?"

"Tomorrow will be fine."

At the lower end of Manhattan on Wall Street, George Mellis was seated at his desk at the brokerage firm of Hanson and Hanson. The stock exchanges were open, and the huge office was a bedlam of noise and activity. There were 225 employees working at the firm's headquarters: brokers, analysts, accountants, operators and customer representatives, and everyone was working at a feverish speed. Except for George Mellis. He was frozen at his desk, in a panic. What he was about to do would put him in prison if he failed. If he succeeded, he would own the world.

"Aren't you going to answer your phone?"

One of the partners was standing over him, and George realized that his phone had been ringing for—how long? He must act normally and not do anything that might arouse suspicion. He scooped up the phone. "George Mellis," and smiled reassuringly at the partner.

George spent the morning taking buy and sell orders, but his mind was on Eve's plan to steal a million dollars. *It's simple, George. All you have to do is borrow some stock certificates for one night. You can return them in the morning, and no one will be the wiser.*

Every stock brokerage firm has millions of dollars in stocks and bonds stored in its vaults as a convenience to customers. Some of the stock certificates bear the name of the owner, but the vast majority are street-name stocks with a coded CUSIP number—the Committee on Uniform Security Identification Procedures—that identifies the owner. The stock certificates are not negotiable, but George Mellis did not plan to cash them in. He had something else in mind. At Hanson and Hanson, the stocks were kept in a huge vault on the seventh floor in a security area guarded by an armed policeman in front of a gate that could only be opened by a coded plastic access card. George Mellis had no such card. But he knew someone who did.

Helen Thatcher was a lonely widow in her forties. She had a pleasant face and a reasonably good figure, and she was a remarkable cook. She had been married for twenty-three years, and the death of her husband had left a void in her life. She needed a man to take care of her. Her problem was that most of the women who worked at Hanson and Hanson were younger than she, and more attractive to the brokers at the office. No one asked Helen out.

She worked in the accounting department on the floor above George Mellis. From the first time Helen had seen George, she had decided he would make a perfect husband for her. Half a dozen times she had invited him to a home-cooked evening, as she phrased it, and had hinted that he would be served more than dinner, but George had always found an excuse. On this particular morning, when her telephone rang and she said, "Accounting, Mrs. Thatcher," George Mellis's voice came over the line. "Helen? This is George." His voice was warm, and she thrilled to it. "What can I do for you, George?"

"I have a little surprise for you. Can you come down to my office?"

"Now?"

"Yes."

"I'm afraid I'm in the middle of—"

"Oh, if you're too busy, never mind. It will keep."

"No, no. I—I'll be right down."

George's phone was ringing again. He ignored it. He picked up a handful of papers and walked toward the bank of elevators. Looking around to make sure no one was observing him, he walked past the elevators and took the backstairs. When he reached the floor above, he checked to make sure Helen had left her office, then casually walked in as though he had business there. If he was caught— But he could not think of that. He opened the middle drawer where he knew Helen kept her access card to the vault. There it was. He picked it up, slipped it in his pocket, left the office and hurried downstairs. When he reached his desk, Helen was there, looking around for him.

"Sorry," George said. "I was called away for a minute."

"Oh, that's all right. Tell me what the surprise is."

"Well, a little bird told me it's your birthday," George said, "and I want to take you to lunch today." He watched the expression on her face. She was torn between telling him the truth and missing the chance of a lunch date with him.

"That's—very nice of you," she said. "I'd love to have lunch with you."

"All right," he told her. "I'll meet you at Tony's at one o'clock." It was a date he could have made with her over the telephone, but Helen Thatcher was too thrilled to even question it. He watched as she left.

The minute she was gone, George went into action. He had a lot to accomplish before he returned the plastic card. He took the elevator to the seventh floor and walked over to the security area where the guard stood in front of the closed grilled gate.

George inserted the plastic card and the gate opened. As he started inside, the guard said, "I don't think I've seen you here before."

George's heart began to beat faster. He smiled. "No. This isn't my usual territory. One of my customers suddenly decided he wanted to see his stock certificates, so I've got to dig them out. I hope it doesn't take me the whole blasted afternoon."

The guard smiled sympathetically. "Good luck." He watched as George walked into the vault.

The room was concrete, thirty feet by fifteen feet. George walked back to the fireproof file cabinets that contained the stocks and opened the steel drawers. Inside were hundreds of stock certificates that represented shares of every company on the New York and American stock exchanges. The number of shares represented by each certificate was printed on the face of the certificate and ranged from one share to one hundred thousand shares. George went through them swiftly and expertly. He selected certificates of various blue-chip companies, representing a value of one million dollars. He slipped the pieces of paper into his inside jacket pocket, closed the drawer and walked back to the guard.

"That was fast," the guard said.

George shook his head. "The computers came up with the wrong numbers. I'll have to straighten it out in the morning."

"Those damned computers," the guard commiserated. "They'll be the ruination of us all yet."

When George returned to his desk, he found he was soaked with perspiration. *But so far so good.* He picked up the telephone and called Alexandra.

"Darling," he said, "I want to see you and your grandmother tonight."

"I thought you had a business engagement tonight, George."

"I did, but I canceled it. I have something very important to tell you."

At exactly 1:00 P.M. George was in Helen Thatcher's office returning the access card to her desk drawer, while she waited for him at the restaurant. He desperately wanted to hang on to the card, for he would need it again, but he knew that every card that was not turned in each night was invalidated by the computer the next morning. At ten minutes past one, George was lunching with Helen Thatcher.

He took her hand in his. "I want us to do this more often," George said, looking at her searchingly. "Are you free for lunch tomorrow?"

She beamed. "Oh, yes, George."

When George Mellis walked out of his office that afternoon, he was carrying with him one-million-dollars' worth of stock certificates.

He arrived at the Blackwell house promptly at seven o'clock and was ushered into the library, where Kate and Alexandra were waiting for him.

"Good evening," George said. "I hope this is not an intrusion, but I had to speak to you both." He turned to Kate. "I know this is very old-fashioned of me, Mrs. Blackwell, but I would like your permission for your granddaughter's hand in marriage. I love Alexandra, and I believe she loves me. But it would make both of us happy if you would give us your blessing." He reached into his jacket pocket, brought out the stock certificates and tossed them on the table in front of Kate. "I'm giving her a million dollars as a wedding present. She won't need any of your money. But we both need your blessing."

Kate glanced down at the stock certificates George had carelessly scattered on the table. She recognized the names of every one of the companies. Alexandra had moved to George, her eyes shining. "Oh, darling!" She turned to her grandmother, her eyes imploring, "Gran?"

Kate looked at the two of them standing together, and there was no way she could deny them. For a brief instant, she envied them. "You have my blessing," she said.

George grinned and walked over to Kate. "May I?" He kissed her on the cheek.

* * *

For the next two hours they talked excitedly about wedding plans. "I don't want a large wedding, Gran," Alexandra said. "We don't have to do that, do we?"

"I agree," George replied. "Love is a private matter."

In the end, they decided on a small ceremony, with a judge marrying them.

"Will your father be coming over for the wedding?" Kate inquired.

George laughed. "You couldn't keep him away. My father, my three brothers and my two sisters will all be here."

"I'll be looking forward to meeting them."

"You'll like them, I know." Then his eyes turned back to Alexandra.

Kate was very touched by the whole evening. She was thrilled for her granddaughter—pleased that she was getting a man who loved her so much. *I must remember,* Kate thought, *to tell Brad not to bother about that financial rundown on George.*

Before George left, and he was alone with Alexandra, he said casually, "I don't think it's a good idea to have a million dollars in securities lying around the house. I'll put them in my safe-deposit box for now."

"Would you?" Alexandra asked.

George picked up the certificates and put them back into his jacket pocket.

The following morning George repeated the procedure with Helen Thatcher. While she was on her way downstairs to see him ("I have a little something for you"), he was in her office getting the access card. He gave her a Gucci scarf—"a belated birthday present"—and confirmed his luncheon date with her. This time getting into the vault seemed easier. He replaced the stock certificates, returned the access card and met Helen Thatcher at a nearby restaurant.

She held his hand and said, "George, why don't I fix a nice dinner for the two of us tonight?"

And George replied, "I'm afraid that's impossible, Helen. I'm getting married."

Three days before the wedding ceremony was to take place, George arrived at the Blackwell house, his face filled with distress. "I've just had terrible news," he said. "My father suffered another heart attack."

"Oh, I'm so sorry," Kate said. "Is he going to be all right?"

"I've been on the phone with the family all night. They think he'll pull through, but of course they won't be able to attend the wedding."

"We could go to Athens on our honeymoon and see them," Alexandra suggested.

George stroked her cheek. "I have other plans for our honeymoon, *matia mou*. No family, just us."

The marriage ceremony was held in the drawing room of the Blackwell mansion. There were fewer than a dozen guests in attendance, among them Vince Barnes, Alice Koppel and Marty Bergheimer. Alexandra had pleaded with her grandmother to let Eve attend the wedding, but Kate was adamant. "Your sister will never be welcome in this house again."

Alexandra's eyes filled with tears. "Gran, you're being cruel. I love you both. Can't you forgive her?"

For an instant, Kate was tempted to blurt out the whole story of Eve's disloyalty, but she stopped herself. "I'm doing what I think is best for everyone."

A photographer took pictures of the ceremony, and Kate heard George ask him to make up some extra prints to send to his family. *What a considerate man he is,* Kate thought.

After the cake-cutting ceremony, George whispered to Alexandra, "Darling, I'm going to have to disappear for an hour or so."

"Is anything wrong?"

"Of course not. But the only way I could persuade the office to let me take time off for our honeymoon was to promise to finish up some business for an important client. I won't be long. Our plane doesn't leave until five o'clock."

She smiled. "Hurry back. I don't want to go on our honeymoon without you."

When George arrived at Eve's apartment, she was waiting for him, wearing a filmy negligee. "Did you enjoy your wedding, darling?"

"Yes, thank you. It was small but elegant. It went off without a hitch."

"Do you know why, George? Because of me. Never forget that."

He looked at her and said slowly, "I won't."

"We're partners all the way."

"Of course."

Eve smiled. "Well, well. So you're married to my little sister."

George looked at his watch. "Yes. And I must get back."

"Not yet," Eve told him.

"Why not?"

"Because you're going to make love to me first, darling. I want to fuck my sister's husband."

30

Eve had planned the honeymoon. It was expensive, but she told George, "You mustn't stint on anything."

She sold three pieces of jewelry she had acquired from an ardent admirer and gave the money to George.

"I appreciate this, Eve," he said. "I—"

"I'll get it back."

The honeymoon was perfection. George and Alexandra stayed at Round Hill on Montego Bay, in the northern part of Jamaica. The lobby of the hotel was a small, white building set in the center of approximately two dozen beautiful, privately owned bungalows that sprawled down a hill toward the clear, blue sea. The Mellises had the Noel Coward bungalow, with its own swimming pool and a maid to prepare their breakfast, which they ate in the open-air dining room. George rented a small boat and they went sailing and fishing. They swam and read and played backgammon and made love. Alexandra did everything she could think of to please George in bed, and when she heard him moaning at the climax of their lovemaking, she was thrilled that she was able to bring him such pleasure.

On the fifth day, George said, "Alex, I have to drive into Kingston on business. The firm has a branch office there and they asked me to look in on it."

"Fine," Alexandra said. "I'll go with you."

He frowned. "I'd love you to, darling, but I'm expecting an overseas call. You'll have to stay and take the message."

Alexandra was disappointed. "Can't the desk take it?"

"It's too important. I can't trust them."

"All right, then. Of course I'll stay."

George rented a car and drove to Kingston. It was late afternoon when he arrived. The streets of the capital city were swarming with colorfully dressed tourists from the cruise ships, shopping at the straw market and in small bazaars. Kingston is a city of commerce, with refineries, warehouses and fisheries, but with its landlocked harbor it is also a city of beautiful old buildings and museums and libraries.

George was interested in none of these things. He was filled with a desperate need that had been building up in him for weeks and had to be satisfied. He walked into the first bar he saw and spoke to the bartender. Five minutes later George was accompanying a fifteen-year-old black prostitute up the stairs of a cheap hotel. He was with her for two hours. When George left the room, he left alone, got into the car and drove back to Montego Bay, where Alexandra told him the urgent telephone call he was expecting had not come through.

The following morning the Kingston newspapers reported that a tourist had beaten up and mutilated a prostitute, and that she was near death.

At Hanson and Hanson, the senior partners were discussing George Mellis. There had been complaints from a number of clients about the way he handled their securities accounts. A decision had been reached to fire him. Now, however, there were second thoughts.

"He's married to one of Kate Blackwell's granddaughters," a senior partner said. "That puts things in a new light."

A second partner added, "It certainly does. If we could acquire the Blackwell account . . ."

The greed in the air was almost palpable. They decided George Mellis deserved another chance.

When Alexandra and George returned from their honeymoon, Kate told them, "I'd like you to move in here with me. This is an enormous house, and we wouldn't be in one another's way. You—"

George interrupted. "That's very kind of you," he said. "But I think it would be best if Alex and I had our own place."

He had no intention of living under the same roof with the old woman hovering over him, spying on his every move.

"I understand," Kate replied. "In that case, please let me buy a house for you. That will be my wedding present."

George put his arms around Kate and hugged her. "That's very generous of you." His voice was hoarse with emotion. "Alex and I accept with gratitude."

"Thank you, Gran," Alexandra said. "We'll look for a place not too far away."

"Right," George agreed. "We want to be close enough to keep an eye on you. You're a damned attractive woman, you know!"

Within a week they found a beautiful old brownstone near the park, a dozen blocks away from the Blackwell mansion. It was a charming three-story house, with a master bedroom, two guest bedrooms, servants' quarters, a huge old kitchen, a paneled dining room, an elegant living room and a library.

"You're going to have to do the decorating by yourself, darling," George told Alexandra. "I'm all tied up with clients."

The truth was that he spent almost no time at the office, and very little time with clients. His days were occupied with more interesting matters. The police were receiving a string of assault reports from male and female prostitutes and lonely women who visited singles' bars. The victims described their attacker as handsome and cultured, and coming from a foreign background, possibly Latin. Those who were willing to look at police mug shots were unable to come up with an identification.

Eve and George were having lunch in a small downtown restaurant where there was no chance of their being recognized.

"You've got to get Alex to make a new will without Kate knowing about it."

"How the hell do I do that?"

"I'm going to tell you, darling . . ."

The following evening George met Alexandra for dinner at Le Plaisir, one of New York's finest French restaurants. He was almost thirty minutes late.

Pierre Jourdan, the owner, escorted him to the table where Alexandra was waiting. "Forgive me, angel," George said breathlessly. "I was at my attorneys', and you know how they are. They make everything so complicated."

Alexandra asked, "Is anything wrong, George?"

"No. I just changed my will." He took her hands in his. "If anything should happen to me now, everything I have will belong to you."

"Darling, I don't want—"

"Oh, it's not much compared to the Blackwell fortune, but it would keep you very comfortably."

"Nothing's going to happen to you. Not ever."

"Of course not, Alex. But sometimes life plays funny tricks. These things aren't pleasant to face, but it's better to plan ahead and be prepared, don't you think?"

She sat there thoughtfully for a moment. "I should change my will, too, shouldn't I?"

"What for?" He sounded surprised.

"You're my husband. Everything I have is yours."

He withdrew his hand. "Alex, I don't give a damn about your money."

"I know that, George, but you're right. It *is* better to look ahead and be prepared." Her eyes filled with tears. "I know I'm an idiot, but I'm so happy that I can't bear to think of anything happening to either of us. I want us to go on forever."

"We will," George murmured.

"I'll talk to Brad Rogers tomorrow about changing my will."

He shrugged. "If that's what you wish, darling." Then, as an afterthought, "Come to think of it, it might be better if my lawyer made the change. He's familiar with my estate. He can coordinate everything."

"Whatever you like. Gran thinks—"

He caressed her cheek. "Let's keep your grandmother out of this. I adore her, but don't you think we should keep our personal affairs personal?"

"You're right, darling. I won't say anything to Gran. Could you make an appointment for me to see your attorney tomorrow?"

"Remind me to call him. Now, I'm starved. Why don't we start with the crab . . . ?"

One week later George met Eve at her apartment.

"Did Alex sign the new will?" Eve asked.

"This morning. She inherits her share of the company next week on her birthday."

The following week, 49 percent of the shares of Kruger-Brent, Ltd., were transferred to Alexandra. George called to tell Eve the news. She said, "Wonderful! Come over tonight. We'll celebrate."

"I can't. Kate's giving a birthday party for Alex."

There was a silence. "What are they serving?"

"How the hell do I know?"

"Find out." The line went dead.

Forty-five minutes later George called Eve back. "I don't know why you're so interested in the menu," he said nastily, "since you aren't invited to the party, but it's *Coquille Saint-Jacques, Chateaubriand,* a bibb lettuce salad, *Brie, cappuccino* and a birthday cake with Alex's favorite ice cream, Neapolitan. Satisfied?"

"Yes, George. I'll see you tonight."

"No, Eve. There's no way I can walk out in the middle of Alex's—"

"You'll think of something."

God damn the bitch! George hung up the phone and looked at his watch. *God damn everything!* He had an appointment with an important client he had stood up twice already. Now he was late. He knew the partners were keeping him on only because he had married into the Blackwell family. He could not afford to do anything to jeopardize his position. He had created an image for Alexandra and Kate, and it was imperative that nothing destroy that. Soon he would not need any of them.

He had sent his father a wedding invitation, and the old man had not even bothered to reply. Not one word of congratulations. *I never want to see you again,* his father had told him. *You're dead, you understand? Dead.* Well, his father was in for a surprise. The prodigal son was going to come to life again.

Alexandra's twenty-third birthday party was a great success. There were forty guests. She had asked George to invite some of his friends, but he had demurred. "It's your party, Alex," he said. "Let's just have your friends."

The truth was that George had no friends. He was a loner, he told himself proudly. People who were dependent on other people were weaklings. He watched as Alexandra blew out the candles on her cake and made a silent wish. He knew the wish involved him, and he thought, *You should have wished for a longer life, darling.* He had to admit that Alexandra was exquisite looking. She was wearing a long white chiffon dress with delicate silver slippers and a diamond necklace, a present from Kate. The large, pear-shaped stones were strung together on a platinum chain, and they sparkled in the candlelight.

Kate looked at them and thought, *I remember our first anniversary, when David put that necklace on me and told me how much he loved me.*

And George thought, *That necklace must be worth a hundred and fifty thousand dollars.*

George had been aware all evening that several of Alexandra's female guests were eyeing him, smiling at him invitingly, touching him as they talked to him. *Horny bitches,* he thought contemptuously. Under other circumstances, he might have been tempted to risk it, but not with Alexandra's friends. They might not dare complain to Alexandra, but there was a chance they could go to the police. No, things were moving along too smoothly to take any unnecessary chances.

At one minute before ten o'clock, George positioned himself near the telephone. When it rang a minute later, he picked it up. "Hello."

"Mr. Mellis?"

"Yes."

"This is your answering service. You asked me to call you at ten o'clock."

Alexandra was standing near him. He looked over at her and frowned. "What time did he call?"

"Is this Mr. Mellis?"

"Yes."

"You left a ten o'clock call, sir."

Alexandra was at his side.

"Very well," he said into the phone. "Tell him I'm on my way. I'll meet him at the Pan Am Clipper Club."

George slammed the phone down.

"What's the matter, darling?"

He turned to Alexandra. "One of the idiot partners is on his way to Singapore and he left some contracts at the office that he needs to take with him. I've got to pick them up and get them to him before his plane leaves."

"Now?" Alexandra's voice was filled with dismay. "Can't someone else do it?"

"I'm the only one they trust," George sighed. "You'd think I was the only capable one in the whole office." He put his arms around her. "I'm sorry, darling. Don't let me spoil your party. You go on and I'll get back as soon as I can."

She managed a smile. "I'll miss you."

Alexandra watched him go, then looked around the room to make sure all her guests were enjoying themselves.

She wondered what Eve was doing on their birthday.

Eve opened the door to let George in. "You managed," she said. "You're such a clever man."

"I can't stay, Eve. Alex is—"

She took his hand. "Come, darling. I have a surprise for you." She led him into the small dining room. The table was set for two, with beautiful silver and white napery and lighted candles in the center of the table.

"What's this for?"

"It's my birthday, George."

"Of course," he said lamely. "I—I'm afraid I didn't bring you a present."

She stroked his cheek. "Yes you did, love. You'll give it to me later. Sit down."

"Thanks," George said. "I couldn't eat anything. I just had a big dinner."

"Sit down." There was no inflection to her voice.

George looked into her eyes, and sat down.

Dinner consisted of *Coquille Saint-Jacques, Chateaubriand,* a bibb lettuce salad, *Brie, cappuccino* and a birthday cake with Neapolitan ice cream.

Eve sat across from him, watching George force the food down. "Alex and I have always shared everything," Eve told him. "Tonight I'm sharing her birthday dinner. But next year there will be just one of us having a birthday party. The time has come, darling, for my sister to have an accident. And after that, poor old Gran is going to die of grief. It's going to be all ours, George. Now, come into the bedroom and give me my birthday present."

He had been dreading this moment. He was a man, strong and vigorous, and Eve dominated him and made him feel impotent. She had him undress her slowly, and then she undressed him and skillfully excited him to an erection.

SIDNEY SHELDON   415

"There you are, darling." She got astride him and began slowly moving her hips. "Ah, that feels so good. . . . You can't have an orgasm, can you, poor baby? Do you know why? Because you're a freak. You don't like women, do you, George? You only enjoy hurting them. You'd like to hurt me, wouldn't you? Tell me you'd like to hurt me."

"I'd like to kill you."

Eve laughed. "But you won't, because you want to own the company as much as I do. . . . You'll never hurt me, George, because if anything ever happens to me, a friend of mine is holding a letter that will be delivered to the police."

He did not believe her. "You're bluffing."

Eve raked a long, sharp nail down his naked chest. "There's only one way you can find out, isn't there?" she taunted.

And he suddenly knew she was telling the truth. He was never going to be able to get rid of her! She was always going to be there to taunt him, to enslave him. He could not bear the idea of being at this bitch's mercy for the rest of his life. And something inside him exploded. A red film descended over his eyes, and from that moment on he had no idea what he was doing. It was as though someone outside himself was controlling him. Everything happened in slow motion. He remembered shoving Eve off him, pulling her legs apart and her cries of pain. He was battering at something over and over, and it was indescribably wonderful. The whole center of his being was racked with a long spasm of unbearable bliss, and then another, and another, and he thought, *Oh, God! I've waited so long for this.* From somewhere in the far distance, someone was screaming. The red film slowly started to clear, and he looked down. Eve was lying on the bed, covered with blood. Her nose was smashed in, her body was covered with bruises and cigarette burns and her eyes were swollen shut. Her jaw was broken, and she was whimpering out of the side of her mouth. "Stop it, stop it, stop it . . ."

George shook his head to clear it. As the reality of the situation hit him, he was filled with sudden panic. There was no way he could ever explain what he had done. He had thrown everything away. Everything!

He leaned over her. "Eve?"

She opened one swollen eye. "Doctor . . . Get . . . a . . . doctor. . . ." Each word was a drop of pain. "Harley . . . John Harley."

All George Mellis said on the phone was, "Can you come right away? Eve Blackwell has had an accident."

When Dr. John Harley walked into the room, he took one look at Eve and the blood-spattered bed and walls and said, "Oh, my God!" He felt Eve's fluttering pulse, and turned to George. "Call the police. Tell them we need an ambulance."

Through the mist of pain, Eve whispered, "John . . ."

John Harley leaned over the bed. "You're going to be all right. We'll get you to the hospital."

She reached out and found his hand. "No police . . ."

"I have to report this. I—"

Her grip tightened. "No . . . police . . ."

He looked at her shattered cheekbone, her broken jaw and the cigarette burns on her body. "Don't try to talk."

The pain was excruciating, but Eve was fighting for her life. "Please . . ." It took a long time to get the words out. "Private . . . Gran would never . . . forgive me. . . . No . . . police. . . . Hit . . . run . . . accident. . . ."

There was no time to argue. Dr. Harley walked over to the telephone and dialed. "This is Dr. Harley." He gave Eve's address. "I want an ambulance sent here immediately. Find Dr. Keith Webster and ask him to meet me at the hospital. Tell him it's an emergency. Have a room prepared for surgery." He listened a moment, then said, "A hit-and-run accident." He slammed down the receiver.

"Thank you, Doctor," George breathed.

Dr. Harley turned to look at Alexandra's husband, his eyes filled with loathing. George's clothes had been hastily donned, but his knuckles were raw, and his hands and face were still spattered with blood. "Don't thank me. I'm doing this for the Blackwells. But on one condition. That you agree to see a psychiatrist."

"I don't need a—"

"Then I'm calling the police, you sonofabitch. You're not fit to be running around loose." Dr. Harley reached for the telephone again.

"Wait a minute!" George stood there, thinking. He had almost thrown everything away, but now, miraculously, he was being given a second chance. "All right. I'll see a psychiatrist."

In the far distance they heard the wail of a siren.

She was being rushed down a long tunnel, and colored lights were flashing on and off. Her body felt light and airy, and she thought, *I can fly if I want to,* and she tried to move her arms, but something was holding them down. She opened her eyes, and she was speeding down a white corridor on a gurney being wheeled by two men in green gowns and caps. *I'm starring in a play,* Eve thought. *I can't remember my lines. What are my lines?* When she opened her eyes again, she was in a large white room on an operating table.

A small, thin man in a green surgical gown was leaning over her. "My name is Keith Webster. I'm going to operate on you."

"I don't want to be ugly," Eve whispered. It was difficult to talk. "Don't let me be . . . ugly."

"Not a chance," Dr. Webster promised. "I'm going to put you to sleep now. Just relax."

He gave a signal to the anesthesiologist.

George managed to wash the blood off himself and clean up in Eve's bathroom, but he cursed as he glanced at his wristwatch. It was three o'clock in the morning. He hoped Alexandra was asleep, but when he walked into their living room, she was waiting for him.

"Darling! I've been frantic! Are you all right?"

"I'm fine, Alex."

She went up to him and hugged him. "I was getting ready to call the police. I thought something terrible had happened."

How right you are, George thought.

"Did you bring him the contracts?"

"Contracts?" He suddenly remembered. "Oh, those. Yes. I did." That seemed like years ago, a lie from the distant past.

"What on earth kept you so late?"

"His plane was delayed," George said glibly. "He wanted me to stay with him. I kept thinking he'd take off at any minute, and then finally it got too late for me to telephone you. I'm sorry."

"It's all right, now that you're here."

George thought of Eve as she was being carried out on the stretcher. Out of her broken, twisted mouth, she had gasped, "Go . . . home . . . nothing . . . happened. . . ." But what if Eve died? He would be arrested for murder. If Eve lived, everything would be all right; it would be just as it was before. Eve would forgive him because she needed him.

George lay awake the rest of the night. He was thinking about Eve and the way she had screamed and begged for mercy. He felt her bones crunch again beneath his fists, and he smelled her burning flesh, and at that moment he was very close to loving her.

It was a stroke of great luck that John Harley was able to obtain the services of Keith Webster for Eve. Dr. Webster was one of the foremost plastic surgeons in the world. He had a private practice on Park Avenue and his own clinic in lower Manhattan, where he specialized in taking care of those who had been born with disfigurements. The people who came to the clinic paid only what they could afford. Dr. Webster was used to treating accident cases, but his first sight of Eve Blackwell's battered face had shocked him. He had seen photographs of her in magazines, and to see that much beauty deliberately disfigured filled him with a deep anger.

"Who's responsible for this, John?"

"It was a hit-and-run accident, Keith."

Keith Webster snorted. "And then the driver stopped to strip her and snuff out his cigarette on her behind? What's the real story?"

"I'm afraid I can't discuss it. Can you put her back together again?"

"That's what I do, John, put them back together again."

It was almost noon when Dr. Webster finally said to his assistants, "We're finished. Get her into intensive care. Call me at the slightest sign of anything going wrong."

The operation had taken nine hours.

Eve was moved out of intensive care forty-eight hours later. George went to the hospital. He had to see Eve, to talk to her, to make sure she was not plotting some terrible vengeance against him.

"I'm Miss Blackwell's attorney," George told the duty nurse. "She asked to see me. I'll only stay a moment."

The nurse took one look at this handsome man and said, "She's not supposed to have visitors, but I'm sure it's all right if you go in."

Eve was in a private room, lying in bed, flat on her back, swathed in bandages, tubes connected to her body like obscene appendages. The only parts of her face visible were her eyes and her lips.

"Hello, Eve . . ."

"George . . ." Her voice was a scratchy whisper. He had to lean close to hear what she said.

"You didn't . . . tell Alex?"

"No, of course not." He sat down on the edge of the bed. "I came because—"

"I know why you came. . . . We're . . . going ahead with it . . ."

He had a feeling of indescribable relief. "I'm sorry about this, Eve. I really am. I—"

"Have someone call Alex . . . and tell her I've gone away . . . on a trip . . . back in a few . . . weeks . . ."

"All right."

Two bloodshot eyes looked up at him. "George . . . do me a favor."

"Yes?"

"Die painfully. . . ."

She slept. When she awakened, Dr. Keith Webster was at her bedside.

"How are you feeling?" His voice was gentle and soothing.

"Very tired . . . What was the . . . matter with me?"

Dr. Webster hesitated. The X rays had shown a fractured zygoma and a blowout fracture. There was a depressed zygomatic arch impinging on the temporal muscle, so that she was unable to open or close her mouth without pain. Her nose was broken. There were two broken ribs and deep cigarette burns on her posterior and on the soles of her feet.

"What?" Eve repeated.

Dr. Webster said, as gently as possible, "You had a fractured cheekbone. Your nose was broken. The bony floor where your eye sits had been shifted. There was pressure on the muscle that opens and closes your mouth. There were cigarette burns. Everything has been taken care of."

"I want to see a mirror," Eve whispered.

That was the last thing he would allow. "I'm sorry," he smiled. "We're fresh out."

She was afraid to ask the next question. "How am I—how am I going to look when these bandages come off?"

"You're going to look terrific. Exactly the way you did before your accident."

"I don't believe you."

"You'll see. Now, do you want to tell me what happened? I have to write up a police report."

There was a long silence. "I was hit by a truck."

Dr. Keith Webster wondered again how anyone could have tried to destroy this fragile beauty, but he had long since given up pondering the vagaries of the human race and its capacity for cruelty. "I'll need a name," he said gently. "Who did it?"

"Mack."

"And the last name?"

"Truck."

Dr. Webster was puzzled by the conspiracy of silence. First John Harley, now Eve Blackwell.

"In cases of criminal assault," Keith Webster told Eve, "I'm required by law to file a police report."

Eve reached out for his hand and grasped it and held it tightly. "Please, if my grandmother or sister knew, it would kill them. If you tell the police . . . the newspapers will know. You mustn't . . . please. . . ."

"I can't report it as a hit-and-run accident. Ladies don't usually run out in the street without any clothes on."

"Please!"

He looked down at her, and was filled with pity. "I suppose you could have tripped and fallen down the stairs of your home."

She squeezed his hand tighter. "That's exactly what happened . . ."

Dr. Webster sighed. "That's what I thought."

Dr. Keith Webster visited Eve every day after that, sometimes stopping by two or three times a day. He brought her flowers and small presents from the hospital gift shop. Each day Eve would ask him anxiously, "I just lie here all day. Why isn't anyone doing anything?"

"My partner's working on you," Dr. Webster told her.

"Your partner?"

"Mother Nature. Under all those frightening-looking bandages, you're healing beautifully."

Every few days he would remove the bandages and examine her.

"Let me have a mirror," Eve pleaded.

But his answer was always the same: "Not yet."

He was the only company Eve had, and she began to look forward to his visits. He was an unprepossessing man, small and thin, with sandy, sparse hair and myopic brown eyes that constantly blinked. He was shy in Eve's presence, and it amused her.

"Have you ever been married?" she asked.

"No."

"Why not?"

"I—I don't know. I guess I wouldn't make a very good husband. I'm on emergency call a lot."

"But you must have a girl friend."

He was actually blushing. "Well, you know . . ."

"Tell me," Eve teased him.

"I don't have a regular girl friend."

"I'll bet all the nurses are crazy about you."

"No. I'm afraid I'm not a very romantic kind of person."

To say the least, Eve thought. And yet, when she discussed Keith Webster with the nurses and interns who came in to perform various indignities on her body, they spoke of him as though he were some kind of god.

"The man is a miracle worker," one intern said. "There's nothing he can't do with a human face."

They told her about his work with deformed children and criminals, but when Eve asked Keith Webster about it, he dismissed the subject with, "Unfortunately, the world judges people by their looks. I try to help those who were born with physical deficiencies. It can make a big difference in their lives."

Eve was puzzled by him. He was not doing it for the money or the glory. He was totally selfless. She had never met anyone like him, and she wondered what motivated him. But it was an idle curiosity. She had no interest in Keith Webster, except for what he could do for her.

Fifteen days after Eve checked into the hospital, she was moved to a private clinic in upstate New York.

"You'll be more comfortable here," Dr. Webster assured her.

Eve knew it was much farther for him to travel to see her, and yet he still appeared every day.

"Don't you have any other patients?" Eve asked.

"Not like you."

* * *

Five weeks after Eve entered the clinic, Keith Webster removed the bandages. He turned her head from side to side. "Do you feel any pain?" he asked.

"No."

"Any tightness?"

"No."

Dr. Webster looked up at the nurse. "Bring Miss Blackwell a mirror."

Eve was filled with a sudden fear. For weeks she had been longing to look at herself in a mirror. Now that the moment was here, she was terrified. She wanted her own face, not the face of some stranger.

When Dr. Webster handed her the mirror, she said faintly, "I'm afraid—"

"Look at yourself," he said gently.

She raised the mirror slowly. It was a miracle! There was no change at all; it was her face. She searched for the signs of scars. There were none. Her eyes filled with tears.

She looked up and said, "Thank you," and reached out to give Keith Webster a kiss. It was meant to be a brief thank-you kiss, but she could feel his lips hungry on hers.

He pulled away, suddenly embarrassed. "I'm—I'm glad you're pleased," he said.

Pleased! "Everyone was right. You *are* a miracle worker."

He said shyly, "Look what I had to work with."

31

George Mellis had been badly shaken by what had happened. He had come perilously close to destroying everything he wanted. George had not been fully aware before of how much the control of Kruger-Brent, Ltd., meant to him. He had been satisfied to live on gifts from lonely ladies, but he was married to a Blackwell now, and within his reach was a company larger than anything his father had ever conceived of. *Look at me, Papa. I'm alive again. I own a company bigger than yours.* It was no longer a game. He knew he would kill to get what he wanted.

George devoted himself to creating the image of the perfect husband. He spent every possible moment with Alexandra. They breakfasted together, he took her out to lunch and he made it a point to be home early every evening. On weekends they went to the beach house Kate Blackwell owned in East Hampton, on Long Island, or flew to Dark Harbor in the company Cessna 620. Dark Harbor was George's favorite. He loved the rambling old house, with its beautiful antiques and priceless paintings. He wandered through the vast rooms. *Soon all this will be mine,* he thought. It was a heady feeling.

George was also the perfect grandson-in-law. He paid a great deal of attention to Kate. She was eighty-one, chairman of the board of Kruger-Brent, Ltd., and a remarkably strong, vital woman. George saw to it that he and Alexandra dined with her once a week, and he telephoned the old woman every few days to chat with her. He was carefully building up the picture of a loving husband and caring grandson-in-law.

No one would ever suspect him of murdering two people he loved so much.

George Mellis's sense of satisfaction was abruptly shattered by a telephone call from Dr. John Harley.

"I've made arrangements for you to see a psychiatrist. Dr. Peter Templeton."

George made his voice warm and ingratiating. "That's really not necessary any more, Dr. Harley. I think—"

"I don't give a damn what you think. We have an agreement—I don't report you to the police, and you consult a psychiatrist. If you wish to break that agree—"

"No, no," George said hastily. "If that's what you want, fine."

"Dr. Templeton's telephone number is five-five-five-three-one-six-one. He's expecting your call. Today." And Dr. Harley slammed down the receiver.

The damned busybody, George thought angrily. The last thing in the world he needed was to waste time with a shrink, but he could not risk Dr. Harley's talking. He would call this Dr. Templeton, see him once or twice and that would be the end of it.

Eve telephoned George at the office. "I'm home."

"Are you—?" He was afraid to ask. "All right?"

"Come and see for yourself. Tonight."

"It's difficult for me to get away just now. Alex and I—"

"Eight o'clock."

He could hardly believe it. Eve stood in front of him, looking just as beautiful as ever. He studied her face closely and could find no sign of the terrible damage he had inflicted upon her.

"It's incredible! You—you look exactly the same."

"Yes. I'm still beautiful, aren't I, George?" She smiled, a cat smile, thinking of what she planned to do to him. He was a sick animal, not fit to live. He would pay in full for what he had done to her, but not yet. She still needed him. They stood there, smiling at each other.

"Eve, I can't tell you how sorry I—"

She held up a hand. "Let's not discuss it. It's over. Nothing has changed."

But George remembered that something had changed. "I got a call from Harley," he said. "He's arranged for me to see some damned psychiatrist."

Eve shook her head. "No. Tell him you haven't time."

"I tried. If I don't go, he'll turn in a report of the—the accident to the police."

"Damn!"

She stood there, deep in thought. "Who is he?"

"The psychiatrist? Someone named Templeton. Peter Templeton."

"I've heard of him. He has a good reputation."

"Don't worry. I can just lie on his couch for fifty minutes and say nothing. If—"

Eve was not listening. An idea had come to her, and she was exploring it.

She turned to George. "This may be the best thing that could have happened."

Peter Templeton was in his middle thirties, just over six feet, with broad shoulders, clean-cut features and inquisitive blue eyes, and he looked more like a quarterback than a doctor. At the moment, he was frowning at a notation on his schedule: *George Mellis—grandson-in-law of Kate Blackwell.*

The problems of the rich held no interest for Peter Templeton. Most of his colleagues were delighted to get socially prominent patients. When Peter Templeton had first begun his practice, he had had his share, but he had quickly found he was unable to sympathize with their problems. He had dowagers in his office literally screaming because they had not been invited to some social event, financiers threatening to commit suicide because they had lost money in the stock market, overweight matrons who alternated between feasting and fat farms. The world was full of problems, and Peter Templeton had long since decided that these were not the problems he was interested in helping to solve.

George Mellis. Peter had reluctantly agreed to see him only because of his respect for Dr. John Harley. "I wish you'd send him somewhere else, John," Peter Templeton had said. "I really have a full schedule."

"Consider this a favor, Peter."

"What's his problem?"

"That's your department. I'm just an old country doctor."

"All right," Peter had agreed. "Have him call me."

Now he was here. Dr. Templeton pressed down the button on the intercom on his desk. "Send Mr. Mellis in."

Peter Templeton had seen photographs of George Mellis in newspapers and magazines, but he was still unprepared for the overpowering vitality of the man. He gave new meaning to the word *charisma.*

They shook hands. Peter said, "Sit down, Mr. Mellis."

George looked at the couch. "Over there?"

"Wherever you're comfortable."

George took the chair opposite the desk. George looked at Peter Templeton and smiled. He had thought he would dread this moment, but after his talk with Eve, he had changed his mind. Dr. Templeton was going to be his ally, his witness.

Peter studied the man opposite him. When patients came to see him for the first time, they were invariably nervous. Some covered it up with bravado, others were silent or talkative or defensive. Peter could detect no signs of nervousness in this man. On the contrary, he seemed to be enjoying himself. *Curious,* Peter thought.

"Dr. Harley tells me you have a problem."

George sighed. "I'm afraid I have two."

"Why don't you tell me about them?"

"I feel so ashamed. That's why I—I insisted on coming to see you." He leaned forward in his chair and said earnestly, "I did something I've never done before in my life, Doctor. I struck a woman."

Peter waited.

"We were having an argument and I blacked out, and when I came to, I had . . . hit her." He let his voice break slightly. "It was terrible."

Peter Templeton's inner voice told him he already knew what George Mellis's problem was. He enjoyed beating up women.

"Was it your wife you struck?"

"My sister-in-law."

Peter had occasionally come across items about the Blackwell twins in newspapers or magazines when they appeared at charity events or society affairs. They were identical, Peter recalled, and strikingly beautiful. So this man had hit his sister-in-law. Peter found that mildly interesting. He also found it interesting that George Mellis made it sound as though he had merely slapped her once or twice. If that had been true, John Harley would not have insisted that Peter see Mellis.

"You say you hit her. Did you hurt her?"

"As a matter of fact, I hurt her pretty badly. As I told you, Doctor, I blacked out. When I came to, I—I couldn't believe it."

When I came to. The classic defense. I didn't do it, my subconscious did it.

"Do you have any idea what caused that reaction?"

"I've been under a terrible strain lately. My father has been seriously ill. He's had several heart attacks. I've been deeply concerned about him. We're a close family."

"Is your father here?"

"He's in Greece."

That Mellis. "You said you had two problems."

"Yes. My wife, Alexandra . . ." He stopped.

"You're having marital problems?"

"Not in the sense you mean. We love each other very much. It's just that—" He hesitated. "Alexandra hasn't been well lately."

"Physically?"

"Emotionally. She's constantly depressed. She keeps talking about suicide."

"Has she sought professional help?"

George smiled sadly. "She refuses."

Too bad, Peter thought. *Some Park Avenue doctor is being cheated out of a fortune.* "Have you discussed this with Dr. Harley?"

"No."

"Since he's the family doctor, I would suggest you speak with him. If he feels it's necessary, he'll recommend a psychiatrist."

George Mellis said nervously, "No. I don't want Alexandra to feel I'm discussing her behind her back. I'm afraid Dr. Harley would—"

"That's all right, Mr. Mellis. I'll give him a call."

"Eve, we're in trouble," George snapped. "Big trouble."

"What happened?"

"I did exactly as you told me. I said I was concerned about Alexandra, that she was suicidal."

"And?"

"The sonofabitch is going to call John Harley and discuss it with him!"

"Oh, Christ! We can't let him."

Eve began to pace. She stopped suddenly. "All right. I'll handle Harley. Do you have another appointment with Templeton?"

"Yes."

"Keep it."

The following morning Eve went to see Dr. Harley at his office. John Harley liked the Blackwell family. He had watched the children grow up. He had gone through the tragedy of Marianne's death and the attack on Kate, and putting Tony away in a sanitarium. Kate had suffered so much. And then the rift between Kate and Eve. He could not imagine what had caused it, but it was none of his business. His business was to keep the family physically healthy.

When Eve walked into his office, Dr. Harley looked at her and said, "Keith Webster did a fantastic job!" The only telltale mark was a very thin, barely visible red scar across her forehead. Eve said, "Dr. Webster is going to remove the scar in a month or so."

Dr. Harley patted Eve's arm. "It only makes you more beautiful, Eve. I'm very pleased." He motioned her to a chair. "What can I do for you?"

"This isn't about me, John. It's about Alex."

Dr. Harley frowned. "Is she having a problem? Something to do with George?"

"Oh, no," Eve said quickly. "George is behaving perfectly. In fact, it's George who's concerned about her. Alex has been acting strangely lately. She's been very depressed. Suicidal, even."

Dr. Harley looked at Eve and said flatly, "I don't believe it. That doesn't sound like Alexandra."

"I know. I didn't believe it either, so I went to see her. I was shocked by the change in her. She's in a state of deep depression. I'm really worried, John. I can't go to Gran about it— That's why I came to you. You've got to do something." Her eyes misted. "I've lost my grandmother. I couldn't bear to lose my sister."

"How long has this been going on?"

"I'm not sure. I pleaded with her to talk to you about it. At first she refused, but I finally persuaded her. You've got to help her."

"Of course I will. Have her come in tomorrow morning. And try not to worry, Eve. There are new medications that work miracles."

Dr. Harley walked her to the door of his office. He wished Kate were not so unforgiving. Eve was such a caring person.

When Eve returned to her apartment, she carefully cold-creamed away the red scar on her forehead.

The following morning at ten o'clock, Dr. Harley's receptionist announced, "Mrs. George Mellis is here to see you, Doctor."

"Send her in."

She walked in slowly, unsure of herself. She was pale, and there were dark circles under her eyes.

John Harley took her hand and said, "It's good to see you, Alexandra. Now what's this I hear about your having problems?"

Her voice was low. "I feel foolish bothering you, John. I'm sure there's nothing wrong with me. If Eve hadn't insisted, I never would have come. I feel fine, physically."

"What about emotionally?"

She hesitated. "I don't sleep very well."

"What else?"

"You'll think I'm a hypochondriac . . ."

"I know you better than that, Alexandra."

She lowered her eyes. "I feel depressed all the time. Sort of anxious and . . . tired. George goes out of his way to make me happy and to think up things for us to do together and places for us to go. The problem is that I don't feel like doing anything or going anywhere. Everything seems so—hopeless."

He was listening to every word, studying her. "Anything else?"

"I—I think about killing myself." Her voice was so soft he could barely hear her. She looked up at him and said, "Am I going crazy?"

He shook his head. "No. I don't think you're going crazy. Have you ever heard of anhedonia?"

She shook her head.

"It's a biological disturbance that causes the symptoms you've described. It's a fairly common condition, and there are some new drugs that make it easy to treat. These drugs have no side effects, and they're effective. I'm going to examine you, but I'm sure we won't find anything really wrong."

When the examination was completed and she had gotten dressed again, Dr. Harley said, "I'm going to give you a prescription for Wellbutrin. It's part of a new generation of antidepressants—one of the new wonder drugs."

She watched listlessly as he wrote out a prescription.

"I want you to come back and see me a week from today. In the meantime, if you have any problems, call me, day or night." He handed her the prescription.

"Thank you, John," she said. "I just hope these will stop the dream."

"What dream?"

"Oh, I thought I told you. It's the same one every night. I'm on a boat and it's windy, and I hear the sea calling. I walk to the rail and I look down and I see myself in the water, drowning. . . ."

She walked out of Dr. Harley's office and onto the street. She leaned against the building, taking deep breaths. *I did it*, Eve thought exultantly. *I got away with it*. She threw the prescription away.

32

Kate Blackwell was tired. The meeting had gone on too long. She looked around the conference table at the three men and three women on the executive board. They all seemed fresh and vital. *So it's not the meeting that has been going on too long,* Kate thought. *I've gone on too long. I'll be eighty-two. I'm getting old.* The thought depressed her, not because she had any fear of dying, but because she was not ready yet. She refused to die until Kruger-Brent, Ltd., had a member of the Blackwell family running it. After the bitter disappointment with Eve, Kate had tried to build her future plans around Alexandra.

"You know I would do anything for you, Gran, but I'm simply not interested in becoming involved with the company. George would be an excellent executive . . ."

"Do you agree, Kate?" Brad Rogers was addressing her.

The question shook Kate out of her reverie. She looked toward Brad guiltily. "I'm sorry. What was the question?"

"We were discussing the Deleco merger." His voice was patient. Brad Rogers was concerned about Kate Blackwell. In recent months she had started daydreaming during board meetings, and then just when Brad Rogers decided Kate was becoming senile and should retire from the board, she would come up with some stunning insight that would make everyone wonder why *he* had not thought of it. She was an amazing woman. He thought of their brief, long-ago affair and wondered again why it had ended so abruptly.

It was George Mellis's second visit to Peter Templeton. "Has there been much violence in your past, Mr. Mellis?"

George shook his head. "No. I abhor violence." *Make a note of that, you smug sonofabitch. The coroner is going to ask you about that.*

"You told me your mother and father never physically punished you."

"That is correct."

"Would you say you were an obedient child?"

Careful. There are traps here. "About average, I suppose."

"The average child usually gets punished at some time or another for breaking the rules of the grown-up world."

George gave him a deprecating smile. "I guess I didn't break any rules."

He's lying, Peter Templeton thought. *The question is why? What is he concealing?* He recalled the conversation he had had with Dr. Harley after the first session with George Mellis.

"He said he hit his sister-in-law, John, and—"

"*Hit* her!" John Harley's voice was filled with indignation. "It was butchery, Peter. He smashed her cheekbone, broke her nose and three ribs, and burned her buttocks and the soles of her feet with cigarettes."

Peter Templeton felt a wave of disgust wash over him. "He didn't mention that to me."

"I'll bet he didn't," Dr. Harley snapped. "I told him if he didn't go to you, I was going to report him to the police."

Peter remembered George's words: *I feel ashamed. That's why I insisted on coming to see you.* So he had lied about that, too.

"Mellis told me his wife is suffering from depression, that she's talking about suicide."

"Yes, I can vouch for that. Alexandra came to see me a few

days ago. I prescribed Wellbutrin. I'm quite concerned about her. What's your impression of George Mellis?"

Peter said slowly, "I don't know yet. I have a feeling he's dangerous."

Dr. Keith Webster was unable to get Eve Blackwell out of his mind. She was like a beautiful goddess, unreal and untouchable. She was outgoing and vivacious and stimulating, while he was shy and dull and drab. Keith Webster had never married, because he had never found a woman he felt was unworthy enough to be his wife. Apart from his work, his self-esteem was negligible. He had grown up with a fiercely domineering mother and a weak, bullied father. Keith Webster's sexual drive was low, and what little there was of it was sublimated in his work. But now he began to dream about Eve Blackwell, and when he recalled the dreams in the morning, he was embarrassed. She was completely healed and there was no reason for him to see her anymore, yet he knew he had to see her.

He telephoned her at her apartment. "Eve? This is Keith Webster. I hope I'm not disturbing you. I—er—I was thinking about you the other day, and I—I was just wondering how you were getting along?"

"Fine, thank you, Keith. How are *you* getting along?" There was that teasing note in her voice again.

"Jus—just fine," he said. There was a silence. He summoned up his nerve. "I guess you're probably too busy to have lunch with me."

Eve smiled to herself. He was such a deliciously timid little man. It would be amusing. "I'd love to, Keith."

"Would you really?" She could hear the note of surprise in his voice. "When?"

"What about tomorrow?"

"It's a date." He spoke quickly, before she could change her mind.

Eve enjoyed the luncheon. Dr. Keith Webster acted like a young schoolboy in love. He dropped his napkin, spilled his wine and knocked over a vase of flowers. Watching him, Eve thought with amusement, *No one would ever guess what a brilliant surgeon he is.*

When the luncheon was over, Keith Webster asked shyly, "Could we—could we do this again sometime?"

She replied with a straight face, "We'd better not, Keith. I'm afraid I might fall in love with you."

He blushed wildly, not knowing what to say.

Eve patted his hand. "I'll never forget you."

He knocked over the vase of flowers again.

John Harley was having lunch at the hospital cafeteria when Keith Webster joined him.

Keith said, "John, I promise to keep it confidential, but I'd feel a lot better if you told me the truth about what happened to Eve Blackwell."

Harley hesitated, then shrugged. "All right. It was her brother-in-law, George Mellis."

And Keith Webster felt that now he was sharing a part of Eve's secret world.

George Mellis was impatient. "The money is there, the will has been changed— What the hell are we waiting for?"

Eve sat on the couch, her long legs curled up under her, watching him as he paced.

"I want to get this thing over with, Eve."

He's losing his nerve, Eve thought. He was like a deadly coiled snake. Dangerous. She had made a mistake with him once by goading him too far, and it had almost cost her l fe. She would not make that mistake again.

"I agree with you," she said slowly. "I think it's time."

He stopped pacing. "When?"

"Next week."

The session was almost over and George Mellis had not once mentioned his wife. Now, suddenly he said, "I'm worried about

Alexandra, Dr. Templeton. Her depression seems to be worse. Last night she kept talking about drowning. I don't know what to do."

"I spoke to John Harley. He's given her some medication he thinks will help her."

"I hope so, Doctor," George said earnestly. "I couldn't stand it if anything happened to her."

And Peter Templeton, his ear attuned to the unspoken words, had the uneasy feeling he was witnessing a charade. There was a deadly violence in this man. "Mr. Mellis, how would you describe your past relationships with women?"

"Normal."

"Did you ever get angry with any of them, lose your temper?"

George Mellis saw where the questions were leading. "Never." *I'm too damned smart for you, Doc.* "I told you, I don't believe in violence."

It was butchery, Peter. He smashed her cheekbone, broke her nose and three ribs, and burned her buttocks and the soles of her feet with cigarettes.

"Sometimes," Peter said, "to some people violence provides a necessary outlet, an emotional release."

"I know what you mean. I have a friend who beats up whores."

I have a friend. An alarm signal. "Tell me about your friend."

"He hates prostitutes. They're always trying to rip him off. So when he finishes with them, he roughs them up a little—just to teach them a lesson." He looked at Peter's face, but saw no disapproval there. Emboldened, George went on. "I remember once he and I were in Jamaica together. This little black hooker took him up to a hotel room, and after she got his pants off, she told him she wanted more money." George smiled. "He beat the shit out of her. I'll bet she won't try that on anyone again."

He's psychotic, Peter Templeton decided. There was no friend, of course. He was boasting about himself, hiding behind an alter ego. The man was a megalomaniac, and a dangerous one.

Peter decided he had better have another talk with John Harley as quickly as possible.

The two men met for lunch at the Harvard Club. Peter Templeton was in a difficult position. He needed to get all the information he could about George Mellis without breaching the confidentiality of the doctor-patient relationship.

"What can you tell me about George Mellis's wife?" he asked Harley.

"Alexandra? She's lovely. I've taken care of her and her sister, Eve, since they were babies." He chuckled. "You hear about identical twins, but you never really appreciate what that means until you see those two together."

Peter asked slowly, "They're identical twins?"

"Nobody could ever tell them apart. They used to play all kinds of pranks when they were little tykes. I remember once when Eve was sick and supposed to get a shot, I somehow wound up giving it to Alexandra." He took a sip of his drink. "It's amazing. Now they're grown up, and I still can't tell one from the other."

Peter thought about that. "You said Alexandra came to see you because she was feeling suicidal."

"That's right."

"John, how do you know it was Alexandra?"

"That's easy," Dr. Harley said. "Eve still has a little scar on her forehead from the surgery after the beating George Mellis gave her."

So that was a blind alley. "I see."

"How are you getting along with Mellis?"

Peter hesitated, wondering how much he could say. "I haven't reached him. He's hiding behind a facade. I'm trying to break it down."

"Be careful, Peter. If you want my opinion, the man's insane." He was remembering Eve lying in bed, in a pool of blood.

"Both sisters are heir to a large fortune, aren't they?" Peter asked.

Now it was John Harley's turn to hesitate. "Well, it's private family business," he said, "but the answer is no. Their grandmother cut off Eve without a dime. Alexandra inherits everything."

I'm worried about Alexandra, Dr. Templeton. Her depression seems to be worse. She keeps talking about drowning. I couldn't stand it if anything happened to her.

It had sounded to Peter Templeton like a classic setup for murder—except that George Mellis was the heir to a large fortune of his own. There would be no reason for him to kill anyone for money. *You're imagining things,* Peter chided himself.

A woman was drowning in the cold sea, and he was trying to swim to her side, but the waves were too high, and she kept sinking under them and rising again. *Hold on,* he shouted. *I'm coming.* He tried to swim faster, but his arms and legs seemed leaden, and he watched as she went down again. When he reached the place where she had disappeared, he looked around and saw an enormous white shark bearing down on him. Peter Templeton woke up. He turned on the lights and sat up in bed, thinking about his dream.

Early the following morning, he telephoned Detective Lieutenant Nick Pappas.

Nick Pappas was a huge man, six feet four inches and weighing almost three hundred pounds. As any number of criminals could testify, not an ounce of it was fat. Lieutenant Pappas was with the homicide task force in the "silk stocking" district in Manhattan. Peter had met him several years earlier while testifying as a psychiatric expert in a murder trial, and he and Pappas had become friends. Pappas's passion was chess, and the two met once a month to play.

Nick answered the phone. "Homicide. Pappas."

"It's Peter, Nick."

"My friend! How go the mysteries of the mind?"

"Still trying to unravel them, Nick. How's Tina?"

"Fantastic. What can I do for you?"

"I need some information. Do you still have connections in Greece?"

"Do I!" Pappas moaned. "I got a hundred relatives over there, and they all need money. The stupid part is I send it to them. Maybe you oughta analyze me."

"Too late," Peter told him. "You're a hopeless case."

"That's what Tina keeps telling me. What information do you need?"

"Have you ever heard of George Mellis?"

"The food family?"

"Yes."

"He's not exactly on my beat, but I know who he is. What about him?"

"I'd like to know if he has any money."

"You must be kiddin'. His family—"

"I mean money of his own."

"I'll check it out, Peter, but it'll be a waste of time. The Mellises are rich-rich."

"By the way, if you have anyone question George Mellis's father, tell him to handle it gently. The old man's had several heart attacks."

"Okay. I'll put it out on the wire."

Peter remembered the dream. "Nick, would you mind making a telephone call instead? Today?"

There was a different note in Pappas's voice. "Is there anything you'd like to tell me, Peter?"

"There's nothing to tell. I just want to satisfy my curiosity. Charge the phone call to me."

"Damn right I will—and the dinner you're gonna buy me when you tell me what the fuck this is all about."

"Deal." Peter Templeton hung up. He felt a little better.

Kate Blackwell was not feeling well. She was at her desk talking on the telephone when she felt the sudden attack. The room started to spin, and she gripped her desk tightly until everything righted itself again.

Brad came into the office. He took one look at her pale face and asked, "Are you all right, Kate?"

She let go of the desk. "Just a little dizzy spell. Nothing important."

"How long since you've had a medical checkup?"

"I don't have time for that nonsense, Brad."

"Find time. I'm going to have Annette call and make an appointment for you with John Harley."

"Bloody hell, Brad. Stop fussing, will you please?"

"Will you go see him?"

"If it will get you off my back."

The following morning Peter Templeton's secretary said, "Detective Pappas is calling on line one."

Peter picked up the phone. "Hello, Nick."

"I think you and I better have a little talk, my friend."

Peter felt a sudden anxiety stirring in him. "Did you talk to someone about Mellis?"

"I talked to Old Man Mellis himself. First of all, he's never had a heart attack in his life, and second, he said as far as he's concerned, his son George is dead. He cut him off without a dime a few years ago. When I asked why, the old man hung up on me. Then I called one of my old buddies at headquarters in Athens. Your George Mellis is a real beauty. The police know him well. He gets his kicks beating up girls and boys. His last victim before he left Greece was a fifteen-year-old male prostitute. They found his body in a hotel, and tied him in with Mellis. The old man bought somebody off, and Georgie boy got his ass kicked out of Greece. For good. Does that satisfy you?"

It did more than satisfy Peter; it terrified him. "Thanks, Nick. I owe you one."

"Oh, no, pal. I think I'd like to collect on *this* one. If your boy's on the loose again, you'd better tell me."

"I will as soon as I can, Nick. Give my love to Tina." And Peter hung up. He had a lot to think about. George Mellis was coming in at noon.

* * *

Dr. John Harley was in the middle of an examination when his receptionist said, "Mrs. George Mellis is here to see you, Doctor. She has no appointment, and I told her your schedule is—"

John Harley said, "Bring her in the side door and put her in my office."

Her face was paler than the last time, and the shadows under her eyes were darker. "I'm sorry to barge in on you like this, John, but—"

"That's all right, Alexandra. What's the problem?"

"Everything. I—I feel awful."

"Have you been taking the Wellbutrin regularly?"

"Yes."

"And you still feel depressed?"

Her hands were clenched. "It's worse than depression. It's—I feel desperate. I feel as though I have no control over anything anymore. I can't stand myself. I'm afraid I'm—I'm going to do something terrible."

Dr. Harley said reassuringly, "There's nothing physically wrong with you. I'll stake my reputation on that. It's all emotional. I'm going to switch you to another drug, Nomifensine. It's very effective. You should notice a change within a few days." He wrote out a prescription and handed it to her. "If you don't feel better by Friday, I want you to call me. I may want to send you to a psychiatrist."

Thirty minutes later, back in her apartment, Eve removed the pale foundation cream from her face and wiped away the smudges under her eyes.

The pace was quickening.

George Mellis sat opposite Peter Templeton, smiling and confident.

"How are you feeling today?"

"Much better, Doctor. These few sessions we've had have helped more than you know."

"Have they? In what way?"

"Oh, just having someone to talk to. That's the principle

the Catholic Church is built on, isn't it? Confession?"

"I'm glad you feel the sessions have been helpful. Is your wife feeling better?"

George frowned. "I'm afraid not. She saw Dr. Harley again, but she's talking about suicide more and more. I may take her away somewhere. I think she needs a change."

It seemed to Peter that there was an ominous foreboding in those words. Could it be his imagination?

"Greece is a very relaxing place," Peter said casually. "Have you taken her there to meet your family?"

"Not yet. They're dying to meet Alex." He grinned. "The only problem is that every time Pop and I get together, he keeps trying to talk me into coming back and taking over the family business."

And at that moment, Peter knew that Alexandra Mellis was in real danger.

Long after George Mellis had left, Peter Templeton sat in his office going over his notes. Finally, he reached for the telephone and dialed a number.

"I want you to do me a favor, John. Can you find out where George Mellis took his wife on their honeymoon?"

"I can tell you right now. I gave them some shots before they left. They went to Jamaica."

I have a friend who beats up whores. . . . I remember once we were in Jamaica together. This little black whore took him up to a hotel room, and after she got his pants off, she told him she wanted more money. . . . He beat the shit out of her. I'll bet she won't try that on anyone again.

Still, there was no proof that George Mellis was planning to kill his wife. John Harley had verified that Alexandra Mellis was suicidal. *It's not my problem,* Peter tried to tell himself. But he knew it *was* his problem.

Peter Templeton had had to work his way through school. His father had been the caretaker of a college in a small town in Nebraska, and even with a scholarship, Peter had not been able to afford to go to one of the Ivy League medical schools. He had been graduated from the University of Nebraska with honors and had gone on to study psychiatry. He had been successful from the start. His secret was that he genuinely liked people; he cared what happened to them. Alexandra Mellis was not a patient, yet he was involved with her. She was a missing part of the puzzle, and meeting her face-to-face might help him solve it. He took out George Mellis's file, found his home number and telephoned Alexandra Mellis. A maid summoned her to the phone.

"Mrs. Mellis, my name is Peter Templeton. I'm—"

"Oh, I know who you are, Doctor. George has told me about you."

Peter was surprised. He would have bet that George Mellis would not have mentioned him to his wife. "I wondered if we could meet. Perhaps lunch?"

"Is it about George? Is something wrong?"

"No, nothing. I just thought we might have a talk."

"Yes, certainly, Dr. Templeton."

They made an appointment for the following day.

They were seated at a corner table at La Grenouille. From the moment Alexandra had walked into the restaurant, Peter had been unable to take his eyes off her. She was dressed simply in a white skirt and blouse that showed off her figure, and she wore a single strand of pearls around her neck. Peter looked for signs of the tiredness and depression Dr. Harley had mentioned. There were none. If Alexandra was aware of Peter's stare, she gave no sign of it.

"My husband is all right, isn't he, Dr. Templeton?"

"Yes." This was going to be much more difficult than Peter had anticipated. He was walking a very fine line. He had no right to violate the sanctity of the doctor-patient relationship, yet at the same time he felt that Alexandra Mellis must be warned.

After they had ordered, Peter said, "Did your husband tell you why he's seeing me, Mrs. Mellis?"

"Yes. He's been under a great strain lately. His partners at the brokerage firm where he works put most of the responsibility on his shoulders. George is very conscientious, as you probably know, Doctor."

It was incredible. She was completely unaware of the attack on her sister. *Why had no one told her?*

"George told me how much better he felt having someone he could discuss his problems with." She gave Peter a grateful smile. "I'm very pleased that you're helping him."

She was so innocent! She obviously idolized her husband. What Peter had to say could destroy her. How could he inform her that her husband was a psychopath who had murdered a young male prostitute, who had been banished by his family and who had brutally assaulted her sister? Yet, how could he *not*?

"It must be very satisfying being a psychiatrist," Alexandra went on. "You're able to help so many people."

"Sometimes we can," Peter said carefully. "Sometimes we can't."

The food arrived. They talked as they ate, and there was an easy rapport between them. Peter found himself enchanted by her. He suddenly became uncomfortably aware that he was envious of George Mellis.

"I'm enjoying this luncheon very much," Alexandra finally said, "but you wanted to see me for a reason, didn't you, Dr. Templeton?"

The moment of truth had arrived.

"As a matter of fact, yes. I—"

Peter stopped. His next words could shatter her life. He had come to this luncheon determined to tell her of his suspicions and suggest that her husband be put in an institution. Now that he had met Alexandra, he found it was not so simple. He thought again of George Mellis's words: *She's not any better. It's the suicidal thing that worries me.* Peter thought he had never seen a happier, more normal person. Was that a result of the medication she was taking? At least he could ask her about that. He said, "John Harley told me that you're taking—"

And George Mellis's voice boomed out. "There you are, darling! I called the house and they told me you'd be here." He turned to Peter. "Nice to see you, Dr. Templeton. May I join you?"

And the opportunity vanished.

"*Why* did he want to meet Alex?" Eve demanded.

"I haven't the slightest idea," George said. "Thank God she left a message where she would be in case I wanted her. With Peter Templeton, for Christ's sake! I got over there fast!"

"I don't like it."

"Believe me, there was no harm done. I questioned her afterward, and she told me they didn't discuss anything in particular."

"I think we'd better move up our plan."

George Mellis felt an almost sexual thrill at her words. He had been waiting so long for this moment. "When?"

"Now."

33

The dizzy spells were getting worse, and things were beginning to blur in Kate's mind. She would sit at her desk considering a proposed merger and suddenly realize the merger had taken place ten years earlier. It frightened her. She finally decided to take Brad Rogers's advice to see John Harley.

It had been a long time since Dr. Harley had been able to persuade Kate Blackwell to have a checkup, and he took full advantage of her visit. He examined her thoroughly, and when he finished he asked her to wait for him in his office. John Harley was disturbed. Kate Blackwell was remarkably alert for her age, but there were disquieting signs. There was a definite hardening of the arteries, which would account for her occasional dizziness and weakened memory. She should have retired years ago, and yet she hung on tenaciously, unwilling to give the reins to anyone else. *Who am I to talk?* he thought. *I should have retired ages ago.*

Now, with the results of the examination in front of him, John Harley said, "I wish I were in your condition, Kate."

"Cut the soft-soap, John. What's my problem?"

"Age, mostly. There's a little hardening of the arteries, and—"

"Arteriosclerosis?"

"Oh. Is that the medical term for it?" Dr. Harley asked. "Whatever it is, you've got it."

"How bad is it?"

"For your age, I'd say it was pretty normal. These things are all relative."

"Can you give me something to stop these bloody dizzy spells? I hate fainting in front of a roomful of men. It looks bad for my sex."

He nodded. "I don't think that will be any problem. When are you going to retire, Kate?"

"When I have a great-grandson to take over the business."

The two old friends who had known each other for so many years sized each other up across the desk. John Harley had not always agreed with Kate, but he had always admired her courage.

As though reading his mind, Kate sighed, "Do you know one of the great disappointments of my life, John? Eve. I really cared for that child. I wanted to give her the world, but she never gave a damn about anyone but herself."

"You're wrong, Kate. Eve cares a great deal about you."

"Like bloody hell she does."

"I'm in a position to know. Recently she"—he had to choose his words carefully—"suffered a terrible accident. She almost died."

Kate felt her heart lurch. "Why—why didn't you tell me?"

"She wouldn't let me. She was so concerned you would be worried that she made me swear not to say a word."

"Oh, my God." It was an agonized whisper. "Is—is she all right?" Kate's voice was hoarse.

"She's fine now."

Kate sat, staring into space. "Thank you for telling me, John. Thank you."

"I'll write out a prescription for those pills." When he finished writing the prescription, he looked up. Kate Blackwell had left.

* * *

Eve opened the door and stared unbelievingly. Her grandmother was standing there, stiff and straight as always, allowing no sign of frailty to show.

"May I come in?" Kate asked.

Eve stepped aside, unable to take in what was happening. "Of course."

Kate walked in and looked around the small apartment, but she made no comment. "May I sit down?"

"I'm sorry. Please do. Forgive me—this is so— Can I get you something? Tea, coffee, anything?"

"No, thank you. Are you well, Eve?"

"Yes, thank you. I'm fine."

"I just came from Dr. John. He told me you had been in a terrible accident."

Eve watched her grandmother cautiously, not sure what was coming. "Yes . . ."

"He said you were . . . near death. And that you would not allow him to tell me because you didn't want to worry me."

So that was it. Eve was on surer ground now. "Yes, Gran."

"That would indicate to me," Kate's voice was suddenly choked, "that—that you cared."

Eve started to cry from relief. "Of course I care. I've always cared."

And an instant later, Eve was in her grandmother's arms. Kate held Eve very close and pressed her lips to the blond head in her lap. Then she whispered, "I've been such a damned old fool. Can you ever forgive me?" Kate pulled out a linen handkerchief and blew her nose. "I was too hard on you," she declared. "I couldn't bear it if anything had happened to you."

Eve stroked her grandmother's blue-veined hand soothingly and said, "I'm all right, Gran. Everything's fine."

Kate was on her feet, blinking back tears. "We'll have a fresh start, all right?" She pulled Eve up to face her. "I've been stubborn and unbending, like my father. I'm going to make amends for that. The first thing I'm going to do is put you back in my will, where you belong."

What was happening was too good to be true! "I—I don't care about the money. I only care about you."

"You're my heiress—you and Alexandra. You two are all the family I have."

"I'm getting along fine," Eve said, "but if it will make you happy—"

"It will make me very happy, darling. Very happy, indeed. When can you move back into the house?"

Eve hesitated for only a moment. "I think it would be better if I stayed here, but I'll see you as often as you want to see me. Oh, Gran, you don't know how lonely I've been."

Kate took her granddaughter's hand and said, "Can you forgive me?"

Eve looked her in the eye and said solemnly, "Of course, I can forgive you."

The moment Kate left, Eve mixed herself a stiff Scotch and water and sank down onto the couch to relive the incredible scene that had just occurred. She could have shouted aloud with joy. She and Alexandra were now the sole heirs to the Blackwell fortune. It would be easy enough to get rid of Alexandra. It was George Mellis Eve was concerned about. He had suddenly become a hindrance.

"There's been a change of plans," Eve told George. "Kate has put me back in her will."

George paused in the middle of lighting a cigarette. "Really? Congratulations."

"If anything happened to Alexandra now, it would look suspicious. So we'll take care of her later when—"

"I'm afraid later doesn't suit me."

"What do you mean?"

"I'm not stupid, darling. If anything happens to Alexandra, *I'll* inherit her stock. You want me out of the picture, don't you?"

Eve shrugged. "Let's say you're an unnecessary complication.

I'm willing to make a deal with you. Get a divorce, and as soon as I come into the money, I'll give you—"

He laughed. "You're funny. It's no good, baby. Nothing has changed. Alex and I have a date in Dark Harbor Friday night. I intend to keep it."

Alexandra was overjoyed when she heard the news about Eve and her grandmother. "Now we're a family again," she said.

The telephone.

"Hello. I hope I'm not disturbing you, Eve. It's Keith Webster."

He had started telephoning her two or three times a week. At first his clumsy ardor had amused Eve, but lately he had become a nuisance.

"I can't talk to you now," Eve said. "I was just going out the door.

"Oh." His voice was apologetic. "Then I won't keep you. I have two tickets for the horse show next week. I know you love horses, and I thought—"

"Sorry. I will probably be out of town next week."

"I see." She could hear the disappointment in his voice. "Perhaps the following week, then. I'll get tickets to a play. What would you like to see?"

"I've seen them all," Eve said curtly. "I have to run." She replaced the receiver. It was time to get dressed. She was meeting Rory McKenna, a young actor she had seen in an off-Broadway play. He was five years younger than she, and he was like an insatiable wild stallion. Eve visualized his making love to her, and she felt a moisture between her legs. She looked forward to an exciting evening.

On his way home, George Mellis stopped to buy flowers for Alexandra. He was in an exuberant mood. It was a delicious irony that the old lady had put Eve back in her will, but it changed nothing. After Alexandra's accident, he would take care of Eve. The arrangements were all made. On Friday Alexandra would be waiting for him at Dark Harbor. "Just the two of us," he had pleaded as he kissed her. "Get rid of all the servants, darling."

Peter Templeton was unable to get Alexandra Mellis out of his mind. He heard the echo of George Mellis's words: *I may take her away somewhere. I think she needs a change.* Every instinct told Peter that Alexandra was in danger, yet he was powerless to act. He could not go to Nick Pappas with his suspicions. He had no proof.

Across town, in the executive offices of Kruger-Brent, Ltd., Kate Blackwell was signing a new will, leaving the bulk of her estate to her two granddaughters.

In upstate New York, Tony Blackwell was standing before his easel in the garden of the sanitarium. The painting on the easel was a jumble of colors, the kind of painting an untalented child might do. Tony stepped back to look at it and smiled with pleasure.

Friday. 10:57 A.M.

At La Guardia Airport, a taxi pulled up in front of the Eastern Airlines shuttle terminal and Eve Blackwell got out. She handed the driver a hundred-dollar bill.

"Hey, I can't change this, lady," he said. "Have you got anything smaller?"

"No."

"Then you'll have to get change inside."

"I haven't time. I have to catch the next shuttle to Washington." She looked at the Baume & Mercier watch on her wrist and made a decision. "Keep the hundred dollars," she told the startled driver.

Eve hurried into the terminal. She half-walked and half-ran to the departure gate marked Washington Shuttle. "One round trip to Washington," Eve said breathlessly.

The man looked at the clock above his head. "You missed this one by two minutes. It's just taking off."

"I've got to be on that plane. I'm meeting— Isn't there anything you can do?" She was near panic.

"Take it easy, miss. There's another shuttle leaving in an hour."

"That's too— Damn it!"

He watched her regain control of herself.

"Very well. I'll wait. Is there a coffee shop around here?"

"No, ma'am. But there's a coffee machine down the corridor."

"Thank you."

He looked after her and thought, *What a beauty. I sure envy the guy she's in such a hurry to meet.*

Friday. 2:00 P.M.

It will be a second honeymoon, Alexandra thought. The idea excited her. *Get rid of all the servants. I want it to be just the two of us, angel. We'll have a lovely weekend.* And now Alexandra was leaving the brownstone, on her way to Dark Harbor to meet George. She was running behind schedule. She had had a luncheon engagement, and it had taken longer than Alexandra had planned. She said to the maid, "I'm going now. I'll be back Monday morning."

As Alexandra reached the front door, the telephone rang. *I'm late. Let it ring,* she thought, and hurried out the door.

Friday. 7:00 P.M.

George Mellis had examined Eve's plan over and over. There was not a single flaw in it. *There will be a motor launch waiting for you at Philbrook Cove. Take it to Dark Harbor and make sure you're not seen. Tie it to the stern of the Corsair. You'll take Alexandra for a moonlight sail. When you're out at sea, do whatever turns you on, George—just don't leave any traces of blood. Dump the body overboard, get into the launch and leave the Corsair adrift. You'll take the launch back to Philbrook Cove, then catch the Lincolnville ferry to Dark Harbor. Take a taxi to the house. Use some excuse to get the driver to go in so that you'll both notice the Corsair is missing from the dock. When you see that Alexandra is gone, you'll call the police. They'll never find Alexandra's body. The tide will wash it out to sea. Two eminent doctors will testify it was a probable suicide.*

He found the motorboat moored at Philbrook Cove, waiting for him, according to plan.

George crossed the bay without running lights, using the light of the moon to steer by. He passed a number of moored boats without being detected, and arrived at the dock at the Blackwell estate. He cut the motor and made the line fast to the *Corsair*, the large motor sailer.

She was talking on the telephone, waiting for him in the living room when George walked in. She waved to him, covered the receiver with her hand and mouthed, "It's Eve." She listened a moment, then, "I have to go now, Eve. My darling just arrived. I'll see you at lunch next week." She replaced the receiver and hurried over to hug George. "You're early. I'm so pleased."

"I got lonely for you, so I just dropped everything and came." She kissed him. "I love you."

"I love you, *matia mou*. Did you get rid of the servants?"

She smiled. "It's just the two of us. Guess what? I made moussaka for you."

He traced a finger lightly across the nipples straining against her silk blouse. "Do you know what I've been thinking about all afternoon at that dreary office? Going for a sail with you. There's a brisk wind. Why don't we go out for an hour or two?"

"If you like. But my moussaka is—"

He cupped his hand over her breast. "Dinner can wait. I can't."

She laughed. "All right. I'll go change. It won't take me a minute."

"I'll race you."

He went upstairs to his clothes closet, changed into a pair of slacks, a sweater and boat shoes. Now that the moment was here, he was filled with a sense of wild anticipation, a feeling of excitement that was almost an explosion.

He heard her voice. "I'm ready, darling."

He turned. She stood in the doorway, dressed in a sweater, a pair of black slacks and canvas shoes. Her long, blond hair was tied back with a little blue ribbon. *My God, she's beautiful!* he thought. It seemed almost a shame to waste that beauty.

"So am I," George told her.

She noticed the motor launch secured to the stern of the yacht. "What's that for, darling?"

"There's a little island at the end of the bay that I've always wanted to explore," George explained. "We'll take the launch over to it so we won't have to worry about rocks."

He cast off the lines and powered slowly out of the slip. He nosed into the wind to raise the mainsail and jib, and the boat fell off on a starboard tack. The wind caught the large sails and the *Corsair* surged forward. George headed out to sea. As they cleared the breakwater, they were met with a stiff force-five wind, and the boat started heeling, its lee rail running under.

"It's wild and lovely," she called out. "I'm so happy, darling."

He smiled. "So am I."

In an odd way, it gave George Mellis pleasure that Alexandra was happy, that she was going to die happy. He scanned the horizon to make certain no other boats were close by. There were only faint lights from afar. It was time.

He put the boat on automatic pilot, took one last look around the empty horizon and walked over to the lee railing, his heart beginning to pound with excitement.

"Alex," he called. "Come look at this."

She made her way over to him and looked down at the cold, dark water racing below them.

"Come to me." His voice was a harsh command.

She moved into his arms, and he kissed her hard on the lips. His arms closed around her, hugging her, and he felt her body relax. He flexed his muscles and began to lift her in the air toward the railing.

She was fighting him suddenly. "George!"

He lifted her higher, and he felt her try to pull away, but he was too strong for her. She was almost on top of the railing now, her feet kicking wildly, and he braced himself to shove her over the side. At that instant, he felt a sudden white-hot pain in his chest. His first thought was, *I'm having a heart attack.* He opened his mouth to speak and blood came spurting out. He dropped his arms and looked down at his chest in disbelief. Blood was pouring from a gaping wound in it. He looked up, and she was standing there with a bloody knife in her hand, smiling at him.

George Mellis's last thought was, *Eve . . .*

34

It was ten o'clock in the evening when Alexandra arrived at the house at Dark Harbor. She had tried telephoning George there several times, but there had been no answer. She hoped he would not be angry because she had been detained. It had been a stupid mix-up. Early that afternoon, as Alexandra was leaving for Dark Harbor, the phone had rung. She had thought, *I'm late. Let it ring,* and had gone out to the car. The maid had come hurrying after her.

"Mrs. Mellis! It's your sister. She says it is urgent."

When Alexandra picked up the telephone, Eve said, "Darling, I'm in Washington, D.C. I'm having a terrible problem. I have to see you."

"Of course," Alexandra said instantly. "I'm leaving for Dark Harbor now to meet George, but I'll be back Monday morning and—"

"This can't wait." Eve sounded desperate. "Will you meet me at La Guardia Airport? I'll be on the five o'clock plane."

"I'd like to, Eve, but I told George—"

"This is an emergency, Alex. But, of course, if you're too busy . . ."

"Wait! All right. I'll be there."

"Thanks, darling. I knew I could count on you."

It was so seldom that Eve asked her for a favor, she could not refuse her. She would catch a later plane to the island. She telephoned George at the office to tell him she would be detained, but he was not in. She left a message with his secretary. An hour later she took a taxi to La Guardia in time to meet the five o'clock plane from Washington. Eve was not on it. Alexandra waited for two hours, and there was still no sign of Eve. Alexandra had no idea where to reach Eve in Washington. Finally, because there was nothing else she could do, Alexandra took a plane to the island. Now as she approached Cedar Hill House, she found it dark. Surely George should have arrived by now. Alexandra went from room to room, turning on the lights.

"George?"

There was no sign of him. She telephoned her home in Manhattan. The maid answered.

"Is Mr. Mellis there?" Alexandra asked.

"Why, no, Mrs. Mellis. He said you would both be away for the weekend."

"Thank you, Marie. He must have been detained somewhere."

There had to be a logical reason for his absence. Obviously some business had come up at the last minute and, as usual, the partners had asked George to handle it. He would be along at any moment. She dialed Eve's number.

"Eve!" Alexandra exclaimed. "What on earth happened to you?"

"What happened to *you*? I waited at Kennedy, and when you didn't show up—"

"*Kennedy!* You said *La Guardia*."

"No, darling, Kennedy."

"But—" It did not matter any longer. "I'm sorry," Alexandra said. "I must have misunderstood. Are you all right?"

Eve said, "I am now. I've had a hellish time. I got involved with a man who's a big political figure in Washington. He's insanely jealous and—" She laughed. "I can't go into the details over the telephone. The phone company will take out both our phones. I'll tell you all about it Monday."

"All right," Alexandra said. She was enormously relieved.

"Have a nice weekend," Eve told her. "How's George?"

"He's not here." Alexandra tried to keep the note of concern out of her voice. "I suppose he got tied up on business and hasn't had a chance to call me."

"I'm sure you'll hear from him soon. Good-night, darling."

"Good night, Eve."

Alexandra replaced the receiver and thought, *It would be nice if Eve found someone really wonderful. Someone as good and kind as George.* She looked at her watch. It was almost eleven o'clock. Surely he would have had a chance to call by now. She picked up the telephone and dialed the number of the brokerage firm. There was no answer. She telephoned his club. No, they had not seen Mr. Mellis. By midnight, Alexandra was alarmed, and by one A.M. she was in a state of panic. She was not sure what to do. It was possible that George was out with a client and could not get to a telephone, or perhaps he had had to fly somewhere and had not been able to reach her before he left. There was some simple explanation. If she called the police and George walked in, she would feel like a fool.

At 2:00 A.M. she telephoned the police. There was no police force on the island of Islesboro itself, and the closest station was in Waldo County.

A sleepy voice said, "Waldo County Sheriff's Department. Sergeant Lambert."

"This is Mrs. George Mellis at Cedar Hill House."

"Yes, Mrs. Mellis." The voice was instantly alert. "What can I do for you?"

"To tell you the truth, I'm not sure," Alexandra said hesitantly. "My husband was supposed to have met me at the house earlier this evening, and he—he hasn't shown up."

"I see." There were all kinds of implications in that phrase. The sergeant knew at least three reasons why a husband could be away from home at two A.M. in the morning: blondes, brunets and redheads.

He said tactfully, "Is it possible he was detained on business somewhere?"

"He—he usually calls."

"Well, you know how it is, Mrs. Mellis. Sometimes you get in a situation where you can't call. I'm sure you'll be hearing from him."

Now she *did* feel like a fool. Of course there was nothing the police could do. She had read somewhere that a person had to be missing for twenty-four hours before the police would even start looking for him, and George was not *missing*, for heaven's sake. He was just late.

"I'm sure you're right," Alexandra said into the telephone. "I'm sorry to have troubled you."

"Not at all, Mrs. Mellis. I'll bet he'll be on the seven o'clock ferry first thing in the morning."

He was not on the seven o'clock ferry, or the one after that. Alexandra telephoned the Manhattan house again. George was not there.

A feeling of disaster began to grip Alexandra. George had been in an accident; he was in a hospital somewhere, ill or dead. If only there had not been the mix-up with Eve at the airport. Perhaps George had arrived at the house, and when he found she was not there, he had gone. But that left too many things unexplained. He would have left a note. He could have surprised burglars and been attacked or kidnapped. Alexandra went through the house, room by room, looking for any possible clue. Everything was intact. She went down to the dock. The *Corsair* was there, safely moored.

She telephoned the Waldo County Sheriff's Department again. Lieutenant Philip Ingram, a twenty-year veteran of the force, was on morning duty. He was already aware that George Mellis had not been home all night. It had been the chief topic of conversation around the station all morning, most of it ribald.

Now he said to Alexandra, "There's no trace of him at all, Mrs. Mellis? All right. I'll come out there myself." He knew it would be a waste of time. Her old man was probably tomcatting around in some alley. *But when the Blackwells call, the peasants come running,* he thought wryly. Anyway, this was a nice lady. He had met her a few times over the years.

"Back in an hour or so," he told the desk sergeant.

Lieutenant Ingram listened to Alexandra's story, checked the house and the dock and reached the conclusion that Alexandra Mellis had a problem on her hands. George Mellis was to have met his wife the evening before at Dark Harbor, but he had not shown up. While it was not Lieutenant Ingram's problem, he knew it would do him no harm to be helpful to a member of the Blackwell family. Ingram telephoned the island airport and the ferry terminal at Lincolnville. George Mellis had used neither facility within the past twenty-four hours. "He didn't come to Dark Harbor," the lieutenant told Alexandra. *And where the hell did that leave things? Why would the man have dropped out of sight?* In the lieutenant's considered opinion, no man in his right mind would voluntarily leave a woman like Alexandra.

"We'll check the hospitals and mor—" He caught himself. "And other places, and I'll put out an APB on him."

Alexandra was trying to control her emotions, but he could see what an effort it was. "Thank you, Lieutenant. I don't have to tell you how much I'll appreciate anything you can do."

"That's my job," Lieutenant Ingram replied.

When Lieutenant Ingram returned to the station, he began calling hospitals and morgues. The responses were negative. There was no accident report on George Mellis. Lieutenant Ingram's next move was to call a reporter friend on the *Maine Courier.* After that, the lieutenant sent out a missing person all-points-bulletin.

The afternoon newspapers carried the story in headlines: HUSBAND OF BLACKWELL HEIRESS MISSING.

Peter Templeton first heard the news from Detective Nick Pappas.

"Peter, remember askin' me a while ago to do some checkin' on George Mellis?"

"Yes . . ."

"He's done a vanishing act."

"He's *what?*"

"Disappeared, vamoosed, gone." He waited while Peter digested the news.

"Did he take anything with him? Money, clothes, passport?"

"Nope. According to the report we got from Maine, Mr. Mellis just melted into thin air. You're his shrink. I thought you might have some idea why our boy would do a thing like that."

Peter said truthfully, "I haven't any idea, Nick."

"If you think of anything, let me know. There's gonna be a lot of heat on this."

"Yes," Peter promised. "I will."

Thirty minutes later, Alexandra Mellis telephoned Peter Templeton, and he could hear the shrill edge of panic in her voice. "I— George is missing. No one seems to know what happened to him. I was hoping he might have told you something that might have given you a clue or—" She broke off.

"I'm sorry, Mrs. Mellis. He didn't. I have no idea what could have happened."

"Oh."

Peter wished there was some way he could comfort her. "If I think of anything, I'll call you back. Where can I reach you?"

"I'm at Dark Harbor now, but I'm going to return to New York this evening. I'll be at my grandmother's."

Alexandra could not bear the thought of being alone. She had talked to Kate several times that morning. "Oh, darling, I'm sure there's nothing to worry about," Kate said. "He probably went off on some business deal and forgot to tell you."

Neither of them believed it.

Eve saw the story of George's disappearance on television. There were photographs of the exterior of Cedar Hill House, and pictures of Alexandra and George after their wedding ceremony. There was a close-up of George, looking upward, with his eyes wide. Somehow it reminded Eve of the look of surprise on his face just before he died.

The television commentator was saying, "There has been no evidence of foul play and no ransom demands have been made. The police speculate that George Mellis was possibly the victim of an accident and may be suffering from amnesia." Eve smiled in satisfaction.

They would never find the body. It had been swept out to sea with the tide. Poor George. He had followed her plan perfectly. But she had changed it. She had flown up to Maine and rented a motorboat at Philbrook Cove, to be held for "a friend." She had then rented a second boat from a nearby dock and taken it to Dark Harbor, where she had waited for George. He had been totally unsuspecting. She had been careful to wipe the deck clean before she returned the yacht to the dock. After that, it had been a simple matter to tow George's rented motorboat back to its pier, return her boat and fly back to New York to await the telephone call she knew Alexandra would make.

It was a perfect crime. The police would list it as a mysterious disappearance.

The announcer was saying, "In other news . . ." Eve switched the television set off.

She did not want to be late for her date with Rory McKenna.

At six o'clock the following morning, a fishing boat found George Mellis's body pinned against the breakwater at the mouth of Penebscot Bay. The early news reports called it a drowning and accidental death, but as more information came in, the tenor of the stories began to change. From the coroner's office came reports that what at first had been thought to have been shark bites were actually stab wounds. The evening newspaper editions screamed: MURDER SUSPECTED IN GEORGE MELLIS MYSTERY DEATH . . . MILLIONAIRE FOUND STABBED TO DEATH.

Lieutenant Ingram was studying the tide charts for the previous evening. When he was finished, he leaned back in his chair, a perplexed expression on his face. George Mellis's body would have been swept out to sea had it not been caught against the breakwater. What puzzled the lieutenant was that the body had to have been carried by the tide from the direction of Dark Harbor. Where George Mellis was not supposed to have been.

Detective Nick Pappas flew up to Maine to have a talk with Lieutenant Ingram.

"I think my department might be of some help to you in this case," Nick said. "We have some interesting background information on George Mellis. I know this is out of our jurisdiction, but if you were to ask for our cooperation, we'd be happy to give it to you, Lieutenant."

In the twenty years Lieutenant Ingram had been with the Waldo County Sheriff's Department, the only real excitement he had seen was when a drunken tourist shot a moose head off the wall of a local curio shop. The George Mellis murder was front-page news, and Lieutenant Ingram sensed a chance to make a name for himself. With a little luck, it could lead to a job as a detective in the New York City Police Department, where the action was. And so now he looked at Nick Pappas and murmured, "I don't know . . ."

As though reading his mind, Nick Pappas said, "We're not looking for credit. There's gonna be a hell of a lot of pressure on this one, and it would make life easier for us if we could wrap it up fast. I could start by filling you in on George Mellis's background."

Lieutenant Ingram decided he had nothing to lose. "OK, you've got a deal."

Alexandra was in bed, heavily sedated. Her mind stubbornly refused to accept the fact that George had been murdered. How could he have been? There was no reason in the world for anyone to kill him. The police had talked of a knife wound, but they were wrong about that. It had to be some kind of accident.

No one would want to kill him.... No one would want to kill him.... The opiate Dr. Harley gave her finally took hold. She slept.

Eve had been stunned at the news that George's body had been found. *But perhaps it's a good thing,* Eve thought, *Alexandra will be the one under suspicion. She was there, on the island.*

Kate was seated next to Eve on the couch in the drawing room. The news had been a tremendous shock to Kate.

"Why would anyone want to murder George?" she asked.

Eve sighed. "I don't know, Gran. I just don't know. My heart breaks for poor Alex."

Lieutenant Philip Ingram was questioning the attendant on the Lincolnville-Islesboro ferry. "Are you positive neither Mr. or Mrs. Mellis came over on the ferry Friday afternoon?"

"They didn't come over on my shift, Phil, and I checked with the morning man, and he didn't see 'em neither. They had to have come in by plane."

"One more question, Lew. Did *any* strangers take the ferry across on Friday?"

"Hell," the attendant said, "you know we don't get no strangers goin' to the island this time of year. There might be a few tourists in the summer—but in *November*? She-e-e-it!"

Lieutenant Ingram went to talk to the manager of the Islesboro airport. "George Mellis sure didn't fly in that evening, Phil. He musta come over to the island by ferry."

"Lew said he didn't see him."

"Well, hell, he couldn't a *swum* over, now could he?"

"What about Mrs. Mellis?"

"Yep. She come in here in her Beechcraft about ten o'clock. I had my son, Charley, run her over to Cedar Hill from the airport."

"What kind of mood did Mrs. Mellis seem to be in?"

"Funny you should ask. She was as nervous as spit on a hot kettle. Even my boy noticed it. Usually she's calm, always has a

pleasant word for everybody. But that night she was in a tearin
hurry."

"One more question. Did any strangers fly in that afternoon
or evening? Any unfamiliar faces?"

He shook his head. "Nope. Just the regulars."

An hour later, Lieutenant Ingram was on the phone talking to
Nick Pappas. "What I've got so far," he told the New York detective, "is damned confusing. Friday night Mrs. Mellis arrived
by private plane at the Islesboro airport around ten o'clock, bu
her husband wasn't with her, and he didn't come in by plane or
ferry. In fact, there's nothin' to show he was on the island at al
that night."

"Except the tide."

"Yeah."

"Whoever killed him probably threw him overboard from a
boat, figuring the tide would carry him out to sea. Did you check
the *Corsair*?"

"I looked it over. No sign of violence, no bloodstains."

"I'd like to bring a forensics expert up there. Would you
mind?"

"Not as long as you remember our little deal."

"I'll remember. See you tomorrow."

Nick Pappas and a team of experts arrived the following
morning. Lieutenant Ingram escorted them to the Blackwel
dock, where the *Corsair* was tied up. Two hours later, the foren
sics expert said, "Looks like we hit the jackpot, Nick. There are
some bloodstains on the underside of the lee rail."

That afternoon, the police laboratory verified that the stain
matched George Mellis's blood type.

Manhattan's "silk stocking" police precinct was busier than
usual. A series of all-night drug busts had filled the prisoners
cage to capacity, and the holding cells were crowded with pros
titutes, drunks and sex offenders. The noise and the stench com
peted for Peter Templeton's attention, as he was escorted
through the din to Lieutenant Detective Pappas's office.

"Hey, Peter. Nice of you to drop by."

On the phone Pappas had said, "You're holdin' out on me, chum. Be at my office before six o'clock, or I'll send a fuckin' SWAT team to bring you in."

When his escort left the office, Peter asked, "What's this all about, Nick? What's bothering you?"

"I'll tell you what's botherin' me. Someone's being clever. Do you know what we've got? A dead man who vanished from an island he never went to."

"That doesn't make sense."

"Tell me about it, pal. The ferryboat operator and the guy who runs the airport swear they never saw George Mellis on the night he disappeared. The only other way he could have gotten to Dark Harbor was by motorboat. We checked all the boat operators in the area. Zilch."

"Perhaps he wasn't at Dark Harbor that night."

"The forensic lab says different. They found evidence that Mellis was at the house and changed from a business suit into the sailing clothes he was wearin' when his body was found."

"Was he killed at the house?"

"On the Blackwell yacht. His body was dumped overboard. Whoever did it figured the current would carry the body to China."

"How did—?"

Nick Pappas raised a beefy hand. "My turn. Mellis was your patient. He must have talked to you about his wife."

"What does she have to do with this?"

"Everything. She's my first, second and third choice."

"You're crazy."

"Hey, I thought shrinks never used words like *crazy*."

"Nick, what makes you think Alexandra Mellis killed her husband?"

"She was there, and she had a motive. She arrived at the island late that night with some cockamamy excuse about being delayed because she was waitin' at the wrong airport to meet her sister."

"What does her sister say?"

"Give me a break. What the hell would you expect her to say?

They're *twins.* We know George Mellis was at the house that night, but his wife swears she never saw him. It's a big house, Peter, but it's not *that* big. Next, Mrs. M gave all the servants the weekend off. When I asked her why, she said it was George's idea. George's lips, of course, are sealed."

Peter sat there, deep in thought. "You said she had a motive. What?"

"You have a short memory span. You're the one who put me on the track. The lady was married to a psycho who got his kicks sexually abusing everything he could lay his fists on. He was probably slapping her around pretty good. Let's say she decided she didn't want to play anymore. She asked for a divorce. He wouldn't give it to her. Why should he? He had it made. She wouldn't dare take him to court—it would touch off too juicy a scandal. She had no choice. She had to kill him." He leaned back in his chair.

"What do you want from me?" Peter asked.

"Information. You had lunch with Mellis's wife ten days ago." He pressed the button on a tape recorder on the desk. "We're going on the record now, Peter. Tell me about that lunch. How did Alexandra Mellis behave? Was she tense? Angry? Hysterical?"

"Nick, I've never seen a more relaxed, happily married lady."

Nick Pappas glared at him and snapped off the tape recorder. "Don't shaft me, my friend. I went to see Dr. John Harley this morning. He's been giving Alexandra Mellis medication to stop her from committing suicide, for Christ's sake!"

Dr. John Harley had been greatly disturbed by his meeting with Lieutenant Pappas. The detective had gotten right to the point. "Has Mrs. Mellis consulted you professionally recently?"

"I'm sorry," Dr. Harley said. "I'm not at liberty to discuss my patients. I'm afraid I can't help you."

"All right, Doc. I understand. You're old friends. You'd like to keep the whole thing quiet. That's okay with me." He rose to his feet. "This is a homicide case. I'll be back in an hour with a warrant for your appointment records. When I find out what I want to know, I'm going to feed it to the newspapers."

Dr. Harley was studying him.

"We can handle it that way, or you can tell me now what I want to know, and I'll do what I can to keep it quiet. Well?"

"Sit down," Dr. Harley said. Nick Pappas sat. "Alexandra has been having some emotional problems lately."

"What kind of emotional problems?"

"She's been in a severe depression. She was talking about committing suicide."

"Did she mention using a knife?"

"No. She said she had a recurrent dream about drowning. I gave her Wellbutrin. She came back and told me it didn't seem to be helping, and I prescribed Nomifensine. I—I don't know whether it helped or not."

Nick Pappas sat there, putting things together in his mind. Finally he looked up. "Anything else?"

"That's everything, Lieutenant."

But there was more, and John Harley's conscience was bothering him. He had deliberately refrained from mentioning the brutal attack George Mellis had made on Eve Blackwell. Part of his concern was that he should have reported it to the police at the time it happened, but mainly Dr. Harley wanted to protect the Blackwell family. He had no way of knowing whether there was a connection between the attack on Eve and George Mellis's murder, but his instincts told him that it was better not to bring up the subject. He intended to do everything possible to protect Kate Blackwell.

Fifteen minutes after he made that decision, his nurse said, "Dr. Keith Webster is on line two, Doctor."

It was as if his conscience was prodding him.

Keith Webster said, "John, I'd like to stop by this afternoon and see you. Are you free?"

"I'll make myself free. What time?"

"How's five o'clock?"

"Fine, Keith. I'll see you then."

So, the matter was not going to be laid to rest so easily.

At five o'clock, Dr. Harley ushered Keith Webster into his office. "Would you like a drink?"

"No, thank you, John. I don't drink. Forgive me for barging in on you like this."

It seemed to John Harley that every time he saw him, Keith Webster was apologizing about something. He was such a mild, little man, so inoffensive and eager to please—a puppy waiting to be patted on the head. It was incredible to John Harley that within that pale, colorless persona there lurked such a brilliant surgeon.

"What can I do for you, Keith?"

Keith Webster drew a deep breath. "It's about that—you know—that beating George Mellis gave Eve Blackwell."

"What about it?"

"You're aware she almost died?"

"Yes."

"Well, it was never reported to the police. In view of what's happened—Mellis's murder and everything—I was wondering if maybe I shouldn't tell the police about it."

So there it was. There seemed no way to escape the problem.

"You have to do whatever you think best, Keith."

Keith Webster said gloomily, "I know. It's just that I'd hate to do anything that might hurt Eve Blackwell. She's a very special person."

Dr. Harley was watching him cautiously. "Yes, she is."

Keith Webster sighed. "The only thing is, John, if I do keep quiet about it now and the police find out later, it's going to look bad for me."

For both of us, John Harley thought. He saw a possible out. He said casually, "It's not very likely the police would find out, is it? Eve certainly would never mention it, and you fixed her up perfectly. Except for that little scar, you'd never know she'd been disfigured."

Keith Webster blinked. "What little scar?"

"The red scar on her forehead. She told me you said you were going to remove it in a month or two."

Dr. Webster was blinking faster now. It was some kind of nervous tic, Dr. Harley decided.

"I don't re— When did you last see Eve?"

"She came in about ten days ago to talk about a problem involving her sister. As a matter of fact, the scar was the only way I could tell it was Eve instead of Alexandra. They're identical twins, you know."

Keith Webster nodded slowly. "Yes. I've seen photographs of Eve's sister in the newspapers. There's an amazing likeness. And you say the only way you could tell them apart was by the scar on Eve's forehead from the operation I performed?"

"That's right."

Dr. Webster sat there, silent, chewing on his lower lip. Finally he said, "Perhaps I shouldn't go to the police just yet. I'd like to think about this a little more."

"Frankly, I think that's wise, Keith. They're both lovely young women. The newspapers are hinting that the police think Alexandra killed George. That's impossible. I remember when they were little girls . . ."

Dr. Webster was no longer listening.

When he left Dr. Harley, Keith Webster was lost in thought. He had certainly not left even the trace of a scar on that beautiful face. Yet, John Harley had seen it. It was possible that Eve could have gotten a scar afterward in another accident, but then why had she lied? It made no sense.

He examined it from every angle, going over all the different possibilities, and when he had come to a conclusion, he thought, *If I'm right, this is going to change my whole life. . . .*

Early the following morning, Keith Webster called Dr. Harley. "John," he began, "excuse me for disturbing you. You said that Eve Blackwell came in to talk to you about her sister, Alexandra?"

"That's right."

"After Eve's visit, did Alexandra happen to come in to see you?"

"Yes. As a matter of fact, she came to my office the following day. Why?"

"Just curious. Can you tell me what Eve's sister came to see you about?"

"Alexandra was in a deep depression. Eve was trying to help her."

Eve had been beaten and almost killed by Alexandra's husband. And now the man had been murdered and it was Alexandra who was being blamed.

Keith Webster had always known he was not brilliant. In school he had had to work very hard in order to achieve barely passing grades. He was the perennial butt of his classmates' jokes. He was neither an athlete nor a scholar, and he was socially inept. He was as close as one could come to being a nonentity. No one was more surprised than his own family when Keith Webster was admitted to medical school. When he elected to become a surgeon, neither his peers nor his teachers expected him to become a competent one, let alone a great one. But he had surprised them all. There was a talent deep inside him that was nothing short of genius. He was like some exquisite sculptor working his magic with living flesh instead of clay, and in a short time Keith Webster's reputation spread. In spite of his success, however, he was never able to overcome the trauma of his childhood. Inside he was still the little boy who bored everyone, the one at whom the girls laughed.

When he finally reached Eve, Keith's hands were slippery with sweat. She answered the phone on the first ring. "Rory?" Her voice was low and sultry.

"No. This is Keith Webster."

"Oh. Hello."

He heard the change in her voice. "How've you been?" he asked.

"Fine."

He could sense her impatience. "I—I'd like to see you."

"I'm not seeing anyone. If you read the papers, you'll know my brother-in-law was murdered. I'm in mourning."

He wiped his hands on his trousers. "That's what I want to see you about, Eve. I have some information you should know about."

"What kind of information?"

"I would prefer not to discuss it on the telephone." He could almost hear Eve's mind working.

"Very well. When?"

"Now, if it's convenient."

When he arrived at Eve's apartment thirty minutes later, Eve opened the door for him. "I'm very busy. What did you want to see me about?"

"About this," Keith Webster said apologetically. He opened a manila envelope he was clutching, took out a photograph and diffidently handed it to Eve. It was a photograph of herself.

She looked at it, puzzled. "Well?"

"It's a picture of you."

"I can see that," she said curtly. "What about it?"

"It was taken after your operation."

"So?"

"There's no scar on your forehead, Eve."

He watched the change that came over her face.

"Sit down, Keith."

He sat opposite her, on the edge of the couch, and he could not keep from staring at her. He had seen many beautiful women in his practice, but Eve Blackwell totally bewitched him. He had never known anyone like her.

"I think you'd better tell me what this is all about."

He started at the beginning. He told her about his visit to Dr. Harley and about the mysterious scar, and as Keith Webster talked, he watched Eve's eyes. They were expressionless.

When Keith Webster finished, Eve said, "I don't know what

you're thinking, but whatever it is, you're wasting my time. As for the scar, I was playing a little joke on my sister. It's as simple as that. Now, if you've quite finished, I have a great deal to do."

He remained seated. "I'm sorry to have bothered you. I just thought I should talk to you before I went to the police." He could see that he really had her attention now.

"Why on earth would you go to the police?"

"I'm obliged to report the attack George Mellis made on you. Then there's that business about you and the scar. I don't understand it, but I'm sure you can explain it to them."

Eve felt the first stab of fear. This stupid, dreary little man in front of her had no idea what had really happened, but he knew enough to start the police asking questions.

George Mellis had been a frequent visitor to the apartment. The police could probably find witnesses who had seen him. She had lied about being in Washington the night of George's murder. She had no real alibi. She had never thought she would need one. If the police learned that George had almost killed her, it would give them a motive. The whole scheme would begin to unravel. She had to silence this man.

"What is it you want? Money?"

"No!"

She saw the indignation on his face. "What, then?"

Dr. Webster looked down at the rug, his face red with embarrassment. "I—I like you so much, Eve. I would hate it if anything bad happened to you."

She forced a smile. "Nothing bad is going to happen to me, Keith. I haven't done anything wrong. Believe me, none of this has anything to do with George Mellis's murder." She reached out and took his hand. "I would really appreciate it very much if you would forget about this. All right?"

He covered her hand and squeezed it. "I'd like to, Eve. I really would. But they're holding the coroner's inquest Saturday. I'm a doctor. I'm afraid it's my duty to testify at that inquest and tell them everything I know."

He saw the alarm that appeared in her eyes.

"You don't have to do that!"

He stroked her hand. "Yes, I do, Eve. It's my sworn obligation. There's only one thing that could prevent me from doing it." He watched her leap to the bait of his words.

"What is that?"

His voice was very gentle. "A husband can't be forced to testify against his wife."

35

The wedding took place two days before the coroner's inquest. They were married by a judge in his private chambers. The mere idea of being married to Keith Webster made Eve's skin crawl, but she had no choice. *The fool thinks I'm going to stay married to him.* As soon as the inquest was over, she would get an annulment and that would be the end of it.

Detective Lieutenant Nick Pappas had a problem. He was sure he knew who the murderer of George Mellis was, but he could not prove it. He was confronted by a conspiracy of silence around the Blackwell family that he could not break through. He discussed the problem with his superior, Captain Harold Cohn, a street-wise cop who had worked his way up from the ranks.

Cohn quietly listened to Pappas and said, "It's all smoke, Nick. You haven't got a fucking bit of evidence. They'd laugh us out of court."

"I know," Lieutenant Pappas sighed. "But I'm right." He sat there a moment, thinking. "Would you mind if I talked to Kate Blackwell?"

"Jesus! What for?"

"It'll be a little fishing expedition. She runs that family. She might have some information she doesn't even know she has."

"You'll have to watch your step."

"I will."

"And go easy with her, Nick. Remember, she's an old lady."

"That's what I'm counting on," Detective Pappas said.

The meeting took place that afternoon in Kate Blackwell's office. Nick Pappas guessed that Kate was somewhere in her eighties, but she carried her age remarkably well. She showed little of the strain the detective knew she must be feeling. She was a very private person, and she had been forced to watch the Blackwell name become a source of public speculation and scandal.

"My secretary said you wished to see me about a matter of some urgency, Lieutenant."

"Yes, ma'am. There's a coroner's inquest tomorrow on the death of George Mellis. I have reason to think your granddaughter is involved in his murder."

Kate went absolutely rigid. "I don't believe it."

"Please hear me out, Mrs. Blackwell. Every police investigation begins with the question of motive. George Mellis was a fortune hunter and a vicious sadist." He saw the reaction on her face, but he pressed on. "He married your granddaughter and suddenly found himself with his hands on a large fortune. I figured he beat up Alexandra once too often and when she asked for a divorce, he refused. Her only way to get rid of him was to kill him."

Kate was staring at him, her face pale.

"I began looking around for evidence to back up my theory. We knew George Mellis was at Cedar Hill House before he disappeared. There are only two ways to get to Dark Harbor from the mainland—plane or ferryboat. According to the local sheriff's office, George Mellis didn't use either. I don't believe in miracles, and I figured Mellis wasn't the kind of man who could walk on water. The only possibility left was that he took a boat from somewhere else along the coast. I started checking out boat-rental places, and I struck pay dirt at Gilkey Harbor. At four P.M. on the afternoon of the day George Mellis was murdered, a woman rented a motor launch there and said a friend would be picking it up later. She paid cash, but she had to sign the rental slip. She used the name Solange Dunas. Does that ring a bell?"

"Yes. She—she was the governess who took care of the twins when they were children. She returned to France years ago."

Pappas nodded, a look of satisfaction on his face. "A little farther up the coast, the same woman rented a second boat. She took it out and returned it three hours later. She signed her name Solange Dunas again. I showed both attendants a photograph of Alexandra. They were pretty sure it was her, but they couldn't be positive, because the woman who rented the boats was a brunet."

"Then what makes you think—?"

"She wore a wig."

Kate said stiffly, "I don't believe Alexandra killed her husband."

"I don't either, Mrs. Blackwell," Lieutenant Pappas told her. "It was her sister, Eve."

Kate Blackwell was as still as stone.

"Alexandra couldn't have done it. I checked on her movements the day of the murder. She spent the early part of the day in New York with a friend, then she flew directly from New York up to the island. There's no way she could have rented those two motorboats." He leaned forward. "So I was left with Alexandra's look-alike, who signed the name Solange Dunas. It had to be Eve. I started looking around for her motive. I showed a photograph of George Mellis to the tenants of the apartment house Eve lives in, and it turned out that Mellis was a frequent visitor there. The superintendent of the building told me that one night when Mellis was there, Eve was almost beaten to death. Did you know that?"

"No." Kate's voice was a whisper.

"Mellis did it. It fits his pattern. And that was Eve's motive— vengeance. She lured him out to Dark Harbor and murdered him." He looked at Kate, and felt a pang of guilt at taking advantage of this old woman. "Eve's alibi is that she was in Washington, D.C., that day. She gave the cab driver who took her to the airport a hundred-dollar bill so he would be sure to remember her, and she made a big fuss about missing the Washington shuttle. But I don't think she went to Washington. I believe she put on a dark wig and took a commercial plane to Maine, where she rented those boats. She killed Mellis, dumped his body overboard, then docked the yacht and towed the extra motorboat back to the rental dock, which was closed by then."

Kate looked at him a long moment. Then she said, slowly, "All the evidence you have is circumstantial, isn't it?"

"Yes." He was ready to move in for the kill. "I need concrete evidence for the coroner's inquest. You know your granddaughter better than anyone in the world, Mrs. Blackwell. I want you to tell me anything you can that might be helpful."

She sat there quietly, making up her mind. Finally she said, "I think I can give you some information for the inquest."

And Nick Pappas's heart began to beat faster. He had taken a long shot, and it had paid off. The old lady had come through. He unconsciously leaned forward. "Yes, Mrs. Blackwell?"

Kate spoke slowly and distinctly. "On the day George Mellis was murdered, Lieutenant, my granddaughter Eve and I were in Washington, D.C., together."

She saw the surprised expression on his face. *You fool*, Kate Blackwell thought. *Did you really think I would offer up a Blackwell as a sacrifice to you? That I would let the press have a Roman holiday with the Blackwell name? No. I will punish Eve in my own way.*

The verdict from the coroner's jury was death at the hands of an unknown assailant or assailants.

To Alexandra's surprise and gratitude, Peter Templeton was at the inquest at the county courthouse.

"Just here to lend moral support," he told her. Peter thought Alexandra was holding up remarkably well, but the strain showed in her face and in her eyes. During a recess, he took her to lunch at the Lobster Pound, a little restaurant facing the bay in Lincolnville.

"When this is over," Peter said, "I think it would be good for you to take a trip, get away for a while."

"Yes. Eve has asked me to go away with her." Alexandra's eyes were filled with pain. "I still can't believe George is dead. I know it has happened, but it—it still seems unreal."

"It's nature's way of cushioning the shock until the pain becomes bearable."

"It's so senseless. He was such a fine man." She looked up at Peter. "You spent time with him. He talked to you. Wasn't he a wonderful person?"

"Yes," Peter said slowly. "Yes, he was."

Eve said, "I want an annulment, Keith."

Keith Webster blinked at his wife in surprise. "Why on earth would you want an annulment?"

"Oh, come on, Keith. You didn't really think I was going to stay married to you, did you?"

"Of course. You're my wife, Eve."

"What are you after? The Blackwell money?"

"I don't need money, darling. I make an excellent living. I can give you anything you want."

"I told you what I want. An annulment."

He shook his head regretfully. "I'm afraid I can't give you that."

"Then I'm going to file for divorce."

"I don't think that would be advisable. You see, nothing has really changed, Eve. The police haven't found out who killed your brother-in-law, so the case is still open. There's no statute of limitations on murder. If you divorced me, I'd be forced to . . ." He raised his hands helplessly.

"You're talking as though I killed him."

"You did, Eve."

Her voice was scornful. "How the hell do you know?"

"It's the only reason you would have married me."

She looked at him, filled with loathing. "You bastard! How can you do this to me?"

"It's very simple. I love you."

"I hate you. Do you understand that? I despise you!"

He smiled sadly. "I love you so much."

The trip with Alexandra was called off. "I'm going to Barbados on my honeymoon," Eve told her.

Barbados was Keith's idea.

"I won't go," Eve told him flatly. The idea of a honeymoon with him was disgusting.

"It will look strange if we don't have a honeymoon," he said shyly. "And we don't want people asking a lot of awkward questions, do we, dear?"

Alexandra began to see Peter Templeton for lunch once a week. In the beginning, it was because she wanted to talk about George, and there was no one else she could discuss him with. But after several months, Alexandra admitted to herself that she enjoyed Peter Templeton's company immensely. There was a dependability about him that she desperately needed. He was sensitive to her moods, and he was intelligent and entertaining.

"When I was an intern," he told Alexandra, "I went out on my first house call in the dead of winter. The patient was a frail old man in bed with a terrible cough. I was going to examine his chest with my stethoscope, but I didn't want to shock him, so I decided to warm it first. I put it on the radiator while I examined his throat and his eyes. Then I got my stethoscope and put it to his chest. The old man leaped out of bed like a scalded cat. His cough went away, but it took two weeks for the burn to heal."

Alexandra laughed. It was the first time she had laughed in a long time.

"Can we do this again next week?" Peter asked.

"Yes, please."

Eve's honeymoon turned out much better than she had anticipated. Because of Keith's pale, sensitive skin, he was afraid to go out in the sun, so Eve went down to the beach alone every day. She was never alone for long. She was surrounded by amorous lifeguards, beach bums, tycoons and playboys. It was like feasting at a wonderful smorgasbord, and Eve chose a different dish each day. She enjoyed her sexual escapades twice as much because she knew her husband was upstairs in their suite waiting for her. He could not do enough for her. He fetched and carried for her like a little lapdog, and waited on her hand and foot. If Eve expressed a wish, it was instantly gratified. She did everything she could think of to insult him, anger him, to turn him against her so that he would let her go, but his love was unshakable. The idea of letting Keith make love to her sickened Eve, and she was grateful that he had a weak libido.

The years are beginning to catch up with me, Kate Blackwell thought. There were so many of them, and they had been so full and rich.

Kruger-Brent, Ltd., needed a strong hand at the helm. It needed someone with Blackwell blood. *There's no one to carry on after I'm gone,* Kate thought. *All the working and planning and fighting for the company. And for what? For strangers to take over one day. Bloody hell! I can't let that happen.*

A week after they returned from their honeymoon, Keith said apologetically, "I'm afraid I'm going to have to go back to work, dear. I have a lot of operations scheduled. Will you be all right during the day without me?"

Eve barely managed to keep a straight face. "I'll try."

Keith was up and out early every morning long before Eve awakened, and when she went into the kitchen she found he had made coffee and laid out all the breakfast things for her. He opened a generous bank account in Eve's name and kept it replenished. She spent his money recklessly. As long as she was enjoying herself, Keith was happy. Eve bought expensive jewelry for Rory, with whom she spent almost every afternoon. He worked very little.

"I can't take just any part," he complained to Eve. "It would hurt my image."

"I understand, darling."

"Do you? What the fuck do you know about show business? You were born with a silver spoon up your ass."

And Eve would buy him an extra-nice present to placate him. She paid Rory's rent and bought him clothes for interviews, and paid for his dinners at expensive restaurants so that he could be seen by important producers. She wanted to be with him twenty-four hours a day, but there was her husband. Eve would arrive home at seven or eight o'clock at night, and Keith would be in the kitchen preparing dinner for her in his "Kiss the Cook" apron. He never questioned her about where she had been.

During the following year, Alexandra and Peter Templeton saw each other more and more often. Each had become an important part of the other's life. Peter accompanied Alexandra when she went to visit her father at the asylum, and somehow the sharing made the pain easier to bear.

Peter met Kate one evening when he arrived to pick up Alexandra. "So you're a doctor, eh? I've buried a dozen doctors, and I'm still around. Do you know anything about business?"

"Not a great deal, Mrs. Blackwell."

"Are you a corporation?" Kate asked.

"No."

She snorted. "Bloody hell. You don't know anything. You need a good tax man. I'll set up an appointment for you with mine. The first thing he'll do is incorporate you and—"

"Thank you, Mrs. Blackwell. I'm getting along just fine."

"My husband was a stubborn man, too," Kate said. She turned to Alexandra. "Invite him to dinner. Maybe I can talk some sense into him."

Outside, Peter said, "Your grandmother hates me."

Alexandra laughed. "She likes you. You should *hear* how Gran behaves with people she hates."

"I wonder how she would feel if I told her that I want to marry you, Alex . . . ?"

And she looked up at him and beamed. "We'd both feel wonderful, Peter!"

Kate had watched the progress of Alexandra's romance with Peter Templeton with a great deal of interest. She liked the young doctor, and she decided he would be a good husband for Alexandra. But she was a trader at heart. Now she sat in front of the fireplace facing the two of them.

"I must tell you," Kate lied, "that this comes as a complete surprise. I always expected Alexandra to marry an executive who would take over Kruger-Brent."

"This isn't a business proposition, Mrs. Blackwell. Alexandra and I want to get married."

"On the other hand," Kate continued, as if there had been no interruption, "you're a psychiatrist. You understand the way people's minds and emotions work. You would probably be a great negotiator. I would like you to become involved with the company. You can—"

"No," Peter said firmly. "I'm a doctor. I'm not interested in going into a business."

"This isn't 'going into a business,'" Kate snapped. "We're not talking about some corner grocery store. You'll be part of the family, and I need someone to run—"

"I'm sorry." There was a finality in Peter's tone. "I'll have nothing to do with Kruger-Brent. You'll have to find someone else for that. . . ."

Kate turned to Alexandra. "What do you have to say to that?"

"I want whatever makes Peter happy, Gran."

"Damned ingratitude," Kate glowered. "Selfish, the both of you." She sighed. "Ah, well. Who knows? You might change your mind one day." And she added innocently, "Are you planning to have children?"

Peter laughed. "That's a private matter. I have a feeling you're a great manipulator, Mrs. Blackwell, but Alex and I are going to live our own lives, and our children—if we have children—will live *their* lives."

. Kate smiled sweetly. "I wouldn't have it any other way, Peter. I've made it a lifelong rule never to interfere in other people's lives."

Two months later when Alexandra and Peter returned from their honeymoon, Alexandra was pregnant. When Kate heard the news, she thought, *Good. It will be a boy.*

Eve lay in bed watching Rory walk out of the bathroom naked. He had a beautiful body, lean and trim. Eve adored the way he made love to her. She could not get enough of him. She suspected he might have other bedmates, but she was afraid to ask, afraid to say anything that might upset him. Now, as he reached the bed, he ran his finger along her skin, just below the eyes, and said, "Hey, baby, you're gettin' a few wrinkles. They're cute."

Each word was a stab, a reminder of the age difference between them and the fact that she was twenty-five years old. They made love again, but for the first time Eve's mind was elsewhere.

It was almost nine o'clock when Eve arrived home. Keith was basting a roast in the oven.

He kissed her on the cheek. "Hello, dear. I've made some of your favorite dishes. We're having—"

"Keith, I want you to remove these wrinkles."

He blinked. "What wrinkles?"

She pointed to the area around her eyes. "These."

"Those are laugh lines, darling. I love them."

"*I* don't! I hate them!" she yelled.

"Believe me, Eve, they're not—"

"For Christ's sake, just get rid of them. That *is* what you do for a living, isn't it?"

"Yes, but— All right," he said placatingly, "if it will make you happy, dear."

"When?"

"In about six weeks. My schedule is full right—"

"I'm not one of your goddamned patients," Eve snapped. "I'm your wife. I want you to do it now—tomorrow."

"The clinic is closed on Saturdays."

"Then open it!" *He was so stupid.* God, she could not wait to get rid of him. And she would. One way or another. And soon.

"Come into the other room for a moment." He took her into the dressing room.

She sat in a chair under a strong light while he carefully examined her face. In an instant he was transformed from a bumbling little milquetoast to a brilliant surgeon, and Eve could sense the transformation. She remembered the miraculous job he had done on her face. This operation might seem unnecessary to Keith, but he was wrong. It was vital. Eve could not bear the thought of losing Rory.

Keith turned off the light. "No problem," he assured her. "I'll do it in the morning."

The following morning, the two of them went to the clinic. "I usually have a nurse assist me," Keith told her, "but with something as minor as this, it won't be necessary."

"You might as well do something with this while you're at it." Eve tugged at a bit of skin at her throat.

"If you wish, dear. I'll give you something to put you to sleep so you won't feel any discomfort. I don't want my darling to have any pain."

Eve watched as he filled a hypodermic and skillfully gave her an injection. She would not have minded if there had been pain. She was doing this for Rory. Darling Rory. She thought of his rock-hard body and the look in his eyes when he was hungry for her. . . . She drifted off to sleep.

She woke up in a bed in the back room of the clinic. Keith was seated in a chair next to the bed.

"How did it go?" Her voice was thick with sleep.

"Beautifully," Keith smiled.

Eve nodded, and was asleep again.

* * *

Keith was there when she woke up later. "We'll leave the bandages on for a few days. I'll keep you here where you can be properly cared for."

"All right."

He checked her each day, examined her face, nodded. "Perfect."

"When can I look?"

"It should be all healed by Friday," he assured her.

She ordered the head nurse to have a private telephone installed by the bedside. The first call she made was to Rory.

"Hey, baby, where the hell are you?" he asked. "I'm horny."

"So am I, darling. I'm still tied up with his damned medical convention in Florida, but I'll be back next week."

"You'd better be."

"Have you missed me?"

"Like crazy."

Eve heard whispering in the background. "Is there someone there with you?"

"Yeah. We're havin' a little orgy." Rory loved to make jokes. "Gotta go." The line went dead.

Eve telephoned Alexandra and listened, bored, to Alexandra's excited talk about her pregnancy. "I can't wait," Eve told her. "I've always wanted to be an aunt."

Eve seldom saw her grandmother. A coolness had developed that Eve did not understand. *She'll come around,* Eve thought.

Kate never asked about Keith, and Eve did not blame her, for he was a nothing. Perhaps one day Eve would talk to Rory about helping her get rid of Keith. That would tie Rory to her forever. It was incredible to Eve that she could cuckold her husband every day and that he neither suspected nor cared. Well, thank God he had a talent for *something.* The bandages were coming off on Friday.

Eve awakened early on Friday and waited impatiently for Keith.

"It's almost noon," she complained. "Where the hell have you been?"

"I'm sorry, darling," he apologized. "I've been in surgery all morning and—"

"I don't give a damn about that. Take these bandages off. I want to see."

"Very well."

Eve sat up and was still, as he deftly cut the bandages away from her face. He stood back to study her, and she saw the satisfaction in his eyes. "Perfect."

"Give me a mirror."

He hurried out of the room and returned a moment later with a hand mirror. With a proud smile, he presented it to her.

Eve raised the mirror slowly and looked at her reflection.

And screamed.

EPILOGUE

Kate
1982

36

It seemed to Kate that the wheel of time was spinning faster, hurrying the days along, blending winter into spring and summer into autumn, until all the seasons and years blurred into one. She was in her late eighties now. Eighty what? Sometimes she forgot her exact age. She could face growing old, but she could not face the idea of growing old and slovenly, and she took great pains with her appearance. When she looked in the mirror, she saw a neat, erect figure of a woman, proud and indomitable.

She still went to her office every day, but it was a gesture, a ruse to ward off death. She attended every board meeting, but things were no longer as clear as they once had been. Everyone around her seemed to be speaking too rapidly. The most disturbing thing to Kate was that her mind played tricks on her. The past and present were constantly intermingling. Her world was closing in, becoming smaller and smaller.

If there was a lifeline that Kate clutched, a driving force that kept her alive, it was her passionate conviction that someone in the family must one day take charge of Kruger-Brent. Kate had no intention of letting outsiders take over what Jamie McGregor and Margaret and she and David had suffered and toiled so long and so hard for. Eve, on whom Kate had twice pinned such high hopes, was a murderer. And a *grotesque*. Kate had not had to punish her. She had seen Eve once. What had been done to her was punishment enough.

On the day Eve had seen her face in the mirror, she had tried to commit suicide. She had swallowed a bottle of sleeping pills, but Keith had pumped out her stomach and brought her home, where he hovered over her constantly. When he had to be at the hospital, day and night nurses guarded her.

"Please let me die," Eve begged her husband. "Please, Keith! I don't want to live like this."

"You belong to me now," Keith told her, "and I'll always love you."

The image of what her face looked like was etched in Eve's brain. She persuaded Keith to dismiss the nurses. She did not want anyone around her looking at her, staring at her.

Alexandra called again and again, but Eve refused to see her. All deliveries were left outside the front door so no one could see her face. The only person who saw her was Keith. He was, finally, the only one she had left. He was her only link with the world, and she became terrified that he would leave her, that she would be left alone with nothing but her ugliness—her unbearable ugliness.

Every morning at five o'clock, Keith arose to go to the hospital or clinic, and Eve was always up before him to fix his breakfast. She cooked dinner for him every night, and when he was late, she was filled with apprehension. *What if he had found some other woman? What if he did not return to her?*

When she heard his key in the door, she would rush to open it and go into his arms, holding him tightly. She never suggested they make love because she was afraid he might refuse, but when he did make love to her, Eve felt as though he was bestowing upon her a wonderful kindness.

Once she asked, timidly, "Darling, haven't you punished me enough? Won't you repair my face?"

He looked at her and said proudly, "It can never be repaired."

As time went on, Keith became more demanding, more peremptory, until Eve was finally and completely a slave to him, catering to his every whim. Her ugliness bound her to him more strongly than iron chains.

Alexandra and Peter had had a son, Robert, a bright, handsome boy. He reminded Kate of Tony when he was a child. Robert was almost eight now, and precocious for his age. *Very precocious indeed,* Kate thought. *A really remarkable boy.*

All the members of the family received their invitations on the same day. The invitation read: MRS. KATE BLACKWELL REQUESTS THE HONOR OF YOUR PRESENCE TO CELEBRATE HER NINETIETH BIRTHDAY AT CEDAR HILL HOUSE, DARK HARBOR, MAINE, ON SEPTEMBER 24, 1982, AT EIGHT O'CLOCK. BLACK TIE.

When Keith read the invitation, he looked at Eve and said, "We're going."

"Oh, no! I can't! You go. I'll—"

He said, "We're both going."

Tony Blackwell was in the garden of the sanitarium, painting, when his companion approached. "A letter for you, Tony."

Tony opened the envelope, and a vague smile lighted his face. "That's nice," he said. "I like birthday parties."

Peter Templeton studied the invitation. "I can't believe the old girl's ninety years old. She's really amazing."

"Yes, isn't she?" Alexandra agreed. And she added thoughtfully, "Do you know something sweet? Robert received his own invitation, addressed to him."

37

The overnight guests had long since departed by ferry and plane, and the family was gathered in the library at Cedar Hill. Kate looked at those in the room, one by one, and she saw each with remarkable clarity. Tony, the smiling, vaguely amiable vegetable who had tried to kill her, the son who had been so full of promise and hope. Eve, the murderer, who could have owned the world if she had not had the seed of evil in her. How ironic it was, Kate thought, that her terrible punishment had come from the meek little nonentity she married. And then there was Alexandra. Beautiful, affectionate and kind—the bitterest disappointment of all. She had put her own happiness before the welfare of the company. She was not interested in Kruger-Brent and had chosen a husband who refused to have anything to do with the company. Traitors, both of them. Had all the pain of the past gone for nothing? *No,* Kate thought. *I won't let it end like this. It's not all been wasted. I've built a proud dynasty. A hospital in Cape Town is named after me. I've built schools and libraries and helped Banda's people.* Her head was beginning to hurt. The room was slowly filling with ghosts. Jamie McGregor and Margaret—looking so beautiful—and Banda smiling at her. And dear, wonderful David, holding out his arms. Kate shook her head to clear it. She was not ready for any of them yet. *Soon,* she thought. *Soon.*

There was one more member of the family in the room. She turned to her handsome young great-grandson and said, "Come here, darling."

Robert walked up to her and took her hand.

"It sure was a great birthday party, Gran."

"Thank you, Robert. I'm glad you enjoyed it. How are you getting along in school?"

"All A's, like you told me to get. I'm at the head of my class."

Kate looked at Peter. "You should send Robert to the Wharton School when he's old enough. It's the best—"

Peter laughed. "For God's sake, Kate, my darling, don't you ever give up? Robert's going to do exactly what he likes. He has a remarkable musical talent, and he wants to be a classical musician. He's going to choose his own life."

"You're right," Kate sighed. "I'm an old woman, and I have no right to interfere. If he wants to be a musician, that's what he should be." She turned to the boy, and her eyes shone with love. "Mind you, Robert, I can't promise anything, but I'm going to try to help you. I know someone who's a dear friend of Zubin Mehta."

The Best OF Bestsellers From WARNER BOOKS

Praise for Anne McCaffrey and Elizabeth Ann Scarborough

"The story is exciting and generously laced with humor, but besides those qualities, the characters—planet, humans, and animals—and their interactions are so well realized as to utterly charm readers."

—*Booklist,* on *Changelings*

"Well-handled far-future speculation on ecological engineering and planetary consciousness . . . [an] agreeably colorful, well-realized adventure."

—*Kirkus Reviews,* on *Powers That Be*

"Anne McCaffrey and Elizabeth Ann Scarborough collaborate seamlessly to tell a first-rate sf adventure with strong male and female protagonists and a life-affirming theme."

—*Library Journal,* on *Power Lines*

"May be the riveting saga's most exciting episode yet . . . The writing and characterization as well as the infusions of Celtic and Inuit lore remain of high quality."

—*Booklist,* on *Power Play*

BY ANNE MCCAFFREY AND
ELIZABETH ANN SCARBOROUGH

Powers That Be
Power Lines
Power Play
Changelings
Maelstrom
Deluge

CHANGELINGS

BOOK ONE OF THE TWINS OF PETAYBEE

ANNE MCCAFFREY
ELIZABETH ANN SCARBOROUGH

BALLANTINE BOOKS · NEW YORK

THIS BOOK IS DEDICATED
TO MARY, KE-OLA, AND KEOKI POOLE

We'd also like to acknowledge the contributions of
Lea Day for her memories of Hawaii and her research
of both print and televised sources of information
about volcanoes, otters, seals, and sea turtles.
Richard Reaser provided valuable feedback and
inspiration as well as consultation on scientific
matters, while Andy Logan provided dinner.
Mary, Ke-ola (the hula consultant), and Keoki Poole
provided valuable information about Hawaiian
culture, language, and customs and generously shared
their own resources with us.

Prologue

PETAYBEE WAS CHANGING. It was always changing. The quakes and eruptions, avalanches and slides, great winds on land and sea, even the ebb and flow of the tide, brought about fundamental changes in the planet's surface, in the way it *was*. The people who lived on Petaybee knew and accepted this. If it had not been for the changes, jump-started and accelerated by a terraforming process begun only a few decades before, no one would have been able to live on Petaybee. The people made songs about the changes, celebrated them.

Their planet, once a cold ball of cosmic rock, was an awakening giant. Each shift, slide, rumble, storm, or explosion was a sign that Petaybee was stretching, growing, continuing to re-form its being into something even grander than it already was. The people and their songs celebrated the changes.

A lot they knew.

If they had bothered to ask their sentient planet just once how *Petaybee* felt instead of always bringing their own hopes and fears, joys and sorrows, into the communion caves where they spoke to the planet and the planet responded, Petaybee would have told them that it sometimes hurt.

All of that grinding of plates, cracking the surface, sloughing away here, washing away there, pushing some bits out and pulling others back, could be painful. Most worlds could take millennia to do what Petaybee did in hours, days, weeks, at the most, years. It was really quite a hectic pace, all this change in such a short time, and Petaybee was not always sure just what was happening to its great self or why.

The planet did know that its function was to be a home for its creatures, its two-legged, four-legged, winged, shelled, finned, and flippered fauna; its leaved, flowered, vined, barked, or grassy flora. It not only made homes for these life forms, it helped them adapt to its conditions so that their fragile husks did not die. The cycle of life formed by all of these living creatures fed Petaybee's vitality even as the planet nourished them. The two-leggeds who had become part of Petaybee's own great being returned its care by keeping the more destructive members of their species at bay, in space, away from their world.

No one was allowed to drill into it or set explosions on its surface to take away bits of its body it might have a use for later. If life was taken, it was replaced by new life.

Though a small planet whose surface consisted of little more than two ice caps and a sea between them, Petaybee had nevertheless made a lot of progress since its terraforming.

But it wasn't enough. Petaybee had to—*had* to—make other kinds of places where more life forms could live. There was too much sea. Too much ice. If there were warm places, dry places, where life could begin, that life could become part of the cycle too and would add its own special gifts to its world. Though Petaybee was a world that could, as humans understood it, think, this idea was not a thought or even a true idea as such. It was a compulsion that expressed itself as a buildup of pressure in one particular area. Here. Land belonged *here*. The sea felt particularly empty and limitless at that point, but moreover, Petaybee actually felt as if it contained a continent within its core. A continent that belonged in this place where now waves rolled on and on. Some shoreline was needed. Some beach. And eventually, some trees and flowers, perhaps, other plants and animals. Yes. As industriously and deliberately as a two-legged dweller might move the furniture inside a house, Petaybee began rearranging its own interior to create what belonged on the surface.

This was not easy, even for an entire sentient planet with a sense of purpose. The landmasses were too far to move them to the empty spot without destroying all of the other life. Besides, the ice would melt and upset everything. The only efficient way to get land in the right spot was to bring it up from the inside, up through the bottom of the sea. And so Petaybee hacked and coughed and spewed and spewed and shot its red hot inner essence up into the sea bed, where some of the minerals within the hot sulfurous gas and magma turned into hollow rock towers that became chimneys for other eruptions.

As the hot vents opened like red mouths, Petaybee swallowed great gouts of seawater. It mixed with the minerals in the molten rock, then, superheated and full of nutrients, it shot back into the sea. When it cooled, it was a warm nutrient for new life. New species of plants and animals sprang up all over. They were not bothered by the sulfurous waters, but thrived in them. Petaybee thought this was as it should be, but then, Petaybee had a very large view of things. It took no particular notice of the *other* life forms lurking near its new cauldron, the ones not of its own creation.

Until that point, the planet's creation had blossomed in relative obscurity—the people had neither navy or civilian fleets, no boats, in fact, but those used for subsistence fishing and hunting. Fly-bys were rare. There was no satellite surveillance. Once, a seal had swum by, pausing to observe the volcano's birth with interest. But he was on his way elsewhere. Only now, with the newest of the life forms in place, was Petaybee's work monitored, though it was done so unobtrusively that the preoccupied planet took no notice.

Gradually, the lava built up the floor of the sea around its chimneys. It was good, but too slow.

Heaving and squeezing, Petaybee pushed magma and gas up through the center of the elevated sea bottom. Once the pressure built up, it would blow a hole big enough to gush rivers of lava out into the sea. It would build up and up and up until it rose above the waves, then begin spreading out until it was a new place, a new home. Though it would be hot and hazardous at first, the seawater and air would cool it until it too was a warm place for life to flourish.

Though volcanoes had created landmasses on Petaybee shortly after terraforming, it had happened very quickly, while the planet was barely awake. This new volcano, this new island, was a conscious effort, Petaybee's greatest work to date. But work it was, a lot of work. As birthing mothers everywhere knew very well, the process of bringing life into the world was called "labor" for a reason.

CHAPTER 1

THE SHONGILI TWINS gave almost simultaneous burps of repletion—the boy on his mother's shoulder and the girl on her father's—and were carefully laid on their backs on their fur-lined cots. Sean and Yanaba made no move to leave the nursery, unable to leave the sight of their offspring, safely delivered just a few hours earlier. The babies looked up at their parents, their dark pewter eyes as brightly focused as those of any bird. Each already wore a soft crown of deep brown downy hair, but Yana would have been hard pressed to decide whose nose or cheeks they had. Everything was still rounded and squashy, unformed and utterly adorable.

Even their contented gurgles sounded for all the world like the chortle of a small and active brook swirling among stones.

"Listen to them," Yana said fondly. "They sound as if they're laughing." Then, "I thought it took longer than that for babies to do things like laugh."

Sean shrugged. "Babies who are always and entirely human perhaps. But a selkie's development is a bit different. Faster in some ways. I don't recall when exactly I developed what, but I do recall being aware of my surroundings almost at once. But as to the details, well, too bad my parents aren't still around to advise us."

But Yana, lost in wonder at the perfection of her children, answered him only with a dreamy glance. "It's almost too much joy for one person to bear," she murmured, feeling tears come to her eyes.

Sean took her in his arms. "Then let's share it. I smell food, and you're still feeding two—one at a time." He gave her a hug and a cuddle and, one arm draped on her shoulders, propelled her gently toward the door of the cube they had hastily attached to one side of the cabin to serve as a nursery. It was spare and spartan except for the furred cots, for it was the custom in Kilcoole to refrain from giving expecting parents items for their unborn children. A superstition really, but since Yana, before conceiving, had thought herself well past childbearing age, it seemed wise to encourage every sort of good luck.

As Sean opened the door, Nanook, his black-and-white track cat, and Coaxtl, his niece Aoifa's snow leopard, slid into the nursery. Nanook took a place under the boy's cot, while Coaxtl, after one long look at her charge, flopped beside the girl's.

"The sentries are on the job," Sean said, and continued to push his wife to the door.

"I just never thought I'd have children," Yana said, looking back over her shoulder at her twins even as Sean closed the door behind her. He left it slightly ajar so they could hear the babies if they cried out or if one of the cats needed to go out or get their attention.

No smells had been able to penetrate the cube from the main part of the house, Yana's old one-room cabin. Now, however, delicious odors of pepper and snow onions, roasting fish and unidentifiable savory spices, wafted from the stove. Over it stood the substantial and comforting bulk of Clodagh, the village's shanachie, singer of songs, bearer of culture, rememberer of history, settler of disputes, healer of wounds, and dispenser of medicines. She had also served as Yana's midwife.

"It's about time," Clodagh said, closing the lid of the pot she had been seasoning. "I thought you'd never think of yourselves. Now, sit and eat. And Yana, use that longie thing," as she pointed a ladle at a chaise longue that had recently made its appearance in their home. There was no proscription against giving an expectant mother a gift for herself. The chaise, which took up a good half of the wall next to the woodstove, had seemed too large and in the way before, but now Yana found it inviting. "Get your feet up and relax. As much as you can, that is," she added in an affectionately derisive tone.

Major Yanaba Maddock-Shongili was quite willing to assume the seat and stretch her legs. Her overtaxed muscles carried her that far mostly because of Sean's support. He rearranged her feet a trifle and sat on the end, folding his arms over his chest and giving a sigh.

"Don't you dare look at your desk," Yana said sternly.

"Even from here I can see the pile of orange flimsies, and they mean urgent."

"Nothing is so urgent as feeding the pair of you up," Clodagh said staunchly, "and there really isn't anything *that* damned pressing that someone else can't handle or defer—preferably until next year."

"But those hydroelectric engineers were supposed to touch down today . . . and you know how eagerly Sister Igneous Rock is awaiting them." Sean referred to the planet's geological expert and its self-proclaimed aco-lyte. The woman and her fellow would-be Petaybean cult followers had surprised Petaybee's longer-term residents by turning out to be quite useful once they discovered they could be of more service to Petaybee practicing their hard-science specialties instead of their misguided attempts at theology.

"Iggierock has 'em and she's dealing with them." Clodagh gave a deep chuckle. "She's near as good as I am . . . at some things. But this stew will give you much-needed energy. And we've more urgent matters to consider, such as the babies' naming song and the latchkay. I'm thinking that tomorrow will be none too soon, if Yana can make it back to the lodge and the communion cave to properly introduce your young by name to their people and their world."

"She can and she will, if I must carry her," Sean said fondly.

"I can handle it," Yana said. Fortunately, those aching muscles of hers were well toned and trained from her years in the Company Corps. "It's the babies we'll need to be carrying."

"Good," Clodagh said. "All of Kilcoole has been waiting for these young ones, but there's a time and place for their gawking and well-wishing and filling your house up with doodads for the babbies. The sooner the better, though. Have you thought of what you'll call them at all?"

She dished up three huge bowls of her concoction, and after serving the new parents, she pulled up one of the new spare chairs to the new huge kitchen table they'd been given by friends who evidently thought they were going to have dozens of children instead of just two.

Clodagh passed rolls just out of the oven, and steaming through the white napkin she had covered them with.

Yana chewed quickly but deliberately, thinking hard. "Of course we've thought about it, but now that they're here, no name seems special enough. Among my mother's ancestors, you know, babies weren't named right away. High infant mortality rate was one reason, but also, her people believed a child didn't get its soul until the first time it laughed."

She and Sean looked at each other over their full spoons and smiled. "Which they've already done, and them only a few hours old," Sean said. "I can tell they're going to be quick, but then, it's well-known that all of the children born to my side of the family are very precocious."

Yana made a face at him. "Oh, in my family too, but our babies are also taught to be modest."

"You two are too giddy by half!" Clodagh mock-scolded, shaking her spoon at them. "Naming is a serious business. It should fit the baby's bloodlines—perhaps we could have names from your mother's people, Yana. There'd be a bit of novelty. It should also tell the world what the child is all about."

"This world knows what the children are about," Yana said. "It's responsible for their selkie nature, after all—well, it and their father," she added with a roll of her dark eyes at her husband. "And how advisable it is to tell the rest of the universe about *that* is debatable."

"No debate about it," Sean said in a tone that brooked no argument. "The universe at large does not need to know that our children mutate into seals when they submerge themselves in water any more than it needs to know that the kids inherited that trait from me."

"Well, the names don't need to come right out and say, 'I'm a selkie,' " Clodagh said. "But they should, for instance, indicate that these children have an affinity for water."

"Born for Water," Yana said with a swallow of soup.

"What?"

She gestured with a piece of roll. "I'm just thinking perhaps we should call them after the Hero Twins my mother's ancestors revered, Born for Water and Monster Slayer. Except at the moment they both seem to be Born for Water and it isn't yet clear who would be Monster Slayer."

"My money is on the wee lassie," Sean said. "She's got something of the look of you in the glint in her eyes and the set of her chin."

"She's barely *got* a chin," Yana said, shaking her head. "No, I think we'll have to go with the Irish side of my family this time. Here in Kilcoole where you're all Irish and Inuit, they'll blend in better with the other children that way anyway. Besides, among the Diné—my mother's people—girls all have war names like mine, and war is the last thing I want my daughter named for. Water's a bit difficult too. The sacred land of Mother's people had very little rain, or standing water either, and so they were extremely short even on fish, not to mention seals and selkies."

She stopped with her spoon halfway to her mouth. "I just had a thought. *Will* the babies be transforming every time they get into water? Any water? If so, I'm going to have a fine old time trying to bathe them and it won't be easy keeping their nature a family secret."

"I used to have the same problem," Sean grinned. "Until I taught myself not to fur up the moment a drop touched me. But I had no da to show me the way, and they do. Meanwhile, if you need help with the family secret, well, we've plenty of family here who know all about it. They'll help. And the four-foots will watch to make sure no outsiders come close enough to learn more than they should."

"You say that, Sean," Clodagh said, speaking quietly into her soup bowl, "but there are outsiders who've seen *you* change, and one of them may take it upon himself to wonder if the twins inherited the ability and need studying." She looked up, her moss green eyes fathomless and deep as one of Petaybee's many artesian springs, seeming troubled. She hated bringing up such worries on what should be a flawlessly happy day. "You know how much scrutiny this planet is under."

"Well, how the hell could they possibly interfere with my family peculiarity when Yana and I have the final say as governors of this planet?" Sean asked.

Clodagh shrugged.

"As long as the four-foots are their guards, no one will get near them," Yana said with far more conviction than she felt. "And Nanook and Coaxtl will keep them from being seen, won't they?" A nervous tic started in her cheek. She rubbed it. "Will the cats follow them into the water?"

"Yes," Sean said positively. "*If* the little ones elude them long enough to get near water, Nanook and Coaxtl would follow them into the mouth of a volcano if necessary. The cats do converse. We just have to make it plain to them how dangerous it would be for the kids to be caught half in, half out. Like I was."

"We'll hope they don't take arrows in their anatomy to induce such a condition," Yana said, referring to what was nearly a mortal wound for him. "And I thought leading training troops on landing parties for the Company Corps was a heavy responsibility!" She shook her head as if to clear it. "We're borrowing trouble. It's not as if shape-changing is a viable occupation."

"Oh, selkies would be real useful on water worlds," Sean argued.

"Yana's right, Sean. There's trouble enough right here and now without borrowing any," Clodagh said in a cajoling tone. "Don't fall into *that* water until the ice breaks up. For now your biggest problem is to decide what these babes of yours are to be called. I will think on it, remember the stories of our peoples, see if there's some appropriate names there. You and Yana should sleep while you have the chance. The cats can't take care of all the needs those babes will have."

THE DRUMMING BEGAN shortly after sunrise. Inside the nursery cube, the twins opened their eyes to the brightness pouring in through the piece of sheeting that covered the cube's single small window. The babies whimpered and wiggled.

Nanook's ears were the first part of him to wake up. They pricked to attention. Coaxtl's tail lashed restlessly before the snow leopard stretched a sleepy paw. The kits had awakened. Both cats stretched and rose, poking their noses over the sides of the cots.

"Rrrow," Nanook told his friend. "I'd cry too if I smelled like that. Where are those humans when you need them?"

"These cubs leak," Coaxtl agreed. "And they've got these things tied around their haunches to hold the leakage in. One wonders how humans come up with such ideas. This arrangement keeps the nest clean but the cubs dirty."

"Sean would not want his kits to be dirty," Nanook said.

"Can one pull these haunch harnesses off so one can clean them?" Coaxtl inquired.

"Yes, they are meant to be removable. But take care with fang and claw. We want to remove the harnesses only, not the kits' pelts. Humans, lacking proper coats, have very sensitive hides."

Nanook's nose touched the kit's leg as he grasped a pinch of cloth in his teeth. The kit stopped whimpering. He looked at it anxiously lest it was merely saving its breath for a good howl, but it was staring at him, wide-eyed and curious. Disconcerting, these human younglings, born with their eyes all open and gawking.

"Hee," the kit said aloud, quite distinctly giggling.

"Hee," the female kit echoed, pumping a plump fist in the air.

Tickles, one of them—the female?—said.

Ma? the other inquired.

No, child, I am Nanook, your keeper. Your mother sleeps. And this one is Coaxtl, also your keeper.

'Nook. Nanook realized suddenly that the boy's more advanced utterances were mental and that it understood as well as transmitted thoughts.

Co'. The female kit was also transmitting thoughts.

Co-ax-tl, the snow leopard said with a dignified fluff of her tufted cheeks. *You may as well get it right to begin with, youngling.*

Co'.

Nanook sat back on his haunches. The harness was too close to the tender skin. "Don't growl, leopard. They will learn. When I was their age, my mother had to lick me to teach me to do what they've already done in their harnesses."

Coaxtl sat back too. "This harness removal is for those with thumbs. The drums call. The time has come to wake the parents. *They* can cope with haunch harnesses."

CHAPTER 2

JUST IN CASE a seventy-five-pound track cat standing over her was not enough of a hint that she should wake, Sean was saying, "Yana, love, it's time to rise. The drums have begun and the babes are hungry again."

"Yes, I got that idea," she said, looking up into Nanook's black-and-white marked face before Sean shooed the cat back to the floor. He had been so good, getting up to change the babies during the night and tucking them in with her so she could breast-feed without disturbing her rest unduly. She attempted to roll out of bed with her customary agility, only to find it sadly lacking. The birthing had not felt too traumatic, thanks to the underwater method Clodagh had employed to ease the way of the children into the world. But what pain had been spared her yesterday seemed to be catching up with her now.

A muted buzz went off in the adjoining cube, which was the main office of the Shongilis. Sean paused halfway to the nursery cube, waiting until a second mechanical noise clicked in.

"It's working?" Yana asked in surprise. This was not the latest or most up-to-date answering machine, but it was the one that worked on their planet. They all listened for a second click, and then a red light appeared on the bar above the door into the cube, indicating a message was waiting. More efficient communication was one of the "improvements" that almost had to be implemented with all of the attention—most of it unwanted—Petaybee received from offworld interests. One com shed could no longer handle all of the messages, now that Intergal communications had pulled out when Space Base was dismantled. The landing area and fueling station had been left intact, and for a small consideration and a trade agreement regarding the fuel for visiting vessels, Kilcoole was allowed to retain it as a civilian concession.

"That thing can wait," Sean said. While recognizing the need for the "labor-saving" device, at the same time he resented its intrusion into what had once been their comparatively peaceful life. "I'll help you with the twins."

First he had to help her hobble into the "nursery." Coaxtl looked up, yawned, stretched, and padded out. One's shift was over, one presumed. Nanook joined the snow leopard, and the two stood by the door until Sean retraced his steps and opened it for them to go out.

The blast of cold air that blew in when the cats departed chilled the overheated room that had been so efficiently warmed by the woodstove and the hot burning Petaybean alder wood. The nursery cube, like the office cube also attached to the cabin, had its own temperature- and humidity-controlled environment, which was why they had chosen it for the twins, in spite of its lack of the individuality that characterized Petaybean dwellings.

Both twins were wide awake and smelly. The little girl held up a fist full of white fur. "Coaxtl got too close to you, I see, my little Monster Slayer," Yana said, pulling off the dirty diaper and cleaning the child with the moistened moss compresses Clodagh recommended for the job. "You need to choose your monsters more wisely, though, my love. Coaxtl is a friend."

"Hee," the little girl said.

"Hee," echoed her brother, spraying his father with urine the minute the diaper was removed and air touched his skin.

"Here now," Sean said. "I think your mummy said your role model was called Born *for* Water, not Born *to* Water!"

"Hee," the baby said again, so of course his sister had to say it again too, so as not to be outdone.

Sean held the boy and walked him around the cabin, talking to him while Yana fed her daughter. Then they switched babies. Finally the little ones were fed, changed, rediapered, and swaddled in clean furs.

Yana had finished washing up and pulled on a pair of old uniform trousers and a fleece top when someone knocked on the door.

She opened it to admit Bunny Rourke, Sean's niece and her closest friend since she had first arrived on Petaybee. Beside Bunny was Aoifa, Bunny's sister. Coaxtl considered Aoifa her two-legged cub.

"Clodagh said we should come to help with the babes while you and Sean get ready."

"Clodagh's reputation as a wise woman is richly deserved," Yana said thankfully. "You missed the messy bits for the time being, but they can use distraction for a moment."

With the help of the girls, the entire family unit was ready to mobilize within an hour. Yana and Sean carried the twins, while the girls followed with their changes of diapers, their packets of moss wipes, and extra furs in case the twins messed the ones they were wrapped in. "We look more like an expeditionary force than a family," Yana remarked.

Sean smiled. "You've not been around all that many families up till now, love. Families with new babies can make expeditionary forces seem underpacked."

"Good thing we brought the snocle," Bunny said. "And a curly coat to carry the gear."

"Have packhorse will go next door," Yana quipped when the girls loaded the supplies on the shaggy little Petaybean horse with its thick curly coat. Sometime during the night it had begun to snow. A blanket three or four inches deep covered the well-tramped path to the river road. Snow still sifted down from a light pewter sky. Soon the sun, which had just risen, would be setting again.

Aoifa led the horse, while Sean and Yana—who were clad in parkas, snow pants, hats, mittens, and mukluks—squeezed themselves and their fur-wrapped offspring into the snocle beside Bunny.

SMOKE POURED FROM the smoke hole of the latchkay lodge, a great plume among the pinion feathers emitted by the chimneys of Kilcoole's other houses. In front of the lodge, men stirred soups and stews in sterilized fuel drums over open fires. The smells didn't travel far in the air, which was so frigid it froze the hairs inside people's nostrils.

The drums drowned out all other noises now, calling the people together. Their beat was so strong the snow seemed to fall in time to it.

The babies wiggled in their parents' arms, wanting to see what all the noise and fuss was about. The thing in which they had been squeezed, the thing that roared and slid, stopped, and suddenly they felt cold air rush in through their furs. It felt wonderful!

Strange and familiar voices mingled all around them. Their parents walked forward until the cold went away and the babies were enveloped in great warmth and felt themselves being passed from their parents to other people. When they were handed back, their furs were removed and their mother had changed from the furry beast she'd transformed into outside back to the soft-slender-dark-haired-sweet-milk-smelling giver of food and cuddles who spoke to them in long utterances and smiled often.

Many faces peered down at them, touching their cheeks and chins, toes and fingers, all of the features of their land shapes. People spoke in odd voices that had "ooo" sounds.

They had slept well and were as curious as the cats who prowled among the people sitting and standing in the hall. The drums stopped for a while as people ate. During the eating, several people stood and spoke, saying things that seemed to make their mother happy.

Then they were both in their father's arms as the one drum began again and their mother stood and danced with other mothers, a slow pacing dance around the center of the big space. Father spoke to them then. He was easier to understand than anyone else, and half of what he said was inside their heads, his meanings confusing and mysterious but clearly important clues to what lay before them. His silvery eyes shone happily down at them as he spoke, and his voice held a lilt of laughter and good feeling.

"Children, we are at your naming latchkay. What's a latchkay? I'm glad you asked. The people of our village and I come from two peoples of Old Earth—the Inuit and the Irish. When something wonderful or important happened, the people would gather to eat and speak, dance and sing together. Among the Inuit, this was called a potlatch. Food and gifts were given to all. Among the Irish, it was a kay-lee, where there was much music and food and drink. We on Petaybee celebrate our occasions with something that mixes the two customs and we call it a latchkay. At this one, people will give us gifts for you. When you are five, we will hold a latchkay to redistribute the baby gifts you no longer use, and you will add gifts of your own to ones we make or barter for. Today your mother and I shall sing and dance with you, and everyone will suggest names and explain why they are good names. Clodagh will probably come up with the best ones. Clodagh was the lady you both saw yesterday, before you saw your mother's face or mine. Your mother has finished dancing now and it is my turn. Any questions?"

"Hee hee," the twins said. Then, " 'Kay."

But their father, passing them to their mother again, didn't hear.

Then Father picked Her up and mother picked Him up and they all danced, a happy jiggly rhythm such as the parents had used to put them to sleep. Two drumbeats, twin hearts, moved the people up and down, back and forth, up and down.

After that there was some more fun. Mother and Father sat down, each still holding one of them, and a round lady not Clodagh brought bright-colored soft things with shiny little round things in pretty patterns all over the front.

"Thank you, Aisling," Mother said. "Carry pouches are exactly what we need. Now the twins can see what's going on too." Mother handed Him to Father and stuck her arms into the bright soft thing she said was "kind of a cobalt blue." Father handed Him back to her, and she put Him into the thing, so that His legs were apart but stuck through the front, His middle held in by the strip with the shiny round things that sparkled in the light, and His head, though cradled between Mother's food-givers, faced forward. He could see everything! Everything!

Father handed Her to Mother too. Mother had a hard time hanging on to Her, because She wanted to see too and tried to twist in Mother's arms. Mother's cuddle wasn't as comfortable as usual because He was in the way.

But Father put on his new soft bright thing, which he said was "Hot pink, not my color, but Hers," and then She too faced forward.

Thus they were able to see all of the gifts. Soft warm things, not furs, for covering during sleep. Moss wipes and haunch harnesses, as the cats called them, though Mother and Father called them diapers. Small versions of Mother's fur-faced thing that made her big when she went outside. Other things like that, garments, clothes, they were called, that their parents held against them or stuck over their arms and legs a little ways to show.

The pile in front of them grew and grew until they couldn't tell one thing from another. Then two men came forward, "Seamus" and "Johnny." If the first thing was the best so far, these last things were best too. They brought between them a cot surrounded by a box that had images of fishes swimming all around it. The bottom had things they took off and put on again.

"Rockers for in the house," Johnny said. "Runners for sledding them over the snows," Seamus said. "Wheels for when it's dry," they both said, attaching round things to the front and back and taking them off again. "And when you're near water and you don't want them in it, use nothing at all on this and it will float tight and dry as any boat."

Best of all, it was not one cot but big enough for two. Mother and Father laid the twins together in it, so they could see each other and snuggle together. It was very nice but the twins did not let them get away with it, of course. Sleep could not come without food.

BEFORE THE LATCHKAY adjourned to the communion place for the Night Chants, the singing was interrupted by the howls of the dogs tethered outside and answered by dogs running toward them. The lodge's doors were flung open and three figures, heavily covered in fur parkas, snow pants, and boots, stamped inside. Bunny and Aoifa Rourke, Diego Metaxos, and young Chugiak rushed out to tend to the newcomers' teams.

"Friends, we're so pleased you've come to honor these children and their parents!"

The first person, now stripped of his parka, was a small dark-haired man. In his plaid shirt and snow pants, he walked in among the celebrants and said, "We are not the only ones to honor them! For weeks the seals have been gathering along the beach, thick as snowflakes. Dolphins and whales come too in great profu-

sion, not to their killing grounds but near our settle-
ments, as if waiting for something to happen. Then
yesterday the ice began to crack and break up as if it
were spring. Finally, a giant wave came rolling in and
crashed onto the shore, carrying fish and other creatures, some we have never seen before, and washed
away half the village. We heard twins were born here in
Kilcoole at the same time the wave rolled in, and the
three of us, who have the fastest teams in our area, were
sent to greet the children and bring them naming gifts."

The twins, seemingly oblivious to the noise, were asleep
in their new cradle when the coastal people arrived, but
by the time the visitors stood dripping melted snow
from their hair in front of Sean and Yana, the little ones
had awakened again.

One man pulled out a length of string and began making figures with it a few inches above the twins' faces.
"A story string to amuse them and help them trap the
best stories in its net. It is made of good strong synweb
too, so they can use it to snare rabbits if they want."

The next person, a woman, handed Yana two knives:
a dagger, and a blade that looked as if it were a quarter
cut from a circle, the point removed and replaced by a
bone handle. "A hunting knife and an ulu, so they will
never go hungry or cold."

The third person, also a woman, handed Yana a large-
eyed steel needle with a cutting end. "My mother always
said a needle was the true magic of our people because
without a needle, we would not be able to make the
clothing we need to survive. Actually, my mother wanted
me to bring you her old treadle sewing machine, but
there wasn't time to load it, even if there had been room
on the sled."

Yana and Sean laughed and thanked them all.

The baby girl reached up and snagged the story string in her tiny fingers.

The man who had been demonstrating its use beamed.

Then the food was served, musicians brought out their rusty instruments, and people began dancing the reels and figure dances from long ago, separated by occasional waltzes.

Marduk, the orange and white striped cat who had adopted Yana when she first arrived at Kilcoole, hopped into the cradle and wrapped himself around the twins' feet, purring when a baby hand patted his magnificent bushy tail. Nanook and Coaxtl reappeared and sat on either side of the cradle. Nanook looked expectantly up at Sean.

"I think that's my cue to ask the mother of the honorees to dance."

Yana was still sore and stiff from sitting so long, but the happiness of the occasion gave her something only a little less earthbound than wings. Taking her husband's arm, she slid to the dance floor and they half waltzed, half polkaed to the plunk and wheeze of instruments that had been frozen and thawed many times and played through many latchkays.

"This has all been a lot of fun, Sean," she said. "Exhausting, but fun. But even though everybody's had suggestions, I still don't know what to call the kids. Do you?"

"Not really. I sort of liked Seamus and Siobhan, but it's a bit too much like Sean and Sinead, and we're not even twins."

"Aisling suggested Murray, which is a sea name, I'm told, and Mairead, but that's not a water name. Muriel is, but I'm afraid we'd confuse them. Murray and Muriel sound awfully close." She dropped her voice so he could barely hear her above the drums. "To tell you the truth, I think those alliterating names for twins are just a bit on the cutesy side."

"It will come to us, love. There's still the Night Chants."

Shortly afterward everyone took a break in the festivities while the dog teams of people from distant villages were hitched up again, the little curly coated horse was loaded with the gifts to be deposited at the cabin on the way, and local people returned home and hitched up their dogs or saddled their curly coats for the trip to the hot springs where the Night Chants were held.

The drummers arrived ahead of everyone else so that drumbeats greeted each new party.

Yana as always was struck by the beauty of the hot springs. You saw the steam first, rising above the snow, and then, between ice-encrusted banks, the curtain of water pouring from the top ledge into a deep pool that cascaded into a second, then a third pool, the water through the steam like jewels behind a sheer veil. That this was the place where she had first made love with Sean and only yesterday birthed her babies added immeasurably to its beauty for her. But the most powerful enchantment it held lay beyond the waterfall, in the communion place.

People stood aside to allow Yana, Sean, and the twins to slip into the cave behind the upper falls. Clodagh was there ahead of them and, surprisingly, the three newcomers from the coast. Soon the cave was crowded with the bodies of neighbors and friends. Yana was a bit surprised to realize that all of these people were from Petay-

bee, most from Kilcoole. None of their offworld friends
were here. She wondered if the naming ceremony wasn't
hastened in order to prevent the attendance of offworld
folk. It seemed a bit discriminatory, especially when some
of them would never have survived some recent events
without the help of those friends.

When everyone arrived and settled, Clodagh said,
"Desmond here is the shanachie of his village. He heard
how we were looking for sea names for the babes and
said he has a song to share."

Desmond spoke so quietly everyone had to be still to
hear him. He also seemed to be well aware of the special
nature of the cave.

"The seals came to remind me of my mother's song
from her mother. The song she sang in its original tongue,
so I will tell you about it before I sing. It tells of a lonely
widow who had lost her husband and her only child to
the sea. Every day she walked the beach and watched
the seals play. One day when she could not go to the
beach because of the rain, a strange mute girl came to
her door to be her daughter. The woman called her
Murel, Bright Waters, and for seven years the mother
and daughter lived together. Then one day when they
walked the beach, a seal called from just offshore. 'Ork
ork ork!' he cried. 'That is Ronan, the little seal,' the
woman told the girl. But the girl knew already. 'Ork ork
ork!' she cried, and the widow knew it was time for her
daughter to return to the sea."

He then began singing quite a long song in a language
that bore only a distant resemblance to the Gaelic people sometimes sang.

Yana didn't pay too much attention, after the translation, because she was pondering the names of the seal

children, Murel and Ronan. Bright Waters and Little Seal. They had a ring to them that she liked. Of course, when the kids got older, she supposed she'd have to figure out how to change the boy's name so it meant big seal, but that could wait. She exchanged a look with Sean over the heads of the twins. By the bioluminescence that made the stone cave walls glow softly and the water wall glimmer, he smiled and nodded.

The cave was warm and cozy, and the bioluminescence had begun to scribe patterns on the cave walls. Desmond's song had a bit of a drone, but the children all liked it when he made the seal sound, which seemed to figure in the chorus. Her own children were no exception. With every ork, the babies squirmed, and for the first time ever she wished the ceremony over and them back at home.

When the song was done, Clodagh turned to them, smiling, her brows raised in question.

"You have the names then, do you, Yana? Sean?"

Yana and Sean nodded once to each other. Then Sean took the little girl from Yana's arms and held her out to Clodagh, who had taken a place of prominence in front of the waterfall. "Right then, pet," Clodagh said softly to the baby. Then she raised her head, her voice still quiet and calm enough to keep from alarming the child but carrying above the roar of the waterfall to everyone in the cave. "People of Petaybee, and our beautiful home, here is Murel Monster Slayer Shongili born to us to live among us."

Yana had been struggling to pay attention but now her eyes snapped open in dismay. "I never. . ." She began to say that she had not seriously meant for Monster Slayer to be part of her daughter's given name, but

Clodagh was passing Murel Monster Slayer Shongili to Aoifa, who sat next to her, and accepting Yana's son.

"And this fine one here, people of Petaybee, is Ronan Born for Water Shongili, born to us to live among us."

But as she turned to hand Ronan to Aoifa, who had been trying to pass Murel to Bunny Rourke, sitting beside her, Aoifa fumbled. That seemed to be the chance Murel had been waiting for. With a fishlike twist, the infant spurted from Aoifa's grasp and into the waterfall. In the confusion, Ronan escaped Clodagh's embrace and dived in after her. "Heeeeee," they cried, followed in a moment by "Ork."

Before anyone could start breathing again, Sean eeled past them and dove into the water himself.

Yana slid to the cave's entrance and ran out, snatching up furs from the snocle as she ran downstream. Behind her, Clodagh commanded everyone to stay put.

By the snowball moon she saw the large sleek head of a seal break water in the lower pool. Using his nose and mouth, he shoved two tiny silvery white seals onto the shore, then climbed out himself, blocking their way to the water while they orked merrily at the prank they'd played on everyone. Yana reached them and flung the furs over her family. Inside the furs, Sean shook himself like a large dog and the little ones instinctively followed suit.

Yana's heart began beating again. Being the only fulltime biped in her family was going to take some getting used to.

CHAPTER 3

A s usual, it was midday of the following day before the latchkay ended. Yana and her family returned home, accompanied by Clodagh, who came armed
with leftovers from the feast.

To her surprise, Yana found she was ravenous again.
After she fed the twins—Murel and Ronan—she sat
down at the table with Sean and Clodagh, knowing that
if she stretched out on the chaise longue she would
drown in her soup.

Clodagh served the rolls and soup. She looked exhila-
rated, as she always did after latchkays, even though
Yana thought they must be somewhat draining for her
too.

"Your message light is still on," Yana observed idly,
nodding to the red light above the door to the office
cube.

"It can wait," Sean said gruffly, and almost savagely
took a bite from his roll, an expression of extreme delight on his face as he chewed. "Featherlight, Clodagh."

"I can't take credit for those. That Aoifa has a real
light hand with bread."

"Indeed. More, please?" And Yana used the last of her

third roll to sop up what little gravy remained on her plate before handing it to whomever would take it.

"Drink that blurry too, Yana. Makes good milk," Clodagh said as she rose to refill her plate and Yana's. The blurry was a special sort of Petaybean beer. One could not drink enough of it to get drunk, but did get pleasantly—well, blurred.

Obediently, Yana took a sip of the dark brew. Actually, it was not her favorite beverage by any means, but she knew of its benefits to a nursing mother, having been told so ad nauseam by every person who had noticed her protruding abdomen in the last nine months.

On the other hand, if she drank enough of the stuff, she might forget which twin she had last breast-fed, though actually she was getting the hang of the rotation bit. Excusing herself from the table, she sought out the chaise and leaned gratefully against its back. Large as it was, it still was the perfect couch for her . . . and even fit her tall body, with room for Sean.

They finished the meal companionably, with Clodagh reciting a list for Sean to write down of the people who had sent messages and congratulations to the new parents from other parts of Petaybee, and another list of the gifts and givers.

"One thing's sure," she finished up, rising to her feet and collecting plates, "they won't lack warm blankets and fur rugs! Nor babysitters. Your nieces have offered their services as their baby gifts. Aoifa said she'd had a lot of experience with babies and kids in Vale of Tears."

Clodagh gave one of her disapproving sniffs for the trials and tribulations of the poor Aoifa, who had been rescued from a most barbaric enclave and the untender mercies of its leader, Shepherd Howling.

Yana scrunched her shoulders into a more comfortable position and sighed with repletion.

"That was splendid, Clodagh."

"Indeed. A fitting end to a very fine naming latchkay, in spite of that little show of independence from the guests of honor."

"I suppose it's just something we'll have to get used to," Yana said. She closed her eyes and saw imprinted on the insides of her lids the incredible patterns the planet had created in the walls of the cave when the twins were recovered and the communion ended. "Even Petaybee seemed proud of them, though." A yawn overtook her and she stretched, jerking her knees up as abused muscles in her abdomen resisted.

"C'mon then, Yana, and get a good night's sleep . . . on your side or your tummy . . ." Clodagh said, and Sean slid his wife's legs to one side of the chaise so she was in a position to rise easily.

"On my tummy, oooh, it feels so good. Yesterday I was too knackered to notice how I lay," she said with a cautious hand on her now unoccupied belly.

"I'll come tuck you in," Sean said, knowing she disliked being too fussed over. "And let you know if that message was anything important."

She gave him a loving smile and stuck out her tongue at his offer to share the message as if it would be a treat. She had already slid into her gown and a dressing robe, so getting ready for bed took little time. Once there, she experimented with positions denied her during her pregnancy to find the most comfortable one. She'd have to get up in about three hours to feed her ravenous babies.

As tired as she was, she found her mind would not

quit whirling as she settled down to sleep. There was so much to think about that she had put on hold the last few days while preparing to birth her babies.

Her babies . . . She was forty-five, and although she had always kept herself fit in the Company Corps, conceiving had been a minor miracle she attributed entirely to Petaybee's healing influence . . . another reason she blessed the planet and resolved to protect it to the best of her ability as joint governor of this fascinating world.

Many of the problems she and Sean had originally faced were sorting themselves out, especially now that Petaybeans, who had been recruited by the Intergal Company for lack of other employment on the planet, were resigning their commissions and returning to their native world, where the training they'd had made them invaluable and very employable in Petaybee's new business ventures.

She would be so relieved when the novelty of the planet faded and it stopped being invaded by all kinds of groups—esoteric, exotic, and daft—who felt they would benefit by time spent here in some capacity or another. Sooner or later word would get around that the planet's wonders were hardly a free lunch for all and sundry. Petaybee took care of its people, keeping them healthy and well fed, but the recipients of those benefits had to endure very cold winters with deep snows and a short and very busy summer with swarms of biting insects attacking any visible flesh. The planet itself had stern criteria that newcomers had to meet.

Yana grinned in the darkened room and twitched a blanket over her shoulder. Where was Sean? Maybe the message was a good one. He said he'd come tuck her in.

She'd need to get as much sleep as she could with the feeding schedule she was now facing.

Sister Igneous Rock had suggested that the planet itself interview candidates. There were several problems with that, but the downside—the candidate had to spend the night in one of the communion places, and some people had very intense reactions to the experience—was sometimes a problem: negative for the applicant, very helpful in weeding out those who had no talents or abilities that the planet needed. There had been some protests by people rejected . . . but that was their tough luck. As word got around that Petaybee was not an easy mark, fewer duds arrived for their entrance exam.

The latest bunch, hydroengineers, had passed with flying colors, and spent more time with Sister Iggierock—as she was called with affection and admiration—who had spent hours reading to the planet so it could decide which types of modernization it would accept.

Now that folk were becoming accustomed to what Clodagh called the "Rock Flock," they were proving invaluable. There had been other "religiously" inclined visitors who'd had to be disillusioned by fact and their interview with the planet on their arrival. So far, of those with determined evangelical zeal, only the Rock Flock had been acceptable to the entity Iggierock still referred to as the Beneficent.

Much had changed, besides the seasons, since Yana first set foot on her "retirement" planet. She hadn't known, but secretly suspected, that her damaged lungs were incurable. That is, until she met Clodagh and had lived through her first winter on the planet. Its curative powers—good food, clean air, and exercise—had restored many to complete good health. The clinic, inaugurated by Farringer Ball, the CEO of Intergal Company and a confirmed sicko who had once been one of the most critical of the company executives, had to increase its beds yet again to accommodate those seeking treatment on organic Petaybee. That clinic promised to be a profitable business now, with the laboratories adjacent to it to have state-of-the-art in equipment. Highly qualified physicians and researchers and equally qualified men and women lined up to take any position available. On his long list of to-do's, Sean added similar clinics for the southern continent and perhaps another facility on the western coast of the main continent.

She heard her door being carefully opened and knew Sean was there to "tuck" her in.

She turned over in the bed and heard his chuckle.

"You were supposed to be asleep," he teased.

"Not until you came to tuck me in. So who was it and what's the new problem?" she asked, having taken a look at his face. She knew him so well now that his expression indicated he needed to talk about whatever that message had been. She pulled her legs to one side so he could sit on the bed, and then she curled her body around his.

"Marmie is coming," he said, as if that explained everything. Perhaps it did. Marmion de Revers Algemeine was one of their most devoted and shrewdest new friends, having been part of a team sent initially to examine the "sentient" claim Sean and Yana had made for their planet. "And she's bringing a top-class lawyer and legal team."

"Why on earth do we need a top-class lawyer and a

legal team . . . apart from those already resident on Petaybee?" Most disputes among the residents were solved by the intervention of shanachies or people like Clodagh who were respected as leaders and wise mentors. The Collective Interplanetary Societies—or CIS—under the guidance of Phon Ton Anaciliact, had helped prove that Petaybee, the planet, was a sentient entity, and Sean and Yana had scrupulously held to the tenets provided by the CIS. So far the planet had been more sinned against than sinning.

"Well, complaints have been lodged by individuals of discrimination by the employer . . ." Sean began, after clearing his throat.

"Oh, those who got rejected," Yana said.

"Exactly." His grin was dour.

"They were interviewed by the main employer and found unsuitable for the tasks available," Yana said, which was basically what the people were told as they were transported to the departures lounge.

"They said the interview was biased and they had not taken any written tests to prove their skills nor asked to produce documents or recommendations to prove their competence. Ergo, they were denied their right to seek employment here."

"Oh, Lordy," Yana said, pushing her hair back from her forehead. "Half of them didn't have working skills but had heard that life on Petaybee was dead easy."

"Most of them also had diseases we do not wish to see circulating here," Sean added. "I asked Petaybee when she started wholesale rejections. Some of the diseases were social, which could be communicated to the entire population. A lot of them were mentally unstable, some criminally insane. Oh, and the discrimination on religious grounds is cited all too often."

"But Petaybee is not religious," Yana said. "I thought we'd cleared that up when we had to limit the number of pilgrims. Mind you, Iggierock and Shale and the others have proved more than useful, but certainly not in any religious circumstances."

"And Marmie says we have to clear that up in legal terms, which must then be presented to would-be immigrants before they take passage here. That won't be hard to do since we control the only transport that is technically admissible in Petaybean space. But we have to set it up, or be continually set upon by lawsuits."

"Who's behind that notion? I thought we'd got rid of Luzon and company."

"Marmie says we're not out of the woods so easily . . . especially since our population is mainly composed of other i.p.'s—inconvenient people. As an Earth-type planet, we are still supposed to accommodate i.p.'s." He grimaced.

"First they have to prove they are not going to remain inconvenient, and so far none of those rejected could."

"There are some iffy cases, Marmion went on to say, which is why we have to sort this problem now. Oh, and more Nakatira cubes are on their way."

"How does she manage that?" Then Yana waved off the need for an answer. She was only too grateful to get all they could of the useful buildings. They came equipped with all mod cons, as Clodagh called it, and required no special foundations or extra facilities, coming complete with solar heating and sanitary bio-conveniences. Their only drawback was a certain characterless sterility, which with a little imagination could easily be imprinted with the individual style of the occupant.

The cubes were manufactured and distributed by a Japanese known to Marmion, and Yana and Sean suspected she had financial connections there as well. They had arrived in what Bunny called the "niche" of time. Building materials alone were precious on Petaybee, and energy to heat them even more so. The cubes were the perfect answer to provide accommodations for an overwhelmed planet that had never expected so many visitors or the need for such things as hotels, schools, offices, and storage space. One of the first to be placed was the cube that was next to Yana's old house and provided the couple with office space and occasional living quarters for legitimate visitors. A second was Kilcoole's school, and others had been placed at the Space Port for essential services and finally for the beginnings of the new hospital. Another cube was now the nursery.

Marmion had warned them that eventually Mr. Soshimi Nakatira wanted to visit this incredible planet and meditate in one of the communion caves. He hadn't yet taken Sean and Yana up on that invitation, but Marmion was certain that he would.

"He's the kind of guy you want to visit and to stay as long as he likes," Marmion had assured them.

At the time, plagued with importunate visitations, Yana had remarked with irony, "Which means he'll arrive in the midst of one of our crises. We'll have to save one cube for him alone."

"Oh, he'll probably bring his own accommodation," Marmie had replied negligently. "He's like that. 'A truly gifted man.'"

"At least we have Soshimi's cube available for the lawyers," Yana said cheerfully.

"Probably the time he'll come for that visit," Sean remarked.

"Now, let's not borrow more trouble," she said soothingly, stroking his hand where it was on her pillow.

"True, love. We'll be looking back on these as the grand old days soon enough. Once Petaybee's midsea volcanoes build up the landmass in the temperate zone, we'll be besieged with even more folk wanting to come to this unspoiled planet to 'improve' it. Without the cold climate to deter them, every planetless soul in the cosmos will be wanting to live here."

"That's far off in the future, Sean," she said. "From what you told me of your journey through that area before, everything is still well below the surface. These things take eons."

"In the natural way of things, that's true. But on a terraformed world like this one, even latent development is much accelerated. I give it a decade, tops."

"For someone not borrowing trouble, you're deep in debt now," she teased.

"Sorry, love, you're quite right. Now you get some sleep," he urged, leaning down to kiss her tenderly. "I want to do a bit more work before I join you. I've let things slide the last few days. Can't think why I've been so distracted."

Yana smiled and squeezed his hand.

"However did I find you in all the worlds I could have gone to?" she asked with a grateful sigh.

"I know you looked long and hard, love," he said, half teasing, half serious, as he pulled the soft fur around

her shoulders and kissed her forehead. "Remember, it'll
be Ronan gets the source this morning."

"I did remember that."

"I'll remind you," he whispered as he left the room.

CLOSING THE DOOR behind him, Sean looked in on the
twins before returning to the office cube. Asleep in their
new dual cradle, they looked as sweet and peaceful, as
peachy and golden, as if they had never turned into little
silvery seals. That trick of theirs this evening showed
him that he would need to be on his guard with these
two slippery characters. He was glad to see the cats had
taken notice too. Marduk had planted himself across the
twins' legs, making a living fur blanket, and Nanook
and Coaxtl stretched out beside the cradle. Nanook
opened one eye, and Sean nodded and closed the door.

He was glad that Yana had been too tired to take in
the end of Shanachie Desi's song, where after seven
years Murel changed back into a seal and swam out to
meet her brother, neither of them ever to be seen again
by her foster mother. It was nonsense, of course. That
was a fairy tale told back on earth about a supernatural
species, not a genetic mutation like himself. All of those
stories involved seals temporarily turning into people
and, when they became seals once more, never being
able to return. They were wild creatures, not part of
families like his. Of course if his children swam away,
they would return. He always had, hadn't he? Becoming
a seal was a gift, an ability, a talent, actually, that allowed him to do certain things others could not.

Still, he was grateful that Yana had not heard the rest
of that song, and he hoped no one would ask her about
it. She had enough to worry about without bringing

in folk tales that had nothing to do with the mutation brought about by Shongili genetic engineering, accident, and Petaybee's own tendency to adapt species to its own needs. With the big cats for babysitters when he himself could not be teaching them about being seals, the kids would be fine; sure they would.

CHAPTER 4

MUREL AND RONAN were quite advanced in most ways. They learned to walk very early, and to run almost as quickly. By the age of three they could sit on the back of a curly coat without being held there. They started school when they were five, and learned to read and write, demonstrating their abilities by reading to each other at home. But by the time they were seven, they were in and out of trouble all the time, the mildest problem being that the teacher was unfairly suspicious when they kept turning in identical test papers written in nearly identical left-handed printing.

The teacher also noted in their student evaluation that Murel and Ronan did not reach out to befriend the other students, especially the newcomers, and spoke mostly only to each other unless asked to recite.

The truth was, they not only didn't reach out to newcomers, they didn't like or trust them much either.

"They come to *our* world because they're sick or other worlds won't have them, and act like they're better than us," Ronan told their mother.

"They're just scared," she said. "It's rough for them, you know. They realize that they're not as well adapted as you are, so they have to act as if they know more in other areas."

"I don't see why," Murel said. "If they were nice, we'd try to teach them stuff about Petaybee, but some of them, especially the older ones, are just nasty and mean. All they do is moan and groan about how bad the com stuff is around here and how they can't always depend on it to reference their lessons or talk to their friends wherever they were before they left. They want to know why we don't have a decent satellite so all the stuff that needs a satellite works better. They don't care about learning about *here*."

When Ronan came home with a black eye and Murel with a cut lip, their father said, "Fighting, were you? Murel too?"

"It wasn't our fault, Da. That Dino Caparthy is a bully. He's really big and he has a gang and they jumped Ronan—I mean all of them. I sorted—I helped Ronan sort them out and sent Dino away with a bloody nose, grabbing his bollocks with both mittens, but they're really a problem."

"So you *did* win then, did you?" he asked. They looked at each other, shrugged, looked back at their father and nodded. He said, "Well, good. I'll speak to their parents and teachers but I'm not sure how much good it will do. They came here from Romopolis on Mingus Prime. It was one of the earliest terraformed worlds and it's not in very good shape. The cities are filthy and the air has been recycled so many times inside the domes that you can cut it as quick as breathe it. Their folks applied to us so they could get their kids out of that environment to someplace more wholesome, and since they've skills we can use, we accepted them. But they're going to have to talk to their kids about cooperating."

"To hear Dino tell it," Ronan said, "Romopolis is a wonderful funfair of a city, and Kilcoole is at the end of the universe and the bottom of the food chain. He said we were all so breaded our chrome was broken and we were mutes with scales."

"Is that insulting?" Da asked, looking puzzled.

"What he *meant*, of course," Murel said in a very careful and grown-up voice, "is that we are *inbred* and our *chromosomes* are broken so that we're *mutants* on the *evolutionary* scale, but he's too dumb to even know how to call people bad things."

Da looked like he was trying to keep a straight face and not smile. He liked it when they used big words, and because he and Mum used them a lot to talk about their work, Murel and Ronan knew how to say the words. And because they wanted to join in the conversation but had to keep asking what things meant, and Mum and Da always told them to go look it up—now—they knew what the words meant. Dino didn't like that about them either. *He* was the real mute with scales.

"And what inspired this lad to call you all of these things he couldn't pronounce?" Da asked.

"Nothing!" they both exclaimed, and Ronan continued, "It was just because we didn't feel bad that the stupid game his uncle sent him won't work here and because he thinks we should have great clattering halls full of fake stuff for him to play with. I can't tell you what he called Petaybee but it had to do with shite and it wasn't nice."

Da nodded, but whether he ever did anything about it, they didn't know. Whatever he did, it didn't work very well. After that, Dino only hit Ronan when he was sure Murel wasn't around. The gang still said horrible, if garbled, things about them and the few other kids actually from Kilcoole, but they said it out of range of Murel's fists, feet, and fingernails.

IF THEIR TEACHER thought the twins were withdrawn, the track cats, Coaxtl, and the curly coats had the opposite opinion of them. It was everything the helpful creatures could do to keep the pair out of trouble. They were insatiably curious, absolutely fearless, and downright dangerous to be around sometimes.

"They keep leaving their outer coats lying around on the riverbank where anyone can find them," Nanook complained. The intrepid track cat was getting a little tired of playing nanny. Nevertheless, he dutifully turned around and used his hind paws to spray powdery snow over the snow pants and parkas the twins had carelessly left lying near their latest ice hole in the river before taking an afternoon dip in seal form.

"It's a very good thing for Sean and Yana that they aren't exactly like the seal people in the old stories," Coaxtl said, settling her white fluffy belly into the snow. She placed her huge paws with their tufts of fur between the toes on either side of the ice hole and watched with flicking fringe-tipped ears for fish swimming across the exposed circle of running water. The water was so deep and cold it looked black at this time of the year.

"Do you recall the song sung at the naming latch-kay?" Nanook asked.

"Many songs were sung," Coaxtl replied. "It was very tiring."

"I mean the one about the seal people who shed their

coats when they became human, not the other way around. If any other human found the sealskin and kept it, then the selkie had to stay on land with that person."

"One recalls something of the sort, yes."

"I fancy Sean and Yana must sometimes wish it were true of the twins so they would have to stay in the nest until they could be safely supervised," Nanook mused. "Of course, humans are a bit silly about that. Their young are sooo fragile and they have only one or two at a time."

"There is no room for those two in any enclosed space," Coaxtl said, and turned her head to lick her shoulder.

At that moment water geysered out of the hole and drenched the snow leopard, who somersaulted backward in surprise.

She twisted and sat up facing the hole. A gray seal slapped front flippers on the edge and pulled its sleek body after it. The cubs' eyes had been silver at birth like their father's but as sometimes happened with kits, the color changed. The eyes of the seal pup looking up at Coaxtl were big and blue and the mouth was grinning.

As soon as the seal was out of the water, it flipped water all over both Nanook and Coaxtl. A childish human laugh pealed from the midst of the spray and a small bare boy stood before the cats. "Gotcha!" he laughed.

Coaxtl gave the boy a withering look and walked two paces forward until she sat on top of the buried snowsuit. *Cold, youngling?* she asked, purring.

"You took my snowsuit! You big fur ball!"

Nanook walked forward and touched a cold nose to the child's bare rump, nudging him back to the ice hole.

If I were you, I'd be a seal again. At least you're dressed for the weather when you're in seal form.

Ronan resisted smacking at, though not on, the black-and-white track cat's icy nose. "Don't get cat snot on me, Nanook. I'm cold enough. I don't want to swim anymore."

Then I suggest you show submission to Coaxtl and beg her to return the property with which you so carelessly littered the landscape. Honestly, child, you never find us leaving our pelts lying around.

"Oh yes we do. During breakup you shed your fuzzy body all over everything."

We remain attractively clad in fur at all times, Coaxtl said. She allowed a sleeve of the snowsuit to poke out from beneath her belly. *You, on the other hand, cover yourself in small bumps, which do nothing that we can see to warm you.*

"I'm going to freeze to death and it will be on your head!" he proclaimed with something of his father's Irish lilt. It was good for dramatic pronouncements.

From the ice beside the hole came a sharp smack and a swoosh, and Murel rose, flashed pink skin, and then ran to the bank and pulled her buried snowsuit and blanket from under a log. She wrapped the blanket around her as she tugged on the suit, then tossed the blanket to her brother.

"Don't tease him, 'Nook," she said. "Can you not see he's about to perish of the cold?"

Perish? It's only minus twenty! Nanook said, but shot a look at Coaxtl, who decamped from atop the clothing while the blanket-clad boy scrambled for it. *Downright sultry weather, I'd call it. It's a wonder the ice is holding. Younglings Petaybean born and bred should be able to*

*withstand this without getting all hissy and breaking out
in bumps.*

Murel bullied her twin often enough when he wasn't
bullying her instead, but she didn't want anyone else to
do it. "Come on, Ronan, don't give the cats the satisfaction next time. I told you to hide your snowsuit. What if
one of the offplanet people was to find it? They'd think
you'd drowned and would have set up a huge hue and
cry and everyone would have to pretend to find you
without letting the off-p's see you as a selkie."

"Oh, would they? If you're that worried about it, you
could have hid mine too. Where would you be during all
of this hueing and crying and searching?"

Murel gave a deep and put-upon sigh and strode as
purposefully toward the village as her seven-year-old legs
would carry her. "Really, Ronan, you are such an infant
sometimes! I can scarcely believe we have the same
birthday. You make any pup in Bunny's new litter look
downright mature by comparison. You just don't *think*,
laddie."

But Ronan had pulled his mittens on and was bouncing the finger pad off the thumb one. "See? This is your
mouth! You just don't *shut up*, do you, lassie?"

He caught up with her and tried to race past her but
she ran even faster when she saw what he was trying
to do.

Kits! Nanook said.

The track cat had meant to bring up the snowsuit
issue with Sean and Yana, but his humans were always
so busy these days, it took actual claws to get their attention. The company and the offplanet people simply
would not leave them in peace. They were always trying
to settle some new group on Petaybee or bring in some

kind of improvements for the good of everyone, as they said, and they kept Sean and Yana hopping night and day just to field all of their chatter. Some of the offplanet people who were settlers were nice enough. Some even settled into Petaybean ways. But most of them came to Petaybee for peace, healing, a clean and simple life, and then wanted to clutter it up with all manner of things they were used to from their noisy, unpeaceful, unhealthy, dirty, and complicated lives somewhere else. That was what Nanook had heard the villagers say anyway. As long as the newcomers didn't bring with them anything that preyed on track cats, he did not concern himself with them.

"What those younglings need is something that can keep up with them swimming," Coaxtl said finally. "They swim farther and farther up the river every time and I'm afraid sometime they'll get in trouble and we won't know because we won't be close enough to catch their cries for help."

AT THE SAME time, Murel and Ronan, having captured their mother in one of her rare moments of leisure, were expounding on the situation to her. "If Da could come with us, it would be fine. We are really too old for baby-sitters now, but if we have to have one, it should be another selkie, or at least someone who can swim with us," Ronan said.

Murel nodded her head, the red tints in her black hair flashing with the firelight from the window in the wood-stove. "Coaxtl can swim and doesn't mind it in the summer but she's really a big wuss-puss about swimming under the ice. All she does is hide Ronan's snowsuit."

"Does she?" Yana asked. "Why doesn't Ronan hide

his own snowsuit? I believe both your father and I have tried to impress upon you—"

"The thing is, Mum, it just isn't practical to have to hide them," Ronan said. "Sometimes we'd like to go explore someplace out of the water but we can't because we don't have a kit to put on when we get out of the water. We need a way to take them with us."

"I suppose we could rig up some sort of harness and a waterproof pack," Yana said, thinking of diving equipment she had used while still in the Company Corps. "It would slow you down a bit but that's hardly a bad thing. I'm not so sure I want you exploring outside the water so far from where you got in."

"Nothing would happen to us, Mum!" Murel said. "Petaybee wouldn't let it. You know that."

"I know nothing of the sort. Petaybee has a good many other functions than providing divine intervention for you when you do something foolish and get yourselves into trouble. And once you're away from the village and our summer campsites on the river, there are all manner of things that could indeed hurt you."

"Not any worse than freezing to death while a snow leopard squats on your protective gear and lectures you," Ronan said with some residual bitterness at the unfairness of those who didn't let him do as he liked, unchecked.

Murel rolled her eyes at her mother and said, "Yes, Mummy, please make Coaxtl stop teasing Ronan. She is just so endlessly tiresome about it, and I'm the one who has to hear it all the time."

"Okay, here's what I can do, kids. Marmion has known about our family secret since you were tiny. I'll see if Marmion can send us some high-tech lightweight snowsuits and waterproof packs and harnesses for you from offworld. One of her companies develops that kind of thing, I think. But meanwhile, you don't go anywhere without hiding your suits and letting Coaxtl and Nanook know where you're going. Meanwhile, I'll talk to your father about finding you a swimming companion. It will pain him, you know. He'd like nothing better than to join you, and the three of you could be off sealing around while I fend off would-be settlers and contractors and answer the wretched com unit."

"Thanks, Mummy, you're the best!" Ronan said, giving her an enthusiastic hug that almost knocked her off her stool.

Murel planted a kiss on her cheek. "We'll look for a swim friend too," she said.

"Someone your father and I approve of, mind you!" Yana said, but she was calling out after their heels as they flashed out the door and down the snowy track between the village's shacks, log cabins, and the incongruous but inconspicuous white Nakatira cubes, which blended into the snow.

SEAN PROMISED THE twins he'd go with them and they could swim as far as the ice floe, farther than they'd ever been before, and look for a friend with flippers or fins who could chaperone them.

The twins were unusually excited when the next ship landed, as it bore the imprint of Marmion's company. Surely she had sent the gear Mother asked for, along with all of these strangers disembarking.

Murel and Ronan hung around until the pilot appeared in the hatchway. "Johnny!" they both cried, and ran to hug Captain Green, one of their family's oldest friends. "Did you bring us anything?" Ronan asked, looking around the pilot for something besides his usual flight duffel.

"I brought you all of those exciting new friends, did I not? What more could you possibly be wanting?" he teased, ruffling Ronan's hair.

"But Marmie promised to send us something," Murel said, hanging on to his belt. "For our birthdays, you know. We're eight today, aren't we, Ronan?"

"We are. And she did say so, Marmie did, said she was sending us this particular item."

"Funny, I don't recall a thing about it," Johnny said with a look of what he intended to resemble wide-eyed bewilderment.

"Maybe you didn't see it get loaded, Johnny. Could you look, *please?*"

Don't overdo it, sis, Ronan told her. *I'm sure he can see through you as well as I can when you bat your eyes at him like that.*

That shows how much you know. If you have any brains, you'll start batting too. He might have to go to a lot of trouble to find it. We'd best be scoring all of the points for adorable that we can.

"Hmm," Johnny said, scratching his chin, although both twins were quite sure it wasn't itchy. "Let me think. You know, there was a lot going on at the time, what with all these folks getting ready to board, but I do seem to remember Marmion mentioning something about you."

"She promised Mum she'd send us something. And you know Marmie would never break a promise to Mum," Ronan said in a sober, man-to-man tone.

"No, no, of course not. But I can't think of anything at all unless it would be those wee ration packets."

"Ration packets?" both twins asked at once.

"Yes, now that I think of it, she handed me the little foil packets and said your mum needed them for you."

"They weren't ration packets, Johnny," Murel said. "You did bring them, didn't you?"

"Oh, aye. Though I hardly thought it worth the trouble. There's plenty of ration packets still left over from when Intergal ran the Space Base. What did I do with them? Gave them to the cook, probably. You'd keep things like that in the galley, you know."

"No, no, they're not ration packets and they were *ours*," Ronan told him.

"We'll go search the galley, Johnny," Murel said. "You needn't bother. How big were they and did the foil have writing on it? We can read that sort of thing now, you know."

"Ah well, I guess they were about as big as . . ." He reached into the pockets on the thighs of his pants and pulled out two packets bright as fish. "And the writing says—this one says, 'for Murel,' and this one says, 'for Ronan.' "

The twins snatched them and Ronan began trying to open his. Murel looked up at Johnny's grin and said, "Thank you very much, Johnny, for bringing them. But Deirdre Angalook is quite right. You're a terrible tease."

"Deirdre said something to you about me, did she?"

"Aye," Murel said, pretending to scratch her own chin. "But I can't quite recall what else it was she said except for the bit about the teasing."

Johnny stabbed a finger to her middle as if to tickle her, but at that moment Ronan figured out the packet and it unfolded, flowerlike, blooming into a metallic-looking suit with what seemed to be very light quilting.

"It's very small and thin," Ronan said, a little disappointed as he felt the cloth.

"Oh, there's directions," Johnny said. "It gets bigger and puffier, I'm told."

"How's that?" Ronan asked.

"See there, that fine print? It says, 'Just add water.' "

Both of them jumped him and there was a lot of rolling in the snow before he finally admitted defeat and said he had to go report in to their parents.

"You two coming along?"

"No," Ronan said. "We need to try these on, test them. So we can show our folks."

CHAPTER 5

WHEN JOHNNY HAD gone, the twins headed directly to the river. It connected the former Space Base with the village. In the winter, its frozen surface served as a road where people drove dogs and snocles back and forth from their ice fishing holes or to go after water.

Ronan compressed his suit again and returned it to packet form, then began removing his snowsuit.

"You're not supposed to take off your clothes where there are people around, or change either!" his sister chided him.

"Well, we have to test them."

"We can go to the spring. And besides, we need to find 'Nook and Co' first anyway."

"No we don't. With these suits, we don't have to worry about getting caught without our clothes anywhere, and that's all the cats really do. Otherwise they just hang around the water hole. I want to test these, Murel. Let's go somewhere fun. Maybe we can find a new chaperone."

"Da said—"

"Didn't you see that load of offworlders? Da will be busy processing and orienting them for days and days. If we can find someone Mum and he like to swim with us, we can go *everywhere*. We won't have to hang around boring old Kilcoole with our skins itching for wet while Mum and Da entertain strangers."

Murel was not above temptation. She wanted to see what was beyond Kilcoole and the familiar waters too. And she knew what Ronan said was true. It seemed like with their parents, what everybody else wanted always came before what they wanted—or even needed. It was very unfair. If they could be a little more independent, or at least not have to wait on their folks or those land-bound cats, maybe they could even help with the work Mum and Da did for Petaybee. After all, they were eight now. That was pretty old.

"Okay," she said. "But not here. That place where they put in the fish wheel in the summer. Nobody is there now and we can strip off and plunge in without getting caught."

They raced through town without drawing much attention since everyone was busy meeting and greeting the new people. Even though a lot of Petaybeans didn't want the offworlders there, Clodagh and the other leaders reminded folk that they had all been from elsewhere originally and these people, like themselves, were just looking for a home to settle down in. Petaybee would either accept or reject them before long. No need meanwhile for Petaybeans to be inhospitable.

But the twins had had entirely too much of that. While they were in town making nice with the refugees, they weren't swimming and playing and teasing their feline nannies.

The stretch of river on the other side of town had another big advantage besides being less public. The hot springs fed into it, so areas of water stayed open year round, and much of the water that did freeze had a far thinner crust than that between the old Space Base and Kilcoole.

The twins found a good, big open place to enter the water, but first took off their clothes and carefully concealed them under some brush on the bank. Then, having located the little straps to their tiny packs, they fixed them over their shoulders so the packs were in the middle of their backs. Then each took a running jump into the water. It was icy at the top but much warmer underneath, and felt warmer still as their transformation took place. By the time they were completely submerged, they were no longer lanky pale children but shorter, fatter, furrier gray seals.

They played hide-and-seek with each other in the patchy ice, then dove deep, as the hot spring's current was diluted by colder streams. They swam for the joy of it, loving the feeling of being in a cave made of river ice, with the bumpy riverbed below and the bumpy ice sheets above. This time of the year there was little sun, but their eyes were excellent in the dark and underwater. They raced each other downstream, stopping once in a while to claw open a breathing hole in the ice with the talons at the ends of their flippers. When they grew hungry, they snacked on fish. They caught the smaller ones just by opening their mouths. The larger ones they had to take to the surface to eat.

When they had swum farther than they'd ever gone before, another hot spring entered the river, making a large area where they could surface and slide up onto the ice and over to the bank. The wind had come up, and it was pretty cold business getting themselves into their new suits. Had they not been native Petaybeans with the special adaptations to supercold temperatures the planet had engendered in its inhabitants, they would have frozen to death long before they got their suits on. However, since they *were* native Petaybeans, they put on their suits very very quickly. Once the shiny thin fabric covered their bodies, including their hands, feet, heads, and all of their faces but their eyes, they found they were quite toasty.

This stuff is amazing! Ronan thought-spoke to his sister, both because that was how they usually communicated with each other and because the fabric covering their mouths made it difficult to speak or to hear someone else speaking through it. *I bet it's what they make ship suits out of.*

Yeah, Murel said, twirling a little in hers, which was fun because the boots were as slippery as her flippers on the ice. *And we could go skating even in human form while we're wearing these.*

Ronan yawned. *What I'd rather do is take a nap. I'm pretty sleepy.*

Me too. Then we probably ought to start back before 'Nook and Co' start stalking us.

So they found a sheltered place among the spindly trees that grew along the bank and lay down beside them. The snow felt soft through their suits, and not the least bit cold. They had barely closed their eyes when Murel sat up. *Did you hear that?*

What?

That chirpy noise. It isn't a bird. I know it's not a bird.

"Hah!" something said, very close to them.

It's coming from the river, Murel said.

"Hah!" it said again, followed by more of the nervous-sounding chirping, like a mother bird missing her chicks.

Almost sounds like a dog driver coming up the trail, Ronan said.

Only not quite. It's coming from under the water.

Yeah?

Listen!

You're right, it is.

They fumbled removing their suits. Ronan left his on the bank and started to slide into the water but Murel stopped him. *No! Strap it on. It's shiny. A bird might take it. Besides, that's what we wanted them for.*

He grumbled but struggled into it while she, with her pack already strapped over her shoulders, slid into the water and transformed. She dove under the ice before her brother hit the water.

It occurred to her to wonder why they heard the sound as a voice if it was underwater. It was a distinct sound that she'd heard, not a thought.

Swimming deeper under, she saw something struggling in the ice. From time to time it made the noises they had heard, but she felt it tiring and sensed it was frightened.

What's wrong? she asked, approaching to see a body with a short thick tail and four furry paws, the back two webbed, struggling in the water. The body ended at the ice.

Caught. Crack opened up and dumped me in then ice trapped my head. Caught. "Hah!"

I see. And your paws are all too far below the ice to be able to help you. We'll see what we can do.

Ronan joined her, and the two of them used their

clawed flippers and noses to push the ice away from the other creature.

A chunk broke off in Ronan's claws, and abruptly the little animal dropped down into the water with a flourish of bubbles that, when they reached the surface, contained the word "Hah!"

But what the creature was thinking was, *Seals? River seals? I never heard of river seals before. Did you free me so you could eat me?*

Of course not, Murel answered.

Why? Ronan asked. *Are you scrumptious?*

No, no, no, the creature answered, its little brain whirling with ideas and images. *Actually, my kind are poisonous to seals. That's why I asked, you see. You two seem like very good sorts for seals and I wouldn't want to make you sick if you tried to eat me, or even kill you.*

What kind are your kind? Murel asked. *Other than poisonous to seals, that is?*

The otter kind, the creature answered, swimming away from them a certain distance. It wanted to escape but its curiosity kept it paddling in the water just under what looked like another hole in the ice. *What kind of seals are you to swim in rivers? You're just pups, I can see that. Did you get lost from your mother?*

How do you know we're seals if you live in the river and seals never swim here? Murel asked.

Otters get around, the little fellow said. He had a round head with a short black nose and very little neck. His eyes were large and shiny, and his mouth curved up into what looked like a smile regardless of what he seemed to be feeling or thinking. *I've been to the coast to visit my cousins. Well, once. But they told me about seals and how they eat—well, I saw some at a distance.*

But they all lived on the beach or the little islands right around. None have ever come into the river before.

We are called Petaybean shepherd seals or selkies, Murel told him, remembering their father's earlier teachings. *We eat fish when we're in the water, but no other creatures. Shepherd seals protect other creatures and help maintain the harmony of the water life on our world.*

Thank you very much, I'm sure, the otter replied. *I'm feeling extremely harmonious, now that I think of it, and very glad not to have my head stuck in the ice anymore. So if you're sure you will not try to eat me—and make your good selves very ill if not dead, of course—I'll just be on my way now.*

The little creature was afraid of them, they could see that, but he was also uncontrollably inquisitive. *Unless, of course, you'd like to play?*

We should be getting back to our vil—to our mother, Murel said.

But we could play for a little while, I guess, Ronan answered, and in an aside to his twin said, *It's only polite not to just run away. Besides, he looks like the sort of chap who could get himself right back into trouble if we don't keep an eye on him.*

You should know all about that, Murel said, as if she were the oldest and didn't get into plenty of trouble herself.

All right then, the otter said. *Hide-and-seek? You two be it and I'll go hide.*

Wait a minute, Murel said before he darted off. *There's only one it. You and I can go hide and Ronan can be it.*

Why don't I go hide with the otter and you be it? Ronan argued.

Don't be such a baby, she told him. *It's just till you find one of us. Then we'll switch. Now close your eyes and count to ten.*

The otter had been about to zip away again, but now, once more, curiosity held him. *What's count?* he wanted to know.

It's how to measure things, she told him. *Like how many of them there are.*

Oh, like how many otters there are in my den? There are many, you know. What count is many?

I don't know. Ten? Forty-seven? A hundred?

What's the most many?

A hundred?

That's it then, that's how many otters are here, all with big sharp teeth to defend themselves against the bad otter-eating seals. *A hundred otters in my family.*

That's a very large family, Murel told him. *Caribou have families that large, but I didn't know otters did.*

My parents were very much in love, he told her. *Besides, we need large families with very big sharp teeth to fend off the bad otter-eating seals.*

I thought you lived in this river and we were the only seals you'd ever seen in a river? she asked.

He swam a couple of strokes and pulled himself up through a hole in the ice, onto more ice.

Look, she said. *We really really don't eat otters, even if they weren't poisonous and if there weren't a hundred with big sharp teeth. If we're going to play together, that makes us friends. Friends don't eat friends.*

Ninety-nine, a hundred! Ready or not, here I come! Ronan called.

"Hah!" the otter said from somewhere she couldn't see. *The other seal knows how many are in my family. He said it.*

No, that's just part of how we play the game. The hole in the ice wasn't quite large enough for a full-grown seal but Murel could just pull herself up through it with only a tiny clawed modification around the edges. She found herself in a low tunnel—good height for an otter and not bad for a seal if she slid on her stomach and just used her flippers to propel her slide forward.

The otter slipped and slid ahead of her, weaving in and out of tunnels as she followed behind. He didn't seem to be hiding exactly, though, so she did. One of the otter's tunnels led to a den dug deep into the thick river ice lining the bank. None of the hundred otters with the big sharp teeth seemed to be using the den, so she hid there waiting for Ronan.

If he found the otter first and the otter got to be it and came looking for them, maybe it would set the little guy's mind at ease about their intentions.

Instead, Ronan came sliding right up to her. "You're it!" he cried aloud.

How?

"Read your mind, silly. Didn't see our friend anywhere."

Otter otter in free! The otter's sending was from way up the river.

You have kind of an unfair advantage in this game, Murel said. *You know where you are and we don't.*

Okay. Let's go sliding then. I've gathered my family. They have agreed not to use their big sharp teeth on you unless you try something funny.

Are you sure? Murel asked, joking. *We know you*

now, but are your relatives maybe those seal-eating otters?

Of course not. Come on! It'll be fun! We can play over the waterfall!

Sounds kinda dangerous.

Not now. It's a seasonal game.

It took Murel and Ronan a long time to find their way back out of the maze of otter tunnels to the hole under the ice.

Then they had to swim back upstream to where the ice was thinner and open another hole so they could surface again without tearing up the otter's home.

They popped their heads out of the water. As long as the rest of their bodies stayed submerged and their heads were wet, they could stay seals.

If we get out now to go play with the otters, we won't be seals anymore, Ronan said.

Oh, bother. Then he'll think we're otter-eating people and we'll have to go all through it again or else those hundred relatives he's trying to scare us with will sink their big sharp teeth into us.

Yeah. As if. But I really want to play with them and I don't want to scare them.

I think we ought to go home now anyway. Let's just send a good-bye to our little buddy and say we were called away by our own family.

Yeah, but, Murel, we needed a swimming buddy and he could be it. If he went swimming with us, we could go all the time maybe.

True. I guess if he agreed to do that he'd find out about us being people part of the time anyway. Let's see what he says. Oh, Otter!

Come, Murel! Come slide with us. You can slide

waaaaay down! It's long and steep but when you get to the bottom you just keep going and going until you slide halfway out to the coast where my cousins live.

We want to come and play, Otter, but we need to talk to you by yourself first. Please. It's a secret.

CHAPTER 6

A SECRET? OTTERS LOVE *secrets! Hey, everybody, I'll be right back. My new friends the seals I was telling you about want to tell me a secret! Maybe they know a secret place where the fish are especially nice.*

They had to wait a long time because he had already taken his first slide and had to climb back up the hill again. When he finally reached them, he dove into the hole they had made.

What is it? What's the secret?

First we want to tell you why you should know about this, Murel said.

Our parents want us to have a friend to swim with, Ronan continued. *Someone who knows the waters and won't get lost and could go for help if something went wrong.*

I can do that. Nobody knows the water like an otter. Your parents don't eat otters either, do they?

No. In fact, our mother isn't like us at all. Our father is like us, but you'd only know it if you saw him in the water. See, Otter, it's kind of hard to explain but our mother is human and our father is, like us, a seal only when he's in the water. On the land he's a human and, uh, so are we.

"Hah!" the otter said. *That's interesting. Show me.*

You won't be scared? Murel asked. *We don't want to scare you. We really want to be your friends.*

Otters don't scare that easy, he said, chittering a bit nervously. *Some of my coastal cousins can turn into people too if they want to. They can even get human beings who aren't like them to turn into otters if they want. Oh, I shouldn't have told you about that. It's a secret too. No, not a secret. It was a lie. I was lying so you wouldn't think otters don't know about turning into humans and—*

It's okay, Murel said. *Just so you're not scared. Come on, Ronan.*

They both jumped out of the water, slid to the bank, and shook themselves off.

"Hah!" the otter said and "Hah!" again. He pushed himself out of the water and slid over to inspect them and said "Hah!" several more times as he circled their legs, which were getting goose bumps. *I don't know why you want to be human. You are all pale and too thin to be warm. You should jump back in and be seals again before you freeze. Being seals isn't as good as being otters, but it's much more practical on the river than being human.*

Good idea, Ronan said, running for the water hole.

Murel turned to show the otter the pack with her shiny suit in it. *If we were going to stay human, we'd put on these suits that are stored on our backs but we—*

"Hah! Hah!" other otters called loudly from down toward the waterfall slide.

"Hah!" their new friend answered. *Wolves!* he told the children. *Wolves have come. Otter-eating wolves. And our den is up here, uphill from where my family is.*

But your family has their big sharp teeth, right? Ronan asked.

Not as big and sharp as wolves', he said, chittering, chirping, and growling aloud in answer to the distress calls from below. *The wolves will eat them all!*

Is there a hole in the ice near the falls? Ronan asked as he teetered on the edge of the ice hole.

Yes, near our slide.

Let's go then! he said, diving in. Murel followed him, and the otter right after her.

Wolves probably eat seals too.

Yes, but we can scare them away when we turn into people, Murel said. But she didn't think that through. She just knew that wolves never bothered her father or her aunt Sinead while they were in the woods. Most sled dogs were part wolf anyway, and she wasn't afraid of them.

It didn't occur to her that nothing had threatened Ronan and her because since they were babies they had been escorted everywhere by a snow leopard and a very large track cat.

A long long dive into the ice cave running beneath the otter tunnels and then, at last, open water. First Ronan surfaced, then the otter, then Murel.

There. There's the slide. Right there. Slide down. Be quick.

Below, the wolves were howling while the otters chittered, chirruped, and hahed as they tried to scramble away. Then one screamed.

Without shaking himself dry, Ronan slid down the long frozen cataract in seal form, Murel and the otter close behind him.

At the bottom he saw a wolf with an otter in its mouth.

The little beast was still alive and snapping its teeth for all it was worth.

The wolves lined the riverbank and blocked the ice downstream. The cataract prevented the otters from climbing back up.

Before she shook herself off, Murel dug a hole in the ice with her claws and told the otter, *Get the others into the water, quickly.*

But that's my mother!

We'll try to save her.

Ronan shook himself dry and instantly was a naked boy. No time to put on the silver suit. *Get your teeth out of that otter right this minute,* he snapped at the wolf, trying to look as menacing as he could, which wasn't very.

Mine, the wolf snarled back.

Look at that, he's already defurred! another pack member, this one about a year-old pup, said. *Can I have him, sire? Can I?*

I don't know, son, the alpha male growled uncertainly. *There's something fishy about those two big ones. They were seals just a minute ago. Now they look like men. Men have firesticks, and besides, you never know what they've been into. They might be bad for you.*

Just let the otter go and be on your way and nobody gets hurt, Ronan told the wolves. *Besides, wolves don't normally eat otters. And we have it on good authority that these ones are poisonous.*

She doesn't smell *poisonous,* the wolf holding the otter argued, slitting her eyes suspiciously.

Neither does he, the young wolf said, slinking closer to Ronan with hindquarters tensed to spring. *He smells delicious.*

By then the last of the otters had popped into Murel's hole and she had changed. While the wolves circled, she put on her silver suit and looked around for a weapon. Ronan's skin was covered with goose bumps. With her entire body protected by the suit, she was better able to defend herself than he.

The female wolf shook the furious snapping otter mother trying to break her neck. Without thinking, Murel took a long slide forward, bowling into the wolf, and smacked her hard on the muzzle with the side of her mitten, making her drop the otter.

Run! she told the smaller creature, but there was no need. The otter hit the water before Murel had formed the thought.

Now there was a new problem. A circle of hungry wolves tightened around Murel and Ronan, so close the twins could smell their breath, which was doggy and rotten at the same time. The wolf who'd had the otter leapt to her feet and with both front feet stiff brought them down sharply in front of Murel, snarling, *Thief!*

Ronan had used the distraction to seal himself into his own silver suit.

Now what is he, sire? The yearling who'd asked permission to hunt Ronan sounded bewildered. *A fish? These creatures can't make up their minds what they are. But they still smell like prey to me.*

And so they are, son, and so they are. Those flimsy shiny hides won't protect them if we all jump them at once. Ready . . . The female wolf waggled her hindquarters, poised to spring. Murel lost her nerve and backed into her twin, who hugged her, and they clung together.

Set . . . the wolf's mate said.

Murel squeezed her eyes tight and hoped she wouldn't

be more than one bite to them so it wouldn't hurt so much. There were no weapons. No fire.

Ronan buried his face in her shoulder, and she did likewise with her twin.

Attack! This order was followed by yipping, snarling, snapping, and growling, but no biting.

The twins were braced, ready to be knocked down by the wolves, but nothing touched them. Instead, they heard familiar voices using feline profanity never before uttered in their presence.

Murel opened one eye in time to see Coaxtl pounce on yet another wolf and ride it like a horse while Nanook sat on his hindquarters, swatting wolf bodies right and left.

The wolves were already on the run when the first shot rang out.

"Go on, you mangy critters, get outta here! Those kids are too fraggin' spoiled rotten for you to eat anyway." Their aunt Sinead's voice sounded so good to them, she might have been promising presents instead of punishment by the time she braked her sled and ran past her spitting track cats to scoop up the children.

She bundled them into the sled and told them, as if talking to one of her team, "Stay."

They tried to tell her about the otters, but she didn't pay any attention to them. Her mouth was compressed in a thin line. The only sounds for several hours were the shushing of the runners and the patter of paws against the snow, the occasional dog stopping to relieve itself, and Aunt Sinead's barked commands. Not even Nanook or Coaxtl spoke. Ronan and Murel were too miserable to communicate with each other. After what seemed like a week but must have been sometime during the night, though it was hard to tell in the winter, the lead dog stopped in front of their house. Sinead stamped on the brake to set it, and ripped off her mittens to release the bindings holding the twins on the sled and under the furs. Her hands were shaking, which was funny since next to their mother, Aunt Sinead was the bravest lady they knew. Silently, she pointed to the door.

When they left the sled, Coaxtl and Nanook stalked them all the way there.

CHAPTER 7

ONLY MUM WAS there, and to the twins' relief, she did not seem upset.

"Where's Da?" Ronan asked innocently.

"Still out hunting for you. I imagine he's on his way home now, though." Mum's voice was smooth and calm, conversational, her face unreadable. But then, her thoughts had never been easily readable to the twins. "Suppose before he gets here you explain to me without benefit of telepathy where you've been and what you were doing that required you to do it so far from home for so long and without the company of Coaxtl and Nanook."

"Well . . . we—There were these otters, weren't there?" Ronan began.

"No, first off, Johnny brought us these suits from Marmie, for our birthday, see—"

"Your birthdays are not until tomorrow," Mum said, lifting one of her raven wing eyebrows. "I should remember. I was definitely there."

"Yeah, well, but we figured it was close enough and we'd be busy on the day and we wanted to try the suits out, that was all," Murel said, feeling it was best to start at the beginning. "Co' and 'Nook weren't around, but we just got excited and wanted to see what the suits were like so we decided to swim for a ways and put them on. They're brilliant, Mum. They kept us as warm and dry as a parka, snow pants, boots, mittens, and a hood with a good ruff, and they're no heavier than long johns."

Their mother sat with her arms crossed under her breasts, and gave a slight nod that they should continue.

"Well, we were just getting ready to come home when we heard this poor little otter crying for help from inside the river. Of course we had to help him. Petaybee would want us to, right?"

Their mother's expression did not change.

"He had his head caught so we got him loose," Ronan said. "Then he wanted to play. Well, you know, we were thinking, here's the new swimming buddy we could have to show us around, like you said we could. So we thought we should get to know him better, didn't we? So we thought just a little longer would be okay. Only the hide-and-seek took a long time in all those tunnels the otters dug, and then he wanted us to slide down the waterfall with his family."

"But before we started down, the wolves came and grabbed his mummy. The otter's, I mean. It was terrible, Mum, the poor little thing chittering and hahing—both our otter friend and his mummy, I mean. We slid down there and there was this big circle of wolves all around them. Ronan was ever so brave."

"I was, rather. I stood there and tried to reason with the wolves while sis dug the otters a bolt hole with her flippers and put on her suit. Then she attacked the wolf with the otter in her mouth while I got on my suit."

"And that held them off until Co' and 'Nook could

wade in and scare off the rest of them," Murel concluded. "Auntie Sinead fired a shot over their heads too, and that convinced them to look elsewhere for prey." Mum still wasn't saying anything, just looking at them. Murel decided to press her luck a little. "So you see, Mum, we were doing a good thing."

"You visited otters and then reasoned with wolves before you attacked them, is that about right?" Mum asked again in that calm voice that wasn't just cool— it was downright cold. This must have been how she sounded when she was an officer for the Company Corps.

They looked at each other, trying to think if they'd left anything out, decided they hadn't, shrugged and faced her again. "Well, yeah."

Ronan added, "It will make a brilliant latchkay song, Mum. We could do harmony."

"Oh yes, I can see that," their mother nodded reasonably. "All about how you almost got eaten one day short of your eighth birthday. Perhaps we could have some wolves howling to accompany the drums? You'd best be quick about writing it, then. Your father and I have discussed this with Clodagh and the village elders and there will be a special secret latchkay held tomorrow in the Night Chant grotto. You are the guests of honor." Her voice was grim now, and tight, as if there were much more she wished to say but would not or could not.

Murel put out a hand, tentatively touching her mother's. "Mum, it's fine. We're fine. We're very sorry we worried you and Da and Auntie and the cats, but we waited and waited and Da never had the time, and really, the suits are all we need to be off by ourselves—"

"Unless there are wolves," her mother said, grasping

her hand and squeezing her fingers so tightly it hurt. "Or bears, or even people who don't know we never hunt seals here. I told you already, you are too young to even imagine the dangers in which your actions placed yourselves, us, the village, and even Petaybee. I love you. Your father loves you. Everybody who knows you loves you, and if they don't know you very well, they love you even better. But, my little ones, despite your lineage from your father, despite your shape-shifting and your ability to talk with all of Petaybee's creatures, you are my children, not wild animals. And you must learn that side of your nature too. I want you to think about that and know that whatever happens, happens for your good. Now off to bed with you. Your father will look in on you when he comes in."

Murel thought that in her sleep she felt her father's kiss on her forehead and a sudden drop of water, warm as it fell into her hair.

Ronan dreamed of wolves and did not realize that the touch brushing his face as lightly as a warm breeze was his father's kiss until it was gone. Then, half awake, he became aware of a strange sound from the other room. It was his mother, so stony-faced earlier in the night, sobbing as if her heart were broken.

MOST OF THE day was suspiciously normal—even better than normal. Father made them a delicious breakfast of blueberry pancakes made with berries stored from the previous summer, caribou sausage, and rose hip tea. Mother was not much of a cook, but after they cleaned up the dishes, she gave them identical presents.

Murel examined the outside of the little hard-bound journal when her mother handed it to her. A diary? It was not very special-looking. But when she opened it, she saw that it was already filled with her mother's writing, including some odd charts and symbols.

"What's this, Mum?" Ronan asked.

"I thought you were old enough for it now. It's everything I know about my side of the family, including the stories about the origin of your middle names and what they were called in my mother's language." She turned to one of the charts. "This is a family tree—two branches, my mother's and my father's. My mother's people consider all of the children and all of the houses and land to belong to the women. Also, everybody belonged to one clan or the other. In the old days, people didn't like to give their proper names because your own personal name is like your arm or your hair or anything else of your person that an enemy could grab onto and hold you with. So they introduced themselves to each other by giving their lineage—who their mother's clan was and who their father's clan was. The way they put it, you were born 'to' your mother's people, as you were most directly tied to your mother. You were born 'for' your father's people because the mother brought her children into the world for the father. Since my father was of Irish descent, I don't have a clan on his side—no 'born for' clan, only a 'born to' clan, that of my mother's relations, the Far Walking Diné. So this is the same clan you have. If you ever meet someone else who is of my mother's people and they know that your mother is half Diné—or Navajo, as our people were known to others—they may ask you about your clans and tell you theirs. What would you tell them?"

"That our mother was born to the Far Walking Diné and born for our Irish grandpa?" Murel answered.

"This is pretty cool!" Ronan said, thumbing through the book before laying it back on the table.

Murel was puzzled. "Why did you write this stuff all down, Mum? We can't even read some of the words yet. I like it when you tell us stories about when you were a little girl and your family and everything. If we meet someone from your mother's people, we would just bring them home to meet you."

Mother's smile faded, and Murel said, "But it's a really great gift. I didn't mean that. It was really nice of you to do this. I just don't understand why is all."

Mother nodded once. "Surely you remember what day it is, pet? It's your birthday, yours and Ronan's. Today you are eight years old. Eight is two times four, which is the number of the four directions, the four elements, and a very special number to my mother's people. It is time for you to know these things."

Their journals lay forgotten at home, however, when Da proposed the most wonderful part of the day. He wanted to go swim with them and have them show him where they'd met the otters and seen the wolves.

Wow, we picked a good time to get born, Ronan told his sister. *I thought they'd punish us for going too far yesterday, and instead, I guess they have decided we're old enough to do what we want to because all of a sudden we're getting everything we've been wanting.*

Yeah, funny, isn't it? And a special latchkay tonight too. Even on our birthday, you'd think they'd make us take naps instead of Da going swimming with us.

The trip downriver to the otter den was much faster now. Not only did they know where they were going, they could predict, more or less, where the ice widened and narrowed, and that helped. Also, during the wide-open stretches, Da raced with them or used the straps holding their suits on their backs to tow them, while his sleek and powerful body carried them so fast, the water streamed through their teeth and left a bubbly wake behind them.

They showed their father the maze of tunnels the otter had led them through the day before, but it was all messed up. The ceiling was caved in the length of the central tunnel and the whole area smelled funny. Not like otters.

Ronan sent out a mental call anyway. *Hey, Otter. It's us, the seals who save otters from otter-eating wolves. We brought our father to meet you. He doesn't eat otters either.*

But there was no answer. Da swam around back and forth, sliding up onto the ice where he could and looking at the entire complex. He sniffed and turned his head to scan the trees on the horizon. But he was also looking at the snow, which was trampled with what looked like human footprints.

Da slid out of the maze back into the water.

Murel ventured a guess. She was pretty sure she was wrong, but maybe it would get Da to tell them what he thought. *The wolves know where they were living,* she said. *So I think they moved.*

These wolves each had two legs and wore military-issue snow boots, Da said. *See there?* He turned his head toward a glint in the trees.

What's that? she asked.

Surveillance equipment of some kind. Did you kids change on the way here at all?

Yes, but only a couple of times, and not for very long.

They know about you, Da said seriously. *Someone*

*told them the circumstances of your birth, and they've
been watching ever since, off and on. That's why we've
always had the cats go with you. Come on, let's get out
of here.*

What did they do to the otters? Ronan asked.

*I don't know. Maybe nothing. Maybe they just scared
them off when they came tramping around looking for
you two. But we need to go now. If they're still watching this spot, they'll be here with dope darts in a moment. Dive below the ice and swim as long as you can.
We'll make new breathing holes on the way upriver too.
Don't want them tracking us with the old ones.*

But before they made their first breathing hole, they
heard a familiar mind-voice.

*Hah! Ronan, Murel! Hah! It's me, the otter who is
friend to brave wolf-scaring river seals who are sometimes human. Wait! Wait! I have a thing to tell you.
Hah!*

Murel somersaulted in the water and swam back to
meet the otter.

*We brought our da to meet you, Otter, but your lovely
tunnels are all messed up. What happened to them?
Where are the hundred otters with the big sharp teeth?*

*Gone, all gone, Murel who attacks wolves. When the
sled woman took you away, we hurried to our dens in
case the wolves decided to return. But then came men
with big feet and big nets and guns that shot sharp
things bringing sleep. Hah! I cried out to warn the others and dove deep but other otters did not. My mother
was taken and my siblings and cousins and grandparents and aunts and uncles on both sides of the family. At
first they bit and scratched, but the men shot them with
sharp things and they no longer moved. The men took*

them, all of my family. Ruined our house and took my family.

All one hundred otters? Murel asked.

All the otters except me. Otters need families, and mine is all gone now. I tried to follow, but the men had those noise-sleds that are fast as an avalanche. Otters are very fast, but I could not catch them.

Da? Ronan turned to his father. *You and Mum are the governors. Make those men bring the otters back, huh?*

I can try, son, but not while you two are with me. Who do you think they really wanted to catch anyway? Probably as soon as they find out that the otters remain otters all the time, they'll let them go. They do, don't they?

What?

Remain otters all the time?

Otter said, "*Oh yes, Father River Seal, my family remain otters at all times. They are always otters. There have been stories about my cousins on the coast, but river otters are different. We are always otters.*

I'll do what I can, Otter. But those men are not acting under my authority. They had no legal right to take your family. I will have to come back later with more men and if possible make them let your family go.

I will go with you then and come back to show you where the men went, Otter told them.

There's no need, Da said. *We'll find you again tomorrow.*

Maybe you will and maybe not, Otter said. *But meanwhile I am alone and have no one to play with. Otters are not supposed to be alone. Otters need to be with others, even if the others are river seals.*

You might not like our part of the river, Da said. He seemed to want to get rid of the otter.

Oh, let him come, Da. He's our friend. We'll take care of him, Murel said.

He can sleep with me, Ronan said. *I'll make a den for him under my covers.*

He's not a pet, Da said. *Your mother—*

Mother will love him, and we know he's not a pet. He's our friend. We have to help him.

I'll help him but he isn't going all the way home with us. He can stay in the river, as he said, and return with my party to find the poachers. Then he'll be with his own family again.

Ronan started to protest. Da was being uncommonly firm and unyielding, and there was something very grim and sad in his thoughts, but it skittered away before Ronan could read it.

That will be good, Murel and Ronan. You can come and play again and I can be your swimming guide, as you asked. And all of my family will guide you too if you bring them back. We will go see my cousins on the coast and they will show you the sea.

Oh, Da, can *we?* the twins asked, but Da swam hard upstream and did not answer.

Otter raced the twins back up the river, and even though they were swimming against the current, they got home only a little after suppertime. Since they'd all snacked on fish throughout the day, none of them were hungry. Outside of town, Da climbed out of the water, shook himself dry, and put on the human clothes he'd hidden in a tree by the riverbank, while Ronan and Murel put on their shiny suits from Marmie. Otter dove down to inspect the riverbank.

Thin ice and many holes in the bank, he reported when he popped his head up again. *Good holes for otter dens. Not as good as the home ones, but good enough for now.*

Good night, Otter, Murel and Ronan said. They turned and waved, and Otter looked at them with large eyes that once more seemed a bit sad. Then he leapt in the air, did a somersault, and dove underwater again.

CHAPTER 8

O NE LAST SURPRISE before the latchkay was that Marmie herself had arrived while they were gone. The tall, elegant woman with the curling dark hair and the impish smile greeted them with hugs.

"The suits fit you beautifully! I was just sure they'd be far too big," she said.

"They work a treat too," Ronan told her. "We didn't get a bit cold after we put them on."

"That was the general idea," she said, laughing.

"I think maybe even wolves can't bite through them," Murel told her, knowing that someone as important as Marmie would like to have useful information about her gift.

"Now, how did you get a chance to learn that, I shudder to wonder?" Marmie asked.

"We were saving otters," Murel said. "But then after we left they were otter-napped by some men. Da's going to make the men bring the otters back, though, probably tomorrow."

"Otter-napping? My goodness, I have *missed* Petaybee. I forgot how exciting it can be here. Well, we don't have any otter-nappings where I live but I bet you'd find it exciting too."

"Do you really live on a space station, Marmie?" Murel asked.

"Yes, a very nice space station. You'd like it. I just had a lovely pool installed at my home. It runs all through and around my house, and there's a big deep part for diving. I had it all landscaped so it looks like a natural stream flowing through the woods."

"That sounds nice," Murel said politely. But she thought it was sort of odd to live on a space station and try to make it look like the woods. Why not just live in the real woods?

Ronan was thinking the same thing. "We can take you to the woods while you're here, Marmie, anytime you want."

She gave him a hug. "You are doing just that. I'm going to the latchkay with you."

"Ronan, Murel, come get dressed," their mother called. "I've things for you to carry."

I wish we could just swim to the springs and go into the latchkay in seal form, Murel said. *We could bring the otter. He's probably lonely out there in the river all by himself without the hundred relatives.*

He might come anyway, if he sees us going. Otters are pretty curious, I think.

They dressed in the furs and fancy bead-embroidered parkas made for them by Aisling, Auntie Sinead's partner, who was the finest sewer in the entire village. The embroidery on both parkas had wiggly blue lines for water and fish of all colors—even purple ones and green ones—swimming around the cuffs, hem, front closure, and ruff of the hood. The matching mittens had fishes swimming in a circle around the wrists.

Mother's parka was blue-green with little pairs of

flowers embroidered for trim. She said the pairs stood for the twins. It was a pretty parka, but that didn't mean Ronan thought he looked like a flower.

Most latchkays were held in the longhouse in the center of the village, and that was usually where the food was served, most of the speeches were made, and the dancing took place. Tonight everybody carried food and gifts with them to the hot springs cave. Usually there was a procession to the cave, but tonight everyone just came out of their houses and started walking.

I wonder why they're doing it this way? Murel said as they walked in the dark, slightly ahead of their parents. Their night vision was very good, and if it hadn't been, the cats walked right in front of them. Besides, they'd been to the latchkay cave many times and knew the path so well they could walk it backward, which Ronan decided to try.

The cats caught his thought and stopped to watch. He stepped back onto Nanook's tail. 'Nook hissed and spat, something he never did around the twins, and Ronan was so startled he slipped and fell, dropping the case he'd been carrying.

Oh boy, Mum will be mad, Murel said, and stooped to help him pick it up. The latch had been jarred open by being dropped, and she opened the lid to put back whatever was in there.

Why did she give you this case with all your stuff to carry? Murel asked.

Don't know. What's in yours?

"Hurry, children. We still have quite a ways to go."

The drums began pounding, telling them that other people had already reached the cave.

"Mum, why is Ronan carrying his clothes and school-books?" Murel asked.

Mum shook her head impatiently and pointed ahead. Murel was pretty sure that whatever the answer was, they weren't going to like it.

The path to the cave was well trod by the time they slipped behind the steaming falls and found seats on the ledge.

The space behind the waterfall was not a cave exactly, because it didn't go back very far. It was more of a room up above the hot springs, and it was the closest place to Kilcoole where people could go to talk to the planet.

Usually when everyone was packed in it felt cozy and snug, with the smell of the smoked salmon and soup floating around the people who had feasted at the latch-kay mingling with the sulfury smell of the hot springs. The warmth of everyone's body heated the grotto so that after a while they removed their furs.

Even in the winter when everything was iced over there was a strong sense of grasses and brambles, berries, and flowering weeds pushing up through the frigid soil, just waiting for the ice to break. Like the ghost of last summer, Murel thought, or the summers before that.

But tonight for the first time ever the twins felt restless and ill at ease in the grotto. The stalactites protruding from the ceiling seemed in danger of falling and stabbing someone, and the stone seat under their bottoms was very hard and very chilly.

Something bad is going to happen, Ronan said. *And it's going to happen to us.*

I feel that way too but how could it with Mum and Da here—and Clodagh, Johnny, and Marmie, besides?

They'll probably give out to us for running off from everyone yesterday—well, swimming off, that's all. I wonder if Da was always getting in trouble like this when he was our age?

Young Desi Sivatkaluk was the lead drummer tonight. Desi was the same age as Aoifa, but his father, Old Desi, had been the lead drummer at the last latchkay. Old Desi and his entire team fell through the ice and drowned while out on a hunting trip only a few weeks before, so now his son played his drum. He must have been practicing a lot because he never missed a beat.

Nanook and Coaxtl stood guard at the edge of the spring, just beyond the watery veil concealing the grotto. Someone uncovered a platter piled high with strips of salty-sweet, pink smoked salmon and started passing it around. When the plate got to Da, he got up and tossed some of the strips to the cats.

When everyone had eaten, Clodagh stood and said, "We have a troubling thing to tell our world tonight. Who will sing the first song?"

Auntie Sinead stood up. She had good songs and usually sang them Irish-style, to old tunes that went with lots of other words. She was the best dog driver, hunter, fisher, and trapper in Kilcoole, and her songs were full of action and adventure. This one she started by saying, "The tune is 'Wild Colonial Boy' and I call it"—she smiled at Ronan and Murel for the first time since their rescue—" 'The Wild Shongili Twins.' I've had only a day to find the words, and some of this I heard from others, but for those of you who did not know of my niece and nephew's recent adventure, I made this song."

She sang, her voice clear and strong:

"*When I was young I ran my traps. My brother Sean
   he swam
As a selkie he could swim much more than human
   men
Now he has two children and as selkies they too
   swim
But now Sean's moored to desk work. No more seal
   swimming for him.*

*Without their Da to roam with them, these children
   swam away
To roam the fields of river ice with otters they did
   play
But wolves find otters tasty and the children almost
   died
Still our Murel she digs a hole, 'Dive, otters, now!'
   she cried.*

*My dogs and I we heard them cry, the big cats made
   all speed
The children now were crying, the wolves poised to
   do the deed
That would have broken my poor heart, Petaybee's
   heart as well
And Sean and his brave wife would find a private bit
   of hell.*

*The cats they leapt, and me I swept the children to
   my sled
But had we not been looking, our twins would now
   be dead.
So I ask you, my neighbors, what will happen when
   again*

The selkie twins go swimming with no one to
   shepherd them?"

"It was only the once," Ronan said when she'd finished and everyone was making appreciative noises.
"We were trying out the warm suits Marmie sent us."

"We didn't mean to be gone so long," Murel said,
looking into the faces of her neighbors, who were regarding them as if they were the tracks of some strange
animals they had never seen before.

Sing them my song, Otter said from somewhere
nearby.

Otters make songs? the twins asked together.

*Of course otters make songs. Otters like fun, and
music is fun. The waters are music to otters, and otters
sing songs to its melody. But I cannot speak to the other
two-leggeds and make myself understood. I will sing to
you and you sing to them.*

Okay, fine. Sing.

Announce us first! the otter said.

Ronan told the other people, "Our otter friend has a
song to share he wants to sing through us."

"You wouldn't be pullin' our legs now, would you,
young Shongili?" Kaiaitok Carnahan asked. Kaiaitok
had the short stocky build and tilted eyes of his Inuit ancestors, but his sparse beard and mustache were bright
red and his eyes green. His hair was red too, but nobody
saw it anymore since he always wore a stocking cap in
winter, a billed cap in summer. He had taken over the
com shed after Uncle Adak retired. Adak said that what
with all the new machines Petaybee had now, communications was getting way too complicated for his liking.

Kaiaitok had gone offplanet to train when he was only a bit older than the twins were now.

If you were going to leave Petaybee, you had to do it when you were a kid. As you got older, your body was so adapted to Petaybee's extreme temperatures and other special properties that you could die if you were offplanet very long. Kaiaitok had left plenty young enough to survive, but he had returned much changed, folk said. He thought the rest of them backward when he first came home, and himself full of learning. All of his learning still didn't keep the machinery and electronic gizmos working when it was minus 150 degrees Fahrenheit. He had to take a snocle or a sled to give people their messages, just like Adak had done before him, only now there were more messages and people on the offworld end expected faster results. Kaiaitok got over himself pretty fast after the first couple of winters and a few latchkays. But however much he communicated with humans, he was not on social terms with four-legged, winged, or finned creatures. Ronan was hazy on whether Kaiaitok had communed with animals before he left the planet. His skepticism about Otter's song didn't seem to trouble the rest of the villagers.

Da relieved any doubts they might have had by saying, "Good. I'm glad the otter could compose on such short notice. I've not been able to do as much myself. Go on, you kids."

Otter's song did not rhyme like an Irish song and did not go with a drumbeat like the songs in the more traditional Inuit style. It had to be danced as well as sung. So the twins acted out their meeting with the otters, and the slide and the wolves and then the coming of the men and the taking of the otters. The words were sung very fast and the dance had to be done fluidly to go with the way the otter was singing it. There were some otter concepts that were difficult to put into human words, and these the twins tried to act out or skip over.

When they finished, Ronan said, "The otter who made this song is staying in the river near the village now, so he can guide us to the men who took his family. So nobody bother him, okay? He's got enough on his mind right now."

Da, Auntie Sinead, Mum, and Clodagh all exchanged looks. The twins couldn't read them, and wondered what it was all about. But they could tell the adults were impressed.

"Anyone else got any songs?" Clodagh asked. When no one spoke, she rose and walked deeper into the cavern. The rest of the village followed her until they reached the central communion room. Behind them, Ronan and Murel slapped hands and practically skipped forward.

We really showed them. We are the first people ever to sing for otters. Or any other four-legged, I'll bet, Ronan said.

Murel could hardly disagree. Life was looking up. Ever since the suits arrived, it had been much more interesting around here. And tomorrow there would be another adventure with Da when he went to get back the otter's family.

Nobody seemed to be mad at them after all, or inclined to scold, and it was past the time when they would.

The singing and talking were over. Now Petaybee would respond. Ronan and Murel always liked this part. It was a little like dreaming, except that the dream wasn't yours exactly, it was Petaybee's. It was also a bit like the way it felt when they became seals and seemed to be part of the water.

But when they got to the entrance of the larger cavern, they were stopped.

As if giant hands were pushing them back from the communion cave, they could not go forward. Murel put a foot out and brought it back right away.

Mum and Da sat down beside Clodagh without noticing the twins weren't with them until Da looked up and called softly to them, "Aren't you coming, kids?"

"Can't," Murel said. "Something's wrong."

Ronan had big tears in his eyes already. "It's like there's a big invisible door, Da."

Clodagh was the one who answered. "There is a purpose in this that you will learn soon. Go to the outer cave but don't go into the water. We will speak again when the planet has spoken."

Bewildered, the twins retraced their steps.

It's not fair. We did good. Is it Petaybee that's mad at us and doesn't want to talk to us?

No, can't be. I mean, it can't be mad at us. We're not offworlders. We're part of the planet just like the rocks are. It can't get mad at itself, can it? Can it?

They fell silent and sat in the outer cave looking longingly at the waterfall. They had never before realized how long the communions took, but it seemed like hours passed. Any moment they expected to hear the footsteps and the very low conversation that sometimes followed communions, but there was nothing.

They're sure taking their time, Ronan said. *I wish Clodagh hadn't said we're not to swim. I would like to go down to the water and talk to Otter a little more. I think we forgot to thank him for his song.*

We don't have to swim to do that. Remember, otters are not afraid of seals who turn into humans. Clodagh didn't say we couldn't go to the water's edge. Just that we shouldn't swim.

They started calling as they took the path out of the cave and down the hill, enveloped in the sulfury and spicy mist from the springs.

But although their new friend had seemed very near when he sang them his song, when he finally answered, it was from far away, with a muffled, *Sleeping. Otters need to sleep.*

Ronan sat down and felt through the snow for rocks to skip across the water, but found nothing. The longer they waited, the more worried and miserable Murel became. Something was really wrong. She knew it but she couldn't think what it was.

Hush, younglings, Nanook's voice, purring and kind, said, as she insinuated her soft furry self between them and lay down with her head cradled on her paws. *No harm will come to you while we're here. We may not be the best swimmers but we are your guardians.*

Sleep. One prefers you when you sleep, Coaxtl said, plopping down behind them to make a plush backrest.

These sometimes grumpy friends had been with the twins since they were babies. Their familiar presence was so comforting that the children fell asleep almost at once, Ronan leaning back against Coaxtl while Murel snuggled with Nanook, her arms around the cat's body and her hands buried in the dense fur.

They awoke to the murmur of voices and looked up from sleepy eyes to see the villagers appear from the mist.

The murmurs were not the kind that normally followed a Night Chant. Clodagh's face, and their parents' faces were very grave indeed. Only Marmion seemed to be smiling.

"Slainté," Ronan said in greeting, sitting up and rubbing his eyes.

Murel stood up and tucked her hands into Clodagh's and Marmie's. Her parents still looked grim.

"So, Clodagh, why couldn't we come into the communion cave this time? Is Petaybee mad at us?"

"I don't know, pet," Clodagh told her. "I don't think so. Perhaps it just wanted to talk to grown-ups tonight."

"Oh." Murel thought that over. "But it's always let us come before. And it *is* our birthday."

Over her head, Marmie exchanged glances with Mum and Da. "*I* have something I'd like to talk to you about, Murel, Ronan."

Ronan arose, giving Coaxtl a pat as he did, and stretched. "What, Marmie?"

"We've been discussing this for some time, your parents and I, and of course, this is only if you'd like to, but I was hoping now that you're old enough to go offworld, you might come and visit me for a while on my space station."

"You mean *now*?" Ronan asked. His eyes were wide open. She had his full attention.

"Yes, well, since you've got your things with you already I don't see why not. I'm sure, as you know from your biology lessons, that the older you get, the harder it will be for you to leave Petaybee for any length of time. And I just had that lovely waterway built at home, so I was so hoping you'd come. I know some other children your age I think you'd enjoy very much, and we have rather a nice school on the station."

"School!" Murel said. "How long a visit are we talking about, Marmie?"

"Well—"

"The thing is, kids, it may be your only chance to see other places," Mum said. "And frankly, your Da and I would like you to get some exposure to human culture on a more sophisticated level than we can provide here."

"Our schools are okay," Murel said.

"Yes, but Marmie's are excellent." Her mother squatted down so that her face was on a level with theirs. "And one day we're going to need your help with managing things here. I don't know how aware of it you are, but your father has been keeping tabs on some midsea volcanoes. They're building up under the sea floor, preparing a new landmass, a warm island, islands, a continent. Lots of people from offworld will want to move here, and perhaps there'll be room for a great many of them. We may need—*Petaybee* may need—your help sorting through them. You need to know something about the offworld universe to be able to cope."

"Right," Ronan said. That sounded good, but if Petaybee needed them to help with something, you'd think it would have let them into the communion cave one last time at least. Mum was just trying to make them feel better. He looked his father full in the face. "This is really about keeping us away from the otter rustlers, isn't it?"

"Among other things, yes, but your mother's reasons are very great concerns as well."

"But we're still going with you tomorrow to get the otters back, right?"

"Son, it's just too dangerous. I think I told you that I'm afraid it was really you those men were interested in when they took the otters. I don't want to give them any more chances to get any closer than they've been to you two already. By the time you're back from Marmie's, we'll have them sorted out and galaxies away, possibly in prison. But I promise you, we will get the otters back if at all possible, and I will send word to you when we do."

Marmie wasn't really asking us, she was telling us, Murel told her twin.

It might be fun except I really wanted to stay here and get to know the otters better, her brother replied.

I don't think we're supposed to. If those men went after the otters because of us, then we just brought them trouble. Besides, Petaybee doesn't want us here anymore. That's why we couldn't get into the communion room. Not just because we're kids.

If Petaybee doesn't want you, it makes you feel worse than that! Ronan argued. *It drives the offworlders crazy and turns their hair white and stuff.*

But they're offworlders. And maybe it's not mad at us, it just wants us to do this now, like Mum and Da and Marmie and Clodagh said.

That's weird. Planets don't take sides, do they?

Petaybee does. I don't think we get to pick this time, Ronan.

"Okay," Ronan said, "we'll go. But as soon as those men are gone, you'll send for us, right? Right?"

Nobody answered, and then Da laid his hands on his

son's shoulders and said, "I can't promise anything right now, but we will send for you as soon as it's time for you to return. Meanwhile, you'll probably be having so much fun with Marmie, you'll be mad at us for making you come home."

CHAPTER 9

A FEW HOURS LATER, the twins watched Petaybee diminish into a blue and white ball and then just another distant dot in the cosmos.

This must be what it's like to swim in the sea, Murel said. Through the fantastic transparent hull of the view deck, they watched as the ship wove through a beaded curtain of star systems, suns with their planets, planets with their moons, all against the deepest blackness.

Yeah, the ship is kind of like a star seal. It's the only thing out here that moves wherever it wants to. Everything else is anchored to an orbit—well, except meteors, I guess. They're kind of wild.

Marmion stood behind them, a hand on each small shoulder. For the time being, the children seemed to have forgotten to be sad at what they saw as their banishment from Petaybee and abandonment by their parents.

Ronan turned suddenly and looked up into her face. "Marmie, do meteors decide where they want to go, do you think, or are they just falling all the time?"

"I don't know that they have a plan exactly—I don't think every random bit of rock is as aware as Petaybee—but they do seem to wander about randomly, getting bits knocked off them here and there."

"But asteroids have orbits, right?" he asked. "And belts. They have belts."

"They travel in belts with lots of other asteroids."

"So the belts are like flocks of asteroids or herds," Murel said.

"Only in the sense that a belt is composed of many asteroids. They aren't animals."

"I know that," Murel said.

The trip was not a long one. Marmie's ship was very powerful and very fast. Meanwhile, when she wasn't on the com unit conducting business, she did her best to entertain them.

When they grew a little dizzy on the view deck, she took them to a large quiet room with a lot of cabinets and a big screen. "This is the ship's library," she told them. "My crew and I pick from the main library on the space station the various media we wish to take on our travels. I pulled some things I thought you two might be interested in before I left."

"Marmie?"

"Yes, Murel?"

"You sent our suits with Johnny and we were gone for a night, but the next day when we came home after swimming with Father, you were there. We've already been on this ship two nights and we aren't at your house yet. When did you leave?"

"About a week ago. I had business to conduct along the way. I think I understand what you're getting at. You think I came to take you away because you got into trouble, don't you?"

The twins exchanged knowing looks, then nodded.

"That's not correct. I have, as I said, been hoping you would come and visit me for some time. As we explained at the hot spring, if you are going to travel, now is the time you must do it. Later you will be so completely adapted to Petaybee that you won't be able to leave safely. Your parents have been worried since you were born that people such as the men who took your otter friend's family might try to kidnap you for study to see what makes you able to change into seals and back again. When your mother contacted me about the suits, I sent them on the next ship, but both she and I realized that the time was coming when your natural wish to explore your environment might lead you into harm."

"You could have come with Johnny, couldn't you?"

"Captain Green's ship was conducting other business for me in other places along the way than what I needed to do myself. Besides, his is a transport vessel and mine is a luxury liner. Much nicer, don't you think?"

They shrugged. "I guess so," Ronan said. The ship had less people and was more spacious while not being much bigger, but he felt like they all sort of rattled around in it. "Any word from Da about the otters?"

"No, but when there is, I'll let you know right away," she promised. She showed them how to use the vid screen, earphones, and other apparatus. "I have a bit more business to conduct and then I'll be back to tuck you in. Enjoy yourselves."

SEAN SHONGILI WAVED good-bye as his children marched sleepily onto Marmion's luxury spaceship, the *Piaf*. Yana turned away as he did and marched straight back to the snocle. He knew she didn't want him to see her crying—again—which was fine with him. She wouldn't see his tears either that way, which would help them both keep control of their emotions in the days to come. Sinead had brought the team up to collect Sean, and the red dogs were straining against their harnesses, ready to be off for a good run.

His sister didn't say anything as he climbed aboard her sled and she shouted at Dinah, the lead dog, to go. Sinead wasn't happy to see her niece and nephew vanish into space either, but she understood the necessity.

Back in Kilcoole they met with Liam Maloney, the borough sheriff. Sinead herself was now Game Warden and Environmental Control Officer. Two of her rangers and two of Liam's deputies brought their teams along as well. Dierdre Angalook, a student of Clodagh's who studied animal healing, rode a curly coat and brought saddlebags full of items for otter first aid.

"Are you all armed?" Sean asked.

"Yes, Guv," Liam answered.

"Can't be too careful with otter rustlers, can we?" Sinead asked.

Sean nodded his head gravely in agreement. "Okay, otter posse, I'll meet you by the shack."

He had an ice fishing shack on the river he used for removing his clothing before dropping through the hole and changing into seal form. Marmion had provided him with a suit similar to the ones she'd given the children. She said she was glad to find something useful to give him for his birthday. Once he transformed, he swam over to the otter's den. *Are you ready, Otter? My friends are on their way.*

Yes, Father River Seal, but where are Murel and Ronan? Otters like brave children. Otters find them very reassuring.

They had to leave, Otter. They are indeed brave children and their mother and I are very proud of them, but they aren't always very wise. I believe the people who took your family did so because they were curious about Murel and Ronan. They must have seen them changing.

"Hah!" the otter said. *When we get my family back, will you send the men away and let Murel and Ronan return?*

As soon as possible, Otter, Sean said.

The dog teams pulled up alongside the bank near the ice fishing shack. Sean surfaced, but the otter stayed under the ice. "The otter tunnels are just before the Chatanika Falls. We'll stop before we reach the tunnels. Keep as silent as possible and be alert for any signs of surveillance from the woods or elsewhere. We'll meet you there."

He and the otter swam on, their noses and eyes barely above the water. They dived under the ice whenever possible. On the banks, the sleds shushed along beside and slightly behind them. Otters and seals were both very fast swimmers, while dogs had to stop to sniff things and take turns yellowing the snow and making their deposits.

Nanook and Coaxtl ranged along with the others, leaving a scallop of tracks along the river as they ran half circles around the dogsleds. Nanook ran along the side of the river where the mushers were, Coaxtl took the opposite side. Away they'd race to the surrounding woods, sniff a few rocks and bits of vegetation, and then return to the river. A half a klick before Sean and the otter reached the ruined tunnels, Nanook spoke to Sean.

There. They are back there. I smell them. I smell otters too. Frightened, angry otters. Now the men will smell like them.

Does the scent grow stronger or weaker the farther downriver we go? Sean asked.

Nanook sniffed for a moment longer, then replied, *Weaker.*

Can you pick up the trail at that point?

I can. I am standing on it now.

Otter, did you understand Nanook?

Cats do not speak as clearly in the mind as otters or river seals, but the cat's meaning was clear. *Do we leave the river now?*

I will, at least. You may stay here if you wish.

No, my family will feel better if I am near to reassure them. Also, other otters may speak to me when we are closer and I can speak to you.

Fair enough, Sean said. He dived, leapt, and landed on the ice, then slid across to the bank, where he shook off the water and donned Marmie's silver warm suit.

It felt almost too warm to Sean but he was glad of the cover and admired the way it kept out the wind that stirred the light dusting of new snow across the ice.

Something low and brown streaked past him. The otter. *Hah! Come, Father River Seal, I'll race you to the cat,* he called.

Nobody races anybody, Otter, Sean told him. *We must go quietly and carefully, stalk these men as if they are prey.*

Fish? the otter asked.

Very slippery fish.

Slippery fish who steal otters.

Keep trying to talk to the other otters. Let me know when you get a response, if they can tell us anything about where they're being held, what kind of condition they're in, how many men there are.

How many? A hundred, Father River Seal. A hundred otter-stealing men all with big tight nets.

I can see this might be a problem, Sean said. Murel had told him about the otter and counting. *Can you get them to say, "the man with the torn coat" or "the man with the beard," and tell us who each of them is that way? Then we'll have a better idea how many there actually are.*

Otters can do that. Otters have good eyes.

And try to stay back here near us, Otter. If you run ahead of us too far, the men might capture you too.

Otters can be very fast, but otters can also be slooooow, like men and dogs and cats.

Carrreful who you call slow, little beast. This cat can run down a caribou herd, Coaxtl grumbled.

The woods were still, as if holding their breath, when the rescue party, dog teams, and the curly coat slipped into the forest almost as silently as falling snowflakes.

The otter chirped and gibbered seemingly to himself, but Sean realized these were the outward manifestations of the little creature's attempts to link minds with his family members.

My mother! She is alive! the otter declared at last. *She did not want me to come because she feared I would be captured too, but at the same time she was thinking that, she was thinking, "Get me out out out." And she did not know until I told her that the father of river seals and his hundred friends with their sharp-toothed dogs and their long-clawed cats are with me. She was afraid of you too until I told her that you are the father of Murel and Ronan River Seal, the friends who attack wolves who try to eat otters.*

I trust she was reassured by the news?

Oh, yes.

Did she give you any idea of how far away the men took her and the others?

Otter didn't answer for a moment, then said, *Not far. Otters had no time to bite through nets before they were put in dens with heavy bars on them.*

Sean considered. Apparently, while he could converse with the otter who was with him, he was not sufficiently attuned to the species to share long-distance inter-otter telepathic communications.

And how many men—can she say what each man there is like?

After another pause, the otter said, *There is man with wind like dead things, man with chin fur, man with wet nose, man with longer chin fur, man with lip fur but no chin fur, young female and old female.*

Is that all?

Mother says yes. Hah! Mother is growling. Man puts hands on her.

Can't have that, now can we? Sean said, and made a sweeping gesture with his arm ending with a point in the direction the track cats were following. The dog teams and the curly coat swung in behind.

Sean took several more strides forward and saw Nanook's tail whipping back and forth across the trail in front of him.

Here, Sean. Otters are here, Nanook told him.

That was immediately evident, as from beyond Nanook came otter chirpings and jabberings and explosive "Hah!" "Hah!" sounds in the voices of, if not a hundred otters, at least fifteen.

And human voices called out suddenly too. "What's

with these specimens all of a sudden? They sound like someone stuck a pin in them and let the air out."

"Omigod, I see what the problem is. They see that big old house cat there. Here kitty kitty . . . kitty like otter meat?"

Nanook growled low in his throat, but Coaxtl let out a roar that sounded as if it came from deep inside a cave instead of a snow leopard's chest.

Sean caught up with the cat. "Slainté. What are you doing with these otters?"

"Uh, studying them."

"Yes, we have seen some unusual creatures on this planet and we want to make sure these otters are the ordinary kind and not some strange Petaybean hybrid."

"What if they are a Petaybean hybrid?" Sean asked. "I don't believe we've met. I'm Dr. Sean Shongili. My grandfather collected and adapted the creatures here on Petaybee. I don't think he'd appreciate it if you attempt to reverse-engineer his otters."

Sinead stepped into the clearing as well. The men kept the otter cages in the open but they had puff tents for themselves. The puff tents were first cousin to the Nakatira cubes. You set them up, opened a valve, and they inflated themselves with a foot of air in walls, floor, and ceiling. Furthermore, they were totally fireproof, so a heating device or even cooking equipment could be used inside them if the occupants were very careful about how they moved. Four of these tents were set up among the spindly trees that were part of the landscape on this part of the planet. Because of the deep ice, even very mature trees reached no great girth. The otter cages were on a table in the center of the clearing, where they would be in full view of the occupants of each puff tent.

"I am Sinead Shongili, and I'm the game warden for this area. I don't recall issuing you an otter-molesting permit, folks. If our creatures need taking care of or keeping track of, my rangers and I see to it. I'll thank you to release the creatures you have in custody. If any of them have been injured or killed while in your care, you must turn them over to me in the name of the Kilcoole Wildlife Council."

"What is it with you Shongilis, coming out here to throw your weight around?"

Liam Maloney stepped forward now. "Dr. Sean and his wife are the co-governors of Petaybee. I am Sheriff Maloney, and you are in violation of ever so many serious statutes. Do as Warden Sinead says and release the otters or we'll be lockin' yourselves up instead."

"I believe I can clear this up, sirs and madam," said the small wizened woman with the dark brown skin and heavily chiseled broad features of an aboriginal New Adelaidian. "I am Dr. Marie Mabo of IGISI, the Inter Galactic Institute of Species Identification. My team and I are here by their authority, so naturally I assumed that our presence and mission were known to and approved by local officials as well. We have been observing these creatures in their wild state for some time and two days ago were privileged to see them interacting peaceably with a pair of seals who seemed to be accompanied by a pair of children who fended off a wolf attack."

"You saw the wolves menacing the children and you did nothing to help?"

"It looked like the wolves were doing fine to me," said the man the otters had identified as the one with fur on his chin.

"That will do, Eric!" Dr. Mabo said. To the Petaybeans, she said, "I apologize that my colleague chooses to display his rather sardonic sense of humor at such an inappropriate moment. I do realize the children must have been yours, Warden, since you and your canines and felines came to their rescue. Had you but known it, we were right behind you, ready to intervene ourselves. We hesitated only because we truly had no wish to shoot the beautiful wolves encircling the children and it seemed we had no alternative. You proved us wrong."

"Did, didn't I?" Sinead said. She stepped forward, her rifle over her arm, and opened an otter cage. There were only three otters in it but they seemed to explode all over the clearing in their haste to get away, and looked like at least ten times their number. No wonder the otter thought he had a hundred family members.

Sinead signaled her rangers to continue opening cages while she opened the puff tents. An anesthetized pregnant female otter lay on a folding table. Her belly was shaved and a needle fed into one of her paws. She was shivering either from shock or hypothermia. Computer equipment in an enclosed thermal shell lined one side of the tent.

Sinead picked her up and folded her inside a special pouch she carried next to her body. She carried the otter in the pouch over to the curly coat where Deirdre Angalook, Clodagh's student, received her, bundling the injured animal to her as if she were a baby. The only other otter to be seen by the time she emerged was the one who had accompanied them from Kilcoole.

"I'm guessin' the only reason you put this little one out was so she wouldn't bite your hand off, right?" she said to Dr. Mabo.

"Actually, we wanted to preserve the specimens as long as possible for more testing," Eric the Whiskers said.

Dr. Mabo whipped around so fast the hood from her parka fell away from her face. "Somebody gag him," she said.

"Nobody will be gaggin' anybody else," Liam Maloney said. "But we'll be cuffing all of you and then taking you back to Kilcoole for deportation, at least until your institute sees fit to consult with us before conducting a study on our four-legged friends."

Deputy Tukaluk walked around the tents and into the forest. "They got a snocle over here, Sheriff. Big one. I never saw one this big. Musta brought it with them when they landed."

"How many will it hold exactly?" Sean asked.

"Six and a driver," Tukaluk said.

"Very well, then. I'll drive and Dr. Mabo can ride in Sinead's sled on the way back."

"Ought to make them walk, Sean," Liam said.

"That would slow us down too much," he replied. "I've business back in Kilcoole. I must tell my children, for one thing, that the otters have been released and are safe."

"Those were *your* children, then, Dr. Shongili?" Marie Mabo asked, but not as if she didn't already know.

"They were. And like my sister the Game Warden, they are extremely protective of the other species on this planet."

"I'd very much like to talk to them and apologize for worrying them," Dr. Mabo said. "They're the age of my grandchildren, and we certainly didn't mean to frighten them."

Sean's heart pounded extra loud for a couple of beats

before he said, "I'm afraid that won't be possible. They've gone to visit a friend offworld. I'll relay your apologies."

After the cuffed prisoners had been loaded into the snocle, Sean took the helm. Sinead had already strapped Dr. Mabo to her sled. Deirdre and the injured otter took off on the curly coat while the other sleds followed. Nobody remembered the single otter that had not run away.

In moments only tracks remained where the rescue party, the offworld scientists, and the captive otters had been. The lone remaining otter returned to the tunnels where he had played with his family and the river seals, but they were still smashed and still abandoned.

CHAPTER 10

A T Marmie's instructions, as soon as the communications officer received word from Kilcoole about the capture of the otter rustlers, she reported straight to Ronan and Murel.

"Oh, good," Murel said absently.

Ronan nodded and said, "Serves 'em right."

If the ship's crew was expecting a big reaction from the children about this bit of news that, according to the boss, the Petaybean kids had been waiting for throughout the trip, they were disappointed.

The twins had eyes for nothing but the viewscreen. Through it they watched the space station, its lights in the darkness of space making it look as if it were decorated for the holidays. Larger and larger it grew until it filled up the screen and only a tiny portion of it was visible. Then that portion, the port hatch, opened like a water lily unfolding to receive the ship into its heart.

"Reminds me of the otter's den," Murel said, smiling to her brother, who grinned back as they raced to their quarters. There, they gathered the few things they'd brought with them, their warm suits and their more conventional parkas, mukluks, snow pants, and mittens for when they went home, plus pouches of Clodagh's remedies and the journals Mum had given them.

When they followed Marmie out of the ship into the docking bay, they looked all around them.

It's huge, Murel said, her neck straining as she looked up and up and up. Flitters, carrying passengers, zipped from a wall to a bit of ceiling to another bit of wall, busy as—well, insects. It didn't matter if they were bees or wasps or mosquitoes.

Yeah, Ronan said. *I bet you could fit all of Kilcoole in just this part.*

His sister nodded mutely.

"Come along, children," Marmie said. "We can do the tour after you've settled in a bit."

A flitter landed in front of them. A very handsome man in a uniform was at the helm.

"Is that your husband come to collect us, Marmie?" Murel asked.

"No, dear, he's one of the chauffeurs, I suppose you might say. There's an entire cadre of them here just to man the flitter fleet."

"Flitter fleet?" Ronan asked, laughing. And had to say it several times over until Murel said privately, *Stop. It's getting annoying. You don't want Marmie to get cross, do you?*

Marmie's not cross. You're the one being bossy. What do you think? Now that we don't have Nanook and Coaxtl to mind us you get to be in charge? Not likely, my girl!

Now you're being snotty. I just want us to make a good impression. Marmie is our friend but she's a very important lady.

So? Mum and Da are governors. That makes them just as important.

Yes, but not us. Mum and Da are our parents. They have to love us. Marmie doesn't.

Maybe she'll get mad at us and send us back, Ronan said. *I wouldn't mind.*

You'd mind by the time Mum got done with you, and once she was through, Clodagh would be after us. We'd bring disgrace to all of Petaybee if Marmie sent us back because we were too big a handful for her.

I don't think that will be a problem. If she gets tired of us, she can just hand us over to the cadre of chauffeurs and their fleet of flitters. With this he began shaking again with another fit of the giggles.

You're impossible, you are, Murel said, and tried to keep a straight face, but then couldn't do it with him tee-heeing all over the place. Apparently, the chauffeur asked Marmie what the children were laughing about, so Ro told Marmie and Marmie told him and he started laughing too, then Marmie. By the time the flitter reached the upper level where Marmie's house was, Murel really had to use the outhouse bad.

But even that was forgotten as she took in as much of Marmie's house as she could.

To begin with, it wasn't a house, it was a whole section of the space station, the upper section. As the flitter rose to cross the garden and fountains, the broad pathways, and, oh yes, the beautiful little river running around the living area, it seemed as if the house was right on *top* of the space station, with no hull around it. Space showed all around them, a night sky made large by proximity to the nearest planet and its moons, which seemed even more huge than moons and the sun on Petaybee.

"Don't you worry that you'll fall off?" she asked Marmie, feeling a little dizzy.

"Cool!" Ronan said, and then thought about it and wondered how the water in the fountains could fall and the river could flow and the flowers grow without atmosphere. How, in fact, were they supposed to breathe?

Marmie dimpled mischievously, then reached forward and touched a button. Instant sunrise. The blackness and the huge planet and moon were eclipsed by a skyscape very much like the one on Petaybee, the sky blue, the sun distant, and everything else had more color too. The flowers became blue and purple, yellow, red, orange, and pink. The grass was green without even a puddle of snow, and the fountains, made of some pretty pink stone, overflowed just enough to cascade into the river.

"How'd you do that?" Ronan wanted to know. He was watching Marmie's hand on the controls instead of looking at the scenery.

"It's just a hologram. What you saw when we came is how it would look with no illusion and no hull. Oh, I do have an observatory—several, in fact, in various strategic locations on different levels. But one feels so closed in living on the station with no real atmosphere or the boundaries of a horizon, so I had the holos created. We can even have weather if you like. Shall I make it snow?"

"Oh, no. Not when it looks like springtime," Murel said. "It would kill your flowers. But—could we have a thunderstorm? Once in a while, right around breakup, Petaybee throws tantrums, so Da says, and they're ever so exciting."

"In that case I suppose we must have one. I like them

too, actually. Do you want lightning or just thunder? Rain? Sheet lightning or the cracked forking variety?"

"Can we have it all please?" Ronan asked.

"With that attitude, you should go far, Mr. Shongili," Marmie said with a smile.

"Could the lightning strike something?"

"Ronan! You want Marmie to burn down her house so you can see how it works?" Murel scolded.

"No need for that. My lightning can only hit virtual trees. We can feel the wind but we will not get wet from the rain or cold from the snow, and once I turn it off, the ground will not be white or wet afterward."

"Oh," Murel said, disappointed. "Then, why do you do it?"

"For a little variety, mood, atmosphere. I can make it rain, you know, by switching the irrigation system from the belowground sprinklers to the overhead ones. And I have a device that will scent the air with that wonderful ozone smell that comes after a rain. So, do you want to see it?"

"Yes," both children said politely. Marmie's fake weather couldn't compete with Petaybee's extremes.

At least, that was how they felt when they first arrived. Everything seemed very tame. The little river was nothing but an oddly shaped swimming pool, with jets in the rocks creating the illusion of riffles or eddies. It never iced over, of course, and there were no other creatures to be discovered along its banks. And there were seldom fish. Even someone with Marmie's resources couldn't keep the artificial stream stocked with enough fish to keep the twins happily catching their own meals for as much as a week.

The only excitement came when Marmie had an unexpected visitor and the twins had to hide their dual nature and talk in a silly way about the "pet" seals they'd brought with them from their home world.

They hadn't known what to expect from Marmie when it came to their education, but as it turned out, they went to classes with the other kids from the space station.

"I could get you tutors, but that would be a bore, don't you think?" Marmie asked. "You must meet these other children, and more than the teachers will instruct you, you will instruct each other."

They were highly skeptical. After all, here *they* were the outsiders, an uncomfortable thought. On the other hand, they weren't the offworlders because on a space station nobody was on a world as such, so they signed up. Instead of books, as they had on Petaybee, they were given individual clipboard-sized screens on which they could receive the text or computerized lesson material for each class. They also carried another clipboard-sized computer for note taking and doing their class exercises and homework.

The flitter let them off on the school level of deck three just in time to join a bunch of other kids pouring in from other flitters, lifts, and staircases.

Murel said, *There's the loo. I'm going before we get to class. Meet you there.*

Yeah, sure, Ronan said, but he was already scanning the doors and the diagram on his text pad, looking for the right room. Looking up and to the side instead of straight ahead, he ran right into a wall and both his pads went flying.

"Hey!" the wall said.

It seemed to be slightly domed and wore floral wallpaper right at eye level. Ronan looked up and stared into the piercing dark eyes and black eyebrows of a boy about three times his size. Oh great. He was in for it now. This guy was way bigger than Dino Caparthy. He so did not want to get beaten up on his first day at Marmie's school.

"S-Sorry, I didn't mean anything. I was looking for my class instead of looking where I was going. I, uh, I have some lunch credits if that will—"

The tall boy put his palms out in front of him. "No, no, little bruthah. I don' want your lunch credits. I hope I didn't hurt you? I was lookin' too and did not look down." He made a sudden move and Ronan jumped back. This guy was enormous! But he had only stooped to pick up Ronan's pads, which he handed back to him. "Good thing these are sturdy, yeah? Where you goin'?"

"Professor Freyasdottur's geography class. You?"

"Same place. I am Ke-ola. You?"

"Ronan. Here comes my sister. Murel, hey, this is Ke-ola."

Murel looked up and then creaked her neck back and looked up a little farther until she met the large boy's friendly grin with one of her own. "Hey. Ke-ola, slainté."

"What's that mean?"

"We say it to mean hello and good-bye," Ronan, now official Petaybean goodwill ambassador, told him.

"Ah, we say 'aloha.' Means a couple of other things too. Slainté. You guys twins?"

"Yeah, we are. You got any brothers or sisters?"

"Ten sistahs, twelve bruthahs. Four sets twins. I had a twin myself but he died when we were born."

"Whew, that's a lot of sibs!" Ronan said.

"Your mum must be tired," Murel said.

"Six sistahs, four bruthahs are half—we got different mamas," he told them.

"Here's our classroom," Murel told him, as if saying good-bye. He reached above her and shoved the door open a little farther.

"Mine too," he said.

As it turned out, the space station school was sort of fun. On Petaybee there were no other kids their own age from the planet. Almost all of the kids in the lower levels were offworlders. Here it was the same, but everyone was in the same boat, or rather, on the same space station. And now Ronan and Murel had journeyed among the stars too, so even though they maybe hadn't seen other worlds like some of the kids had, they had more in common with them than they did with the offworld kids back home.

Also, they weren't the littlest kids here. Many of the others were younger than they were and several were their own age. A couple of them had never been off the space station.

They were friendly too, if a little too curious for comfort sometimes.

"Hey, twins, I heard you brought your pet seals with you," a younger boy named Dewey said. "Madame built them a pool up at her house, is what my mom said. Can I come and play with them?"

What shall we say? Murel asked.

We can say we had to send the seals home, Ronan suggested.

Yeah, but then if anyone sees us accidentally in seal form we won't have any way to explain it, Murel said. Finally she told Dewey, "You know, the reason we brought them with us, Dewey, is that they're really shy—

even around our parents. They hide if they know anybody else is around. They're, uh—"

"They're rescue seals," Ronan said. "They were going
to be killed by offworld fur trappers when they were
babies. The trappers already killed their families and
everything. It was terrible. Our aunt Sinead is the Game
Warden and she gave them to us to raise but they never
have wanted to be around any other humans, only us."

"Oh," Dewey said. "Well, maybe when you've been
here awhile and they get a little older they'll get used to
us too, if you have us up to Madame's a lot."

"Yeah, maybe so," Ronan said. But to Murel he said,
Like we're going to be away from Petaybee that long.

They had one teacher overall for each age group, and
that teacher supervised all the computer classes that
made up the bulk of their studies. But since they had
several very prominent scientists on board the station,
Marmie had talked some of them into teaching classes in
their specialties in the school too.

Dr. Freyasdottur, their geography teacher for this class,
was also a sociobiologist and an environmental systems
engineer, responsible for the weather system on Marmie's
level, among other modifications on the space station.
She was a sturdy young-looking blond woman with a
round face, dancing blue eyes, and large teeth that
showed a lot because she smiled often. Her hair was cut
short and by the end of the class stuck out in all directions because she often grabbed at it, stuck pencils in it,
or pulled at it for emphasis.

She employed a lot of holos as models and teaching
tools and hopped enthusiastically around each, pointing
out the features of systems full of planets that had
worlds within worlds. The holos showed people work-

ing in fields blooming with crops or picking fruit from trees, manufacturing parts for electronic equipment, or mining minerals. Each planet had a different skyscape, and after they studied one, Dr. Freyasdottur would zip it back into its star system to show them where it fit in the cosmic scheme of things.

"Now then," she said at the end of class one day, "for your homework, I want you all to design a holo of your own home world. Yes, yes, I know a few of you are station born and bred and have never been dirtside, so you will need to ask your parents for help locating, gathering information about, and depicting their worlds of origin. If they are from one of the older planets, you may place your focus on the country from which they come, its language, if other than Standard, customs as they deviate from those in station life, imports and exports, and contributions to the Federation. If you or your parents come from one of the planets terraformed by Intergal to house the inhabitants of Old Earth and some of the other older worlds, then we'd like to know what life is like there.

"Focus on how your world has been developed and what it's like for boys and girls who grow up there. If possible, compare their lives with yours here on the station. You will be sharing your holos with the rest of the class in two weeks. In the meantime, this class period will be devoted to learning to design holos. My assistant, Top Tech Wayans, will be helping you develop the technical end of your projects."

Murel's hand shot up and Dr. Freyasdottur called on her. "What if there's two of us from the same planet? Can we do our holo together?"

"Certainly, Murel. In fact, most of you here have

other family members in class. Even if you share a holo, you will each have to do a presentation of a different aspect of your planet's culture, environment, or social structure, of course."

Marmie's eyebrows rose when they told her about the assignment. "Alors! That should be extremely challenging for children your age, but no doubt you will all learn a lot about each other as well as other places in the universe and how to design a holo."

The twins were so involved in their own project, they didn't realize how truly Marmie had spoken until the other kids began their presentations.

"This is Wurra-Wurra, where my folks came from," a boy named Rory said. His skin was very dark, almost black, and his features looked like the ones some of the old men carved with chain saws out of tree stumps. His eyes were a brilliant and startling blue. He opened his program, and a stretch of salmon pink sky and blowing sand that looked like a spray of blood under two glowing suns spun out before them. Tall rusty spires rose in clusters here and there. "It's got two suns, see, and they dry everything up. So it's desert, right?"

"Are those tall things the buildings of your cities?" Lan Huy, a girl a year or two older than the twins, asked.

Rory laughed, a sharp little yip. "Not our cities, Lan. They are cities, though. The ants that live there could probably tell you all the best places to get tea or go shopping."

"So—you're not the dominant species on your planet?" Ke-ola asked curiously and with no hint of humor or mockery. In school he spoke more correctly than he did when he was just messing around with the other kids, Murel noticed.

"We think so. Don't know what the ants think. Stay away from them, my folks said, much as possible."

"Where's your water?" Murel asked.

"Underground, what there is," Rory said. "Mum says you have ter dig for it."

Murel said, "Underground water is the *only* water you have? We have underground water too, but we've got regular rivers and seas and such as well."

"You'll have your turn soon enough, Murel," Dr. Freyasdottur said. "Go on, Rory."

Rory finished up.

Ke-ola was next. He shuffled to the front and tapped in his program, picked up his laser wand. As soon as he started his presentation, Murel and Ronan realized there was even more to their large friend than there appeared to be. Three worlds started spinning.

"I am Ke-ola O'honu-aumakua. On Old Earth my people lived on islands in the warmest of the two great oceans, the Ocean of Peacefulness. Originally we ate what the islands brought us, fish from the sea, fruit from the trees. The climate was mild and warm, and except for volcanoes erupting at times, or monsoon rains, our lives were peaceful. Then other people came to the islands with things and ideas they said would make our lives better. Some things seemed to but others did not. Finally came the day when Intergal came to the few of us who were left and still in possession of some of the islands in our chain. They told us they now owned our island and we could not live there any longer but would be moved to a better place. We did not quite believe them because, although the islands were not as good in many ways as they had been before the new ideas and things came, they were still a very good place to live.

The new place was a specially prepared world that much resembled our own. We brought with us the seeds to some of our trees, and the eggs and young of our fish and animals. My family brought the eggs of the sacred Honu, the sea turtle that is our special animal. Our last name means 'people of the sea turtle.'

"For a time we lived in the new place fairly contentedly, though it was a new place and never home and we still sang to each other of the old islands lost to us. Then the company came and told us that our new place, which they already owned, had been found to have a rare mineral they needed for a vital manufacturing process, but that another place had been prepared for us and we would be moved again.

"This time, the new place was not as well prepared as the other, and though we brought our plants and animals with us again, they do not thrive in this new place. Neither do we. The gravity is greater, the weather is colder and more changeable, and our animals must be kept in artificial pens and tanks, our plants in big houses with artificial sunlight. Once, on the old world, and to a lesser extent on the second one, we were scientists and singers, ranchers and dancers, teachers and creators of beautiful and useful items."

He paused, pointed the wand to the first globe and drew up a picture of what looked like a hat made of flowered fabric with a pineapple-shaped container strapped to either side of it. Ke-ola suddenly grinned, a warm and funny expression that seemed totally at odds with the serious and even sad look he'd worn throughout the rest of his recitation. "Well, some of the items were ugly and useless too, but the outsiders seemed to want them so we sold them to them." Then the grin went away as if it had never been and he continued in the same slightly sing-song voice, "We were healers, lawgivers and musicians, makers of food and purveyors of goods. We have become a people of zookeepers and gardeners.

"The company tells us that we are ungrateful for everything they have done for us and that our people must learn new jobs and new ways to be more productive to repay the kindness of the company. And so I have been sent here to school on a special scholarship to learn more about how to maintain space stations. I cannot tell you of imports or exports—everything my people have they have brought with them or have had provided for them, at a cost, by the company, who may take back whatever they need, including us. Fortunately, even though the heavy gravity is very hard on the mamas when they give birth, our families have become large with little to do but grow food and children. We don't manufacture much anymore or work away from home much either. Mostly the older people tell the younger ones stories and teach us our old songs and dances so we don't forget who we are or what we had a long time ago. That's all good, but as you can tell, we don't always have enough to eat." He patted his round stomach. "So probably it is a good thing I am here among you, my classmates, where I don't get so skinny I blow away on the wind. Makes more food for my family at home too."

As he talked, he spun the worlds and brought up the animals, trees, volcanoes, fish, and turtles of the first world, and showed people like him doing the jobs he described. The second world he showed had less of everything, and the new one had a lot of the same things, only in containers set on stark landmasses.

That's terrible that they just kept taking his people's

homes away from them, Murel said. *They're i.p.'s too, just like us—the inconvenient peoples Intergal moved to terraformed worlds from places the company had a better use for.*

Yeah, that's kind of what the older people were afraid of about Petaybee, that once the company realized how good our world was, they'd try to move us off of it. That was before Mum and Da straightened it all out, Ronan replied.

"That was excellent, Ke-ola, and far exceeded the assignment," Dr. Freyasdottur said. "Your holos turned out so well I'm afraid you may have raised the grading curve on this assignment."

The big kid flushed and grinned but to their surprise said, "Don' do that, teachah. I cheated a little."

"You did? You mean you didn't make those holos?"

"I did. But I made two of 'em a long time ago, back on three world. Auntie Kimmie Lee, oldest lady living, she learned to make them to sell to visitors back on two world a long time ago. She taught us kids to keep us out of trouble, she says. Also, it shows us what it was like on those two worlds. What we were like. So I just uploaded the old ones I made for fun for the assignment. I did do the last one though, just like you said."

"Oh well," Dr. Freyasdottur said. Both twins could see she was trying hard not to giggle. "I won't raise the curve then if you cheated, but I'll just grade you on the new one. By the way, maybe instead of bothering Top Tech Wayans the next time we do holos, you must share your unfair advantage with the other students and teach them how to make their holos the way you did. Am I clear?"

"Yes'm," he said, and sat down, trying to look suitably chastised.

Chesney Janko gave her presentation next. She was a year and a half younger than the twins and had grown up on a large industrial planet that was a company headquarters. Her family had moved to the station when her parents left the company's employment to take a job with Marmie. She seemed to list imports and exports for hours. "Computer chips and antibiotics and guidance systems and butter and laser rifles and . . ." She listed them as they occurred to her and not in any particular order or with any particular interest.

Lan Huy had grown up on the station. Her father was one of Marmie's top engineers. She said that at one time, a very long time ago, her father's people had come from a small client country that paid tribute to a very large one. Some of the animals in the larger country were dragons, horned beasts that sounded a little like the curly coats, and birds called phoenixes that self-destructed and rebuilt themselves from ashes. She had seen evidence of these things, but had never encountered any herself except sometimes in dreams. Her presentation seemed to be mostly made up of imaginary stuff, which she said was legend, because although her people were once the most numerous on Old Earth, a catastrophic plague had all but wiped them out.

By the time it was their turn, the twins were both feeling even luckier than usual to be Petaybeans. They looked forward to showing their new friends what a proper planet should have.

But when they were finished, Rory made a big display of shivering. "Brrr, sounds cold to me."

"It is cold, but we don't mind really. Everyone is used to it and our bodies are adapted to it," Murel told him.

"How'd they do that?" asked Chesney.

"The planet did it," Ronan said. His sister looked away. She wished he hadn't said that. She didn't think it was a good idea to tell offworlders any more about Petaybee than they might already know.

"How could it do that? It's not like planets think," Rory scoffed.

"Petaybee does," Ronan said. "It's like it's this really big person we all live on." The holo spun on his computer screen.

"Looks like an ice ball to me," Chesney said, shaking her head.

"It is an ice ball," Murel said, her brows lowering and coming together to make a fierce expression, had she been able to see it. "But it's *our* ice ball and at least it has ground water."

"Now then, young'uns," Dr. Freyasdottur said. "This lesson was to help you learn about one other's home planets, not to criticize them or brag about your own. Please continue, twins."

They did, but it was hard to give the other kids the right feeling about Petaybee when they couldn't talk about winter swims without at least hinting that they could turn into seals. And they just couldn't do that. They understood that much about what Da and Mum were trying to protect them from.

But at least the assignment let them know more about the other students and gave them some idea of how many different kinds of worlds and peoples there were on them.

By the end of the week they had heard from kids

whose planets were desert, jungle, rich farmland, or mostly water.

"Nobody else seems to be able to talk to their world, though, Marmie," Ronan said when their hostess asked them how their presentation went and how they liked the others. "Is Petaybee the only one that's—you know— alive?"

Marmie shrugged. "I very much doubt it, mon petit. Perhaps it is just that Petaybee is more gregarious than the others. More outgoing. Or perhaps your people are simply more in tune with the world they were placed upon than others are elsewhere. It's a great mystery."

"Yes," Murel said. "But I still think it would be cool if sometime some of those other worlds started letting their people know whose surface they were living on, don't you?"

"Very cool, my darling. Very cool indeed," Marmie agreed, fluffing Murel's hair with her hand. "Perhaps, given enough time, they will."

CHAPTER 11

FOR THE FIRST few months, the twins were able to talk to their parents often. At first it was every day, and then one of the expensive relays went down and the com systems had to be rerouted, so it was only possible to talk face-to-face every week. Then Petaybee began emitting electromagnetic interference so that half the time neither one could make out what the other was saying, or see the other either.

"How come it's more that way now than when we left?" Murel asked.

"Lots of reasons," Marmie replied. "Sunspots, the increased activity from the midsea volcanic region your father mentioned. You remember him saying that on his last recon swim he felt the heat in the water and smelled the sulfur much earlier than he had on previous trips?"

"Yeah," Ronan said, "He said it was just a matter of a couple of years now before it surfaces. I hope we can go home by then. I want to see! Besides, if we can't talk to them . . ."

The face-to-face calls finally became impossible, and the messages had to be routed through a number of different stations. It was hard to say anything important, much less be silly or share a joke, with so many people between you. Petaybee, Kilcoole, the people of their village, and their family began to feel very far away. Fortunately, school was interesting and they liked the other kids and most of their teachers; and of course they had each other, so they could forget to be homesick for long periods of time.

One day toward the end of the first term, Marmie asked them, "What flavor cake do you two like best?"

"Chocolate," "Raspberry," they answered at the same time.

"Chocolate raspberry it shall be then. Your parents cannot come for your birthday, but they've sent gifts and I've invited all of your classmates here for a party. I thought, if it was all right with you, we could make it a theme party and set it up as if it were a latchkay on Petaybee. How would that be?"

Ronan looked at Murel and Murel looked at Ronan.

Marmie said, "You do not care for the idea? Would it make you too homesick?"

"Oh, it's a good idea, Marmie," Murel said. "It's just—we don't think the other kids are really ready for Petaybee yet. I don't think some of them liked our holo."

Marmie gave an elegant lift and fall of her shoulders, with her hands outstretched, palms up. What Mum called a "Gallic shrug." It said, basically, What is a sensible person supposed to do when other people are being so silly?

"Your holo was very nice," she said finally. "Those who did not care for it were foolish. But a holo and Petaybee are different, yes?"

"Still. . . ," Murel said, and let her voice drift off as

she looked at Marmie, hoping she'd understand the rest without her actually trying to say it.

"We'd like to keep the Petaybee part of our birthdays private, I guess," Ronan said finally. "I'm sorry. It's really nice of you to want to give us a party, Marmie, but we don't have to have one. We could have the cake anyway, couldn't we?" He looked at his sister. "And presents?"

Marmie laughed, and it sounded like bells jingling on sled dogs' harnesses. "Yes, yes, we must have cake and presents and a party too. But the Petaybee part, that will be our own little celebration, after the others have left. I know! Everyone must come as a creature from their planet that either swims or flies."

"Wouldn't we be a little too realistic as seals?" Murel asked, wincing. She hated to keep shooting down Marmie's ideas, but felt their friend got carried away with enthusiasm before thinking about how wrong things could go. Lately, it seemed to the twins that they'd had a lot of experience with how wrong things could go.

"Ah, but you will not be seals!" Marmie said.

"We will be if we go swimming," Ronan said grimly.

"Only if you swim in the water. I am thinking you will not be swimming in the water, you will be swimming in the air."

"Yes, but we can't do that," Murel said.

"You can in zero g," Marmie told her. While they were thinking that over, she asked, "So, what will you be? Eagles? Fishes? Whales?"

"Otters," they said at the same time. "We'll be otters."

EVEN AFTER THE humans rescued his family, Otter stayed in the small den in the riverbank, waiting for his friends the river seals to return. But winter ended and the ice melted and still they were gone and did not come home. Finally, Otter went to the dwelling he had seen them enter and sent his thoughts on the matter to the Father River Seal.

Father River Seal, where are your children? Shouldn't they be back by now? Otters have many more games to play with them and things to show them. Marvelous things they will enjoy very much. Otters know lots of good secrets. Where are your river seal children?

What the . . . ? Father River Seal's thought was fragmented and startled.

It's me, Otter, Father River Seal. Do not be afraid, Otter told him.

Laughter came into the Father River Seal's thoughts. *I was not afraid, Otter. Merely thinking of something else.*

Not thinking of your children? Although they are not here?

Always thinking of my children, Otter. Their mother and I both miss them very much, but we sent them somewhere they would be safe from the kind of people who took the other otters.

Those people are gone. The good people took them away. Why have your children not returned? No danger now!

A smile came into Father River Seal's thoughts. *No danger for otters. But for my children, yes, there is still danger and their mother and I have been working hard to see to it that the danger such offworld scientific groups present will never threaten our children again.*

That is good, the otter said, for he could think of nothing else to say. His friends the river seal children were safe, but they were not in the river and so could not play with otters. *I will return to my family now but later I will come back here.*

I'll tell Ronan and Murel you were asking for them, Otter, Father River Seal said, and went back to thinking his deep, unsealy thoughts and doing the unsealy things he did when in human form.

Otter was surprised, when he returned home again where the ice maze was in the winter, that none of his family were at play on the banks or in the river. *Where have all the otters who are not me gone?* he asked. He was asking himself but unexpectedly received an answer from the otters who were not there when he found a scent message.

Scent messages between river otters were quite complex, and in a way that would have astounded humans or river seals. River otters could write entire tomes with one spritz from the proper area or a rub from another. And there were dialects of scents understood only by otters of the same colony, as well as nuances of meaning, idiomatic expressions or slang of particular families, that only otters in the same colony could fully grasp, or smell.

It was fortunate that otters had excellent memories for scent too, because great otter romantic literature had been composed in scent messages, as well as geography texts and adventure stories.

The message that Otter found that day was somewhat simpler. It said, "Kinsman Otter who Plays with River Seals, we do not care for this place any longer. Too many wolves and too many men with otter cages. We are moving closer to the sea to seek solidarity with our cousins the sea otters. See you by the sea!" Otters could pun in scent messages too. The language of otters was full of puns. Not the same ones humans used, but otter puns, which were very funny because otters enjoyed laughing. Like humans, however, otters had similar sounds for the big water *sea* and what otters did with their eyes *see*.

It was a long swim to the sea, especially all alone. The message was three days old, which meant the family was probably already at the shore. But it meant swimming with the current, and the weather was pleasant, as most weather was for otters, and so in a single day Otter caught up with part of his family, which had stopped at a particularly tempting mud slide. It was very long, slick, and muddy, and gave them a little "Whoop!" before they went splashing into the river, cleaned off the mud, and climbed back up the hill to slide again.

They had been playing for some time and were ready to join the rest of the family, so Otter had time for only a few slides—certainly not hundreds—before he resumed swimming again.

At last, after much swimming, with a few games along the way, they were reunited with the rest of the family on the banks of the river at the mouth where it spilled into the sea.

Where are our cousins the sea otters? Otter asked his mother.

You see that island over there? she replied, indicating a large landmass squatting amid the waves rolling onto the shore beyond their river camp. *They live there. It is full of sea otter dens, and you can see them lying on the rocks eating clams. Some have been coming over to show us where the best places to build dens might be here. We do not swim in that salty stuff they call water, but they say that in the winter, when the ice is in, we could walk to their island, though of course we would not do so unless asked. Like us, sea otters protect their homes with great ferocity.*

She bared her teeth in a suitably ferocious way, and Otter backpaddled away from her a little. He knew his mother's teeth and claws very well from times when she had been greatly ferocious about how her offspring should behave.

The river otters moved into their comfortable new dens in the wide river mouth. There were low hills nearby that made passable mud slides, once the otters removed the rocks at the bottom, which they did with great efficiency. These were useful in breaking open the delicious shellfish they found on the shore, which was technically their cousins' territory, though the cousins did not use it much, preferring their island.

Otter loved the new delicacy and hunted on the shore as often as he could, keeping a careful eye on the island, lest ferocious cousins come and attack him for his boldness. Then one day he noticed that there were no longer any sea otters to be seen on the island. Not one. Not anywhere.

"Hah!" he said. *Where have they gone?* He alerted his family, and they all came to the beach to see for themselves. They could see he was right. No sea otters on the island's narrow beach, no sea otters in the water, no sea otters on the shore, no sea otters higher up on the island. No sea otters anywhere.

Later in the day, all of the sea otters returned. To Otter's surprise, three of the cousins swam straight to the shore. Otter was afraid at first, thinking that he'd been caught stealing their shellfish.

"Hah!" he said, greeting them. *Cousins, where did you all go? You disappeared. Otters who live in the river saw no otters who live in the sea all day.* Otter hid the shell of the fish he had just eaten behind him while pushing forward three rocks. *Otters came to the shore to bring you gifts but we did not see you on your island. Here are the gifts. Rocks for shell cracking.*

Sea otters cannot possibly have too many rocks! his cousins said, accepting the rocks as if they were better than shellfish. *Rocks are for preparing food and also for leaving messages.*

Like scent messages? Otter asked.

Scent messages are for river otters. Rock talk is for sea otters. You live in the riverbanks and the water. We live almost always in the water, and scent would wash away. Rocks are better.

To himself, Otter thought that rocks could wash away too and that otters who lived always in the water had to come out of it to pile rocks and leave messages and to find piles of rocks and read the messages. *I would like to see a rock talk message,* he said.

The sea otters had a lot of fun stacking the rocks first one way and then another, adding one kind of rock and then another, going from just a few rocks to—well—probably hundreds! Each time, they made him guess what the message said and translate it into scent for them. Each time, they agreed among themselves that, yes, rocks were definitely better. Otter did not disagree with them. They were the bosses of otters here, and besides, they had rocks.

Instead Otter tried to learn what he could about their rock messages. They were so pleased that they agreed he surely must have some sea otter ancestors.

Shall we tell this smart river otter our secrets? one cousin asked another.

Yes, he is our cousin and gives good gifts. Besides, we were going to tell all our cousins the big secret.

Before Otter knew it, his family surrounded him, all of them waiting to hear the big secret of the sea otters.

The planet is making a new home for us, said the sea otters. *It's a bit hot, but it will be a wonderful home when it is done.*

How will we know when it is done? Otter asked.

It will come up out of the water and cool off and not smoke or make fire anymore, said a cousin. *At least, that is what Senior Sea Otter says, and Senior Sea Otter has lived a long long time and spoken to many creatures who have lived much longer. A few of the oldest have seen this thing happen in other places, long ago. Others have heard of it happening from their grandparents and their grandparents' grandparents. And now it is happening again and sea otters can watch!*

So you go to watch it being made?

And to eat! Everything in the sea is attracted to the new home and many delicious fish already live near it, sheltering in it.

Suddenly, right under his paws, Otter felt the ground tremble. It did that sometimes but it always startled him. "Hah!" he said nervously.

Do not be alarmed, cousin. That is what the planet does when it is making the home.

That is an extremely fine secret, Otter said, impressed. *Is there another secret?*

We have found a new branch of the family.

New branch?

Yes, before there were always you river otters and us sea otters. Now there are other otters.

What otters are these? How different are they?

They are deep sea otters. They can live under the water and have a home there. It is too deep for us to dive but they say it is the kind of home deep sea otters like. They sang us wonderful songs of deep sea otters and wanted us to sing them sea otter songs too. We sang of you, little cousin, the River Otter who Plays with River Seals. It is not a sea otter song but it is a very good song. It was the best song we know and we know many good sea otter songs. You will not bite us for singing your song?

Hah! Bite you! You are our cousins and now our neighbors. You share these very fine secrets. You may sing my song to other otters whenever you like.

Good. But we will all sing it together soon. The deep sea otters say that one day when we come again to see the new home the planet is making, they will swim back with us. They wish to hear your song from you.

All Otter could think of to say to that was, "Hah!"

CHAPTER 12

HOLOGRAMS WERE HANDY things. They could be lessons or environments or costumes, if you needed them to be. It was a little hard to keep them in place in zero g, but everyone seemed to have a good time swimming or flying, depending on what they were supposed to be. Ke-ola was a sea turtle, a big one. Lan Huy was a dragon. Rory was a shark, which was a little scary, especially for Chesney, who was a lake gull. She flapped her arms so hard she ended up hitting Dewey, who came as a monkey, in the nose, which made him cry until Marmie had him come out to help her bring down the cake.

"I thought Marmie had people who did things like baking cakes and carrying them around for her," Ronan said.

"She does. I think she wants to do this personally because it's, you know, for us. Letting Dewey help instead of one of the people who work for her keeps him from crying. Have you noticed how if one person starts crying, pretty soon everybody else does too?"

Suddenly, Ronan wasn't having any fun anymore. He faked being an otter sliding but since he didn't go down, no matter what, it didn't look right. By the time he stood back up, he saw that Murel's eyes were glistening, and he felt a lump in his own throat. But then a voice on the intercom said, "All members of the Shongili birthday party please report immediately to Ms. de Revers Algemeine's deck for cake and ice cream."

Rory, sharklike, burst through the hatch and fell with a clunk into normal gravity on the deck outside.

Ronan did a halfhearted otter slide and landed on his butt, without his holo-costume. Murel slid down beside him. "Your costume is still flickering on and off," Rory told her. "But you're barely ottered at all!"

Murel just groaned and rolled her eyes, and Ronan pretended he was puking.

Aboard the intrastation transfer flitter, however, they saw someone who lifted their spirits. "Look!" Murel said aloud, pointing. "It's Johnny!"

You think he's come to take us home? Maybe as a surprise?

Why else would he be going to Marmie's on our birthday? Murel asked.

They kept it to themselves, though, thinking Marmie meant it to be a big secret, which they didn't want to spoil. Johnny and Marmie ate cake and ice cream off to one side and watched while Ronan and Murel opened their gifts. Rory gave them each a shark's tooth he swore had been dug out of somebody's leg. He didn't say if the leg had still been attached to the person when the teeth were removed. They were strung on thongs for the twins to wear around their necks.

"Do you like it?" the boy from Wurra-Wurra asked.

"It's awesome," Murel replied.

"Yeah," Ronan said, almost forgetting to be sad or anxious about what Johnny was doing there. Rory was turning out to be okay after all.

Lan Huy gave them a scroll that turned out to be a blueprint of the space station. "There's lots of interesting ways to get where we're not supposed to go," she leaned forward and whispered. "You just have to study it a bit."

Chesney gave them free passes to see the new vids the last supply ship had delivered. Her dad was the morale and recreation chairman.

"Gosh, thanks, Chez," Murel said. "I've been wanting to see the one about the explorer who finds the ancient civilization filled with the remnants of a highly advanced race."

"They never find the ruins of ancient civilizations filled with the remnants of a buncha complete eejits, do they?" Rory observed.

"Probably no ruins left because complete eejits wouldn't have figured out how to build an ancient civilization in the first place," Ke-ola said.

Ke-ola handed them each a saucer-sized flower from the ponics garden then helped Murel stick it behind her ear.

"There's no music at this party so far," he said. "What, nobody sings to you on your birthday?"

Under Chesney's direction, the other students dutifully sang a round of "Happy Birthday."

Ke-ola groaned. "That's lame, man. You got to have real music at a party. You twins say on your world you sing at the parties all the time. So okay, I'll tell you what. I'm gonna make you an old-style song, my little bruthah and sistah, the kind we sing at home. You other kids, you can sing with me."

"That's great, Ke-ola, but we don't know your language."

"Don't matter. Just do what I do and say what I say after me. You can do the dance and hum the words if you want to. "

"Dance?" Rory made a face. "That's sissy stuff."

"Yeah? Okay, you don't have to do it then if it's sissy. I didn't know that. We do sissy stuff at home all the time I guess."

"No offense, man," Rory said. He didn't want to make the big guy mad.

"No offense," Ke-ola said, shrugging. Then he jumped, stomped, bellowed, snapped bent knees back and forth, and chanted in a language that had lots of great rhyming and repetitive sounds that seemed vaguely funny sometimes and beautiful at others. Murel thought he was choosing the words that would be the most fun to say, to get the other kids to say them too, and it worked. Some of the movements he made, which were a kind of sign language, looked like they might be something rude, and others looked like waves or stars twinkling or wind in the trees.

"I don't see how all of that could be about us," Murel said. "But thanks."

"You're right. It's not all about you. You haven't been around long enough for it to be all about you. It's about where you come from, where you are now, and how you managed to land where you get to hang out with such great people like us."

Then he told them what the gestures meant and some of the words he said the most.

"That's a lot like Petaybee songs," Ronan told him, "except we use drums a lot."

"We use drums too," he said. "Come here, Rory, man.

Bring your empty head so I can show you all some drumming."

But Marmie's butler, who'd been watching everything onscreen inside the house, came out bringing a drum that usually acted as a side table in Marmie's main living room. Ke-ola looked at it critically, then started in on a beat that sounded a lot like a heartbeat and went perfectly with the chant he sang in quite a different tone from the last one. Periodically he danced along with his drumming, stomping for emphasis between drumbeats. Pretty soon everybody was doing it, even Rory.

"What's that one about?"

"Oh, it's just a song we do a lot on birthdays at home," he said vaguely. "It's the men's part. You do one now."

So first they sang the otter song, then Murel sang one about mosquitoes.

Ke-ola laughed. "You want to see what dance my people do about mosquitoes?" he asked, and when they said they did, he did a rhythmic chant that involved slapping himself silly on his thighs and chest, belly and forearms, the back of his neck and his face, even the soles of his feet.

"Wow, you must have bigger mosquitoes than we do even," Ronan said.

The kids started trying to make up their own dances then for a while, but they got pretty silly. Ke-ola jumped into the fake river and floated there like a contented island.

And Dewey was in a much better mood. He helped serve the refreshments, and now sat beside the fake river, his pant legs rolled up and his bare feet kicking back and forth in the water. The lights from below lit up his toes so they looked all white and corpsey. Or at least, what Murel thought corpse toes would probably look like.

"Do you guys swim here?"

"Uh, no," Murel said. "We, uh, we're afraid of the water."

"How deep is it?" he asked.

"Oh, it's different in different places," Murel said casually. Actually, it was a good five feet deep in some places, and more in others.

"How about right here?"

"I dunno. I could get a line to measure it, though, if you really want to know."

"I got a better idea," he said, and slid off the edge, and sank. Bubbles blew up from his mouth, but his face looked really white and corpsey now. Murel didn't even think about the secret. She just dove in after him, clothes and all. *Ronan, help! No, don't you come in too. Just stand there and wait,* she said. *Try not to let anybody else see me.* Fortunately, Dewey hadn't realized he was in trouble until it was too late to scream, so maybe nobody else noticed.

She caught the neck of Dewey's ship suit in her mouth, since she now had flippers poking out of her sleeves, and hauled him up to the surface where Ronan began pulling him up onto the "bank" of ponics-grown turf.

Ronan was not quite alone, though. Ke-ola and Rory helped, Ke-ola pulling Dewey the rest of the way to his feet. Murel flipped the water off her head and hands and turned her back on everyone.

"I thought you were afraid of the water?" Dewey said between chattering teeth.

"I was more afraid you'd drown," she replied, as soon as her muzzle turned back into a separate mouth and nose again, which fortunately didn't take but a second. "I mean, I *can* swim, I just don't like to."

Lan Huy said, "Wow, you had a whole nother holo, Murel. Cool one! You looked just like a seal carrying Dewey in her mouth!"

"Yeah," Murel said. "So now *this* seal is flapping back inside to change into something dry."

That sort of broke up the party. Marmie directed a flitter to return the other kids to their quarters.

By the time Murel came out, Ronan was staring at the packages Johnny carried and thinking that if these were from home, it meant that he and Murel weren't going to get to go back to Petaybee now.

"I'm sorry," Murel said, apologizing before she reached the place where their chairs were clustered around a realistic holo of a blazing fireplace. Enough heat came from it to dry her hair into the long wild red-brown Irish curls that distinguished her from Ronan now. His hair was Inuit or maybe Navajo, straight and black. You couldn't tell them apart in the water very easily, though. "The water's ten feet deep there, and the silly git doesn't know how to swim. Someone should teach him."

"I'll speak to his parents," Marmie said. "That was very brave of you, cherie. No harm done. The others thought you had a good second holo."

Murel smiled, but it faded as she saw the presents.

"You don't even know what's in them," Johnny exclaimed. "Why the long face?"

"We thought maybe you had come to take us home," Ronan said. "I know Marmie said not now, but we thought maybe Mum and Da had changed their minds."

"No, my pets, I'm afraid you're stuck with me for the time being," Marmie said.

But she didn't say what the time being might be.

That year, their gifts were new journals from Mum. She had kept them all year long to let the twins know what was happening between the rare times when they could talk via the com units. Da sent them carvings he had made of otters, each carving wrapped with a clam-shell. Clodagh sent them a big plastic tub of her rose hip preserves and loaves of zucchini bread. Aunt Sinead and Aisling sent them "Eskimo yo-yos"—moose-hair-stuffed hide sewed into balls, beaded by Aisling and attached to a long thong. You twirled it and then threw it at a bird, to either knock it out of the sky or snag its feet. They didn't have any birds to try them out on and got in trou-ble if they used the yo-yos on other kids, so finally they each sort of left them somewhere and forgot about them.

CHAPTER 13

THE FOLLOWING YEAR, when they turned ten, went much faster. They'd made friends, together and separately, and did a lot of visiting away from Marmie's deck, studying in the excellent multimedia library, playing nonwater sports, studying martial-arts moves, and hanging out at the large shopping mall, the holo deck, and the homes of their friends. Marmie also welcomed the other kids to her compound, but the twins were worried that their friends would want to go swimming. Marmie's private waterway was a treat for the others since the station only boasted a single large pool complex, which was packed all the time. The twins made excuses not to go into the water but hated not to join in. It was fine to swim alone on the waterways, though awfully tame after the rivers around Kilcoole, but it would have been fun to play water games with the other kids.

"I wish we could control the change a little more," Murel said one day, watching the sparkling drops spraying up from the usually still pool as their friends splashed each other. They had said they had sinus infections and weren't supposed to go in.

"Yeah, swim like people sometimes, or be seals on dry

land. That might be good once in a while," her brother agreed.

A well-known geneticist had arrived at the station and would teach the children during the next round of classes. "It's my granny," Rory said proudly. "She's retired now and come to live with us, she says. But she's been all over the universe with her institute, studying all the different species on all the different worlds. She's really interested in the new ones."

"What new ones?" Ke-ola asked.

"You know, the mutants that form because of conditions on one planet or the other. Seems the worlds terraformed by Intergal to house different races from Old Earth change things."

"Like how?" Ke-ola asked, trying not to sound too interested.

"Oh, one of them has a special disease that people who work the soil get. It killed off a lot of them, but then they found a drug to help it, and the ones that get it now are okay but they shed their skin every year."

"Like snakes?" Ke-ola asked.

"No, not all in one piece. They shed it in big flakes or scales, kind of like some trees lose their leaves."

"Don't their insides fall out then?" Chesney asked.

"No, of course not, 'cause they have new skin underneath," Rory said, looking at Chesney as if she were a silly little girl, which, actually, she wasn't.

When the twins told Marmie that Rory's granny was a famous scientist and was going to be one of their teachers, she seemed pleased, but was distracted by business. They realized that though she tried to act interested in their school and what they were doing, she was as busy, or maybe even busier, than Mum and Da.

Marmie had lots of people working for her and doing things for her, but that gave her even more problems to solve. Often when they talked to her, she nodded and smiled or made appropriate noises, but wasn't really listening. And of course, she didn't personally pick out the teachers or have a lot to do with the school. She was too important for that.

"I think she liked us better when we were little," Murel said later.

"Nah, she still likes us. She's just used to us now," Ronan told her. "She knows she doesn't have to worry about us all the time. Why should she? We know our way around now and who to go to for stuff. We know how to keep people from finding out about us. We're almost adults, when you think about it."

"True. And it's not as if she's our mother or even a real auntie," Murel said a little bitterly. She had wanted to tell Marmie about them wanting to ask the new teacher if she could help them learn to control their shapeshifting. But Murel knew she could have said they were going to jump off the station into space without the benefit of suits and Marmie would have probably replied, "Bon, cherie. Très bon. You are so clever."

"Really," Murel told her brother, "she's sort of a glorified babysitter. Only not as furry as 'Nook and Co'."

Mentioning the cats' names made her homesick. She longed to bury her face and hands in their fur, feel their raspy tongues on her cheeks and fingers—or flippers as the case might be—hear their thundering purrs or even their disdainful scolding. She missed mind-talking with them, missed talking with other creatures who were not her twin brother.

The first day of class, Rory's gran strode into the room

after they were all seated. She was dark-skinned, like Rory, with the same rough-carved features and broad nostrils. Her eyes were not blue like his, but sparkling black, like anthracite at the bottom of a cold and flowing stream.

"So," she said. "You are all my grandson's classmates. Do not think, because Rory is my grandson, that I am a daft old woman who will sit here knitting while you throw spitballs at each other."

They all laughed. Professor Mabo had a great smile, with shiny white teeth and dimples, and when she spoke, her voice had kind of a song to it. It rose and fell and did little tweaks and twirls that made what she had to say more interesting. And it turned out to be plenty interesting already.

She took out some pictures that looked like the ones the twins had seen in Rory's parents' quarters. They were very stylized and looked kind of like X rays of animals, with pictures of other things inside of them. "Do you know what these are?" she asked.

"Rory's screensaver?" Ke-ola asked.

"Is it?" Professor Mabo asked her grandson.

"Yeah, Gran, I have the wombat design as a screensaver."

"It will be Professor Mabo to you too, Rory, while class is in session," Rory's gran told him. "As for you, young man, you are apparently correct. Rory does have this sort of artwork as a screensaver. So you are familiar with the design, but do you understand what it means?" Rory raised his hand, but very cautiously. He wasn't looking nearly so pleased to be in a class where his grandmother was the teacher now. Murel thought it would have been nice if the grandmother had told Rory before class started what he was supposed to call her.

"Anyone but you, Rory. This art comes from our culture, so you should know already what it means. But I want to know if anyone else can figure it out."

"I think I know," Ronan said at the same time he raised his hand.

"Yes. It's Ronan, is it not?" But she looked as if she knew exactly who he was.

"Yes, ma'am. I think the drawings inside the bigger drawing are the story that explains the bigger creature. Some of the art of our Inuit ancestors is a bit like that."

"Most perceptive, Ronan. That is indeed part of the reason for the inner drawings. They also serve to depict the essentially dual nature of all creatures."

"All creatures, Professor?" Murel asked.

"Oh yes. You will always find the remnants in every living thing of the thing it was before it became the thing it is now."

"But most creatures are only one thing at a time, aren't they? I mean, they used to be something else maybe, but now, in this time, they are what they look like."

"Most creatures? That is an interesting way to phrase your question, my dear. Most *students* would feel that *all* creatures are as you describe, not merely most."

"Oh well, we don't know about *all*, do we?" Dewey asked. "I mean, none of us have seen all the creatures there are to see. That's what Murel meant, right, Murel?"

She nodded slowly, which wasn't exactly a lie.

"I think in the future—Dewey, is it not?—you must allow Murel to clarify her own comments. Yes?"

"Okay, Professor. Sorry."

"The other interesting feature of this art form is that it

demonstrates a certain knowledge of the anatomy of these creatures. It was probably influenced by the earliest dissections, at least insofar as shown by bone structure, organ placement, and the relationship of the parts to each other. Therefore, we will be doing dissections in this class—hands-on ones, not via computer or videotape. Since there is no extraneous animal life aboard this space station, when I learned I was to have a teaching position here, I brought specimens from my last laboratory. We will begin tomorrow. For now, you are to read the first two chapters in your text, and we will discuss them tomorrow."

She dismissed the class. Murel and Ronan stood up to leave, but Rory stopped them. "My mum said I should ask you two if you'd care to come for dinner tonight. She's making a special meal in honor of Gran. Can you come?"

"Sure. We'll have to ask Marmie, but I don't think she'll mind," Ronan said.

Marmie met them at the flitter when they came home that afternoon. She had a small bag in her hand. "I have been called away on business for a couple days, children. While I am gone, Petronella will look after you. You must not annoy her. She is not as tolerant as I am, and is much better at hand-to-hand combat, so I trust you will behave." Petronella Chan was Marmie's chief of domestic security, in charge of the mansion, grounds, and in fact the entire deck housing Marmie and her staff. She reported only to Space Station Security Chief Fadeyka Petrovich, but he also reported to her. They worked together to ensure that the station, and especially their employer, was safer than most fortresses. Neither twin had been in an actual fortress, but knew they were supposed to be really safe. Pet was a tough cookie, but she also baked great cookies, and the twins liked her a lot.

"We always do behave, Marmie," Murel said.

"Rory wants us to come to his place for dinner tonight," Ronan said. "Is it okay? Will Pet let us?"

"I shall call her and tell her I authorize it," Marmie answered, and bent to give them each a double-cheeked kiss before boarding the flitter and buzzing off to the docking area.

Rory's folks were quite nice and had sponsored class events before, though they'd never invited the twins to their quarters.

His mother, Elizabeth, was a scientist, a biologist like her own mother, Professor Mabo. Rory's father was an engineer. Everyone was bustling around like mad when the twins got there. Dinner was cooking, and it smelled delicious, all spicy and vaguely like roasting meat.

Rory's da carried a large chair and set it down in front of Ronan and Murel, emitting a huff as he did so. "Have a seat, one of you. Or better yet, pick up something and set it on its chalk mark."

"Is it a game?" Murel asked Rory.

"Nah," he said. "They moved us into bigger quarters now that Gran is with us. She has an apartment of her own next door, but there's a connecting door. Our other place wasn't set up that way. They just told my mum today."

"That's fast," Ronan said.

He and Murel helped to put things where they were supposed to go. Finally, Rory's mum called out that they should stop and told Rory to go next door and get his grandmother so they could eat.

Professor Mabo was the only one who didn't look overheated and sweaty. Rory's mum and dad rushed around trying to get the food on the table, but the professor took a seat and stayed there. "Seniority has its privileges," she told Murel and Ronan, showing her dimples as she smiled at them as if it were a big joke.

"Sure," Ronan said. "I bet you had to run around like this to take care of stuff when Rory's mother was little too."

"Oh no, I had assistants to do these things. Unfortunately, Elizabeth has not attained the stature I had even as young as I was, and so she must raise Rory and entertain his friends with no help except that of poor Bram, who as you can see is not quite up to the task."

That's a nasty thing to say, Murel told her brother.

At least she isn't being nasty to us, Ronan answered.

"Rory, go back to my apartment and fetch the book on my dresser," his gran said. "There are pictures in there I want to show you all."

Rory had just settled into his chair and was helping himself to the first ladle of food from one of the steaming dishes.

"Can't it wait until after dinner, Mother?" Rory's mum asked. "The food is hot now."

Ronan and Murel exchanged nervous looks. Rory's mother sounded as if it took all of her courage to speak up to Professor Mabo.

I think I'm not so sorry we don't have a grandma after all, Ronan said.

They're not all like her. We know lots of nice grandmas in Kilcoole.

But Professor Mabo looked at the two of them and changed her tone. "I'm sorry. How thoughtless of me.

Of course we must eat your lovely meal while it's hot. Rory can get the photos afterward or perhaps we can all go to my quarters to look at them while you and Bram clean up. My rooms are more spacious and comfortable anyway."

She smiled at the twins and Rory, and everybody dug in. Professor Mabo seemed to relax during the meal and even told some funny stories about collecting species on various planets and her other work with the institute. " 'What kind of a rat is that?' the man asked me, and I said, 'It's a bear, actually.' He said it was no wonder he had sustained so many injuries while trying to catch them with cheese."

The twins offered to help with the cleanup, as they'd been taught, but Rory's mother seemed relieved to have everyone out from underfoot. "No, no, you go. It's quite an honor for you that Mother wants to share her work— or at least its history—with you."

"Yeah," Rory said, frowning. "She never showed *me* any of that stuff before."

By then, Professor Mabo was waiting impatiently by the door, so the three of them caught up with her.

Rory acts like he's mad at us, Ronan told Murel, with a big question mark hanging over the thought.

Well, she's his grandma but she's being nicer to us than she is to him. I wonder why?

'Cause we're so cute? Ronan asked.

Does Professor Mabo seem like the kind of person who cares about cute to you?

No, not exactly. Why, then?

I dunno. Maybe we'll find out pretty soon.

Professor Mabo's place didn't look very grandmotherly at all, or even homey. It was bare of pictures and personal touches. In the center of the living room there was a long white table with chairs around it, as if prepared for a meeting. Her computer was at one end. Instead of knickknacks, she had specimen jars. They seemed to contain small pickled creatures or parts of them.

I don't think I want to see what's in the fridge, Murel said.

"Now then, children, have a seat and I will bring out my album," Professor Mabo said. When she came back out, she was wearing a shawl over her ship suit and fuzzy slippers, as well as a pair of reading spectacles, an old-fashioned touch.

She sat down with the album in front of her and asked Murel and Ronan to pull up chairs on either side. Rory had to peer over her shoulder.

After showing them a number of creatures that were variations on lions, tigers, bears, and camels, she displayed a picture of two different sorts of lizard. "Now this is a Sorrysaurus," she told them of the first one. "Guess what this one is?"

"Dunno," Rory said.

"Me neither," Ronan said.

Murel shook her head.

"Just guess."

"Can't," they all three said.

"It's a Sorrysaurus too."

"They look really different."

"It's a chameleon of sorts," Professor Mabo said. "It not only changes colors, it actually changes shapes according to its environment."

"Weird," Rory said.

"Not at all," she said. "It's simply a natural adaptation, quite practical under the circumstances. The world on which the Sorrysaurus lives changes not only its climate, but the complete environment of its landmasses from one season to the next. The first picture, in which the creature is yellow-green, is a warm-season Sorrysaurus. The second picture, in which the creature is white and spiked, is the cold-season version. Not only does the creature survive the entire year, but also, only one creature of its sort inhabits the same territory year round, which limits predation to some degree."

"If you say so," Ronan said. "It sure looks different, though."

"Many creatures in the universe change their colors or shapes—for some it is a question of time. You are not the same shape you will be when you are a man, for instance, Ronan. Nor is Murel the same shape she will be when she is an adult woman. For others it is a question of season or environmental coloration. The Sorrysaurus is only one of the slightly more extreme versions. There are many others. I find them fascinating, don't you?"

"Oh yeah," Rory said.

Murel and Ronan both nodded cautiously. "How can they do that exactly?" Ronan asked.

"It is so simple it's a wonder more things don't change form more often," the professor said. "We are all of us made up of various particles. The important thing about this—whatever the theory, whatever the physicists call them—is that all of these particles, relative to their size, are very very far apart. They have great latitude of movement. If they are somehow manipulated, by whatever science or force, to move in certain ways, the nature of the object or being they compose will also alter. Human beings have known this for many years before they knew about science. Always, throughout history, even before it was written down, there are stories of men or beasts who are first one thing and then another. Once, this was thought to be superstition, but I have made a study of the way life forms are altered, particularly on these new, terraformed planets, and I have seen, as you see here with the Sorrysaurus, that such transformation is not only possible but actually occurs."

There was a knock on the door then. When Rory opened it, Pet Chan stood there.

"Dr. Mabo? The doctors Upfield say that Ronan and Murel are visiting you. It is time for them to return to their compound and go to bed."

"Very well. Run along now, children, but do come and visit me again."

"Thanks," Murel said. "Maybe Rory could come up and visit us tomorrow. Would you, Rory? We've got a new card game but it takes at least three."

Rory looked as if he was about to refuse. He was clearly miffed about the preference his grandma showed for his friends, but it wasn't as if Ronan and Murel had tried to *make* her like them. And it didn't really make a lot of sense that Murel could see either.

"Please, Rory," Ronan added. "Marmie has some great vids, and we'll ask Pet to make us some of her chocolate fudge bomb cookies."

"Right you are, mate," Rory said finally, with a brief version of his usual grin. "I'll ask the folks."

"I'm sure it will be fine, Rory," Professor Mabo said, waving good-bye as the twins hopped into the flitter.

That night before they went to sleep, the twins had a swim and played in seal form, as best they could in such a tame environment.

Did you feel any particles moving around when you changed? Murel asked her brother.

Maybe I do. Maybe hand particles turning into flipper ones or something, but I never really thought about it. It's good she knows about this stuff and that she's our teacher. And I'm glad she likes us because she's not very nice to her own family, and if she didn't like us, she could really make us miserable.

Yeah, but it might be better if she did that than make Rory miserable and think it was all our fault. I'd hate it if Mum or Da acted like they liked some other kid better than they did us.

Not that they've shown any signs that they really do like us recently, Ronan replied. *Can you even remember what they look like, when they're not on the com screen? It's kind of hard. Sort of like their particles keep shifting around in my head.*

He was joking, but it was one of those jokes that was too true to be funny. It was almost three years since they'd seen their parents in person, or been on Petaybee. He felt tears welling up and tried to choke them down.

But hey, who needs all that cold and stuff? Here we can make the weather any kind we want, we get to see all kinds of vids and meet all kinds of people. Important people are our teachers, not somebody we're not supposed to bother. And Marmie has new surprises for us all the time.

Yeah, that's right, Murel agreed. *It's great here. No wolves to worry about when we swim, or otter poachers even. Of course, there's no otters, or track cats, or snow leopards, or curly coats, or even sled dogs or house cats. And the weather isn't exactly real. And Marmie can't change into a seal. But hey, Da can do that, but he stopped doing it with us most of the time, so that doesn't matter, does it?*

No way. We're a lot better off here. Our parents were right. They were doing us a big fat favor sending us here.

Yeah, Murel agreed. *That is all so true. Which makes me feel like a real head case because, aw jays, Ronan, I really really miss them.*

Me too. I miss Petaybee. I miss the caves and the rivers and the otters and the other critters and Clodagh and latchkays, and I miss Mum and Da something terrible.

Me too. But they don't want us there right now. Maybe when we're better prepared for life and can handle ourselves better.

Yeah, like when we're twenty or something really old like that.

I want to go home now. I don't want to wait till I'm twenty.

Me too.

They didn't cry. Murel crawled into her bunk and Ronan into his. Without talking about it, each of them rolled toward the other and held out a hand. They linked fingers and finally fell asleep swapping mind pictures of their favorite things back home. It wasn't much of a swap, since they'd shared everything from the time they were born, but it was the best comfort they had.

CHAPTER 14

"ALL I CAN say is that I certainly hope the planet knows what it's doing," Yana said to the committee composed of herself, her husband, Dr. Whittaker Fiske—the originator of the terraforming process used on Petaybee—Clodagh, and Dr. Frank Metaxos. Sister Igneous Rock, a geologist and one of the cult of originally misguided religious fanatics who had come to Petaybee thinking to worship it—before the planet declined their worship—was also in attendance.

"Of course Petaybee knows what He or She or possibly They are doing," Sister Iggierock chided her. "We should praise Petaybee's name for its compassion for those among us who need a more temperate zone in which to live. A zone where one need not dress like a polar bear and live in darkness most of the year, as we do now. Your children and your children's children will be able to live in a place where they can enjoy greenery year round. The entire planet will have a source of nourishment from gardens and farms growing fresh fruits and vegetables—even a broader range of medicinal plants, Clodagh—than is now possible with our limited growing season."

"That would be beneficial, yes," Yana said, "*if* our children and their children were ever able to enjoy it."

"Oh well, perhaps I should have said descendants," Iggierock conceded. "These things do take time, even for a brilliant sentient world like Petaybee. It will be centuries—millennia, actually—before the new landmass extruding from the sea will be stable enough and cool enough for people to live on it."

Dr. Whittaker Fiske cleared his throat. "That is not exactly true in Petaybee's case, Sister," he corrected her. "The process that accelerates Petaybee's development also accelerates the maturation process. Once the volcanic mass surfaces, it will begin to stabilize. It will probably be ready for habitation within the next twenty years at the latest. Of course, with Petaybee it is always difficult to say. For a couple of generations, we've believed that the terraforming process was completed and that two large polar landmasses would be the extent of the planet's habitable area, and that was stretching the definition of habitable. However, from what I've learned of Petaybee, you are all being more accurate than whimsical to imply that the planet is choosing to present an island, at the very least, at this time. As all of you know, our usual instrumentation is impeded by the electromagnetic fields emanating from Petaybee, from the sunspots currently mucking up our communications equipment, and from the extremes of temperature it is subjected to on this planet. Although we know that at least one volcanic mass is arising from the sea near the equator, we have little idea of its ultimate extent or what we may expect in the way of seismic activity."

"That's why I'm going to explore underwater," Sean said. "It's easier for me than for divers, and besides, all that equipment would need to be imported, as well as the personnel. We haven't trained a lot of human divers here for obvious reasons. And if you all could see the stacks and lists of individuals and groups and whole displaced populations applying for immigration to Petaybee, you'd understand why we wish to know the potential of the new landmass ourselves before letting outsiders have a look at it."

He began his journey the next morning, leaving poor Yana with the paperwork and such electronic communiqués as were able to reach them these days. They didn't mind so much being cut off from the more sophisticated offworld amenities such as direct audiovisual contact between callers from space to ground or from planet to planet, but they sorely missed being able to talk to the kids. When sending the twins to Marmie's space station, they had not anticipated being unable to have face-to-face, voice-to-voice contact with their children on a weekly if not daily basis, no matter the cost. Marmie had generously agreed to foot most of the bill. Secondhand messages and written notes were simply not the same. Yana was not the type to pine over anything, but she missed the children so badly that her appetite was off, despite all of Clodagh's remedies.

Sean felt as if part of himself was missing, floating off somewhere inaccessible. His thoughts did not all want to stay in his head—they kept wandering off in search of the twins' thoughts, but those were no longer there. No smooth rounded baby arms to hug him, or flippers either for that matter. But with them wanting to swim freely so much that they ran into constant danger, he and Yana simply couldn't risk having them near. They were too precious, too important. He would have to free the planet of all of those outside dangers like the one the otters had faced. He'd have to look into this new development at sea and figure out what to do with those who wanted to exploit it. Best keep the kids clear of that one too. But he missed them.

Well, the sooner started, the sooner finished. He dove into the running river, free of ice but still chilling and powder-gray with glacial runoff.

Of course, he could have easily ridden a curly coat to the coast, but actually, in seal form, he swam faster than a curly coat could navigate the spongy tundra or the swampy banks where the channels branched and re-braided themselves before reaching the sea. Besides, this mission was a confidential one, and the fewer people—even their people—involved, the better.

When he paused for air, he enjoyed the wild lupine and fireweed turning the riverbanks purple and magenta against the background of a thousand greens. The river teemed with fish, so he could have gorged himself if he'd wanted to, but he preferred to take only what he needed to maintain his energy and not get loggy trying to digest too much food.

When he first pulled out of the water to sleep he was grateful for the suit Marmie provided for him. He had small caches of clothing along the riverbank, but this way he could stop where he needed to without worrying about that. Once he was dressed in the suit, he located his clothing downstream from it and wore that until he was ready to dive back into the water. He wanted to look as normal as possible to any people he might meet, and a shiny silver suit didn't help him blend.

On the second day, he pulled himself out of the water and onto land that was part riverbank and part seashore. A small island lay offshore, perhaps two hundred meters away, but otherwise the horizon was coral-red with the setting sun, the water beneath the color of salmon meat.

Tonight he would rest well, because tomorrow's swim would take him too far from shore to sleep.

He found a dry sandy place and curled up to sleep, but as he began nodding off he heard, *Hah! Father River Seal, why are you here? Have you come to tell otters that your children are coming home?*

He opened his eyes and looked into a round brown furry face with bright black eyes and breath that smelled, pleasantly to Sean, like fish.

What is a river otter doing so close to the sea? he asked the otter.

My question first! I asked first! Are the river seal children coming home? Is that why you're here—oh, no, I suppose not since you did not expect to see otters here. You could not be bringing otters a message if you did not know otters would be here to receive it. So why are you here? Not that you are not very welcome. We have told our sea otter cousins all about our brave river seal friends who are the protectors of otters, and they will welcome you also. But why?

I'm exploring, Sean told the otter.

Otters.

At least a dozen more otters had joined the kids' friend, boldly standing right next to his prone body. Another half-dozen pairs of bright eyes focused on him from the water.

He doesn't look so big now, the river seal man, one said.

No, but he is very fierce. You saw him carry away the

humans with cages, he and his family. He must like otters very much to have followed us all the way here.

Are you hungry, seal man?

Do you want to play, seal man? There is a nice mud slide just over there.

Their voices chittered and chattered in his head so busily he had trouble focusing.

I came exploring, he said to the colony at large. *I want to bring my children home but I have to make sure conditions here won't bring more dangerous people to harm them and, er, otters too.*

He barely had the thought out, however, before they had plucked an image from his mind. One forgot to guard against that sort of thing when surrounded by otters.

You're going to the New Home! He's going to the New Home! Where the sea otter cousins go. It's very far and rather deep for a river seal.

I should think it would be out of bounds for river otters, Sean replied.

Hah! It is much too far through that salty liquid for river otters. We are not going there. We are staying right here.

Sean had been so absorbed in river otter thoughts that he hadn't noted the arrival from the darkened sea of the other species of otters—the cousins of whom Otter was so proud.

Sea otters go check out the construction of the New Home, one of these said. To the river otters he said, *This looks like a man. You are sure it is the father of river seals from your song?*

"Hah!" Otter said. *Of course we are sure. Father*

River Seal and his family are close personal friends and protectors of river otters.

So you sing, the sea otter said. *Does he come to visit you often? Does he need to be fed?*

I am not hungry, thank you, Sea Otter, Sean said. *I did not know river otters were here, or sea otters either, but I'm pleased to see all of you. I came to see the New Home. My people want to know what our world is doing out there in the ocean.*

It is very interesting and rather tasty, the sea otter told him. *We will take you there. It is also a bit dangerous, so we can show you where to go and where not to go. But first we all sleep.*

The river otters chittered among themselves so quickly Sean couldn't read their thoughts. The otter said, *You have no den. We could enlarge one for you. You will be cold out here although it is summer.*

We could offer you our kelp beds to wrap your seal-self in and keep you afloat, as we do when we sleep, the sea otters, not to be outdone in hospitality, quickly counteroffered.

I'll be grand right here, Sean told them all.

Well, if you're sure, the sea otters said, sliding back into the water, their thoughts washing away on the tide.

Good night then, Father River Seal, the river otters said as those on the edge of the group disappeared into the riverbanks.

Sean lay down again murmuring, *Good night* to the river otters.

Hah! Otter said. *This is not right. Father River Seal will be cold and lonely without his family. Otters will keep you warm.* And with that Otter snuggled in next to the back of Sean's neck and at once fell asleep. Others, close family members including six of Otter's brothers and sisters, his mother and grandmother, four aunts and two uncles, also snuggled next to Sean. He lay warmly immobilized in a living furry blanket for the rest of the night. He fell asleep hoping he would not need to get up and relieve himself and disturb his hosts or squash one of them.

THE NEXT MORNING before school, the twins made it snow. Marmie had showed them how to do it, but most of the time they left it up to her. Now, however, Murel typed with one hand while holding her breakfast bar in the other. "How heavy do we want the snow?" she asked.

"Real heavy. Not a blizzard, but so it stacks up. And wind. Let's have some wind so we can have drifts."

"What velocity?"

"Doesn't have to be a gale to blow snow," he said, and scooped a spoonful of cereal from his bowl.

"I wish we could put some river ice on the waterway," Murel said.

"Yeah, but it's heated all the time. We could make a rink on one of the flitter pads, though. You can adjust ground temperature by pressing Control GT."

"Cool."

"Yeah, it will be. We won't even need skates. We can just skate in our shoes. We'll have to shovel the snow first."

"Good. I want to."

That was all they had time to do before school, but by the time the flitter picked them up, the sky was white with snow and the flakes fell like broken crystals. You could tell they weren't real flakes, though. They were all the same.

Their class with Professor Mabo was in a lab that had been set up near the school complex for her use. It was small but there were tables with stools and a desk, besides all of the standard lab equipment for biology, chemistry, and general science courses.

Professor Mabo looked up from the desk. She was wearing a lab coat over her silver ship suit. Her teeth flashed pleasantly as she greeted the students, and her large silver hoop earrings matched the ship suit.

Three boxes sat in front of her, two of them open and full of shiny objects, one closed.

"As you come in, please select an item from each box. Box A contains scalpels. The blades are attached but sheathed. Please do not cut yourself, as taking time to clean up your blood will deprive the other students of lab time and possibly contaminate your specimens. Box B contains hemostats. Box C contains your specimens. You may use the synskin gloves beside the box to extract your specimen and conduct your dissection. You will work in pairs, one specimen to each pair of students."

Ronan, Rory, and Murel were the first students to enter, and each of them did as directed. Then Ronan lifted the cover from the large specimen box and his eyes widened.

"Nothing to be afraid of, boy. They're quite dead. They won't bite," the professor said.

Dead frogs, Ronan told his sister. *She wants us to cut up dead frogs.*

Murel came to his side and peered into the box. "Professor, how did the frogs die?" she asked.

"Of old age," the teacher snapped. "While waiting for squeamish students to do as they're told."

"Oh, sorry, I just wondered," Murel said. "It's just that on Petaybee, animals come to specific places when they're sick or old so that they can be killed kindly and their bodies used for food or clothing or whatever the hunter needs."

Rory flinched, and Murel realized he was waiting for his grandmother's wrath to come down on his friends the way it usually did on him.

The professor's face contorted for a moment, as if she were about to turn into something else, but the contortions ended in a wise smile. "Fascinating, my dear. Thank you for that enlightening explanation. In fact, it ties in nicely with our lesson today. How indeed did these frogs die? How would we learn that sort of thing? By examining their remains. That is how, and that is what we will be doing today. So, as I said, each of you take your instruments and your frogs and find a place at the table so we may begin."

Murel and Ronan chose spots adjacent to each other, but once everyone had a place, Professor Mabo said, "Murel, please trade places with Chesney. Neither she nor Ke-ola obtained a frog, and both you and Ronan have one."

Murel nodded and did as she was told.

She just wants to split us up, Ronan said. *We could have always given Chesney and Ke-ola one of our frogs.*

Of course, the professor had no way of knowing that the two of them could communicate telepathically. Nobody knew that except maybe Marmie, and if she knew, it was only from observation. They had learned early on that their private line into each other's minds was a bigger advantage when nobody around them realized they had it.

Who was she trying to kid? Ronan asked about half-way through the session. *This frog was perfectly healthy until someone killed it.*

She probably didn't think we'd know how to tell, Murel said. *She thought we were just squeamish. She doesn't know about us helping Da do this kind of thing in the lab.*

Professor Mabo had been circling the classroom and stopped to stand behind Ronan. "Very good work, Ronan. Very precise. I believe your technique is almost as good as mine."

Ronan ducked his head, as if he were bashful. *She has no idea what Auntie Sinead would have said if we'd spoilt the meat or hide on one of her kill after she showed us how to clean and skin it,* he told Murel.

No, or how Clodagh has always taught us that we're supposed to use every possible piece of the animal as wisely as possible out of respect for the gift of its body for our benefit.

"Murel, what is taking you so long?" Professor Mabo said. "Give Chesney a turn, or however that frog died, it will have been for nothing." She had circled behind Murel while Murel was exchanging thoughts with Ronan. Murel jumped, and the knife slipped, slicing her finger, so that blood dripped onto the table, the frog, and the other instruments.

"Ouch!" Murel said, and dropped the scalpel to hold her finger with her other hand.

"You are supposed to dissect the frog, Murel, not your hand," Professor Mabo scolded. Chesney produced a grubby tissue, but it quickly turned bright red and the blood kept dripping. "I think you had best seek medical attention. You may finish your dissection tomorrow."

The professor didn't seem to notice that Ronan had dropped his scalpel and started to hold his hand, then quickly picked up the scalpel again and tried not to look pained as his twin hurried off to the station's infirmary. *He* noticed, however, that the professor, after handing Murel a fresh tissue, pocketed the bloody one before she handed Chesney a towel with which to mop up his sister's blood.

Murel was home when Ronan got there. She hadn't needed stitches but she sported a big plaskin on her index finger, and it leaked once in a while if she put too much pressure on it.

THAT EVENING, PET made some of her cookies and Ronan fixed Murel a cup of the orange spiced tea Clodagh brewed for special occasions. They sat at the window watching it snow until bedtime.

Professor Mabo doesn't seem to like me anymore, Murel said. *Did you see how she snuck up on me? That's why I cut my finger.*

Yeah, well, having her like me doesn't feel like any great honor either, Ronan said. *There's something really strange about her. I wonder why she stuck your bloody tissue in her pocket. There was a trash chute right next to the table.*

Do you think she was collecting a specimen?

Possibly. I'm not sure what she could tell by it, though. Maybe we should ask Pet how to send a secure message to Da. He'll know if there's anything in our blood that would tell her how different we are.

CHAPTER 15

WHEN MARMIE RETURNED, though she said nothing about the deep winter into which the twins had plunged her home, the weather changed. When they returned from school, they found Marmie taking a swim in tropical conditions, sunny, warm, and balmy, with a slight breeze scented with exotic flowers.

When it was time for student evaluations, toward the end of the term, Professor Mabo requested a personal interview with Marmie.

"I feel that Ronan and Murel have a great deal of potential," she said. "They are extraordinarily quick and bright. But perhaps they impede each other's intellectual growth. I think if they were in separate classes, they might do better."

"They have an A-plus average," Marmie pointed out. "I scarcely see how they can improve on it."

"For their age group, of course they get high marks. But they are each capable of functioning far beyond their age group."

"Well, be that as it may, splitting them up is not an option," Marmie told her firmly. "For one thing, it would break their hearts, and they have already been through a great deal, being separated from their parents and their home. For another thing, it can hardly have escaped your notice that ours is a small educational facility with only one class for each age group."

"Yes, yes, I know all that," Professor Mabo said, barely managing to keep the impatience out of her voice. "But I have a suggestion. I think Ronan would benefit by doing an extra lab class with me, as my assistant. I have been trying to teach my grandson to do it but he is not an apt student. Initially the twins disliked the dissections, but now they seem to tolerate them well. I believe that with additional exposure, Ronan may turn into a fine little scientist."

"He's only ten years old, Dr. Mabo," Marmie said.

"Immaterial."

Ronan and Murel had been listening, with the collusion of Pet Chan, on the intercom, and now Marmion said into it, "Pet, would you have the twins join us in the observatory tearoom please?"

The professor was dressed in an elegant long scarlet robe over her ship suit. She seemed to be trying to appear relaxed, but the twins weren't fooled.

"The professor seems to feel you two should study independently of each other for a while and has offered you, Ronan, the opportunity to be her lab assistant. What do you think?"

Careful, Murel said.

I know. I don't trust her any more than you do, but we've got to start learning more about this stuff, Murel, if we're ever going to be able to control our own shapes. Da could—

We're not with Da, are we? He's too busy to help us figure this out, and besides, if he knew how, he probably

would do a better job of it for himself. Remember their
story about how he got shot when he was half changed?

Their message to their father for advice about the blood
sample so far had gone unanswered. Pet's advice about
making the message they sent their father secure was not
reassuring. "There's all kinds of ways to secure information, and there's also all kinds of ways for data thieves to
hijack it. The safest way to do this, if it's really important, is to set up a code with the recipient—a personal
code, that is—and encrypt your message using that.
Even so, data pirates have strange minds that seem to
read yours and they've been hijacking passwords and
codes for centuries. Really, the very safest thing is to
hand-deliver the message by a courier both you and the
recipient know and trust. If it was really imperative that
the message not fall into enemy hands or be hijacked,
that's what I'd do. Of course, I have been accused of
being overly paranoid, but this is the same advice I give
to Madame and the procedures we follow in extreme
circumstances. Of course, you understand that my du-
ties include only her personal communications. Corporate and station security are the responsibility of other
personnel."

Since they had set up no code in advance, they wrote
out the message. When Johnny stopped by prior to his
supply run to Petaybee, Murel tucked it into his hand.
"It's top secret, Johnny, but really urgent. Ask Da to give
you the answer before you leave."

"I'll do my best to corner him, Murel."

"*Really* important," she stressed.

Johnny had several other stops to make, however, and
hadn't returned as yet, nor had Da answered in any
other way.

I'm going to do it, Murel, Ronan said. *She's snoopy and cranky, but she is still an expert in what we need to know about. Maybe we'll even get to be friends and I can ask her directly sometime.*

Don't! Murel warned.

I'll talk to you before I do, don't worry, he promised. Aloud, he said, "I think I'd like to be your lab assistant, Professor, but except for that, Murel and I don't like being split up. Can we stay together in class if I work for you alone afterward?"

"I suppose so," she said. "But in my professional opinion—for your own good, mind you—you two need to work on developing some independence of thought and opinion. I realize the bond between twins is supposed to be quite close, but too much interdependence is unhealthy, particularly when they are of different genders, as you two are. You are entering puberty now, after all."

Marmie frowned but said only, "Very well. Ronan, I'll place a flitter at your disposal for you to return here after you finish working with Dr. Mabo each day."

"That won't be necessary," the professor told her. "You have kindly placed a flitter at my disposal as well. The least I can do is to give Ronan a ride." She turned and regarded him with clinical interest that made Murel shudder.

I bet she asks you to climb up on a slide and scoot under a giant microscope lens right away, Murel said.

She's not going to try anything when Marmie knows right where I am. Besides, station security wouldn't let her do anything to me.

I still have a really bad feeling about this, Ronan.

*   *   *

SEAN SWAM WITH the sea otters, one large gray seal among their smaller forms, gliding through the water with ease for many kilometers.

He had no trouble telling when they began swimming across the volcanic ridge since a very warm column of water bubbled to the surface. Anticipation bubbled through the otters at the same time, and suddenly they all dived at once. Sean followed.

Look at them! the senior otter exclaimed, his thought filled with blissful anticipation. *Such clams! Petaybee must really love otters to give them this food.*

Although the seal in Sean could certainly have eaten something, the clams were not so interesting by themselves as they were as part of the underseascape.

They had to dive quite deeply, but Sean was somewhat surprised to find it was not as deep as he would have thought. Normally, seals and otters would not be able to dive to the most extreme depths of the ocean, but it was comparatively shallow here. The volcanic activity had built up the ocean floor, forming a sort of mountain range that would build the farther south it went. Sean had observed this from a distance on other swims, but he hadn't realized the planet was in such a hurry to produce its new landmass.

The water around them was milky blue, the color, as Sean knew, coming from the minerals and bacteria in which volcanic areas were rich.

Tall black rocky chimneys rose up from the ocean floor, which was paved with flowing billows and pillows of black lava rock. Each crevice and crack of the lava was stuffed with the foot-long clams. White crabs scuttled along over the blackness, going about their business. Like little gardens of animals, each of these communities had as its centerpiece huge clusters of exceptionally long tube worms, bursting like enormous red flowers among the other creatures.

Surfacing for air again, Sean told himself he had to return with a scientific team sometime and see what was down there. He was certain there were all manner of life forms that Intergal, the company that had ordered the planet terraformed, had no idea were there. He just wanted a quick look in seal form. All around him sea otters surfaced carrying large clams, though not the largest.

Are they good? he asked the nearest otter conversationally.

Delectable. Bright red meat and lots of it. But opening them is tricky. They're not of a size you can crack open on your chest without cracking otters as well as clams.

When we get back, I'll change into man form and get a heavy rock to open them for you, he promised.

You will? The sea otter's round eyes got, if anything, rounder in his round face. *Did you otters hear that? Go for the big ones! The river seal will help us open them and there will be feasting for us all!*

The surface thrashed with otter bodies diving down and popping up with clams bigger than their heads. Each otter could carry only one clam. Soon, Sean knew, they'd be ready to return. *I'll just swim ahead a little and circle back and catch up with you,* he told them. *I want to see the New Home where it is building the quickest.*

There's not as much food there, an otter told him. *Too hot, too busy. Hey! No fair slipping out of otter paws! Come back you!* And his sleek rump surfaced for a moment before it smoothly vanished under the waves. For the first time Sean noticed that off in the distance what had seemed to be low cloud cover was actually rolling smoke. Petaybee surely was cooking with gas now.

He swam swiftly forward. The bubbly warm spots grew more frequent, until the entire ocean seemed to be warmer by many degrees. He caught fish simply because he had to swim through so many of them to proceed and it was easier to catch some than to go around them.

The water grew warmer and warmer, like bathwater and not unpleasant. The seawater cooled the molten lava almost at once, though that would not be the case once the volcano grew until it erupted on the surface. He wondered how close that was. He'd been feeling a bit foolish for deciding to reconnoiter by swimming over the site, but with the smoke and ash piling up on the horizon, aircraft would be in danger of getting their motors and other sensitive parts clogged.

Soon he realized that he'd left the otters far behind. He could see the bottom of the ocean beneath him now simply by looking down. The piping black smokers and the gentle lava pillows stuffed with clams and other sealife had long ago given way to some true volcanic mounds with vents in the middle. Diving down, he could see a long way into them, into the heart of Petaybee.

He got so busy looking down and diving to swim around the vents and examine the life forms there that he forgot to look up and ahead until the entire ocean shook like jelly, sloshing him about. He was startled to see that a real mountain loomed ahead of him, the summit just below the ocean's surface.

It was brilliant! What a wonderful opportunity. He wondered why he had seen no larger animal life so far, whales or dolphins. They would all love the fish and other animal and plant life as much as the otters. But he did not hear them or sense them. Perhaps the change in the depth and temperature of the water had caused them to shy away. The mineral content was much different around the vents too, some of it toxic. He trusted his seal nose to keep him away from the dangerous parts. The otters, with their curiosity, seemed to be the only mammals venturing close enough to be harmed. But they had been very clever about diving, snatching up what they wanted, and surfacing again.

The sight of the billowing smoke sobered him. It had been foolish to come out here as a seal, he thought. Better to come with machinery and instruments. Petaybee giving birth was not likely to be tolerant. For that matter, Yana, who loved him, hadn't been in the best of moods while in labor. One more dive and then he'd call it quits and follow the otters back to shore.

His dive took him to the base of the underwater mountain. Quake after quake, at first small and then larger, shook the water and sent rocks tumbling down from above.

The water was murky here from all of the sediment. Circling the mountain's base, he tried to gain some idea of its size and shape. Then, in a deep rift below the mountain's base, he spotted something curiously angular and shining, despite the sediment and rock. He surfaced, caught his breath, and dived again. It could hardly be a shipwreck since Petaybee had never had large ships on her waters. The ports were all icebound too much of the year to make it feasible. It could have been a space vessel or even the wreck of a station, but there had been no report he could recall of such a crash. And it would have been noticed. The impression he had was of something as vast as a city.

He forced himself to dive deeper than he had done so far on this journey. The area in question was indeed filled with what seemed to be manufactured structures—angular, architectural, though indistinct because of the opacity of the water. Lying in the rift as it was, it could even be the ruins of some ancient Petaybean civilization, from the look of it.

But before Intergal had terraformed the planet, it had been little more than a ball of ice and rock, and for all anyone could tell, had never been inhabited by sentient life prior to its colonization.

Of course, as his people knew, the planet was itself a sentient being, but still, it didn't build cities, or at least had never been known to do so.

But maybe eons ago there had been other life here and they built this city and perhaps others, still buried under the sediment on the ocean's floor. Although the mountain above him rumbled and shook and showered more rocks and debris so they shot into the water like deadly missiles, Sean dived a little deeper.

Yes, it could be a ruin, although everything looked remarkably intact and—there seemed to be lights. Perhaps it was just molten lava glowing up from beneath, in which case this ruin would be ruined once more in very short order. But it didn't have the red glow of lava, or the green or blue iridescence Petaybee often displayed. No, this light was brighter, whiter, less natural-looking.

He could go no farther without another breath. He shot for the surface, thinking of the lights and what appeared to be buildings where none should be. Though his mind was occupied, his eyes saw the boulder crashing toward him from the murk, and his seal reflexes responded. Those reflexes were fast, and sent him into a dive, but they were not fast enough to evade the impact. A single boulder avalanche smashed into his body, and the pain of it was the last thing he knew.

CHAPTER 16

HOW'S IT GOING? Murel asked from class, as Ronan pushed a broom around the laboratory.

So far all I'm doing is housework, he told her. *She won't even let me ask any questions. I think we were worried about nothing. She's like every other scientist we've ever met, so wrapped up in what she's doing when she's working that she doesn't even think about other people.*

Yeah, that sounds familiar. She loaded us down with homework too. But so did the others.

After a while Murel stopped checking in with him, which gave Ronan a lonely feeling. Professor Mabo kept him for a couple of hours every afternoon after classes mostly picking up after her and tidying the lab.

DURING THE FIRST week Ronan worked for Professor Mabo, Murel had the feeling she'd forgotten or had lost something. She wasn't used to being alone, even in her own thoughts, and it felt weird.

She went back to Marmie's alone the first couple of afternoons, but it was just too lonesome with nothing to do but try to get Ro to tell her what *he* was doing. She knew how lame that was. Other kids could spend five minutes without their brothers around. What did *they* do?

She made the mistake of whining about it to Pet Chan, who said, "For pity's sake, Murel! Here you are on a space station with a computer that holds the knowledge of the universe in its data-banks, holo decks to play on where you could be anything and do anything, and you're *bored* because your brother has to work after school? Give me a break!"

She made a mental note that security personnel, even those who made great cookies, were disinclined to be sympathetic about catastrophes that didn't actually involve explosions, break-ins, beatings, or murders. But she had one more whine coming. "Yes, but I don't know how to use half this stuff. Remember us, the hick kids from the low-tech world? How do you turn on a holo deck anyway?"

She thought she had shamed Pet into feeling sorry for her. Maybe the security woman, who did after all sometimes make those great cookies, would see how mean she was being to a poor twinless girl and would put aside what she was doing and take her down and make up some story to play with her on the holo deck. People did that, Murel knew. She just didn't know how they did it exactly.

Pet did turn aside from the security cameras, and for a moment Murel thought she was going to get her way, but then Pet said in a tone worthy of Nanook or Coaxtl, "Not my problem, child. I understand there's a whiz kid student aide on call, so call, already, and let me get my work done."

Murel scrubbed tears from her eyes as she climbed into the flitter that took her to the holo deck. She'd do that. She'd show Pet and Ro and all the rest of them. She'd make up some holo where they were all getting chased down by polar bears and if they screamed loudly, she might decide to rescue them. Maybe. Maybe not. She was pretty sure the bear would probably eat Dr. Mabo before she could be rescued. Of course, that wasn't a very good thing to do to the bear. Probably break its teeth on the stringy old bat.

She flounced in, not paying much attention. Most of the time the holo lab was a big blue grid, but now there was a sandy beach and huge blue waves breaking off it. Ke-ola sat on the beach playing some kind of a little guitar while people danced a swaying dance with a lot of hand motions and sang beautiful songs and ate roast pig. Everybody had flowers around their necks. It looked like a lot of fun, but Ke-ola was sitting apart from everybody else, his fingers barely touching the instrument, staring out to sea. He wasn't in a good mood either, for the first time since she'd met him. Maybe it was something in the ventilation system that day. Big tears were rolling down his broad brown cheeks.

"Hey, Ke-ola, can I come to your party?" she asked.

"Better you go away, little sistah," he said. "This luau is just for us ghosts."

"Ghosts? You're not a ghost." He really *was* in a bad mood.

"Oh yes, I am," he said. He clapped his hands, and now they were standing on a dirty street between two tall buildings. The sea was still out there but it rolled in a sluggish way and it was a muddy brown color. Where they had been before, with all the happy people, was an island clearly visible from where they stood now.

"You know what happened there, to that place? That second place where we lived?"

"You said there was something there the company wanted so they made you move," she said.

"No. This," he said. And suddenly a blinding light flashed. When she could see again, the island was bare of people and palms, and the sea and sand were slimy with bits of dead fish and seaweed. "What our new home had that they wanted so much we had to go? It was far from other places. So they set off bombs there to see how much damage they did. Better to blow it up than to let us live there."

"That freezes," she said.

"We have this kinda luau now," he told her, and flipped a couple of buttons on the little guitar, which was actually the remote for the holo suite. It changed into a pokey little room with no color, no sea, no sand, and a bunch of ragged, discouraged-looking people tending some anemic plants.

He switched it off and they sat in the blue-gridded room she remembered.

"I'm sorry, Ke-ola. But that's all past, isn't it?"

"Is it? That's no place for us. Only place good for us is too good for us, the company says. Madame brought me here, but so what? Where my family lives now, they're gonna die. They live in little boxes and little fake ecobubbles. We are people of the sea bubbles, not ecobubbles. I miss my family, Murel. I love them. But I got no place with them. One more mouth, one more breather, one more kid to hear the ghost stories about what all of us used to be."

He never sobbed, but the tears kept rolling until they didn't. Murel patted him on the shoulder, feeling helpless. His questions didn't have any good answers that she could think of. The funny thing was, he was mourning a place he'd never been as much as he he mourned the family that was too big to hold him now. She felt that way about being away from Petaybee sometimes, except she knew she and Ro would be going back sometime soon. Wouldn't they?

WORKING WITH DR. Mabo was frustrating. Ronan thought that once she got used to him, she'd be ready to teach him the things she hinted that only she knew. But usually, even after several weeks of working together, when he tried to ask her a question, she'd grunt impatiently and wave him aside.

Boredom was what finally forced him to confront her. He couldn't take much more beaker washing, computer dusting, or floor sweeping. "Professor Mabo?"

"Um?"

"I have a really important question to ask you. It's the reason I wanted to work with you, so I'd appreciate it if you'd be kind enough to give me your attention for a few moments."

"I'm very busy, Ronan. Can this not wait?"

"It cannot, Professor. Well, I mean, I suppose it could, but you are always very busy, Professor, and if I'm to give up my free time to help you, the answer to this question is what I would like in return."

She sighed and pushed back from the worktable. "Go on," she said, with a grimace that he thought was supposed to pass for a smile.

"It's about your research, Professor. I—well, Murel and I both—are really interested in shape-shifters. We have some species on Petaybee that shift shapes, and we were wondering—do they ever get to control when they turn from one thing to another or is it strictly environmental or what?"

"Gracious, boy, I don't know how to answer that. For one thing, it surely varies from species to species. But as far as I know now, the change is always triggered by something environmental. A full moon is a classic example, although how susceptible species who live on planets that have more than one moon respond to that is not something we've had much chance to study. Tidal or seasonal differences are another influence. But I have not been able to document much of this material—a lot of what has been written about shape-shifters is more folklore or myth than science. Probably, back on Old Terra, the stories were exaggerated or untrue. Sometimes they were about an illness that afflicted certain people. The only creatures it's ever been said that totally control their own shape-shifting are vampires. Which is, of course, a totally silly and romantic notion that is a combination of a misunderstanding of the nature of certain flying mammals and a high incidence of live burials during epidemics way back in the ancient history of European Terra. None of these things have conscious control, Ronan. None of them are capable of such complex thought."

"But how about the ones that change from human to something else—some animal maybe?"

"Human to animal? Like a werewolf? Oh, child, these things don't occur with humans. We are far too complex in our physiology and too complicated in our mental and emotional makeup to translate easily into some other beast of lesser intelligence. Why, if a human were to transform into a beast, most likely the person would stay the beast because it would not know what to do to change back again, unless by accident. I thought your question was a serious one, Ronan." She waved him away with an air of dismissal. "Now, finish your sweeping while I finish this entry, and I will call the flitter so I can take you home."

Ronan was only too happy to oblige, and that night he confided in Murel that at least they didn't have to worry about the professor suspecting their own shape-shifting abilities since she didn't believe it ever happened to humans.

"She was really scornful about it," he said.

"It could be just an act," Murel said.

"Well, if it is, she did a good one," he answered. "She thinks it only happens to what she calls lesser beasts. She's not so bad, really. I know she doesn't seem to like *you* anymore, but she was decent to me. It was boring, but when I came right out and asked her, she gave me a straight answer right away."

"Don't trust her," Murel said. "You're not as good at figuring people out as you think."

"Well, neither are you. You always think you're cleverer than I am, and you're just jealous because I got picked instead of you."

"I'm not either. I certainly don't want to spend all of my free time slaving away for a teacher I don't even *like*. And you do realize, don't you, that she had promised before she came that Rory could be her assistant, then gave the job to you?"

"Not my fault. Rory isn't that keen on the subject anyway, and I am."

"Yeah, now that she's chosen you as her favorite."

"Look, let's not fight about this, okay? I'm finding out

stuff we need to find out, and that's the only reason I'm doing it. It's for both of us, and Da too. I wish we'd hear from him soon."

"Me too. Marmie said Johnny had been delayed on Petaybee but he's due back in a couple of days. He ought to be bringing us an answer then."

PROFESSOR MABO WAS unusually nice to everyone in class the next day, and when she met Ronan in the lab, she wore a rueful smile. "My boy, I realize I was unfair to you yesterday. You had every right to ask the very intelligent questions you asked, and I—what is the expression?—blew you off. One of the reasons I chose you as my assistant is that I noticed you displayed an interest in these mutant shape-shifting or bimorphic life forms. I had a headache yesterday and was in pain, and therefore in an unreceptive mood."

Ronan wondered if she had a headache every day then, since she hadn't seemed any more grumpy yesterday than every time he'd seen her since she arrived. Even if she was nice to him, she was always cutting to someone—usually Rory, although lately she'd been picking on Murel too.

"As a matter of fact, your questions anticipated our experiments for today. I was vague on the subject of the shape-shifters, or bimorphs as we call them. Today we will be working with one."

"Live?" he asked.

"Certainly. I could not very well expect it to alter its shape if it is already dead."

Ronan perked up. "What is it, then?"

"A Honokuan sea turtle is its common name. Or one of them."

"What other names does it have?" Ronan asked. Did she mean scientific names or something like Seymour the Sea Turtle? He was afraid to ask. Although Dr. Mabo seemed to be in what, for her, passed for a talkative and friendly mood, she definitely believed there was such a thing as a stupid question.

However, she continued explaining. "That is what we shall discover today," she said. "I have it on good authority that this creature is able to alter its shape into quite another species altogether. Once we properly stimulate it to perform its metamorphosis, then we will know what other names would best describe it."

"Like what?"

"For instance, if we discover that the turtle turns itself into one species of—oh, bear, for instance, we would naturally name it 'chelonia mydas trans ursidae Mabo,' to indicate me as the first to identify it."

Ronan thought about that for a moment. That would make him and Murel what? Pinnipedia; Phocidae Sheperdus trans homo sapiens Shongili? Since Da was a scientist too and the first selkie on Petaybee, so the first to "discover" their species. Whatever. Just so they never had to be named after Dr. Mabo. "What if it just stays a turtle?" he asked before he could stop himself.

She snorted a snort that clearly accused him of lacking the proper attitude.

"Well, where is it?" he asked.

She pointed to a long metal tank he had mistaken for a covered sink before. He wondered why the tank wasn't glass if she wanted to observe the creature. "Please fetch the turtle for me. You will have to open the front of the tank by sliding the panel upward and encouraging the creature to emerge. Careful, it is rather large and heavy, although it is relatively young. A fully mature adult may weigh as much as 115 kilograms, or 253 pounds, but this one only weighs roughly eleven kilograms, or about twenty-five pounds. A sturdy lad like you should have no problem managing that much. Still, it has a nasty beak. If it bites you, nothing will make it let go short of death."

Ronan wanted to ask if she meant the death of the turtle or his own death but figured he shouldn't push his luck. Instead he said, "I thought they just pulled back into their shells when they're scared. I never heard of attack turtles before."

"These turtles do not have the ability to retreat into their shells," she told him.

"So they turn into something else?" he asked.

"Apparently so. I have witnessed the phenomenon briefly, but it was all rather a blur and unfortunately my photographic equipment was not yet unpacked at the time."

"Before I open the tank, I'd like to know what it changes into," Ronan said, hanging back. "If it's really a bear or maybe a crocodile or something, I don't think I want to see it very much."

"Of course it's not a crocodile, you silly boy. I would not have a crocodile on a space station. And I postulated an ursine transformation only as an example. If it were to change into anything aggressive, it probably would have done so previously. It is a vegetarian and not dangerous, except, as I said, for the beak. Mostly it is like others of its kind, torpid and lazy. The tank is kept at fifty-five degrees Fahrenheit, so the cold-blooded creature is quite lethargic now."

"Okay then," he said, and lifted the panel by the handle at its top. From inside he heard a slight scrabbling, then, inside his head, a plea. *Help me.*

It's okay, he told the creature. *I'm a friend.*

You understand! Oh, joy! I thought I would never again know communication. Are you a Honu also?

No, I'm a human. Mostly.

Mostly?

I change shapes. The professor says you do too.

So you are also a captive?

No, I'm her assistant. She doesn't know about me and my sister. At least, I don't think she does. Anyway, she told me she wants you alive. She just wants to see you change.

Oh, yes, I'm aware of that. Please don't let her torture me. I may have a hard shell but I'm not very good at withstanding pain.

I don't think she wants to hurt you.

"Is it coming out, Ronan?" the professor asked.

Are you coming out?

You will protect me?

Yes. I will. And my sister will too. And Marmie. You'll be safe. All you have to do is change and she'll probably want you to go right back into the tank.

You speak as if it were a small matter for me to transform before her, and yet you say she does not know that you also transform. So, if I understand you correctly, you are wishing me to do something you yourself are afraid to do?

I'm not afraid. It's just that our changing is a secret, not just ours. It belongs to the place where we live.

You do not live here?

Well, yeah, we do right now, but—Never mind. Are you coming? You won't bite me, will you?

Only if you provoke me.

The turtle crawled very slowly from the sand-strewn floor of the tank, struggling out onto the metal table on which the container rested. *Uh-oh! Owww, oooh, my aching flippers! Oh, my shell and scales, I think I've broken something. Oh, mercy! I'm sorry, boy, but I can go no farther.* Far more quickly than it had emerged, the turtle backpedaled into the sandy-bottomed tank.

Ronan felt sympathy pangs in his own arms and legs. He did not weigh as much in proportion to the size of his flippers, when in seal form, as the turtle did, but dry surfaces that didn't slide or give were more difficult for seals to navigate too. Of course, for him and Murel, it posed no problem since they could quickly morph to their human form so flippers were no longer an issue.

"What is the matter with the wretched creature?" the professor asked.

"Looks like maybe he's too heavy to take all his weight on his flippers where there's no give to the surface," Ronan told her, thinking that if she was such a hotshot biologist she ought to know stuff like that. "I'll go find some more sand or dirt or something in the 'ponics garden."

"You will do no such thing," his teacher said. "We'll flip the thing over onto its shell and examine its underside. If its flippers are a problem for it, then perhaps on encountering a situation where the flippers are of no use, it will take its alternate form, which is presumably one that does not have flippers."

Oh, cruel! Oh, pain and agony! Oh, anguish! The turtle groaned, and big tears rolled down its face. *Please don't let her put me on my shell. It's humiliating and I'm so helpless.*

She doesn't listen to me real well, but maybe when she grabs you, you should bite her. Not me, mind you, her.

I abhor violence.

Why? Ronan asked. He didn't underestimate creatures who were not human, but he didn't ascribe codes of morality to them either.

I'm not fast enough to get away when it starts, usually, the turtle replied.

Yeah, I can see where that makes sense. But if you could lower your standards long enough to just bite her and hang on, then you won't have to be fast enough to get away from violence because you'll be the one being violent. And besides, she sort of expects you to.

No, no. If I bite her, she will retaliate when I finally have to let go. But if I don't come out at all, she'll have no choice but to go away and pick on someone else. I hope. Saying this, the turtle retreated all the way back into the box.

"Never send a boy to do a scientist's job," Professor Mabo said. She shoved Ronan aside, shoved the metal tank to the end of the metal table, kept shoving it until half of it was suspended over the floor, then upended it.

Uh-uh-uh-oh! the turtle cried as it slid out and tumbled, flippers and feet over shell, onto the floor. *Now I'm done for. Don't let her torture me too long, boy.*

Ronan stooped down, picked up the shell in both hands and gently righted the turtle. *I'd tell you to run for it but I don't imagine that's a practical suggestion,* he said.

"Now that it's out in the open, we'll immerse it and see if that causes it to change," Dr. Mabo said. "Pick it up, Ronan. Come on now, what's the matter with you? Afraid of a little turtle bite?"

He wasn't, actually. He was just trying to pick the poor creature up without harming its flippers or any of its tender bits. The professor slid a wall panel aside to reveal two tanks, each about eight feet deep and just as wide, side by side.

One was clearly freshwater, since it was, well, clear. "In here first," the professor said. Ronan climbed a metal ladder up to the top of the tank, not an easy thing to do with his hands full of turtle. "Release it!" she snapped. Ronan did, and the turtle first sank like a stone then struggled to right itself. To the professor's disgust, however, it remained a turtle. It was a very angry and frightened turtle but that was all. It did not change into anything else. It did demand of Ronan, *What is this stuff? It feels like water but there's no buoyancy.*

Ronan said, "Professor, if this is a saltwater turtle and people where it comes from claim that it changes, don't you think that it probably does its changing in salt water, since that's where it lives?"

"I suppose so, but we must be thorough in exploring which stimulus is the one that activates the change. Scientific method, my boy, scientific method." She handed him a sturdy net to fish the turtle out of the freshwater tank, which he did, and directed him to release the creature into the saltwater tank instead.

The turtle, so clumsy on land, was graceful as an otter or a seal in the salt water. Its flippers flowed beside it like wings as they propelled it around the tank. It was in raptures. *Oh, oh, my dear boy, you are a wonder! This is fantastic! Look! Backward roll! Forward roll! Sideways flip!*

By then it was quite late, and the professor said, "We can leave it there for now. Tomorrow afternoon we'll try electrical stimuli and a few other methods to see if we cannot persuade the specimen to display its alternate form."

Not if I can help it, Ronan thought, and Murel answered.

Huh?

Professor Mabo locked up the lab with the old-fashioned key, grumbling because she didn't have access to the high-tech facilities of the station guarded with "proper" retinal scan locks. The flitter waited for them in the corridor outside.

Climbing into the vehicle beside the professor, Ronan sent his sister images of the turtle, telling her, *We have to help it escape.*

Where does a turtle escape to on a space station? she asked.

Eventually back to its home world, if we can manage.

Where's that?

I dunno, but he said something about a place called Honuania.

That's on Ke-ola's world! Murel said. *Remember his holo? I think he even mentioned the turtles, come to think of it. Called them "the sacred Honu."*

Great, I wonder if he'd have some idea how we can get the turtle back where it belongs.

Marmie could make Professor Mabo return it, couldn't she?

Maybe, but I'm not sure it would be good to try to make her do anything. She thinks the turtle is her personal property and refers to it as "the specimen." She might just kill it if Marmie told her she couldn't have it here. She plans to "stimulate" it with electric shock tomorrow, Murel. She's trying to make it change into an-

other shape, but the turtle doesn't understand what she's talking about. I have to help it get away.

No, you were right the first time, bro. We have to help it get away. Just because we're not together all the time anymore doesn't mean I don't still care about the same things you do. I haven't ever met a sea turtle before, but I'm sure I'd like him. And I'd help him escape torture and maybe death even if I didn't. You used to know that.

Aw, sis, I still do. I'm just worried. And the professor is right here next to me in the flitter so I can't think straight.

I can. Has she got the key to the lab on her? Can you nick it?

Yeah, as a matter of fact, I think I can. It's in the pocket of her lab coat. Sometimes you're really quite brilliant, you know. I suppose that's why I keep you around.

Yeah, yeah. Now all you have to do is sneak the keys away from her.

Oh, well, if that's all. His thought was accompanied by an image of him rolling his eyes.

Look, when the flitter lands, Murel said, *I'll create a diversion. I've been watching lots of vids. Creating diversions is how people always manage to swipe things. There's an accomplice or two, and while one person creates a diversion, another one does the actual stealing.*

Mum and Da are going to be really pleased to know they've sent us here so far from home just so you can study how to lead a life of crime.

Do you want to save the sea turtle or not?

As the flitter set down, Murel ran up to it. Her eyes were red as if she'd been crying, though Ronan suspected an onion had more to do with it, and she seemed very upset. "Professor Mabo," she whined, poking her head into the flitter and blocking Ronan's exit. The professor leaned forward to hear her over the flitter's motor.

"What is it, Murel?"

"When do I get to be your assistant? Ronan and I always share everything, and now he gets to do all this interesting stuff and—and—you don't let me do anything. It's not fair! I'm just as smart as he is. I'd be just as much help." Murel reached in and grabbed the professor's hands.

Now, she told Ronan.

The old-fashioned keys were outlined by a bulge in the lab coat pocket nearest Ronan's fingers. The way Professor Mabo was leaning toward Murel, the pocket was practically in his fingers. He slipped the key from her pocket as easily as he slipped through the water in seal form.

When the professor snatched her hands away from Murel's grasp with a cutting remark, Ronan jumped out of the flitter.

CHAPTER 17

JOHNNY GREEN KNEW something was wrong the moment he saw Yana Maddock-Shongili waiting at the dock, her hands folded behind her at parade rest, her eyes first on the ground, then looking up as he climbed off the gantry. Her jaw was set and her eyes were blazing.

"Yana, how good it is to see you. And how is Sean? Busy as always, I imagine." He always talked too much when something made him nervous, and women wearing that look—especially women with advanced training in sophisticated weaponry—definitely made him nervous.

"He's not here at the moment, Johnny," she said, her voice as tense as her jaw looked.

"What a shame. I've a message for him from the children."

"They sent their father a message, but not me? Why? Is it in seal-speak or something?"

"Worse. It's about biology and genetics and such."

"I know a bit about that too after all these years on Petaybee. And I am their mother."

"Yes, Yana—"

"Whatever anyone thinks, I *am* their mother. Petaybee may have given them to me, but it's a planet. If it had children, they're—let's not get into that right now, actually. But my kids are mine too, and they're half human. I never meant, in sending them off to Marmie, that they should stay three years. I would never have agreed to that."

The normally taciturn Yana was babbling like a brook let loose from the winter ice. He knew something else was bothering her too, though. It wasn't just the kids' absence.

"You can send for them at any time, Yana, you know that. Marmie would never keep them from you. She is only trying to help you keep them safe."

"Well, their father and I have a disagreement about that. I thought, after they'd been attacked by wolves and almost snatched by those otter-napping biologists, that they'd be safer away. But the truth is, Johnny, I can take care of my children better than anyone else. I'm trained to be able to care for the people under my—you should pardon the expression—command. They are safer with me than anywhere else."

"I'm sure they'll be glad to hear you feel that way. You see, the message I had for Sean concerns their own worries about some security issues. I don't know if you can answer for him, but once the kids are back here, they can ask him themselves."

"Fine. But we have to find him first."

"Where is he?" Johnny asked.

"He went for a long swim. Out to the coast, and then to explore a new volcanic mass building up at the equator. He's been gone ten days now and we've heard not a word. That little otter the kids are so fond of seemed to come looking for him, but I am the only member of my family who doesn't speak otter, so I haven't a clue what he wants."

"I don't speak otter either, Yana, but I do fly helicopters. Has anyone gone out to have a look?"

Yana nodded. "Scads of people. I've gone out there too. But the ash and steam are so bad out that way you can't see anything. Divers can't get near the place. I don't know why the man thinks that just because he's a man who turns into a seal and vice versa that it makes him superseal or something. He's a mortal man and a mortal seal, and I am mortally afraid he's got himself into more than he can handle."

"He's been in scrapes before, I'm sure. Superseal he may not be, and mortal man he may, but he is a most resourceful fellow and wise in the ways of this world."

"Yeah, I know, and too cocky by half about it sometimes. Clodagh has been petitioning the planet for news, and Sinead and her posse have joined up with the coastal folk to patrol the shoreline looking for—in case Sean swims ashore. But so far all they seem to be doing is annoying the local wildlife, including some otters. Possibly that's what the kids' little buddy is here about." She gave a small smile that bloomed on her anxious face like a flower in the snow. She had a sense of whimsy, did Yana, and a connection with natural things that had come with her to Petaybee despite her offworld life. "He wants to protest the human invasion of his territory to the Petaybean government officials."

"Or perhaps he's just looking for his friends."

"Yes. I can't blame him there. As for fly-bys, Bunny has tried it in Frank Metaxos's single-engine plane, and Aoifa organized the divers right off. But the bloody volcano is hampering any efforts they have to make a good search."

"It can't hurt if we go out there again, Yana. You still have a chopper available?"

She shook her head. "Not until the last one that went out searching returns. I can try to get them on the radio, but the com unit has been fried by the quakes and the electromagnetic waves Petaybee is putting out. I guess I could feed you while we wait."

Johnny had eaten Yana's cooking in the past. "Let's just go see if Clodagh has had any luck with the planet, shall we? She could tell us over dinner."

CLODAGH SEEMED OUTWARDLY as imperturbable as ever, large, round as Petaybee, moving about her cabin with a fluid grace that seemed strange in such an enormous woman, as if she were swimming through the air instead of constrained by gravity like the rest of them. Though her eyes lit with welcome when she saw him, Johnny felt she had known all along he'd be showing up at her door. Yana had already told him that she'd been haunting Clodagh when she wasn't haunting everyone else.

Clodagh dished each of them up a huge bowl of rabbit stew and served it with blueberry bread and rose-hip jelly. As soon as she served the food, however, she slung her pack onto her shoulder and went to the door. "You can leave those things and I'll clean them when I get back, Yana."

"Going to the spring?"

"Yes."

"Wait and we'll come with you," Johnny said. "Unless you'd rather be alone."

"No, you should come. Petaybee is pretty excited right now. I have a hard time getting any attention. We should have a latchkay, but folks are too busy looking for Sean to get organized. A couple more voices might get heard better than just mine."

On the way to the spring and the communion cave, Johnny nearly fell twice with the force of the quakes shaking the ground. Petaybee had always been prone to earthquakes and volcanic activity, the legacy of its comparatively recent rebirth by terraforming, but this was quite energetic shaking, even so.

"Is it safe in the cave, Clodagh?" he asked.

She shrugged. "I guess."

Johnny was more reassured by that than he would have been were he not a native-born Petaybean. He was a brave man, the veteran of many years of military service in the Company Corps and numerous hazardous missions on behalf of his civilian employer. Still, he found himself reluctant to step into the tunnels leading deeper into the planet's grumbling bowels, which sounded as if Petaybee could use a dose of antacid and a nice cup of tea.

However, though the walls shook and the footing was uncertain, though the water sloshed and rolled in the little hot pool as if it were a miniature ocean, they reached the communion cave without incident. The major pieces of rock all seemed inclined to remain where they were.

Clodagh pulled out a thermos and four cups, as if she'd read its mind about the planet needing tea. "There now, just you simmer down, love," she murmured to Petaybee.

Yana smiled and said quietly to Johnny, "Clodagh's

talking to the planet like she did to me when I was going into labor with the twins."

"Our Sean is still missing," Clodagh said conversationally, not to Johnny or Yana. "We'd like him back safe, please."

After a while other people began filing into the cavernous room, people with drums and other instruments.

They started singing songs. Yana and Johnny sang a couple too, then Yana said, "I can't sit here. We have to go look. Call Marmie and have her send another chopper if we must, but we have to go back out there. He could be hurt, clinging to a log or something."

But one of the search copters had returned by then, and the pilot, who had been out since daybreak, was more than willing for Johnny and Yana to take the evening shift. With summer, evening was very long—it lasted until twilight, and somewhere around midnight the sun, which had only taken a slight dip in the sky, began to rise again.

Even so, the weather was hardly bright. Debris in the air almost obscured the sun entirely. Johnny didn't expect to be able to find anything farther away than the copter's nose.

Unfortunately, his expectations were fulfilled. He and Yana ventured as close as they could get to the steaming smoking vent in the ocean, closer than they should have gone, but to no avail. They spent hours circling it, waiting while the quakes grew greater and subsided, backing off as the rumbling grew more intense and edging closer when it stilled, but they couldn't see more than the surface of the water, and even then infrequently. They had to return to refuel twice, and both times he could almost hear Yana fretting that they had missed Sean at the very moment when they might have saved him.

At her insistence, they did the same thing after the next crew went up, and again the following day. They spoke very little the entire time. Yana's focus was total and she could not seem to bear a word to break into her thoughts.

But finally, after the third search shift, Johnny said, "I think I'd best give you the children's message, Yana, and you pass it on."

At once her eyes snapped to his like an eagle fixing claws on its prey.

"They want to know if people can tell about their selkie nature from a blood sample. Their new science teacher, Dr. Mabo, was seen to pocket a handkerchief Murel bled into after cutting herself in lab class. They thought it suspicious and figured their father would know."

They were on their way back to the helicopter, but Yana turned and pointed in the direction of Johnny's ship. "Go get them now and bring them home, Johnny," she said, and as an afterthought added, "Please."

"I guess the answer would be yes to that question then?"

"I don't know about the blood, but a Dr. Marie Mabo was one of the scientists—the head one, if I remember correctly—Sean and Sinead arrested for, as Sinead put it, 'unlawful detention of river otters.' Mabo and the rest were deported. It may not be the same person, but I don't want to even entertain the possibility that the woman might be anywhere near my children. Losing Sean is bad enough."

"I'll go then," he said, his hand on her shoulder

squeezing a little, trying to be reassuring. "But you've not lost him yet. He may have swum to the other pole to get out of the way, for all you know. Communications haven't been the best so we wouldn't necessarily know. But I'll get the kids nonetheless. They'll be glad to be returning."

CHAPTER 18

THE TWINS WERE tired by the time they reached the laboratory. First they had to convince Marmie that they were too sleepy to stay up and play a game with her, as she suggested, but needed to go straight to bed. Then they had to wait until all was quiet and they were sure she'd retired to her quarters before they crept out of the house.

Marmie had set the weather for fall. Holo leaves fell from holo trees and wind gathered them in breathy gusts into holo piles along the banks of the fake river, from which a holo deer was drinking. Realistic rattling and rustling sounds accompanied the whistle of the wind as if an overly friendly ghost were trying to get their attention.

They made it through the garden without arousing Pet or the security staff, and reached the utility stairs leading to the next level. Stairs and elevators honeycombed the vast station, though most people chose to use the flitter fleet.

The stairs were metal, grated, and zigzagged back and forth in a seemingly endless sawtooth between Marmie's deck and the next one. Every step the twins took clanked and clattered, but it didn't make a lot of difference since most of the station's nonresidential areas operated continuously, were brightly lit, and had people coming and going at all hours.

The third level, where the school and Professor Mabo's science lab were located, was an exception. The white-tiled hallways that were so brilliantly lit during school hours were now dimly lit tunnels demarcated by strip lighting running the length of the hallway where the floors met the walls.

Each footstep seemed to them to echo as loudly as a blacksmith's hammer on an anvil as they tried to creep forward toward the lab.

When they reached the lab door, Ronan pulled out the keys. *This is it. You keep lookout.*

Out here? By myself? The whites of Murel's eyes seemed very white indeed as she peered down the maze of hallways.

Sure, what are you afraid of? If there are any wolves around here, you can trust Professor Mabo to have them locked up in cages.

Professor Mabo makes the wolves look gentle and friendly as sled pups, Murel said. *I don't mind admitting I'm a bit afraid of her. What if she decides to come back?*

Oh, she won't do that, Ronan said with more certainty than he felt, once he had a moment to think it over. *She doesn't plan to do any more work until tomorrow, when she tortures the turtle.*

Well, go on then. And make it snappy, will you? We have a lot of stairs to carry a turtle up before it's time to get ready for school again.

Ronan fitted the key, gave Murel a thumbs-up sign, opened the door and let it snick gently closed behind him. The lights in the lab immediately flared into brilliance. They did that when anybody walked in. It wasn't so—sudden—during school hours, but now he felt as if a spotlight had been focused on him. He shook himself a little, as if misgivings, like water, could be dispersed that way.

The lab seemed huge now, the tables with the chairs upended over them for the custodian to clean the floors, the racks of beakers and bottles above each table. His footsteps and even his breath sounded unnaturally loud.

He had not pulled the curtain over the front of the water tanks again, but even so, he couldn't see much but the ladder at the top of the tank and the glint of water among the chair legs and beaker racks as the light sparked white from its surface. As he drew nearer, he could see more of the tank walls, and expected to see the turtle by the time he'd drawn close enough to touch the tanks and could see their bottoms. To his surprise, however, both tanks appeared empty.

He couldn't see the turtle at all. True, the saltwater tank did seem a bit murkier than it had before, the sandy bottom stirred into the water making it cloudy, but that shouldn't have kept him from seeing the turtle. He checked the freshwater tank and the tank in which the Honu had been housed to begin with, but both were empty. *Turtle? Honu? You there? Where are you? It's me, Ronan. I came to—*

Heeeelp, a feeble thought reached him. The turtle sounded weak and frightened. *Help me, Ronan. I'm stuck.*

Stuck? Where? Ronan pressed hs face to the glass, cupping his hands around his eyes to try to see into the tank more deeply without interference from the lights in the room. They cast his reflection back at him so that he got in his own way when he tried to see.

Down here. In this cave.

Cave? The tank was glass, not natural landscape. Why would there be a—*Oh, you mean a drain, I bet. How did you get in there?*

Tried . . . escape . . . but . . . I . . . am too big. No air here. Need air.

Sea turtles, like seals, needed to breathe every few minutes, Ronan knew. He and Murel had done a search for the Honu's species in the station's extensive computer databanks. They'd learned some other interesting things about the Honuian sea turtles too, while trying to figure out what they would feed the turtle and where the best place would be to keep him once they rescued him.

Hang on, Ronan said, and began stripping off his clothing. *Murel, the turtle got stuck in the drain. I have to dive in and pull him out. I'm not sure how I'm going to do that, of course, when all I have to use are flippers, so you may have to come into the room and help us.*

Now?

No, wait till I tell you. Keep lookout meantime.

He climbed up the ladder to the top of the tank, poised over the edge for a moment, and dived in. His vision underwater and in the dark was much better as a seal than as a human. Diving to the bottom of the tank, he spotted the back half of the turtle's shell and its tail and rear flippers sticking out of a round hole in the rear wall.

Ronan swam all around the drain and the turtle, wondering why the hole hadn't been covered. He tried the claws on his flippers to tear at the portion of the drainage pipe farthest from the turtle's body. It was made of much sterner stuff than ice and he quickly gave it up.

I'm going to take hold of the edge of your shell and pull, he told the turtle. *Your tail doesn't look sturdy enough to withstand my claws or teeth.*

Oooh, I should say not! The turtle's thought came out with a sort of squeak. *Be careful to bite only the shell. I'm quite tender underneath. And ticklish.*

That was a problem. Ronan couldn't get his teeth to lock tightly enough on the turtle's shell to pull at it. His teeth kept sliding off the slippery carapace. He tried first one side, then the other. Once he thought he felt the turtle slip a little and intensified his efforts, but Honu remained as stuck as ever.

Okay, let's try one more thing. I'm going to ram, er, nudge you from each side and hope to jar you loose. I'll try not to hurt you.

The turtle winced. Ronan felt it, though he neither saw nor heard any physical change in the trapped creature. Backing up as far as the small tank allowed, he swam at the turtle from the left, bumped into the back of the shell and felt it move a little. He did it again. When there was no further movement, he swam up under the trapped creature and butted it from below. Then he attacked from the right and started over again. Gradually, the vibrations his movement set up caused the turtle's shell to separate from the lip of the drain. The turtle felt it too and its tail began to bob like a rotor warming up while its rear flippers started to backpaddle.

Someone's coming! Murel sent a warning thought.

We're alllllmost there, Ronan told her. *But you're going to have to come in now. I need you to lift him out and*

help me out of the tank so I can change back enough to
climb down the ladder.

Before he finished the thought, he heard the clanking
of feet knocking the rungs of the ladder against the side
of the tank. As he pulled the turtle free, he looked up to
see Murel peering down at them.

Come on. Hurry, she urged.

The turtle popped loose of the drain and lay on the
bottom of the tank for a moment, the movements of its
tail and back flippers twitchy instead of purposeful. One
of the front flippers looked like it had a small tear.
Ronan hoped he wasn't responsible.

The turtle's thoughts were fainter than ever and dis-
jointed. Ronan carefully picked up the shell and bal-
anced it between his front flippers and his body.

You can make it, Turtle, Murel coaxed. *That's it. The
tank's not that deep. Just a bit farther.*

Finally, the water splashed just above Ronan's nose
and the weight was lifted from his flippers and neck as
Murel said, *Gotcha!*

The turtle's thought was something like the turtle
equivalent of *Ahhh.*

Ronan thought he was making a lot of noise, or Murel
was, clanking against the tank, when all of a sudden the
turtle plummeted back into the tank and Murel fell in
after, her body striking Ronan's and driving him downward with the force of her plunge. She changed shapes
as she fell so that the fall turned into a less than graceful
dive.

Looking down at them, where Murel's face had been
a moment before, was the small dark face of Professor
Mabo. She wore a gloating expression. "I do not know
what I am going to do with that assistant of mine," she

said. "I thought I told him to clean the tank, but although it is not growing algae, it seems to have grown two seals since I last looked. Hello, Shongili twins. I trust the water is fine."

Neither of them could answer her or ask how she had known they'd be there, but she told them anyway. "You couldn't resist trying to steal my specimen, could you, Ronan? You are too much your father's son. He wouldn't allow me to study the otters either. Perhaps he realized I'd rather be studying you. And here you are. I have my wish. Little Murel has even granted me some immediate gratification by changing shape before my very eyes. I know you thought you were being clever, Ronan, with your questions about the causative factors of transformations. Now you and your sister will have the opportunity to help me answer those questions and more, in earnest."

Ronan was exhausted from struggling to free the turtle. He had not been able to get a breath himself before Murel and the turtle came back down on top of him. But Murel was angry. He could feel her anger although she said nothing. But the anger spewed her upward like a slippery furry geyser from the bottom of the tank straight up to Dr. Mabo. Ronan saw his sister's sharp seal teeth snap and Dr. Mabo shriek and fall away from the ladder.

Murel dived back down into the tank with a big sealy smile stretched across her muzzle.

Did you bite her? Ronan asked.

No, but I scared her, didn't I?

"Thank you, Ronan or Murel, as the case may be." Marmion's voice reached the twins from beyond the tank. Actually, her words were a bit garbled by the water, but they also caught her thought. It was clearly projected and easy to pick up, although they could not normally read people other than each other and sometimes their father.

The water in the tank quivered and the glass vibrated with what felt like a herd of moose galloping across the lab floor. Not moose, of course, but people! Help? The ladder clanked and groaned as someone clambered up it again.

"Get away from there!" Dr. Mabo's voice, muted by the water, was still nasty. "What are you people doing here anyway? Madame, I insist on privacy to conduct my experiments. You students have no business here without my permission."

Other voices, both male and female, obscured hers until they all sounded like they were speaking through layers of cloth.

Then Johnny Green's friendly face appeared at the top of the tank where Mabo's sneering one had been before Murel scared her off the ladder.

"Okay, kids, come along," Johnny said, holding out his arms. "You're safe now."

The man will lift you out, Ronan told Honu. *He is a friend.*

Honu shot to the surface while Ronan surfaced long enough to watch and catch his breath. Johnny lifted the creature gently and handed him off to someone else standing behind and below him and blurred by the water.

Johnny was not strong enough, however, to lift either twin in slippery seal form. Pulling them out of the water and up over the ladder while they changed would be difficult.

The tank was small for two half-grown seals, and there wasn't much room to swim. Besides which, the turtle, having caught his breath, told them that he wanted to return to the water too. Their rescuers had set the turtle on the floor beside the tank, and the weight on its flippers was more than it could bear. Ronan kept bumping the glass next to the turtle to try to alert Johnny and their other rescuers, whoever they were, of the turtle's needs.

Then Ke-ola, previously hidden by the rungs of the ladder while he stood at its foot, bent over, picked up the turtle and lifted it back up to Johnny.

"The sacred Honu wishes to return to the water," Ke-ola told him. Johnny grunted and shook his head but set Honu loose again inside the tank.

Ahhh. The turtle once more emitted the turtle equivalent of a sigh.

The people outside the tank looked in as the turtle dived back down toward the seals. Ke-ola had come in answer to the distress broadcast by the Honu. Johnny Green, Marmion, and Pet Chan were there because Rory alerted them to what his grandmother was doing to the twins.

"So," Johnny said. "The turtle is back but the kids aren't out. I don't see how we're going to do this unless we just break this sucker open." He gave the side of the tank a little kick.

"The children could be injured by fragments, assuming we found something strong enough to break the glass," Marmie said. "It is shatterproof, laser proof—"

"Etcetera. I understand. Very well then, what do you suggest? The kids can't stay in there forever."

"How about a crane?" Pet Chan suggested. "It could

hoist them out of the water with no problem. I'll just call down to the hangar and have them send up a small one with a basket on it, shall I?"

"We don't have to do that, ma'am," Ke-ola said, kicking off his shoes. "I can help. If you'll move alongside there, Captain Green, sir, I'll just dive to the bottom and boost the seals up to you."

"Can you do that?" Marmie asked. "You have no diving equipment."

"Excuse me, Madame, but my people have been deep-sea divers for eons. We hold our breath almost as long as the sacred Honu. The water will make the seals light as long as we're submerged."

"Hmm," Pet said, "I believe I'll just get that crane anyway, in case."

Johnny climbed down and Ke-ola swarmed up the ladder in his bare feet. He wore only a pair of shorts. Like the turtle, he looked heavy and lumbering on dry land, but in the water, even so little water, he was strong and graceful. Blowing a fine stream of bubbles, he dived down to the seals, met their eyes, and jerked his head toward the top of the tank.

RONAN WAS REASSURED by Ke-ola's calm presence when he entered the water with them. As his classmate gave the signal, Ronan swam to the surface. Ke-ola boosted him up toward Johnny as effortlessly as an otter might heft a clamshell. Ronan was surprised that Ke-ola was *that* strong. He was also surprised to see Rory's face and his arms reaching for him along with Johnny's from the top rung of the ladder, which Rory now shared.

Johnny had a towel with him and began patting Ronan dry as soon as he was half out of the water. When

Ronan's upper half began to change so that his hands were free to help himself, Rory scooted down the ladder. Then with Johnny's support, Ronan held on to the ladder with his hands, pulled his sleek flippered back end free of the water and let Johnny pat that dry until the flippers turned to feet again.

Rory was looking up at Ronan with eyes so wide, white showed around his pupils.

Ronan, human again, grinned down at him, said, "Thanks, Rory. I can take it now and help Johnny fetch Murel up. Good of you to come to our aid, though."

Rory nodded but looked a little hurt and a lot puzzled. Pet Chan returned with the crane but it wasn't necessary. Johnny and Ronan repeated the previous procedure with Murel, though she kept the towel closer to her than her brother had.

Rory handed lab coats up to them both, since Murel's clothing was at the bottom of the tank, torn during her transformation after Dr. Mabo pushed her in. Ronan picked up his own discarded clothes and put them on, stealing glances at the others. Marmie, Johnny, Pet, Rory, and Ke-ola were there, he confirmed when, fully dressed, he turned to face them. Dr. Mabo was not.

Murel caught his thought before he spoke and said, "Hey, where's Mabo?"

"Oops," Johnny said. "Guess she slipped away while we were all helping you kids and the turtle. Oh well, she can't have gone far."

Pet Chan pulled the radio from her belt and spoke into it. "Chan here. Put out an APB on Dr. Marie Mabo. Arrest and detain her until I can arrive to take custody. Charges of kidnapping and possible child and animal abuse."

"Sorry, Chan, but she's gone. Her shuttle departed a few minutes ago. You want us to launch a posse?"

Marmie shook her head sadly. "There is no need to risk our personnel. She will not return to trouble us again."

"Good," Rory said when Pet had passed on the order and clicked off the com unit. "I thought it would be so great to have a grandma, and she just kept Mum upset all the time."

Marmie turned to the twins. "You've Rory to thank for alerting us to your danger," she said.

Rory waved his hand in dismissal, "Nothing, really. I went to take her something and caught the old cow watching you on the labcam in her quarters as you entered and dived into the tank, Ronan. I backed out before she saw me, but I knew she was up to no good so I called Madame and raced down here to see if I could help you."

"You're a good pal, Rory."

"Not so much," he said, shaking his head and looking as if he'd just opened what he thought was a fresh can of milk and found it had gone sour.

"Rory," Marmie said, "you cannot hold yourself to blame for your grandmother's actions. If I had realized the connection between her and the twins, I'd never have allowed her on the station. You are not responsible for who your relatives are. It's how you treat your friends that matters."

"What connection, Marmie?" Murel asked. "Mabo said something about Ronan being Da's son like she knew Da or something. She said something about him keeping her from studying the otters and that he knew she'd rather study us."

"Yes. Of course, we knew a group of scientists had

been deported from Petaybee after you left, but no one sent any details, just that the otters were safe and their captors had been dealt with."

"When I gave your mum your message about Dr. Mabo keeping a sample of Murel's blood, she was horrified," Johnny told them, speaking carefully. Ronan thought he was measuring his words so he didn't say the wrong thing. What wrong thing could he possibly say now? But Johnny kept talking, as if to ice over the cracks between his words. "Your folks thought they were sending you to safety. They never figured Mabo would follow you here."

"Bad luck for the twins, us being here for my lovin' granny to latch on to as cover," Rory said.

"It's not your fault, Rory. Marmie's right," Murel said, putting a slightly moist arm around him. "If you hadn't been here, she'd have come up with some other excuse since she was so determined to trap us."

"How'd you know to come tonight, Ke-ola?" Murel asked.

"Once I knew the sacred Honu was here, I opened my mind to accept his bidding. He bade me come here double quick and help him, but you got here first," Ke-ola said, his shoulders rolling in a shrug that was like the tide coming in and going out again.

"So what will happen to him now?" Ronan asked. "Will you take him home?"

Before Ke-ola could answer, Johnny Green spoke up.

"Speaking of returning to your native habitat," he said to the twins, "you two need to pack up your belongings and say good-bye to your friends here. You're coming back to Petaybee with me."

"We're going home?" Murel asked. "Just like that?"

"Just like that," Johnny said, trying to sound cheerful, but again there was a cautious note in his voice that neither of the twins cared for. Something was fishy, and it wasn't the edible kind.

Ke-ola said, "The sacred Honu and I come with you."

"Oh, no, Ke-ola," Murel said. "It's much too cold on Petaybee for Honu. Probably for you too. Not that we wouldn't like you to visit."

"The sacred Honu says a home is being prepared for him and his kind. I will send a message to my family. They will find she who is to be the mate of the Honu and bring her to him."

"You mean on Petaybee?" Johnny asked, looking puzzled. "How would a turtle from here and parts beyond have any idea what might or might not be happening on Petaybee?"

Ke-ola gave him a pitying look. "The Honu are not sacred for nothing. They know many things."

"If he knows about Petaybee and this home he thinks is being built for him, why didn't he know my gran was going to turtle-nap him and experiment on him?"

"I said the sacred Honu and his kind know many things, not all things," Ke-ola said, and after a sigh, added, "They are somewhat more likely to know of distant things and future things than what is right under their flippers, perhaps."

Murel said, "Well, whatever the reason, I think it's brilliant that he's coming to Petaybee with you! I was just thinking that what Petaybee needs are some sea turtles."

"Do they really change, Ke-ola?" Ronan asked. "*She* said they were shape-shifters."

Ke-ola smiled a smile that made him look every inch

of his height and girth. It was a very superior kind of smile. "That is for the sacred Honu to tell if he wishes."

"Do you know, though?"

"That is for me to tell if I wish, and I do not wish at this time."

CHAPTER 19

MARMIE WAS GOING with them, which surprised the twins. They were more surprised to see several helicopters and small submarines and a lot of diving equipment being loaded onto the ship.

"That going to Petaybee, is it?" Murel asked Marmie as they boarded.

"Yes, it is."

"Our folks want all that and us too or did you make them take us back if they wanted all the tech stuff?" Ronan asked, teasing.

They were inside the ship and strapped to chairs in the lounge before Marmie answered. "It's search and rescue equipment. Remember how everyone was thinking Petaybee was building a new landmass?"

"Yeah, is that what's happening? The volcano is erupting? Cool! But why the need for rescue equipment? Nobody lives anywhere near there," Ronan said.

"It's probably also for scientists to go study it, isn't it, Marmie? Good ones like Sister Iggierock."

Marmie started to say something, then closed her mouth again and said, "Something of the sort."

"Okay, Marmie, what's going on really?" Murel demanded. "We haven't had any sleep and a tiring time of it lately. You're holding out on us. Why?"

"I wasn't going to tell you or let Johnny tell you either," she said, shaking her head regretfully and smoothing her skirt across her knees. Marmie almost never wore ship suits. She usually wore something elegant and flowing. Today it was iridescent blue synsilk. The rings on her fingers twitched a little, which was unlike her. She was something like an old-time queen, making all sorts of decisions every day. It wasn't like her to act nervous and uncertain. Seeing her that way gave Murel a sick feeling, and she felt the same trepidation from Ronan. "It seems unkind to make this journey last longer for you than need be, when we can have no news between now and the time we land. But your father has gone missing."

Neither of them said anything, but each felt the other reeling. They'd never thought, when they left Da on Petaybee, that he might not be there when they returned. Then Ronan said staunchly, "Good job Mum's sent for us then. We can find him."

"Non!" Marmie said. "What I mean is, I don't think your mother will want to risk you two as well. I certainly wouldn't in her place. The volcano is very active. It could completely blow at any moment. Johnny says there's almost no visibility even in Kilcoole."

"We don't need visibility," Murel said. "We can hear our da in our heads."

"I'm sure you won't be able to go near enough to do it."

"We hear pretty good," Ronan said, "and at least we could tell your searchers how to look—better yet, if you *really* want to find him, we should be leading."

But Marmie was shaking her head again. She unstrapped herself, rose and left the lounge. After that, when they tried to talk to her, she pretended not to hear them or ignored them or changed the subject.

Ke-ola, who stayed close beside the tank containing Honu, watched one of these encounters with a little twist of his lips. "That Madame is very stubborn," he said.

Murel crossed her arms on her chest and glared at nobody in particular. "She's not the only one," she said. "He's our da."

WHEN AT LAST the ship set down on Petaybee, the twins saw their mother pacing the ground, waiting while they climbed down the gantry to meet her. It was in some ways as if they'd never been away at all, and in some ways as if they were coming here for the first time and didn't know anyone.

She's so little, Ronan told his sister. *She always looked so tall and straight.*

Could be because you're looking down on her from about forty feet, dopey, Murel said. Then relented. *But I know what you mean. And, well, Petaybee isn't as pretty as I remembered it, even in summer, but it feels good to be here.*

Can't tell if it's pretty or not with all that stuff in the air, Ronan replied, swatting at the space in front of his face as if to clear the air of the smog that turned everything gray. *At least our river is still there.*

Murel stopped on the step she'd just set foot upon. *Even if our da is not.* Her throat hurt suddenly, and not just from all the particles in the air. Her heart felt as if it twisted up inside her not to see her father standing there, and Ronan felt it too.

We'll get him back, Mur. You'll see. We will. We'll show them all.

Of course we will, she sniffed, and started down again. Fortunately, she still held firmly to both rails of the gantry because suddenly it and the ship shuddered and jumped, and when it stopped, their Mum and Marmie, who was already down, were picking themselves off the ground and looking anxiously up at the twins.

After that they hurried down. But when she reached the foot of the gantry, Murel waited for Ronan, and the two of them walked over to their mother and let her put her arms around them. After a moment they each put an arm around her too.

Marmie smiled, wiggled her fingers in a "See you later" gesture, and returned to the dock, where she helped Johnny Green supervise the unloading of some extremely large crates, boxes, and uncrated hunks of equipment. Among the large things was the Honu's tank, with Keola sometimes walking along, sometimes crouching, beside it, apparently soothing the Honu.

"Marmie told you why Da isn't here?" Mum asked them. Left to her own devices, Mum never was one to beat around the bush. The more difficult or distasteful something was to discuss, the sooner she'd bring it up. Da was the one more likely to wait for the proper moment.

"She did," Murel answered.

"And you're not to worry, Mum. We'll get him back," Ronan said.

"Yes, we will," she replied. "I'll brief you on what we know already on the way back to the village. As soon as you've had a chance to settle in and have been brought up to speed, we'll fly back out again."

The twins exchanged looks. "You'll let us help?" they asked incredulously.

"I'm counting on it," Yana told them. "Not that you're to take any unnecessary risks, of course, but if anyone who speaks the human tongue can find him, it's you kids."

Just then Clodagh, surrounded by orange cats, strode up the river road toward them. The twins squealed and raced forward to embrace her. Clodagh smiled and patted them on the heads, said how big they'd grown, and disentangled herself, continuing on to the ship. The Honu's tank was being loaded aboard some sort of a wheeled barge, and Clodagh stopped there, bending over to peer into the tank for a moment before straightening to clasp Ke-ola in a huge hug and even exchange cheek kisses with him.

In spite of their excitement over their own homecoming, the twins couldn't help being distracted by this uncustomarily effusive display on the part of Kilcoole's shanachie. Almost as surprising was the way the often taciturn Ke-ola seemed to be brimming over with things to tell the woman he'd just met.

Well, I guess we don't have to worry about making Ke-ola and the Honu feel welcome, Murel said.

I didn't know Clodagh was so keen on sea turtles, but you'd think she'd been dying to meet one her entire life.

Mum hadn't noticed their lapse of attention. She pointed to where three curly coats, now shedding badly, stood flanked by Nanook on one side, Coaxtl on the other. "When I told Sinead you were coming home, she sent Chapter and Page here to help you get around on the ground. They were born last year to Book and Novella. Can you tell your aunt has been doing her bit to support the Petaybean literacy program?"

Page, it's them! It's really them! The twins. They've come to be our humans.

Semihumans, old chap.

Close enough for the likes of you younglings, Coaxtl growled at the colt, then stretched and regarded the twins with narrowed eyes. *Grrreetings, Ronan and Murel. One had hoped it would have been more peaceful without you to guard, but this has not been so.*

Nanook was not so droll. He rose from his haunches and rubbed each twin so hard with his body that he nearly knocked them over. Then he rubbed the side of his mouth against each of them, marking them as his while they stroked him.

Murel almost forgot that she couldn't be entirely happy, what with their father missing. It was good to be home again. She gave Nanook's neck a hug and kissed Coaxtl between the ears before mounting Page.

They rode slowly along the river from what used to be Space Base, the former Intergal toehold on Petaybee, toward Kilcoole.

"You guys are as tall as I am," Mum said. "When did you do that?"

It wasn't a question that needed an answer, but they had other questions that did.

"So, I get the impression Da was in seal form when he disappeared?" Murel asked.

"Yes. He wanted to swim out to the volcanic ridge where a landmass has been developing. I can only guess that he may have wished to talk to the ocean creatures and get their impressions of what was happening."

"That gives us a starting place then," Murel said. "We can put the word out and see if anyone knows what happened to Da or where he might be."

"Johnny thought Sean might have fetched up on the southern continent, but no one there has seen him. He's swum that far before but I know he'd find a way to let me know that he's safe."

At the river bend just before town, they saw a once-familiar sleek brown form diving into the water.

Otter? Murel asked.

"Hah!" The otter popped almost entirely out of the water. *River seals! You are here now. Before, you were gone. I looked for you hundreds of times, but Father River Seal said you were gone.*

"Mum, it's Otter!" Ronan said, sliding off Chapter and stooping at the edge of the river, reins still in his hands. Murel did the same.

"So I see. I don't suppose I can compete with that. Just make it snappy, will you? I want to make one foray to the volcano with you aboard before we lose any more light, okay?"

Mum looked all tight through the back and military again, so Murel handed the reins to her brother, caught up with her and touched her calf. "Mum, sorry, we really are glad to see you, but Otter might know something about Da. They talked too, you know."

Mum's expression warmed a bit and she put her hand on the top of Murel's head. "I know, sweetie, I know. Visit your friend, gather your intelligence, and come home, okay?"

"Right, Mum. Love you. Can't believe we're home again."

"Me too, sweetie. Me too."

Coaxtl and Nanook lay a discreet distance away from Chapter and Page, and Murel turned their way for a moment to give them each a stroke.

But Nanook asked, *What's he doing?* and bounded away.

Ronan had his shoes and shirt off and one foot in the river.

Good question, Murel said. *Ro, wait! No fair turning when we just got here. We can play with Otter later.*

He saw Da, Mur. He swam off with some sea otters. I want to go talk to them.

Swimming to the sea will take too long, she said, shaking her head as she ran to the bank in case her brother decided to jump in before they'd finished talking it over. Otter watched them, first one face and then the other, with a wary eye cast in Nanook's direction. *Otter,* she said, *we are flying out to the sea in a little while. Do otters like to fly?*

Hah! Otters love to fly. Otters always fly when they can.

So you've flown before, then, have you?

I would have flown hundreds of times when I could, but I never could, Otter admitted finally.

Well, river seals have flown hundreds of times too. If an otter flew with river seals, that otter would see things no otters have seen before and we would make sure he was very safe and went home to his hundreds of relatives.

But why fly? River seals can swim. Swimming is fun, and there are mud slides along the way and fish to eat. Are you sky seals as well as river seals?

Nooo, but humans fly all the time. We are sky humans. We fly because flying is very very fast, much faster

*than swimming, and we want to talk to those other ot-
ters about our da, the father river seal.*

Hah! Flying, huh? On a smelly man thing?

*Smelly and noisy, but we could carry you personally
with us so you could just put your nose inside a shirt
and not have to smell anything but river seal. And it is
very fast, as I said.*

You could be the first and only sky otter, Ronan said
slyly.

*Hah! That would make the other otters of all other
kinds very impressed. Yes, this otter will be a sky otter.*

"THE THING IS, Mum, Otter trusts us and maybe his relatives do too, but the sea otters don't know us and
they're the ones who were with Da. So we should talk to
them ourselves, without you or the copter or anything
around. If you drop us off by the river upstream from
the shore, we'll swim with Otter to meet the cousins,
and maybe they'll even show us where Da went. It's a
lead," Ronan said.

"What I'm thinking is that you two have this psychic
contact, right?"

The twins looked at each other, shrugged, looked
back at their mother and nodded. "Uh-huh."

"Well, then, how much distance can there be between
you before you lose it, have you any idea?"

"It's pretty strong," Murel said. "I could hear him from
Marmie's when he was levels and levels away."

"Yeah," Ronan said.

"And it works underwater too?"

"Especially there," Murel said.

"And you've the same thing with your father?"

"Yeah, but maybe not quite as strong because we aren't

with him as much as we're with each other," Murel said after pausing to think about it and trying to remember.

"Well, then, my strategy would be for one of you to go with the otter and get the goods on where your father is, while the other one stays in the copter with me and relays information from below. That way I don't lose contact with you both at once, and if one of you gets in trouble, the other can help us with the finding. If you both got in trouble, I'd have no way of knowing it unless I went with you, and I'm not really a diver."

"Well, I guess so," Ronan said. "I'll go with Otter and Murel can stay with you."

"I wanted to go with Otter!" his sister protested at once.

"He had dibs," their mother said, settling it. "Now let's go collect the otter and get out to the helipad."

CHAPTER 20

SINCE RONAN WAS to be the one swimming with Otter, Murel insisted on holding the little creature on the way to the ocean. Otter had other ideas.

Otters do not need to be held. Otters can stand on their own paws, Otter told her as they settled into the helicopter. He ran to the window and put his front paws on the glass.

Then the blades started rotating, *chuck-a, chuck-a, chuck-a,* and in a moment the aircraft lifted up, tipping slightly and spilling Otter onto the floor. He leapt back into Murel's lap and buried his nose in her armpit for a good deal of the rest of the trip.

When they reached the broad river delta, all ice for most of the year but now with braided channels of free flowing water, the copter set down, Mum grabbed Ronan for a quick hug, and he opened the copter door.

You can come out now, Otter. We're going to swim.

Otter disentangled himself from Murel, who combed her fingers through his soft thick fur as he left. *Hah! Yes, swimming is good, though sky otters can also fly.*

Ronan ran to the water, shucked off his outer clothes and, with the suit that Marmie had given him so long ago strapped in place on his back, dived into the water and emerged in seal form. Otter splashed him happily and swam off downstream.

Murel felt aggrieved. *No fair. I haven't even got to swim since we arrived,* she said.

Ronan barked a laugh. *This mission is much too dangerous for a female river seal. Only males and sky otters can do this bit.*

She sent him an image of her sticking out her tongue at him. She supposed she was being silly. This was a serious mission, after all, and the point was to find Da and bring him back safely. It didn't matter which one of them talked to the otters. The other one could hear and ask questions too. She just preferred to be there than up here above everything.

It was even more frustrating that they couldn't even fly out to the volcano where Da had said he was going until Ronan finished interviewing the appropriate otters. It took quite a long time too. Otter etiquette, which seemed to involve a lot of rocks changing paws, had to be observed. Ronan held back during this part of the negotiation, as the river otters all gathered around and declared themselves pleased to see him, though he could tell by their thoughts that some of them hadn't a clue as to who he was. Otters were live-for-the-moment creatures. Their otter friend was exceptional in that respect.

Murel caught all of this from Ronan and Otter's internal conversations and passed it along to her mother, to make the time go faster, if nothing else, since it was hardly the sort of information they'd come for. She liked to think she could have moved things along more quickly had she been in Ronan's place.

The thought escaped somehow, and Otter answered her

directly. *Hah! Murel could not make sea otters come. Sea otters come when they wish to come.*

Where are they, do you think, Otter? she asked.

They live on the island—there. She received a slightly distorted otter-generated image of an offshore island and also Ronan's image of the same place. *But sometimes they are gone. They go back to where they lost Father River Seal, back to where they gather the big big clams.*

Big big clams?

Yes, and very large white crabs as well. They are easy to catch if you are a sea otter. They cannot see and they are easy to find against the black rock sea bottom.

I never heard of white crabs and giant clams before, she told him.

The sea otter's song says the crabs and clams live in the folds of the black rock sea floor beneath the tall black rocks that puff hot bubbles.

It took a lot of river otter chatter and a few turns on the mud slide—which made Murel, who thought she'd outgrown such foolishness, feel sharply envious of her brother—but at length Ronan and Otter spotted the sea otters swimming from the offshore island. One of them carried a giant white clamshell. It was almost as big as the sea otter carrying it, Ronan told her.

It made everything easier that the twins were famous among the otters. *Where is the other river seal?* the sea otters wanted to know. *This river otter—*

Hah! Sky otter, Otter corrected. *Now there is a sky otter. Me.*

Sky otter?

Ronan explained. *My sister, the other river seal, is in a sky machine with our mother, who is not a river seal but a human all the time. The sky otter bravely rode with us to the sea so we could meet you and ask you about our father.*

What sky machine? the sea otters asked, swiveling their heads from side to side, to the back, up, and back down to face Ronan again.

I will call it so you can see, Ronan told them.

Murel told Mum what he'd said, and she spoke to the pilot, who lurched the copter skyward and flew to the shore to hover a little ways away from the otter colony.

Can your sister come and play with us too? We want to hear her song as well.

Hah! Murel said. *I can.* To her mother, she said, "Excuse me, Mum, but if you'll have the pilot fly a little lower so I can dive in, I have to make an appearance as a river seal for the benefit of my otter public. They know about two river seals, the song is about two river seals, and two river seals are more believable than one."

"Fine. Meet the otters, but then tell them you have to be a sky seal when Ronan goes to find your father." Mum let a small smile play at the corners of her lips, though her eyes were still sad and anxious.

Murel didn't like seeing her mother sad, but then again, she didn't mind leaving her in the copter either. After all, Mum had sent them away for three long years without even asking what they wanted, so now her mother could get left when she herself wanted to go. The girl shucked her clothes and dived out the copter door into the sea. No need for her suit since she would be returning to the copter.

The water was cold cold cold after the warm and regulated pool at Marmie's, but it felt wonderful, especially when her skin covered itself with its seal coat. It smelled fresh and exciting and full of life and adventure and—

fish! She gobbled three small ones as she swam toward the otters. Delicious! Nothing like Petaybean fish.

Feeling like some sort of a seal celebrity—the kind that never appeared on the vids available on Marmie's station—she joined Ronan and the otters.

Yes, that is right, Otter said, being the official spokes-otter either for them or for his relatives. *Now there are both river seals and that is the right number. Ronan is not enough river seals.*

Gee thanks, she said. Then she and Ronan listened as Otter sang the song he'd made about them again. It was no good for them to sing their own song because it was in the human language and lost a lot in the translation. Otter's version was far more appropriate to the audience at hand, or paw or flipper.

The sea otters then favored them with a song of their own, about finding the great clams and leading the father river seal to the beds. Ending the song, the sea otters sang, *But he swam away. He did not want clams and had no paws to hold them. He swam toward the great smoke and the thing beneath it. He swam to the great mystery and the otters who guard it.*

Otters guard it? Murel asked.

Yes, the sea otter said, sounding a bit nervous.

But is it not a big fiery underwater mountain? Why would it need otters to guard it?

That is a mystery.

Surely not to the otters who guard it. Do you know them? Are they a related clan of sea otters?

We have seen them, we have spoken with them, we have shared food with them, but we do not know them. They are not sea otters like us. They are deep sea otters and live beneath the waves.

Beneath the waves? But otters are—otters need air like seals, don't they? Otters cannot always live beneath the water.

The deep sea otters do, the sea otter told them. *They can stay above the water too but have to go down into it to breathe the same way we have to come up above the water to breathe. It is very strange.*

Are you sure they're otters?

Oh yes. They look just like us only they live beneath the sea.

Weird, Ronan said. *But if they live near the big volcano and that's where you think Da was swimming, then they may have seen him. Will you take us to them?*

We will take you as near as the clam beds and call to them. If the smoky mountain is very busy, they might not hear.

That would be good, Ronan said. *My sister and mother will follow us in the sky machine, okay? That way they can help us if there is trouble.*

Your mother who is not a seal nor any of your human people can know about the deep sea otters, the sea otter said. *They are very shy. They do not want to be taken by scientists for study as the river otters say they were.*

I suppose if they stay below the waves, Mum wouldn't see them. But she and Murel do need to follow. It's entirely possible nobody but Mur and me will be able to tell one sea otter from another. Do they look much like you?

They look almost exactly like us. Maybe larger.

Then nobody will know. Besides, there's no one here now to give any of you sea otters or your larger friends the kind of trouble Dr. Mabo gave the river otters.

"Hah!" Otter said. *Sea otters do not know about that*

trouble the way river otters do. But river otters cannot swim in the sea, so if sea otters and river seals are in trouble, this otter and his hundreds of relatives cannot help them out of it.

Murel heard the disappointment in Otter's thought. *A river otter may not swim in the sea but a sky otter could fly over it if he wanted to,* she said. *Then if the kind of help a river or sky otter could give was necessary, that otter would be there.*

"Hah!" Otter said, and at once she knew that although he had no real wish to go up in the copter again, he was now a sky otter, and having said so of himself, his relatives would expect him to want to go into the sky. *That is true. Sky otters could go.*

Of course, they might have better things to do, Murel said, to give him an out.

But Otter said staunchly, *River seals help river otters, and river otters who are also sky otters help river seals.*

The little guy was trembling as Murel carried him back into the copter. At her signal, it had landed once more on the shore. The hundreds of relatives—there were actually probably less than twenty—chittered and chattered anxiously as she and Otter climbed aboard the noisy, smelly, wind-blowing machine and rose into the sky over the ocean. Otter himself kept saying "Hah!" a lot.

Mother smiled at her and nodded to Otter as if he were a respected acquaintance.

Ready when you are, Murel told Ronan.

Okay then, sea otters, shall we swim?

You realize that we are very tired, having just come from there, the one they'd been speaking to said. *However, some of us did not get clams, and these otters will return to the lava beds with you, river seal, because of your song.*

Without further fanfare, the sea otters knifed into the waves and Ronan followed.

Murel put her earphones on and heard Mum say to the pilot, "Just keep them in sight. We don't want to frighten the otters. They might be able to lead us to Sean."

Murel thought her mother was awfully brave. Da had been missing for more than a week now. Where would he go in the middle of the ocean that he might be safe? He was all alone unless those deep sea otters knew where he was. Murel didn't want to think about it where anyone could read her, but she didn't see how Da could still be safe. There was no way, really. And yet, if he were gone for good she was sure she would know, sure that Mum would know, and Ronan too. *Da?* she called experimentally, and imagined her thought sending out ripples in the waves, ripples in the air like a very special kind of father-seeking sonar.

It rippled away into nothingness though, if she didn't count Ronan's irritated, *You think I haven't been trying that?*

I think you're doing what you show me you're doing, she told him.

We're still not to the place where the sea otters lost him, so you may as well save your energy.

Within another four hours, however, there was a different kind of energy crisis. The pilot's voice boomed and crackled inside Murel's earphones. "We're going to have to go back to refuel pretty soon, ma'am."

"Frag," Mum said, pounding her knee with her fist in frustration. "How close are we now, Murel?"

It had been a long time since Ronan had sent her pictures of anything but waves rolling around his ears, or diving under ice, or otter hind ends. The sea could be very boring if you weren't actually in it. And it wasn't as if they could see much of anything in the copter. You couldn't even make out the otters swimming right below. The farther they flew, the worse the fog became.

In fact, Murel realized she'd been dozing when the pilot's voice awakened her.

So, Ro, how are we doing down there? she asked her brother.

Good! The water is a lot warmer here and it smells like rotten eggs, which seems about right for a place with volcanic vents, from what we studied in science class. The otters have been getting more and more excited, and making me hungry talking about those delicious red clams.

River otters like those too, Otter said suddenly. He'd been very quiet, and Murel thought he might have been napping.

Ooops, there goes an otter bottoms up, and another. We must be there. I'm diving too.

"Well?" Mum asked impatiently. Murel had almost forgotten about her.

"We're at the clam beds now. The sea otters say this is where Da left them."

"Tell your brother to steer clear of those vents. They have sulfuric acid coming out of them."

"We know all that stuff from school, Mum. Besides, we can smell the difference in the water. So can the otters."

"We have to turn back now, ma'am," the pilot's voice

boomed into their earphones once more. "Just enough fuel to make it back."

"Let me get out, Mum. We'll lose Ronan and the otters otherwise."

"I don't want to risk losing you both. Besides, what about your little friend here? Didn't you say he doesn't do salt water?"

Another voice crackled into the headphones. "This is Captain Johnny Green aboard the amphibious yacht *Melusine,* registered to Lady Marmion de Revers Algemeine of Versailles Space Station. We are desperately seeking Petaybean Chinook-class helicopter zero-seven-three-niner-penguin-tango-bear, newly renamed the *Flying Otter.* Lady Marmion wants to know, 'Is that you, Yana? Have you found him? Do you need fuel because the *Melusine* is equipped with a helipad and a fueling station.' "

"Yes, no, and *merde alors*! Marmie, but you think of everything," Mum replied.

Johnny and their copter's pilot exchanged coordinates—normally you could see from a copter, but the smog from the volcano kept that from happening. The result was that soon the copter banked to the left, flew for a while, then settled down toward the sea like a bird fluffing down into her nest.

"Hah!" Otter said. *We have left Ronan and the sea otters, Murel. Where are we?*

The Flying Otter *needs fuel,* she told him.

Yes, even flying otters get hungry, but there will be clam meat later.

I didn't mean you. They've renamed the helicopter after you. It's called the Flying Otter *now. And I was thinking. We always think of you, and you refer to your-*

self, as Otter. But with so many other otters around, and you being our special friend, maybe you would let us call you a special name. How about Sky?

Hah! Sky! Hah! Of course this otter is called Sky by his friends the river seals. Other otters know each other only by individual scent names, but Sky has friends who are not otters and must make sure it is their friend who hears them. Yes, this otter is Sky. Sky is a good name. A high name for an otter so special that even flying machines are named for Sky the sky otter.

Murel had to smile. Otter—Sky—was obviously well pleased with the distinction he had picked up simply by flying with them.

Well, at least things were going well for someone.

Ronan, can you still read me?

Yeah, but I can't hear you anymore. Where did you guys go?

We have to refuel, but Marmie brought her special refueling yacht she packed with her aboard the ship when we came here. So we're not far. Any news of Da yet?

No, mostly just the sound of breaking clamshells and otter bodies diving back down for more goodies. They got a little sidetracked.

CHAPTER 21

W*HAT IS THAT?* Sky asked, as Murel opened her arms to let him leap from the copter to the pad on the deck of Marmie's yacht.

Sky was looking through the puffs of smog and smoke at the Honu's tank, and Ke-ola beside it.

Oh, that's Ke-ola and the sacred Honu. Honu is a sea turtle. We don't have them here on Petaybee but he wanted to come and see it.

Loving greetings, Otter of the Skies, Honu's thought voice said.

Greetings, shelled creature who comes from space and is not for eating by river otters. Or sky otters. What brings you to our world and waters?

My kind love the places where the ocean bed is closest to the heart of the world and this is such a place. Your world is giving you a new land place, and my two-legged family is in much need of such a place. I have come to examine its suitability for us all, and ours for your world. I go now with my grandson Ke-ola to swim. Would you swim with us?

River otters, even when they are also sky otters, do not swim in salt water, Sky said regretfully.

Murel walked over to Ke-ola. "Ronan is already in

the water with some of the sea otters, looking for our father. I'd dive in with you but I can't change in front of so many people. Besides, Mum needs me here to let her know what's going on with Ro."

"That's okay, sistah. The Honu and I will look. I think we will see more below than we can up here." He inhaled deeply, throwing his arms out and drawing them back to his chest. "But, ahhh! The air smells wonderful here."

Murel wrinkled her nose. "You're kidding! It smells like rotten eggs!"

Ke-ola just grinned. He liked the smell. Maybe it was some ancestral memory of volcano fart in his bloodlines, she thought.

Marmie's crew had lowered the tank into the hold of the yacht far enough that Ke-ola could simply reach in and lift out the sacred Honu, which he did. He stood on the deck where there was no railing.

"Slainté, Ke-ola," Murel said softly.

Ke-ola paused. "You told me slainté meant hello and good-bye."

"It also means 'to your health,' " she said.

"Slainté, Murel," he said. "Slainté, Sky."

In her mind she heard Sky and the Honu echo the sentiment, and then Ke-ola, with Honu under one large arm, held his nose between the fingers of the other hand and happily dived feetfirst into the water.

THE SEA OTTERS were restless. After each of them dived to get a clam and returned, some empty-pawed, they were ready to swim back to the shore again. Ronan couldn't blame them. He had never been swimming in the ocean before this and wasn't used to tides and waves. He thought it would be way more fun than rivers but this was no fun at all. Even the otters were finding swimming conditions difficult. When they led him to the first of the lava beds, he'd been able to see the tall rock chimneys pumping out their smelly bubbles and smoke, could feel from the warmth of the water where the black smokers lay beneath him.

But now, just a short distance farther, everything had changed.

A hot wind blew out of nowhere, whipping the waves high over his head. He couldn't even see the otters most of the time. Every once in a while the whole ocean would shudder and shake.

Hey, Ronan called out to the sea at large. *We should call those deep sea otters now. I don't think we can go much farther.*

No farther at all, River Seal! the closest sea otter said. Ronan couldn't see him through the smoke. *Going home now. No deep sea otters today.* Then suddenly he saw the crest of a wave bearing three sea otters riding the swell. One was floating on his back and almost sinking from the weight of the clam held to his chest with his front paws. *Water is too rough to play, food too hard to get. Wait for better seas and not so much smoke.*

Good idea, but my da is out here somewhere. You guys promised to help me. Otters were great playmates but except for Sky himself they didn't seem to be very reliable. *Could you just call them, though?*

If they are near enough to feel us calling, they'll already know we're here, the clam bearer called back, finally flipping over and releasing his prize before undulating away into the waters.

Yes, but . . . How did you argue with otters?

No sense trying. He had come all this way to find Da, and he wasn't about to go back after nothing more than a fishing expedition on the part of his trusty native guides. No way was he calling this off on account of waves.

This was as far as the otters had come with Da anyway, and they said he'd swum out to sea a little farther— toward the large and active volcano, which would mean swimming into thicker smoke at the very least.

He started to let Murel know, then thought better of it. He knew this was the right thing to do if he was going to find Da, but Mum might not allow it. Or Mur might try to come with him. She was now on Marmie's yacht, however *that* got here. He gathered it was some distance away, so he'd have to wait for her to catch up. The air quality here was terrible, and he could almost breathe water better than he could breathe the air. He didn't think it was going to improve and he didn't know how much longer he could hold out, so if he was going, he'd better go while the getting was good.

He tried drawing a diving breath but kept choking on the air. Swimming Petaybee's clean rivers, he had never had this problem before, but he thought full-time seals probably did sometimes. He wouldn't be such a baby. He'd do what he'd come to do. Finally, he took in what air he could and dived. He wouldn't be able to stay down long, but though the water was churning with mud, ash, and other debris, it was cleaner than the air.

By repeatedly diving and barely surfacing enough for his nose to suck in air before he dived again, he made some progress. He thought he did anyway. Actually, he didn't even know which direction he was going except he thought the smoke and debris were worse, and the water smelled worse and burned at times, not a hot burn so much as an irritating one. He thought surely he must be drawing nearer to the big volcano.

So, good for him. The only problem was, he could hardly see his own flippers, much less another seal or person in all this muck. He'd dive just a little deeper and then he would have to turn around. Mum and Mur would never forgive him if he got himself killed while trying to help Da.

That was such a grim thought that he dived deeper than he intended, and ended by touching the ocean floor—which was quite a bit closer than he'd supposed it might be.

He glided forward, his belly grazing the smooth lava bottom, where already plants were fringing up from the cracks, tickling his fur and flippers.

This was as far down as he could go. No way could he comb the entire ocean floor looking for—well, for what was left of Da. He didn't like to admit it, but Da could not have survived this for many hours, much less days or weeks.

His air was giving out. Little spots sparkled before his eyes, turning into dazzling stars, blinding after so much darkness. Then, to his surprise, his eyes adjusted—not to hallucinatory spots, but to real light, coming from what looked like real windows. In front of him and towering above him were what seemed like buildings, domes, towers—a gateway.

MUREL KNEW HER brother was in trouble right after Keola hit the water. Sky felt it too. *The sea otters have gone. Your river seal brother is alone.*

Usually the twins communicated directly with each

other, but Ronan wasn't doing that. Still, Murel felt from the tight constriction of her chest, the heaviness of her limbs, and the stuffiness in her nose that these sensations were Ronan's, not hers.

She found Mum talking to Marmie and tugged at her arm. "Mum, you need to cover for me. I have to change and go to Ronan. He's become separated from the otters and he's not well."

"Not well how?" Mum asked.

Quickly, impatiently, Murel described what she was feeling. Marmie whirled around and began gathering items and thrusting them at her.

"Even seals aren't safe in the sea at times like these, dear," Marmie told her. "You will need a respirator, a hard hat, probably a line to help you haul your brother to safety, and, oh yes, a homing beacon. And really, you should wear protective clothing and carry a knife as well."

"I don't know how to break this to you, Marmie, but seals don't have pockets or anything to carry that stuff with, and the little packet my suit fits in won't hold it all. Just cover for me so the others don't see and I'll change *now*."

"No," Mum said. "You will take these things or I will take them and dive with you."

"Mum, you'd slow me down. Ro's in *trouble*."

"And if you go without taking the proper precautions you will be too."

Finally everyone was satisfied—except Sky, who wanted to go too but still didn't think river otters could swim in salt water. Murel put on the protective gear, with straps for the knife, rope, and hat. Then she cut the arms and legs out of the clothing to make room for her flippers, which would need the room once she was in the water. She dove in and made her change under the yacht. The hard hat was slippery on her seal's head and ended by sort of dangling around her neck.

"We'll be right behind you," Mum called through the earpiece that was the other item they insisted she wear. They'd wanted her to wear a voice mike too, but she pointed out that they probably wouldn't understand her until she was back somewhere where she could speak without barking. The earpiece would probably float out of her ear once she started swimming.

Okay, Ronan, where are you and what kind of a jam are you in? she asked, but received no reply. So she struck out toward the lava beds where the otters and her brother were last seen. She called and called but although she continued to get the sensation that he was in deep trouble, he didn't respond.

Ronan, Ronan Born for Water Maddock-Shongili, where in the water are you? she cried in exasperation.

Come and see for yourself, sis, he replied. *You're not going to believe this!*

What do you see? Keep in contact. I'm on my way and Mum and Marmie and the yacht are following. I've a locator beacon so we'll find you.

It's some kind of an underwater city, Mur. Not too far from the main volcano cone.

Is it a ruin, you think? Maybe from way back before Petaybee needed terraforming.

It's a pretty lively-looking ruin. There are lights and things moving around.

She swam as quickly as she could, undulating toward where she felt him to be. *The moving things could just be sea creatures swimming through it, but the lights? Bi-*

oluminescence, do you suppose? Petaybee exhibited that kind of thing in many places, inside the caves, sometimes along the inner banks of the river, but it hadn't ever gone so far as to light up buildings, not that she knew of. Usually you had to use at least a candle or a lantern or something.

No, no, you'll just have to see.

Don't go in yet unless you have to. Wait for me.

Suddenly the entire ocean gave a violent shudder and she was buffeted back and forth by the swell before she could proceed onward with any speed. On the surface, rocks rained into the water, which told her she was getting closer to the cone. Below her the water was warm, sometimes uncomfortably so. She knew the vents spewed acid, and could only hope it was diluted enough by the water that she wouldn't suffer burns to her exposed flippers and face. She was very glad now to have all the silly equipment Mum and Marmie had insisted on loading onto her.

The respirator especially was coming in handy now when she surfaced, even though it didn't fit a seal's snout very well. Mum forgot her seal daughter didn't have hands to adjust the darn thing.

Funny, with all the smoke it looked like the weather was stormy, but really, back on the boat the sky had been blue where you could see it beyond the smoke.

She dived again and swam on, calling and calling. Behind her she heard the engine of the *Melusine*. She surfaced and looked back. Mum, Marmie, and some of the other people aboard the yacht stood on deck wearing hard hats, protective coats, and respirators. There were human divers on board too, and they were prepared to help, but Murel had asked that they stay aboard the boat until she located Ronan. No sense in muddying the waters any more than they were already muddied, and besides, it would be impossible to keep their secret from all those divers.

ALTHOUGH RONAN LOOKED up to the tops of the towers of the city stretching out before him, the city's base was beneath the place where he stood, sunken into a wide volcanic caldera that glowed cherry red all around the edge of the city.

How could people live there? Well, maybe they didn't. There were lights and shadows, flickering and movement, but he couldn't identify what was causing the movement. After staring at it for a while, he wasn't even convinced it was real. It could be a hologram, he decided, although why anyone would project one in an isolated undersea spot near a volcano was beyond him.

Then he realized the lights were changing colors—that a progression of colors beginning with white turned to yellow, lime, emerald, teal, aqua, brilliant blue, purple, red, orange, and back to yellow. From the bottom of the towers to the top and back down again, from the spires closest to him to those farthest away, the lights ran their rainbows.

Fascinated, he swam forward, thinking to explore the streets that surely ran between the towers, but instead of swimming straight ahead, he found himself swimming to the surface, there to be assaulted by more rock showers. Lightning bounded through the smoke in front of him. Taking as much air as he dared, he dived again, but although he thought he was swimming into the city, he reached the ocean floor pretty much where he had been before.

He surfaced and dived many more times, each time drawing shallower breaths and growing more light-headed. He should turn back, he thought, try to meet Murel, but he didn't want to lose sight of the city for fear that he wouldn't find it again. He half thought it was an illusion. Each time he went up for air, he tried to dive at a different angle, but always he was off to one side of the city. Perhaps it was farther than it looked, though he could feel the heat from the glowing crater beneath it.

It wasn't just that the city had a hypnotic effect on him, he thought. No, he could break away from that if he wanted. It was just that if this were a real place, it was the best hope that Da was still alive and well. Unless, of course, whoever ran the city was evil or something.

Ronan? Ro? Where are you? Murel's mind-voice was very close to him now.

Here, he said, but even to his own mind his thought was not projecting very well. *I'm here, by the city.*

By the—what are you on about anyway? Have you been eating funny seaweed?

He didn't answer. He felt her glide up next to him. More distantly there was a rumbling. He thought it was the volcano again but then felt the churning of the water and heard echoes of other human thoughts.

Oh. I see, Murel said, her body hanging lengthwise in the water beside him as she looked into the city. She looked very funny, wearing a hat on the back of her head and neck and something weird and mechanical over her nose. She also had on some kind of clothing, not becoming to a seal. Though it was comical, he didn't feel like laughing. He just stared at her for a moment then back at the city. *That's incredible. I bet Da is in there somewhere. Have you tried calling to him?*

Uh, not yet, Ronan replied, feeling incredibly stupid. *I was—was waiting for you.*

Let's get some air, then we'll try, she said, but she had begun to sound less direct and certain and more as if she too had been mesmerized by the city and its lights.

This time when they surfaced, he was aware of the yacht, a slightly darker shape through the smoke, with figures moving purposefully about there.

River seals! River seals! Sky called to them. *Have you found the deep sea otters? Have they seen your father?*

No, but Ronan has found something else very strange, Murel said. She was about to suggest that they return to the yacht to tell their mother about the city when there was a splash that sounded more like otter than rock, and presently the sleek brown head of Sky peered at them out of the smoke.

I thought river otters didn't swim in salt water.

Normally we don't but this was just a short swim, just a little ways and besides, if there are deep sea otters here, maybe they only speak to otters. Maybe they don't know that river seals don't eat otters.

What we've found isn't exactly deep sea otters, Murel told him. *Come.*

The three of them dived back down to the city, which was still there.

It's almost like it's not real, Ronan said. *I tried over and over again to swim into it but I couldn't.*

BUT SKY WAS not interested in the city as much as he was in contacting its inhabitants. Standing on the ocean floor on his hind paws, he moved the top of his body to the right and then to the left, then back again, inspecting the entire thing. Finally he sent out his message, *Deep sea otters, deep sea otters, it is your cousin Sky the River Otter who is also a sky otter, calling you. Our cousins the sea otters say that you live here. This otter has braved the salt water, which is not the element of river otters, to find you. Please answer. Your cousins have a problem and seek your help.*

From within the city came the first thought any of them had sensed. *Do you think deep sea otters are so easily tricked, little cousin? We know you brought that boat full of scientists to study us. We know there are seals out there with you.*

Hah! That is so. But the boat is full of rescue people and family members, not science people looking for you. The seals are only partly seals. Partly they are two-legged children. Their father, also only partly a seal, is missing and was last seen swimming your way. Did you see him? Do you know what became of him?

Maybe. The thought was cautious. *We don't want boats and seals around our den, though. Those seals, especially the one, have been here staring into our den for a long time.*

Murel said, *It's a pretty exotic-looking den, deep sea otters. We were just wondering how it got there and if our father might have found shelter there.*

If he did, if deep sea otters helped him, then his children wouldn't tell the scientists about our den?

If you don't want us to, we won't, Murel said. *Nobody wants to hurt you or molest you, and we won't let anybody study you if you don't want to be studied. We just want our father.*

You will tell no one else about us? No two-legged people?

No one, she said.

Not even Mum, Ronan promised.

River Otter, you believe these seals? the alleged deep sea otter asked.

These are the seals that save the lives of otters. They do not lie. They do not tattle. But they will keep searching until they find their father, and so will the big boat. There are other men too. Men who can enter the water and swim like otters.

Deep sea otters are very shy, the thought came to them, but to Murel, it sounded more sly than shy. *No men must come and find our den.*

They won't come if we don't tell them to, Murel replied. *But we need to find our father. He is a very important man to this world and none of us will rest until we know where he is and how he is. If we don't find him,* she warned, *there will be more men and women here than any deep sea otter has ever seen before.* It was a safe threat. Since no people had ever seen deep sea otters that she knew of, it stood to reason that deep sea otters had never seen all that many people either.

Above them, through the murky water, she saw two new shadows—a large human-shaped one and a round one, which she recognized as being turtle-shaped. *One of our friends is seeking us now,* she said. *You know what?*

She received an image of otter ears pricking forward as if to say "What?"

I think you know where our father is. I think you found him and took care of him in your secret den and he is still alive. That would be very good for deep sea ot-

ters, you know. It would make my brother and me and the sky otter here and even all the men who don't know about you owe you big-time.

She got the impression of confused inter-otter chittering. *We would be your friends and wish you well and maybe do something for you sometime.*

You must keep us a secret, the thought returned clearly. *If you do this, we may be able to help you with what you seek.*

Great. She looked up and saw the Honu and more of Ke-ola than she had before—hands and upper torso gaining shape. *Oh look! One of the divers is coming now! What do you say? Shall we keep him away? He'll go away if we say so.*

Yes. He must not find our den, the spokes-otter replied quickly, though again she felt there had been some excited consultation before he spoke.

Okay then. We're all going to surface for air now and to keep our friend up there from finding you. You otters think it over.

She conveyed this, and the three of them lofted themselves toward the surface. It was none too soon, as the ocean floor rolled and fiery liquid belched beneath the city/den. Strangely, the eruption didn't seem to hurt or move the odd collection of lighted towers in any way, but it splashed upward. Had they delayed another moment, they would have been burned.

The three of them rose straight up underneath Ke-ola and the Honu, nudging Ke-ola back up into what could now only loosely be called fresh air.

"Ronan and Murel! River Otter! The Honu felt that you were in danger. We came to help you. We must go back to the boat. The Honu and I would be fine but the boat could sink from the falling rock. It's very hot, you know."

They couldn't answer him. The waves swelled like angry cats and attacked them, driving them apart and spinning them around with the force of the tormented water.

Hah! River otters are not meant for salt! River otter fur is full of dirty ashen stuff that stinks and stings. Sky was fretting, but neither Murel nor Ronan could see the otter or each other because of the water and the steaming ash.

Only the Honu bobbed on top of the waves, sliding down them and riding back up.

But more than anything they were actually experiencing was the pressurized sensation that something ominous was building very near them, something about to explode.

Why is Petaybee so furious with us? Murel couldn't help but wonder.

Not furious. Spawning, the Honu told her.

Well, as soon as the planet's between contractions we should dive one more—

At that moment something bobbed up beneath her, bumping her underside. Murel rolled off it and down and saw another seal. *Da!* she cried. But the other seal did not answer her. It bounced helplessly with the waves, not moving a flipper to help itself.

Then suddenly the ocean seemed to fly apart as a torrent of water plummeted from high up in the sky, smashing into her body with more force than a speeding snocle.

CHAPTER 22

THIS CAN'T BE *happening. It's too weird and too un-fair.* Murel sent the message to all and sundry as a wave slammed her under, the force of it almost driving her back to the ocean's shallow bottom. She choked on dirty ashen water and tried not to breathe until she fought her way to the surface again. Wherever that was!

The whole world rumbled and roared louder than a giant snocle. Clumps of burning rock pelted her and she kept dodging scalding steam. *Da? Ronan? Otter? Sky? Honu?* she called silently.

"Murel! Ronan!" Mum's voice called out to them somewhere very near.

Murel heard the thought as much as the words and struggled toward her mother's voice.

Here you go, little seal, came another thought, and she felt herself snatched clean out of the water and handed up, so that she tumbled onto a hard, knobby surface.

Almost immediately something huge and heavy was dumped on top of her. She tried to roll sideways but there was very little room. Before she could pull herself entirely clear, something else was dumped on top of the other thing. The things wiggled and breathed, and, of course, when her vision cleared, she saw that they weren't things at all. It was Ronan and Da. Mum and Johnny sat at the bow and the stern of a lifeboat with the three of them in the middle. Nobody was rowing, and Murel feared they'd be swamped. But as she dragged herself out from under her relatives, she saw that there were lines attached to the lifeboat tied to the *Melusine*. The boat was being towed back toward the yacht by all hands on deck, fighting the swamping waves and the swell.

Something else, small and wriggling, flopped into the boat. "Hah!" Sky said, his favorite otter expression mingling indignation and relief in the same puff of breath. "Hah!"

Finally one more object landed in the boat, clattering on the side. *I could have made it myself, foolish boy,* the sacred Honu said. *I was swimming before you were an egg.*

"Ke-ola, get in!" Mum cried. "You're exhausted."

"No room!" he bellowed back up at her. "Sink . . . you. Hang . . . onto . . . hull."

A huge wave slid the lifeboat back to the yacht, smashing into it and dumping everyone back into the raging sea. The crewmen were tossed backward, to sprawl on the deck, and the ropes went flying. The lifeboat, its hull splintered, sank beneath them as they scrambled for safety.

Murel saw Mum thrown against the yacht's hull and swam over to break her fall. Ke-ola grabbed Johnny, who, being unhurt, shook him off. Da started to sink with the lifeboat, but Ronan fetched him up again.

Otter clung to the Honu's tail.

The lines were tossed over the side once more. Mum,

Johnny, and Ke-ola caught them. Then Ke-ola boosted
Murel up on a rising wave so that she practically washed
onto the yacht. He did the same thing with Da and
Ronan. Mum, who was shaken but didn't seem injured,
tried to help, but Ke-ola nodded to her own rope. Seeing
that he had matters in hand, she climbed aboard and
was helped on deck by Johnny, who had by that time
helped Marmie pull Da and Ronan onto the deck. Sky
scampered up across Mum's back and hair to safety.
Johnny turned to pull Ke-ola aboard but the Kanaka
boy rode another wave up and clung to the deck.

Darkness descended on them almost as quickly as the
waves. Marmie bundled them all in blankets, which were
soaked but not so thoroughly that the seals couldn't
change back into Shongilis.

Wanting to stay human for a while, and unsure that
they would do so if the waves kept washing over them,
the twins tugged on their waterproof suits, pulling
up the hoods.

Johnny tried to stuff Da into a waterproof suit too. Da
struggled to sit up, saw Mum's face and said, in a voice
much the same as the one they'd heard him use when
he'd drunk a bit of the blurry at latchkays, "Jayz, dar-
lin', what are you doing out here? The weather's terrible."

Mum made a funny half-sobbing noise Murel could
barely hear as Da finally managed to sit up and pull on
his own suit.

Because of the darkness and the fact that only their
family and closest friends were helping, the selkies' secret was preserved as much as possible. They couldn't be
sure, of course, but none of the crew members said,
"Hey look, those seals they hauled up just turned into a

couple of kids and their old man!" so it seemed their secret was intact.

But that kind of exposure was the least of their worries. Marmie and Pet Chan helped everyone but Sky and the Honu lash themselves with ropes—lines—to the sturdier and more permanent features of the yacht. Although Murel wondered how sturdy the boat could actually be since apparently it had come off the spaceship in pieces with some assembly required. "All secured, Captain," Pet told Johnny.

Johnny in turn shouted to the crew, "Okay, give her full throttle and get us out of here."

"Uh, Captain?" the nearest crew member said.

"Yes? Wait a tick. We are supposed to be idling. I know it's noisy here but we're not idling. Why are we not idling?"

"Not actually sure, sir, but the engineer said something about ash clogging the fuel pumps."

"That's just—" Another huge wave washed over the deck. Murel felt paws wind tightly into her hair. When the water subsided with the yacht miraculously still right side up, she saw Ke-ola leaning over the railing, apparently communing with the Honu, who was in the water. "—brilliant," Johnny finished.

Sky, you're pulling, Murel told the otter.

Grooming, the otter mumbled through a mouthful of hair.

Da and Mum were hanging on to each other literally for dear life. Murel felt rather than saw her father staring at her and Ronan as if he could hardly believe they were there. *How long have you been home?* he asked.

Dunno, Ronan replied. *Feels like not very long and nearly forever at the same time.*

What happened to you, Da? Murel asked. *Everyone thought you were a goner.*

Far as I knew, I could have been. The last thing I recall was something falling on me, and then I woke up floating in the water beside you two.

So you don't remember anything about otters, for instance?

Oh, the sea otters were having a grand time bringing up clams from the lava beds when I left them but I finally swam onward. Not all that clever of me, really. It would have been a better job for people with two legs and equipment. It's dangerous around here, in case you haven't noticed.

We noticed.

Who's the big lad being chummy with the turtle? And for that matter, how did the turtle get onto Petaybee? No turtles were authorized that I recall.

That's Ke-ola, one of our classmates from the station. The sacred Honu is the turtle. I believe they're considering immigrating. Ke-ola just saved the lot of us, pulling us out of the water and sticking us in the lifeboat, so I think you might want to give their request special consideration.

Should Petaybee allow us to live through this, I promise to do that very thing, Da said.

The sun, having disappeared for half an hour or so, once more swung around on the horizon until it was over the ocean. Of course, nobody on the boat could actually see it, but they knew that it had because the rays shined through the shroud hanging over the ocean and dyed it brilliant scarlet, fuchsia, and tangerine.

Almost as if the sun's rising soothed the volcano's temper, the rumbling quieted and the seas became comparatively calm. With the yacht's motor out, the loudest noises were the tinkering and swearing that could be heard clearly from the engine room. The twins and their parents loosened their lines enough that the twins could turn around and give their father huge hugs.

"You took that business of being hero twins seriously, didn't you, kids?" he asked aloud. "Your mum says it was you who came to fetch me from what I can only presume was almost a watery grave."

"Much as we'd like to take credit for that, Da, it was actually Sky—"

"Sky?"

"Otter. Now that he's ridden to your rescue in a helicopter, he is a sky otter instead of merely a river otter, so we've given him an appropriate name and he likes it."

"It is more original than Otto or something of the sort," Da agreed. "And it was good of him to come along. River otters do not go to sea, as a rule."

"So he's told us. But in your case he made an exception. And it's a good thing he did," Murel said. "He's the one who, uh—found where you were for sure."

"But you two got me out? How did I survive?"

"There seemed to be air pockets or something—maybe the volcano created a kind of grotto with an air tube to the surface?"

"Which, providentially for me, did not turn into a lava tube? Petaybee was being extremely thoughtful there."

"Pity that mood didn't continue," Mum said.

Lookit Ke-ola, Ronan told Murel while their parents were discussing Petaybee's moods.

Ke-ola stood on deck staring straight out at the tip of

the cone, becoming slightly visible above the water at times, when the steam wafted up and away from the rim. His expression was thoughtful. A dome bulged in the cone like an egg about to hatch. Although the volcano was quiet for the moment, once more they could feel the pressure building.

"Whatcha think, Ke-ola?" Murel asked.

"I was just thinking about my twenty nieces and twenty-five nephews," he said.

"Are you worried you will never see them again?" she asked sympathetically. At least she and Ronan were back home with their parents and their friends, even if it only meant they wouldn't die alone. Not a happy thought. Murel choked up in spite of herself. She didn't want to die, but the dome inside the crater was bright red and pulsing.

Sky was puzzled. *Is there not enough water here for you?*

We were thinking of our families, Sky. Ke-ola was remembering his relatives who are not here.

He has many?

Hundreds, like you.

Many Ke-olas. Good. Honu likes Ke-ola. Sky otters like Honu. Sky looked over the side, where Honu was swimming back and forth beside the yacht.

Johnny Green returned from belowdecks and reported to Marmie.

"How long?" she asked.

"Too long, I'm afraid," he replied, shaking his head. "They're clogged as bad as if they'd been poured full of concrete. The lads are working as fast as they can but they'll be no match for Herself," and he nodded to the volcano. He turned to Marmie. "There's one lifeboat left. You and Pet, Yana and the kids—"

"Not us," Murel said. "We're better off as seals now that we're rested, right, Da?"

"Yes, but I'll be alongside the boat where your mother is."

"Mother isn't going in any lifeboat," Mum said. "There's room enough for Marmie, Ke-ola and the crew. Too many people depend on Marmie for her to be lost this way. She's been Petaybee's number one outside ally. You'll need her help."

"*We'll* need her help, luv."

"He's right, Yana. I'm the captain, not you. I'll go down with the bloody ship if anyone does," Johnny said.

"No, Johnny. Marmie needs you too . . . and I outrank you."

"Not anymore, you ridiculous baggage. Get in that boat, and that's an order."

"You can't talk to my wife that way, Johnny. I'll do it," Sean said. "Get into that boat, Yana, and stop being such ridiculous baggage. You're the mother of our children and *they* need *you*."

Meanwhile other sailors, more practical and less noble, had lowered the remaining lifeboat over the side and were climbing in. Pet Chan practically forced Marmie in along with the crewmen. Once Pet was seated, there was room for two more passengers.

"Not the way they need you," Mum argued with their father. "You understand them. You can all speak without words. I—"

"No time for this nonsense, Yana," Da said, and tried

to lift and manhandle Mum over to the lifeboat. When he proved too weak to do it, Johnny scooped her up but she fought them both off.

"Hey, Mama," Ke-ola said, padding barefoot over to the three of them and separating the men from the twins' furious mother. "You don't gotta do it, lady. I'll go now. I know what has to be done. It's in the oldest chants. Your keikis need you, your man, your world."

"Petaybee does not seem highly attached to any of us just at the moment," Mum snapped, and turned on Ke-ola, her dark eyes flashing. "And where is it you think you're going, young man?"

"Ke-ola knows all this old stuff from when his people lived near volcanoes, Mum," Ronan told her.

"Yeah, I bet they had some really neat way of dealing with eruptions and stuff, didn't they, Ke-ola?" Murel asked.

"Yeah," he said. "That's right. Those old ones knew that if you were gonna have life, there had to be death so somebody had to give themselves to Pele—our volcano goddess. I'm not afraid. There's too many people where I come from anyway. I'll do it, then the volcano will quiet and you all can go home." He turned and walked to the rail, and in another fraction of a nanosecond would have slipped into the waves. Ronan and Murel exchanged looks and ran up beside him, stripping off their dry suits. He gave each of them a chagrined look. "Little bruthah, little sistah, you should understand!"

"Are you out of your *mind*?" Mum demanded. "Johnny, Sean, someone brain this child before he does something monumentally stupid."

"I don't care what your chants said, Ke-ola, if they told you to jump into a volcano, they were wrong,"

Murel told him. "I thought that was a good place you came from to begin with. Why would your volcano want anyone to jump into it?"

"Yeah, it's not hungry, for pity's sake," Ronan added. "It's trying to pump stuff out, not take stuff in. You'd just be polluting it. We'd have Ke-ola bits all over the nice new island Petaybee's trying to make. Honestly, I know it looks bad, Ke-ola, but nobody has to die here. If anyone does, it will be an accident, and Petaybee, well, I think Petaybee will be really sorry. You were the one who said the planet wasn't angry, it was just giving birth and a little out of control."

Murel had a flash of insight. *I think that's what Mum understands, maybe without knowing she does. She sort of knows what Petaybee's going through. It was hard enough for her to have twins. Think what it must be like to try to have an island. Ugh. I don't ever want to have any kids.*

"I honestly think you misunderstood those chants, guy," Ronan said earnestly.

"That's what you think, do you, little bruthah?" Ke-ola asked with maybe a little of his old twinkle returning.

"It is. You're our friend, you know, partly because you were the one kid at school who kind of understood about Petaybee. I think you're supposed to live here, not die here."

Murel realized that she thought the same thing, but she didn't see how that was going to happen. The lifeboat had not yet completely detached from the yacht, Mother and Father and Johnny were still arguing, the yacht was still dead in the water, and the waves began slapping ominously against the side of the hull again. *Slap-slap, slap-slap.*

She hoped it was her imagination that made the dome look bigger—and as if it were throbbing steadily.

"Shite on a shingle," Mum said. "Here comes another contraction."

Steam jetted up suddenly from vents around the dome, and the sea started shaking again, rumbling as if it were full of bones. Which it could be pretty soon if they weren't careful.

"A contraction." Ke-ola smiled and turned to them, asking casually, "Maybe I got to thinking of the wrong chant at that. You remember that one song I sang at your party—the one I didn't translate?"

"Which one?"

"The one with the stomps. Like this." He stomped, bringing the opposite leg up sharply, then stomped again so the rhythm was *stomp-stomp, stomp-stomp*, like the *slap-slap* of the ocean against the boat. The stomps shook the whole boat.

"Oh, yeah, that one! I like that," Ronan said. "It's fun. Only—maybe not now."

"Now is a real good time, I think," Ke-ola replied. "You do it too. You too, Mama and Papa and Captain," he called back, continuing the stomp.

"Like a heartbeat!" Murel said.

"That's it, sistah. Because it's a birthing chant. Like I told you, all we got to do on that asteroid where we live now is make babies, and because of the gravity, it ain't easy. So everybody has to help the mamas. The men's part, with the stomping, goes something like, 'Swim swim,' to the baby, with the stomps being like canoe paddles. To the mama we say 'Breathe breathe,' until it's time to 'Push push,' and the verse that just repeats is something like, 'Have no fear your men are here. We will protect you,' to put it in your language, which is, sorry, really not good for poetry. There's a women's part that goes something like, 'Take it slow, sistah, take it easy, be calm, breathe easy, the birth is a beautiful dance, bring your child into the sunshine so he can dance with his relatives.' Or something like that. But I think if you just clap, soft, like this," he showed her, "in the same time, that will get it across."

"Okay," Murel said. "So, you think we should do this now?"

He shrugged tidally once more. "Can't hurt. If your world is as willing to listen to you as you say, maybe we can make her hear, before she's making too much noise again." He kept stomping and shouted again at the twins' parents and Johnny, "Mama, Papa, Captain, do what we do. You folks in the lifeboat, drum on the side. Paddlers, strike the sea with your oars."

More fumeroles gushed steam, Petaybee exhaling through her teeth. The sea rocked the yacht, but Murel liked to think that the stomping feet and clapping hands steadied it somehow.

Ke-ola called out the first words of the chant, addressing the laboring volcano not as a goddess, but as he probably already had sung many times to his mother, aunt, or sister. He waved his hand to Murel and Ronan and sang the words to them. They repeated them after him as loud as they could, matching his beat. Then he called out some more. This time he added a little lilt and melody to the words.

The dome swelled and throbbed, the fumeroles spewed

and steamed, and the column of steam and ash rose into the coral sky, deepening its hue to bloodiness.

The rumbling got louder, but not as loud as before.

Ke-ola stamped and chanted. Murel and Ronan, and soon their father and mother, stamped and chanted after him, their words finding an unbidden harmony with his, so accustomed were their voices to songs in a mode more familiar to their world. Marmie and most of the people in the lifeboat drummed on its side or with paddles against the sea. Johnny didn't join in, nor did the chief engineer. They chose the more pragmatic path of going below and trying to fix the engine with the time they hoped the chant might be borrowing for them.

Ke-ola looked straight out at the volcano the whole time, his head held high and his body erect as an arrow, shooting his words into the horizon. His bare feet alone shook the entire yacht. Amplified by the stamping of the other feet, the sound gave a heartbeat to the rising waves, measured the rising smoke with its cadence.

The twins stamped and sang until not only their feet, but their knees hurt. The throbbing dome could burst at any moment and send a fountain of lava into the sea and onto the yacht, but it didn't.

But their throats began to burn with the singing and with the little particles of ash that should have made them cough but didn't.

Ke-ola did not cough or falter in his singing either.

They stamped until their hips ached and their soles began to bleed. Their throats longed for water but they could not stop singing.

From the corner of her eye Murel saw Sky dive into the sea. Following him, she watched him swim after the Honu, both of them toward the cone being joined slowly in the middle of the ocean by other cooling lava being spewed by the lesser volcanoes around it.

Honu and Sky swam back and forth, back and forth, and before long it seemed other creatures were swimming as well. Among them were some sea otters and great shoals of fish, dolphins, orcas, and larger whales that came right up under the boat without touching it. Instead of swimming back to the boat, however, these creatures swam to either side of the cone and onward. Only Sky and Honu went back and forth. Soon Murel realized their journeys were in prolonged counterpoint to the stamping.

The dome could have blown, should have blown, all at once, but didn't. It seemed to recede a little, the throbbing developing into a regular pulse. When it opened, the top of the dome didn't blow. Instead its sides opened and pumped rather than spewed the lava into the sea, to be cooled almost at once by the water.

As the volcanoes blew and the islands formed and joined, it seemed to Murel that the sea itself was working with their party, a pathetically puny bunch of humans, occasionally some seals, plus an otter and a sea turtle. Instead of swamping the boat, the waves picked it up and carried it away from the volcano. They had been perhaps a mile away from the throbbing dome to begin with, but soon the swells carried them two miles, then five, then ten miles farther from it. By the time the cone's pumping escalated into the fountain they'd been expecting, they were safely away from it. The lifeboat, still attached to the yacht, was also carried to safety. Honu and Sky ceased swimming back and forth and watched as the other sea creatures paraded past, greeting the new arrival, which would breed food and shelter for them in time to come.

Ke-ola did not stop singing and stamping, however, and neither did the twins or anyone else, though they badly wanted to. Surely it was safe now? But maybe not. There were still those volcanic beds beneath the sea even this far out. Murel thought they would be agitated too.

But she got out only another half-dozen stomps and another line of chanting that she wasn't even sure got from her sandpapered throat to her mouth. Then her legs gave out and she sat down on the deck. To her surprise, she saw that Mum and Da were also both sitting down and no longer chanting. Ronan almost fell on top of her. Still, the rhythm and melody of the chant rolled on toward the volcano, as strongly as ever, and the beat seemed even stronger. Maybe the people in the lifeboat, sitting as they were, could carry on with more force?

But as she glanced back she saw that something different was happening. A line of fishing boats bobbed along on the yacht's port side, and more were fighting the waves to reach them, the paddles keeping time with the chant. No motors were running now. With the ash in the air, they would suffer the same fate as the yacht's engines.

Everyone seemed to be carrying the melody of Ke-ola's chant, which was a good thing, because strong as he was, their classmate was beginning to droop a little.

But reinforcements came just in time. Clodagh climbed over the side of the boat, as always amazingly graceful despite her great size, and, singing and stamping as she went in a kind of a dance, she joined Ke-ola, singing the same words he sang. The first time he faltered, she touched his shoulder to signal him to sit.

She sang only a few lines more before the cherry red of the volcano faded to orange, then yellow. The rumbling quieted, the smoke cleared, and a shallow star of land rose above the ocean's surface, its rays spreading from the central crater, while the sky's bloody fever receded to a rosy blush.

CHAPTER 23

ABSOLUTELY NOTHING HAPPENED next, because nobody who was at the volcano was able to talk or move around much for the next couple of weeks.

The fishing boats rescued the yacht crew and passengers and relayed them back to shore. The copter, which Johnny had left near the river otter dens when he and Yana finally joined up with Marmie and the yacht, once *its* motor was also cleaned, returned them all to Kilcoole.

But nobody talked, because nobody could. It was even too much trouble to thought-speak for a long time because the chant was burned into their brains. Murel's feet hurt up to her tonsils.

Clodagh's student, Deirdre Angalook, under the drooping eyelids of her teacher, made up salves, tinctures, syrups, and packs for everyone's lungs, throats, and muscles. By the time she had everyone dosed, she needed sleep and the muscle salve herself.

Finally, Murel, Ronan, and their dad were able to walk as far as the river and change to seal form, which was easier because then they wouldn't have to walk and their seal muscles were configured differently. The river was silvery and cool, the slender trees on the banks a hundred shades of green—evergreen, or variegating from silver green to grass—as they flipped back and forth in the wind. Mum put on a wet suit and joined them since even in the summer the water of the Kilcoole River was too cold to brave for long in just human skin. The sky was the blue of a glacier, with fluffy clouds and no hint of smoke or steam, but the light faded far more quickly than it had just two weeks before. Some of the leaves on the deciduous trees were already yellowing where the sun lingered on them the longest.

A little after the twins and their parents entered the river, Clodagh, Dierdre, and Ke-ola ambled down to meet them. Ke-ola actually looked great for a guy who'd done all that stomping around.

"Did Dierdre give you extra salve while you've been staying up at Clodagh's?" Murel asked him when she'd dragged herself out of the river, dried off, and put on the change of clothes she'd brought along. Her voice was still a bit husky, but at least audible now.

"Naw, it's that gravity thing," he said, sounding almost normal. "I'm used to being heavier so I'm way stronger than you wimpy Petaybee guys. I could go back out and talk to Pele Petaybee some more right now if I wanted to."

Ronan was out of the water now too, and said, although he was once more in human form, "I flash my furry seal butt at you, big fella, and flap my hind flippers in your general direction. I don't want to see anything hotter than a teakettle for the rest of my life."

Ke-ola laughed and waded in, turned the color of the sky and waded out again.

"We can take you to the hot springs if you fancy a dip," Murel offered. "And there's parts of the river warmer than this, but this was the closest place with any privacy."

He nodded and lay back on the grassy bank with his head cupped in his palms.

Mum used the newcomers' arrival as an excuse to escape the water. She did her best, but she just wasn't a watery person at heart. "Clodagh, I need to know something."

Clodagh lifted her eyebrows. She never used words where an expression or action could do the job, and seldom used two words when one would do.

"Why did all of you show up in the fishing boats the way you did, when you did, and how did you learn Keola's chant?"

"Petaybee told us," she said simply.

It was Mum's turn to raise her eyebrows. "It did?"

"Sure. We were all down in the caves when the drumming started coming through the walls, and the words. We knew you were out there with that volcano, so that was the only place it could be coming from. Petaybee echoing the words back was a good sign that the planet liked what you were doin', so we joined you." She shrugged. "That's all."

"Well, of course," Mum said. "Silly me. Who wouldn't mount a major rescue operation on the basis of an echoed chant heard inside a cave from hundreds of miles away. Why didn't I think of that?"

Clodagh patted her on the shoulder. "It's okay, Yana. You're not a cheechako anymore, but you didn't grow up here. You'll get used to our ways one of these days."

A wistful look spread across Ke-ola's big face, but he said, "You folks think I could borrow a boat to go check on the Honu?"

Clodagh surprised him. "Not now. Maybe later. Fall latchkay time now. Lots of people coming and we gotta get ready."

He nodded but Murel could see he was disappointed.

"But latchkays are wonderful, Ke-ola. You'll like them and—Ke-ola gets to come, doesn't he, Clodagh?"

"Sure. Marmie isn't leaving until after so you can all come."

I don't like the sound of that, Ronan said. *What does she mean "all"?*

They wouldn't make us go back to the space station now. Not after we saved Da and everything. They can't! And Ke-ola saved all of us. They can't send him back too. He likes Petaybee. I know he does.

It's too cold for him, sis, and winter's coming.

Well, but—well, it just wouldn't be fair. He should get to pick.

WHEN THE HUMANS returned to Kilcoole, Sky and the Honu stayed behind so the Honu could swim and commune with the sea otters and absorb more information about the place he felt would become his new home. Sky had remained behind to tell his hundreds of relatives and the sea otters all about his adventures,

Sky otters, he told his hundreds of relatives, now including the sea otter cousins, *know all kinds of creatures, like this big shell one. He is not a big clam and he is not to eat. He is a turtle and a very important creature. He came with his own human from a place far away that is not our home. But he helped keep the volcano from killing everybody, otters, humans, everyone, so he must belong here. So otters can play with him and talk to him but not harm him.*

What happened out there after we left? the sea otters wanted to know. And Sky had a long and enjoyable time of it telling them in great and colorful—and because he was an otter, somewhat smelly—detail of the adventures they missed.

While the others prepared for the latchkay, Johnny Green and Marmie accommodated Ke-ola by taking him out to visit the Honu. When they returned, Sky came with them.

Ke-ola was looking a little more satisfied. Sky scampered off the copter ahead of him.

Ke-ola had no fancier clothing than his bright colored ship suit and the flowered shorts he swam in, but Clodagh said she thought he could wear some of her things.

However, when the drumming began at the longhouse and everyone filed past the stew steaming in the cleaned-out fuel drum heating over the open fire, Ke-ola wore his ship suit. One of Clodagh's extra snow shirts was draped over his lap, humped up in the middle.

"We looked for you all day long but couldn't find you anywhere," Murel whispered fiercely. "Where *were* you?"

"I had stuff I had to do," he said, his lower lip squashing into his upper one as he looked down at her to see if she bought it. There was a ghost of the old twinkle in his eye. He was still pretty tired, she guessed, and also sad. He'd miss the Honu. Maybe Marmie would let him swim in her river sometime. Maybe they'd all end up swimming in it together. She decided not to think about that.

Speeches were made, and Clodagh said there would be songs to sing about the volcano, but everyone's throat was still very sore right now, so that night no one would sing of it, except for one repeat of the chant, for those in the village who had not come.

Ke-ola laid aside the snow shirt and what was under it and obligingly sang the chant and stamped the rhythm, as did all of the others who had been there. Then it was time for the smoked salmon to get passed around and a few more speeches.

But finally Ke-ola stood up himself and said, "I want to do something before it's time to go. This is something my people used to do all the time, and now only at special times, and with special people. These aren't what we usually use but I did what I could with them."

He lifted the shirt, under which was a mound of flowers, purple and magenta fireweed and lupine, pink wild roses, white wild daisies. Only the flowers, none of the stems. It must have taken him hours and hours, since the fireweed was a cluster flower. Lifting a few in his fingers, he brought up a long necklace made of them and put them around Clodagh's neck, kissing her on both cheeks and saying, "Aloha, Auntie."

He did the same for Marmie, Johnny, Yana, and Sean, and last for Ronan and Murel. The wild roses were for Murel, and she stroked the already wilting petals.

"These are flower leis. In old times they were made of plumeria, frangipani, and other beautiful flowers from our islands, to welcome people. But I made these to thank you for your hospitality."

"No dance tonight," Clodagh told everybody. "Meet in the communion cave in an hour."

People murmured among themselves. Some folks had traveled from as far away as Harrison's Fjord to attend this latchkay, and the amenities were being dispensed with. Everything was so hurried up these days, what with the offworlders here. Even Clodagh seemed to be losing her feeling for the stateliness of the old ways.

Murel and Ronan grabbed Ke-ola's arms and immediately headed with him down to the hot springs. They knew he'd enjoy a nice warm swim, and they wanted to show off the beautiful waterfall and steaming pools, one falling into the other, where their parents told them they had fallen in love.

The twins dived and splashed for a while but soon fell into the same mood as Ke-ola, who floated on his back and admired the new night sky.

Before long the others began arriving and filing into the waterfall, with the cave behind its shimmering curtain.

The three of them got out, dried off, and dressed. Marmie and Johnny, Mum and Da, Clodagh, Dierdre, and Dr. Fiske were just arriving. Mum put her arm around Ronan, Da around Murel, and Johnny Green clapped Ke-ola on the shoulder. They walked straight through the outer cave and down the winding path into the innermost one.

They stepped cautiously forward as they reached the inner cave. Murel let out a sigh of relief. Ronan said, *Much better than last time, yeah?*

Much. Petaybee is glad we're home. I almost feel like the planet is giving us a lei too.

Yeah, like we're being honored or something. As we should be. Really, we've been wonderful.

She batted at him. *We did good, but Ke-ola was really the hero. He's such a good guy, Ro, and he's just sort of lost.*

Yeah, well . . .

They all sat, and Murel was afraid she was going to

have to explain things to Ke-ola, but when the planet began talking, he just snuggled back against the rocky cave wall with a huge grin on his face. So Murel relaxed and gave herself up to the experience.

Maybe it was just the recent volcanic activity, but Petaybee seemed more excited than usual, stimulated, happy even. The cave walls glowed with the cherry red of lava, and Murel felt the beat of her own feet on the shipboard and seemed to hear the chant resounding through the stone. A breeze blew through the cave, the scent of flowers on it—surely not the flowers Mum and the others still wore with their leis? These flowers were as heavily and sweetly perfumed as anything Murel had ever smelled before. She felt something soft under her fingers and looked down. Sky lay beside her, his head cradled on her leg, looking utterly peaceful and happy.

Paradise. Petaybee was already very good, but tonight it felt like paradise. Which, she realized, was a concept from ancient religions found mostly in old books these days. But it meant that a place was the best of all possible places, an ideal place. Tonight Petaybee showed them how it could make a place with no ice, where the water was warm and the wind was balmy.

Great round rolling waves seemed to break at her feet, which felt as if they were bare and buried in something pleasantly hot and gritty. The roar of the water was as great and as oddly comforting as Coaxtl's purr. These rhythmic swells had a completely different feeling than the fierce and frightening crescendos of water that had pounded the yacht.

Then, gradually, the sense of being beside the lovely sea faded, and the only watery roar she heard was that of the waterfall at the mouth of the communion cave.

Murel caught one last fleeting impression of foamy pearls left glistening in front of her toes before the seaside sensations washed away entirely.

People began to stir and move. Clodagh was the first to rise.

She smiled beatifically. "Well, Petaybee has spoken. Did everybody get the message?"

People nodded to each other, though some a little doubtfully.

Murel wondered what the shanachie meant, since usually the communion was somewhat different from person to person. Mum and Da, for instance, were so tightly entwined they seemed to entirely forget where they were.

Ke-ola opened his eyes, blinking, then rubbing them.

"You, young man, you understand what our world is saying?" Clodagh asked.

He shrugged. "I—I think so."

"I hope you do, because Petaybee told *me* that you, of all the people here, are the one who understands the need for the warm landmass and the one who wants it. You were the one to welcome it with your song. Soon Marmie's ship will be flying back into space, and before you go, Petaybee has a question. Did you get it?"

He blinked and shook his head uncertainly.

"You, Murel and Ronan, did *you*?"

They exchanged looks, widened their eyes at Clodagh and shook their heads too.

Clodagh began to laugh. She turned to Marmie. "I thought these kids were getting an education up there in your sky house, Marmie, but they don't even seem to see the obvious."

Ronan, who didn't have much patience and knew

when he was being teased, prompted, "Which *is?* You're the wisewoman, Clodagh. You tell us."

"It's dead simple, boy. Petaybee loves your new friend and wants you all to find out if there are any more like him out there that you can bring home."

Epilogue

I'M NOT SURE which one will take longer," Da told the twins and Ke-ola, "Petaybee, building its landmass, or the Federation red tape we have to cut through to invite Ke-ola's people to join us."

Three months had passed since the latchkay. Summer was at an end and freeze-up would begin soon. Neither Ke-ola nor the twins had returned to school.

Mum, back from her helicopter trip with Dr. Fiske and Dr. Metaxos to check on the volcano, said, "My money is on Petaybee finishing first. As for inviting Ke-ola's people, a lot of that paperwork is just nonsense they use to keep the punters at bay and the pencil pushers employed, love. Have you never heard that it's easier to ask forgiveness than it is to ask permission?"

"It's my ancestral family motto, actually," Ke-ola said.

"Which makes it ours too," Ronan put in.

"See there?" Da told her. "We're setting a bad example for the children. Pay us no mind, kids. We're just frustrated by the communication glitches. With the equipment banjaxed every other week or so, having to send messages by passing ships is ponderous. Really, you do have to wait for permission for some things. To make it official. To keep from bringing the wrath of the heavens down upon our humbled heads. We've yet to hear back from the Federation or Intergal about our proposal. Neither is there any response from Ke-ola's people."

"Da, why don't we just go get them?" Murel asked. "I don't see why we need permission to issue an invitation or why they would need permission to come and see if they like it here or not."

"They'll like it," Ke-ola said. "But they're probably not even getting the messages. The Company Corps monitors traffic in the area, and besides, we have communications problems of our own. Lots of meteor showers. Very hard to keep a com relay up when the sky keeps falling."

"See what you started?" Da asked Mum playfully.

"Me?" she asked, hand to breast in make-believe innocence.

"No, seriously," Murel said. "I don't see why not."

"We have no spacecraft of our own," Da pointed out.

"Marmie has lots."

"Those things cost a great deal to operate, dear," Mum said. "Marmie has been a wonderful friend to us and to Petaybee, but we mustn't ask her to beggar herself."

"We could pay her back. Probably," Ronan said.

"Besides," Da said, "there's no hurry. Winter is coming and Ke-ola's folk don't care for the cold, from what he says. The volcanic area is still way too unstable for them to try to occupy it."

"But it won't be for very long, right, Mum?"

"We have no way of knowing that, kids. We can't be inviting Ke-ola's people to come and cohabit with active volcanoes."

"Pardon me, ma'am," Ke-ola said, "but that's how

my people used to live. That's what they remember from way back. They liked it. It's how we learned the chants I showed you. How we could help Petaybee and everybody else who lives here. If some volcanoes are left all alone, or with people who don't understand them, they get wild, explode all over the place, shake the whole world and make huge waves higher than the treetops, kill everybody."

"But Ke-ola, your people haven't lived near volcanoes for many generations," Mum said.

"Don't matter. Honus remember. Some people remember stories and songs. They can help the others."

"Well, you're certainly optimistic, I'll say that," Mum said, sounding the opposite of optimistic.

"What's it like out there now, Mum?" Murel asked. The twins hadn't been allowed to swim in the area since they returned, and Da didn't seem inclined to do it either. Sky had returned to his hundreds of relatives on the coast, and the twins hadn't heard from him, or Ke ola from the Honu, for almost a month. The twins had spent the time teaching Ke-ola to ride a curly coat and showing him around the woods and villages surrounding Kilcoole. When the days were chilly, they swam at the hot springs. But this time they had not ventured beyond the area where their parents said they could wander. Almost losing their father had been an eye-opener. If they got into trouble, he'd come looking for them again, and he or other people in a rescue party could get hurt even if they themselves and Ke-ola were fine. So the twins obeyed the restrictions, though they chafed under them.

Mum said, "The smoke kept us from seeing a great deal, but the central crater is now elevated to approximately a hundred feet above sea level."

Da gave a low whistle.

"It is not the only vent, however. What we haven't seen in the past is that another crater has surfaced about fifteen klicks south of the primary one, and there is some activity from a third another forty miles south of that. The landmass surrounding the primary crater covers something like five square miles at the moment, but of course there's still pyroclastic flow from the crater, pumping steadily from it as if it were blood from the heart. I didn't think volcanoes worked that way."

Da, who had been sitting at his desk while the kids stood around him, reached up, meaning to pat Ke-ola on the shoulder, but only reached his elbow, so he patted that instead. "Petaybean ones apparently do—especially one that has had a good coach." With an apologetic glance at the twins, he added, "Or coaches."

"Has the planet given Clodagh any idea how long this might take?" Ronan asked.

"I don't think Petaybee wears a watch, Ro," Murel said.

Ronan colored and said, "I *meant* that Petaybee seemed to be pretty clear about wanting Ke-ola and his people to live there. I don't think the planet would have been that specific if it didn't have some notion that the land would be ready in Ke-ola's lifetime."

"The Honu might know," Ke-ola said.

"How?" Murel asked.

Ke-ola shrugged. "Honus know many things people don't. Especially about weather and disasters and natural events."

"It can't hurt to ask," Murel said. "And I miss Sky. If the volcano is behaving itself, Mum, don't you think it would be okay if we swim out there to see them?"

"In a couple of days I could take you in the copter," Mum replied.

"But we want to swim!" Ro protested. "Ke-ola can swim with us—he's not a selkie or an otter but he's a really good swimmer. Please?"

Mum was looking at Da, but he shook his head. "I'll never get all this paperwork sorted if I take off now. I see no harm in them going, though. After all, they've already been through quite a bit out there and got through it all right. In fact, the rest of us, especially me, might not have made it without them."

Mum tilted her head and looked at him questioningly. He smiled and shook his head. "No, love, I still don't remember what happened or how I survived. I suppose that will always be a mystery."

Da, Ronan asked. *You don't suppose maybe some special kind of animal who lives under the sea found you and took you into its city—its shelter—and took care of you, do you?*

Now, why would I suppose something like that, son? You have quite an imagination on you, boyo. No, what I suppose, between you and me, is that Petaybee somehow knew it was me in trouble—and me its first selkie and father of the selkie twins—and somehow led me into a safe place with enough air to keep me going until the fireworks were done or you found me.

Yeah, I guess that makes more sense at that, Ronan said.

Murel shot him a look. They had promised the deep sea otters that if they gave Da back, no one would learn of the strange city or its mysterious inhabitants. But Ronan hated keeping a secret from Da, especially one that concerned him and Petaybee. So he'd sort of given his father a chance to remember what really happened. Which he hadn't. Also, it seemed that Da wouldn't have believed them if Ronan and Murel had sworn to what they had seen, so it was okay not to push it. Ronan's conscience was clear.

"So we can go?" Murel asked hurriedly.

"Yes, but take your dry suits. And Ke-ola, you'll want to wear a wet suit. The water is far too cold this time of year for you to swim unprotected. I'll fly out in the copter and pick you up Wednesday afternoon, so be right there at the otter colony. Got it?"

"Got it," the twins said, and bounded off, Ke-ola in their wake.

I'M DYING TO *know if the deep sea otters and that strange city of theirs survived the eruption,* Ronan told his sister.

Me too, but we promised not to go back there.

Yes, but Sky didn't promise. The Honu didn't promise.

The Honu doesn't know about them.

Are you sure? Ke-ola says the Honus know about many things. And Sky might have told the Honu about them. Nobody said anything about not telling animals about them—just no humans.

The three of them had been swimming hard all day, with one break to portage themselves in human form to the foot of the falls. Fun to slide down when frozen, the cascade was much too dangerous to tackle even for seals and certainly for Ke-ola.

The twins pointed out the site of the former otter dens to their friend before everyone plunged back into the water. Ke-ola dived in first, to give Murel privacy to change from her suit into her sealskin. He was also a little slower than they, so he would find the head start useful.

Poor Ke-ola wasn't much good at eating raw fish either, so he didn't have the benefit of frequent energy-boosting snacks that they did.

Finally they could smell the salt in the freshwater and saw the river broadening as its mouth opened to feed the sea. It came much sooner than they expected and was much broader than they remembered.

I guess the shoreline has risen permanently here, because of the water displaced by the volcano, Murel said.

We're lucky we were out swimming when the waves hit, Ronan agreed. *There used to be a lot more trees here—a lot more lots of things. And look at the sea otter island. It only barely sticks up out of the water now. A lot of it was flooded.* They hadn't noticed any of these things when returning from their harrowing encounter with the volcano, but now, in calmer times, the changes in the landscape were downright unsettling. Perhaps all of the changes hadn't taken place immediately after the first major eruption. The steady pumping of lava Mum described could have accounted in part for the higher water level. What if the otters had lost their dens, become afraid to live here, and moved somewhere else?

The twins began sending mental calls to Sky. It was a good idea to announce their presence and identify themselves anyway, so as not to alarm the hundreds of relatives, lest the three of them be attacked as invaders by angry otters. *Sky, it's us, Murel and Ronan! Can you hear us yet?*

Hah! River seals! The river seals have come! Sky's thought sang out, and before the twins quite knew where they were, they were surrounded by eager, not angry, otters, who immediately wanted to show them a new mud slide they had made.

Ke-ola was also surrounded, but at first the otters weren't too sure about him. "Hey, what is this with the small, cute, and menacing?" he asked aloud. The twins started to translate for Sky but their otter friend had already assessed the situation.

Mother, sisters, brothers, cousins, aunties, and uncles, do you not recall my story about the Honu? What did I say about this Honu?

Hah! Not food! A sister three litters behind him answered.

Yes! Did I not also tell of the Honu's brave human protector? One who does not eat otters and is friend to the river seals? What did I say about him?

Hah! Not food? asked his uncle five litters before his mother.

Not food and not to be harmed. Friend. Like river seals.

Friend? asked another much younger brother.

Family member who is not an otter, Sky said quickly. He had evidently given the concept considerable thought since being introduced to it.

At that, the otters around Ke-ola relaxed. One brushed gently against him in apology. The little sister dived down and resurfaced holding a rock in her paws, which she dropped into the water near Ke-ola's hand. He caught it. "Thank you," he said, but she didn't hear. She watched him catch it, then dived back under the surface again.

Sky! Murel exclaimed mentally, and dived under him and resurfaced to show her pleasure. *We were afraid you'd moved your dens again, that maybe the bigger waves and higher tides had washed them out.*

Hah! Old dens are all underwater. Sea otter dens too. But riverbank is full of holes. Otters dig holes larger, have new homes. Have to get more rocks, though, he said. *And the sea took back hundreds of clamshells.*

I'm sorry, Murel said. *Maybe we can help you gather more.* The twins pulled and flopped themselves onto the riverbank and shook off the water, then put on their dry suits.

Did the sea otters make new dens too? Ronan asked. *I see their island is mostly underwater now.*

"Hah!" Sky said. *Sea otters don't have dens. They need only the sea. Their back feet are flippers and they blow bubbles in their fur to make it warm and waterproof. When they are on land it is just for hunting food in pools on the beach. They sleep in the sea, wrapped in kelp. They mate in the sea. They have strange ways, but they are our cousins.*

And—the deep sea otters, Sky? Murel asked. *What of them? Have the sea otters seen them since the volcano?*

"Hah!" Sky chittered a moment, plainly disturbed. *No deep sea otters. No deep sea otter strange bubble den. All land now. Underwater land, under volcano land. But no deep sea otters. No.*

Oh, Ro! Murel said.

Looks like we got Da out just in time, Ronan said.

But we didn't save the deep sea otters, or whatever they were. They helped Da, saved his life, and now they're extinct and we didn't even try to help them.

We sort of had our hands full. And they didn't want help. They wanted secrecy, remember?

She couldn't help it. She started crying. Everything had turned out fine for everyone except the heroic creatures who had saved their father, and it wasn't fair, it just wasn't.

Ke-ola, who had been sending his own silent calls to the Honu, turned back from the sea in alarm when he heard her sobs. He swept her up in a huge and all-enveloping hug that nonetheless only circled her lightly within his arms, to comfort her but not break her. "Little sistah, why do you cry? Did someone bite you?"

"No, no, it's just too sad, Ke-ola," she said. And she told him about the deep sea otters and what they had done and what had become of them. "If they hadn't been so afraid of us, maybe they would have saved themselves. They wanted everything secret—well, I told you now, but I guess it doesn't matter since they're all dead."

"I would never tell," he said.

So she blurted out some of the rest of it, and Ronan finished. While they were talking, the sun completely disappeared and the moon rose. Its shaft fell on the mouth of the river, and within it they saw the head and shell of the Honu swimming toward them. He looked awfully sacred right then, his shell sheened by moonglow and his wet head glistening with light.

"Except for the Honu, of course," Ke-ola amended. In a moment he sighed and said, "And that's okay. The Honu knew all about the deep sea otters. He says we should take them flowers."

"We can't go," Murel said. "We promised Mum."

"I didn't promise," Ke-ola said. "The Honu didn't promise."

Sky, who had been following the thread through the twins' thoughts, piped up, *Sky did not promise. Deep sea otters did not think Sky could tell scientists about them, since otters cannot talk to two legs who are not river seals.*

"You should wait till morning," Murel said aloud to Ke-ola and Ronan. "We won't be able to find flowers to make leis until then anyway."

They don't want flowers, Sky said again. *Otters have no use for flowers. Why flowers?*

Because—because they're pretty, Sky, Murel answered, feeling even as she said it that the answer didn't make much sense. Otters weren't great flower fanciers unless they sometimes nibbled certain varieties. And then, she doubted the beings that had helped Da and inhabited the strange city were otters of any kind. Maybe some ancient pre-terraforming denizens of Petaybee preserved by their city and resurrected with the opening of the volcanic vent. Maybe aliens. But they were good, whatever they were, because they saved Da, and if the Honu thought they deserved flowers, then they did.

Rocks. Clams. Food. These are good gifts. Pretty gifts. Deep sea otters would like these gifts. Not flowers.

"He's got a point," Ronan said aloud. To Ke-ola, he said, "Sky thinks the deep sea otters wouldn't appreciate a flower lei as much as one made out of something otters value—like rocks or clams."

"But we can't make a rock lei or a clam lei—can we?" Murel asked.

"Clamshells," Ke-ola said. "They used to make leis from shells sometimes. We could net them with seaweed."

Sky and all of the other otters, including the sea otters who had congregated by the shore to see what all of the excitement was about, agreed that clamshells were best. Dead otters ate no clams but would enjoy the pretty shells. Living otters would have to eat the clams *for* the dead otters. It made sense to them. The tide pools, beach, river mouth, and sea soon frothed around diving otter butts, the owners of which made short work of the whole clams and deposited the shells into huge piles. These they basketed in strands of kelp and other seaweed, enclosing each shell in three or four strands, then tying another strand at top and bottom. It took a very long time. The twins weren't very good at it, so in the end, Ke-ola ended up with three leis, one from each twin and one from their father, which he, the Honu, and Sky would carry to a place as close to the deep sea otters' "den" as Sky could guess.

Murel didn't think the leis were pretty at all, but she only thought it, so as not to insult Ke-ola.

Sky disagreed. *Pretty. Much pretty. Hundreds pretty.* All of the other otters agreed that the leis were hundreds pretty.

So that was all right. If the otters liked the leis, the self-proclaimed deep sea otters would have liked them.

The day was half gone before Ke-ola, the Honu, Sky, and an otter escort set off for the volcano. Ronan and Murel swam out part of the way with them, but kept their promise and didn't go near the volcano. Well, not very near. Actually, it was hard to judge because, what with all the building up it had done, the volcano sort of met them earlier than they expected to encounter it. At least, the underwater part that was the skirt of the island extended until it was much closer to the northern mainland than they remembered.

It didn't matter anyway. Once they came to the place where the lava flow had cooled on the ocean floor, building it up until the water was comparatively shallow there, nobody stood much chance of getting anywhere near the place where the deep sea otters had so recently dwelled in their peculiar city.

That being the case, the twins watched when the Honu suddenly stopped swimming and turned back to Ke-ola, treading water, and Sky. *Otters talk to other otters best,* the Honu told Sky.

The twins felt relief from Sky. The little river otter had not wanted to go back to the volcano, because it was a long swim, because he was not a sea otter and didn't like salt water very much, and because *his* sort of otter had the intelligence to avoid erupting volcanoes. After a number of "Hahs," he dropped his clamshell lei into the sea with the thought, *Deep sea otters, here are your presents—nice shells, only you are not here and are probably dead.* The thoughts were accompanied by vocalized chitterings and mumblings that were otter verbalizations.

To the twins' surprise, the Honu and Ke-ola swam back to them.

"As long as you're here, you may as well represent yourselves," Ke-ola said, pulling the clamshell lei off over his head and dropping it over Ronan's. The Honu came close enough for Murel to take his lei.

Since the twins were naturally in seal form, Ronan barked acknowledgment, then dived, letting the lei drop over his head to drift slowly downward before he rose once more to the surface. *Thanks for giving our Da back,* Ronan thought.

Murel followed him, letting her lei drop over her head as he had.

Yes, thanks, she said. *And we're awfully sorry you didn't make it too. You could have come with us. I hope*

you knew that. Whatever you were, you saved our fa-
ther. We'd have been glad to help you too.

Then they turned around and returned to the river
mouth. Halfway back, they were met by their mother's
helicopter. It shadowed them back to the river, where the
twins and Ke-ola withdrew from the water and the
twins reassumed human shape and pulled on their dry
suits. There was no one there to see but Mum, who recently had recertified as a copter pilot, updating the
training she had received while in the Company Corps.

Murel expected Mum to be at least a little angry that
they had gone out to the volcanoes, but she didn't mention it. "Get in," she said to the two of them and to Ke-
ola. "Marmie and Johnny should be docking the *Piaf* in
another hour. You'll need to get ready to go."

*Oh, no! Back to school no matter how much more in-
teresting things are at home,* Ronan said.

But then Mum surprised them by saying, "Your father
asks if Sky would like another helicopter ride and suggests perhaps the Honu might like to come along on this
trip as well."

Ke-ola's face filled with thunderclouds, but he called
the Honu, who had been swimming just offshore, and
politely lifted him into the copter and sat holding his
shell so the flippers would not have to bear the turtle's
weight on dry ground. It wasn't a lot of weight even yet,
though the Honu was several inches larger in diameter
than he had been when he arrived, but the flippers were
delicate.

Mum had her headphones on the whole way so they
had no more opportunity to quiz her about why Sky and
the Honu needed to come, unless it was to say good-bye.

Of course, there was always the chance that Marmie's

school might be starting special classes for airborne otters and psychic sea turtles with extrasensory knowledge
of natural disasters, but it didn't seem likely.

The copter set down at the space port just as the *Piaf*
was landing. Da and Aunt Sinead arrived, and Clodagh
too. They seemed to be trying to look as if they had just
been in the neighborhood, saw the spaceship landing,
and decided to come and see what was going on, but the
twins noticed that their bags and Ke-ola's were strapped
across the back of Da's mount. Page and Chapter were
nowhere to be seen, nor were other mounts for Johnny
and Marmie. But when Mum, Da, Clodagh, and Aunt
Sinead dismounted, Coaxtl and Nanook appeared from
behind them, split up and sat down flanking them, one
on each side, like good guardian beasts.

Other than the refueling crew, no one disembarked
from the *Piaf* except Johnny and Marmie, who waved
and hurried toward them.

"Ah," Marmie said, "I see the delegation has arrived.
What's it to be then, Your Excellencies?" she asked
Mum and Da.

Delegation? The twins exchanged startled looks.

Before they could ask, Mum answered Marmie. "We
haven't had a chance to discuss it with them yet." She
turned back to the twins and Ke-ola, "Sorry, but with
the communications problems, Marmie wasn't able to
get through until this morning to let us know about
this."

"What?" the twins and Ke-ola asked at once. The
Honu was not exactly struggling in Ke-ola's hands, but
seemed to want to go somewhere, and poked his head
toward the ship first at one angle, then another, his flippers paddling as if he would swim through the air to

reach it. Sky stood beneath him, the lower part of his body still but the upper part bobbing inquisitively from side to side as he too watched the ship.

"Are we going back to school then, Mum? What's all the fuss?" Murel asked.

Mum shook her head, and now she did seem a bit angry. "No. I'm dead set against it, mind you, but Marmie has been pulling all the strings she can and this seems to be the only way. We've received permission from the Federation, though not from Intergal, to send a native Petaybean delegation to invite Ke-ola's people to visit us, and live with us if everyone is mutually agreeable."

"So, is that what Marmie and Johnny are doing here? Have they found some way you and Da can go after all?"

"Of course not," Mum snapped, then relented, realizing she was acting angry at a time when she most wanted to be loving. She continued in a more patient and reasonable tone. "You know that. We're too acclimated by now to leave the planet for any length of time. And we're too old. To my way of thinking, you are too young. And what with everything happening, we haven't had much time to catch up or for you to enjoy being home again. But still, if you're willing . . ."

"We need you to be Petaybee's emissaries," Da said aloud. "It's a lot to ask of youngsters, but Ke-ola is your friend, after all, and you brought him and his Honu to Petaybee's notice. Besides, it will be a fine opportunity for you to travel, see other places. I've never been able to do that myself, you know. And of course, Ke-ola must go to introduce you."

"You mean we're going to go see Ke-ola's people and

bring them back?" Ronan asked. "We don't have to go back to school?"

"Not right now," Mum said.

"Though I have brought a nice selection of vid courses with me and you can study those if you find yourselves hungering for knowledge on the journey," Marmie said.

"No!" they both said, but Murel added diplomatically, as befitted her new appointment, "That is, a journey to a distant world and a real mission to perform seems educational enough for now, thanks."

"So you don't mind then?" Marmie asked.

"When do we start?" Ronan replied.

Sky suddenly streaked toward the *Piaf*. Otters run very quickly when they want to, as he had told the twins. The Honu's swimming motions seemed to be dragging Ke-ola in the same direction. "You still got the sacred Honu's tank, Madame?" Ke-ola asked Marmie.

"A bigger one," she said. "Of course, if your people or some of them come, we hope they will bring others of his species with them."

Da handed Marmie a sheaf of paperwork, and Johnny handed the twins some as well. "Maps and such," he said. "So you'll know where we are, and if communications clear up, can get in touch. It's a bit out of the way, on the fringes like Petaybee, but another fringe. Yana, you know—"

"Yes, of course," she said. There were hugs all around and head butts and rubs from Coaxtl and Nanook, then Da took the packs off the curly coat and handed them to the twins, and Clodagh handed them another.

Da held out Ke-ola's, but the Kanaka boy was already halfway to the ship, so Ronan took it.

More hugs and, amazingly, tears from Mum and Clodagh. Sky streaked back to them, then back toward Ke-ola and the Honu.

"Better we take off pretty quick," Ke-ola called. "The Honu wants to go *now*."

Johnny frowned. "He seems to be on a tight schedule. I never thought to see a turtle in such a hurry."

"Better go now, then," Clodagh said, waving the twins toward the ship. They turned toward it, and her bemused comment followed them. "Honus know things."

READ ON FOR AN EXCERPT FROM

MAELSTROM

The newest novel of Petaybee from
Hugo and Nebula award–winning authors

Anne McCaffrey

and

Elizabeth Ann Scarborough

Available in bookstores everywhere
from Del Rey

THE TWINS AND KE-OLA were on the bridge watching as the *Piaf* approached Halau. It was a large planet, orbited by two moons and an asteroid belt. As Ke-ola had intimated, it didn't look like the pretty pictures on Intergal's vid clip. Its surface was as pocked and colorless as someone in the last stages of a contagious illness.

It didn't look like a place anyone would want to visit, much less live. Nevertheless, the *Piaf* was not the only ship in the vicinity. In the huge viewport, plainly visible between them and the asteroid belt that partially obscured the pitted planet, another ship hung in space.

The comscreen lit and suddenly another bridge with another life-size crew was looming above the deck of the *Piaf*'s bridge. A woman with dark almond-shaped eyes and strawberry blond hair bobbed asymmetrically across her forehead and down one cheek to just below her ears was looking straight at them. She wore a uniform similar to the one that hung in a bag in Mum's wardrobe. Company Corps. Of course, she was only a lieutenant, and Mum had been a Colonel by the time she quit for good.

"This is the InterGalactic Enterprises Company Corps carrier *George Armstrong Custer*," the woman announced. "You have entered restricted InterGalactic Enterprises airspace. Please identify your vessel."

The *Piaf* had a com officer too, Steve Guthe, who spoke twenty-seven languages and could sing in even more, but Johnny spoke up instead. "This is the passenger liner *Piaf*, flagship of Algemeine Intergalactic Enterprises. Captain John Greene speaking but Madame herself is aboard if there's a problem you and I can't sort out between us."

"No problem, sir, and nothing to sort out. Your ship must reverse course and leave this area immediately. Even under normal circumstances, unauthorized vessels are not allowed to visit this world. And at the moment Halau is experiencing a condition red emergency. We're standing by to be of assistance."

"I think you will find that as a senior council member of the Federation, Madame has clearance, as does this vessel, to visit just about anywhere in the known cosmos she wishes. Maybe if you fill us in on the emergency, we might be of assistance too. We're quite handy, you'll find, for civilians."

"No doubt, sir, but it's none of your concern, or Madame Algemeine's. Halau routinely experiences meteor storms. Such a storm is in progress at this time. We are standing by until our instruments indicate that it is safe to land and render aid to the inhabitants, if necessary."

"Where are the hits?" Ke-ola asked urgently. "What coordinates?"

The woman took in Ke-ola, who was peering over Johnny's head, with no sign of surprise. "I don't have that information at this time. From your appearance,

I surmise that you may be a native of Halau, is that correct?"

"My people live there now, yes," Ke-ola said. "Can you tell me if the area around New Puna has been hit?"

"I'm sorry. I do not have access to that data at this time," the woman said.

"Perhaps you could obtain it, then," said Marmie, sweeping onto the bridge, dressed dramatically in a flowing scarlet robe with a tall black collar, trim in front and around the hem, and deep black cuffs folded back on a wide sleeve. She looked elegant, even regal, Murel thought. "My dear friend Ke-ola is naturally concerned for the welfare of his family."

Don't you love it when Marmie throws her weight around? Ronan asked telepathically. The twins had been able to speak to each other without words since they were small, and could communicate with nonhuman animals in that fashion as well. Usually the only other human they could talk to was their father, who was also a selkie, but sometimes people surprised them.

I love it that she's important enough to let us do things we wouldn't be able to without her help and that she's willing to do it, Murel answered a bit primly.

I wasn't being disrespectful, Sis. I just think it's fun to see her sail in and take charge. She's awesome. Like a queen.

She is in a way, only of a company instead of a country. She's got presence, Adrienne says, and of course it's backed up with a lot of real power and money.

The com officer on the Company Corps ship was enough of a soldier to know superior fire-power when she saw it. "Colonel Cally can better assist you with that information, ma'am."

"Then I'll thank you to fetch the officer in question," Marmie said, not in a snooty voice but as if she would be truly grateful to the com officer for doing her job. One thing the twins had noticed about Marmie was that she never bullied the "little people" unless they were acting like total idiots.

When a very official-looking man with an iron gray crewcut and colonel's leaves on his uniform stepped up to the com screen, the corporal sat back, looking relieved.

"Madame Algemeine, I presume?"

Marmie nodded regally.

"Colonel Zachariah Cally at your service, ma'am. As my lieutenant has already informed you, this is restricted space and the best service I can render you is to advise you to return to the other pressing matters that no doubt compete for your attention and leave the current crisis to us. We are trained to deal with these things."

"Indeed?" Marmie asked. "As I explained to your corporal, one of the pressing matters to which you refer involves accompanying my young ward Ke-ola home to his family. If they are, as your officer indicated, in danger, then it is very much my business to do all that I can to make sure they come to no harm, as that would cause my ward considerable distress. Would it not, Ke-ola?"

"Oh, yes, Madame, I would be very much distressed. My brothers and sisters and aunties and uncles and cousins are all there—and the sacred Honu's family too. That is why I want to know where these meteors are landing. I am hoping they are not landing on my family."

"I'm sure Colonel Cally can understand your concern, Ke-ola, and mine. For of course we can surmise that since the company has sent a ship to aid the inhabitants, they must be in danger. It is a very large planet, and with very little, from the look of it, that could be harmed other than the people who have been settled there."

The colonel remained unruffled. "That's true, Madame Algemeine. We have feeds from the surface that indicate a large strike in the very midst of the largest settlement. And yes, I believe that's locally known as New Puna."

"Is that all? Have you had no communication from the inhabitants, no maydays or other requests for help?"

The colonel ran his tongue around his lips as if his mouth had suddenly gone dry. "Yes, we have. But right now, with the meteors still falling, it is far too dangerous to take a ship down there. While the situation is unstable, we would only be risking our people along with those below."

"I see. So no aid has been dispatched at all? No medical team or help in evacuating people to a safer location?"

"They have medical people of their own and we hope sense enough to leave the area while the sky is falling." His tone was snappish but he smiled, remembering to whom he was speaking.

"Yes, well," Marmie said, her accent more pronounced, drawled with a pursing of her mouth and a narrowing of her eyes that somehow conveyed that she was exercising great tolerance, "my ship has excellent shields and sensors for deflecting projectiles. I shall see to it at the next council meeting that we discuss having similar ones installed on the military vessels so you can take a more active role in this sort of emergency. If you would care to transfer some of your personnel to my vessel, we will be happy to give you safe transport to the planet's surface so you may carry out your mission with greater safety and so that Keola's people will receive help as soon as possible."

Bright patches of read appeared on the colonel's close shaven cheeks and traveled down his neck. "I'm afraid I cannot allow—"

"Mr. Guthe," she said to her own com officer, "do patch me through to the High Command so they can provide authorization for the colonel to make use of our resources."

The colonel turned away for a moment. Murel and Ronan were certain it was to get control of his temper. When he turned back to face them, he did seem to have regained a measure of composure.

"That won't be necessary, ma'am," He said smoothly. "It's very good of you to offer your help. However, I've just received word from our link to the surface that the meteor bombardment seems to have stopped for the moment so we can all proceed."

He had his navigation officer provide landing cordinates for Johnny and communications termnated while the *Custer* darted toward the pockmarked planet, the *Piaf* following.

As they neared the surface, the landscape before them looked even less habitable than it had from the air. Murel had done some computer research on volcanoes while aboard ship, wanting to learn more about the one forming Petaybee's newest landmass. One of the pictures of the field inside the volcanic crater had looked something like Halau's surface. There were large craters with emberous pimples of meteor rock. The comparatively level bits of ground looked back at them with thousands upon thousands of bloodshot eyes, and the air was still spangled with fiery rain.

Ke-ola, his finger trembling, pointed out what had been New Puna.

"You see that big hole there? That is where we had the gardens. And that one over there? That is where the pool was that held the Honu's relatives."

"And your relatives, Ke-ola? Where are they?"

He scanned the viewport in a slow deliberate way then shrugged. "I don't see the home dome, where the people lived. Not even a splinter. That big hole with the m-melted edges? That's where it used to be."

Johnny quietly placed a hand on Ke-ola's shoulder.

As quickly as it was humanly possible they suited up and prepared to leave the ship. The soldiers and Johnny at first wanted Ronan and Murel to stay aboard but the twins were adamant.

"Since we *are* Petaybee's ambassadors," Murel said. "I think we really do have to be in on everything."

"You are only ten years old," Marmion said. "It could be very upsetting out there."

"We won't be any more upset than Ke-ola or his bruthahs and sistahs," Murel said, pronouncing the words the way Ke-ola did, out of respect for what seemed to be a colloquial language mutation, rather than ignorance of the way everyone else said it. "We're here to help and that's that."